THE MAMMOTH BOOK OF

New Comic Fantasy

FOURTH ALL-NEW COLLECTION

Edited by Mike Ashley

CARROLL & GRAF PUBLISHERS
New York

Carroll & Graf Publishers
An imprint of Avalon Publishing Group, Inc.
245 W. 17th Street
New York
NY 100115300

AVALON
publishing group incorporated

First published in the UK by Robinson,
an imprint of Constable & Robinson Ltd 2005

First Carroll & Graf edition 2005

ISBN-13: 978-0-7394-5786-3

Printed and bound in the U.S.A.

CONTENTS

CONTENTS

COPYRIGHT AND ACKNOWLEDGMENTS

"A Rude Awakening" © 2005 by Gail-Nina Anderson. First publication, original to this anthology. Printed by permission of the author.

"Yo Ho Hoka!" © 1955 by Fantasy House, Inc. First published in *The Magazine of Fantasy and Science Fiction*, March 1955. Reprinted by permission of Ralph M. Vicinanza, Ltd. as agent for the authors' respective estates.

"The Sea Serpent Syndicate" by Everard Jack Appleton. First published in *The Royal Magazine*, April 1905. Copyright expired.

"The Strange Affair of Mr Corpusty" © 1932 by George A.A. Willis. Reprinted from *The Prince Who Hiccupped and Other Tales* (Benn, 1932) by permission of the author's estate.

"The Blue Magnolia" © 2000 by Tony Ballantyne. First published in *The Third Alternative* #22 (January 2000). Reprinted by permission of the author.

"The Great Wish Syndicate" by John Kendrick Bangs, first published in *Jack and the Check Book* (New York: Harper, 1911). Copyright expired.

"The Power and the Gory" © 2005 by James Bibby. First publication, original to this anthology. Printed by permission of the author.

"The Kaluza-Klein Caper" © 2005 by Damien Broderick. Originally published in a different form as part of the novel *Striped Holes* (New York: Avon Books, 1988). Printed by permission of the author.

"Bad Timing" © 1991 by Molly Brown. First published in *Interzone*, December 1991. Reprinted by permission of the author.

"Fractal Paisleys" © 1992 by Paul Di Filippo. First published in *The Magazine of Fantasy & Science Fiction*, May 1992. Reprinted by permission of the author.

"Sweet, Savage Sorcerer" © 1989 by Esther Friesner. First published in *Amazing Stories*, January 1990. Reprinted by permission of the author.

"Forbidden Brides of the Faceless Slaves in the Nameless House of the Night of Dread Desire" © 2004 by Neil Gaiman. First published in *Gothic!* edited by Deborah Noyes (Cambridge, MS: Candlewick Press, 2004). Reprinted by permission of the author and Candlewick Press.

"A Drama of Dragons" © 1980 by Craig Shaw Gardner. First published in *Dragons of Light* edited by Orson Scott Card (New York: Ace Books, 1980). Reprinted by permission of the author.

"Almost Heaven" © 2004 by Tom Gerencer. First published as "Almost (But Not Quite) Heaven" in *Realms of Fantasy*, October 2004. Reprinted by permission of the author.

"I Married a Robot" © 1999 by Ron Goulart. First published in *Analog Science Fiction and Fact*, November 1999. Reprinted by permission of the author.

THE WONDERS TO BEHOLD

Mike Ashley

It was a dark and stormy night. Deep in the forest, just within earshot of the Walderslade bypass, a young, virile but care-worn man sat hunched over a pile of manuscripts.

"Now, what have we here?" he muttered to himself as the winds battered against his window and the trees formed eerie tracery against the scudding clouds. He began to leaf through the stories in front of him, recalling their pleasures.

"Ah, yes, the intelligent alien banana turned detective, the teddy-bear pirates, the computerized shoes, the high-energy trousers that threaten the universe, the Neighbourhood Watch and the forces of Beelzebub, the missionary who underesti-mates an aboriginal ritual, the talking moose head . . ."

Hang on, hang on. What's all this?

"Ssshh – don't interrupt."

What are you doing?

"Go away. You'll spoil everything."

You're not doing another of your Introductions, are you?

"Of course not. This is the story of a forgotten genius and his great works."

Forgotten genius! What's this: "young . . . virile!"

"Be quiet. You'll ruin it."

Look, we had all this out last time. No one reads Introductions. I bet they're already halfway through the book. They can find out what everything's about themselves.

"No, no, I must reveal what wonders lie before them. All the hard work that went into the book. That there are eight brand new stories and some very rare reprints. And about the politically incorrect bits . . ."

Ah, that sounds good. I must look out for those.

". . . and the significance of the title."

Why, what have you called it this time? The Enormous Book of Strenuously Comic Fantasy? The Huge Book of Rib-tickling Fantastica?

"No I haven't. It's now become a standard title."

A what?

"Look, never mind. Go away and let me explain everything properly."

You don't need to explain everything. It spoils the magic.

"That's true, I don't want to spoil the magic. But there's still so much I want to say."

Why not save it for those story blurbs you write?

"No, no, I'm not doing story notes here, because I want the stories to flow together. I've arranged them so that they're kind-of connected."

Really?

"Well, sort of."

That's good. So there's even less of your ramblings.

"No. I've done a note on contributors at the back of the book."

Good, say what you want there. Now can we get on with it?

"Well, yes, I suppose so."

At last. Take it away, Neil. Get this show on the road.

Mike Ashley
February 2005

FORBIDDEN BRIDES OF THE FACELESS SLAVES IN THE NAMELESS HOUSE OF THE NIGHT OF DREAD DESIRE

Neil Gaiman

I

Somewhere in the night, someone was writing.

II

Her feet scrunched the gravel as she ran, wildly, up the tree-lined drive. Her heart was pounding in her chest, her lungs felt as if they were bursting, heaving breath after breath of the cold night air. Her eyes fixed on the house ahead, the single light in the topmost room drawing her toward it like a moth to a candle flame. Above her, and away in the deep forest behind the house, night-things whooped and skrarked. From the road behind her, she heard something scream, briefly – a small animal, that had been the victim of some beast of prey, she hoped, but could not be certain.

She ran as if the legions of hell were close on her heels, and spared not even a glance behind her until she reached the porch of the old mansion. In the moon's pale light the white pillars seemed skeletal, like the bones of great beast. She clung to the wooden doorframe, gulping air, staring back down the long driveway, as if she were waiting for something, and then she rapped on the door – timorously at first, and then harder. The rapping echoed through the house. She imagined, from the echo that came back to her that, far away, someone was knocking on another door. muffled and dead.

"Please!" she called. "If there's someone here – anyone – please let me in. I beseech you. I implore you." Her voice sounded strange to her ears.

The flickering light in the topmost room faded and vanished, to reappear in successive descending windows. One person, then, with a candle. The light vanished into the depths of the house. She tried to catch her breath. It seemed like an age passed before she heard footsteps on the other side of the door, and spied a chink of candle-light through a crack in the ill-fitting doorframe.

"Hello?" she said.

The voice, when it spoke, was dry as old bone – a desiccated voice, redolent of crackling parchment and musty grave-hangings. "Who calls?" it said. "Who knocks? Who calls, on this night of all nights?"

The voice gave her no comfort. She looked out at the night that enveloped the house, then pulled herself straight, tossed her raven locks, and said, in a voice that, she hoped, betrayed no fear, "'Tis I, Amelia Earnshawe, recently orphaned and now on my way to take up a position as a governess to the two small children – a boy, and a girl – of Lord Falconmere, whose cruel glances I found, during our interview in his London residence, both repellent and fascinating, but whose aquiline face haunts my dreams."

"And what do you do here, then, at this house, on this night of all nights? Falconmere Castle lies a good twenty leagues on from here, on the other side of the moors."

"The coachman – an ill-natured fellow, and a mute, or so he pretended to be, for he formed no words, but made his wishes known only by grunts and gobblings – reined in his team a mile or so back down the road, or so I judge, and then he shewed me by gestures that he would go no further, and that I was to alight. When I did refuse to do so, he pushed me roughly from the carriage to the cold earth, then, whipping the poor horses into a frenzy, he clattered off the way he had come, taking my several bags and my trunk with him. I called after him, but he did not return, and it seemed to me that a deeper darkness stirred in the forest gloom behind me. I saw the light in your window and I . . . I . . ." She was able to keep up her pretence of bravery no longer, and she began to sob.

"Your father," came the voice from the other side of the door. "Would he have been the Honourable Hubert Earnshawe?"

Amelia choked back her tears. "Yes. Yes, he was."

"And you – you say you are an orphan?"

She thought of her father, of his tweed jacket, as the maelstrom seized him, and whipped him onto the rocks and away from her forever.

"He died trying to save my mother's life. They both were drowned."

She heard the dull chunking of a key being turned in a lock, then twin booms as iron bolts were drawn back. "Welcome, then, Miss Amelia Earnshawe. Welcome to your inheritance, in this house without a name. Aye, welcome – on this night, of all nights." The door opened.

The man held a black tallow candle; its flickering flame illuminated his face from below, giving it an unearthly and eldritch appearance. He could have been a Jack O'Lantern, she thought, or a particularly elderly axe-murderer.

He gestured for her to come in.

"Why do you keep saying that?" she asked.

"Why do I keep saying what?"

"*On this night of all nights.* You've said it three times so far."

He simply stared at her for a moment. Then he beckoned again, with one bone-coloured finger. As she entered, he thrust the candle close to her face, and stared at her with eyes that were not truly mad, but were still far from sane. He seemed to be examining her, and eventually he grunted, and nodded. "This way," was all he said.

She followed him down a long corridor. The candle-flame threw fantastic shadows about the two of them, and in its light the grandfather clock and the spindly chairs and table danced and capered. The old man fumbled with his keychain, and unlocked a door in the wall, beneath the stairs. A smell came from the darkness beyond, of must and dust and abandonment.

"Where are we going?" she asked.

He nodded, as if he had not understood her. Then he said, "There are some as are what they are. And there are some as aren't what they seem to be. And there are some as only seem to be what they seem to be. Mark my words, and mark them well, Hubert Earnshawe's daughter. Do you understand me?"

She shook her head. He began to walk, and did not look back. She followed the old man down the stairs.

III

Far away and far along the young man slammed his quill down upon the manuscript, spattering sepia ink across the ream of paper and the polished table.

"It's no good," he said despondently. He dabbed at a circle of ink he had just made on the table with a delicate forefinger, smearing the teak a darker brown, then, unthinking, he rubbed the finger against the bridge of his nose. It left a dark smudge.

"No, sir?" The butler had entered almost soundlessly.

"It's happening again, Toombes. Humour creeps in. Self-parody whispers at the edges of things. I find myself guying literary convention and sending up both myself and the whole scrivening profession."

The butler gazed unblinking at his young master. "I believe humour is very highly thought of in certain circles, sir."

The young man rested his head in his hands, rubbing his forehead pensively with his fingertips. He sighed. "That's not the point, Toombes. I'm trying to create a slice of life here, an accurate representation of the world as it is, and of the human condition. Instead, I find myself indulging, as I write, in schoolboy parody of the foibles of my fellows. I make little jokes." He had smeared ink all over his face. "Very little."

From the forbidden room at the top of the house an eerie, ululating cry rang out, echoing through the house. The young man sighed. "You had better feed Aunt Agatha, Toombes."

"Very good, sir."

The young man picked up the quill pen and idly scratched his ear with the tip.

Behind him, in a bad light, hung the portrait of his great-great grandfather. The painted eyes had been cut out most carefully, long ago, and now real eyes stared out of the canvas face, looking down at the writer. The eyes glinted a tawny gold. If the young man had turned around, and remarked upon them, he might have thought them the golden eyes of some great cat or of some misshapen bird of prey, were such a thing possible. These were not eyes that belonged in any human head. But the young man did not turn. Instead, oblivious, he reached for a new sheet of paper, dipped his quill into the glass inkwell, and commenced to write:

IV

"Aye . . ." said the old man, putting down the black tallow candle on the silent harmonium. "He is our master, and we are his slaves, though we pretend to ourselves that it is not so. But when the time is right, then he demands what he craves, and it is our duty and our compulsion to provide him with . . ." he shuddered, and drew a breath. Then he said only, ". . . with what he needs."

The bat wing curtains shook and fluttered in the glassless casement as the storm drew closer. Amelia clutched the lace handkerchief to her breast, her father's monogram upwards. "And the gate?" she asked, in a whisper.

"It was locked in your ancestor's time, and he charged, before he vanished, that it should always remain so. But there are still tunnels, folk do say, that link the old crypt with the burial grounds."

"And Sir Frederick's first wife . . . ?"

He shook his head, sadly. "Hopelessly insane, and but a mediocre harpsichord player. He put it about that she was dead, and perhaps some believed him."

She repeated his last four words to herself. Then she looked up at him, a new resolve in her eyes.

"And for myself? Now I have learned why I am here, what do you advise me to do?"

He peered around the empty hall. Then he said, urgently, "Fly from here, Miss Earnshawe. Fly while there is still time. Fly for your life, fly for your immortal aagh."

"My what?" she asked, but even as the words escaped her crimson lips the old man crumpled to the floor. A silver crossbow quarrel protruded from the back of his head.

"He is dead," she said, in shocked wonderment.

"Aye," affirmed a cruel voice from the far end of the hall. "But he was dead before this day, girl. And I do think that he has been dead a monstrous long time."

Under her shocked gaze, the body began to putresce. The flesh dripped and rotted and liquefied, the bones revealed crumbled and oozed, until there was nothing but a stinking mass of foetor where once there had been a man.

Amelia squatted beside it, then dipped her fingertip into the noxious stuff. She licked her finger with her tongue, and she made a face. "You would appear to be right, sir, whoever you are," she said. "I would estimate that he has been dead for the better part of a hundred years."

V

"I am endeavouring," said the young man to the chamber-maid, "to write a novel that reflects life as it is, mirrors it down to the finest degree. Yet as I write it turns to dross and gross mockery. What should I do? Eh, Ethel? What should I do?"

"I'm sure I don't know, sir," said the chambermaid, who was pretty and young, and had come to the great house in mysterious circumstances several weeks earlier. She gave the bellows several more squeezes, making the heart of the fire glow an orange-white. "Will that be all?"

"Yes. No. Yes," he said. "You may go, Ethel."

The girl picked up the now-empty coal-scuttle and walked at a steady pace across the drawing room.

The young man made no move to return to his writing-desk; instead he stood in thought by the fireplace, staring at the human skull on the mantel, at the twin crossed swords that hung above it upon the wall. The fire crackled and spat as a lump of coal broke in half.

Footsteps, close behind him. The young man turned. "You?"

The man facing him was almost his double – the white streak in the auburn hair proclaimed them of the same blood, if any proof were needed. The stranger's eyes were dark and wild, his mouth petulant yet oddly firm.

"Yes – I! I, your elder brother, whom you thought dead

these many years. But I am not dead – or perhaps, I am no longer dead – and I have come back – aye, come back from ways that are best left untravelled – to claim what is truly mine."

The young man's eyebrows raised. "I see. Well, obviously all this is yours – if you can prove that you are who you say you are."

"Proof? I need no proof. I claim birth-right, and blood-right – and death-right!" So saying, he pulled both the swords down from above the fireplace, and passed one, hilt first, to his younger brother. "Now guard you, my brother – and may the best man win."

Steel flashed in the firelight and kissed and clashed and kissed again in an intricate dance of thrust and parry. At times it seemed no more than a dainty minuet, or a courtly and deliberate ritual, while at other times it seemed pure savagery, a wildness that moved faster than the eye could easily follow. Around and around the room they went, and up the steps to the mezzanine, and down the steps to the main hall. They swung from drapes and from chandeliers. They leapt up on tables and down again.

The older brother obviously was more experienced, and, perhaps, was a better swordsman, but the younger man was fresher and he fought like a man possessed, forcing his opponent back and back and back to the roaring fire itself. The older brother reached out with his left hand and grasped the poker. He swung it wildly at the younger, who ducked, and, in one elegant motion, ran his brother through.

"I am done for. I am a dead man."

The younger brother nodded his ink-stained face.

"Perhaps it is better this way. Truly, I did not want the house, or the lands. All I wanted, I think, was peace." He lay there, bleeding crimson onto the grey flagstone. "Brother? Take my hand."

The young man knelt, and clasped a hand that already, it seemed to him, was becoming cold.

"Before I go into that night that none can follow, there are things I must tell you. Firstly, with my death, I truly believe the curse is lifted from our line. The second . . ." His breath now came in a bubbling wheeze, and he was having difficulty speaking. "The second . . . is . . . the . . . the thing in the abyss . . . beware the cellars . . . the rats . . . the – *it follows!*"

And with this his head lolled on the stone, and his eyes rolled back and saw nothing, ever again.

Outside the house, the raven cawed thrice. Inside, strange music had begun to skirl up from the crypt, signifying that, for some, the wake had already started.

The younger brother, once more, he hoped, the rightful possessor of his title, picked up a bell and rang for a servant. Toombes the butler was there in the doorway before the last ring had died away.

"Remove this," said the young man. "But treat it well. He died to redeem himself. Perhaps to redeem us both."

Toombes said nothing, merely nodded to show that he had understood.

The young man walked out of the drawing room. He entered the Hall of Mirrors – a hall from which all the mirrors had carefully been removed, leaving irregularly-shaped patches on the paneled walls, and, believing himself alone, he began to muse aloud.

"This is precisely what I was talking about," he said. "Had such a thing happened in one of my tales – and such things happen all the time – I would have felt myself constrained to guy it unmercifully." He slammed a fist against a wall, where once a hexagonal mirror had hung. "What is wrong with me? Wherefore this flaw?"

Strange scuttling things gibbered and cheetled in the black drapes at the end of the room, and high in the gloomy oak beams, and behind the wainscoting, but they made no answer. He had expected none.

He walked up the grand staircase, and along a darkened hall, to enter his study. Someone, he suspected, had been tampering with his papers. He suspected that he would find out who later that evening, after the Gathering.

He sat down at his desk, dipped his quill pen once more, and continued to write.

VI

Outside the room the ghoul-lords howled with frustration and hunger, and they threw themselves against the door in their ravenous fury, but the locks were stout, and Amelia had every hope that they would hold.

What had the wood-cutter said to her? His words came back to her then, in her time of need, as if he were standing close to her, his manly frame mere inches from her feminine curves, the very scent of his honest labouring body surrounding her like the headiest perfume, and she heard his words as if he were, that moment, whispering them in her ear. "I was not always in the state you see me in now, lassie," he had told her. "Once I had another name, and a destiny unconnected to the hewing of cords of firewood from fallen trees. But know you this – in the escritoire, there is a secret compartment, or so my great uncle claimed, when he was in his cups . . ."

The escritoire! Of course!

She rushed to the old writing desk. At first she could find no trace of a secret compartment. She pulled out the drawers, one after another, and then perceived that one of them was much shorter than the rest, which seeing she forced her white hand into the space where the drawer had been, and found, at the back, a button. Frantically, she pressed it. Something opened, and she put her hand on a tightly rolled paper scroll.

Amelia withdrew her hand. The scroll was tied with a dusty black ribbon, and with fumbling fingers she untied the knot, and opened the paper. Then she read, trying to make sense of the antiquated handwriting, of the ancient words. As she did so, a ghastly pallor suffused her handsome face, and even her violet eyes seemed clouded and distracted.

The knockings and the scratchings redoubled. In but a short time they would burst through, she had no doubt. No door could hold them forever. They would burst through, and she would be their prey. Unless, unless . . .

"Stop!" she called, her voice trembling. "I abjure you, every one of you, and thee most of all, oh Prince of Carrion. In the name of the ancient compact, between thy people and mine."

The sounds stopped. It seemed to the girl that there was shock in that silence Finally, a cracked voice said, "The compact?" and a dozen voices, as ghastly again, whispered "The compact," in a susurrus of unearthly sound.

"Aye!" called Amelia Earnshawe, her voice no longer unsteady. "The compact."

For the scroll, the long-hidden scroll, had been the compact – the dread agreement between the Lords of the House, and the denizens of the crypt in ages past. It had described and enumerated the nightmarish rituals that had chained them one to another over the centuries – rituals of blood, and of salt, and more.

"If you have read the compact," said a deep voice from beyond the door, "then you know what we need, Hubert Earnshawe's daughter."

"Brides," she said, simply.

"The brides!" came the whisper from beyond the door, and it redoubled and resounded until it seemed to her that the very house itself throbbed and echoed to the beat of those words – two syllables invested with longing, and with love, and with hunger.

Amelia bit her lip. "Aye. The brides. I will bring thee brides. I shall bring brides for all."

She spoke quietly, but they heard her, for there was only silence, a deep and velvet silence, on the other side of the door.

And then one ghoul-voice hissed, "Yes, and do you think we could get her to throw in a side-order of those little bread-roll things?"

VII

Hot tears stung the young man's eyes. He pushed the papers from him, and flung the quill pen across the room. It spattered its inky load over the bust of his great-great-great grandfather, the brown ink soiling the patient white marble. The occupant of the bust, a large and mournful raven, startled, nearly fell off, and only kept its place by dint of flapping its wings, several times. It turned, then, in an awkward step and hop, to stare with one black bead eye at the young man.

"Oh, this is intolerable!" exclaimed the young man. He was pale and trembling. "I cannot do it, and I shall never do it. I swear now, by . . ." and he hesitated, casting his mind around for a suitable curse from the extensive family archives.

The raven looked unimpressed. "Before you start cursing, and probably dragging peacefully dead and respectable ancestors back from their well-earned graves, just answer me one question." The voice of the bird was like stone striking against stone.

The young man said nothing, at first. It is not unknown for ravens to talk, but this one had not done so before, and he had not been expecting it to. "Certainly. Ask your question."

The raven tipped its head onto one side. "Do you *like* writing that stuff?"

"Like?"

"That life-as-it-is-stuff you do. I've looked over your shoulder sometimes. I've even read a little here and there. Do you enjoy writing it?"

The young man looked down at the bird. "It's literature," he explained, as if to a child. "Real literature. Real life. The real world. It's an artist's job to show people the world they live in. We hold up mirrors."

Outside the room lightning clove the sky. The young man glanced out of the window: a jagged streak of blinding fire created warped and ominous silhouettes from the bony trees and the ruined abbey on the hill.

The raven cleared its throat.

"I said, do you enjoy it?"

The young man looked at the bird, then he looked away and, wordlessly, he shook his head.

"That's why you keep trying to pull it apart," said the bird. "It's not the satirist in you that makes you lampoon the commonplace and the humdrum. Merely boredom with the way things are. D'you see?" It paused to preen a stray wingfeather back into place with its beak. Then it looked up at him once more. "Have you ever thought of writing fantasy?" it asked.

The young man laughed. "Fantasy? Listen, I write literature. Fantasy isn't life. Esoteric dreams, written by a minority for a minority, it's –"

"What you'd be writing if you knew what was good for you."

"I'm a classicist," said the young man. He reached out his hand to a shelf of the classics – *Udolpho, The Castle of Otranto, The Saragossa Manuscript, The Monk* and the rest of them. "It's literature."

"Nevermore," said the raven. It was the last word the young man ever heard it speak. It hopped from the bust, spread its wings and glided out of the study door into the waiting darkness.

The young man shivered. He rolled the stock themes of fantasy over in his mind: cars and stockbrokers and commuters, housewives and police, agony columns and commercials for soap, income tax and cheap restaurants, magazines and credit cards and streetlights and computers . . .

"It is escapism, true," he said, aloud. "But is not the highest impulse in mankind the urge towards freedom, the drive to escape?"

The young man returned to his desk, and he gathered together the pages of his unfinished novel, and dropped them, unceremoniously, in the bottom drawer, amongst the yellowing maps and cryptic testaments and the documents signed in blood. The dust, disturbed, made him cough.

He took up a fresh quill; sliced at its tip with his pen-knife. In five deft strokes and cuts he had a pen. He dipped the tip of it into the glass inkwell. Once more he began to write:

VIII

Amelia Earnshawe placed the slices of wholewheat bread into the toaster and pushed it down. She set the timer to dark brown, just as George liked it. Amelia preferred her toast barely singed. She liked white bread, as well, even if it didn't have the vitamins. She hadn't eaten white bread for a decade now.

At the breakfast table, George read his paper. He did not look up. He never looked up.

I hate him, she thought, and simply putting the emotion into words surprised her. She said it again in her head. *I hate him.* It was like a song. *I hate him for his toast, and for his bald head, and for the way he chases the office crumpet – girls barely out of school who laugh at him behind his back, and for the way he ignores me whenever he doesn't want to be bothered with me, and for the way he says "What, love?" when I ask him a simple question, as if he's long ago forgotten my name. As if he's forgotten that I even have a name.*

"Scrambled or boiled?" she said aloud.

"What, love?"

George Earnshawe regarded his wife with fond affection, and would have found her hatred of him astonishing. He thought of her in the same way, and with the same emotions, that he thought of anything which had been in the house for ten years and still worked well. The television, for example. Or the lawnmower. He thought it was love.

"You know, *we* ought to go on one of those marches," he said, tapping the newspaper's editorial. "Show we're committed. Eh, love?"

The toaster made a noise to show that it was done. Only one dark brown slice had popped up. She took a knife and fished out the torn second slice with it. The toaster had been a wedding present from her Uncle John. Soon she'd have to buy another, or start cooking toast under the grill, the way her mother had done.

"George? Do you want your eggs scrambled or boiled?" she asked, very quietly, and there was something in her voice that made him look up.

"Any way you like it, love," he said amiably, and could not for the life of him, as he told everyone in the office later that morning, understand why she simply stood there holding her slice of toast, or why she started to cry.

IX

The quill pen went *scritch scritch* across the paper, and the young man was engrossed in what he was doing. His face was strangely content, and a smile flickered between his eyes and his lips.

He was rapt.

Things scratched and scuttled in the wainscot but he hardly heard them.

High in her attic room Aunt Agatha howled and yowled and rattled her chains. A weird cachinnation came from the ruined abbey: it rent the night air, ascending into a peal of manic glee. In the dark woods beyond the great house, shapeless figures shuffled and loped, and raven-locked young women fled from them in fear.

"Swear!" said Toombes the butler, down in the butler's pantry, to the brave girl who was passing herself off as chambermaid. "Swear to me, Ethel, on your life, that you'll never reveal a word of what I tell you to a living soul . . ."

There were faces at the windows and words written in blood; deep in the crypt a lonely ghoul crunched on something that might once have been alive; forked lightning slashed the ebony night; the faceless were walking; all was right with the world.

THE BLUE MAGNOLIA

Tony Ballantyne

Bogart stands before the bar, Hepburn is serving drinks. Cary Grant sits in a chair nearby.

"You've got to choose," says Grant, his eyes hard.

"I can't! Not now!" says Hepburn, shaking her head in despair. Bogart lifts the shot glass to his lips and knocks his whisky back in one. You can tell by his stance that he resigned himself to this moment long ago. He pulls back his sleeve as if to look at his watch, but his eyes never leave Hepburn's. Hepburn's dark, wide eyes, filling with tears.

"Hell. Is that the time?" he murmurs. "I've got to catch my plane."

He turns to leave. Hepburn calls after him.

"No! Wait! We must . . ."

Bogart stops at the door, by the hatstand.

"Damn. Can't find my hat."

We can see it hanging there next to him.

"We'll mail it," says Grant. He's looking at the floor. Ashamed.

"Don't go like this! I . . . I can explain!" says Hepburn.

"No need. Why explain things to a man who's not there?" He looks into the distance and speaks reflectively.

"I guess a man who lives his life alone is never really a part of the world."

He closes the door gently as he leaves. Close up on the hat, Hepburn's gift to him in happier times, from their trip to Majorca. The music swells in the background.

Recognise it? It's a scene from *The Blue Magnolia*. Once upon a time it was a classic film. And I mean a real classic, one of the top ten all-time greatest, not one of these modern hype-driven instant classic features that leave you feeling you've spent the last two hours sitting in a bath of electric jelly watching a strobe light in an echo chamber.

No. A Classic with a capital "C".

It can't be called that now, of course. Now it's just a cheap piece of tawdry entertainment, something designed to appeal to the lowest common denominator as any modern 3D flick. And whose fault is that?

I write this as a confession. I must hold up my hand and accept the blame. I destroyed *The Blue Magnolia*.

The fault was mine.

Hepburn is laughing as she hands Bogart the hat.

"Think of me when you wear it," she says. He puts it on and adjusts to a slight tilt. For the first time, his face splits into a smile and Hepburn flings her arms around him in delight. Laughing they walk through the hot dusty streets of Majorca.

Suzie, the salesperson, was wearing a smart red leather suit that creaked and squeaked as the zoom train rocked back and forth in its tube. She was watching *The Blue Magnolia* with me, an attentive smile on her face as the characters moved through their roles on the carpeted back of the seats before us. I'd called the shop from the office, later that day and they had retroactively arranged for her to board the train with me as I set out for work that morning. Now she turned to face me and pushed a strand of blonde hair away from her face.

"I've never seen this before. It's a good film."

Her leather suit creaked as she spoke.

"A classic," I said. "So, can you help me?"

"No problem. You don't even need one of the expensive models. An entry-level machine should meet your needs. I've got one here."

Suzie pulled a blue crackly box from the pocket of her red leather jacket. I looked at it in astonishment.

"Is that a time machine?" I whispered.

"After a fashion," she replied. "You press the button and think about what you want to be until the light comes on."

The train jolted and she swayed closer to me for a moment. She smelt of perfume and leather.

I reached across and took the machine carefully in my hand. Its touch on my hand was like the feel of a fizzy drink in the mouth. I made to press the button and she held out one hand.

"Payment first," she said. "Do you permit withdrawal of the funds from your account?"

"I do," I replied, and then pressed the button and thought about what I wanted to be. A red light came on.

"But nothing's happened!" I said. All around me was the same soft cream leather of the swaying zoom tube, the same early morning commuters, the same flicker of movement behind the windows. Suzie gave a delightful smile.

"Don't worry about it," she said. "Nobody ever remembers the trip."

It worked: I saw the proof on channel 36B that night. I was just having a drink to congratulate myself when the phone went. My stomach sank when I heard the voice at the other end.

"Oh. Anderson. It's you," I said.

Anderson's voice was full of easy enthusiasm

"Hey, Calverley, I saw you! What a brilliant idea!"

"I don't know what you mean," I lied.

"Oh, don't be so modest! Channel 36B. *The Blue Magnolia*. The back of the bar in the classic "hat" scene. You were just sitting there taking a drink. It was brilliant. Didn't I say it was brilliant, dear?"

"You did, dear," said a voice in the background. I shuddered as I recognised the tones of Emerald Rainbow, Anderson's wife. I gave a cautious reply.

"I'm pleased you liked it, Anderson."

"How did you think of it?" he said, a little too quickly.

"Well . . ." I began, but he interrupted me. Anderson never gives you time to answer his questions.

"Never mind. We think it's such a good idea we're going to join you. Me and Emerald Rainbow."

"No! Anderson, it's a quiet bar. The essence of that scene is we are all, as human beings, alone. You join me at that table, you'll crowd it, you'll ruin the effect."

There was a pause. I heard Anderson and Emerald Rainbow whispering together. They seemed to reach a conclusion. Anderson came back on the line.

"You know, Calverley, Emerald thinks you have a point. We'll have to think about this, but quickly. We've already booked a time machine for tomorrow morning. They're showing *The Blue Magnolia* tomorrow at thirty-five hours. Watch it! We'll be there."

"Anderson. No, wait!"

There was a note of panic in my voice, but it was too late. Anderson had already hung up. I slumped forward in my chair, my head in my hands at the enormity of what I'd done. Nobody is more convinced of Anderson's talent than Anderson. He thinks he has discerning taste in movies. Odd that it never expresses itself until he's read the reviews.

The next night I was in the entertainment tank half an hour before the movie. Just me, half a bottle of Irish whiskey, a block of feta cheese, some black olives and a terrible sense of foreboding. I ate the cheese and spat the olive stones into a little glass dish that danced in the reflected flicker of the projectors. The film started at thirty-five. I was tense, sipping at the whisky and refilling my glass. Sipping and refilling. The movie progressed normally and I relaxed. Maybe Anderson had changed his mind. His fads seldom lasted. Maybe it would be okay.

I should have known better.

The movie came to the Hat scene. Bogart and Hepburn were standing at the bar, gazing at each other. Cary Grant speaks softly from his chair.

"You've got to choose."

The camera pans slowly around the room, taking in Grant, Hepburn and Bogart. If you look carefully you can see me sitting alone at a table in the background, sipping whisky and looking kind of world weary. The camera pans back to Grant and then across to Anderson and his wife. Anderson is drinking a cocktail with umbrellas in it. Both of them are grinning at the camera.

The phone started ringing. My eyes still glued to the screen, I snatched up the receiver in anger. There could be no doubt who it was.

"Anderson!" I shouted.

"Can you see us? There, on the table in the middle! Do you see us? Subtle, don't you think?"

"Subtle? Anderson, you . . . you moron!"

Thinking back, this was unfair. It actually was quite subtle for Anderson. There was a pause. When he spoke again he sounded hurt and indignant.

"You're just jealous. Emerald Rainbow thought the cocktail was a great touch." Emerald Rainbow would. "Don't you think so? It had blue curacao in it."

"Because the film is called *The Blue Magnolia!*" called Emerald Rainbow in the background.

I found myself speechless. My mouth moved silently as Anderson resumed speaking.

"They're showing it again tomorrow on 5B at twenty-six hours. Look out for us."

He hung up before I could speak. The door announced there was someone outside. I answered it to find Suzie, the woman from Timex-Swatch standing there, holding out the blue crackly box.

"You phoned me, fifteen minutes from now," she explained. "You know how it works, don't you?"

"Yes. You showed me this afternoon."

"I haven't got there yet," she said, and gave a little grimace. "We're rushed off our feet at the moment."

"Oh? I would have thought you had all the time you needed," I said absently, taking the box from her.

I pressed the button and concentrated until the red light came on.

"Okay?" said Suzie. "All done?"

"Why can I never remember going back?" I said.

"You don't actually go back in time," said Suzie. "You just

move across to another reality where what you thought about actually took place. Actual time travel costs a lot more."

I looked confused. Suzie straightened herself and half closed her eyes as she recited her sales pitch.

"Timex-Swatch offer a range of products tailored to meet the demanding lifestyle of the modern consumer. We have determined that model X46 best meets your needs. This model makes use of the quantum uncertainty model to provide a range of universe choices appropriate to your situation."

I shook my head, still confused.

Suzie faltered for a moment. She closed her eyes fully, no doubt trying to recall a lecture from her induction course.

"Well, it's like this: Schrodinger's Cat shows that situations can arise where you have a cat that is both alive and dead at the same time. Obviously, that can't happen: it doesn't make sense. It is far more probable that the Universe splits in two every time an event with multiple outcomes is about to occur."

"Are you sure?" I said, frowning. It didn't sound very likely to me.

"Oh yes," she said, nodding seriously. "I mean, it stands to reason. It's far more likely that there are millions of new Universes forming every second than for a cat not to exist until you look at it. That's the whole basis of time travel."

I didn't understand this, and she knew it. She smiled and shrugged her shoulders with a delicious creak of red leather.

"Got to go. See you tomorrow."

"Okay. Bye," I said. I watched as she walked away around the corner and then the thought occurred to me.

Tomorrow? Surely she meant this afternoon?

The classic Hat scene. The eternal triangle. A woman must choose between two good men, and she must choose the wrong man. They all know it. They all feel sympathy for Bogart, who must allow his duty to come before his personal feelings.

"You've got to choose."

Hepburn never acted so well as in that scene. Those dark, confused eyes. The panic and the pain. Bogart is as world-weary and knowing as only he can be. I'm sitting at my table drinking my Jack Daniels. A drunk in a bar, oblivious to the scene around him. Grant is wearing the look of a man who has won and wishes he hadn't. A pyrrhic victory. A bamboo screen stands in front of a table, cutting two imbeciles off from view. My doing.

Bogart stands by the door. By the hatstand.

"Hell. I can't find my hat."

"It's hanging by the door," calls a voice from behind the screen.

"Anderson!" You can see the surprise on my face, there on the screen. Bogart is a true professional. He ignores the voice. Grant grits his teeth.

"We'll mail it," he says.

"There's no need," says the voice from behind the screen. "It's right next to him. It's the nice brown one she bought him in Majorca, remember? It's there by my wife's red beret."

The phone started ringing. I was too shocked to answer it. Bogart had just taken his hat and was walking out of the door, a dazed expression on his face. The scene was ruined. The film was ruined. Anderson would pay for this.

Every movie ever made is shown every day. Every song recorded, every painting, every book is displayed in some way. The entertainment corporations make sure that they are pumped into entertainment tanks in strict rotation every twenty-four hours. All of them. From the sublime to the ridiculous, the culture of the last twenty centuries is constantly broadcast to the world. Are we any richer for the experience?

No. Not when morons such as Anderson call me in the middle of the night and say: "Did you like it? I think it gives the scene more . . . poignancy."

"Like it?" I shouted back. "You've ruined the whole scene. You've destroyed the meaning of the film."

"I improved it. It needs a happy ending."

"What?" I squeaked. I took a few deep breaths to allow my voice to return to normal and then began, very patiently, to explain.

"Anderson. The whole point of the film is that sometimes life is hard. Sometimes the right decision to make is the one that makes us unhappy, but we go ahead and make it anyway because it's just that. The right decision. The film lays out the best and the worst of the human condition in ninety glorious minutes. The ending is supposed to be unhappy."

"Oh no," said Anderson cheerfully. "You always need a happy ending."

"Anderson!" I shouted. "You arrogant moron! What gives you the right to change the original concept?"

"Oh come on," said Anderson. "It is the duty of every modern artist to improve on the past. Only by constant revision can a work of art eventually achieve perfection. Do you think you are the first person to use a time machine? They give us the opportunity to realise perfection even after the artist's death. To realise perfection with the benefit of modern enlightened viewpoints."

"Anderson. What the hell are you talking about?"

"I'm going back again to complete my reconstruction of *The Blue Magnolia*. Emerald Rainbow will be with me."

"Listen . . ." I shouted, but it was too late. He'd hung up. I held my head in my hands. Suzie rubbed my shoulders sympathetically. She had been sitting eating peanuts on my sofa for over an hour now, time machine at the ready.

The Blue Magnolia showed on channel 17W at forty-six. It was unbelievable.

"You've got to choose." Hepburn's dark eyes, full of tears. The camera begins to pan . . .

Grant. Hepburn. Bogart. Me. Bamboo screen hiding two buffoons. Bogart by the door.

"Hell. I can't find my hat."

"It's – Gmmph." That was me thumping Anderson, just out of shot.

"We'll mail it." Cary Grant, of course.

"Don't go like this. I . . . I can explain."

Hepburn's brown eyes are filled with tears of despair. She looks so lost, so unsure. She's probably wondering why

Anderson's pet Labrador has just walked across the room, wagging its tail.

"No need," says Bogart, kicking at the dog. "Why explain things to a man who's not there?" There is a noise off camera as Emerald Rainbow hits me.

"I guess a man who lives his life alone is never really a part of the world," says Bogart. Anderson appears in the shot.

"Me and the wife are going by the airport, Mr Bogart," he says. "We'll give you a lift."

"There's no need," says Bogart.

"That's okay, it's not a problem," smiles Emerald Rainbow.

"Yes, it is," says Bogart through gritted teeth.

"Just ignore him," says Anderson. "He's bound to be in a bad mood, considering."

"I am not in a fucking bad mood," shouts Bogart. He stomps out of the room. Anderson and Emerald Rainbow follow him.

You can see me sitting at a table crying softly to myself when Anderson reappears. He grins at the room sheepishly.

"I just came to get the hat," he explains. "He's forgotten it again."

Me and Anderson slugged it out for a few more days, but my heart wasn't in it. The film was ruined and, no matter what I tried, it couldn't be fixed. It's been moved to the back of the schedules, to the most distant channels. No one wants to know any more.

Anderson insists he's not to blame, that these things happen all the time. He says everything is in a constant state of flux since the invention of the reality re-integrators. (I think he means the time machines.) All I understand is that I'm trapped in a timeline where *The Blue Magnolia* is ruined. Suzie tells me not to despair, there is a near infinite number of timelines where the film goes on as normal. Then again, I haven't the money to reach them, unfortunately.

Still, at least I get to see Suzie now, which is some consolation.

And as for Anderson, well. Have you seen *Star Wars*? You

know that bit at the end when they fly down the trench on the Death Star? If you look closely you can see my car driving along the bottom. If you look very closely you might be able to see Anderson running along in front of it.

COLQUITT'S HIGH-ENERGY TROUSERS

Steven Pirie

Dean Withers tossed darts at Colquitt's photograph pinned to the back of his office door. Colquitt did things with quarks. Unwholesome things, the dean said; things that left a ring of scum around the high-energy building's bathtub and caused the bristles of the dean's toilet brush to glow sunset pink. He'd done odd, entropic things to the dean's best rubber duck so that now it floated lop-sided in the water. He'd forced relativistic effects upon the dean's slippers until the dean could only walk in circles in them. Now, the rumour was that Colquitt's high-energy trousers were an offence to common decency.

The dean aimed. He was deadly with a dart where Colquitt's picture was concerned. He hardly ever spiked Maureen's features smiling pictorially at Colquitt's side.

Tap . . . tap. "There was, um, something you wanted, Dean Withers?"

"Ah, Colquitt." The dean fought the urge to fling the last of his darts at the lithe figure framed by the doorway. Colquitt's teeth were dangerously straight, and his manly jaw far too jutting for the dean's comfort. "Come in. Sit, sit."

The dean drew a calming breath against the unsettling effect of *the trousers*. Sparks leapt from Colquitt's inside leg. The hair on the dean's scalp lifted and fell. Trickles of current electrified his fillings. The air smelled of fire and soot and singed fabric. "I see you've not managed to remove the trousers, Mr Colquitt."

Colquitt coughed. "No, Dean."

The dean leaned forward across his desk and wagged an accusing finger. "There have been complaints, Mr Colquitt. Your trousers are interfering with Miss Rogers' attempts at radio astronomy. Mr Ling keeps thinking he's discovered new gamma ray bursts every time you pass his window. You're doing unpleasant things to Professor Hedge's pacemaker."

"I'm trying all I can to control my trousers, sir."

"Do you have a theory yet as to what happened to them?"

Colquitt toyed with his perfect hair. "I think there was a fault with the particle accelerator. Mrs Hopkins believes we're drawing dark energy from a fifth dimension. She thinks we've entangled the protons of the trousers' fabric with some exotic matter."

The dean glanced sharply to the bulge in the pocket of his overcoat hung upon its peg below Maureen and Colquitt's dart-riddled photograph. He nodded, though nobody truly understands such a thing as quantum entanglement. The dean wondered what the denizens of other dimensions would think of having Mr Colquitt's legs thrust upon them. He'd seen Colquitt's legs at the university sports day. As far as he could tell, they were not *nice* legs, even in four dimensions. It was a mystery why the typing pool girls talked so fondly of them.

And drawing off the other dimension's energy would likely make their light bulbs flicker and annoy them. It was the stuff of wars.

"And you've tried simply removing the trousers?"

"Mrs Carson tried to pull them off." Colquitt looked uncomfortable. "She's, um, recovering, Dean, and should walk again, given time. Mr Beecham suggested poking them with a copper earthing rod, and I believe I'm still providing power to the west wing. Personally, I think we should . . ."

Colquitt's words trailed away. Dean Withers frowned. Being dean, he had dealt a lot with trailing words in his time. He knew that following such trails was apt to lead to an unhappy end. Usually, extra funding was involved – the purchase of special, intrinsically safe hammers for the geologists, or lead safety underwear for the hot-plasma scientists, or trips to exotic locations where the science often seemed secondary to the investigation of women in grass skirts or of olive-skinned, thick-muscled men named Carlos.

"Go on," said the dean, slowly.

"Well, Dean, it seems to me that if my trousers really are in quantum entanglement with matter from other dimensions, then we have a golden opportunity to test all manner of current theories – teleportation, faster-than-light communication, time travel, quantum gravity."

The dean was not convinced. "You think your trousers may reveal such mysteries?"

Colquitt crossed his legs and the dean's table lamp dimmed. "I've learned not to underestimate high-energy trousers, Dean. They're, um, very pinching in, um, tender places. Besides, it's hard to walk when one has the energy of the sun in one's pants."

"Then we should proceed at once, Colquitt."

"Indeed, sir." Colquitt loosened his collar. "I have pressing biological needs to get the damned things off as soon as possible, Dean. Today, if we may."

The dean grinned. Of course, *proceed at once* could be such a relative term should he want it to be. "It might take weeks, Colquitt."

"But I've a date with Maureen, tonight. She'll not like her candlelit dinner spoiled by the wattage from my trousers, sir."

"No, Colquitt, Maureen won't." The dean sighed. His thoughts wandered amongst clandestine, candlelit encounters, heady with the hint of indiscretion and the thrill that would surely follow the pudding course. He'd heard Maureen did a fine "Death by Chocolate". And that she was very inventive with whipped cream. "Very well, in the morning, then. I shall instruct Mrs Hopkins to cancel all reservations of the accelerator and we shall see what we can do about removing your trousers."

The following morning, Colquitt was strapped to a makeshift target at the far end of the particle accelerator tunnel. Using the words *strap* and *target* in conjunction with *Colquitt* brightened the dean's mood considerably.

"The trousers seem particularly active this morning, Mrs Hopkins," said the dean, watching as Mr Colquitt's trousers flared in the monitor upon the high-energy control panel. On a second monitor, lines traced the spiralling dance of subatomic debris flung from the hotter regions around Colquitt's thighs. A nearby Geiger counter counted a frenzy of Geigers.

Mrs Hopkins spun her chair around to face the dean. "Aye, and the funny thing is we've not switched on the beam yet, Dean Withers. Mr Colquitt's trousers appear to be disobeying the laws of cause and effect. They're decaying before their time."

The dean often felt like that, decaying before his time. It was a thankless task being dean of the high-energy physics department. People were distrustful of folk who claimed to spend their day delving in ten dimensions. He was never invited to the best parties. Unlike Rogers of Chemistry who could synthesise Viagra from a couple of teabags and half a doughnut; or Evans of Biology who had a full set of *Joy of Sex* videos; or even Morris of Geology who could chip ice cubes into rude shapes with his trusty hammer. Physics was so often the study of the unfeasibly small or the unimaginably large, and folk who held parties with Viagra, sex videos, and rude ice cubes weren't interested in that sort of thing. Only Colquitt went to those kinds of parties, because things *happened* to Colquitt; interesting things like high-energy trousers.

The dean smiled. "Are you saying there's even more damage to be done if we turn the beam on?"

Mrs Hopkins hesitated. "Surely not, Dean? It might be hard to control the collisions. We could strip off Mr Colquitt's electrons. We could turn him into a Bose-Einstein condensate, or a soup of Buckminsterfullerines, or even into a singularity."

"I want some of your pointiest protons turning on right away, Hopkins. There's science to be done." The dean rubbed his hands together. "And get some more magnets around Colquitt's pants. I want that beam focussed."

"Is that ethical, Dean?"

"Don't talk to me of ethics, Hopkins. The bugger ruined my slippers."

Soon, Colquitt's face was twisted upon the monitor screen. His voice wavered over the loudspeaker. "I, um, think the trousers are unravelling, Dean. And I can't feel my legs. Or rather, I can."

The dean waved a hand that Mrs Hopkins should turn the power knob further. "Talk sense, Colquitt," he said. "What do you mean you can't but you can?"

"I think my legs are in two places at once, Dean, and neither of them starts at my bum. I think I'm being interfered with. It feels like there're a couple of Higgs bosons in my pocket. I think my nether regions are experiencing wave-particle duality on a macroscopic scale."

This subject unsettled the dean. The girls in the typing pool had talked admiringly of Colquitt's nether regions just that morning and the dean had felt insecure. No one ever mentioned *his* regions. Certainly not in the way the typing pool girls did Colquitt's. The dean's were regions of unexplored country. The only woman ever to stand at his frontier was Maureen, and she did so only until Colquitt came by with his teeth and jaw and swagger and style and *interesting* things. Whisked away before his hormones, she'd been, and the dean had sworn . . . what . . . vengeance? Science? A tinkering with the particle accelerator that might render *somebody* into a person with high-energy trousers?

"We're going up to full power, Mr Colquitt," said the dean. "Perhaps you should keep a tight hold on your bosons."

Smoke billowed from Colquitt's trousers. Mrs Hopkins rose from her seat as if to protest, her mouth open, her hands covering her ears as the whine of the accelerator grew. The dean shook a fist at the monitor. He felt the flush of madness upon his cheeks. "That'll teach him," he raged. "That'll teach the womaniser to run off with my Maureen."

It was a quiet morn, the following day, as the dean sat pensive at his desk. The high-energy trousers had been found in Aberdeen. Seven hundred and three miles, they'd flown; a

streak of fire that had outshone the sun. No one knew how far
Colquitt had gone.

Tap . . . tap.

"Yes, Mrs Hopkins?"

"I thought you might like to know they've found one of Mr
Colquitt's shoes, Dean."

"Oh?"

"In Norway."

"Ah."

"And Mr Pike the builder thinks he can repair the high-
energy building's roof, though he's refusing to go anywhere
near the black hole that's fizzing about in the accelerator
tunnel."

The dean shuddered. Had he really allowed his emotions to
unleash such retribution upon Colquitt? Surely such a thing
was beyond a cold, analytical, scientific mind? Now, bathed by
the bright, morning sunlight that angled through the office
windows, the dean wasn't even sure if Colquitt was the
problem. *He*, Dean Withers, was no different. A large part
of the plan was that *he*, Dean Withers, *would* be different with
Colquitt out of the way. And thus far Maureen had not swung
open the door and leapt naked into his arms. Thus far the
typing pool girls had not swooned as he'd passed by. All *they*
talked about was the missing Colquitt, squirming in their seats
as if fond reminiscence of his libido alone were potent enough
to transcend black holes, as if he could give them multiple
orgasms even from other universes.

"And the gravity waves?"

Mrs Hopkins shook her head. "Mr Ling has nailed down
everything that moves, but the west wing of the university is
still edging toward the east wing at three inches per hour. He
thinks Chemistry and Earth Sciences will collide in days."

"Won't the buildings collapse before then?"

"Time and space are warping, Dean, and Mr Ling thinks
the world itself will probably collapse before the west wing.
The university survived Hitler's best efforts, so Mr Ling
reckons it will stand an amble across the cloisters."

The dean shuddered once more. Maureen was in Earth

Sciences – as tender a goddess as ever chipped away at an igneous intrusion – what would she do if the louts of Chemistry were forced upon her? And who could know that the world was such a fragile thing?

"Then I've ruined everything," said the dean. He stood and took his coat from the peg behind the door. Colquitt's face smiled back at him under its barrage of darts. The dean felt for the bulge in his coat pocket. "There's something I must do, Mrs Hopkins. I may be some time in doing it."

The black hole swirled. It was grey, in reality, because contrary to the dean's prior beliefs stuff did escape from its event horizon. It wouldn't be noticed, otherwise, and a fundamental law of the universe is that the things in it *want* to be noticed. It fizzled and crackled as he neared its rim. The gravity gradient between the front and back of his head was bringing on an awful headache. The dean cupped his hands about his mouth. "Colquitt?" he called into the singularity's depths.

He listened.

Colquitt's reply came faint and stretched. "Dean? Is that you?"

"It's poor science to disappear up one's own black hole, Colquitt."

"Yes, Dean, though I think perhaps you had something to do with it."

"Oh?"

"Your screaming of Maureen's name as I slipped beyond made me wonder."

"Ah."

"Still, never mind, sir, it was fun science whilst it lasted."

The dean sighed. Even stuffing the bastard into a black hole didn't ruffle him. And the shame was that so much else was connected – the gravitating of the various university wings, for example. It was as if duelling a rival, in particle physics, was apt to take along the bloke who counted out the paces before the turn and fire, too. And the podium upon which he stood. And the forest clearing, and half the castle wall beyond, and . . . ultimately, the world.

"Then I suppose I should get you out of there, Mr Colquitt," said the Dean.

"Surely that's impossible, Dean?"

The dean patted the bulge in his coat pocket. He reached in and removed a jam jar. A fog swirled within its glass. "Not when I have the protons you were entangled with."

"Um, teleportation, sir?"

"Shut up, Mr Colquitt, and brace yourself."

The west wing didn't collide with the east wing. Even the universe couldn't befriend chemist and geologist. Without Colquitt leaching dark energy from the fifth dimension, the black hole in the basement fizzled out. Maureen, it turned out, was not unresponsive to the odd *playful* threesome now and then, and so the dean's hatred of Colquitt diminished, particularly when Colquitt presented him with a new pair of non-relativistic slippers. Sadly, the rubber duck imploded before help could arrive.

But it was on the day the dean overheard the typing pool girls talking fondly about *his* nether regions that he realised fully the subtle changes that had taken place when matter and energy were flinging about near the black hole. He had, of course, wondered at his newly found confidence, particularly where the fairer sex' was concerned. Rumours about the campus suggested he was about to be promoted to Chancellor, and that opened up to him the kind of parties that Colquitt could only dream of. He felt *different*. Vibrant. Alive.

He felt . . . *Colquittish*.

"Have you seen Colquitt lately, Dean?" said Mrs Hopkins, as the two smoked a post-coital cigarette one evening in June.

The dean chose to ignore his dart-pocked photograph stuck to the bedroom door above Mr Hopkins' housecoat peg. It wasn't his fault if Mr Hopkins wasn't up to standard as far as Mrs Hopkins' *needs* were concerned. The dean took the search for G-spots seriously. The typing pool girls would vouch for that. And Maureen had tipped her sponge cake into her lap, such now was his expertise.

"No, not for a while, Mrs Hopkins. He seems to have gone a

little introverted. Spends his time skulking about his dormitory room, so I'm told."

"He's changed," said Mrs Hopkins. "In polarity, for a start. His electrons are spinning the other way. I noticed just yesterday when he passed by the magnetron. His *up* quarks have turned *strange*."

The dean raised himself to his elbows. He wondered if all that was some sort of euphemism for repressed homosexuality. Funny, but he'd never thought that Colquitt might be *riding on the other bus*. And he'd always hated it whenever the girls in the typing pool made the same suggestion about himself during the shy, dark, unhappy, pre Colquitt's high-energy trousers days.

Mrs Hopkins stubbed her cigarette out in one of Mr Hopkins' slippers. "Oh, and he mentioned he'd like you to meet him at the hot plasma field generator in the morning, Dean."

"Oh?"

"He said something about some new science or other he's up to. Asked me to find him half a dozen jam jars and a pair of oversized underpants for an experiment. I wonder what all that's about."

The dean dressed quickly.

He liked the new spin of his electrons just fine.

The Dean's Hot-Plasma Underwear was not for him.

A DRAMA OF DRAGONS

Craig Shaw Gardner

(1)

A good magician should always subscribe to the highest purposes, and nothing should dissuade him from these lofty goals, except, perhaps, that he has to eat, and it is nice to put a little away for retirement.

> – from *The Teachings of Ebenezum*
> Volume III

I could no longer bring myself to gather firewood. My world had ended. She hadn't come.

I sat for far too long in the sunlit glade where we always met. Perhaps she didn't realize it was noon; she had somehow been delayed; her cool blue eyes and fair blonde hair, the way her slim young body moved, the way she laughed, how it felt when she touched me. Surely she was on her way.

But I didn't even know her name! Only her interest in me – a magician's apprentice. She'd once called magicians the closest things to play actors she knew in this backwater place, said she'd always admired the stage. And then she laughed, and we kissed and –

A cold breeze sprang up behind my back. Winter was coming.

I gathered what logs and branches I could find and trudged back to my master's cottage.

In the distance I heard a sneeze. My master Ebenezum, no doubt one of the world's greatest magicians until an unfortunate occurrence involving a demon from the seventh Netherhell. My master had succeeded in banishing the foul creature, by far the most powerful he had ever faced, but his triumph was not without its costs. From that moment onward, Ebenezum found that, should he even approach something of a sorcerous nature, he would fall into an immediate and extended sneezing fit. This malady had put something of a crimp in Ebenezum's wizardly career, but my master was not one to accept defeat easily. Just this moment, he had probably made another attempt to read from one of his magic tomes. Hence the sneeze. Why else?

Unless there was something sorcerous in the air.

Perhaps there was another reason besides my mood that the world was so dark around me, another reason that she hadn't met me as we'd planned. The bushes moved on my right. Something very large flew across the sun.

I managed the front door with the firewood still in my arms. I heard the wizard sneeze. Repeatedly. My master stood in the main room, one of his great books spread on the table before him. I hurried to his aid, forgetting, in my haste, the firewood that scattered across the table as I reached for the book, a few miscellaneous pieces falling among the sneezing Ebenezum's robes.

I closed the book and glanced apprehensively at the mage. To my surprise, Ebenezum blew his nose on a gold-inlaid, dark blue sleeve and spoke to me in the calmest of tones.

"Thank you, 'prentice." He delicately removed a branch from his lap and laid it on the table. "If you would dispose of this in a more appropriate place?"

He sighed deep in his throat. "I'm afraid that my affliction is far worse than I imagined. I may even have to call on outside assistance for my cure."

I hastened to retrieve the firewood. "Outside assistance?" I inquired discreetly.

"We must seek out another magician as great as I," Ebenezum said, his every word heavy with import. "Though to do that, we might have to travel as far as the great city of Vushta."

"Vushta?" I replied. "With its pleasure gardens and forbidden palaces? The city of unknown sins that could doom a man for life? That Vushta?" All at once, I felt the lethargy lift from my shoulders. I quickly deposited the wood by the fireplace.

"That Vushta." Ebenezum nodded. "With one problem. We have not the funds for traveling, and no prospects for gaining same."

As if responding to our plight, a great gust blew against the side of the cottage. The door burst open with a swirl of dirt and leaves, and a short man wearing tattered clothes, face besmirched with grime, staggered in and slammed the door behind him.

"Flee! Flee!" the newcomer cried in a quavering voice. "Dragons! Dragons!" With that, his eyes rolled up in his head and he collapsed on the floor.

"I have found, however," Ebenezum said as he stroked his long, white beard, "in my long career as a magician, Wuntvor, if you wait around long enough, something is bound to turn up."

(2)

Dire creatures from the Netherhells should always be faced directly, unless it is possible to face them some other way, say from behind a bush, in perfect safety.

          – from *The Teachings of Ebenezum*
                      Volume V

With some water on the head and some wine down the gullet, we managed to revive the newcomer.

"Flee!" he sputtered as he caught his breath. He glanced about wildly, his pale blue eyes darting from my master to me to floor to ceiling. He seemed close to my master in age, but there the similarity ceased. Rather than my master's mane of fine, white hair, the newcomer was balding, his hair matted and stringy. Instead of the wizard's masterful face, which could convey calm serenity or cosmic anger with the flick of an eyebrow, the other's face was evasive; small nose and chin, a very wrinkled brow, and those eyes, darting blue in his dark, mud-spattered face.

"Now, now, good sir," Ebenezum replied in his most reasonable voice, often used to charm young ladies and calm bill collectors. "Why the hurry? You mentioned dragons?"

"Dragons!" The man stood somewhat shakily. "Well, at least dragon! One of them has captured Gurnish Keep!"

"Gurnish Keep?" I queried.

"You've seen it," Ebenezum murmured, his cold grey eyes still on our guest. "'Tis the small castle on yonder hill at the far side of the woods." Ebenezum snorted in his beard. "Castle? 'Tis really more of a stone hut, but it's the home of our neighbor, the Duke of Gurnish. It's a very small dukedom. For that matter, he's a very small duke."

Our visitor was, if anything, more agitated than before. "I didn't run all the way through Gurnish Forest to hear a discussion of the neighborhood. We must flee!"

"Gurnish Forest?" I inquired.

"The trees right behind the hut," my master replied. "Surely the Duke's idea. Everyone else knows the area as Wizard's Woods."

"What do you mean, Wizard's Woods?" the newcomer snapped. "This area is Gurnish Forest. Officially. As Gurnish Keep is an official castle!"

"'Tis only a matter of opinion," Ebenezum replied, a smile that could charm both barbarians and maiden aunts once again upon his face. "Haven't we met somewhere before?"

"Possibly." The newcomer, who was somewhat shorter than my master's imposing frame, shifted uneasily under the wizard's gaze. "But shouldn't we flee? Dragons, you know."

"Come now, man. I wouldn't be a full-fledged wizard if I hadn't dealt with a dragon or two." Ebenezum looked even more closely at the newcomer than he had before. "Say. Aren't you the Duke of Gurnish?"

"Me?" the smaller man said. His eyes shifted from my master to me and back again. "Well – uh –" He coughed. "I suppose I am."

"Well, why didn't you say so? I haven't seen you since you stopped trying to tax me." Ebenezum's smile went to its broadest as he signaled me to get our guest a chair. The duke obviously had money.

"Well, this whole situation's a bit awkward," our honored guest said as he stared at the floor. "I'm afraid I feel rather undukeish."

"Nonsense. A run-in with a dragon can unnerve anyone. Would you like some more wine? A nice fire to warm you?"

"No, thank you." The duke lowered his voice even more than before. "Don't you think it would be better if we fled? I mean, dragons. And I've seen other things in the forest. Perhaps if your powers were –" The duke coughed again. "You see, I've heard of your accident."

Ebenezum bristled a bit at the last reference, but the smile more or less remained on his face. "Gossip, good duke. Totally blown out of proportion. We'll deal with your dragon in no time."

"But the dragon's taken over Gurnish Keep! He's immense, bright blue and violet scales, twenty-five feet from head to tail. His wings scrape the ceiling of my great hall! And he's invincible. He's captured my castle and beautiful daughter, and defeated my retainer!"

Beautiful daughter? My thoughts returned to the girl of my dreams. Where had she gone? What had kept her away?

"Only a child!" the duke cried. "No more than seventeen. Fine blonde hair, beautiful blue eyes, a lovely, girlish figure. And the dragon will burn her to a crisp if we don't do his bidding!"

Blonde? Blue? Figure? I had a revelation.

"Come now, man," Ebenezum remarked. "Calm down. It's common knowledge that dragons tend to be overdramatic. All the beast's really done so far is to overwhelm one retainer. I assume you still only had one retainer?"

She hadn't deserted me! She was only held prisoner! All the time she and I had spent together, all those long, warm afternoons, that's why she would tell me nothing of herself! A duke's daughter!

The duke glared at my master. "It wouldn't be like that if my subjects paid their taxes!"

A duke's daughter. And I would rescue her! There'd be no need for secrecy then. How magnificent our lives would be!

A fire lit in Ebenezum's eyes. "Perhaps if certain local nobility were not so concerned with extending the borders of his tiny dukedom –" The wizard waved his hands and the fire disappeared. "But that's not important. We have a dragon to evict. As I see it, the elements here are quite ordinary. Dragon captures castle and maiden. Very little originality. We should be able to handle it tidily."

The duke began to object again, but Ebenezum would have none of it. Only one thing affected his nose more than sorcery – money – and the smell of it was obvious in the cottage. My master sent the duke outside while we gathered the paraphernalia together for dragon fighting.

When I had packed everything according to my master's instructions, Ebenezum beckoned me into his library. Once in the room, the wizard climbed a small stepladder, and, carefully holding his nose, pulled a slim volume from the uppermost shelf.

"We may have need of this." His voice sounded strangely hollow, most likely the result of thumb and forefinger pressed into his nose. "In my present condition, I can't risk using it. But it should be easy enough for you to master, Wuntvor."

He descended the ladder and placed the thin, dark volume in my hands. Embossed in gold on the cover were the words "How to Speak Dragon".

"But we must be off!" Ebenezum exclaimed, clapping my shoulder. "Musn't keep a client waiting. You may study that book on our rest stops along the way."

I stuffed the book hurriedly in the paraphernalia-filled pack and shouldered the whole thing, grabbed my walking staff and followed my master out the door. With my afternoon beauty at the end of my journey, I could manage anything.

My master had already grabbed the duke by the collar and propelled him in the proper direction. I followed at Ebenezum's heels as fast as the heavy pack would allow. The wizard, as usual, carried nothing. As he often had explained, it kept his hands free for quick conjuring and his mind free for sorcerous conjecture.

I noticed a bush move, then another. Rustling like the wind pushed through the leaves, except there was no wind. The forest was as still as when I had waited for my afternoon love. Still the bushes moved.

Just my imagination, I thought. Like the darkness of the forest. I glanced nervously at the sky, half-expecting the sun to disappear again. What was so big that it blotted out the sun?

A dragon?

But my musings were cut short by a man dressed in bright orange who stood in our path. He peered through an odd instrument on the end of a pole.

I glanced at the duke, walking now at my side. He had begun to shiver.

The man in orange looked up as we approached. "Good afternoon," he said, the half frown on his face disproving the words. "Could you move a little faster? You're blocking the emperor's highway, you know."

The duke shook violently.

"Highway?" Ebenezum asked, stopping mid-path rather than hurrying by the man in orange.

"Yes, the new road that the great and good Emperor Flostok III has decreed —"

"Flee!" the duke cried. "Dragons! Dragons! Flee!" He leapt about, waving his hands before the emperor's representative.

"See here!" the orange man snapped. "I'll have none of this. I'm traveling to see the Duke of Gurnish on important business."

The duke stopped hopping. "Duke?" he said, pulling his soiled clothing back into place. "Why, I'm the Duke of Gurnish. What can I help you with, my good man?"

The man in orange frowned even deeper. "It's about the upkeep of the road . . ."

"Certainly." The duke glanced back at us. "Perhaps we should go somewhere that we can talk undisturbed." The duke led the man in orange into the underbrush.

"They deserve each other," Ebenezum muttered. "But to business." He looked at me solemnly. "A bit about dragons. Dragons are one of the magical sub-species. They exist largely between worlds, partly on Earth and partly in the Netherhells, and never truly belong to either. There are other magical sub-species —"

Ebenezum's lecture was interrupted by a commotion in the underbrush. Large arms with a thick growth of grayish-brown hair rose and fell above the bushes, accompanied by human screams.

"Another sub-species is the troll," Ebenezum remarked.

I let my pack slide from my back and firmly grasped my staff. They would eat my true love's father! I had never encountered trolls before, but this was as good a time as any to learn.

"Slobber! Slobber!" came from the bushes before us. A rough voice, the sound of a saw biting into hardwood. I assumed it was a troll.

"Wait!" another voice screamed. "You can't do this! I'm a representative of the emperor!"

"Slobber! Slobber!" answered a chorus of rough voices.

"Let's get this over with!" Another voice, high and shaky. The duke?

Although the voices were quite close now, it was getting difficult to distinguish individual words. It just sounded like a large amount of screaming, punctuated by cries of "slobber!" I lifted my staff over my head and ran forward with a scream of my own.

I broke into a small clearing with four occupants. One was the duke. The other three were among the ugliest creatures I'd seen in my short life. Squat and covered with irregular tufts of greybrown fur, which did nothing to hide the rippling muscles of their barrel-like arms and legs. Three pairs of very small red eyes turned to regard me. One of them swallowed something that looked a good deal like an orange-clad foot.

The sight of the three hideous creatures completely stopped my forward motion. They regarded me in silence.

"Oh, hello," I said, breaking into the sinister quiet. "I must have wandered off the path. Excuse me."

One of the trolls barrelled towards me on its immensely powerful legs. "Slobber," it remarked. It was time to leave. I turned and bumped into my master, who ignored me as he made a mystic gesture.

"No slobber! No slobber!" the trolls cried and ran back into the heart of the woods.

I picked myself up and helped the wizard regain his feet as well. Ebenezum sneezed for a full three minutes, the result of his actually employing magic. When he caught his breath at last, he wiped his nose on his robe and regarded me all too evenly.

"Wuntvor," he said quietly. "What do you mean by dropping all our valuable equipment and running off, just so you can be swallowed by –"

The duke ran between the two of us. "Flee! Flee! Dragons! Trolls! Flee!"

"And you!" my master said, his voice rising at last. "I've had enough of your jumping about, screaming hysterical warnings! Why do you even worry? You were surrounded by trolls and they didn't touch you. You lead a charmed life!" He grabbed the duke's shoulder with one hand and mine with the other and pushed us back to the trail.

"Come," he continued. "We will reach Gurnish Keep before nightfall. There, my assistant and I will deal with this dragon, and you, good duke, will pay us handsomely for our efforts." The wizard deposited us on the trail and walked briskly towards the castle before the duke could reply.

"Look!" The duke pulled at my sleeve. There was a break in the trees ahead, affording a clear view of the hill on the wood's far side. There, atop the hill, was Gurnish Keep, a stone building not much larger than Ebenezum's cottage. Smoke poured from the Keep's lower windows, and once or twice I thought I saw the yellow-orange flicker of flame.

"Dragon," the duke whispered. I hurriedly reached into my satchel and pulled out *How to Speak Dragon*. The time to start learning was now.

I opened the book at random and scanned the page. Phrases

in common speech filled one side. Opposite these were the same phrases in dragon. I started reading from the top:

"Pardon me, but could you please turn your snout?"

"*Sniz me heeba-heeba szzz.*"

"Pardon me, but your claw is in my leg."

"*Sniz mir sazza grack szzz.*"

"Pardon me, but your barbed tail is waving perilously close . . ."

The whole page was filled with similar phrases. I closed the book. It had done nothing to reassure me.

Ebenezum shouted at us from far up the trail. I ran to follow, dragging the Duke of Gurnish with me.

We walked through the remaining forest without further difficulty. The woods ended at the edge of a large hill called Wizard's Knoll or Mount Gurnish, depending upon whom you spoke with. From there, we could get a clear view of the castle. And the smoke. And the flames.

The duke began to jabber again about the dangers ahead, but was silenced by a single glance from my master. The wizard's cool grey eyes stared up towards the castle, but somehow beyond it. After a moment, he shook his head and flexed his shoulders beneath his robes. He turned to me.

"Wunt," he said. "More occurs here than meets the eye." He glanced again at the duke, who was nervously dancing on a pile of leaves. "Not just a dragon, but three trolls. That's a great deal of supernatural activity for a place as quiet as Wizard's Woods."

I expected the duke to object to the wizard's choice of names, but he was strangely quiet. I turned to the pile of leaves where he had hidden.

The duke was gone.

"Methinks," Ebenezum continued, "some contact has been made with the Netherhells of late. There is a certain instrument in your pack . . ."

My master went on to describe the instrument and its function. If we set it up at the base of the hill, it would tell us the exact number and variety of creatures from the Netherhells lurking about the district.

I held up the instrument. My master rubbed his nose. "Keep it at a distance. The device carries substantial residual magic."

I put the thing together according to the wizard's instructions, and, at his signal, spun the gyroscope that topped it off.

"Now, small points of light will appear." Ebenezum sniffled loudly. "You can tell by the color of –"

He sneezed mightily, again and again. I looked to the device. Should I stop it?

Ebenezum sneezed to end all sneezes, directly at the instrument. The device fell apart.

"By the Netherhells!" Ebenezum exclaimed. "Can I not perform the simplest of spells?" He looked at me, and his face looked very old. "Put away the apparatus, Wunt. We must use the direct approach. Duke?"

I explained that the duke had vanished.

"What now?" Ebenezum looked back towards the forest. His cold grey eyes went wide. He blew his nose hastily.

"Wunt! Empty the pack!"

"What?" I asked, startled by the urgency of my master's voice. Then I looked back to the woods, and saw it coming. A wall of black, like some impenetrable cloud, roiling across the forest. But this cloud extended from the sky to the forest floor, and left complete blackness behind. It sped across the woods like a living curtain that drew its darkness ever closer.

"Someone plays with great forces," Ebenezum said. "Forces he doesn't understand. The pack, Wunt!"

I dumped the pack's contents on the ground. Ebenezum rifled through them, tossing various arcane tomes and irreplacable devices out of his way, until he grasped a small box painted a shiny robin's egg blue.

The magician sneezed in triumph. He tossed me the box.

"Quick, Wunt!" he called, blowing his nose. "Take the dust within that box and spread it in a line along the hill!" He waved at a rocky ridge on the forest edge as he jogged up the hill and began to sneeze again.

I did as my master bid, laying an irregular line of blue

powder across the long granite slab. I looked back to the woods. The darkness was very close, engulfing all but the hill.

"Run, Wunt!"

I sprinted up the hill. The wizard cried a few ragged syllables and followed. He tripped as he reached the hilltop, and fell into an uncontrollable sneezing fit.

I turned back to look at the approaching blackness. The darkly tumbling wall covered all the forest now, and tendrils of the stuff reached out towards the hill like so many grasping hands. But the fog's forward motion had stopped just short of the ragged blue line.

There was a breeze at my back. I turned to see Ebenezum, still sneezing but somehow standing. One arm covered his nose, the other reached for the sky. His free hand moved and the breeze grew to a wind and then a gale, rushing down the hill and pushing the dark back to wherever it had come.

After a minute the wind died, but what wisps of fog remained in the forest below soon evaporated beneath the bright afternoon sun. My master sat heavily and gasped for breath as if all the air had escaped from his lungs.

"Lucky," he said after a minute. "Whoever raised the demon fog had a weak will. Otherwise . . ." The magician blew his nose, allowing the rest of the sentence to go unsaid.

A figure moved through the woods beneath us. It was the duke.

"Too exhausted to fight dragon," Ebenezum continued, still breathing far too hard. "You'll have to do it, Wunt."

I swallowed and picked up *How To Speak Dragon* from the hillside where it lay. I turned to look at Gurnish Keep, a scant hundred yards across the hilltop. Billows of smoke poured from the windows, occasionally accompanied by licks of flame. And, now that we stood so close, I could hear a low rumble, underlining all the other sounds in the field in which we stood. A rumble that occasionally grew into a roar.

This dragon was going to be everything I expected.

The duke grabbed at my coatsleeve. "Dragon!" he said. "Last chance to get out!"

"Time to go in there," Ebenezum said. "Look in the book,

Wunt. Perhaps we can talk the dragon out of the castle." He shook the quivering duke from his arm. "And if you, good sir, would be quiet for a moment, we could go about saving your home and daughter. Quite honestly, I feel you have no cause for complaint with the luck you've been having. Most people would not have survived the evil spell that recently took over the woods. How you manage to bumble through the powerful forces at work around here is beyond . . ." Ebenezum's voice trailed off. He cocked an eyebrow at the duke and stroked his beard in thought.

The rumble from the castle grew louder again. I opened the thin volume I held in my sweating palms. I had to save my afternoon beauty.

I flipped frantically from page to page, finally finding a phrase I thought appropriate.

"Pardon me, but might we speak to you?"

In the loudest voice I could manage, I spat out the dragon syllables.

"Sniz grah! Subba Ubba Szzz!"

A great, deep voice reverberated from within the castle. "Speak the common tongue, would you?" it said. "Besides, I'm afraid I don't have a commode."

I closed the book with a sigh of relief. The dragon spoke human!

"Don't trust him!" the duke cried. "Dragons are deceitful!"

Ebenezum nodded his head. "Proceed with caution, Wunt. Someone *is* being deceitful." He turned to the duke. "You!"

"Me?" the Gurnish nobleman replied as he backed in my direction. Ebenezum stalked after him.

They were squabbling again. But I had no time for petty quarrels. I firmly grasped my staff, ready to confront the dragon and my afternoon beauty.

The duke was right behind me now, his courage seemingly returned. "Go forward, wizard!" he cried in a loud voice. "Defeat the dragon! Banish him forever!"

"Oh, not a wizard, too!" cried the voice from within the castle. "First I get cooped up in Gurnish Keep, then I have to capture your beautiful daughter, and now a wizard! How dull! Doesn't anyone have any imagination around here?"

I came to a great oak door. I nudged it with my foot. It opened easily and I stepped inside to confront the dragon.

It stood on its haunches, regarding me in turn. It was everything the duke had mentioned, and more. Blue and violet scales, twenty-five feet in length, wings that brushed the ceiling. The one oversight in the duke's description appeared to be the large green top hat on the dragon's head.

I saw her a second later.

She stood in front and slightly to one side of the giant reptile. She was as beautiful as I'd ever seen her.

"Why, Wuntvor," she said. "What are you doing here?"

I cleared my throat and pounded my staff on the wom stone pavement. "I've come to rescue you."

"Rescue?" She looked up at the dragon. The dragon rumbled. "So father's gotten to you, too?"

The duke's voice screamed behind me. "I warned you! Now the dragon will burn you all to cinders!"

The dragon snorted good naturedly and turned to regard the ceiling.

"The game is up, duke!" Ebenezum called from the doorway, far enough away so that the dragon's magical odor would not provoke another attack. "Your sorcerous schemes are at an end!"

"Yes, father," my afternoon beauty said. "Don't you think you've gone far enough?" She looked at my master. "Father so wanted control of the new Trans-Empire Highway, to put toll stations throughout the woods below, that he traded in his best retainer for the services of certain creatures from the Nether-hells, which he'd use to frighten off anyone who stood in the way of his plans."

She turned and looked at the dragon. "Luckily, one of those creatures was Hubert."

"Betrayed!" The duke clutched at his heart. "My own daughter!"

"Come, father. What you're doing is dangerous and wrong. Your greed will make a monster of you. I've been worrying what my future was with you and the castle. But now I know." She glanced happily back to the dragon. "Hubert and I have decided to go on the stage."

The duke was taken aback.

"What?"

"Yes, good sir," Hubert the dragon remarked. "I have some small experience in the field, and, on talking with your daughter, have found that she is just the partner I have been looking for."

"Yes, father. A life on the stage. How much better than sitting around a tiny castle, waiting to be rescued by a clumsy young man."

Clumsy? My world reeled around me. Not wishing to be rescued was one thing, considering the situation. But to call me clumsy? I lowered my staff and walked towards the door.

"Wait!" my afternoon beauty cried. I turned quickly. Perhaps she had reconsidered her harsh words. Our long afternoons together still meant something!

"You haven't seen our act!" she exclaimed. "Hit it, dragon!"

She danced back and forth across the castle floor, the dragon beating time with its tail. They sang together:

"Let's raise a flagon
For damsel and dragon,
The best song and dance team in the whole, wide world.
Our audience is clapping,
And their toes are tapping,
For a handsome reptile and a pretty girl!"

The dragon blew smoke rings at the end of a line and breathed a bit of fire at the end of a verse. Six more verses followed, more or less the same. Then they stopped singing and began to shuffle back and forth.

They talked in rhythm.

"Hey, dragon. It's good to have an audience again."

"I'll say, damsel. I'm all fired up!"

They paused.

"How beautiful it is in Gurnish Keep! What more could you ask for, damsel, than this kind of sunny day?"

"I don't know, dragon. I *could* do with a shining knight!"

They paused again.

"Romance among reptiles can be a weighty problem!"

"Why's that, dragon?"

"When I see a pretty dragoness, it tips my scales!"

They launched into song immediately.

"Let's raise a flagon

For damsel and dragon –"

"I can't stand it any more!" the Duke of Gurnish cried. "Slabyach! Grimace! Trolls, get them all!"

A trapdoor opened in the corner of the castle floor. The trolls popped out.

"Quick, Wunt!" Ebenezum cried. "Out of the way!" But before he could even begin to gesture, he was caught in a sneezing fit.

The trolls sauntered towards us. I bopped one on the head with my staff. The staff broke.

"Slobber!" exclaimed the troll.

"Roohhaarrr!" came from across the room. The dragon stood as well as it was able in the confines of the castle's great hall. It carefully directed a thin lance of flame towards each troll's posterior.

"No slobber! No slobber!" the trolls exclaimed, escaping back through the trapdoor.

"Thank you," Ebenezum said after blowing his nose. "That was quite nice of you."

"Think nothing of it," the dragon replied. "I never sacrifice an audience."

(3)

The best spells are those that right wrongs, bring happiness, return the world to peace and cause a large quantity of the coin of the realm to pass into the wizard's possession.

> – from *The Teachings of Ebenezum*
> Volume IXX

"I finally got our good Lord of Gurnish to listen to reason," my master said when we returned to our cottage. "When I mentioned how close to the palace I might be soon, and that I might find myself discussing the region, the duke saw his way to hire me as a consultant." Ebenezum pulled a jangling pouch from his belt. "The duke will now most likely receive clearance to build his toll booths. Pity he no longer has the money for their construction."

"And what of his daughter and the dragon?" I asked.

"Hubert is flying to Vushta with her this very instant. I gave them a letter of introduction to certain acquaintances I have there, and they should find a ready audience."

"So you think they're that good?"

Ebenezum shook his head vigorously. "They're terrible. But the stage is a funny thing. I expect Vushta will love them.

"But enough of this." The wizard drew another, smaller pouch from his bag. "Hubert was kind enough to lend me some ground dragon's egg. Seems it's a folk remedy among his species; gives quick, temporary relief. I've never found this particular use for it in any of my tomes, but I've tried everything else. What do I have to lose?"

He ground the contents of the pouch into a powder and dropped it in a flagon of wine.

"This might even save us a trip to Vushta." He held his nose and lifted the concoction to his lips. My hopes sank as he drank it down. With the duke's daughter gone, a trip to Vushta was the only thing I had to look forward to.

The wizard opened a magical tome and breathed deeply. He smiled.

"It works! No more sneezing!"

His stomach growled.

"It couldn't be." A strange look stole over the wizard's face. He burped.

"It is! No wonder I couldn't find this in any of my tomes! I should have checked the *Netherhell Index!* It's fine for dragons, but for humans —" He paused to pull a book from the shelf and leaf rapidly through it. He burped again. His face looked very strained as he turned to me.

"Neebekenezer's Syndrome of Universal Flatulence!" he whispered. A high, whining sound emerged from his robes.

"Quick, Wunt!" he cried. "Remove yourself, if you value your sanity!"

I did as I was told. Even from my bed beneath the trees, I could hear the whistles, groans and muffled explosions all night long.

We would be traveling to Vushta after all.

PEST CONTROL

Adam Roberts

1

Des pulled up the handbrake and clambered out of his van. The property was an unusual one: a long, low-roofed building set in many acres of unfarmed land; land that looked more like wilderness than anything else. There hadn't even been a tarmac road for the last two miles, and the wheels of the van were clogged with mud.

Des pulled his workbag from the back of the van and made his way to the large oaken front door. There didn't seem to be a bell. He knocked.

It was more than a minute before the door opened.

"Afternoon," said Des. "Mr – Wulf, is it?"

"That's me," said the man. He was a blond-haired, broad-chinned man, his body a chunk of muscular torso from which jutted muscular limbs. He had a strange, rather startled expression on his face. "And you are?"

"Des Hannigan. I'm from King and Kegan, Mr Wulf. Pest Control. You called us?"

"Ah you've come," said the large man. He ushered Des inside. "Excellent. Excellent. Yes, we have a small – infestation. Your guarantee?"

"We guarantee to clear your domicile of infestation completely or your money back," Des recited. "It's in the small print of the contract. What sort of infestation are we dealing with sir?" Des looked around. The interior of the building appeared to be one giant, dimly-lit space; it was a huge hall rather than a space divided into rooms. A central fire smouldered in its gleaming cinders in the very centre of the space. There were – it was hard to see – supine figures lying on the floor.

"Excellent," said Wulf, following Des's gaze. "Them? Don't worry about them."

"They're – asleep?"

"Sleeping it off, yes. Best not wake them. Best not. If you just follow me I'll show you the . . . the, um, problem."

Des allowed himself to be led through the cavernous space. It was all wooden, all very dark. "Mind the steps down," said his guide.

"Could we, perhaps, turn the light on?" Des stepped down half a dozen steps, crossed a plane and then stepped up half a dozen steps. "I'll need to have more light to work in, sir," he said. "To see where to lay the traps. I'm right in thinking we're dealing with rats?"

"It's out here," said Wulf, pushing at a wooden door on the far side of the building. "In the garden?"

"The garden?" repeated Des. "Really? We don't usually deal with garden pests."

The door swung away and daylight fell on Des's face again. Standing amongst the unmown grass was a huge creature, half as high again as a man; a beast of malign and potent hideousness. Its fatly muscled shoulders and arms were covered in tightly interlocking chainmail-like scales. Its hands were tipped with blood-red claws. Its head had the texture of a carved and sanded lump of gristle. Gleaming red eyes glinted beneath its snub-browed forehead. As it breathed its reptilian lips parted just enough to display catlike teeth, sharp as thorns.

"Right," said Des, apprising the situation. "Not rats, then?"

"Did I say rats?" asked Wulf, nervously.

The beast man looked at them both with malignant evil in its eyes.

"You did, sir, yes. On the phone you said rats. Definitely rats you said."

"I'm not sure I did . . . I mean, it wasn't a very good line . . . phone line I mean . . ."

"To be precise," said Des, "you said wasps first off. I distinctly remember. Wasps, you said. When I asked how many, you changed your mind and said rats."

"No, I'm *sure* I mentioned the huge scaly beast-man Grendel in the garden," said Wulf, keeping the Pest Controller's body between himself and the creature. "Didn't I?"

"No, sir," said Des.

"Must have slipped my . . ." said Wulf. "Slipped my . . . Look, I definitely meant to. I really did." The beast man grunted, and his shoulders twitched. Wulf jumped and let out a little scream, half under his breath.

"I came with my rats case," said Des sternly. "You told me rats, and rats is what I've come prepared for."

"Well," said Wulf, "there may well *be* some rats. In fact I'm pretty sure there *are* some rats – in the hall, somewhere. Nibbling at the sacks of grain. Squeaking. That sort of thing."

"And do you want me to exterminate these rats?" asked Des.

"Well you *could* do that, you *could* do," said Wulf. "Be nice to get rid of them, always scrabbling about. But, well, to be honest with you, Mr Hannigan, now that you're here, I wonder if you couldn't . . . you know . . ." He finished the sentence by nodding at the Grendel.

"Well, I ain't got the right equipment for Grendels," said Hannigan. "I brought the rats case, and just to be on the safe side I brought an insect kit as well. But that'd hardly do for a Grendel, now, would it?"

"Oh," said Wulf, in a disappointed tone of voice.

"A Grendel," said Des, in a slow and determined voice, "not being a insect, do you see."

"I suppose not. I suppose it's not. It's just that – since you're here, I thought that maybe . . . maybe you could just *polish off* the Grendel . . ."

"I can definitely do yer rats for you," said Des firmly.

"Let me be absolutely honest, Mr, er, Mr Hannigan. The rats don't bother me overmuch. They're not nice, I don't deny it. The squeaking and scrabbling about, that's not nice. But, to speak frankly, the rats aren't the ones bursting into my hall into the middle of the night, devouring my men in groups of three and running out leaving trails of blood all over the floor."

"Hhhrrrgg," said the Grendel, shifting its weight from one hideously beclawed foot to another. Wulf flinched again, and pulled back to the doorframe.

"You're supposed to deal with these yerself," said Des, tutting. "I mean, speaking strictly. Haven't you a sword?"

"Ah, yes," said Wulf. "Sword, yes, right. Well obviously that's a good idea. Only, well, you know. I may have strained my shoulder in the, well, mead-drinking competitions we have. In the hall."

"You've strained your shoulder," repeated Des.

"Some of the jugs of foaming mead are terribly, well, big. Heavy. The constant lifting of jug from table to mouth . . ." He mimed the action. At the motion of his arm the Grendel grunted and shifted its weight back from foot to foot. Wulf yelped and shrank further back. "Besides," Wulf continued, his voice more high-pitched and his delivery more gabbly, "besides my sword has got a bit rusty, a tad rusty . . ."

"You're supposed to oil it and wrap it in a rag, like," said Des, schoolma'amishly.

"I know, and I feel simply terrible, I can assure you . . . it's frankly negligent, I know . . . but, under the circumstances . . . isn't there anything you can do?"

Des sighed. "You called the council?"

"They refused to come. Said it wasn't their responsibility. Refused flat out."

Des sighed again. "Look," he said. "Tell you what I'll do. I can leave a couple of my traps about. Only don't tell my supervisor I done this, or he'll have my guts for garters and no mistake."

"Thank you," Wulf gushed. "Thank you, thank you so much. So these traps – they'll . . . um . . . How do they work?"

Des unbuckled his bag and went into his spiel. "I'd advise you to keep all domestic pets, cats and other animals, out of the house for at least forty-eight hours. King and Kegan can accept no liability for death of same, should they ingest any of the arsenic patty."

"Excellent, excellent," said Wulf, keeping a wary eye on the beast. The sun was sinking slowly down over the grassy downs beyond the hall; shadows were thickening and lengthening; a ruddy tint was creeping into the green of leaf and blade. Soon it would be dark, and then the Grendel would wake from its torpor, and become a nightmare of pouncing claws and fangs and an anaconda grip of steely musculature. "And this arsenic will . . . will kill it?"

"Oooo, shouldn't think so," said Des. "Big strong Grendel like this? Nah. No, what would be good is if you could, you know, *persuade* it to stick its *head* in – you know, *tempt* it, taunt it, something like that – persuade it to stick its *head* in one of them. Then when it's stuck in there, just –" he made a chopping gesture with his free hand "– just chop it off with a axe."

"Axe," said Wulf, backing away through the door into the darkness of the hall. "Excellent. Thank you so much, Mr – Mr – Mr Hannigan. You've been – eek!" This last noise was occasioned by the Grendel shaking itself suddenly, growling and taking a step forward. Des shook his head. Good half hour before dusk; nothing to worry about just yet. Some people get so jittery.

2

Des was halfway through the crossword and thinking of an anagram for "what" when the phone rang. He picked it up and cradled it between his left ear and shoulder. "Thaw" wouldn't do. Wouldn't fit with the "horrible" of seven across.

"King and Kegan Pest Control," he said. "How can I help?"

"Mr Hannigan?" came the squeaky voice. "Is that you? This is Wulf here. Do you remember, you were round ours yesterday? Laid some traps down for me?"

"I remember," said Des. "Rats, wasn't it?"

"It was more along the lines of," said Wulf in his jittery voice, "a Grendel. We had a slight Grendel problem. If you remember, I explained it to you. A certain amount of slaying, a touch of devouring and running out leaving blood spatters everywhere. Just a bit, at night only."

"Yeah, I remember. Did you get the little critter?"

"He stuck his arm in, is what he did," said Wulf. "Not his head like you said. An arm. Still, we managed, six of us together, to chop it off. Then he ran away."

"That'll do for him," said Des with authority. "They're rubbish without their arms, those Grendels. He'll probably lie down in a field somewhere and bleed to death."

"We were rather hoping something like that has happened. But since then we've another problem."

Des's heart sank. "Yeah? What's that?"

"It's a Grendel's-mother."

"Oh blimey."

"I know. I know, it's awful. She's much bigger than her son, and she's active in daytime *and* nightime both. The slaying is much worse than it used to be. The body count is more than twice what it was before. Morale is fairly low, I don't mind telling you."

"I'm sorry Mr Wulf, there's really not much I can do. For Grendel's-mothers you need heavy lifting gear, and we ain't licensed. You could call the council . . ."

"Please, Mr Hannigan. You've got to help us."

"My hands," said Des, stretching in his chair, "are tied, Mr Wulf."

"But your guarantee . . ."

"Don't apply in this case, Mr Wulf," said Des smoothly. 'It only covers the removal of the pest specified on the contract. The Grendel's-mother is a totally different . . ."

"I'm begging you, Mr Hannigan."

Des paused. He was too soft hearted. He knew it. "Well, Mr Wulf," he said. "I'm afraid my hands really are tied. I'm not able to tell you – you got a pen there?"

"Pen?" Wulf sounded confused.

"Yes, sir, I cannot advise you to pick up a pen, even to write down a hypothetical set of instructions, of the sort I'm not allowed to pass on to you regarding the extermination of a Grendel's-mother infestation."

"I don't understand, Mr Hannigan."

Des sighed. "Pick up a pen, Mr Wulf."

There was a pause. "Right, yes," said Wulf. "I've got a pen."

"Now, I didn't tell you to do that."

"Yes, you did."

Des looked at the office door. His supervisor, Mr Alfred, was out on a job – the burial of four horses and a chariot under a patio feature – but he could be back any time. He really didn't want to get into hot water with Alf. He should have just turned this Wulf down flat, washed his hands of the whole affair.

"You really did," Wulf was saying, earnestly. "I heard you say quite distinctly . . ."

"I'm also *not* telling you," said Des, "to chase the Grendel's-mother back to the nearby lake in which it lives."

"Does it live in a lake?"

"Nine times out of ten, if you trace an infestation of Grendel's-mothers back to their nests you'll find them at the bottoms of lakes," said Des. "Now, I *didn't* just tell you that."

"Mr Hannigan," said Wulf, rather primly. "I don't know if you think you're playing some sort of game with me, but I'll tell you straight out I'm finding it rather confusing. You *did* just tell me that."

"I think you're misunderstanding, sir," said Des. He could hear the sound of a van pulling up in the drive outside the main portacabin. It was probably Alf. Des dropped his voice and cradled the telephone receiver closer to his mouth. "When I say I didn't tell you that," he hissed, "I don't mean that I *literally* didn't tell you. It's my way of informing you that I'm passing on information regarded as illicit by my employers, and for which therefore I require a plausible deniability. In effect I am saying that, in the event that my supervisor calls you and asks you, 'Did Mr Hannigan tell you such-and-such,' you can reply, 'No, he didn't'."

"But you *have* been telling me such-and-such," pointed out Wulf.

"I may have been, I concede that, but immediately afterwards I have said that I haven't just told you that."

It took Wulf long moments to digest and decipher this. "So the fact that you say 'I didn't just tell you x' is supposed to make it legitimate to repeat that you didn't tell me x, even if you did tell me x?"

"Exactly."

"But you see," said Wulf, warming to his topic, "this is my problem: your supervisor is unlikely to ask me, 'Did Mr Hannigan *tell you that he had told you* about x?' He's much more likely to ask, more simply, 'Did Hannigan tell you about x?' In the case of the former interrogative, the fact that you had appended a 'I didn't tell you x' to your previous telling me of x might indeed give me the sophistical loophole of denial. But in the latter case . . ."

"I think we're getting bogged down here," interrupted Des. "Do you want me to tell you how to get rid of your Grendel's-mother or not?"

"Aren't you going to come round and sort it yourself, Mr Hannigan?"

"No, I'm not."

The pause that followed lasted exactly long enough for a man to give up a fondly held hope. "Oh," said Wulf. "That's a disappointment."

"Now, do you want me to tell you how to get rid of the infestation yourself? I have to tell you, Mr Wulf, that when my supervisor comes through the door here in the office I'm putting the phone down, because I'm not supposed to be talking to you about this. We're not licensed, you see?"

"Go on then," said Wulf, in a defeated voice.

"Trace the Grendel's-mother back to its lake. It'll probably be the one nearest your domicile. Then you need to follow it under the water, and on the lakebed . . ."

"What – sorry? I'm to go underwater?"

"Yes. Take your sword. Don't forget it, or you'll be well jiggered."

"How long will I be down there?"

"Ooh, half an hour minimum. Depends on your swordarm. The problem is swinging the sword under water. It's a pig swinging a sword under water."

"There's a pig?"

"There's an *expression*, that's what the pig is," said Des, becoming more exasperated. "Is a way of saying it's *hard work* swinging a sword under water."

"But how am I going to breathe?"

Des paused. "You what?"

"I mean – should I rent scuba gear, or . . ."

"Hold your breath, I would. Or get an aqualung, if you really want to, but that's only going to push the cost up."

"Get," said Wulf, scribbling the words as he spoke them, "An. Aqualung. Right. Got that. What next?"

"Next you chop its head off. Be sure'n carry it up out of the lake with you. Pin it over the mantelpiece, would be my advice."

"And that's it?"

"That's it."

"Only I was wondering . . ."

Wearily: "What, Mister Wulf?"

"Well, I was wondering if it had to be the head? Having managed to cut off the Grendel's arm – which amputation killed the monster, after all – I'm thinking, perhaps I might just cut off the Grendel's-mother's arm too. That might be the easier option."

"I'm sure that would work just fine too Mr Hannigan. I really have to go now. I can hear my Supervisor coming up the portacabin steps."

3

Much later that day, in a slow half-hour between jobs, Des found his mind wandering back to the Grendel infestation. It was a rare enough call-out, that. When Alf stepped out for a crafty puff, Des picked up the phone and rang his friend Dave from X-Terminate Inc. They exchanged the long-time-no-see variety of pleasantry for a few minutes.

"Dave," he said. "I've a question. Grendels."

Dave sucked in a fierce breath over his teeth. It sounded like a slashed tyre deflating. "What about them?"

"Had a client with a infestation of Grendels," said Des.

"Thought your firm didn't have the licence?"

"Well, strictly speaking, we don't, no. Strictly speaking. Speaking strictly I'd have to say, no, the licence for Grendel extermination, we don't have. But I didn't want to leave this geezer in the lurch, did I? There he was with a steaming great Grendel standing on his back lawn."

"Ooh, you gotta be careful with Grendels," said Dave, in a warning tone.

"They're all right provided you cut their heads off, I thought."

"Yeah, granted, cut their head off, you deal with them. But you want to make sure it is the head. If it's the arm, then you got problems."

"You have."

"Yep. Cut off an arm or a leg and you prompt a rapid cellular regeneration and they turn into Grendel's-mothers."

Des swallowed. "You don't say?" he replied.

"And they're buggers to get rid of, Grendel's-mothers," said Dave. "You got to track them down to the lakebed and everything."

"Yes, I heard that. Under the water. Still, a beheading will dispose of them, no?"

"Oh, yeah, that's true. Provided you separate the head and body. But, *eeesh*," (this last sound was an inexpressibly eloquent noise formed by drawing the mouth very widely and half-breathing, half-grunting through the slot). "If you chop an arm off of a *Grendel's-mother*, well, you don't want to know."

"What happens then?"

"Reduplicated rapid cellular regeneration. Before you know it the whole property will be absolutely over-run with ga-lumphing great fire-breathing dragons. Very nasty. Very nasty indeed."

"Oh," said Des.

"Still," said Dave. "You wouldn't be so daft as to cut off a Grendel's-mother's arm, now would you?"

"Course not," said Des, weakly. "Thanks for that, Des. I'll speak to you soon." He hung up, sat back in his chair, and looked out the window, wondering whether he needed to worry. He'd definitely told Wulf to cut off the monster's head. *Definitely.* And that, surely, is what he'd do. There'd be no further complications, that would end it. He smiled, and let a breath out. Des, he told himself, you worry too much. He got up, went over to the kettle, and set it boiling. Nice cup of tea, he thought. Draw a line under the whole business. After all, he thought, chuckling a little to himself, he wouldn't want this case to *drag on* at all, would he? "You're a droll cuss, Des Hannigan," he told himself, as he popped a teabag into the cup. And just at that moment he heard, distant but clearly audible, carried on the cold breeze from the direction of the lake, the unmistakeable, tiger-roar-run-through-the-tape-player-backwards howl of a young dragon tasting the air for the first time.

"Oh," said Des, to no one in particular, in a low voice, "shit."

WRONG PLANET

Tom Holt

"Bugger," said the first man to set foot on Mars, a fraction of a second before his toe touched the dust. "Wrong planet."

35 million miles away, Mission Control nearly swallowed its mike.

"Mission control to Excelsior," it said, trying to sound unconcerned, "we're having trouble reading you, please clarify. Repeat –"

"Oh, be quiet," snapped the first man on Mars. "And for pity's sake stop calling me Excelsior. My name's George. You should know that by now."

The thought of ten billion eavesdroppers on seven continents didn't do much for mission control's composure. Not good television, it thought, staring dumbly at a screen that showed a hazy space-suited figure apparently booting a small pebble across a chartreuse desert. "Well, um, George," was all it could think to say. "And how does it feel to be, like, the first man on Mars?"

"Disappointing."

"Ah." The hazy figure was, apparently, turning round and heading back to the landing module. "You wouldn't say, for instance," persisted mission control, "that it was a small step for a man but a giant . . ."

"Wild goose chase. Yes, that puts it pretty bloody well." A million-dollar boot stepped onto the first rung of the ladder. "Not to mention a rather spectacular waste of money. Hey there, all you people watching this at home, have you the faintest idea how much this is costing you? Well, to the nearest billion –"

All over Earth, TV screens went blank; and a moment later, a slightly hysterical voice explained that due to technical problems the uplink to Excelsior was temporarily offline, but it was being fixed; in the meanwhile, here's a favourite episode of the *Mary Tyler Moore Show* . . .

After that, life was interesting for a while in Houston, Texas. The President of the United States, calling in for an update, was politely informed that his call was being held in a queue, he could either hold or try again later. Representatives of the major TV networks and high-ranking Pentagon officials met to discuss the feasibility of blasting Excelsior out of the heavens with a stockpiled Reagan-era laser-beam as a damage limitation exercise. The slipstream caused by plummeting aerospace shares roared through the streets of New York and Tokyo like Dorothy Gale's cyclone. In Fleet Street, editors roared "Hold the second page!" across frantic news-rooms (the front page, of course, was reserved for SEX CHANGE VICAR IN GAY ROMP WITH TV VET, thereby demonstrating that one nation, at least, retained a sense of perspective).

Back on Mars, the first man clambered back into the module and flopped down on his bunk. Serves me right, he thought, for getting my hopes up. Should know better by now. Oh, well, never mind. At any rate, it helped pass the time.

"You are starting to feel sleepy," said the voice. "You are completely relaxed. Your toes are relaxed. Your feet are relaxed. Your ankles are relaxed . . ."

Alice gritted her teeth. Compared to her, a cheesewire was limp spaghetti. The more the voice told her to relax, the more she wanted to scream –

"Your calves are relaxed," the voice lied to her, "your kneecaps . . ."

Oh, sure, Alice thought. If I relax any more, I'll strangle myself with my own neck tendons. Not, she added, that I'm hostile or anything; and I really do want this to work or I wouldn't be here, I mean, this is costing me sixty quid of my own money, dammit, sixty pounds just to be told the little hairs in my nose are relaxed when they palpably aren't – sod it, you could play my nose like a bloody violin, so how dare he say I'm feeling relaxed when it should be perfectly bloody obvious – "Your wrists are relaxed," the voice said, obviously not aware how close it was getting to being shoved down its owner's neck, "your fingers are relaxed . . ."

On the other hand, Alice forced herself to remember, I haven't had a cigarette now for, oh, thirty-five hours. Thirty-five hours, sixteen minutes and twenty-three seconds. No make that thirty-five hours, sixteen minutes and twenty-six seconds; thirty-five hours, sixteen minutes and twenty-nine seconds –

Whereupon her eyes suddenly went blank, her head lolled sideways and she began to breathe deeply and regularly, like someone else's cat on the lap of a cat-hater. The voice, which had just got past her collar-bone, was silent for a moment.

Zwz, thought Alice. *Hwa* . . . ?

"Now you're fast asleep," the voice said, in a slightly brisker tone. "Now I want you to think about how nasty your mouth tastes first thing in the morning, when you've just woken up . . ."

"Who're you?"

The owner of the voice sat up sharply. He didn't know who'd said that, but he was morally certain it wasn't Alice Fennel, his patient, even though the words had sort of jostled their way out of her mouth. Completely different age, accent, inflections –

The hypnotist grinned. One of them, he thought. Yay.

He glanced down at his watch; forty minutes before the next patient was due. It'd take, what, two minutes to do the usual nasty-smelly-cigs routine (which reminded him, he was gasping for a smoke; add on three minutes for a cough and a drag out on the fire escape between appointments); that left him at least half an hour to explore the regressive personality he'd just apparently stumbled on. He just hoped Ms Fennel wouldn't turn out to have been Cleopatra in her previous existence – that would make sixteen Cleopatras this week, and a man can only stand so many barge-trips down the Nile.

"Who are you?" he asked.

"Alice," replied the voice. "Who're you?"

"That's not important," he replied soothingly, "it's you that's interesting. What year is it?"

The other Alice was quiet for a heartbeat or so. "I'm not sure, actually," she said. "Let's see; King Richard died the year before last –"

"Excuse me. Which King Richard?"

"*The* King Richard of course, silly. King Richard of England. How many king Richards do you think there are?"

Three, the hypnotist didn't reply. Instead he said, "You mean Richard the Lion-Heart, don't you?"

Other-Alice giggled. "We don't call him that in our village," she said. "We're supposed to call him that, or at least the priest tells us to, but we don't, not when he isn't listening. We call him Richard Got-His-Balls-Bit-Off-By-A-Camel –"; at which Other-Alice laughed so much he was afraid she might wake up.

Hey, said the hypnotist to himself, authentic twelfth-century humour. Gosh, aren't I the lucky one, to be sure. "That's really funny," he said aloud. "All right, can you tell me where you live?"

"In the village."

The hypnotist scowled. Ask a twentieth-century question, get a twelfth-century answer. Served him right. "And what's the village called?" he said.

"Birmingham."

"Right. Is it a big village?"

"Oh, yes. Huge. There's more'n thirty houses."

"Wow," the hypnotist said, "that's a lot. Can you tell me how old you are?"

"Course I can," said Other-Alice. "I'm seven. But quite soon I'll be eight."

Children. Another damn child. Why can't I ever get a bloody grown-up?

"That's a very good age to be," he said. "All right, what's your daddy's name?"

"George."

"What a nice name. And what does your daddy do?"

"Sits around a lot."

"I see. And how old is your daddy?"

Other-Alice hesitated, as if rehearsing a difficult speech. "Two thousand, five hundred and six," she said, "come Michaelmas."

"I see," said the hypnotist patiently. "Well, there we are, then. Have you got any brothers and sisters?"

Over the course of the next half hour, the hypnotist learned something he hadn't realised before; namely that eight-hundred-year-old seven-year-olds are just as hard to have intelligent conversations with as their modern counterparts. All in all, he was glad when the time was up and he could fill Ms Fennel up with the usual anti-weed stuff, wake her up and boost her out into the street without feeling guilty about not making the most of a unique transtemporal opportunity. Thanks to this wormhole in chronology, he'd learned that Alice had two brothers and a sister, didn't like boiled leeks and had a pet rabbit called Fern. It was almost as good as having a time machine.

"Zwz," muttered Ms Fennel, as she came round. "Is that it? Did it work?"

"Let's hope so," the hypnotist said.

"Right," grumbled Ms Fennel. "My left arm's gone to sleep."

"Try rubbing it. That'll be sixty pounds, please."

Standing in a fuzz of blue smoke on the fire escape, watching Ms Fennel in the street below frantically searching her pockets for her lighter, the hypnotist sighed. It'd made a pleasant change from all those confounded Cleopatras, and the sheer triviality of it all convinced him it was genuine; but was it too much to ask that once, just once –

My daddy's two thousand five hundred and six years old. An odd thing for a child from any era to come out with; but that's kids for you. Say any old thing, kids. It was probably her way of saying he was the wrong side of thirty. Oh well.

His next client wasn't there yet, so he went into the back office and switched on the little portable TV, to check Ceefax for the long range weather forecast. Just before the screen changed, he caught the tail end of some story about the mysterious disappearance of one of the Mars astronauts. He grinned, remembering the *Mary Tyler Moore Show*; nothing too mysterious about that, he thought. If I'd pulled a stunt like that, I'd be putting an advert in the Exchange and Mart for a forged Bolivian passport and growing a beard right now. That was one guy whose brain he'd love to unpack – what was it he'd said? Disappointing? The first man on Mars?

The hypnotist frowned. He'd also said wrong planet – now there was a thought to conjure with (Oh, Mr Porter, far beyond the stars; I wanted to go to Jupiter but they've taken me on to Mars . . .) Assuming that it wasn't a simple case of falling asleep on the bus, what the hell had he meant by that? There was, of course, a perfectly rational explanation; but after twenty years in the brain trade, he could generally spot an eccentric-as-a-hatter in the first eighth of a second. The first man on Mars may have been many things, but insane? No. If anything, the reverse. Possibly to excess . . .

She didn't see him until the last moment. Correction; she didn't see him until the moment after that – by which point he was halfway up her windscreen and accelerating dramatically.

She stood on the brake; and the car, after trying its best to fold up like a concertina, dug its tyres in and stopped. The windscreen was frosted with shatter-lines.

A small, obnoxious voice in the back of her mind proposed the motion that she should start the engine, punch a hole in the screen to see through, and drive away. The man, whoever he was, was most decidedly dead; there was nothing she could do for him. Running away was about the only thing in the universe that could make matters worse than they already were. She got out of the car, shivering. Somebody had re-possessed her knee tendons, which made walking difficult.

Absolutely no excuses. None. She'd not been looking at the road, because she'd been looking down, lighting a cigarette (a cigarette she shouldn't have been attempting to light, not after going to the hypnotist; the small, obnoxious voice, her inner lawyer, tried to make out a case for it all being the hypnotist's fault, but nobody was listening). Well, she thought, that's that. My life, down the drain. Shame, dishonour, prison. And it can't have been all fun and games for him, either.

"Don't just stand there, you stupid bitch," said a voice. "Help me out."

It was as if the angels were singing to her. "Hello?" she squeaked, her throat too tight for anything except Piglet impersonations.

"Help me out," the voice repeated.

It was coming from a gorse bush at the side of the road; into which, she discovered, a man had been inserted. All the engineers in the world, she couldn't help thinking, would be hard put to it to duplicate the experiment; he'd gone in head-first, like a high-diver, and was hanging upside-down, his weight marvellously supported by thousands of gorse-prickles lodged in his clothing. It was like something from the ashram of a Yoga master, a position symbolising opposing forces poised in space, or something of the sort.

"All right," she said doubtfully. "I – It's a bit awkward," she said.

At this point she noticed the lack of something; namely, blood. A man who's just been hit square-on by a Ford Fiesta doing 60 m.p.h. and thrown thereby into a dense tangle of thorns oughtn't to be quite so blithely monochromatic. Either the shock had made her temporarily colourblind, or he wasn't bleeding.

"Are you all right?" she asked, peering.

The man laughed. "It's all right," he said, "private joke. Look, are you going to help me out of here or do I have to wait till my clothes rot?"

"I'm sorry," she said, quite truthfully, although she was beginning to find him rather annoying. The fact that she effectively owed him her life for not being dead and that her immortal soul was presumably in his debt for the next twenty thousand years still didn't mean she had to like him. "I'm really sorry, but I don't know what to do."

"What? Oh, forget it, then." His manner and tone of voice

were definitely getting on her nerves. "Just stand back and don't get in my way, all right?"

He sort of wriggled; then he squirmed a couple of times in a thoroughly scientific manner; then he somehow fell out of the gorse bush onto the palms of his hands, did a double hand-stand and landed neatly on the soles of his feet about eighteen inches away from her. She stared at him.

"How the hell did you do that?" she asked.

He sighed. "Years of practice," he replied, examining some of the more spectacular rips in his jacket sleeves. "Bye."

He was walking away.

He was also – she'd already noticed it, but the information had taken its time registering – the most amazingly, stunningly, breathtakingly, incredibly handsome-looking man she'd ever seen in her entire life.

"Wait," she burbled.

He turned his head, flashing a profile that surely couldn't be legal in peacetime. "What?" he said, and frowned.

She still didn't like him very much, but she had to say something. "I'm – well, I'm sorry," she said. "Are you sure you're okay?"

"Never felt better. Is that it?"

He sounded as if he was talking to something he was in the act of wiping off his shoe. Not a nice man, in spite of the profile. "Can I give you a lift somewhere?" she mumbled.

"The way you drive," he said, "I think I'll pass. Try looking at the road this time. It's the long, darkish-grey thing with the white stripe up the middle."

"Yes, all right," she replied. Her inner lawyer was urging her to smack him round the head, and for once was not without a degree of support. But she couldn't stop staring. "Well," she said, "I'd better let you get on, then."

"Jolly good," he said.

"At least let me pay for the suit."

He stopped again. "That's terribly sweet," he said, as if talking to a small, irritating child, "but you can't afford it, and I can. Secretary, right?"

"I'm sorry?"

"Don't be. It's an honourable calling, and if you stick at it for twenty years you might just make office manager. Meanwhile, any suit you could afford to buy me I wouldn't be seen dead in. Another private joke," he added, "don't worry about it. Run me over again in 2026 and then maybe we can do business."

Possibly, just possibly, he was being deliberately objectionable out of a chivalric urge to smother her natural feelings of distress and guilt and replace them with good, healthy loathing. But he didn't seem the type. "All right, then," she said. "If you're sure."

"No, I only said it to practise my vocabulary. Now please go away and ram a tree or something."

He was moving away again. She ran after him and grabbed his sleeve, which came away in her hand.

"Neat trick," he said. "But I'm still not letting you buy me a new one."

"Why aren't you hurt?" she shouted at the top of her voice. "You went flying up in the air. You smashed my windscreen."

"Ah. Now there's something I could buy for you."

"Stop being so bloody annoying and answer me!"

He looked at her, and shook his head. "No," he said. "Keep the sleeve."

"You . . ."

"I think you'd better move your car," he said. "There's people trying to get past."

"What? Oh . . ."

Of course she couldn't see anything through the screen, and when she tried to bash a hole in it she hurt the side of her hand quite badly. In the end, she guessed, and kept on creeping forward till she came up against something – a tree or a fence-post, she couldn't care less. When she climbed out again and ran up the road after him, there was no sign of anybody.

"Damn," she said, looking around. There were a couple of field gates he could have hopped over, but the thought of wading around in muddy fields looking for him was more than she could cope with. On the way back to the car she picked up a reasonable-sized stone that made a perfectly adequate port-hole in the windscreen and also helped her relieve her feelings to a moderate extent. Of course, the driver's seat was now covered in bits of glass, but that was probably the least of her problems.

Maybe I imagined the whole thing, she thought, as she sat and looked at the world through the frosty-edged hole. Maybe I'm still three parts hypnotized, and having hallucinations. A moment later she noticed a lit cigarette between her fingers; she threw it out through the hole, and lit another one a second or so later. If I imagined the whole thing, what happened to the car? Hit a tree? Suppose I must have done. Either I knocked a drop-dead gorgeous, invulnerable pain in the bum into a gorse bush, or I hit a tree. I think I must have hit a tree.

She drove the last six miles at a steady fifteen miles an hour, parked the car and sat down on her front doorstep, trying to find the energy to fish out her keys and open the door. Hit a tree, she told herself, mindlessly chewing the words like gum, I hit a tree, I hit a tree. There was a tree, really there was, and I drove into it. Wham crash tinkle. Really and truly, there was a tree . . .

She stood up. She felt fine. When I hit the tree, I bashed my head. That's why I imagined that I hit him, not a tree. But it was a tree I hit, not him. I know him from somewhere.

She opened the door and let herself slump through it. Of course I think I know him from somewhere, because he was a hallucination, brought on by hitting my head when I hit the tree. When you hallucinate, you make up the picture from someone you know. That's why I thought he looked familiar. But really, I hit a tree.

Depressingly, she'd never felt better in her life; but that was probably a side-effect of the concussion too. Ought to see doctor, if bad concussion, seeing things. Too ill to see doctor. Best place for her was in bed; then, tomorrow, the doctor. Then the garage. Lots of incredibly tedious, boring things to do. Thinking about them made her feel a little better – nothing like extreme inconvenience to bring you back down to earth –

and she managed to crawl into bed and close her eyes. She couldn't sleep, so she tried counting sheep. Then trees.

At half past three in the morning, she woke up out of a dream she instantly forgot. "Not him," she said aloud, "tree."

She knew who he was. Except he wasn't. No trace of a resemblance; not physical, behavioral or verbal. Never seen him before. Complete and total stranger.

"Daddy?" she said.

There were 26,865 messages on his answering machine when he got home. He wiped them all without listening to any of them, got undressed, brushed his teeth and went to bed. He'd have to be up bright and early in the morning, before NASA and the Europeans and the Chinese and all the rest of them figured out where he'd sneaked off to. He had a long way to go. He needed a few hours' sleep.

Which wouldn't come, no matter what. Overtired, he realized. Jetlag – no, timelag; ought to be used to it by now, it wasn't the first time he'd indulged in faster-than-light travel and arrived home after a six-week journey three hours before he'd set off. It had been a slice of luck, of course, picking up a lift on Mars from a passing Ostar survey ship ("You want to go where? Seriously? Oh, you live there. . ."); it had spared him the unspeakable tedium of a voyage home via human technology, as well as giving him a head start on his erstwhile colleagues, who wouldn't be expecting him home until the stub end of the rocket went splash in the Indian Ocean, in approximately eight weeks' time. He grinned briefly, imagining the look on their faces when they popped the hatch and found him absent; their shock, horror and disbelief as it slowly dawned on them that they were going to have to find someone else to blame . . .

The hell with them, and all that. It had been a pretty fatuous hope to begin with; that the silly little red ball of dust and rock the humans called Mars would turn out to be his home. But, fatuous or not, it had also been his last, best shot, the culmination of centuries of hard work, subtle manipulation, unendurable patience and almost continuous tongue-biting.

No small task he'd set himself, back in the dawn of European prehistory; to nudge, suggest and puppy-train Homo Sapiens into a state of technological achievement sufficient to enable the building of a space-going vessel capable of reaching that dusty red rock in the sky – and that had been a thin sliver of Battenburg compared with the job of creating a society enlightened, educated, scientifically curious and above all, gullible enough to want to send a rocket to the stars, all without letting anybody suspect that they were being used, or that the using had been done, from start to finish, by the same unknown and uncredited individual.

On balance . . . Well, quite. On balance, he'd have been better off, three and a third millenia ago, settling down and getting a job. Never too late to plan for your retirement, the TV ads were forever screeching at him; just think. If he'd planned ahead – He frowned, did sums on his fingers. If he'd pulled his finger out the day he'd arrived on Earth, consulted an independent financial adviser and taken out an endowment mortgage linked to a with-profits term life policy, by now he'd have paid off the final instalment and be the owner of the entire planet.

Instead; well, the first hundred years had been a gas, a riot, a ball. Soon as he'd realized that in this miserable little planet's atmosphere he was effectively immortal, ageless and invulnerable, he'd been off in a whirl of larking about that had irrevocably altered history, founded half a dozen religions and left him with a permanent taste for dry white wine, feta cheese and impersonating supernatural entities. Good fun, until the homesickness cut in and he found himself staring bleakly at the raw fact that he'd done everything, been everywhere, sampled every experience that this cramped little pebble could possibly offer; and meanwhile, back home, Real Life was tapping its foot, glancing at its watch, wondering where the hell he could possibly have got to, with the implied proviso that if he was much longer, it would have no choice but to go on without him. If his calculations were accurate, a century on Earth was very roughly equivalent to a month back home. The general rule, essential in a spacegoing culture, was that once you'd been missing off-planet for eighteen months and your family and employers had no reason to believe you were still alive, the court declared you legally dead; your possessions were sold off, your dwelling unit was reassigned, your union memberships and Book Club subscriptions were automatically cancelled and your back pay was donated to the Ministry of Justice Probate Division Social Club and Beer Fund, to defray the expenses of your Statutory Wake. Once you were legally dead, of course, that was that. The Ministry of Justice hadn't tamed a turbulent warrior species and established an ideal society by letting mere facts get in the way of presumptions of law.

Eighteen months – eighteen hundred years, Earth time – and he'd be irrevocably screwed; his life as he knew it would be over, his spouse would be free to recouple with her loathsome cousin the insurance broker, and his unique collection of Strange Animal Noises vids would be split up and dissipated across the length and breadth of the Spinning Rose. Disaster.

Just thinking about it made him wince, even now. It's only when you watch what you've got slipping away through your fingers that you realize it was actually rather a lot, verging on unalloyed bliss; certainly when compared with what he had on rotten stinking Earth, in the company of fifty billion barely planet-trained hairless primates. Even when the deadline had passed, he was painfully aware that he'd give anything to be back home, living the half-life of a legal ghost, barred from owning property, contracting marriage or joining a video library, rather than be stranded here among the monkey people. If anything, his efforts to guide humanity became more feverish in their intensity. The camshaft, moveable type, democracy, the blast furnace, high-carbon alloy steel, the telescope, income tax, electricity, science fiction, the rocket motor, one by one he'd cunningly smuggled them into the sum of human knowledge and experience; hoping all the while that the planet they called Mars was indeed the Spinning Rose, just because Mars looked sort of reddish too . . .

Wrong planet. He'd got there eventually, but it was the wrong bloody planet. Pity, really. Final crowning irony of ironies, that he should have set foot on Mars at precisely the moment when another space-travelling race, one with the technology to take him to the very furthest edge of the galaxy, was just about to leave – and that that race should be the rotten bloody Ostar . . . Nice enough blokes in their way, delighted to help out a fellow sentient being in any way they could, with just the one unfortunate exception; that they believed without question that the Spinning Rose was the planet where all their race's lawyers went to when they died, which meant that nothing under the stars would ever induce them to go within fifty thousand light-years of it.

Spiffing. Just for a split second he'd toyed with the thought of asking them for a lift to Ostar Prime; but he'd been there, many years ago, and remembered that their entire culture was based around a game in which twenty-two Ostar chased an inflated egg-shaped bladder round a flat grass square. The hell with that. Suddenly, Earth hadn't seemed quite so bad after all.

He yawned, rolled over onto his back, stared at the ceiling. Tomorrow, he told himself, would be the first day of the rest of his everlasting life. Oh, what joy.

"Daddy?" she repeated.

Sitting up in bed, gormless expression on face, feeling about as bright and chirpy as a troll who's forgotten that the clocks go forward; Daddy? Nah, can't have been. *Think*, you stupid girl, *think*. Last time you saw Daddy was twenty-five years ago, when he would have been somewhere around thirty and you were two. Therefore it follows, as the night the day, that a man you bump into twenty-five years later who looks exactly, down to the last hair, like Daddy looked twenty-five years ago, cannot, in the very nature of things, be him. Besides, if it had been Daddy, he'd have had a newspaper; because the last thing he'd said to Mummy before he disappeared was that he was just nipping down the road to get a paper; and by now he must've found one he liked, surely – Her face hardened just a little. Of course it hadn't been Daddy; but if it had been, she'd missed out on a wonderful opportunity to show him how much she loved him by reversing back over him a few times and parking her car on his head.

But it hadn't been him, it was just a tree. Tree. Big tall wooden thing with leaves. Big tall wooden thing with leaves that doesn't suddenly piss off when you're two and not come back. And therein lay the difference. She quite liked trees.

Time to get up, dress, eat breakfast, go to work. She was at the office and taking the cover off her keyboard when she remembered she was completely out of cigarettes. Not that it mattered a damn, since she'd given up smoking for good, permanently and for ever nine hours, fourteen minutes and thirty-five seconds ago.

"Won't be a moment," she trilled at the office manager, as she grabbed her coat off the hook. "Just got to nip out to the shop."

The office manager pulled a face like a basilisk with toothache, but by then she was halfway down the stairs.

Outside the newsagent's, he opened the paper and scowled.

They'd spelt his name wrong, of course; even more annoying was the fact that they'd announced that he was dead. Huh. If only.

Astronaut Dead in Mars Probe Horror. Yes, well. He had mixed feelings about his apparent immortality. On the one hand, anything had to be better than life on Earth. On the other hand, what if he died and got bundled off by default to some human-specific afterlife, which would inevitably consist of everything he found most objectionable about the planet, only more so? The eternity aspect of it wouldn't be so terribly different to what he was going through now, but human beings floating on fluffy white clouds playing harps –

Interesting line of speculation, nonetheless, and one he'd toyed with before. So far, in over three thousand years of boisterous activity, he hadn't found anything on Earth that could kill him, or even give him a mild headache. Even so, just because he hadn't found it yet didn't mean to say it didn't exist; and besides, he was limiting himself rather with that implied on-Earth proviso. He might be tougher than Clint

Eastwood's stunt double, but . . . He turned the page of his
newspaper. A light flipped on inside his head, and he grinned.

The headline on the top left of page three was something
about some arms limitation initiative somewhere; presumably
an effort to prevent the possibility of the planet getting blown
to rubble as the result of an unfortunate misunderstanding.
Yes, he thought, what about that? If he'd learned one thing
about humans, it was that they were distinctly touchy about
certain things – borders and airspace violations and stuff like
that – and also perfectly capable of blasting out the baby with
the planetary bathwater over matters of ideological principle.
Just suppose . . . If the planet got blown into space-dust,
surely even he couldn't be expected to survive that – or even if
he did, surely a minute or so in the interplanetary void could
be relied on to do him in. Furthermore (and this was the clever
bit); if there was no planet Earth and no human race, would
there still be a human heaven and/or hell (as far as he was
concerned, the two would be interchangeable) waiting to
snaffle him as soon as his soul broke out of his body? Logic
would seem to suggest not. He had no idea how these things
were supposed to work, but he'd been around for the rise and
fall of more human religions than a millipede could count on
its fingers, and they'd left him with the distinct impression
that once people stop believing in them, gods die and heavens
fade. Switch off the power at the mains, therefore, and
inevitably the screen must go blank.

Yay, he thought. Easy peasy. The tricky part over the last
century or so had been stopping his unwitting proteges from
exterminating each other, at least until they'd built the
manned Mars rocket. Just a little bit of encouragement, a
few tugs on the chain here and there, and he could be out of
here inside a month – He looked up, suddenly aware that he
was being stared at.

"Oh," he said. "Hello."

"You."

Some female; he was rather good at monkey-faces, but after
watching so many generations go by, he couldn't help getting
just a little bit confused sometimes. He was pretty sure he

recognized this specimen, but it was entirely possible that she was the spit and image of her great-great-great-grandmother, who might have been the waitress who spilt hot soup in his lap back in 1854.

"You," she repeated. She'd just lit a cigarette, and the forgotten match burned down and scorched her fingers. She hardly noticed. "I –"

"Ah yes." He remembered now. "You're the silly cow who rammed me with a car last night." He grinned. "You got home safely, then, after all?"

"Me?"

"Yes. Not," he added with a sweet smile, "that I give a shit, because fairly soon, if everything goes the way I'm hoping it will, all that sort of stuff'll be largely academic anyhow." He grinned. "Private joke," he explained. "See you around." And, before she could say anything, he'd crossed the road without looking and walked round the corner, out of sight.

"You are starting to feel sleepy," said the voice. "You are completely relaxed. Your toes are relaxed. Your feet are relaxed. Your ankles are relaxed . . ."

Balls, she thought; but her eyelids dropped anyway, and her mind started to drift, in the way which had by now become familiar. Waste of time, she thought, waste of money, this is pointless, doesn't work – Oh, she thought.

Rationalizing after the event, she decided it must've been because her second encounter with the strange, unpleasant man was still fresh in her subconscious mind, his face still plastered all over the screen there; so, when the brakes of consciousness were taken off and she started gently freewheeling through her own hidden preoccupations, the sight of the same face in a completely different context must've pulled her up sharp.

Very different context, or series of contexts; her mind was now a bank of split screens, each showing the same face, his; each one as radically different as one century from another, one lifetime from another. Much, much better value for money than drowning or falling off a tall building; because instead of just one past life flashing in front of her eyes, there were *dozens* . . .

Turned out she'd been – let's see, she thought; in this life, a humble secretary in a government office. In her previous incarnation, by contrast, she'd been a professor of nuclear physics; before that, the wife of a world-famous astronomer; before that, a humble New England schoolteacher; before that, the widow of a wealthy industrialist; before that – oh, all sorts of things, right back to a little girl standing in the sun in a dusty courtyard watching a bald old man drawing lines in the dust with a stick, pointing something out to him – ooh look, uncle, the square on the hypotenuse is equal to the squares on the other two sides, just fancy that –

So many lives. All different. All me.

All not so different as all that.

Maybe if she'd been awake, she wouldn't have been able to join the associational dots; too much would've got in the way. But as she watched the images flick past, the basic shape of the plot stared out at her like a turd in a bowl of salad; and quickly, intuitively, she put the story together.

Each time round, he'd been her father. Each time, he'd suggested or argued or pressured her into a way of life – marriage, career, whatever – and each time round she'd been the vital link in the chain. As a scientist, she'd made the crucial breakthrough; before that, she'd drawn her husband's attention to the little speck through the telescope that he'd overlooked; before that, she'd invested some of her late husband's fortune in the company that went on to refine the necessary alloy; before that, as a schoolma'am, she'd imbued the child prodigy with his lifelong passion for mathematics; before that, talking her husband into bankrolling Hernan Cortes and his wild dreams of exploration. Each time around one more little step (and every time, nobody taking the slightest bit of notice, because after all, she was only a woman . . .) on the way to bringing about the grand design of her serial father. Daddy's little girl.

I'd like to wake up now, please, she screamed; but her mouth and lungs were fast asleep, while the hypnotist droned

on about how much she hated the smell of tobacco smoke
(liar). So instead she stepped back until she could make out the
broad, bold lines of the big picture.

Whereupon she understood.

A rich, full day.

He hadn't been able to bring himself to do it, of course;
mostly, he realized, because it would've been too bloody easy –
too depressingly, predictably, disappointingly simple. A few
calls, whispers in a few ears, some lies, some half truths, and he
could have had a thousand bombers in the air before the pubs
opened. But then, he'd thought. If it's so easy, I guess there's
no rush. I can do it tomorrow, or the next day, or the day after
that. If I really want to. Which I –

Which I don't, he admitted. And I'd really rather not dwell
on the reasons behind that. The very idea that I'm going soft,
going native, turning into one of *them* – well, might as well
grow a tail and put in a bulk order for bananas. He slipped his
key into the lock and let himself in.

"Hello."

This time it was his turn to say, "You."

She nodded to him; distant, polite. "Hello, Dad," she said.

He frowned. "You what?"

"Also," she went on, "hello grandad, great-grandad, great-
great-grandad, and great-grandad to the power of twelve
recurring. You bastard," she added, with feeling.

"Ah," he replied. "Got you. Sorry, I didn't recognize
you."

She shook her head. "I quite understand," she said. "After
all, I look different each time round, and you haven't seen me
this time since I was two. Did you get your paper, by the
way?"

"My what?"

"Newspaper. The one you were just nipping out for, last
time I saw you. Ah yes, there it is in your side pocket."

"Oh," he said. "Look, I'm sorry about that –"

She thew an ashtray at him. It shattered against his forehead. She scowled.

"Didn't hurt, did it?" she said.

"Well," he admitted, "no."

"I thought not. Pity. Is there anything that hurts you? Anything at all? Because –"

He smiled. "Only being stuck on this planet," he replied. "Ignore me," he added. "Private –"

"Yes, private joke," she interrupted. "Only, not any more. You see, I've remembered. All of it, or all of them, whatever. Sheer fluke," she went on, "regression under hypnosis, which I'm having to help me quit smoking, which I only started doing because of the stress I was under at home, because my mum's a complete emotional *wreck*, because –"

He nodded. "Chains of causality are bitches, aren't they?" he said. "Any point in asking how you found me? This address is meant to be – well, private, and . . ."

"Yes," she said icily, "but I seem to have inherited some of my dad's low cunning and utter ruthlessness, so I hacked into the Department's database and there it was. You should be very proud."

He thought about that for a moment. "Not really," he said. "Would you like a cup of tea?"

"I couldn't have your liver raw on a slice of toast instead?"

He shook his head. "Scalpels snap on me," he replied, "and I just seem to absorb industrial lasers. But I happen to have some chocolate mini-rolls in the fridge, and since they're my favourite, it's a fair bet you like them too . . ."

An unslakeable thirst for revenge is one thing, but chocolate is something else. "Go on, then," she said. "But I still hate you to death."

"Me too," he said with a mild grin, and filled the kettle.

"So there I was," he said, half an hour later, "alone, stranded under the glare of an alien sun, who knows how many thousands of light-years away from home, with no prospect of escape, doomed to an eternity of exile on an inhospitable planet at the mercy of a race of savage primitives." He sighed. "And all because my evil friends though it'd be a good stag-night prank to get me drunk and lock me in the hold of an unnumbered deep space probe on the night before my wedding. If ever I get my hands on them –"

"Hardly likely," she interrupted. "That was three thousand years ago, they'll all be dead by now."

He sighed, and explained about the relativistic distortions. "So really," he went on, "I've only been away, what, twenty-five Home years. And since where I come from we don't start drawing our pensions till we're 200 . . ." He shrugged. "Not that it matters a damn," he continued, "because it's bloody obvious, I've finally accepted it, I'm not going home. Not ever. Damn it, I don't even know where home is." He paused. "Why are you looking at me like that?"

"But of course you know," she said.

He shook his head. "No, I thought I knew; Mars, because it's sort of red-coloured, and so's the Spinning Rose. But I was wrong, as I found out just the other day. So –"

"Oh!" She stared at him, then giggled. "You thought that, did you?"

"What do you mean?"

"You thought Mars was your homeworld? Really?"

"Yes."

She sniggered. "*Really?*"

"All right, there's no need to be offensive. I got it wrong, I admit that –"

"But it's so *obvious*," she interrupted. "Where it is, I mean. Your planet."

He frowned. "Really? And how the hell would you know?"

She smiled. "Because you had me figure it out for you, silly," she explained patiently. "In 1894; you know, when I was married to that incredibly boring astronomer person. All those hints you dropped when I was a kid; all those stories about the planet far away in the sky where the elves live. You were feeding me everything you could remember about your home, so I'd grow up with a lifelong ambition to find it. And I did."

He stared. "You what?"

"I found it. With George's telescope. And then I told him, and he wrote it up for the journals, said he'd found it himself, of course, and they made him a Sir and a Regius professor and everything." She looked at him. "You mean to say," she said, "I went to all that trouble, and you didn't even realize?"

He shook his head. "No," he said. "I'm sorry. I was so convinced it was Mars, and –"

"And all you wanted was a son-in-law with a really powerful telescope you could borrow at weekends, and of course anything *I* came up with couldn't have been important because I'm only a girl . . ."

He didn't say anything.

"Fine," she said. Then suddenly she grinned. "That explains the other thing that was puzzling me. I mean, why you were so dead keen to go fooling about on a stupid little sub-light rocket ship poking around the solar system, when I'd already invented a faster-than-light stardrive –"

The sound he made couldn't actually be produced by a human larynx; the nearest equivalent would be something like *tweep*, but a good deal of the effect is wasted in transcription.

"A faster-than-light stardrive," she repeated. "Last time round, when I was a scientist, remember? Oh sure, you just wanted me to solve the artificial gravity thing so you wouldn't have to pee down a straw all the way to Mars, so obviously once I'd done that you lost interest. And," she admitted, "it didn't help that I died the day after I finished the design –"

"And nobody bothered to read through the papers you left behind, because you were just –"

"Exactly." She clicked her tongue. "But I did take the precaution of bequeathing all my notes and stuff to the University of Florida, and I *know* they won't have chucked them out or anything because they're so historically important. Because of all the really famous *male* scientists I worked with over the years –"

"All right, yes." He pulled a face. "Point made and duly hammered into the ground. And now, perhaps," he added, "you can see why I'm not so desperately fond of this planet and its dominant species. Well?"

She looked at him for a moment, then nodded. "Quite," she said.

Forty-three years and six months later, on the day when she was due to retire as McConnell professor of applied microphysics at MIT, she got a postcard. It was slightly creased; and the gum on the back of the stamp contained at least seven elements not known to Earth science, though the post office probably hadn't spotted that. It read –

Well, I'm back. Ride a bit bumpy – lost a phase integrator coupling relay in a paraspatial vortex just outside the Crane nebula, and all the condensed milk curdled, but better than walking nonetheless. Home's much the same as when I left, except of course I'm legally dead, which means I'll be lucky to get a job flipping burgers, and I can't murder my best man and groomsmen after all, because they died last autumn in a freak ashslide. Also, I'd forgotten just how damp and miserable this rotten planet gets in winter. Like England, only worse.

Even so. Thanks.

Cordially,
Dad.

She grinned. "No worries," she said, and put the card on the mantelpiece, behind the clock.

RETURN OF THE WARRIOR

Laird Long

In the Province of Sull, in the Kingdom of Ronn, all seemed right with the world – the potters potted, the sculptors sculpted, the painters painted, and the scriveners did whatever their name implies. For Sull was home to the kingdom's artisans, a colourful colony of creative cranks who used well their artistic endowments, for satisfaction of the soul, and sale. And they toiled truly and profitably.

But beneath the placid, pleasant exterior of the province and the people, lay a seething resentment bubbled to near-surface boil by the erratic, practicality-impaired nature of the creative personality, and the indolence of a King who listened not to ill-formed complaints some two hundred leagues removed. A prickly current of unrest sparked and shocked the citizenry, for many held the opinion that the provincial governor, the Wizard Kadil, was in no uncertain terms fudging the books, collecting taxes beyond what the law allowed. And though the people of Sull claimed to be moved primarily by muse, so, too, were they moved by a love of the good old gold stuff.

The Wizard Kadil ruled the Province of Sull at the pleasure of King Dorn, a fatted lion of an emperor who oversaw his vast and vibrant kingdom with the sure and sleight-handed aid of Zaric, Wizard of all Wizards, to whom the wizard governors reported directly. And foremost amongst the Wizard Kadil's tools of governance, beyond the merciless armies of Dorn, was the Tithle – the ancient, righteous code of tithes and taxation written by those wise sages whom first trod the fair plains and lush valleys, climbed the craggy mountains, and forded the blue lakes and turgid rivers of the Kingdom of Ronn. These founding deities well-knew that a fair and just system of levies would serve to cornerstone the advanced civilization that they envisioned, just as the hand-hewn dung bricks, stenched though they may be, still serve as the cornerstones of the true and sturdy homes of the kingdom's citizenry.

So it was that this code of taxation, embodied in the Tithle and enforced by the army, served to unite the kingdom, furnish it with communal roads and bridges and dungeons, furnish the King and his wizards with a lifestyle befitting their status. As certain as death and taxes, the non-payment of the latter summoning forth the former, was the smooth governance and functioning of the Kingdom of Ronn.

"We are gouged!" Aynd the actor railed, in a back-rows voice much larded with indignation.

Jodd the juggler supped at his grog and glanced nervously about the dim tavern. "You can't be sure," he whispered, twirling one bar of his mustaches. "How can you be sure?"

The subject of heathen coin never failed to fire the fine-tuned temperaments of the artisans, like flame to flower, not only because of their unspoken love for the stuff, but more so because of their abysmal ignorance of the handling and the bookkeeping of it, their impotence in the face of matters monetarily technical.

"The Tithle is being abused!" Aynd yowled, in exquisite profile, causing shaggy heads to rise from their gourds of inspiration. "I know for a fact that my brother Wass, in the Province of Dramm, is paying far less to his wizard than I am paying to ours." Aynd uplifted his arms in supplication. "Yet he earns much more than I, as a mule-brusher and stall-sweeper of many years experience."

"Hmmm," Jodd mused, tugging now on his twin strands of facial hair. "But – but the founding principle of the Tithle is that each shall pay according to their earnings."

"Yes!" Aynd roared, his sensitive eyes registering a much baser emotion, one coined in gold.

Jodd chugged at his grog, choked on it, his face burning as

red as the copper drachma. "But how can we – you prove this
gouging of which you and you alone speak? The Tithle is
thousands of parchments long, written in a scrip so cramped
even Blan's seeing-eye dwarf could hardly read it. And complex? T'would be easier to swim naked and unscathed through
the rock-bladed rapids of the snake-filled Kaidel River than it
would be to comprehend the Tithle and all it contains. That is
why a tax wizard is needed." Jodd shrugged, defeated. "We
are artisans, after all, and know no more of numbers and
clauses and calculations than a sloth knows of busywork."

"True enough," Aynd agreed, his voice dropping to the
level of conspiracy, his lips leaking it. "But we now have
among us one who can wrestle sense out of the Tithle, rebates
out of the Wizard Kadil."

Jodd's blackened eyes widened. "Who?"

Aynd held the suspense a perfect ten beats, then tapped the
right flank of his equine nose. "Ihor!"

Jodd dropped his gourd. "What!? You can't be serious! Can
you? The newcomer who dwells in the burnt-orange cottage at
the lee end of Sunset Road? He is but an ironmonger, with the
thew-thick arms and shoulders to prove it."

"Once was tax warrior," Aynd commented wryly, nodding
both of his gourds.

Thus it was that the Province of Sull, in the Kingdom of
Ronn, grew abuzz with the prospect of tax relief, as a swarm
of bees grows agitated at the sight and the scent of a field of
goldenrod, the prospect of pollination and the honey that
will come of it. The people began to believe that if only the
massive, mysterious stranger known as Ihor could be ca-
joled into challenging the Wizard Kadil, then the truth
could be revealed, and more importantly, the artisans
refunded.

"You must help us – help yourself!" Aynd argued, at the
head of the twenty-strong delegation – Artisans for Account-
ability – that had marched on Ihor's cottage. They stood as a
group under a blazing noonday sun that set their fair skin to
burning and weeping, anxious for an answer.

Ihor shook his boulder-like head. "I am but an iron-monger," he protested, platter-sized paws full of tongs and bellows, "hammering out abstracts and objects d'art – an artisan like yourselves. Matters of money and the taxation of money are beyond my realm and beneath my dignity."

"As an artisan, yes," Aynd agreed, the delegation, in turn, nodding their collective, somewhat pointed heads. "But we know that you were once a mighty tax warrior, Ihor, a cruncher of numbers and a counter of beans, a holy disciple of the sacred Tithle."

The stave-thick thews on Ihor's tree-trunk arms corded and uncorded, and a bloated, purple-pink worm of a vein throbbed in his temple. "How do you know?"

Punt the painter spoke up. "My cousin, Zalt, tells tales of how you fought, alone and armed but with a magnifying glass, through the maze-like fine print of the Regulations of Roinder, to forge better trade ties with the Kingdom of Nann!"

"And my father saw you rush from the customs offices of Azul, howling at the head of a team of tax warriors, during the Ronn–Azul tariff wars of many moons past!" Natd the needle-pointress pointed out, her eyes uncrossing ever so briefly.

Ihor's instruments of forging artistry thudded to the ground. "I – I –"

"And look at your hands!" Aynd wailed, grasping the he-man's fearsome fists and flipping them over.

The assemblage oohed and then aahed, as they saw for themselves the baby's-bottom palms of the giant, pale palms tinted with streaks of ledger ink – the unmistakable signs of accountancy.

Ihor sighed as bellows sigh when fully deflated, his mammoth body sagging. He had painstakingly built up a physique of sun-burnished sinews, worn it like a suit of armor in order to shield him from his past, but his bookish hands had betrayed him, subverted his desperate attempt to broach the cavernous gulf between a career of destruction and one of creation. "You think the Wizard Kadil is cheating you?" he said, in a voice grown low and weary with the remembrance of grueling account examinations past.

The delegation roared.

So it was that the reluctant warrior – armed only with a razor-sharp charcoal stick, a blood-red beaded abacus, and a brass-bound folio loaded with seven-column parchment – and his self-serving entourage trod the dusty, hallowed ground that led to the imposing castle of the Wizard Kadil. Once arrived, Ihor pounded on the drawbridge, his tacit supporters scuttling to safety in the surrounding shrubbery.

Kadil appeared at a parapet, looked down at the giant, the frightened eyes peering out of the bushes. "What is it you want!?" he asked, in a voice both foul and fearsome, his rancid breath stirring the warrior's night-shaded locks, and nostrils.

"I am demanding an examination of your records!" Ihor replied, implacable and erect.

Kadil stroked his wattled, wart-laden jowls and considered. The wizard collected taxes on all manners of citizens' incomes and transactions and usages in the Province of Sull, under authority of the King, in full compliance with the terms of the Tithle, it was understood. But it was the right of any citizen to inspect their wizard-kept records, consult one of the ten handcalligraphed copies of the Tithle that resided at the wizards' castles. But no citizen ever did, for all knew that none but a tax wizard, schooled and steeped in the ways of the Tithle, could ever hope to come to grips with the sheer immensity of material, the complexity therein.

"Surely you jest," Kadil finally replied.

"I jest not!" Ihor bellowed. "I demand entrance and audit!"

"Audit!?" Kadil was shaken to the fawn-skinned bottoms of his pointy, ankle-high boots – such a word was anathema to the financially ignorant colony he ruled. "W-well . . . come in!" he hissed eventually, the sleeves of his monochrome tunic already writhing with the tricks that they held.

Ihor and the band of artisans followed the wizard deep into the booklined bowels of the granite, gold-fixtured fortress, through wending, spike-walled hallways, down tottering, kindle-dry staircases, across open, leech-thick plumbing, till at last, with half of the group still somewhat intact, they came upon the entrance to a small, stuffy, single candle-lit room crammed to the cobwebbed rafters full of sharp-edged parchment and paper, splintery chunks of pulpwood, stone-heavy journals and ledgers, and reams and reams of bland, boiler-plate forms bearing scrawls and figurings in what was supposed to be the language of numerology. And there, amidst the dangerous disorder that threatened to break into chaos, nesting in a towering, bristling stack of papyrus atop a wobble-legged desk of flammable balsam minus its chair companion, lay a copy of the Tithle – all ten thousand, two hundred, and forty-eight word-cramped, onion-skinned pages of it, complete with two hundred and fifty-seven attached appendices, shoulder-to-shoulder with one hundred and forty-nine companion volumes of euphemistically entitled Clarifications.

"All is as it should be. At your disposal," Kadil cackled, spreading wide his pasty, pixie-thin arms at the unholy mess. He waded through the crinkly flotsam, pages disintegrating and sheaves sticking to his charged robes as he did so, and tried to heft the mightily-engorged Tithle, and failed. "I assume it is with this tome that you'd like to begin?" he brayed, caressing the unwieldy, rusty-hinged volume of revenue procurement regulations.

"You know what happens when you assume, don't you?" Ihor replied, both rhetorically and insolently. "I am already familiar with all that lies between the covers of that manual, Wizard."

Kadil gasped. "What!? What is this!?" he jabbered, his jaundiced orbs darting around the muscled periphery of the giant, striking the delegation of artisans cowering behind. They vanished yet further into the wake of their gargantuan representative. "How can one such as yourself be familiar with what lies within the Tithle – an artisan!?"

Ihor did not respond, for he was keenly observing Kadil, seeking physical manifestations of malfeasance, the scent of fear a thing sharp to his sensitive nose, the body-language of deceit a thing naked to his shrewd eyes.

"You have one week," Kadil gritted.
And the battle was joined.

The Wizard Kadil behaved as any resentful being being audited would behave, which is to say, badly. And as someone arrogantly used to getting his own way, to unquestioning obedience, he behaved that much worse. He was recalcitrant in addressing even the simplest of Ihor's questions, such as where documents lay and journals were to be found, misdirecting his inquisitor to the appropriate ledgers, then feigning ignorance and absentmindedness, and then outright hearing impairment.

Ihor was undeterred, however, and he dug through the mountain of material on his own, sifting and shovelling, exhuming the items he would require for a thorough examination. Kadil saw Ihor's expert documentation-gathering techniques, his unflagging processes of polished audit evidentiary accumulation, and he went into action. He commenced showering the giant with paperwork, in a confusatory, perverted spirit of cooperation, tearing open drawers and cupboards and cabinets and flinging out chits and chats and receipts and invoices, whole anvil-weighted subledgers packed with notations and numbers, foot-wide logs thick with spidery figures, calculations arcane and convoluted, striving to bury Ihor and his clarity of thought and purpose in a blizzard of apocryphal records, some germane to the warrior's purpose, most obfuscatory.

And when still Ihor slogged onward through the fibrous onslaught, his brow furled like a sweat-stained battle flag, his teeth clenched as the steel jaws of a trap are clenched upon their hapless prey, his eyes gleaming with the bloody zeal of the battle-hardened number-disciple driving ever-forwards on the rocky, ragtag audit trail – checking and rechecking and crosschecking, calculating and comparing, balancing and booking – Kadil gripped his flowing, eunuchian robes and swirled them about, as if in disgust, the real purpose being to send the entire chattered heap of documentation swirling about tornado-like, the slashing, ink-jotted paper spinning and spinning, sorting and resorting, coming together and apart without rhyme nor reason either.

But Ihor stood his ground inside the dervish of debris, bleeding copiously from paper cuts yet unbowed, snagging and hauling down the scraps of information he sought, cunning orbs scouring pages and columns for relevancy and revelation. He did not compromise nor did he skimp, performing his examinary tasks fully and completely, with a dour doggedness that would have left lesser men dulled and lifeless.

The artisans stared from behind their oak-ribbed door shield, in dumbfounded awe, never before dreaming that the world of accounting and taxation could be so violent and variable. They cheered lustily when Ihor ticked, clapped gustily when he bopped, watching wide-eyed and wonderstruck as their heroic warrior reaped the pulpy, number-scrawled whirlwind.

"Finding everything you need!?" Kadil howled above the tumult. "Everything agreeing!?"

"So far," Ihor replied, nonplussed, his fleet fingers manipulating the beads of his abacus with blinding speed, scratching down figures in his folio fast and furious and on the fly. His abacus and charcoal, and the brilliant mind that drove them, were the weapons of Kadil's possible math destruction.

Hours and then days dragged by, the battle raging on and on, Kadil unleashing his full arsenal of audit-thwarting techniques. He counted out loud, over and over, playing havoc with Ihor's mental arithmetic, his powers of concentration, reciting random numbers in a shrill, sing-song voice that had the dead-tired delegation clutching their ears in stultified terror. And to Ihor's legitimate and legal inquiries of clarification, Kadil responded in a tongue as forked as a serpent's, his answers doubling and trebling back upon themselves, meandering around and around and going nowhere, their points blunted and lost, in a voice now hale now hushed. Still Ihor plucked out the gems of information and assurance he needed from the fractured responses and fractious paperwork, his spirit strong, his senses heightening rather than fading.

Six days so passed, each grinding hour like the one preceding, the world of life and light beyond the stale, stone walls a long-forgotten thing. The Wizard Kadil grew desperate. Ihor was tying things together as surely as a butcher binds a pig to a spit and then fires it into oblivion, inching unrelentingly ever-closer to conclusion, questions becoming answers, to do points resolving, calculations being proved. So, Kadil sneezed, and sneezed again, imparting from his suddenly runny nose, his treacherous nostrils, a mystical secretion that settled like a fine mist over the maelstrom, blurring everything within the cloistered compartment. The figures on the documents Ihor was studying, the numbers in his folio, seemed to fade and jumble, mix and mismatch, rendered shapeless and potentially meaningless.

Ihor looked at the wizard and gave his rugged head a shake, clearing the cobwebs of confusion. Then he grinned a rave-nous grin, his bloodshot eyes clouded now only by wretched remembrance. "I've seen all such tricks before, Wizard," he snarled. "And more. I've pieced together ledgers frozen by icy coughs and shattered to shards of their former selves, been swept out to sea in roiling red ink swells engendered by the waves of a wizard's arms, and had lead-jacketed account books rained down upon me like square-shaped hail by the telepathic wobbling of dry-rotted shelves. I've seen it all and worked through it all, till, by Gods, I got my audit satisfaction! And now I render my opinion on your records, Kadil!"

The musty, paper-strewn room was suddenly shrouded in silence, the delegation of artisans pricking up their ears, the wily Wizard Kadil clutching a trembling hand to his quivering lips.

"It is a qualified audit opinion!" Ihor intoned, passing a doomsday judgment, a wizardly death sentence. He threw aside his charcoal and abacus and advanced on Kadil, con-sulting his notes. "I give, as but one example, the June 23rd transaction between Ewt the engraver and Wund the whittler, wherein Ewt performed engravement on one of Wund's whittled wind instruments, and you, Wizard, applied a 2.5 per cent transaction levy on the sale of service, as per the Tithle."

"As per the Tithle," Kadil breathed.

"Then you rebated Wund at the rate of 3.25 per cent of the 2.5 per cent levy that he'd paid, again as per the Tithle."

"As per the Tithle," Kadil chanted, mesmerized.

"But then Wund subsequently sold the whittled wind instrument to Mord the musician, the 2.42 per cent remaining levy now forming part of the cost of the blowpipe. And yet you had Mord pay the full 2.5 per cent transaction levy on his purchase – on the full cost and mark-up of the product without giving credit for the input tax already paid! Tax on tax! Double-taxation, Kadil! Something expressly forbidden by the Tithle!"

Kadil recoiled in horror, and the enraged mob surged forward.

Zaric, Wizard of all Wizards, fled to the throne room of King Dorn upon receiving news of Kadil's treachery, of the burgeoning tax revolt in the Province of Sull. The King, however, had already been informed, and he greeted Zaric with his palace guards, who promptly seized the wizard.

"What is this, my lord!?" Zaric shrieked, struggling in vain to free himself.

Dorn shrugged his heavy, fur-mantled shoulders and said, "Your wizard in Sull has been proven a tax cheat, Zaric. He lies dead and the province lies in rebellion. And his failure is, of course, your failure, and thus you, too, must be executed, as his superior and collaborator." Dorn smiled reassuringly. "But fear not for the Kingdom of Ronn, for I have dispatched an army to crush what little revolt the artisans can muster, and the tax warrior, Ihor, will soon be impressed back into my legion of accountants. All will then be well again."

"What about me?" Zaric wailed. "I knew nothing of Kadil's treachery!"

"And, indeed, you should have."

Dorn waved one of his jewelled hands and his guards dragged the kicking and screaming Zaric away, to the chopping block, for a mandated tax cut. The King then shook his crown-mantled head and chuckled, reflecting ruefully on the vast sums of money lost to him in the form of kickbacks, now that the Wizard Kadil's scheme had been exposed. "Death and taxes – inevitable, indeed," he mused.

CHRISTMAS GAMES

David Langford

Christmas at Shambles Hall! It was a picture of Olde English festivity, of Yule logs and paper chains and the traditional tree with all its ornaments, candles and festoons. The fireplace in the great entrance hall sent out endless pulsing warmth and cheer. Outside, the local robin strutted in the snow . . . the seasonal snow that filled up the estate and draped the leafless trees on either side of the long carriage-sweep. The unmarked snow.

"Of course," murmured Felicity as she snuggled against the Hon. Nigel in the window-seat, "we are quite, quite cut off from the outside world. If anything were to *happen* . . ."

Over the mantelpiece in the lofty dining-room hung the one statutory reminder built into every sequence: here, a probe's impression, done into oils, of the dim landscape to be expected on a certain world circling Barnard's Star. It was topped with a sprig of mistletoe.

Lord Blackhat the City financier had ruined countless men and tried hard to ruin as many women, yet he had a lingering sentimental streak and always invited his victims to Christmas at Shambles Hall. It was his whimsical way of dicing with Fate. He never troubled to remove or secure any part of the weapon collection from his youthful, sporting days which so extensively adorned the oak-panelled walls. Broadswords, crossbows, rapiers, shotguns, bludgeons, morningstars, garrottes and vials of prussic acid were always to hand at the Hall. Today he had added spice to the festive season by blackmailing the crusty old Colonel and forbidding his own son's intended marriage to Felicity.

This year, the Duchess of Spong's fad was fortune-telling with a wicked pack of cards. As an old family friend who had swindled her out of her inheritance, Lord Blackhat liked to humour her. "This covers you, this crosses you," she intoned as she dealt out the pattern. "This is your heart and this is your head and this your destiny as of approximately supper-time."

"Funny," said his lordship without real surprise, "how all of them seem to be the ace of spades."

The Colonel and the Professor were taking a turn along the Yew Walk, swapping anecdotes of relativistic physics and the tiger hunt at Poona. "My God," said the Professor suddenly. "These seem to be . . . the footprints of a gigantic hound!"

"Lodge-keeper's dog, I believe. Bloody great animal."

"For a moment I thought that, even though it is Christmas Day, some sinister element might yet enter our revels, ha ha."

The Colonel laughed shortly. "Someone here'd make short work of any mystery, Prof. Funny thing, really, that we should have with us as a fellow house-guest the eminent amateur detective Chester Dix who's sent so many foul murderers to the dock!"

"Oh, yes, in my absent-minded way I had almost forgotten. But Colonel, surely Dix couldn't be here on . . . business?"

"Nonsense! Balderdash! Pull yourself together, man!"

The Professor started. "Er . . . what was that?"

"Just an ominous magpie, Prof. Flying across our path. Symbol of sorrow and bad luck, they say, like those thirteen black cats over there."

"The scientific mind is above such nonsense," the Professor said conscientiously, walking under a ladder. From within the Hall came a crash as the tween-maid broke another mirror.

"Such a thing as overdoing the atmosphere," muttered the Colonel. "Oh well, it's only Christmas once a subjective year."

★   ★   ★

Chester Dix examined himself in the dressing-table mirror. Waxed moustache, deerstalker, monocle, magnifying glass – all seemed adequate. "One employs the little grey cells," he said experimentally. "By Jove, what? When you have eliminated the impossible, then what remains, *no matter how improbable* . . ." Losing the thread, he began again.

"Mortimer," said the dashingly handsome but amnesiac stranger who had so mysteriously turned up at Shambles Hall before thick snow isolated it for all practical purposes from the nearby village of Mayhem Parva. "Sebastian. Cholmondeley, pronounced Chili. It was something like one of those."

"Aldiborontiphoscophornio," Felicity suggested at random. "Chrononhotonthologos, pronounced Chris. You ought to recognize your own *name* when you hear it."

"I'm sure I shall. Fred. *Fred*! No . . . no, not Fred."

The Hon. Nigel Scattergood, son and heir to the tainted Blackhat fortune, stared moodily into the great fireplace. "Four bloody Christmases since launch day. I wish someone else got a chance to play detective just for once."

Felicity said, "Well, he *is* the infosystems chief, darling."

"Victor. Vitamin. Vitellus. Virtual Reality," muttered the stranger. "No, I'm fairly sure that isn't it either."

"Can we all try to stay a trifle more in character?" said Felicity. She tweaked at the hem of her short skirt. "Nigel, I shall be seriously annoyed with you if you don't *do something* about Lord Blackhat's pig-headedness. I want to marry a *man of action*. I . . . was that someone listening at the door?"

"That amnesiac chap," mused the Professor to the Duchess, "reminds me oddly of our host's younger brother; you know, the one long thought dead under suspicious circumstances in that Antarctic expedition from which only one survivor, Blackhat himself, returned. Odd how one gets these fancies."

"Another odd thing that few people know," said the Duchess, "is that identical twins run in that family."

*   *   *

The Christmas dinner was excellent as ever: the turkey vast and succulent enough to feed a family for a fortnight, the plum pudding flaming in brandy, the crackers exploding with satisfying bangs which, this year, did not once serve to cover a pistol-shot. But there seemed to be a strange atmosphere at the merry table. After pulling crackers with all twelve guests, Lord Blackhat idly unfolded the screw of paper bearing the last amusing cracker-motto. It proved to have been constructed from letters cut from a newspaper and pasted down, reading: "yOU *will* DiE to *NIGHT*".

The other eleven were substantially the same.

"One recognizes, does one not, the characteristic Baskerville typeface of the *Wessex Methodist Gazette*?" murmured Dix at his elbow. "*Alors*, my friend, we progress."

"Bah, humbug," said his lordship, and beckoned to the butler. "Starveling, I shall retire to the library and pass the evening altering my will. You might look in towards midnight with a whisky-and-soda, and see that I am . . . in good health."

"As your lordship pleases," said Starveling.

Firelight flickered in the dining-room where Chester Dix, brilliant amateur detective, brooded with steepled fingers and half-closed eyes over the remnants of the feast. No doubt each member of the party in turn would be paying a deviously motivated visit to the library. In due course there would follow a resounding crash of silver tray and shattered glass as the impeccable Starveling strove to be surprised at what he found slumped over the antique mahogany desk in Lord Blackhat's library. And then the investigation would . . .

There was a frightful discontinuity.

"Lightning?" said the Professor.

"In a dead clear sky?" said the Colonel.

Upstairs, Felicity and the Hon. Nigel had been busy failing to establish a convincing alibi. "Did the earth just move for you?" she asked.

"Dash it all, I'd hardly touched you."

In the smoking room, the amnesiac stranger explained to

Starveling, "I had it, I had it right on the tip of my tongue, and then that earthquake distracted me."

"Most regrettable, sir."

Alone in the Heliotrope Room, the Duchess turned over the thirteen fateful cards and found that all of them were Mr Bun the Baker. She frowned.

Lord Blackhat, caught unawares in mid-disinherit, felt himself all over. He seemed intact. "Thought they'd got me with an electrified codicil that time. Be a damned clever notion . . ."

"I have gathered you here," spluttered what seemed to be the brilliant amateur sleuth Chester Dix, "because one of you is guilty. Before twenty-four hours have passed I shall name the guilty person." He had a shaky, semi-transparent look.

Starveling bowed imperceptibly. "Sir," he said, "the fiendish criminal who so cunningly struck down Lord Blackhat in his prime has . . . er . . . has not done it yet. There would appear to be no crime."

"*Nom d'un cochon! Merde!* It is *I* who have been murdered, and I will know the reason why!"

"I say, the game's afoot, what?" marvelled the Colonel. "This is a new one."

The VR system, making the best of it, was seen to be maintaining two versions of Dix: the angrily gesticulating one, and an evident corpse slumped among the dessert plates and port glasses on the great oaken dinner-table.

Climbing with some difficulty out of her character as a bright young debutante, Felicity said: "This is the spare you talking, right? The machine analogue you programmed in. So the real you's gone to sleep in the VR tank or something. So what?"

The sleuth twirled his moustache with a flourish. "Mademoiselle will kindly employ her little grey cells. Chester Dix does not 'go to sleep' during an investigation. Archons of Athens! There has been foul play."

"All right, all right, game's over," snapped the Hon. Nigel. "Terminate. Terminate. If something's happened to Chester we need to go realside and take a look. Sorry to spoil the fun, everyone. Terminate, terminate. – Why the hell isn't it terminating?"

"A thousand pardons. I have taken the small liberty of activating a, how you say, a gamma-gamma override. *No one shall be permitted to leave Shambles Hall until this mystery she is solved.*"

He stalked haughtily from the room.

"Jesus Christ," said Felicity.

"Anyone for tennis?"

"That's not funny, darling," said the Hon. Nigel, shivering in a chill like interstellar space. They were using the racquets as improvised snowshoes and had made it almost half a mile down the empty white lane. Although (as the Professor had pointed out) the benefits of reaching the police station in the village were extremely unclear, it seemed something that had to be tried.

"*While the snow lay round about, Deep and crisp and eeeven,*" Felicity chanted. "Cut off, indeed. It's not six inches deep anywhere."

Then they rounded a corner of the sunken lane and met an infinite wall that somehow hadn't been visible before, rising forever, the colour of the dark behind one's eyelids.

"That's what I call cut off," said Nigel gloomily.

"That's what I call shoddy programming," said his companion.

The suspects gathered in the library while the detective was occupied taking plaster casts of the strange new footprints he had found leading down and back up the snow of the carriageway.

"I don't understand," said the Duchess.

"Then I shall explain the situation to you as though you knew nothing of it," the Professor began.

The Hon. Nigel broke in hastily. "It's obvious. Chester dropped out of the gamesmaster link – that was when everything sort of quivered – and this bloody stand-in program of his took over. We'll need to give it some kind of solution to get out of this. Someone will just have to confess."

They cut cards for it, and the mysterious stranger lost.

"But I still don't even know my name," he whimpered.

"Constraint of the scenario," said the Professor helpfully.

The Hon. Nigel fiddled irritably with the carvings on the library's old oak panelling, and one of the wooden roses sank into the wall at his touch. At once a tall case of Agatha Christie titles swung aside to disclose a secret passage.

"Oh *f* –" Nigel began before the scenario constraints stopped him. "I mean, oh dash it all."

"I am in fact Lord Blackhat's identical twin brother, with our close resemblance disguised by plastic surgery," the supposed stranger said with growing confidence. "In my extensive travels in South America I acquired a quantity of an arrow poison compounded from tree frogs and almost unknown to science. This I planned to administer in the special Stilton cheese reserved for Lord Blackhat, who unfortunately took the precaution of exchanging his plate by sleight of hand with that of the person next to him, the unfortunate sleuth Chester Dix. Meanwhile I had established an alibi with a fake telephone message from Warsaw, actually my confederate speaking on the extension phone in the butler's pantry. Now I see you are hot on my trail and my only option is to confess. It's a fair cop."

"An amusing fantasy," smiled the detective. "But you have failed to explain the singular incident of the dog in the night-time."

"What was the curious incident of the dog in the night-time?"

"It was spelt backwards." The great sleuth looked momentarily confused. "Ah. Never mind that. There is one fatal error in your story, my friend. I have examined the body minutely. You know my methods. It is clear that the unfortunate victim has suffered a cerebrovascular accident, a stroke. Not, I fancy, a little-known arrow poison . . ."

"He's got access to the ship systems," Felicity whispered.

"*That's* what happened to poor old Chester. I always thought he must have fiddled the physicals, you know, to get passed for this trip."

"Natural causes!" said the Hon. Nigel, pouncing. "There has been no murder. The case is closed."

"That, of course, is what the killer would *like* us to think. We are dealing with a very clever criminal, my friends. I see half of it now – but only half."

"Oh . . . botheration," Felicity paraphrased.

A loose group had formed around the glittering Christmas tree in the great entrance hall. "If we all committed suicide . . ." the Duchess suggested vaguely.

"Would just go non-interactive," Lord Blackhat grunted. "Used to like that bit the best, drifting round like a ghost and watching you all hash up the investigation."

"Then the case might never be solved," said the Hon. Nigel. "Would the scenario terminate if it recognized an insoluble problem?"

Felicity pouted. "God knows. Well, only God and Chester."

"Dammit," said the Colonel, "one of us will just have to be caught red-handed. No time for more fooling around. Got a starship to run."

"Ah, a second murder!" Nigel snapped his fingers. "Time to draw lots again."

"Ought to be me who's bumped off," said the mysterious stranger. "The person suspected of the first murder should always be the second victim. It's part of the classic unities."

"No. Build-up was for Blackhat," rumbled the Colonel crustily.

The Duchess sighed and broke the seal on a fresh pack of cards.

"Oh!" cried Felicity in synthetic alarm as the library door creaked open. "Oh! I was just passing by and happened to pick up the knife, forgetting everything I know about not touching anything at the scene of the crime. . . . Who would have thought the old man had so much blood in him?"

(The silver fish-slice had been an awkward choice of weapon, but Nigel thought it rather picturesque. "It's more of a blasted blunt instrument," Lord Blackhat had groaned irritably as he expired.)

The great detective took in the scene at a single hawk-eyed glance.

"No," said Felicity. "It's no use. This huge bloodstain on my dress . . . the six witnesses in the corridor outside who will swear that no one but myself has entered this room since his lordship was last seen alive . . . I can't conceal my blatant guilt from you."

Alternately puffing at a huge pipe whose stem curved like a saxophone and sipping at a rummer of priceless old liqueur brandy, the sleuth made his way along the floor on hands and knees. Then he rose and touched a place in the panelling. The secret door opened on well-oiled hinges.

"Burn and blister me! Not quite a locked room after all, I fancy. Now I have just one question for you, my dear girl. *Whom are you shielding?*"

Felicity pronounced a word under her breath.

Shortly afterwards: "Is there not," said the Professor with a certain academic distaste, "a criminal device known in the literature as a 'frame'? Now what I propose . . ."

Starveling the butler made a pathetic corpse in his pantry. He was only a program construct and not a live player, but the Hon. Nigel had felt a pang of real remorse as he did the deed and arranged the evidence.

"*I done it. I can live with myself no longer. Farewell cruel world. Tell the maid to decant the '49 port for Boxing Day,*" the investigator read aloud to the suspects. "Very determined of the fellow to write all that in his own blood on the table, after shooting himself through the heart. Using a disguised hand, too."

"Ah," said Nigel guiltily.

"Yes, what the murderer forgot was, firstly, that yellow stitchbane is not yellow at all but a pale mauve . . . and secondly, that Starveling *was left-handed.*"

Nigel gave a muffled exclamation, laden with even more guilt.

"Fortunately my snuff-box is invariably charged with fingerprint powder . . ." To an accompaniment of impatient shufflings, forensic science proceeded on its remorseless way.

"No! There must be some mistake!" cried Nigel unconvincingly.

"God, Captain, you're a lousy actor," Felicity whispered.

"Satisfactory. Most satisfactory. And what do we deduce from this exact match between the prints on the automatic and those of the Hon. Nigel Scattergood? Why, of course, that he must have handled the gun innocently at some earlier time, else he would have taken care to wipe it clean!"

The Colonel made some feeble suggestion about doublebluff, but the sleuth was happily launched on a flight of deductions about the unknown murderer's careful manipulation of the gun in a wire frame that left the prints undisturbed . . .

"We're being too rational," said Felicity. "This imitation Chester is soaked and saturated in detective stories just like the real one. We can't out-subtle him."

"Thanks so much, darling," said the Hon. Nigel with venom. "Thanks for explaining that things are utterly hopeless."

"Ah, but if we could use the ship-system AI it could fudge up a super-clever pattern that any Great Detective would fall for."

"If, if," grunted the Colonel. "If pigs could fly we could all make a getaway on porkerback, if we had some pigs."

"Wait," said Felicity. "As *he* would say – when you've eliminated all logical solutions you have to try something that's stark raving bonkers. Duchess dear, where's the ouija board from our séance on Christmas Eve that gave us all those thrillingly sinister and atmospheric warnings?"

After prolonged searching the apparatus finally came to light under a pile of anonymous letters.

"This is ridiculous," complained the Hon. Nigel as the

planchette began to slide across the lettered board. Under all their fingertips it moved uncertainly at first, then with more seeming decision. "Is it spelling anything out?"

"L-O-G-I-N," said Felicity. "That looks promising. Now we're going to need a *lot* of pencil and paper."

They were busy through the small hours, placing a wild variety of clues everywhere the Astral Intelligence had advised.

Bleary-eyed and feeling hungover, the Hon. Nigel lifted the silver cover of the largest dish on the sideboard. It contained, perhaps inevitably, red herrings. He settled for bacon and egg. The others were already gathered about the breakfast table, and after an early-morning hunt for evidence the world-famous sleuth was clearly ready to hold forth.

"This has been one of the most baffling and complex cases that I have ever encountered. Even I, Chester Dix, with my sixteen heraldic quarterings and unparalleled little grey cells . . . even I was stretched to my deductive limits by the satanic cunning of this crime. But now I have the answer!"

Felicity led a discreet patter of applause.

"What first drew my attention was that the seemingly false alibi with the phonograph record of the typewriter was a clever decoy. Second came the realization that when the tween-maid glimpsed the clock through the window of the supposedly locked room, *she saw the clock-face in a mirror* . . . producing an error of timing that has literally turned this case upside down. Next, the drugged cigar-cutter . . ."

The breakfast party found the thread a little hard to follow: there was mention of the legendary Polar Poignard or ice dagger that melted tracelessly away, of a bullet misleadingly fired from a blowpipe and a hypodermic filled with air, while disguises and impersonations were rampant. Keys were ingeniously turned from the wrong sides of doors, and bolts magnetically massaged. In the end it seemed on the whole that Lord Blackhat himself was the villain, having faked his own murder and posthumously blackmailed Starveling into doing much the same.

"Didn't quite follow the bit about the murderous dwarf hidden under the cover of the turkey dish," said the Colonel.

Felicity explained that that notion had been seen through by the detective as a diabolical false trail. She thought.

"And so, ladies and gentlemen, you are all free to depart. Merry Christmas!"

"Merry Christmas! I've never looked forward so much to boring old shipboard chores. Until next year –" said Felicity, and winked out. The others followed suit.

Alone again in the great dining-room, deep in the ship-system's bubble memory, the sleuth smiled a small, secret smile. He moved to the telephone and lifted the receiver. "Get me Whitehall 1212. Inspector Lestrade? . . . I have solved the mystery at Shambles Hall. Yes . . . In the end I deduced that, unprecedentedly, *every member of the house party* conspired to commit the original crime. The method, I fancy, was suffocation – it was their good fortune that the victim suffered a stroke when part-asphyxiated. All of them were in it together. The ingenuity of their false clues proves it. *Sacre bleu*, they think me a fool! Being outnumbered, I lulled their fears most beautifully by announcing the solution they wished. They will return here – do we not know that the criminal always returns to the scene of the crime? – and we shall set a trap. . . . Yes. Yes, that murderous gang will not find it so easy to escape Shambles Hall *next* Christmas!"

STEPHEN SKARRIDGE'S CHRISTMAS

Frank R. Stockton

'Twas Christmas eve. An adamantine sky hung dark and heavy over the white earth. The forests were canescent with frost, and the great trees bent as if they were not able to sustain the weight of snow and ice with which the young winter had loaded them.

In a by-path of the solemn woods there stood a cottage that would not, perhaps, have been noticed in the decreasing twilight, had it not been for a little wisp of smoke that feebly curled from the chimney, apparently intending, every minute, to draw up its attenuated tail, and disappear. Within, around the hearth whereon the dying embers sent up that feeble smoke, there gathered the family of Arthur Tyrrell – himself, his wife, a boy, and a girl.

'Twas Christmas eve. A damp air rushed from the recesses of the forest and came, an unbidden guest, into the cottage of the Tyrrells, and it sat on every chair, and lay upon every bed, and held in its chilly embrace every member of the family. All sighed.

"Father," said the boy, "is there no more wood, that I may replenish the fire?"

"No, my son," bitterly replied the father, his face hidden in his hands; "I brought, at noon, the last stick from the wood-pile."

The mother, at these words, wiped a silent tear from her

eyes, and drew her children yet nearer the smouldering coals. The father rose and moodily stood by the window, gazing out upon the night. A wind had now arisen, and the dead branches strewed the path that he soon must take to the neighboring town. But he cared not for the danger; his fate and heart were alike hard.

"Mother!" said the little girl, "shall I hang up my stocking to-night? 'Tis Christmas eve."

A Damascus blade could not have cut the mother's heart more keenly than this question.

"No, dear," she faltered. "You must wear your stockings – there is no fire – and your feet, uncovered, will freeze."

The little girl sighed, and gazed sadly upon the blackening coals. But she raised her head again and said,

"But, mother dear, if I should sleep with my legs outside the clothes, old Santa Claus might slip in some little things between the stocking and my skin; could he not, dear mother?"

"Mother is weeping, sister," said the boy, "press her no further."

The father now drew around him his threadbare coat, put upon his head his well-brushed straw hat, and approached the door.

"Where are you going, this bitter night, dear father?" cried his little son.

"He goes," then said the weeping mother, "to the town. Disturb him not, my son, for he will buy a mackerel for our Christmas dinner."

"A mackerel!" cried both the children, and their eyes sparkled with joy. The boy sprang to his feet.

"You must not go alone, dear father," he cried. "I will accompany you."

And together they left the cottage.

The streets were crowded with merry faces and well wrapped-up forms. Snow and ice, it is true, lay thick upon the pavements and roofs, but what of that? Bright lights glistened from every window, bright fires warmed and sof-tened the air within the houses, while bright hearts made rosy and happy the countenances of the merry crowd without. In some of the shops great turkeys hung in placid obesity from the bending beams, and enormous bowls of mince-meat sent up delightful fumes, which mingled harmoniously with the scents of the oranges, the apples, and the barrels of sugar and bags of spices. In others, the light from the chandeliers struck upon the polished surface of many a new wheelbarrow, sled, or hobby-horse, or lighted up the placid features of recumbent dolls and the demoniacal countenances of wildly jumping jacks. The crop of marbles and tops was almost more than could be garnered; boxes and barrels of soldiers stood on every side; tin horns hung from every prominence, and boxes of wonders filled the counters; while all the floor was packed with joyous children carrying their little purses. Beyond, there stood the candy-stores – those earthly paradises of the young, where golden gumdrops, rare cream chocolate, variegated mint-stick, and enrapturing mixtures spread their sweetened wealth over all available space.

To these and many other shops and stores and stalls and stands thronged the townspeople, rich and poor. Even the humblest had some money to spend upon this merry Christmas eve. A damsel of the lower orders might here be seen hurrying home with a cheap chicken; here another with a duck; and here the saving father of a family bending under the load of a turkey and a huge basket of good things. Everywhere were cheerful lights and warm hearthstones, bright and gay mansions, cosey and comfortable little tenements, happy hearts, rosy cheeks, and bright eyes. Nobody cared for the snow and ice, while they had so much that was warm and cheering. It was all the better for the holiday – what would Christmas be without snow?

Through these joyous crowds – down the hilarious streets, where the happy boys were shouting, and the merry girls were hurrying in and out of the shops – came a man who was neither joyous, hilarious, merry, nor happy. It was Stephen Skarridge, the landlord of many houses in that town. He wore an overcoat, which, though old, was warm and comfortable, and he had fur around his wrists and his neck. His hat was pushed down tight upon his little head, as though he would shut out all the sounds of merriment which filled the town. Wife and child he had none, and this season of joy to all the Christian world was an annoying and irritating season to his unsympathetic, selfish heart.

"Oh, ho!" he said to himself, as one after another of his tenants, loaded down with baskets and bundles, hurried by, each wishing him a merry Christmas; "oh, ho! there seems to be a great ease in the money market just now. Oh, ho, ho! They all seem as flush as millionaires. There's nothing like the influence of holiday times to make one open his pockets – ha, ha! It's not yet the first of the month, 'tis true; but it matters not – I'll go and collect my rents to-night, while all this money is afloat – oh, ho! ha, ha!"

Now old Skarridge went from house to house, and threatened with expulsion all who did not pay their rents that night. Some resisted bravely, for the settlement day had not yet arrived, and these were served with notices to leave at the earliest legal moment; others paid up to their dues with many an angry protest; while some, poor souls, had no money ready for this unforeseen demand, and Stephen Skarridge seized whatever he could find that would satisfy his claim. Thus many a poor, weeping family saw the turkey or the fat goose which was to have graced the Christmas table carried away by the relentless landlord. The children shed tears to see their drums and toys depart, and many a little memento of affection, intended for a gift upon the morrow, became the property of the hard-hearted Stephen. 'Twas nearly nine o'clock when Skarridge finished his nefarious labor. He had converted his seizures into money, and was returning to his inhospitable home with more joyous light in his eyes than had shone there for many a day, when he saw Arthur Tyrrell and his son enter the bright main street of the town.

"Oh, ho!" said Stephen; "has he, too, come to spend his Christmas money? He, the poor, miserable, penniless one! I'll follow him."

So behind the unhappy father and his son went the skulking Skarridge. Past the grocery store and the markets, with their rich treasures of eatables; past the toy-shops, where the boy's eyes sparkled with the delight which disappointment soon washed out with a tear; past the candy-shops, where the windows were so entrancing that the little fellow could scarcely look upon them – on, past all these, to a small shop at the bottom of the street, where a crowd of the very poorest people were making their little purchases, went the father and his son, followed by the evil-minded Skarridge. When the Tyrrells went into the shop, the old man concealed himself outside, behind a friendly pillar, lest any of these poor people should happen to be his tenants, and return him the damage he had just done to them. But he very plainly saw Arthur Tyrrell go up to the counter and ask for a mackerel. When one was brought, costing ten cents, he declined it, but eventually purchased a smaller one, the price of which was eight cents. The two cents which he received as change were expended for a modicum of lard, and father and son then left the store and wended their way homeward. The way was long, but the knowledge that they brought, that which would make the next day something more like Christmas than an ordinary day, made their steps lighter and the path less wearisome.

They reached the cottage and opened the door. There, by a rushlight on a table, sat the mother and the little girl, arranging greens wherewith to decorate their humble home. To the mute interrogation of the mother's eyes the father said, with something of the old fervor in his voice:

"Yes, my dear, I have brought it;" and he laid the mackerel on the table. The little girl sprang up to look at it, and the boy stepped back to shut the door; but before he could do so, it was pushed wide open, and Skarridge, who had followed them all the way, entered the cottage. The inmates gazed at him with astonishment; but they did not long remain in ignorance of the meaning of this untimely visit.

"Mr Tyrrell," said Skarridge, taking out of his pocket a huge memorandum-book, and turning over the pages with a swift and practised hand, "I believe you owe me two months' rent. Let me see – yes, here it is – eighty-seven and a half cents – two months at forty-three and three-quarters cents per month. I should like to have it now, if you please," and he stood with his head on one side, his little eyes gleaming with a yellow maliciousness.

Arthur Tyrrell arose. His wife crept to his side, and the two children ran behind their parents.

"Sir," said Tyrrell, "I have no money – do your worst."

"No money!" cried the hard-hearted Stephen. "That story will not do for me. Everybody seems to have money to-night; and if they have none, it is because they have wilfully spent it. But if you really have none" – and here a ray of hope shot through the hearts of the Tyrrell family – "you must have something that will bring money, and that I shall seize upon. Ah, ha! I will take this!"

And he picked up the Christmas mackerel from the table where Arthur had laid it.

" 'Tis very little," said Skarridge, "but it will at least pay me my interest." Wrapping it in the brown paper which lay under it, he thrust it into his capacious pocket, and without another word went out into the night.

Arthur Tyrrell sank into a chair, and covered his face with his hands. His children, dumb with horror and dismay, clung to the rounds of his chair, while his wife, ever faithful in the day of sorrow as in that of joy, put her arm around his neck and whispered in his ear, "Cheer up, dear Arthur, all may yet be well; have courage! He did not take the lard!"

Swiftly homeward, through the forest, walked the triumphant Skarridge, and he reached his home an hour before midnight. He lived alone, in a handsome house (which he had seized for a debt), an old woman coming every day to prepare his meals and do the little housework that he required. Opening his door with his latch-key, he hurried upstairs, lighted a candle, and seating himself at a large table in a spacious room in the front of the house, he counted over the money he had collected that evening, entered the amount in one of the great folios which lay upon the table, and locked up the cash in a huge safe. Then he took from his pocket the mackerel of the Tyrrell family. He opened it, laid it flat upon the table before him, and divided it by imaginary lines into six parts.

"Here," said he to himself, "are breakfasts for six days – I would it were a week. I like to have things square and even. Had that man bought the ten-cent fish that I saw offered him, there would have been seven portions. Well, perhaps I can make it do, even now – let me see! A little off here – and the same off this – so –"

At this moment something very strange occurred. The mackerel, which had been lying, split open, upon its back, now closed itself, gave two or three long-drawn gasps, and then heaving a sigh of relief, it flapped its tail, rolled its eyes a little, and deliberately wriggling itself over to a pile of ledgers, sat up on its tail, and looked at Skarridge. This astounded individual pushed back his chair and gazed with all his eyes at the strange fish. But he was more astounded yet, when the fish spoke to him. "Would you mind," said the mackerel, making a very wry face, "getting me a glass of water? I feel all of a parch inside."

Skarridge mumbled out some sort of an assent, and hurried to a table near by, where stood a pitcher and a glass, and filling the latter, he brought it to the mackerel. "Will you hold it to my mouth?" said the fish. Stephen complying, the mackerel drank a good half of the water.

"There," it said, "that makes me feel better. I don't mind brine if I can take exercise. But to lie perfectly still in salt water makes one feel wretched. You don't know how hungry I am. Have you any worms convenient?"

"Worms!" cried Stephen, "why, what a question! No, I have no worms."

"Well," said the fish, somewhat petulantly, "you must have some sort of a yard or garden; go and dig me some."

"Dig them!" cried Stephen. "Do you know it's winter, and the ground's frozen – and the worms too, for that matter?"

"I don't care anything for all that," said the mackerel. "Go you and dig some up. Frozen or thawed, it is all one to me now; I could eat them any way."

The manner of the fish was so imperative that Stephen Skarridge did not think of disobeying, but taking a crowbar and a spade from a pile of agricultural implements that lay in one corner of the room (and which had at various times been seized for debts), he lighted a lantern and went down into the little back garden. There he shovelled away the snow, and when he reached the ground he was obliged to use the crowbar vigorously before he could make any impression on the frozen earth. After a half-hour's hard labor, he managed, by most carefully searching through the earth thrown out of the hole he had made, to find five frozen worms. These he considered a sufficient meal for a fish which would scarcely make seven meals for himself, and so he threw down his implements and went into the house, with his lantern, his five frozen worms, and twice as many frozen fingers. When he reached the bottom of the stairs he was certain that he heard the murmur of voices from above. He was terrified. The voices came from the room where all his treasures lay! Could it be thieves?

Extinguishing his lantern and taking off his shoes, he softly crept up the stairs. He had not quite closed the door of the room when he left it, and he could now look through an opening which commanded a view of the whole apartment. And such a sight now met his wide-stretched eyes!

In his chair – his own arm-chair – by the table, there sat a dwarf, whose head, as large as a prize cabbage, was placed upon a body so small as not to be noticeable, and from which depended a pair of little legs appearing like the roots of the before-mentioned vegetable. On the table, busily engaged in dusting a day-book with a pen-wiper, was a fairy, no more than a foot high, and as pretty and graceful as a queen of the ballet viewed from the dress circle. The mackerel still leaned against the pile of ledgers; and – oh horror! – upon a great iron box, in one corner, there sat a giant, whose head, had he stood up, would have reached the lofty ceiling!

A chill, colder than the frosty earth and air outside could cause, ran through the frame of Stephen Skarridge, as he crouched by the crack of the door and looked upon these dreadful visitors, while their conversation, of which he could hear distinctly every word, caused the freezing perspiration to trickle in icy globules down his back.

"He's gone to get me some worms," said the mackerel, "and

we might as well settle it all before he comes back. For my part I'm very sure of what I have been saying."

"Oh, yes," said the dwarf; "there can be no doubt about it, at all. I believe it, every word."

"Of course it is so," said the fairy, standing upon the day-book, which was now well dusted; "everybody knows it is."

"It couldn't be otherwise," said the giant, in a voice like thunder among the pines; "we're all agreed upon that."

"They're mighty positive about it, whatever it is," thought the trembling Stephen, who continued to look with all his eyes and to listen with all his ears.

"Well," said the dwarf, leaning back in the chair and twisting his little legs around each other until they looked like a rope's end, "let us arrange matters. For my part, I would like to see all crooked things made straight, just as quickly as possible."

"So would I," said the fairy, sitting down on the day-book, and crossing her dainty satin-covered ankles, from which she stooped to brush a trifle of dust; "I want to see everything nice, and pretty, and just right."

"As for me," said the mackerel, "I'm somewhat divided – in my opinion, I mean – but whatever you all agree upon, will suit me, I'm sure."

"Then," said the giant, rising to his feet, and just escaping a violent contact of his head with the ceiling, "let us get to work, and while we are about it, we'll make a clean sweep of it."

To this the others all gave assent, and the giant, after moving the mackerel to one corner of the table, and requesting the fairy to stand beside the fish, spread all the ledgers, and day-books, and the cash, bill, and memorandum books upon the table, and opened each of them at the first page.

Then the dwarf climbed up on the table and took a pen, and the fairy did the same, and they both set to work, as hard as they could, to take an account of Stephen Skarridge's possessions. As soon as either of them had added up two pages the giant turned over the leaves, and he had to be very busy about it, so active was the dwarf, who had a splendid head for accounts, and who had balanced the same head so long upon his little legs that he had no manner of difficulty in balancing a few ledgers. The fairy, too, ran up and down the columns as if she were dancing a measure in which the only movements were "Forward one!" and "Backward one!" and she got over her business nearly as fast as the dwarf. As for the mackerel, he could not add up, but the fairy told him what figures she had to carry to the next column, and he remembered them for her, and thus helped her a great deal. In less than half an hour the giant turned over the last page of the last book, and the dwarf put down on a large sheet of foolscap the sum total of Stephen Skarridge's wealth.

The fairy read out the sum, and the woeful listener at the door was forced to admit to himself that they had got it exactly right.

"Now, then," said the giant, "here is the rent list. Let us make out the schedule." In twenty minutes the giant, the dwarf, and the fairy – the last reading out the names of Stephen's various tenants, the giant stating what amounts he deemed the due of each one, and the dwarf putting down the sums opposite their names – had made out the schedule, and the giant read it over in a voice that admitted of no inattention.

"Hurrah!" said the dwarf. "That's done, and I'm glad," and he stepped lightly from the table to the arm of the chair, and then down to the seat, and jumped to the floor, balancing his head in the most wonderful way, as he performed these agile feats.

"Yes," said the mackerel, "it's all right though to be sure I'm somewhat divided –"

"Oh! we won't refer to that now," said the giant; 'let by-gones be by-gones."

As for the fairy, she did not say a word, but she made a bounce to the top of the day-book which she had dusted, and which now lay closed near the edge of the table, and she danced such a charming little *fantaisie* that everybody gazed at her with delight. The giant stooped and opened his mouth as if he expected her to whirl herself into it when she was done; and the mackerel was actually moved to tears, and tried to wipe his eyes with his fin, but it was not long enough, and so the tears rolled down and hardened into a white crust on the green baize which covered the table. The dwarf was on the floor, and he stood motionless on his little toes, as if he had been a great top dead asleep. Even Stephen, though he was terribly agitated, thought the dance was the most beautiful thing he had ever seen. At length, with a whirl which made her look like a snow-ball on a pivot, she stopped stock-still, standing on one toe, as if she had fallen from the sky and had stuck upright on the day-book.

"Bravo! bravo!" cried the dwarf, and you could hear his little hands clapping beneath his head.

"Hurrah!" cried the giant, and he brought his great palms together with a clap that rattled the window-panes, like the report of a cannon.

"Very nice! very nice, indeed!" said the mackerel. "Though I'm rather di –"

"Oh, no, you're not!" cried the fairy, making a sudden joyful jump at him, and putting her little hand on his some-what distorted and certainly very ugly mouth. "You're noth-ing of the kind, and now let's have him in here and make him sign. Do you think he will do it?" said she, turning to the giant. That mighty individual doubled up his great right fist like a trip-hammer, and he opened his great left hand, as hard and solid as an anvil, and he brought the two together with a sounding whang!

"Yes," said he, "I think he will."

"In that case," said the dwarf, "we might as well call him."

"I sent him after some worms," said the mackerel, "but he has not been all this time getting them. I should not wonder at all if he had been listening at the door all the while."

"We'll soon settle that," said the dwarf, walking rapidly across the room, his head rolling from side to side, but still preserving that admirable balance for which it was so justly noted. When he reached the door he pulled it wide open, and there stood poor Stephen Skarridge, trembling from head to foot, with the five frozen worms firmly grasped in his hands.

"Come in!" said the giant, and Stephen walked in slowly

and fearfully, bowing as he came, to the several personages in the room.

"Are those my worms?" said the mackerel. "If so, put them in my mouth, one at a time. There! not so fast. They are frozen, sure enough; but do you know that I believe I like them this way the best. I never tasted frozen ones before."

By this time the dwarf had mounted the table, and opening the schedule, stood pointing to an agreement written at the bottom of it, while the fairy had a pen already dipped in the ink, which she held in her hand, as she stood on the other side of the schedule.

"Now, sir!" said the giant, "just take your seat in your chair, take that pen in your hand, and sign your name below that agreement. If you've been listening at the door all this time, as I believe you have, you have heard the contents of the schedule, and therefore need not read it over."

Stephen thought no more of disobeying than he did of challenging the giant to a battle, and he therefore seated himself in his chair, and taking the pen from the fairy, wrote his name at the bottom of the agreement, although he knew that by that act he was signing away half his wealth. When he had written his signature he laid down his pen and looked around to see if anything more was required of him; but just at that moment something seemed to give way in the back of his neck, his head fell forward so as to nearly strike the table, and he awoke!

There was no longer a schedule, a fairy, a dwarf, or a giant. In front of him was the mackerel, split open and lying on its back.

It was all a dream!

For an hour Stephen Skarridge sat at his table, his face buried in his hands. When, at last, his candle gave signs of spluttering out, he arose, and, with a subdued and quiet air, he went to bed.

The next morning was bright, cold, and cheering, and Stephen Skarridge arose very early, went down to the large front room where his treasures were kept, got out his checkbook, and for two hours was busily employed in writing.

When the old woman who attended to his household affairs arrived at the usual hour, she was surprised at his orders to cook, for his breakfast, the whole of a mackerel which he handed her. When he had finished his meal, at which he ate at least one-half of the fish, he called her up into his room. He then addressed her as follows:

"Margaret, you have been my servant for seventeen years. During that time I have paid you fifty cents per week for your services. I am now convinced that the sum was insufficient; you should have had, at least, two dollars – considering you only had one meal in the house. As you would probably have spent the money as fast as I gave it to you, I shall pay you no interest upon what I have withheld, but here is a check for the unpaid balance – one thousand three hundred and twenty-six dollars. Invest it carefully, and you will find it quite a help to you." Handing the paper to the astounded woman, he took up a large wallet, stuffed with checks, and left the house.

He went down into the lower part of the town, with a countenance full of lively fervor and generous light. When he reached the quarter where his property lay, he spent an hour or two in converse with his tenants, and when he had spoken with the last one, his wallet was nearly empty, and he was followed by a wildly joyful crowd, who would have brought a chair and carried him in triumph through the town, had he not calmly waved them back.

When the concourse of grateful ones had left him, he repaired to the house of Philip Weaver, the butcher, and hired his pony and spring cart. Then he went to Ambrose Smith, the baker (at whose shop he had stopped on his way down-town), and inquired if his orders had been filled. Although it was Christmas morning, Ambrose and his seven assistants were all as busy as bees, but they had not yet been able to fill said orders. In an hour, however, Ambrose came himself to a candy store, where Stephen was treating a crowd of delighted children, and told him all was ready and the cart loaded. At this, Stephen hurried to the baker's shop, mounted the cart, took the reins, and drove rapidly in the direction of the cottage of Arthur Tyrrell. When he reached the place it was nearly one o'clock.

Driving cautiously, as he neared the house, he stopped at a little distance from it, and tied the horse to a tree. Then he stealthily approached a window and looked in.

Arthur Tyrrell sat upon a chair, in the middle of the room, his arms folded and his head bowed upon his breast. On a stool by his left side sat his wife, her tearful eyes raised to his sombre countenance. Before her father stood the little girl, leaning upon his knees and watching the varied expressions that flashed across his face. By his father's right side, his arm resting upon his parent's shoulder, stood the boy, a look of calm resignation far beyond his years lighting up his intelligent face.

'Twas a tableau never to be forgotten!

Able to gaze upon it but a few minutes, Stephen Skarridge pushed open the door and entered the room. His entrance was the signal of consternation. The wife and children fled to the farthest corner of the room, while Arthur Tyrrell arose and sternly confronted the intruder.

"Ha!" said he. "You have soon returned. You think that we can be yet further despoiled. Proceed, take all we have. There is yet this," and he pointed to the two cents' worth of lard, which still lay upon the table.

"No, no," faltered Stephen Skarridge, seizing the hand of Arthur Tyrrell and warmly pressing it. "Keep it! Keep it! 'Tis not for that I came, but to ask your pardon and to beg your acceptance of a Christmas gift. Pardon, for having increased the weight of your poverty, and a gift to celebrate the advent of a happier feeling between us."

Having said this, Stephen paused for a reply. Arthur Tyrrell mused for a moment; then he cast his eyes upon his wife and his children, and, in a low but firm voice, he said:

"I pardon and accept!"

"That's right!" cried Skarridge, his whole being animated by a novel delight; "come out to the cart, you and your son, and help me bring in the things, while Mrs T. and the girl set the table as quickly as possible." The cart was now brought up before the door, and it was rapidly unloaded by willing hands. From under a half dozen new blankets, which served to keep

the other contents from contact with the frosty air, Stephen
first handed out a fine linen table-cloth, and then a basket
containing a dinner-set of queensware (third class – seventy-
eight pieces with soup-tureen and pickle-dishes) and a half-
dozen knives and forks (rubber-handled and warranted to
stand hot water). When the cloth had been spread and the
plates and dishes arranged, Arthur Tyrrell and his son, aided
now by the wife and daughter, brought in the remaining
contents of the cart and placed them on the table, while, with
a bundle of kindling which he had brought, and the fallen
limbs which lay all about the cottage, Skarridge made a
rousing fire on the hearth.

When the cart was empty and the table fully spread, it
presented indeed a noble sight. At one end a great turkey; at
the other, a pair of geese; a duck upon one side and a pigeon-
pie upon the other; cranberries, potatoes, white and sweet;
onions, parsnips, celery, bread, butter, beets (pickled and
buttered), pickled cucumbers, and walnuts, and several kinds
of sauces, made up the first course; while upon a side-table
stood mincepies, apple-pies, pumpkin-pies, apples, nuts, al-
monds, raisins, and a huge pitcher of cider, for dessert.

It was impossible for the Tyrrell family to gaze unmoved
upon this bounteously spread table, and after silently clasping
each other for a moment, they sat down, with joyful, thankful
hearts, to a meal far better than they had seen for years. At
their earnest solicitation Mr Skarridge joined them.

When the meal was over, and there was little left but empty
dishes, they all arose, and Skarridge prepared to take his leave.

"But before I go," said he, "I would leave with you a further
memento of my good feeling and friendship. You know my
Hillsdale farm, in the next township?"

"Oh, yes!" cried Arthur Tyrrell; "is it possible that you will
give me a position there?"

"I make you a present of the whole farm," said Skarridge.
"There are two hundred and forty-two acres, sixty of which
are in timber; large mansion-house, two good barns, and cow
and chicken houses; a well, covered in; an orchard of young
fruit-trees, and a stream of water flowing through the place.

The estate is well stocked with blooded cattle, horses, etc., and all necessary farming utensils. Possession immediate."

Without waiting for the dumb founded Tyrrell to speak, Skarridge turned quickly to his wife, and said: "Here, madam, is my Christmas-gift to you. In this package you will find shares of the New York Central and Hudson (sixes, of 'eighty-three), of the Fort Wayne (guaranteed), and of the St. Paul's (preferred); also bonds of the Delaware, Lackawauna, and Western (second mortgage), and of the Michigan Seven Per Cent. War Loan. In all these amount to nine thousand and eighty-two dollars; but to preclude the necessity of selling at a sacrifice, for immediate wants, I have taken the liberty of placing in the package one thousand dollars in greenbacks. And now, dear friends, adieu!"

But the grateful family could not allow this noble man to leave them thus. Arthur Tyrrell seized his hand and pressed it to his bosom, and then, as if overcome with emotion, Mrs Tyrrell fell upon her benefactor's neck, while the children gratefully grasped the skirts of his coat. With one arm around the neck of the still young, once beautiful, and now fast improving Mrs Tyrrell, Stephen Skarridge stood for a few minutes, haunted by memories of the past. Then he spoke:

"Once," said he, his voice trembling the while, "once – I, too – loved such a one. But it is all over now – and the grass waves over her grave. Farewell, farewell dear friends!" and dashing away a tear, he tore himself from the fervent family, and swiftly left the house.

Springing into the cart, he drove rapidly into the town – a happy man! . . .

Did you ever before read a story like this?

SING A SONG OF SIXPENCE

Robert Loy

If you are not handsome at twenty
If you are not strong at thirty
If you are not rich at forty
If you are not wise at fifty
You never will be.
— Nursery Rhyme

She was blonde. She was tall. She had smoky-cool green eyes that — although I would have bet all eleven dollars of my life savings it was impossible — were compelling enough to pull my attention away from that plunging-to-paradise neckline of hers.

She was also a princess — *the* princess — and the next queen of our country if her mother-in-law, Queen Charismatic, ever gets tired of hogging the throne.

"Princess Ella," I said, wishing I had thought to wear that necktie I almost bought a couple years ago, "come on in. 'Scuse the mess; I wasn't expecting company."

"Ever?" she asked, delicately handkerchiefing away the knuckle dust she had accumulated when she knocked on my door.

My association with majesty was limited to a disbelieving gape at a royal flush that my oversexed friend George Porgie folded cuz he had a hot date to get to. I wasn't sure if I was supposed to bow or curtsy, kiss her hand or tug my forelock, so I stayed where I was, seated behind my desk. I did stub out my cigarette. But that was more of a safety precaution than etiquette. With the hair spray and the perfume she just exuded flammability.

Not to mention the way she crossed her legs.

"Mister Nimble?" my guest said.

"No," I told her, indicating the broken and dusty but still legible – if you looked at from the right angle – nameplate on the door. "My name is Jack B. Goode. Private investigator. At your service."

"Hmm, that's strange. Somebody told me your name was Jack B. Nimble."

My face reddened, but I wasn't sure if it was because I was blushing or because I put too much bourbon in my morning coffee again.

"I'm afraid that's just a nickname a gratified girlfriend gifted me with some years ago."

"Well, now I am really confused." Her hand fluttered up and lit softly on her alabaster cheek. "But I shouldn't be, I suppose. You probably have lots of names. Now that I think of it, I could swear another friend told me your name was Jack B. Quick."

I didn't see any reason to explain that this moniker was another nickname from the same gossipy no-longer-gratified girlfriend after we broke up, so I asked the princess what it was I could do for her.

"I'm worried about my husband," she answered.

"You mean Prince Charming?"

She nodded her head and when she spoke again it was in a slower more school-teachery voice.

"Well, yes, he's the only husband I have."

"Go on," I told her.

"I think somebody's trying to kill him."

"What makes you think that?"

"He has a terrible sweet tooth, always insists on a slice of blackberry pie before he goes to bed. Lately somebody has been putting blackbirds in his pie."

"Putting what in his pie?"

"Blackbirds."

"So what? A lot of politicians have to eat crow. Kinda goes with the territory, doesn't it?"

My little joke fluttered over her head and out the window to its death.

"But the Prince is extremely allergic to anything avian. It's already happened two dozen times. Robert Shaftoe, the head of the palace guards is completely at sea about this; you're our only hope. There was an anonymous letter baked in with the last one threatening dire consequences if he didn't stop doing you know what."

"No, I don't know. What?"

"I don't know. That's what the letter said: You know what."

"Oh, well, that's different." I excavated through three or four strata of desk junk and emerged with a spiral notebook.

"Well," I said, licking the point of my pencil stub, after deciding it wasn't worth risking rabies to dig down deep enough to where there might be a pencil sharpener, "if he's doing you know what, he must be doing it with you know who. So who?"

Princess Ella's cheeks turned even rosier and she raised her voice maybe five or six decibels. I guess this is what princesses do when they're angry.

"Mr Goode, are you implying that my husband might be committing the sin of adultery?"

"Yes, Yer Highness, that's exactly what I'm suggestin' and I'll need all the usual info – names, addresses, favorite positions. Glossy color 8 × 10 pictures if you can get 'em."

"Why on earth do you need all of that?"

"I'm lonely," I told her. "Now what can you –"

Now she stood up and tapped her little size double zero foot on the floor. I thought she might be patting a cockroach on the head, but it turns out this is how princesses throw a temper tantrum.

"Sir, you are barking up the wrong dog. It's true that his father the old King was something of a merry old soul, loved a party with lots of wine, women and tobacco, but Prince Charming is nothing like that old reprobate Cole."

⋆   ⋆   ⋆

Well, I wasn't going to argue with a princess. Maybe it becomes second nature to try and protect the family name. Maybe she really didn't know her husband had a wandering eye and a body that was willing to follow. After all, not everybody reads the same high-class tabloids I do.

And maybe the Princess was right. Maybe Charming was faithful. Maybe for the first time in the history of mankind "You know what" referred to something asexual.

One way to find out. I dropped by to see my favorite informant, Bill Winkle. Short and gruffer than a billy goat, Winkle runs a newsstand and he really knows his business. And since he is also a dedicated busybody he knows everybody else's as well.

"Hey, Bill," I said.

"Hi, Jack, find ya a Jill yet?"

"Still looking, my friend. I'm thinking she must have found herself one heck of a hiding place."

Winkle scowled. "Fah, by the time you find her you'll be so far over the hill you won't remember what you're supposed to do with her."

"Say, Bill," I said, "you got a little time for me?"

"Sure, Jack, *Time, Newsweek*, whatever you want."

"How about Playboy? As in Prince Charming following the philosophy?"

Winkle scowled. "How many times have I told you don't believe everything you read. This stuff about the prince's philandering is just a little hard to swallow," He said, straightening up a row of *Reader's Digests*. "I happen to know the Prince likes nothing better than staying home and organizing his collection of clodhoppers."

"So you're saying he's the model husband?"

"No, the Prince has his faults but he's not the scoundrel some of your less-respectable publications would have you believe."

"So, that's it? No dirt."

"Well, nothing new. Everybody knows he's got that funny thing about feet. Whaddayacallit? A fetish. That's how he used to pick all his girlfriends back in his bachelor days; never even looked at their faces, just their dogs. You remember that crazy old woman over in Wellington actually lived in a giant shoe? For a while Charming was dating one of her daughters, even though she was uglier than homemade sin, just so he could hang around that big old brogan building. His brother, Prince Winsome, digs the lower digits too. He had his eye on that same girl – same foot, I should say. For a while there he and Charming were arch enemies."

"What was the name of the girl he was dating?" I asked, thinking I might finally have a lead here.

"I don't know, there was so many of them. And the house is all boarded up now. Turns out the mother was abusing the kids something awful. Terrible sad story.

"Say, wait a second," he interrupted himself. "I do know something about the Prince. Ambassador White took the Prince to dinner one night a month or so ago. I hear she wanted to ask some special favors for that dopey miner coalition she represents. I happen to know that she kept your friend Charming out till way after midnight."

My ears perked up.

"Yeah, where were they?"

"I toldja, they were having dinner. That's all – dinner. The point is that the sleep you get before midnight is the best and they got none that night."

Winkle is a real believer in the early-to-bed philosophy. In fact he's a fanatic about it. It's his whaddayacallit – fetish.

"The real story is about the Princess."

"You got some dirt on her?"

"There used to be a lot of dirt on her. She's a gutter-snipe, comes from some bourgeois family out in the sticks. Father dead, stepmother mean as hell, same old story. Charming only fell for her cuz she had those tee-tiny feet he's so crazy about. Course they've since discovered that it's tough to base a relationship on a cute instep. But I'm pretty sure the Prince is still toeing the line. I mean, I really don't think he's got a tootsie on the side. He's not that kind of a heel."

*   *   *

I called the palace to see if I could get an appointment to see Prince Charming, but I was told that although he was too busy to see me just yet he would be in touch with me soon to set up an appointment.

At least I assume that's what all that laughing meant.

So the only thing I could think to do was root around Princess Ella's family tree. It was easy to see why she didn't go around bragging about her background. Her family lived in what was probably a nice house once, in a neighborhood that could still have passed for respectable if this house had been in a different one. Their mailbox was down and the yard was filled with junk and trash. I guess they were having a hard time finding help since Ella went to live in the palace.

The woman who answered my knock was grey-headed and starting to stoop, but still with a fire in her eye. I handed her my card and asked if I could come in for a few minutes.

"Jack B. Goode?" she said, studying my card. "I'm sorry, Mr Goode. We don't do much planting these days, and even if we did I wouldn't be interested in buying any beanstalks."

"Then we'll get along just fine," I told her, as I stepped in the door. "Since I'm not selling any beanstalks."

The house smelled like mildew and stale popcorn. Dirty out-of-date party dresses and shoes were strewn everywhere. So were pizza boxes and microwave dinner trays. The only part of the house I could see that wasn't filthy was the fireplace and it sparkled.

"Girls, clear off that table, we've got company," my hostess yelled into the dark kitchen. "A gentleman caller."

It took my eyes a few seconds to adjust to the gloom, but when they did I saw two women lost somewhere in their thirties, playing an ironic hand of Old Maid – and arguing – at the kitchen table. Their hair was in curlers, where it looked like it had been for weeks, and their bellies roiled out over the strained waistbands of their moth-eaten sweat pants.

My eyes continued downward, and I made a bet with myself that soon I would find dirty off-brand sneakers, but I lost that wager because what they actually had wrapped around their lower extremities was some sort of system of rags and wooden braces. It was obviously an attempt to emulate our oriental friends and make their feet petite.

But I could have told them it was a painful waste of time. For one thing their ankles were already sailing along on size 12 dinghys, and for another if by some weird chance another prince did come to this house looking for a mate, he probably would not be as kinky as Charming.

The news of a gentleman caller did not impress either of these young ladies. There was a bowl of milk that had curdled on the table, and one of the sisters did shove this out of the way so I could sit down, but a tarantula had beaten me to the seat, so I passed.

"You cheated," said the ditch water-brunette one. "That is not the card I meant to draw."

Her sister made an even funnier face than the one God gave her – another bet I would have lost – and said, "Well, it's not my fault if you're clumsy."

"Cheater."

"Lummox."

Mamma cuffed them both in the back of the head.

"Girls, say hello to Mr Jack B. Goode. Mr Goode, these are my daughters, Emberita and Sparkimberly."

Neither of them got up, but Emberita rolled her eyes at me and said, "Didn't you kill a giant or something? I know I've heard of you."

"Frame-up job," I told her. "I never killed anybody bigger than a bread box."

"Can I get you something to eat?" Momma asked me. "We've got some leg of lamb that our neighbor Mary lost – I mean gave us."

I did the rub-your-belly-and-pretend-like-you-just-ate-a-big-meal "No-thanks." number. I'd already learned all I could here without asking a single question. Prince Charming was certainly not having an affair with any of the yetis in this house. And no doubt they could dish up plenty of dirt on Ella if I asked, but how much of it would be fact and how much plain old jealousy would take too long to figure out.

Just for the hell of it I decided to see if I could start a family feud before I left. Everybody's got a fetish. Charming's was feet. I'm betting that Mamma's was a clean fireplace.

"I'm not hungry," I said. "But there is a chill in the air. Would you mind if I started a fire?"

Now both girls jumped up.

"I'll make you some coffee – hot coffee," said Sparkimberly.

Emberita pulled on my arm. "And I'll get you a blanket and a coat. Although I don't know why I should care – it's her turn to clean the fireplace."

"Liar," was her sister's oh-so-clever retort. "It's your turn and you know it."

Momma grabbed a broom, but I snuck out the back door and didn't see if she swatted her daughters with it or flew off on it to her coven meeting.

By now it was 2:00 in the afternoon, and I thought about spending the remainder of the day whiskey diving at the Gosling's Mater, and the night wandering around trying to figure out where the heck my house had gone. But then I remembered that Princess Ella was paying me by the job and not by the hour, so I bought a newspaper and took a seat at the Silver Spoon coffee shop to plan my next move.

The place had changed. Instead of the usual gossip and clamor, there was musical entertainment, some unseen jazz cat manqué torturing a fiddle somewhere. Worst of all, instead of the redhead I usually flirted with, some greasy-haired guy came over to take my order.

"Good afternoon, sir," he sang. "My name is Tommy Tucker; and I'll be serving you supper. Our special this afternoon is a porridge made from pease meal; and you can have that hot or already congealed. We also have it specially aged for –"

"You bring me anything green – especially porridge – especially old green porridge, and you'll have to get all your music transposed to a higher register."

"Sorry, sir. Perhaps you're more in the mood for something sweet. Our baker Patty's cakes are quite the treat."

"Just bring me coffee. Black. And say, kid, what happened to the little girl that used to work here? Red hair. A real dish."

"Oh, she quit. Took a month's advance on her salary and vanished." He looked around before adding in a whisper – "Took most of the silverware with her when she went."

I gave him my card to give to the manager in case he wanted me to track down the fork filcher.

The coffee was hot and for some reason tasted like peas. While I waited for it to cool off enough to pour into the potted plant, I perused the paper.

The news was too depressing, the crossword puzzle was too hard and the comics were dull, so I gravitated to the classified ads.

Right under a plaintive plea from somebody named Peep looking for some lost livestock was this:

> **WANTED**: Pastry chef, must be honest
> and hard-working. No bird-watchers.
> Apply at Her Majesty's Royal Palace.

Hmm, I haven't been undercover since those horrible humiliating days I spent disguised as a hog, waiting for Tommy Thomas, the bagpiper's boy, to purloin another piggy. Of course, I don't know the difference between a pastry and a g-string, but with any luck – and surely I must be due for a dose – I'll have this case solved before I have to do any actual baking.

Going to work at the palace was a lot easier than I thought it would be. I didn't have to pass any tests or fill out any forms. I just hopped over the moat, banged on the back door of the castle and introduced myself.

"Hi, I'm Jack B. Goode and I'm –"

"Come in, come in," the old lady who answered the door grabbed me and pulled me into the kitchen. "Jack Goode, did you say? I thought you were a much skinnier man. How is your wife, still as obese as ever?"

"I don't have a –" But she just shoved a tall white hat and an apron at me and dragged me over to meet my mentor, an amiable, buck-toothed fella named Simon.

"Simon," she said, flinging open cabinet doors, "I thought I told you to restock these shelves. These cupboards are bare."

"I'm sorry, Mrs H. I'll take care of it as soon as I get a chance." Simon sounded dog tired.

"Don't I know you from somewhur?" he asked me, after the boss lady left. "You look awful familiar."

I wasn't in the mood to explain that I wasn't whatever National Enquirer freak named Jack he thought I was, so I ignored his question and asked about the turnover rate in the royal kitchen.

"Oh, we never make turnovers. Charming can't stand 'em."

Once I had clarified my query, I learned that the royals have been having a hard time keeping anybody in the position, what with one after another getting blamed for poisoning pies, and they were now drafting people into kitchen service. Simon was roped into the position when he couldn't afford to pay a traveling pie man for the treat he ate. Kind of ironic, I guess, that his sweet tooth led to him becoming indentured.

"If you can tell the difference between a blackbird and a blackberry you should be fine. It's not hard, even I can do it and I'm not very bright," Simon said. "But if you mess up and put a blackbird in there, heads will roll – and I'm not using that as a figger of speech. I mean heads will roll – laterally.

"But don't worry, we're not making blackberry pies yet," Simon said. "We're starting off today making tarts. You know how to make tarts, dontcha?"

I started to worry that I might be in over my head here, but Simon told me not to worry.

"Just do whatever I do," Simon said.

"Does Prince Charming ever get down here?" I asked, thinking that if I could just get a quick man-to-man word with the Prince, he might know who was trying to poison him.

"The Prince? Down to the kitchen? Are you kidding?" Simon asked. "He's way too busy playing golf and polo and . . . uh, you know, being a prince."

It turns out that tarts are really just little pies with no crust on the top. My job was to knead and roll out the dough so Simon could shape it into little pie pans and send it on down the line to be filled with what looked like Granny Smith apples but for all I knew could have been blackbird guts.

Don't let anyone tell you that kneading dough is easy work. I was just about to ask Simon what time we got our bourbon break when some fool behind me blew a trumpet or a bugle or some other loud scary wind instrument, and Queen Charismatic herself sauntered into the kitchen.

Everybody cast down their eyes as she passed, but I don't know why. She wasn't the show-stopper that her daughter-in-law was, but she wasn't all that ugly for an old broad. Still, me and some old one-eared grey kitchen cat, who had been toying with a trio of sightless mice he'd captured, were the only ones brave enough to actually look at the Queen.

"I'm here to inspect the tarts," she sniffed regally.

"Does she usually inspect your work?" I asked Simon, but he was standing silently at attention. He might have nodded but I'm not sure. Once again, I followed Simon's lead, straightened my spine and unfocused my gaze.

The tarts weren't the only thing she inspected. As we all stood there, an unblinking grease-covered army, General Charismatic walked in front of and then behind our ranks. We stood there without moving for what seemed like ever. My legs were itching and I was wishing I remembered how to do those bird calls I almost learned when I was a lad.

"Where are the tarts?" shrieked the Queen.

Her henchman nodded to release us from suspended animation, and we turned to where the tarts were laid out, but they weren't. There, that is.

My co-workers really came alive now. We were looking in the pantries, up the chimney, everywhere we could think of for the missing tarts – or a way out of the castle.

"He did it," the Queen shouted. "I saw him! Grab that knave!"

I turned and gave me the guy behind me a what-kind-of-miserable scalawag-would-sink-so-low gaze, but it was a bluff. And a pretty pitiful one at that. I knew she was pointing at me.

So did her troops. The guards grabbed my arms and pulled my hands behind my back. The Queen yelled for somebody to get the Prince; the captain of the guards yelled for somebody to get the royal executioner; and I wished I had hit the snooze button on my alarm clock a few hundred more times this morning. Either that or hit Princess Ella up for money. If I'd known I was going to end up losing my head I woulda charged her at least twice what I did.

Some harried-looking lackey burst in with a prince – Prince Alluring, the youngest royal. From the way the underling's knees were knocking, I think he had a sneaking suspicion this was not who Charismatic had in mind.

"Where is Charming?" she sniped at the guy.

"I called him just like you said, Your Majesty," he sputtered, "but the Prince is in the counting room, counting up his slip-ons. He said he didn't want to be disturbed."

"Why, that lazy loafer, I ought to –" She turned her royal attention back to me. "You are accused of stealing tarts. The penalty is death for you and several of your coworkers. How do you plead? Guilty or what?"

"Yer Majesty," I said, "I gotta tell ya the truth, I did steal a tart. Once. From my best friend Phil. But it was a long time ago and as soon as I found out what kind of girl she was I gave her back. Pilfering pastries is really not one of my vices."

"Hah! You stole them, and I bet you tried to poison Prince Charming. Everybody turn and face the doorway, so that you can hail the Prince when he arrives. I am going to inspect these blackberry pies."

It was at that moment as my captors spun me around away from the blackberry pies I had not even seen yet, that I decided to become a socialist – or a communist or Buddhist or whoever it is that don't have these royal pains in the neck.

I knew Prince Charming was not coming. So did Queen Charismatic. I knew I didn't steal any tarts or put any bird parts in pies. So did Queen Charismatic. I also knew why she wanted us to turn our backs.

There was a "skritch-skritch" sound as one of the blind

mice escaped from its tabby tormentor and scurried up a hickory grandfather clock. It wasn't much of a diversion, but it was gonna have to do.

"Look over there," I shouted. "It's Prince Charming. Behind us."

Everybody turned around but what we saw was not Prince Charming but Queen Charismatic. She was not just inspecting our pies, she was flavoring them.

It took a moment or two before she realized that her youngest son as well as her entire kitchen staff had just seen her pull a big dead black bird out of her purse and put it inside a pie crust.

To her credit she didn't try to bulldoze her way out of it. She said, "I . . . I never put enough in there to actually hurt him. I just wanted to make him see that being monarch is a serious job. He won't grow up and stop playing, and I'm tired, I want to step down."

Nobody knew what to do now. Technically, it's not against the law for royals to break the law. Just when it looked like we were all going to spend the rest of our lives there, playing the who-can-look-the-stupidest game, the Queen took command.

"Let him go," she said to the guards holding me. "You can keep your head but not your job. You're fired."

Turning to the guards who had escorted into the kitchen, she sighed and said, "Well, come on, let's get back to the throne room. I guess this reign is never going to go away."

As I was untying my apron and wondering if I had enough money to buy a bottle of rye to celebrate wrapping up this case, Simon stuck out his hand for me to shake.

"Wow," he said, "you are a great detective, I mean great. You solved one of the biggest mysteries of our time."

"You think so?"

"Yeah, I mean, I always wondered what she was lugging around in that purse of hers."

I handed him my card and he looked at it for a minute.

"Jack B. Goode? Now I know where I know you from," Simon said. "You can play a guitar just like a ringin' a bell, right?"

It was started to dawn on me why everybody thought of Simon as simple.

"I'm sorry," I told him. "I have no idea what you're talking about."

THE KALUZA-KLEIN CAPER

Damien Broderick

A mind-crackingly ugly woman named Hsia Shan-yun was all set to blow the crap out of the major personal records filing installation in the West Pacific Zone when a monitor Bug put the arm on her.

Shan-yun was a horrifyingly tall Valkyrie, just under two metres from her size-ten track shoes to the top of her wildly flowing black mane. Eyes of slashing jade green glared out at the world she despised under slanting, Oriental eyelids. Her mouth was ripe and full, hardly the neat, demure pallid line esteemed by leading fashion experts of the 23rd century.

I won't even talk about her breasts, or the violent animal swing of her muscular body, or the way her legs stretched most of the way from earth to sky and her arms seemed fitted by evolution to a role quite other than punching data into a terminal fifteen hours a day. A detailed list would be disgracefully sexist, whether by our standards or hers.

Take it from me. Hsia Shan-yun was outstandingly unattractive.

Her benighted parents, the world's last Confucian Scientologists, had hidden her in a small shielded bottle during the Reconstruction Phase, when genetic engineers in geosynchronous orbit had broadcast whole-body altering messages to the gonads and onboard fetuses of the entire planet. In consequence, the unfortunate creature looked like an abominable throwback to that peak epoch of nutrition-driven Brute Expressionism – the 20th century.

Naturally, Shan-yun compensated for her atrocious looks by denial and fantasy. Day and night she read forbidden books (all books, of course, being forbidden, but some being incredibly more forbidden than others, and it was this kind she crammed into her perverted brain).

The books she sought high and low were about the 20th century, that sink of degradation and physical excess.

Best of all, she loved books about inner-city fun running.

In the depths of the empty municipal sewers, during darkest night, aided only by the light from her Watchplate tuned to an empty channel, she pounded out the klicks in her handmade track shoes, until inhumanly shaped muscles swelled in her legs.

Next of all she loved books about working out with weights.

Staring with a swollen heart at flat photographs of Bev Francis and Arnold Schwarzenegger in their heyday, she hack-squatted and bench-pressed, chest-flyed and lat-extended, leg-lifted and bicep-curled. What this did to her already distorted atavistic frame can only be left to the imagination, because I really couldn't stand the aggravation.

How did the robot Bugs know what Shan-yun had been up to? She'd taken every precaution. The whole thing had been planned out in exquisite detail for nearly fifteen months. She'd gone over every single detail of the operation a dozen times, from the initial routine of getting a job in Pacific Data Central to the final step of smuggling her home-plaited Striped Hole into the terminal terminal.

She hadn't been able to find a flaw in the plan but obviously there'd been a flaw you could drive a Bug through.

The robot cop rolled up beside Shan-yun just as she was entering the Personal Information Bubble Banks, as she had every right to do, being assistant trainee data slibber.

She watched it coming at her from the corner of her slitted, tilted, jade-glowing eyes and kept walking.

Even though she was by now very, very good at running, running would not have helped, as it turned out.

A cloud of gossamer filaments belched from the Bug's chest spigots and settled on her like acid rain.

"Shit!" cried Hsia Shan-yun, proving yet again that she was an evil lowlife throwback.

Tiny itching threads coated her from head to foot, leaving uncovered only her eyes, ears and nostrils. Achieving that effect had consumed a decade of nonstop dedicated research in the National Goo Laboratories, but Hsia Shan-yun was not impressed. She hissed with rage. She spat. There wasn't much else she could do, because the filaments put their tiny hands together and squeezed, tightening into a body-hugging plastic shell. Just enough slack was left around Shan-yun's hideously overdeveloped rib cage and chest for her to breathe, but only just enough.

She started to fall flat on her face. Before the statue-like form she now was could topple to the tiles and shatter, the monitor Bug whipped out metal tentacles and nestled her carefully against its own hard torso.

"Citizen Hsia," the thing intoned, "it is my unhappy duty to take you into protective custody, for both your own highest good and that of the republic."

"Mmmnbbn," Shan-yun explained. "Gmmngb."

"I regret the temporary restraint on your freedom of speech," the tin cop said unctuously, "but rest assured you will be permitted full range of expression as soon as we arrive at Medical Six. And how," it added with a low chuckle, and spun about, accelerating out of the Bubble Bank.

"We intend to indict you for conspiracy against the State," it re-added for good measure. "Appropriate remedial steps will follow forthwith. Oh my, yes."

Did this unwelcome mechanical badinage affect the apprehended criminal?

What do *you* think? Shan-yun was rather miffed.

No, that doesn't quite capture it. She was seriously alarmed at her prospects.

Actually, she was in a turmoil of panic. Not to put too fine a point on it, she was ready to shit herself.

The monitor Bug rolled swiftly though the foyer of Data Central with Shan's rigid torso tucked against it like a huge ungainly swaddled baby, except that they didn't deal that way with babies anymore.

When her head happened to tilt that way, Shan-yun had no difficulty in seeing people scurrying out of the way. The chief slibber, coming in from a lunch of chives, peatgrowth, and yogurt sausages, blenched and turned aside without a word.

"Fair-weather friend," Shan tried to shout bitterly, but it came out as another collection of vowelless unpalatalized consonants.

Outside the building, machine and captive swung down a ramp to a thoroughfare marked MEDICAL ONLY.

In 197 years' time, that's a sign to make your blood run cold. Well, I suppose it is already, to be brutally frank.

The monitor jacked without hesitation into a high-speed conveyor unit, thoughtfully raising a shield to keep the wind out of Shan's eyes.

The harsh violet lights of the tunnel went blurry with speed. Shan-yun's tummy tried to sneak away, but her backbone wouldn't let it. Half a minute later it got its revenge.

"All still in one piece, I hope, dear," the machine said in Shan's reeling ear. "Here we are. Have a nice day, now."

The monitor coasted into the aseptic whiteness of a medical bay. You can always tell, 197 years from now, when you've reached a medical bay. The atmosphere reeks of such a high-toned blend of purity and righteousness you want to throw up.

Two crisp blue-garbed apes stepped out of a lift. Mental health and social adjustment radiated from their every pore.

"Citizen Hsia!" cried the one on the right. "Welcome to Medical Six."

His demeanor blended professional cheeriness with personal stoic resignation to the iniquity of social deviants with Striped Holes tucked inside smelly parts of their bodies.

"Kindly place the citizen on the couch and return to your post," said the one on the left.

Still locked solid in her plastic cocoon, Shan-yun was positioned carefully on a form-fitting cot. The Bug rolled away whence it had come without a word of farewell.

The mind-crackingly ugly woman stared up at her doctors and tried to set off the Hole. Nothing happened. Her fingers would not bend. The muscles in her belly spasmed but she lay motionless. The Hole spun uselessly inside her, quite beyond her control.

"Well, Ms Hsia," the first ape told her, "you've certainly got yourself into a peck of trouble."

"Yep. No double ungood untruth there. Let's hope for your sake we can straighten you out, ethics-wise, without having to reduce you to a vegetable."

Under the plastic skin, cold sweat jumped from Shan's forehead in almost exactly the way moisture develops on the inside of a loaf of plastic-wrapped bread. It was a disgusting and depressing sensation.

"Brainscrub . . ." one of the creatures said reflectively. "You can't use it, you gotta lose it."

"It's a tragedy, though, Frank, she's a person of evident resource. How many of us could plait a Striped Hole without being picked up at the nudge-horizon stage? That's skill, Frank, whether or not we care to admit it. Talent."

"Yet we mustn't forget that she's abused her abilities to the detriment of the State."

"I'd never let that slip my mind, Frank, but it seems our fellow citizen must have done so." He peered down into Shan's eyes with a look of loathing and concern. Shan's eyes by now were brimming to overflow with tears of fury and terror. In fact, Shan's eyes took the opportunity to try to leap from her head and tear the ape's sanctimonious tongue from his head, but being organs ill adapted by evolution to that function, they had to content themselves with bulging in red-shot hatred.

"You should have recognized your own sickness," Frank told her. "You ought to have boldly stepped forward for voluntary treatment."

The threads of the cocoon tightened and the ape shook his head ruefully.

"Relax, Ms Hsia. Anger is a wasteful and antisocial emotion. A good case has been made for the view that all emotion is wasteful and antisocial, but I don't subscribe to that view. Live and let live, I say."

A colorful board of indicators flashed and chimed. Shanyun seethed.

"We'll be sending you through to the Analyst any moment now, Ms Hsia, and I've got to tell you, it won't look good on your record if you're harboring resentment."

A muffled series of explosive noises came from the cocoon.

A melodious tone sounded from the lift.

"Ah, there we are now. No need for anxiety, Ms Hsia. Truly. You'll go straight through for analysis and judgment as soon as the techs have removed the cocoon and that Striped Hole you inserted into yourself."

The other ape nodded vigorously, leaning across Shan-yun with an aerosol can. "Absolutely correct. Remember – our job is to get you *well*." He squirted spray into her nostrils. The room tilted and banged the side of her head.

She was not quite unconscious as the apes began to push the couch and her numb body into the lift. "Candidly, Ted," she heard Frank say, as the darkness ripped her mind into silly small shreds, "these deviants give me the gol-durned *creeps*."

The cell Hsia Shan-yun woke up in was dank, foul, almost lightless, and, she decided with horror, very possibly rat-infested.

This was impossible, of course.

The future's not like that. You know that and I know that.

The people who live in the future know it better than either of us.

Gosh, if a single fact has been established once and for all, surely it's that the future is *clean*.

It's sanitized. Everyone's shoes are tucked neatly under the bed before they go to sleep, which they do at 10:15 or earlier.

The future's no banana republic. Granted, there's that little spot of bother immediately up ahead, with the ayatollahs and the pastors and so on, but nothing's perfect, not even utopia.

There simply can't be rat-infested cells with rusty chains and dried marks down the stone walls looking suspiciously like old blood (not all *that* old). The unions, the government, and the public service would not put up with it. The future is the last redoubt of *niceness*.

Hsia Shan-yun knew that as well as we do, which is why she

sat there quivering with her hands jammed into her mouth and her white even teeth clamped into the skin of her knuckles.

She stopped after a rather commendably brief interval, and sat up straight on the wooden bench and stifled a cry.

She'd got a splinter in her bare ass.

Hsia Shan-yun shook her head to clear the fog out of it. A faint trace of illumination straggled through the tiny mud-caked barred window high in the opposite wall. It glistened from a rivulet of authentic dank running down the rough-hewn and palpably iron-hard blue blocks of stone of which the wall had been built, obviously by convict labor.

"Absurd," Hsia Shan-yun muttered. Shivering, as you will when you are naked and you have lived all your life in centrally heated buildings and there's a nasty draft coming in some-where, she dropped her tootsies to the ground.

This was her next mistake, and she regretted it bitterly and at once.

The walls were not the only feature of the cell which were dank. The floors were danker.

Hastily, Shan-yun tucked her befouled soles back under her haunches and hugged herself tight to ward off the chill.

Hugging herself was something, it must be confessed, which she'd had a fair amount of practice in. Nobody else in her exceptionally silly world would give her a hug, so she'd had to develop a knack for doing it herself. Nobody hugs ugly people if they can possibly avoid it, and the people in the future were even better than we are at avoiding doing what might be nice for other people but grossly unrewarding for ourselves.

"Slimy floors," Hsia Shan-yun muttered in disbelief. "Barred windows."

What Hsia Shan-yun was experiencing has been described by the social psychologist Leon Festinger as *cognitive disso-nance*. There was a big gap between what she believed and what she experienced.

After all, it's evident that Hsia Shan-yun found her ambient social order so entirely and unredemptively corrupt that she'd gone to the shocking length of planning to blow the crap out of its major data stores with a Striped Hole secreted within her own person.

Now, true, this desperate remedy was facilitated by her total lack of any sense of physical self-worth. If people often give you hugs when you're blue, or because they think you're nice, or just for the fun of it, you start to attend to the care and maintenance of your body. Blowing it to shreds to make a political point is the last thing that would occur to you.

Still, in her wildest vituperations against the State, in her maddest anarchic fantasies, Hsia Shan-yun had never imagined that they had become this barbaric.

"You evil malefactors," she suddenly screamed at the top of her voice, leaping from the bench into the slimy muck of the floor and beating uselessly against the unyielding stone walls, "let me out of here!"

This outburst was greeted by an equally sudden scream at her back.

All the tiny wild black hairs at Hsia Shan-yun's neck went rigid and tried to throw themselves overboard but got their feet caught.

She lurched around in the penumbral gloom. A second bench stretched out behind hers, depending from the wall opposite on thick rusted chains.

A dim figure, she now saw, huddled there also, naked and panic-stricken.

"Keep away from me, you fiends, or I'll tear your eyes out!" cried the voice, distorted by terror. Abruptly it broke, gave way to terrible wrenching sobs. "Do what you like to me, but leave my *mind* alone, you broggish snaggers."

Shan-yun was amazed and appalled. The dim figure was a breeding male in full heat!

She crossed the room in two athletic bounds, scarcely aware of the loathsome grime and squelching muck and pullulating pustules of decay and skin-crawlingly horrible fragments and so on stuck to the floor.

"Hey, calm down," she said urgently. "I'm a prisoner, too, honey-pong. Just woke up."

"Stay away," shrieked the breeder, arching his fingers into

claws. He was quite a specimen, she saw. They must have been pumping testosterone into him for weeks.

"Flibble out, manjack," she said soothingly, trying to approach him in the skilled way a trained librarian deals with a maddened overdue borrower. She padded through the unspeakable vileness underfoot, sat on the creaking, swaying bench, started to put a comforting arm about the man's shoulders.

The claws flashed out and raked her face.

Fortunately, his nails were short and blunt. Even so, he nearly hooked out Shan's left eye with his pinky.

She slapped his flailing arm aside, caught both his slender wrists in one large hand, shook him heavily with the other.

"Listen, tooter, get a grip on yourself. I'm not a doctor and I'm not a State spy, and it looks to me as if we're both in the same flivver."

"A likely story," the brute snivelled.

Patiently, she said, "My name's Hsia Shan-yun and I'm here because I tried to do in a data store with a Striped Hole." That should give him pause. "What's your excuse?"

"You should know, you mendacious swine," he mumbled.

He was a nerdish little wimp, of course, due to the DNA-altering satellite radiations that had solved the world's problems fifty years before by making everyone kindly, socially responsible, aggressively peaceful, noncompetitively self-regarding, and incapable of forgetting to give flowers on Mother's Day. Even so, Hsia Shan-yun now thought she detected a steely grace in his wimpish face, which was, for the reasons just adumbrated, fairly uncommon.

He looked at Shan-yun with watery eyes through which could be glimpsed some small spark of salvageable human worth. It was a wildly arousing sight for Hsia Shan-yun, given the narrow range of her experiences to this point in time.

"No, I don't know your name," she told him patiently, "and I don't see how we can be friends if you won't even tell me that much about yourself." There was no answer from the ruttish but miserable male. "Well, what *sign* are you?"

He still clearly supposed that she was lying.

"You and your henchmen must have been right through my brain by now! Why are you toying with me like this? Are you nothing but sadists? Get it over and done with, damn you. *Turn* me into a zombie. Rip out my brain and crush it in a *food* processor. Burn out my frontal lobes and peel all my other lobes down like *onions.* Ravage my –"

"Hey, ease up already."

"Shred my reticular activating system and unravel my cortical rind, do it! *do it!* and then just let me go – at least I'll be out of this horrible place."

And he was weeping again, wrenchingly, rackingly, with the bitterness of newly found courage confronting archaic fears, of bravery facing down cowardice in the depths of the archetypal psyche, of ancient instincts battling with comparatively recently inculcated and historically untested utilitarian social values, of good against evil and sweet against sour.

Hsia Shan-yun spent several minutes wiping away the salty tears he'd got all over her quite large chest.

Even profound emotional breakthroughs into openness and trust must, sad to say, end.

Actually, Shan-yun's justifiably paranoid mind was starting to latch onto the idea that maybe this breeding male was the spy he accused her of being, that this primitive horror was some kind of carefully arranged and elaborate double-bluff to soften her up, damage her defenses, and cause her to spill out the names, addresses, @s, urls and datacodes of her confederates (which she didn't have any of anyway).

She didn't get a chance to voice this unkind suspicion. Brain-fryingly bright lights glared on with a sizzle of ozone.

The wall – blue stone, dried blood, rusted chains, mud, slime, ichor, and all – slid gratingly up, one monumental piece, into the cobweb-matted ceiling.

A huge authentically ugly monitor robot hummed there on its knurled metal wheels, ruby dials flashing with menace.

The Bug ignored Hsia Shan-yun. It fixed all seven of its nasty beady glowing red photoreceptors on the quivering person of the breeding male cowering behind her under his wooden bench.

"Ex-citizen Turdington Jimbo, it is my grave duty to inform you –"

"Aargh, aargh, *not the brainscrub machine!*" howled Hsia's companion.

"– that a final analysis has been made of your deviation," the monitor ground on in its unfeeling, non-Rogerian way. "In view of your intransigent recidivism –"

"My *what*?"

"You did it once," Shan-yun said helpfully, "they figure you'll do it again, given half a chance."

"Oh. Gotcha."

"– you are to be taken to a place of correction where your unsavoury personality will be expunged and replaced by one more to our taste."

"*No! No! Not the scrub, you fiends!*"

Ignoring every outburst, the Bug extended a small document featuring a really rather flattering three-dimensional picture of Turdington Jimbo with some of his friends at a take-out Japanese Nooky bar. No text was visible, firstly because by 197 years from now nobody (other than intransigent recidivists like Hsai Shan-yun) could read, and secondly because robot Rugs see mainly at the ultraviolet end of the spectrum.

"You are to surrender this notification of intent to the officiating medic. Heavy penalties will attend unauthorized folding, bending, spindling, or mutilation of the card. Kindly follow me."

The machine spun majestically and rolled slowly away into the brightly lighted corridor.

Since one of its metal tentacles was firmly attached to the shrieking man's arm, Turdington Jimbo skidded across the foul, dank, slippery cell floor, kicking and banging with his spare arm.

The wall started back down again, with the clear intention of resealing Hsia Shan-yun inside the cell.

"*Hold* it, buster!" Outrage and disbelief made her own voice squeak. She hurled herself forward without waiting for that refreshing cortico-thalamic integration pause recommended by leading mental health authorities.

What you are about to witness is unadulterated thalamus at work. Brute beast.

Shan-yun rolled bruisingly into the corridor a split second before the wall blasted down into its groove with a crash that rocked the Bug on its tracks.

"Take your tentacles off him, you tin retard!"

The Bug spun about with dazzling speed, incidentally jerking Turdington Jimbo off his feet and slamming him against the corridor wall, which at least was smoother of surface than the cell's barbarous bluestone.

"Ex-citizen Hsia Shan-yun," it cried in a particularly official tone, training a scanner at her, "I discern that you are at liberty without lawful authorization. Have you taken leave of your senses? Return to your cell at once."

The bluestone wall at Shan-Yun's back screeched back up again into the roof.

Shan glanced over her shoulder. The cell looked even less inviting than it had when she was pent up in it. She waited for the robot monitor to activate its spigots.

Watch closely, for we have come in this pivotal and revealing moment to one of the intrinsic limitations of artificial minds: They are easily scandalized. Some courses of action simply strike robot monitors as beyond the bounds of probability. I mean, would *you* leave your cell without proper authorization?

The Bug sat there humming, patiently waiting for Hsia Shan-yun to trot obediently back into durance vile.

The astonishingly tall, ugly, powerful woman again took advantage of this epistemologico-ethical programming flaw without conscious thought.

Robots have no thalamus, which might be why in the 1,482,965 worlds in the local arm of the Milky Way known to possess life, only one (Alpha Grommett) is governed exclusively by machine intelligences. Even that exceptional case can be explained, since it is now known that all mechanical life on Alpha Grommet evolved from an autonomic mousetrap discarded on the radiation-hot planet by a visiting Bargleplod seven million years ago.

Doubled over to reduce her profile, Shan-yun sprinted past the Bug and pelted up the stark white hallway.

With an efficient whine the monitor reversed, started after her.

Shan-yun dug her heels in, skidded to a stop, caromed off a wall, and headed back the way she'd come.

As her thalamus had hoped, the monitor had let Turdington Jimbo loose before it came after her. It could hardly hare off in pursuit with a living human person attached only by one arm, for though monitors had a disagreeable amount of discretion and no high regard for organic life systems *per se*, assault and battery was not part of their charter.

As a matter of fact, Hsia Shan-yun was betting her life on the truism, never to her knowledge publicly tested, that robots had an express prohibition against irreparably killing a human being built into their core chip.

She was almost upon it when it fired its cloud of goo.

The stuff passed over her head, for at that very moment her thalamus had caused her to somersault forward, throwing her directly in the path of the monitor's heavy treads.

"Hsia!" the male screamed, hands pressed hard against his bloodless cheeks. "Oh, no! You'll be killed so badly they won't be able to fix you!"

Of course, the robot had jammed on its brakes the moment it worked out what was what, which as you can imagine happened pretty fast, given the niftiness of today's Moore's Law-accelerated chips and extrapolating forward 197 years from that.

Even so, it had acted too late. The Bug was right on top of her. It did the only thing left to it. It lifted its entire torso into the air on its telescoping wheelbase, like something out of *Inspector Gadget*.

Hsia Shan-yun's thalamus was not working blind in precipitating this chain of events, because she had seen robots perform the same stunt to clear unexpected obstacles when moving at high speed. (I thought you'd like to be reassured that there was nothing gratuitous or *ad hoc* in her methods.)

She made herself snake-thin, or as close to it as a woman designed like Shan-yun could manage, by tightening her rib cage.

Treads clanked and banged and thundered past on either side.

She reached up convulsively and clamped her arms and legs to its underbelly, then clung on for dear life.

All manner of knobs and levers festooned the Bug's belly. Chortling merrily, Shan pressed, pulled and tampered with as many as she was able to reach with one hand, clinging the while to her haven. The monitor could hardly shoot goo at her while she stayed in this position, but the depressing possibility remained that it might drop back down to normal profile and sandwich her across the floor.

A very bad noise went through her body then, like the bell of the Hunchback of Notre Dame being put through a suitably sized garden mulcher. This was followed by an equally abrupt ghastly silence.

The Bug stopped with a jolt.

Hsia Shan-yun fell off, banging her spine.

Somewhere farther up the corridor, the breeding male was venting strange muffled sobs. Shan rolled up her eyes, sighed, shook her head, eased out from under the motionless machine, and sat up to blow her nose.

Turdington Jimbo was not weeping with terror, as she had supposed. He sat in the middle of the corridor doubled up with mirth.

He was trying to hide his unseemly mirth behind his hand. When Shan-yun scowled bitterly, he only laughed the harder, shaking his own head in explanation and apology and gesturing for her to look behind her.

The monitor's twenty-seven utility tentacles stuck straight out from its torso like the quills on a porcupine. Its lights were off.

She'd killed it stone dead and turned it into a pincushion.

"Hsia," the man began.

"Call me Shan." To her amazement and almost without waiting to notify her brain, the stomach cramp of terror switched to a top-class pulse of sexual excitement.

"Turdington Jimbo," the breeding male said, covering his chest gallantly with his outspread hand.

"Hi. That's not –?"

"That's Jimbo."

"Gotcha."

Turdington Jimbo's eyes were shiny with the lust of the reprieved. The erogenous zones of them both were inflamed, engorged, and highly visible. They were employing a form of signaling evolved by human people back in the days of *Australopithecus boisei* but hardly ever used to full advantage any longer because of the widespread custom of wearing clothes over most of them.

Instead of falling into an absent-minded fit of procreation, though, Shan-yun ran to his side, grabbed his hand, pulled him to his feet. "Up, man. We've got to move fast."

"Don't be a spoilsport," Turdington Jimbo said sulkily. "Let's tango. Let's get it on. We could be big, really big. Let's talk this over. I know a great place where some actors go after the show, we could eat, maybe take a bottle of Chianti, or the house white's fine if you'd rather try something different, dance a little –"

Shan-yun slapped him hard about the chops. He staggered, touched his bleeding lip, shook his dazed head, averted his gaze.

"Sorry. You know how it is. I'd just like it to be the last thing I remember before they burn my brain out." He sat down again on the hard white synthetic flooring and started to cry.

At that moment the lights went out and the entire wall at the far end of the corridor lit up with the huge face of a gray-haired bureaucrat.

As enormous lips moved, an amplified voice like planks of wood being slammed over and over against the sides of your head told them:

"Do not make the slightest move! Nerve crunchers are trained on you both from every side. You will never escape!"

"Run, Jimbo!" Hsia Shan-yun cried. Hand in hand, lust and self-pity momentarily displaced from the centre of their attention, they sprinted toward the huge projected face.

With a really awful teeth-grating whine, the nerve cruncher came on.

Hsia Shan-yun and Turdington Jimbo instantly crashed to the floor, while utmost agony knotted every muscle in their bodies into a macramé of incandescent thermite wire.

"Release the prisoner."

Hsia Shan-yun battled her way free of the lashing coils of boiling pain and sat up, looking blurrily at the gray face that loomed over her from the holovision screen. Its huge lips pursed in distaste.

"You cannot escape, Ms Hsia. Mr Turdington, to your feet, if you please."

Strangely unhurt, Turdington Jimbo climbed sheepishly to his feet and began to back away from his twitching companion.

"Sorry, babe. I know we could've swung, you dig? If we'd met in more propitious, like, you know . . . Love your glands, kiddo, no shit."

Shan-yun stared from the magnified image to the scuttling breeder and back again. She shook her head, which still felt as if it were connected to her neck by hot wire and staples.

"Ms Hsia, I am your doctor. This psychodrama has confirmed beyond any doubt the analysis of obdurate deviation produced by the computers during your interrogation."

"What! You lying maniac, I haven't been interrogated! I only just woke up in that filthy cell —"

"The questioning was conducted while you were unconscious, naturally. This was praiseworthy efficiency, since the techbots had to anaesthetize you in any case to recover the Striped Hole you had secreted about your person."

Turdington Jimbo continued to skulk furtively down the corridor. Hsia stared at him with slowly dawning understanding.

"Jimbo! Is this prick telling me that you —"

"Just doing my job, honeyroll," he screeched. She was

almost on him in one convulsive arm-swinging vengeful leap
when part of the corridor wall bubbled, irised, put out a
tentacle, and pulled him through, legs kicking in wild alarm.

The huge gray mouth in the screen pursed, sighed. "You
see? Utterly uncontrolled. You are a pitiful atavism, Ms Hsia,
a genetic error that we must set right."

Shan glared wildly up and down the corridor, prying at the
walls and flooring with her strong fingers. The bubble was
gone, sealed over. She was trapped, pinned down by the
doctor's eyes, at their merciless mercy. Shan-yun's skin
seemed rigid, her muscles shimmered, she seemed to feel
every nerve picked out in blue and red and crackling with
electricity. She looked like a wild beast with an IQ of 150.

"It is beyond the power of 23rd-century mental hygiene
conditioning to cure you. I have only one recourse left to me.
You are to be taken from this place and –"

"Brainscrubbed!" The word burst like blood from her
mouth.

"Certainly not! Do you take us for savages?"

Shan's lips did that rictus which cheap pulp writers describe
as a mirthless smile. It's certainly true that she didn't have
much to chuckle about right at that moment.

"'Brainscrub,' so-called, is merely a convenient fiction,
serving as a public deterrent to deviation. We are not monsters, despite the detestable claims of your twisted philosophy."

"Your robot Bug said –"

"The KS-749 unit was programmed for the psychodrama
that tested your fidelity to the State. Allow me to continue.
You leave us no alternative but Hyperspatial Morphology
Restructuring."

You must have noticed the aggravating way bureaucrats and
politicians love to simplify the genuinely difficult, handing out
their jackass Golden Fleece Awards to people whose imagination and powers of thought leave the jackasses limping badly in
the rear of the van of history, while inflating the commonplace
with their orotund bombast.

In ordinary terms, what Hsia Shan-yun's doctor had in

mind for her amounted to amputation of most of her limbs, surgical removal of all those items of her anatomy that distinguished her from her drab fellows, blurring of the eye's cornea to reduce her visual acuity, drugging and numbing of her mind, and in general changing her from the mind-crackingly ugly creature she was into a standard wimp of the 23rd century.

"When your physical state has been ortho-retro-fitted, you are to be taken to the Pacific Zone starport and from there removed to a place of permanent exile from the Earth, namely the Prison World ZRL-25591.

"In the company of other confirmed deviants you will live out what remains of your life in the perpetual absence of those advantages and regulations of civilization which you find so irksome. Judgment has been rendered."

The man's face dwindled to a single point of light and, then even that faded. The corridor lights went out, leaving Hsia Shan-yun in total darkness. There was a hiss of gas. It didn't make any difference to Shan. Even when you're in a state of hyper-arousal, ready to fight and die, red in tooth and claw, thalamus and cortex locked into synch, some prospects are simply too tacky to face while you're awake.

Having all your major bits trimmed off to fit you on the Procrustean bed is an example of one such challenge.

Even as the gas eddied into the corridor, Hsia Shan-yun was already out cold as a mackerel.

If you ever find them coming at you with a Hyperspatial Morphology Restructurator, I can only advise you to run as fast as your legs can carry you in the opposite direction.

While you're running, search your pockets for a cyanide capsule.

If you find one, place it between your teeth and crunch down hard. With any luck, you should be dead inside a couple of minutes and beyond their reach.

Hsia Shan-yun was not that lucky.

She awoke stiff and sore. When she ran her hand over her aching face, nothing fit.

There are no makeup mirrors in a space-hulk, but after her eyes finally came as close to focusing as anyone can reasonably expect eyes to do when they've just had their corneas hyper-spatially scratched out, she saw at once that the surgeons had really earned their fees while she was blotto.

Her legs were now slightly less than half their previous length, and effectively clubbed at the ends.

Shaking, she raised her hands in front of her weakened eyes.

Claws. Bird claws. Shrivelled, enfeebled things, the hands of a woman of 122.

Hsia Shan-yun moaned and tried to push herself to a standing position.

Every part of her body was out of whack. She tottered backwards, unbalanced.

When she looked down, a gust of shocked grief burst through her. Her breasts were *gone*. Under the rough convict sack, her chest was flat as a normal attractive 23rd-century woman's.

Shan-yun started to cry. She slid woozily down to the metal deck and hunched there, puny arms folded over her poor depleted flesh. She sobbed with loss, then with growing anger, and finally with great noisy howls of furious defiance.

"Attention! Attention! We are now in orbit about Prison World ZRL-25591."

The throbbing in her head was not helped by the speaker blaring in her left ear. She covered the sides of her mutilated face with the mean little hands they'd left her, but the voice cut through like a surgeon's scalpel.

"Prepare for immediate disembarkation. When the doors open, leave your cells. Follow the green line to the shuttle pod. Attention!"

Howling with rage, Shan-yun shoved herself off the cold, damp metal plating and waited shivering for the snick of the door's lock. She was starvingly hungry. Her breath stank as it bounced back to her from the scratched, graffiti-covered door.

The door grated open. She burst out into the gangway and slammed into a surly woman with swarthy skin. Bristling, Shan raised her hands angrily.

And stopped.

Her entire physical relationship to the rest of the human world had turned on its head.

The other woman was centimeters taller than she, and tough with it.

Hsia Shan-yun dropped her hands and croaked, "You a fellow felon?"

The other woman lowered her own fists and frowned. "Freda Odell," she said. "'Felon' is right. I was caught programming the teaching machines with subversive material."

Shan-yun was impressed. "Wormhole theory?"

"Nah. History."

They smiled and hugged each other with spontaneous warmth.

"Move along! No loitering!"

A green arrowhead flashed imperiously along the scarred metal bulkhead. Shrugging, the women followed it to the shuttle pod.

Seven other sociopaths were already there, looking lost. Nobody was speaking to anyone else until Shan and Freda arrived, and they'd hardly begun to liven the party with introductions and outbursts of grievance when another PA system started up.

"Enter the shuttle in orderly procession! Strap in at once for immediate re-entry. Hurry it up. A nerve-crunching for the tardy!"

"In a pig's eye!" Her moment of rational humility firmly behind her, Shan-yun started along a side corridor looking for someone to kill with her feeble new hands. Worried, Freda lingered at the entrance. The rest filed in obediently.

"Back to the shuttle, deviant!" yelped the PA. "At once!"

A single jolt from the nerve cruncher convinced Shan that she was in neither position nor shape to seek immediate restitution. Somewhat cowed, she limped back to the shuttle and allowed Freda to strap her in to an acceleration couch.

The trip down to the surface was done under power, a monstrous buffeting racket that lasted ten minutes or ten hours and more or less precluded conversation, plotting, thinking about sheep or indeed any activity more demanding than being dead.

Hitting dirt in a shuttle is like having a golf club slam your spine, though this simile would not have occurred to Hsia Shan-yun. Golf was outlawed under the All Islamic-Christian Decency Interregnum as morale-sapping, and never regained its popularity owing to the brief but concentrated use of major greens for disciplinary rallies.

Shan did wonder, though, how many uses the authorities got from a shuttle before the bloody thing fell into small pieces from sheer mechanical fatigue.

Nauseated, the six women and one man in the convict landing detail, assuming I have the penological-cum-military terminology correct, stumbled from their landing couches and lurched down a creaking plastic ramp for their first look at the place of exile.

The planet was *hideous*.

"Hubbard's E-meter!" Freda was appalled. Her fists tightened at her sides, and Shan-yun could hear the knuckles cracking. "It's . . . it's –"

Hardened subversive that she was, covertly trained in the lore of the history of human people on and off planetary bodies, Freda could not bring herself to express such an indecency.

Shan gritted her teeth and forced out the words Freda Odell was looking for.

"Open. It's *open!*"

She could hardly breathe. The blue, white-splotched, hazy ceiling infinitely high above them was, she decided through her viscera-clutching panic, what the people of Earth used to call "sky".

Just thinking the word was enough to throw her into a tizzy.

The insane visual distances on every side put her already blurry eyes completely out of kilter. She simply could not conceive of so much open, unroofed, unused space.

Browns and greens and yellows and other blotches of visual stimuli lay here and there with no sense to them.

Hsia Shan-yun was experiencing the exact opposite of the Ontological Pre-eminence of Symbol. Here and now, brute empirical reality was crashing over her sensory input systems, bypassing the usual interpretative codes and grids.

She saw stuff she couldn't name. In fact, she saw stuff she couldn't, strictly speaking, even *see*.

"Give it time," she murmured desperately, trying to hold Freda vertical as the larger woman toppled toward her in a faint. "Our ancestors dealt with this. We're just as tough. Freda, there are some people coming toward us. Freda, I think we're going to have to be on our toes, kiddo."

The human people walking in their direction across the uneven dirty floor had come, Shan finally appreciated by dint of a bout of sheer intellectual effort, from the squarish slope-topped boxes a few hundred paces distant.

Buildings, those things were. Dwellings constructed *outside* from dried organic tissues. *Wood*, that was it.

Most of the advancing party of human people were males, and each of them looked approximately the way Hsia Shan-yun had looked before the surgeons had got to her. True, they were not two-metre-tall Valkyries, but their limbs were visibly swollen with muscle. Compared with the shuttle wimps, they could have been a different species.

A tremendous screaming thunderous racket burst through the air.

Shan spun on her heel, which hurt rather a lot, and what she saw took the last bit of gristle from her backbone.

The shuttle – the sole decent, human, metal, *manufactured* object visible on the entire planet – was blasting off from the surface.

Freda shrieked. The man in their group keeled over and lay face down in the dirt.

The flame-cupped shuttle soared like an ancient god, diminished from mere human ken until it was a bright dot immensely high in the blue.

Freda too quietly slumped to the ground and curled up like a fetus.

"Hey, come on, snap yourselves together!"

The strangers, by one of those incomprehensible tricks of perspective, were abruptly in their midst, pushing through the group, pulling and slapping and roughly punching the newcomers to their senses. Shan-yun stared.

Cracked faces, seamed from exposure to the open environment. Eyes like archival holograms of animal eyes, startlingly bright in the raw sunlight.

One of the men shook her shoulder. In disgust, she threw off his hand. He wore garments made from dried animal skins and woven vegetable fibres. Shan felt tiny creatures, real or imaginary, scuttle out of the clothes and crawl all over her own bruised skin.

"Right, you motley crew." The oldest of them, a man whose face was half covered by an appalling wild growth of pubic hair and whose sunburnt scalp was covered by an equally appalling huge patch of baldness, stationed himself in front of them, fists braced on hips.

The male convict, awakened and tottering, took his first close-range look at the kind of creature he was now doomed to become, and spontaneously vomited into the dirt.

"Clean the bastard up and get him to the med shed," the leader snarled to a subordinate. "Now listen up, you people. I know what you're going through, so I won't be too hard on you straight off. We've all been through it. You'll live – unless, that is, you die, which isn't impossible." He smirked. "We haven't got the spare personnel or the resources to coddle you. Everything you eat, your housing, your antibiotics, your drugs, your entertainment – you'll make them yourselves."

"I don't *know* anything about any drugs," one of the convicts wailed pitifully.

" 'Housing'? What's 'housing'?" asked another, with a sob.

"You'll specialize, naturally," the old man said. "What you don't know now you'll learn – or you'll die." He seemed to relish this prospect, smacking his lips. "There's no place in this outfit for crybabies and lily-livered liberals. You'll have to be tough – tough, and determined to *survive*."

He stared from one convict to the next, squinting in the

bright light. Hsia Shan-yun felt as much like vomiting as I do. But she met his gaze when his eyes reached hers.

He locked on to her, tried to stare her down. Shan's pupils shrank and her whites boiled with blood. He grinned with satisfaction and pointed at her.

"You. Round them all up and bring them across to the Great Hall when they're ready. We have to get back to the harvesting. The Big Wet's due any day now."

With a gesture to his companions he turned and started back toward the wooden buildings.

"Just a moment," Shan-yun said loudly. To her ears, her voice seemed attenuated, an auditory shadow of its former power. Was it the atmosphere of this world, she wondered, or yet another atrocity wrought by her doctors?

The man paused elaborately, glanced over his muscular shoulder, narrowed his sun-dazzled eyes.

"I take it you're addressing me"

"I want to know your name," Shan yelled.

"My name's Anson. You can call me 'Boss.' We'll talk later." He turned away again.

"Hold it, damn you." Shan-yun tried to stride like a tiger toward him and managed a dwarfish totter. Even so, he stiffened, and his men moved in on either side of him. "What's the escape plan?"

Anson grinned sardonically, then slapped her painfully on the arm.

"I like your style, sweetheart, even if you do lack a little something in the looks department. I think you're going to do all right here on Paradise – if you learn some manners."

"The escape plan, Anson."

"No escape, lady. The shuttle comes here once a year. Remote control from orbit, Bug driver, nerve crunchers from New Year's to Christmas. There's no escape. What was that name again?"

"Hsia Shan-yun, snotsucker."

He grinned, and she recoiled at the sight of his thin hard yellow gums, his missing teeth. No cosmetic dentistry on Paradise.

"Unless you just happen to know how to plait a Striped Hole, my dear foulmouthed ex-citizen Hsia, you're *here* until you die. Until you rot and we put you in the ground."

Shan-yun ran her tongue around the inside of her mouth. By an odd oversight the surgeons had left her all her own teeth. She bared them happily at Anson, and strolled away to round up her companions from the shuttle.

Seasoned long-distance travellers know there is only one thing worse than waiting at the carousel for your luggage.

This is *giving up* waiting at the carousel because the swine have lost it all between Djakarta and Cairo and you know you'll never see it again.

Hsia Shan-yun, Freda Odell and the rest of the criminals from the shuttle trudged across the vile, open face of the planet Paradise without their luggage, indeed with no possessions whatever except the tatty gowns they wore.

"Essential supplies we can't grow or make for ourselves are dropped in from orbit," a bearded man told Shan, currying favor. Everyone looked at her with a whole lot more respect after her tiff with Anson. "Comes in on 'chutes, no human contact, not even an onboard monitor Bug. Absolutely no machines permitted down here on the surface."

Shan grunted, looking gloomily at the hairy green stuff on the ground and wishing her toes were slurping instead through the foul muck of the dear little brutal cell she'd shared with her close friend Turdington Jimbo.

She felt like crying, but once you've earned a rep as the tough kid on the block you forfeit your right to a recuperative howl.

The moment of pleasure that had burned through her veins was well behind her. Knowing how to plait a Striped Hole is one thing. Having the raw materials and the opportunity to tangle the threads one over another through ten dimensions in Kaluza-Klein spacetime is another.

"I'm stuck here," she muttered pitifully to herself. "I'll never escape. I'll be a flat-chested dwarf to the end of my days."

In fact, it wasn't until another nine and a half years had dragged by, as measured on Paradise, without any further shuttle-delivered prisoners due to temporary suspension of the programme, years of power struggles and attempted rape, of chilly, snow-buried mornings and debilitating forty-five-degree centigrade summer noons, of raising high roof-beams and seeing them crushed by gales of soot, of laughter, somehow, deep and true in the face of adversity, and tears at the loss of loved companions, of getting and spending, remembering and forgetting, taking up the fight and laying down the law, that a passing galactic holiday cruise sponsored by the ladies' auxiliary of the Gamma Globulin combined football leagues landed at the east pole of the convict world Paradise and liberated the pitiful remnants of the prison colony.

The lady lizards' cruise ship, half a million tonnes of squishy lanoline-soaked urdat and runny glass, lingered for an entire month at the delightful east pole, the ladies taking the waters and admiring the views. The brontomegasaurs of Gamma Globulin, being a race of excess longevity, never rush their tours.

A party of haggard, desperate human people finally swam, rappeled, white-watered, portaged, and orienteered its frantic way to the plateau where the cruise ship *Snardly Blint* lay crushing a square kilometre of delicious weevilwart blooms and a few thousand small vertebrates.

Shan-yun, of course, was among the party's number, though on this occasion the rough frontier democratic vote had declined to select her as band leader, which was okay with her. Instead, she was point scout.

"Hey!" she yelled, sighting the cruise ship.

Puffs of smoke were rising from the cruiser's stacks.

A fearful presentiment clutched at her heart.

A weird, ear-hurting mechanical scream was rising from the cruiser's off-side Hyperspatial lifters.

Dazzling beams of multihued elementary particles splattered with motes of exploding photons were rising from the cruiser's pleasure domes.

"Hey! You snotsuckers!" screamed Hsia Shan-yun, running and tripping under the weight of her depleted supply gunnies and handmade fire-hardened machete and bow-and-arrow set.

The cruiser *Snardly Blint* lifted lightly and musically into the frighteningly pellucid sky of Paradise, streamers flying and passengers snug in their acceleration couches.

On board, the captain and her crew played cards and started in on the long drunk that always filled the tedious weeks in Hyperspace between ports of call. None of them – tendrilled, boll-eared, infrared sensitized, locally telepathic – attended to the remote skin microphones that picked up Shan's cries for succor.

This is the way of it with the Bargleplod, a sentient species that has plied the star lanes for upward of seven million years without either taking control of the Milky Way in an outburst of drum-beating imperialism or wiping themselves away in nuclear squabbles.

You'd imagine the Bargleplod would be the envy of everyone, for their relaxed insouciance has guaranteed their survival well beyond the parameters given by the late Carl Sagan's analysis of interstellar culture. In fact, they're too sloppy and stolid and besotted and dull for anyone sane to envy or emulate.

Hardly surprisingly, it was a Bargleplod who left behind the autonomic mousehunter on the green sweet world Alpha Grommett once was.

Hsia Shan-yun watched incredulously, her enraged, wind-reddened eyes bulging like peeled hard-boiled eggs, as the Bargleplod cruise ship whiffled away into the sky and vanished with an ear-shattering clamor of brute force.

Freda, lithe as a lath, hardened by adversity, hardened indeed by a history more immediate than any she'd ever subversively programmed into the teaching machines back on Earth, pounded up, breath rasping, and fell against Shan's side.

"Oh, shit," she whimpered. "They've gone. They've left us here. We'll never get free now, never, never . . ."

Hsia Shan-yun had been indulging exactly these sentiments, but getting it in the lughole from a friend she'd trusted to have more gristle got right up her nose.

"Come on, Freda, it's not the end of the world. It's just a spaceship flying away. Where there's one visiting alien spaceship there's bound to be another, in a few years, a few decades. Hell, kiddo, we've pulled through this far, haven't we? We've each got five fine kids, and the hospital's almost finished, and if we can get the harvest in before the Big Dry we should see our way to autumn okay. I mean, it's not as if the Sun is going out or something."

She slapped with by-now-automatic vigilance at her leg. The animals of Paradise are not always friendly. Anson, for example, had been badly mauled by a wet thing that dropped on his back from a tree and sucked out his brain with an awful slurping noise before anyone could get to it and bash it to death.

Shan gave a cry then, looking down to check on what had tried to bite her.

A small bright machine was casting back and forth, blindly through the grass.

It was the first actual, real, metal machine they'd seen on Paradise since their prison shuttle roared away back to orbit.

"Oh! The poor little thing's lost."

"Can it be a –"

"Hubbard's E, Shan, I think it's –"

Shan-yun's hard-boiled eyes bugged with gratitude and pleasure. She started after the cute little scuttling mechanism, brought it to the ground in one practiced pounce, and began to dismantle it.

"An autonomic toaster!"

Freda licked her lips. "If only we had some real sliced bread, the sort they had in the old days back on Earth, came in plastic bags, I can taste that wonderful mould now. If you don't mind my saying, Boss, don't you think it'd function more efficiently if you leave its legs on?"

Shan-Yun sniggered happily.

"Forget the bread, Freda. Don't you see yet what this means?"

Her quite intellectually gifted but less handy colleague's jaw gaped. Blood drained from her cheeks and other places less visible.

"You don't mean . . . ? Surely you can't –"

Shan beamed up at her.

"Yup. With the quark powerpack in this lovely little guy, and a few tufts from its wiring, I'll have a Striped Hole plaited in about three days."

She shot a worried look at the sky. The light was fading, but with any luck she'd have the job well started before dark.

"Watcha got there? Hey, gang, lookit, a *machine!*"

Freda held her finger to her lips, and the arriving party pushed and jostled a bit less noisily, watching the deft weaving fingers of the woman who was about to build them a Hyperspatial wormhole pathway home to Earth and their long-delayed revenge.

"You're sure it won't blow up on us?"

"Of course I'm sure. Hold that light steady."

"It'd make a terrible mess."

Shan-yun said nothing, squinting through her scratched-out corneas at the wobbling skein of energy. She licked her lips and pushed another string into the blistered surface.

"I mean, that's what you were sent here for, isn't it? Trying to blow everything up."

Shan blew up.

"Listen, I've been working two centimetres from this singularity for five days now and my patience is just about worn right through, so if you want to *walk* home, you squawking, blathering, onion-breathed, interfering –"

"All right, all right." The felon backed away from the fire, muttering and scowling sullenly. "Just don't blame me, too-ter," Shan-yun thought she heard him start to add, but there was nothing she could do about leaping up and boxing his ears for him because if she let go of the almost completed Striped Hole everything really *might* blow.

Freda said quietly in her ear, "How long now?"

"Dunno. Couple of minutes."

"I'll get everyone formed up."

The children were pushed into line, thin and scrawny, in handwoven clothing that would certainly draw unfavourable attention when they suddenly materialized back inside some part of the State on Earth.

Still, their prospects were better on the home world than here, because for the first time in some dozen decades there was going to be gathered in one place an entire community of rebels, people who'd come through the fire and been tempered in it, people who knew how to work and plan and survive together against all odds.

The tip of Shan-yun's tongue protruded from the corner of her mouth as she slotted the final superstring into place.

Like a blue ball of charged plasma, the Striped Hole hung in the air beside the camp fire. It was an extrusion into human-perceivable spacetime from a higher realm, and in minutes everyone on the planet Paradise was going to step into its insane Hyperspatial wormhole and plunge infinitely faster than light, along its slippery slide, back to Earth.

"I'm not going," old Harry suddenly declared in his mulish way. "Won't get me into one of them damn fangled contraptions."

Before panic could spread, Shan-yun beckoned the oldtimer close and leaned toward his ear. As he bent to her, she tripped him and sent him across her shoulder in a perfect judo fall.

Harry struck the seething surface of the Hole and dopplered in so fast not even his scream of protest got away.

"Works okay," Shan muttered darkly. There was a belated round of applause, and she was borne about the campfire on everyone's shoulders. Before they could break out the last of the wart-wine for a celebration binge, she kicked and wriggled back to her feet and hollered for attention.

"I can't guarantee the stability of this mock-up. We have to follow Harry right now."

A ripple of fear rippled fearfully through the frightened gathering.

"I'll lead the way," resolute Freda said before they could all get out of control.

She stepped forward, holding one hand in a careless gesture under her chin to stop her teeth chattering. "Come on, kids, last one in's a jumbled genotype!"

The Striped Hole gulped her down without a belch. One by one the pitiful remnants of the prison planet stepped forward and took their dive.

When the last one was gone Hsia Shan-yun looked about with bittersweet happy sadness at the world that had been all of freedom to them, and all of hell too.

Were they right in abandoning this frontier world where they owned a kind of artless liberty?

Might they bring salvation from oppression to their brothers and sisters on Earth?

Or would the invincible robot Bugs be waiting, ready to ensnare them in projected goo the moment they materialized?

The cold night air brought only strange unearthly odours and no answers!

Wiping away a tear, Shan put out the last fire on the planet Paradise, raked the hot cinders over with dirt, and stepped into the Striped Hole, pulling it shut behind her.

SHOES

Robert Sheckley

My shoes were worn out and I was passing a Goodwill store so I went in to see if they had anything that would fit me.

The assortment you find in places like this is not to the most exacting taste. And the sizes they get don't fit a normal foot like mine. But this time I lucked out. A pair of lovely heavy cordovans. Built to last. Looking brand new, except for the deep gouge on top of one toe, a mark that had undoubtedly resulted in the shoes' disposal. The outer leather had been scraped away – maybe by some indigent like myself, outraged at so expensive a pair of shoes. You never know, it's the sort of thing I might have done myself in one of my darker moods.

But today I was feeling good. You don't find a pair of shoes like this every day, and the price tag read a ridiculous four dollars. I removed my ragged K-Mart sneakers and slipped into the cordovans, to see if they fit.

Immediately I heard a voice in my mind, clear as a bell, saying, "You're not Carlton Johnson. Who are you?"

"I'm Ed Phillips," I said aloud.

"Well, you have no right to be wearing Carlton Johnson's shoes."

"Hey look," I said, "I'm in a Goodwill, these shoes are priced at four bucks, they're here for anyone to buy."

"Are you sure?" the voice said. "Carlton Johnson wouldn't have just given me away. He was so pleased when he purchased me, so happy when I was enabled to give him the maximum in shoe comfort."

"Who are you?" I said.

"Isn't it obvious? I am a prototype smart shoe, talking to you through micro-connections in my sole. I pick up your subvocalizations via your throat muscles, translate them, and broadcast my words back to you."

"You can do all that?"

"Yes, and more. Like I said, I'm a smart shoe."

By this time I noticed that a couple of ladies were looking at me funny and I realized they could hear only one side of the conversation, since the other side seemed to be taking place in my head. I paid for the shoes, which offered no further comment, and I got out of there. Back to my own place, an efficiency one room apartment in the Jack London Hotel on 4th near Pike. No comment from the shoes until I reached the top linoleum-covered step of the two flight walk to my apartment, the elevator being a non-starter this evening

The shoes said, "What a dump."

"How can you see my place?"

"My eyelets, where the laces go, are light-absorbing diodes."

"I realize you were used to better things with Carlton Johnson," I said.

"Everything was carpeted," the shoes said wistfully, "Except for expanses of polished floor left bare on purpose. It paused and sighed. "The wear on me was minimal."

"And here you are in a flophouse," I said. "How have the mighty fallen!"

I must have raised my voice, because a door in the corridor opened and an old woman peered out. When she saw me, apparently talking to myself, she shook her head sadly and closed the door.

"You do not have to shout," the shoes said. "Just directing your thoughts toward me is sufficient. I have no trouble picking up your subvocalizations."

"I guess I'm embarrassing you," I said aloud. "I am so terribly sorry."

The shoes did not answer until I had unlocked my door, stepped inside, turned on the light and closed the door again.

Then it said, "I am not embarrassed for myself, but for you, my new owner. I tried to watch out for Carlton Johnson, too."

"How?"

"For one thing, by stabilizing him. He had an unfortunate habit of taking a drink too many from time to time."

"So the guy was a lush?" I said. "Did he ever throw up on you?"

"Now you're being disgusting," the shoes said. "Carlton Johnson was a gentleman."

"It seems to me I've heard entirely enough about Carlton Johnson. Don't you have anything else to talk about?"

"He was my first," the shoes said. "But I'll stop talking about him if it distresses you."

"I couldn't care less," I said. "I'm now going to have a beer. If your majesty doesn't object."

"Why should I object? Just please try not to spill any on me."

"Whatsamatter, you got something against beer?"

"Neither for nor against. It's just that alcohol could fog my diodes."

I got a bottle of beer out of the little fridge, uncapped it and settled back in the small sagging couch. I reached for the TV clicker. But a thought crossed my mind.

"How come you talk that way?" I asked.

"What way?"

"Sort of formal, but always getting into things I wouldn't expect of a shoe."

"I'm a shoe computer, not just a shoe."

"You know what I mean. How come? You talk pretty smart for a gadget that adjusts shoes to feet."

"I'm not really a standard model," the shoe told me. "I'm a prototype. For better or worse, my makers gave me excess capacity."

"What does that mean?"

"I'm too smart to just fit shoes to people. I also have empathy circuitry."

"I haven't noticed much empathy toward me."

"That's because I'm still programmed to Carlton Johnson."

"Am I ever going to hear the last of that guy?"

"Don't worry, my deconditioning circuitry has kicked in. But it takes time for the aura effect to wear off."

I watched a little television and went to bed. Buying a pair of smart shoes had taken it out of me. I woke up some time in the small hours of the night. The shoes were up to something, I could tell even without wearing them.

"What are you up to?" I asked, then realized the shoes couldn't hear me and groped around on the floor for them.

"Don't bother," the shoes said. "I can pick up your sub-vocalizations on remote, without a hard hookup."

"So what are you doing?"

"Just extracting square roots in my head. I can't sleep."

"Since when does a computer have to sleep?"

"A fault in my standby mode . . . I need something to do. I miss my peripherals."

"What are you talking about?"

"Carlton Phillips had eyeglasses. I was able to tweak them up to give him better vision. You wouldn't happen to have a pair, would you?"

"I've got a pair, but I don't use them much."

"May I see them? It'll give me something to do."

I got out of bed, found my reading glasses on top of the TV, and set them down beside the shoes. "Thank you," the shoe computer said.

"Mrggh," I said, and went back to sleep.

"So tell me something about yourself," the shoes said in the morning.

"What's to tell? I'm a freelance writer. Things have been going so well that I can afford to live in the Jack London. End of story."

"Can I see some of your work?"

"Are you a critic, too?"

"Not at all! But I am a creative thinking machine, and I may have some ideas that could be of use to you."

"Forget about it," I told him. "I don't want to show you any of my stuff."

The shoes said, "I happened to glance over your story 'Killer Goddess of the Dark Moon Belt.'"

"How did you just happen to glance at it?" I asked. "I don't remember showing it to you."

"It was lying open on your table."

"So all you could see was the title page."

"As a matter of fact, I read the whole thing."

"How were you able to do that?"

"I made a few adjustments to your glasses," the shoe said. "X-ray vision isn't so difficult to set up. I was able to read each page through the one above it."

"That's quite an accomplishment," I said. "But I don't appreciate you poking into my private matters."

"Private? You were going to send it to a magazine."

"But I haven't yet . . . What did you think of it?"

"Old-fashioned. That sort of thing doesn't sell any more."

"It was a parody, dummy . . . So now you're not only a shoe adjuster but an analyst of the literary marketplace also?"

"I did glance over the writing books in your bookcase."

By the sound of the thoughts in my head, I could tell he didn't approve of my books, either.

"You know," the shoe said later, "You really don't have to be a bum, Ed. You're bright. You could make something of yourself."

"What are you, a psychologist as well as a shoe computer?"

"Nothing of the sort. I have no illusions about myself. But I've gotten to know you a bit in the last few hours since my empathy circuitry kicked in. I can't help but notice – to know – that you're an intelligent man with a good general education. All you need is a little ambition. You know, Ed, that could be supplied by a good woman."

"The last good woman left me shuddering," I said. "I'm really not ready just yet for the next one."

"I know you feel that way. But I've been thinking about Marsha –"

"How in hell do you know about Marsha?"

"Her name is in your little red phone book, which I happened to glance through with my X-ray vision in my efforts to better serve you."

"Listen, even my writing down Marsha's name was a mistake. She's a professional do-gooder. I hate that type."

"But she could be good for you. I noticed you put a star after her name."

"Did you also notice I crossed out the star?"

"That was a second thought. Now, on third thought, she might start looking good again. I suspect you two could go well together."

"You may be good at shoes," I said, "but you know nothing about the sort of women I like. Have you seen her legs?"

"The photo in your wallet showed only her face."

"What? You looked in my wallet, too?"

"With the help of your glasses . . . And not out of any prurient interest, Ed, I assure you. I just want to help."

"You're already helping too much."

"I hope you won't mind the one little step I took."

"Step? What step?"

My doorbell rang. I glared at my shoes.

"I took the liberty of calling Marsha and asking her over."

"YOU DID WHAT?"

"Ed, Ed, calm down! I know it was taking a liberty. It's not as if I called your former boss, Mr Edgarson, at Super-Gloss Publications."

"You wouldn't dare!"

"I would, but I didn't. But you could do a lot worse than go back to work for Edgarson. The salary was very nice."

"Have you read any of Gloss's publications? I don't know what you think you're doing, but you aren't going to do it to me!"

"Ed, Ed, I haven't done anything yet! And if you insist, I won't. Not without your permission!"

There was a knock at the door.

"Ed, I'm only trying to look out for you. What's a machine with empathy circuits and excess computing ability to do?"

"I'll tell you in a moment," I said.

I opened the door. Marsha stood there, beaming.

"Oh, Ed, I'm so glad you called!"

So the son of a bitch had imitated my voice, too! I glanced down at my shoes, at the gash in the cap of the left one. A light went off in my head. Realization! Epiphany!

"Come in, Marsha," I said. "I'm glad to see you. I have something for you."

She entered. I sat down in the only decent chair and stripped off the shoes, ignoring the shoe computer's agonized cry in my head of "Ed! Don't do this to me . . ."

Standing up again, I handed them to Marsha.

"What's this?" she said.

"Shoes for one of your charity cases," I said. "Sorry I don't have a paper bag for you to carry them in."

"But what am I going to do with –"

"Marsha, these are special shoes, computerized shoes. Give them to one of your down-and-outers, get him to put them on. They'll make a new man of him. Pick one of the weak-willed ones you specialize in. It'll give him backbone!"

She looked at the shoes. "This gash in one of them –"

"A minor flaw. I'm pretty sure the former owner did that himself," I told her. "A guy named Carlton Johnson. He couldn't stand the computer's messing around with his head, so he disfigured them and gave them away. Marsha, believe me, these shoes are perfect for the right man. Carlton Johnson wasn't the right man, and I'm not either. But someone you know will bless the ground you walk on for these, believe me."

And with that, I began herding her toward the door.

"When will I hear from you?" she said.

"Don't worry, I'll call," I told her, revelling in the swinish lie that went along with my despicable life.

THE DAY WE PLAYED MARS

Maurice Richardson

THIS is the story of how Engelbrecht, the Dwarf Surrealist Boxer, wins his Global Football Cap. It's a story the oldest members still whisper in the Ghost Room of the Surrealist Sportsman's Club, a story of indomitable courage, and no little cunning, winning through against overwhelming odds.

Engelbrecht has never played surrealist football before and his delight at finding his name, just above *Engels, F.*, in the list – a sizeable work in many volumes – of the team to play Mars in the Final of the Interplanetary Challenge Cup, leads to a celebration in which we all take part.

The Final of the Interplanetaries is played off on the Moon, and months before the kick-off all sorts of vehicles – everything from ordinary space-ships to beams, dreams, mediums, and telepathic wave-patterns – start arriving with the players. There's a pause for rest and reorientation; then they begin trooping into the vast Metamorphosis or Changing Room. Engelbrecht and I blow in in a rocket with the usual party of our Skipper's intimates. We've been training strictly on hashish and mescaline, and by the time we arrive on the Ground it's a job to sort us out from our hallucinations.

The Lunar Twickenham is a boundless plain of glassy black lava pitted with craters. The Larger Ball is considered *de rigueur*. It has to be something pretty sizeable to keep in play at all, though, as Charlie Wapentake says, it's a bit nightmarish trying to dribble with a thing like a Roc's egg.

Dreamy Dan, our old-time surrealist umpire, is thought to

be too biased, as well as a trifle slow for such a commando-type operation. The new referee is Cecil B. de Mille, picked for his crowd work. Presently he sends a message to ask the Id to scrabble along and meet the Martian Skipper in a neutral crater for final briefing. So off the Old Master trots, accompanied by Chippy de Zoete, his Vice. When they come back they're shaking all over and Chippy de Zoete's chest-wig, which he had made at Clarkson's to strike terror into the opposing forwards, has turned white as fleece. From which we deduce that this year's Martian team includes some pretty formidable Entities. So tough, indeed, does the opposition appear that it's decided to try a very unorthodox ploy and put the full side, the entire human race, into the field straight away.

The opening ceremony is held as usual. There's a silent tribute to the honour of William Webb Ellis, that Glorious Precursor of Surrealist Sport, the Rugby Schoolboy who first ran with the Ball. Then the Band strikes up the Supersonic Symphony – a rather unfortunate choice for it brings half the Grandstand down with a crash. After which we take the Field.

Even I, old hand as I am, haven't quite bargained for the procession of Giant Monstrosities that come filing out of the Visitors' Entrance. When Lizard Bayliss, Engelbrecht's pessimistic manager, catches sight of them he tries to beat it back to the Changing Room, but the crush of characters is too thick.

It's our kick-off. It takes a bit of doing to sort us all out, but by the next full moon de Mille has us well in hand. I've been given a cosy little assignment, narking to the Central Captain's Committee on the Wing Forwards, so I take Engelbrecht under my wing and pilot him.

The whistle blows and Melchisedek takes the kick. Nebuchadnezzar follows up and gathers it. He passes to Nero, Nero to Attila, Attila to the Venerable Bede, the Venerable Bede to Ethelred the Unready, who knocks on into a crater. De Mille screams for a scrum. Engelbrecht tries to climb down into the thick of it. "You keep out of that," I tell him. "The ideal! A Dwarf trying to scrum down between Henry VIII and Cetewayo. You'd get pulped."

De Mille rolls the ball down an inclined plane right into the centre of the great heaving mass. Anak and Harold Hardrada, our hookers, get their toes round it. But our frail human forwards are too light for those great Martian thugs. We can't possibly hold them. Our only hope is to heel out quickly before they can crush us against the sides of the crater. It doesn't take Charlie Marx, our scrum-half, long to twig this, and as we peer down over the lip we can hear his harsh bark of "Heel! You *teufels!* Heel in the name of History!" And heel they do, but only just in time. As Charlie Marx gathers the ovoid from Bismarck's boot, our front line breaks and the Martian phalanx comes crashing through. Marx slings it back to Fred Engels, his fly-half. Then he's down in a sea of boots and backsides. "You've got to hand it to old Charlie," says Tommy Prenderghast, "he may be nasty tempered but he's the nippiest scrum-half in this world or the next. Well, we'd better be heading for Goal. Can I give you chums a lift?"

But Fred Engels has seen it coming and had time to get his life-line organised. He passes it up to Gladstone who makes a present of it to Blondin. And before you can say "I told you so," Blondin's away out on his tightrope with the Giant Ball at his feet. It's a great moment, one of the greatest in the history of the game. The field is in a frenzy and the Band can think of no more fitting token than to strike up the Second Movement of the Supersonic Symphony, which brings down the other half of the stand.

We're out of the crater but still on the defensive. Unfortunately, it's not been possible to fix Blondin's tight-rope to a strategic point, and he has to find touch. Still, we recover a good bit of ground, and it's a lovely run of Blondin's, especially when you remember that for the last five miles he's being worried by a pack of pterodactyls loosed from a string-bag by a Martian bobby-soxer.

At the line-out it's our ball, but it falls into bad hands. Stavisky catches it and passes it to Bottomley, Bottomley to Jabez Balfour, Jabez Balfour to Charlie Peace, and Charlie Peace to Jonathan Wild, losing ground all the way. Jonathan Wild slings a long one to Judas Iscariot, who sells the pass to the Martian Threequarter line, and they get into their stride. For a surrealist football-fan, no doubt it's a lovely sight to see this far-flung line of giants racing across the jet-black surface of the Moon with the Ball flashing from one wing to the other and back again. For us, who're supposed to stop them, it's slightly different. I'm too busy taking notes of shirkers' names myself, but Engelbrecht insists on showing what he's made of. With a grunt of defiance he hurls himself through the air and catches hold of a Martian Three Q's bootlace. He hangs on like grim death, taking fearful punishment as he's dragged over the lava.

There's nothing to stop them now except Salvador Dali, our Full Back. Some of us doubt the wisdom of our skipper's choice of such an *avant-garde* type for such a die-hard position. But we've got to hand it to old Salvador. He tries Everything. As a last attempt to stop them he even camouflages the Goal Posts as a Giant Gallows with some very tasty objects from his studio strung up from the cross-bar. Neither – though some of his less charitable team-mates say this is because he's got stuck in the chest of drawers with which he's been protecting his person – does he flinch from the ultimate sacrifice of a flying tackle. Useless, of course. A brief splintering crash. Then the Martian Three Q touches down between the goal posts.

As we all crowd together in the Goal Mouth there's a multitude of doleful faces such as never was seen since the Last Trump. I've just handed in my list when Charlie Wapentake jogs my arm and points to the Id and Chippy de Zoete chatting to Pierpoint, the Public Executioner. We know what that means. Somebody's going to swing for it.

The Martians convert and we migrate back to midfield. Soon after the kickoff Vivekananda finds touch. But our luck's out. At the line-out Zerubabel tips it back to Origen, but Origen passes to Julian the Apostate, who starts running back. Luther and John Huss trip him up and start a plucky dribble. They're joined by Calvin who picks up and passes to Wesley. For a glorious moment it looks as if we're going to get somewhere. Wesley jinks like a rabbit, sells the dummy to three enemy forwards. But he hasn't got the legs. He passes, and one of the Plymouth Brothers knocks on. This time the enemy forwards get the ball and wheel with it. Charlie Marx empties his pistol again and again into the back row of our scrum in an attempt to stop the rot.

10 – nil, and the game's only in its first light-year. Some poets start a passing movement. Chatterton passes to Keats, Keats to Shelley, Shelley to Byron, Byron to Wilde, who muffs it. There's a lot of tittering in the loose. The Martians get it back to their Three Q's, and there's no stopping them. They run through us like a dose of salts, cock snooks at the Easter Island statues which Dali has brought up to guard the Goal Mouth, and score again.

After that it's a procession and they score as they please. Full backs are tried by the dozen only to have rings made round them.

At half-time the score is astronomical, and Wing-forwards are being shot in batches in the Changing Room.

Towards the end of the Interval, Engelbrecht, Lizard Bayliss, his manager, and I, are reclining in our bivouac, toasting our toes at the core of a crater, when Charlie Marx and Fred Engels limp past. "There's only one way, *knabe*," we hear Charlie say. "We must give them the old Trojan horse." "All very well," says Fred, "but there's not much room in there." "Room for a little 'un," says Charlie. His eye lights on Engelbrecht. "How about it, *junge?*" he says, raising an eyebrow. "Care to volunteer for an interesting mission in History's service?" And before we can remonstrate he marches off to the Changing Room.

We come out for the second half dizzy and defeatist. But the moment they kick off it's clear that a change has come over the game. The Ball is taking a hand. It won't roll right for the Martians nohow. They muff pass after pass and in the scrum our hookers get it every time. It's as if it's grown a little pair of legs of its own. Soon comes our first try. Charlie gathers it clean as a whistle and passes to Fred, who punts for the open field. Stenka Razin and his band trap it and take it on with their feet. There's a fierce loose scrummage in a crater, but

Guy Fawkes has got a map of the Underground. The Ball seems to beckon him on. They surface just in front of the Goal, and Jack Cade slips over for a touch-down. Goliath, the new full back, takes the kick. The Ball grazes the cross bar, but instead of bouncing off it seems to hang there in the air. Then it drops over.

The Score is 5555–5. Things are looking up. The Id commutes the sentences of one in ten of the doomed Wing Forwards to Life in the Scrum. Soon after the kick, Hannibal gets it and blunders right through with his footballing elephants. Goliath converts.

All that epoch the same tactics are repeated. We're using our feet like dancing masters. It's 5555–5550 now. Not long to go. Some unlikely characters have scored, even Heliogabalus, Bishop Berkley, and Aubrey Beardsley.

De Mille is looking at his travelling clock. He's lifting the whistle to his lips with both hands. Sorrowfully, Lizard Bayliss folds up the special edition of the Fly-Paper with Engelbrecht's Obituary notice and wipes away a tear. "If only he could have lived to see this," he says.

Charlie Marx is giving the forwards their final pep-talk. "A Spectre is haunting Football!" I hear him bark. "The time has come to convert the Feet of History into the History of Feet! Forwards of the World! Pack Tight! You have nothing to lose but your Shins!"

The Martians try hard to find touch with a terrific root, but the Ball drops back into play. There follows one of the sweetest pieces of combination in History. Lecky passes to Gibbon, Gibbon to Tacitus, Tacitus to Josephus. Josephus slings a long pass to Isaiah, who punts ahead. Samuel catches it and passes to Lot, Lot to Noah, who gives it to Cain. Cain tries to keep it but it slips sideways out of his fingers. Abel dribbles it over the line and Adam falls flat on it.

Goliath has strained a tendon and the Id orders Dali out of the Morgue to take the kick. He asks me to place for him.

As he adjusts the angle to his liking I hear Engelbrecht's voice speaking to me from inside the Ball. "What's the score, chum?" it says. "I've rather lost count."

That night, at a little private ceremony in the Changing Room, attended only by Charlie Marx, Arnold of Rugby, and the Politbureau of the Selection Committee, Engelbrecht receives the highest award of Global Football, the crypto-Cap.

As soon as the ceremony is over he's smuggled out of the Changing Room in a tiny coffin.

FOWL PLAY

Steve Redwood

When I woke up in a cage that, judging from the smell, might have just come from a poultry farm, my mind was at first completely blank. I knew I had never before been in this room, illuminated by hundreds of candles, and with walls decorated with unusual and somehow sinister-looking symbols.

I didn't recognize the woman staring in through the bars, or the blindfolded man sitting beside her, with an expression of malevolent triumph on what I could see of his face. I had a feeling, though, that I might have seen them both before, perhaps even recently.

Could the woman be my wife? Had I perhaps refused to do the washing up? Or performed my conjugal duties too perfunctorily? I didn't want to ask her directly because, if she *were* my wife, she would surely be offended that I wasn't aware of the fact, and might nag me: a mere cage is no bar to a woman's tongue.

Perplexed, I scratched my cheek. As I did so, I felt a deep curved scar gouged into it, and I noticed that my lips were terribly hard and swollen. So bad had been the wound that some skin was still hanging loose.

Ah, this was a clue to my identity! The scar pleased me. It showed I had lived dangerously. I felt a tremor of excitement. Perhaps I had fought a duel. Could I conceivably be Robin' Darktree, the notorious unforgiving highwayman? Or Spermicidal Whiskers, the infamous pirate whose one-eyed glare could unman the most virile enemy? Perhaps I had fought *many* duels, in which, due to my speed and uncanny dexterity, I had never so much as received a scratch. Except for that one occasion, I suddenly seemed to remember quite clearly, when I had been challenged by an enigmatic, deadly, and mercilessly sensuous woman – much like Catherine Zeta-Jones in *The Mask of Zorro* – because of some classically tragic misunderstanding. My code of honour, of course, wouldn't allow me to raise my sword against a poor defenceless woman.

"Never," I had declaimed, my voice liberally sprinkled with nobility, "will I raise my sword against a poor defenceless woman!"

"Villain!" cried the feisty daughter of Don Diego de la Vega, "hiding behind a fictitious code of honour when what is really holding you back is my deliciously decadent décolletage and the flashing-dragonfly-wing flimsiness of my attire which, in this rather pretty clearing in the forest coming down to the sea, in the early morning light, with the frost glinting on the bark of phantasmal beech trees like a poignant memory, and the sun straining to get round the trees in order to caress me with its lascivious rays, barely hides my maddeningly provocative curves from your marvelling eyes! *En garde!*"

Yes, it was chivalry which had stopped me defending myself when she had lunged with her delicate rapier.

Or had that sun deliberately got into my eyes?

A sudden wild idea brushed me, like Kandinsky having an afterthought: there was something about that woman sitting in front of me, watching me from behind those dark glasses, something about her stance and fulminating figure . . . Could she be the same one who had given me my scar? Could she be Elena de la Vega herself? Had her heart been won by the way I had stood there, my grey eyes calm and ironic, ignoring the blood gushing from my left cheek?

But immediately that memory was submerged by another.

I was actually an astronaut! Captain Pilchard Stopdrooling. Yes, now it all came back to me. My God, that had been a tough life! Defending Earth from the scum of the universe is not all quips, noises in a vacuum, and strange hair styles. I remembered those sadistic bastards Kuiper and van Allen giving our ship a damn good thrashing; catching a hacking cough in the Oort Cloud and then falling into a coma; getting slimy diseases in worm holes; developing suppurating accretion discs; suffering from an excess of trapped solar wind.

But, on the other hand, the things we had seen! Pulsars, quasars, binaries, gas giants, blue giants, red giants, red dwarfs, yellow dwarfs, white or "degenerate" dwarfs . . .

I felt a flush of fear! Of all the degenerate dwarfs, Engelbrecht had been the worst. There was so much bad blood between us that people slipped and slid in it if they came near. A sinister squat pugnacious interstellar assassin who had no choice but to keep his head low and his ear close to the ground, a real heavy who came from a dwarf star with a ridiculously eccentric orbit which had rubbed off on him, and who had vowed never to be eclipsed by lesser luminaries. He'd had to change his somewhat right-wing politics after an acute red shift in his adopted star system. His first exploit had been to capture and cork a Betelgeusian ghost, which had greatly aided spectral classification. He'd just returned cock-a-hoop with one of the rings of Saturn, but the lack of oxygen there hadn't gone to his head, and, drunk on sidereal time and spiritual vacuum, he told tall stories and boasted that there was nothing he couldn't do. So he had been challenged to bring back a mythological creature, so that it could be stuffed and put in the Sages Hall of the Surrealist Assassins Club in Smallsphere, his home planet.

But then that memory was replaced by another. No, I must have been confused. At last I realized who I really was: Squeeze Thews, the new Hemingway, the international sportsman and celebrated breaker of records, wind, and hearts, with a ransom on my rakish testicles that increased with every balcony successfully and swashbucklingly scaled. I deliberately sported a rum-hither look to intrigue and intoxicate the maidens. I had melancholy muscles and terminally romantic toes and tendencies. Ladies nipped at my lip, and napped on my lap, and complied when I implied. Other adventurers cried out, "Kiss my steel!", but *they* weren't naked. I preferred to miss meals and steal kisses. I climbed

trees and had epic conker fights with Baron Cosimo while
Calvino wasn't looking. I dived and goggled at mermaids as
they passed by with the fluidity of elusive dreams, and pursued them with pumping thighs and frantic flippers. I hunted
down universally infamous villains and, now and then,
wrestled leap years to the ground. For relaxation, I challenged
disabled snails to races, or tramped mountain ranges looking
for lost valleys and mythologies, and fairies shyly embracing
inside four-leafed clovers or snuggling up in old boots. I
nibbled nuts gingerly where the condor flies, and sipped
carajillo, and curried favour with spicy South American ladies.

Yes, yes, and I now remembered I had a half-brother,
Hymen Simon, who used music and poetry and romantic
tales where I used muscle and endurance. His weapons were
languorous lutes and impetuous mandolins. He minstrelled his
way into women's hearts and parts with a broken harp
dropped by a weeping Fallen Angel. He ardently pursued
women round the world, a tireless retiarius seeking to ensnare
them with nets woven from the fervid fibres of his poetic soul,
hoping to bring them down with lassos of whirling words and
lariats of lush swirling compliments! He promised nights of
passion in Vienna, Sienna, Rome, Paris, Bangkok, Mecca . . .
But one night he was arrested in Rio, and accused of being a
Troublesome Troubadour. They cunningly paraded Copaca-
bana beauties in front of him, and when his frumious tongue
was hanging out far enough, snipped it off, snicker-snack,
hoping to turn his soaring *cynghanedd* metres into plodding
feet of iambic clay. They used the gold to make rings, one of
which now adorns the delicately shy finger of a sleeping
princess. But the words and music still gushed relentlessly
out of his eyes, so they had to pluck them too, notes, motes and
all. They left him writhing on the ground, in pain as they
thought, but a passing entomologist pointed out that the man's
seemingly random movements suspiciously resembled a bee's
courtship dance. He was therefore further charged with
"Apiarian Aping Without Due Authority", and had his legs
broken. He now had neither honeyed words, glances, or tics.

As I shuddered at the thought of those twitching limbs, I

was suddenly jerked back to the present. The blindfolded man moved the malevolent triumph from his face to his tongue.

"Ah, Mr Isk," he said, "I suppose you're wondering what's happening. People who find themselves in cages at the beginning of stories often do that. Well, you are the victim of a fiendishly convoluted plot hatched up by myself and a wench I was generous enough to tumble a long time ago, Catherine Meaty-Zones here, now a powerful witch, whom you mistook for a lady of similar name and bosom. You're in a cage because you've been turned into – forgive me, I really don't know how to break this gently – a chicken, destined to be my dinner for the next few days. Spermicidal Whiskers, Pilchard Stopdrooling, Squeeze Thews, Engelbrecht the Degenerate, and so on, are all characters I've invented. I poured the stories into your ear while you were drunk, so that you would forget who you really were, and therefore be unable to resist a Transformation Spell. Still, they have also helped you to forget your predicament for a few hours: dreams to help you pass the time; it's quite an Aboriginal idea, you must admit."

"I'm a chicken? Then I'm not a writer or a lunatic?" I wasn't sure whether to be relieved or not. So what I'd thought was an enormous scar was in fact part of my beak and the loose skin my wattle! I scratched my comb in dismay, producing a rather tuneless twang, like Bob Dylan on a foggy Monday.

"Pah, you have the desire without the fire, the quills but not the skills. Your stories creak more than Mr Flay's knees in *Gormenghast* or the Queen's smile after a right royal eructation during her Christmas Day Speech. Your most rounded characters are still as flat as old beer. *I'm* the only decent writer around here. My name is Stark Antonym Zanahoria, as I'm sure you now remember. Everywhere I am lionized, and roar my appreciation. I thrive on contradictions, and glow with red hair, crude wealth, and logical impossibilities."

"A chicken?" I tried to stop bobbing my head.

"Yes, Cat here did the Spell, and put you in this cage. Remember that article you wrote in *Rhondda Quarterly* last month? Saying that my work wasn't worth chicken shit, and that more nuggets were to be found in a dilapidated McDo-

nalds than in the whole of my work? Didn't you wonder why
so many of your 'memories' concerned ships or spaceships?
It's because you had unknowingly taken my ideas *on board*.
But brilliant ideas in the head of a hack are like listeners to a
Fidel Castro speech: they get bored and shuffle towards the
back of the crowd, and in your case they've reached the edges,
and are slipping out through your comb! You've come a
cropper, bach! The few ideas of your own that you still have
are hopelessly half-baked, so it's time to wring your neck, I'm
afraid, and then finish cooking you. Though your prose is
notoriously indigestible, I'm hoping your thighs are not."

"But why? What have I done to deserve this?"

"Written so badly, so predictably, so unimaginatively, that
there was a serious danger that *you* might have got elected to
the Swansea Literary Academi instead of me, since the last
thing they want is internal competition. That's why they
praise Dylan Thomas so much, so no one will notice the
new poets and novelists. I intend to murder you, to make
sure I get the only vacant seat, and because I've never liked
you. But murdering humans, even ones as mortally tedious as
you, is frowned upon, and punishable by law, even in Wales.
There's no penalty against killing chickens, though."

"Why are you wearing a blindfold?" I squawked, playing
for time.

"It was Cat's idea. She knows I'm a sensitive soul, and so
she suggested I put it on before you woke up, in order not to
see myself spilling your blood. It is easier to live with oneself
when one does not witness one's crimes. I'm surprised more
murders aren't committed by blind people, or at least cross-
eyed ones. I know I'm a toad, but I'm not going to risk you
crossing me, or pushing me into a hole. Proffer me the plump
or scrawny neck of that chicken-livered coward, please, Cat,
that I may kill, cook, slice, and dice him."

But now, suddenly, I really did remember everything. The
poor fool didn't know that the *real* conspirators were Cat and
myself!

I gave an evil laugh, and curled my beak with contempt.

"Ha, Zanahoria! Your commination I have allowed, but

comminution is going a midge too far! Cat, remove his blind-fold!"

"Just a minute!" cried the witch imperiously. She reached behind her, and produced a thick manuscript, which she held under Stark's head. She then tore off his blindfold while I stuck my head through the bars of the cage.

Stark Antonym saw me, was immediately sick all over the manuscript, and staggered around in agony before collapsing to the floor.

"Take that, carrot-face!" I cried. "I am no broody rooster, but a moody monster! Didn't you notice my name? Basil Isk? I am a cockatrice!"

"O clucking shell!" he groaned. "But that's impossible!"

"Not logically, only empirically so!" I crowed.

"Mendacious meretrix!" gurgled he, fixing his seared eyes on Cat. "May slugs beget bugs in your double-D dugs!"

"Silence, loquacious loony!" she snapped back, glaring at him with scorn and fury. "In my youthful innocence I wor-shipped you, Stark Antonym, and your writing, full of flame and fantasy and frowning opposites: I grew giddy with desire chasing after twists and turns in your stories, where juicy metaphors lurked in silk-bed ambush behind every sensuous simile. My only desire was to surrender my tender flesh to you and live with you for ever; I even loosened my virtue a little bit beforehand, so that you would have no difficulty finally relieving me of it. But when the moment came, all you did was furtively fumble me on the Mumbles, breathlessly mount me on the Brecon Beacons, and then abandon me to pursue and bedazzle rich *salon* hostesses all over Europe. Had you left me anywhere else, the sandpaper of time might have smoothed away my spleen and filed down my fury, but you left me in Swansea! Swansea! I vowed then not to simply measure out my life with coffee and love spoons, but to take revenge on you. It took a long time, but eventually I became a witch.

"Knowing that both you and Basil Isk would be in Swansea to present your latest works in the hope of getting elected to that seat in the Academi, which really belongs to another, I arranged to meet you both for a drink in *The Englishman's*

Severed Head. I pretended I had forgotten your crime against me. My whole object was to get you at my mercy – which, by the way, is also a fictitious quality, but in this case a winning one!

"Of course, you and Basil pretended, in front of me, to be delighted to see each other, and claimed you had only really come to Swansea hoping to have the pleasure of witnessing the election of the other to the vacant seat.

"But before we met, I had told Basil my plan: to pretend to turn him into a chicken, but in reality to turn him into a cockatrice. He confessed he was too afraid to lay a hand on you himself, but that he felt he could see his way to *looking* you to death! Just as you, Stark, said you feared to murder a man in cold blood, but that killing a chicken, especially when blind-folded, was no crime.

"So when we met up, and while you two were smiling with false camaraderie, slagging off all the other Academi members, we got Basil drunk, as he had already agreed. You filled his head with your stories to take away his remaining personality, and then you helped me carry him back here to my home. I sent you off to the kitchen to prepare the cooking sauces and mix the stuffing, while I did my Transforming. I told you that after eating him, and keeping back a bit of chicken soup for our souls, we could then recline together on a soft luxurious bed made of his plucked feathers. "Yes," you joked, thinking yourself very witty, "as the bluesman Mississippi John Hurt almost sang, 'Make me down a pullet on your floor'."

"But instead of a chicken, I really created a cockatrice – my contact lenses and rather sexy *Dolce & Gabbana* glasses protect me from its gaze – and now its hideousness has, as I planned, caused you to vomit all over your manuscript, which you dare not now present to the fastidious judges. In any case, you are unlikely to live more than a few hours."

As my rival groaned and shuddered in the corner, I cackled with delight.

"That'll teach him! Now you can transform me back like you promised, Cat, *I'll* get the Academi seat, and then we can marry in church and live happily ever after, and have two children, maybe three, and send them to a good school where they wear respectable uniforms, and bring them up properly to learn their catechism and know their place, and then we'll have pretty blue-eyed grandchildren and a garden and poodle and lace curtains."

I fluttered my wings and waggled my wattle suggestively, and stuck my beak through the bars to give her a little peck on the cheek.

"Back, hack!" she shouted, "or I'll break your drum sticks! You will never lay a hand on me, or an egg *in* me, either! Away, fowl creature!"

"But what's this? What about our agreement? What have I done?"

"What have you done? Stark Antonym just told you! You have less imagination than an undarned grey sock! Oh, if you knew how I suffered at school because of you! Your insipid *Liking Among The Dandelions* was a set text, as was your eye-closing *Behind the Scenes in Milton Keynes.* Three teachers resigned, rather than have to teach it, and another actually died of a fatal yawn in front of us while trying to explain the hidden significance of Ethel's daily shopping trips. We girls read Richardson's *Pamela* in the toilets for a bit of excitement, and underlined the naughty bits in Jane Austen. Your soulless works ruined romance for me, delayed my first period by a year, and gave me inverted nipples! My life was meaningless until I met Hymen Thews at a fencing class."

"Hymen Thews? You mean Hymen Simon, don't you? Or Squeeze Thews?"

"No, I don't. Stark Antonym has a strong imagination, that I can't deny, but his soul, like yours, is devoid of romance. Only rabbits and turnips really excite him. On principle he is all negative, nihilistic. Hymen Thews on the other hand is a *real* writer who not only never got the recognition he deserved, but is also the most romantic man alive, the only one worthy to lay his craggily exciting head on my savage Welsh breast. So much larger than life is he that Stark in his fiction unconsciously divided him into two, the Cloven Lover: Squeeze Thews the man of action and Hymen Simon the poet-musician. And so great was his jealousy that in his stories he always had them bumped off – in one novel, Squeeze died of gingrene from too many biscuits, and Hymen, while his legs were still broken, was tied down in the sun until his back was bright red, and then, naked, forced to join in the Pamplona bull run."

"But . . . you're saying all my 'memories' were real, then, even though they weren't my own? But Captain Pilchard Stopdrooling can't be real! Or his arch-enemy Engelbrecht the Degenerate Dwarf!"

Her smile was more sinister than a chess board in a badly-financed operating theatre.

"Oh yes they are! After countless skirmishes, they decided to fight it out once and for all, man to dwarf. They stared each other up and down – Pilchard finished first – took deep valiant breaths, and were dropped in the local Grudge Crater on the Moon. But Engelbrecht, coming from a dwarf star, was so heavy, even there, that with each movement he sank more and more into the lunar surface, and as for Pilchard, he didn't dare get too close to the dwarf for fear of being trapped in his gravitational pull. They were too intelligent not to recognise zugzwang, so they agreed to a stalemate, and were taken back on board the Referee's spaceship, where they took another deep breath and to each other, expressed mutual admiration for a gallant opponent, and became the best of friends.

"Which is why I chose to take my revenge in this particular way. Since Pilchard just happens to be my uncle, he asked me if I had any ideas on how to help out his newfound chum. Engelbrecht was finding it difficult to locate any mythological beings in his part of the galaxy – apparently, they're a delicacy on certain planets, and have been hunted to extinction – and was in danger of being thrown out of the Smallsphere Surrealist Assassins Club. The back-stabbing there takes place *after* public exposure and expulsion, and all members, friends or foes, are expected to join in. That's another reason why I turned you into a cockatrice instead of a mere chicken. But you should feel honoured: I told Pilchard to tell Engelbrecht that I had hatched you from one of the *fatal eggs* laid by Bulgakov.

So, although it is obvious to all you are not a great writer, you can at least claim to be the progeny of one."

"Oh vile villainess! But I'm not afraid. You said yourself Engelbrecht is too heavy to move even on the moon, so here he'd be as helpless as a boiled foreskin on a hook in a damp vestry."

I realised I was still infected by Stark.

"That was some time ago. Engelbrecht went on a diet for this mission. First he tried losing electrons, but found after a week his weight was just the same, of course. So then he cut down drastically and pluckily on carbohydrates and protons, and after losing about 300 septillion of the latter – that's a good 300,000,000,000,000,000,000,000,000 amu – he found he'd lost about a pound. Which, being a dwarf, was a fair percentage. He tested himself out last week in a boxing match, and clocked up a resounding victory against a remarkably sprightly grandfather clock. I don't think a mere cockatrice will give *him* much trouble. I'm pretty sure your lethal gaze won't work on extraterrestrials, though I've bought him a few pairs of short contact lenses, just in case.

"Anyway, I'm only keeping my promise to you: I told you that I had influence in the Academi, and that if you helped me in my plan – since Transformation Spells only work if the subject isn't resisting – I would make sure you went far. Well, so you shall! With Engelbrecht! He should be here soon. If you're lucky, he might get here before Stark starts to reek."

So saying, she picked up my cage with one hand, and hurled me through the door behind her. A moment later, Stark Antonym's still-twitching body landed on top of me. I looked up, and then had to squeeze shut my eyes. Oh horror of horrors! It was a hall of mirrors! If I so much as opened my eyes for a second I would be violently ill at the sight of myself. Trapped in a cage, and as good as blind, how could I hope to resist capture?

I had one last hope. If Engelbrecht and Pilchard and Hymen Simon and the rest were all real, then that meant Spermicidal Whiskers and Robin' Darktree also existed. I could expect little help from the former – he would be useless against women, except unborn ones – but if *I* hadn't been the one to receive the enormous scar from Catherine Meaty-Zones, then I must have been reliving the memories of Darktree the scandalously pitiless highwayman. He might, faced, fazed and amazed by her décolleté, have forgiven her in the chivalric heat of the moment, but when he got home and tried to shave, he would almost certainly have painfully nicked his underlying pitilessness. What if he were on the way here now, seeking dire revenge? If he killed Cat, her spell would be broken, and Engelbrecht would see that I was just a hapless hack, and leave me in peace.

A poultry hope, it is true.

At that moment, triumphant laughter came from the other side of the door, followed by what sounded exactly like a particularly treacherous witch being passionately kissed by a man with melancholy Machiavellian lips and a Brazilian-sounding limp.

And pretensions to literary respectability.

THE DEATHS OF ROBIN HOOD

Rhys Hughes

Nina, the Queen of the Amazons, wants to go somewhere different this year. She is bored with Lake Karatis, despite its giant snakes. She has wrestled most of them anyway. She uncorks her little god and whispers into the jar: "Any suggestions for a holiday?"

The shape inside heaves like a bosom. "The Forest of Sherwood."

"Where in all Scythia is that?"

"Beyond its western horizon. Cross the Caucasus and follow the Black Sea coast with the Pontine Mountains on your left. Turn sharp right at Byzantium. I don't know the way from there. You'll have to ask. Perhaps the Emperor can help you."

She frowns and rattles the jar. "Not in Scythia, you say? Well that's original. But what's so special about this Sherwood Forest?"

"It's the home of an outlaw."

"But I'm always catching those and poking them with spears!"

The shape within seems to chuckle. "This one is different. He is the Prince of Thieves. He steals from the rich and gives to the poor. You are very rich and so he will try his luck with you. He is fearless and has the luck of a legend. A good match."

"You are right, little god! It has to be better sport than monstrous serpents. I shall pack my things at once. But how do you get to learn of such strange people and events? After all, you're stuck in there all day."

"I dream about them, mistress. I was the Khazar god of dreaming before you captured me. Now my people never dream. And they are too tired to sleep."

Nina replaces the cork. She is almost excited.

The Sheriff of Nottingham is a villain, but he just follows orders, so it isn't his fault. Following orders is much harder than following a road. You have to leap from one instruction to the next, never knowing where they are taking you, like stepping stones over a river of scorpions, either marching packed tight down a dry channel, or else floating on broad leaves, depending on the season, but a difficult feature to cross all the same, and always a suspicion that the next stone will tip up and throw you greaves over helm into the torrent of sting. And the poison forming little tributaries.

"Guy of Gisborne! Come in here at once!"

"Yes, your Sheriffness?"

"Can you guess what I'm doing now? Three guesses!"

"Um, being a villain?"

"Damn it! How do you keep winning this game? Take a draught of mead as your reward. Now then, I have a problem. I can't follow *these* orders."

"King John asked you to dress in lingerie again?"

"Would to heaven he had! No, Guy, this is far more awkward than that. See this letter I'm holding? No, not in that hand, which is under the table. This hand! That's right, in front of your face. I know these Norman helmets make you cross-eyed with their nose-guards. Anyway, it was delivered a few minutes ago, don't ask how, all right carrier pigeon if you must know, and it has come all the way from the Emperor of Byzantium, Isaac II Angelos."

"Oh, him. We don't owe him any allegiance, do we?"

"I wish we didn't, because he has asked me to expect an honoured guest, the Queen of the Amazons. I'm supposed to

put her up here in my castle and introduce her to the outlaw
Robin Hood. She wants to challenge him to a fight."

"That will save us the trouble, won't it?"

"No, no, no! Don't you remember? You mortally wounded
him yesterday!"

Robin Hood is dying in a comfortable bed with Maid Marian
and Little John in the same room. They made the bed. Little
John always has difficulties with duvet covers, he's so clumsy.
Robin can feel lumps in the bedding pressing down on his
wounds. It's not so merry. He is delirious and mutters strange
phrases.

"Go take a Frying Tuck at the moon!"

"What's that he's saying?" asks Little John.

Maid Marian shrugs. "Probably connected with forest
business. That's all he ever thinks about. Greenwood this,
greenwood that. Bash a holy man on the head, rummage his
surplice for his surplus. Code of honour, squirrels."

"Red or grey?"

"I don't believe the latter have been introduced yet."

"No I meant the holy men. Cardinal or monk."

"Ah, bishops mostly. But you know that surely? You did
it!"

"I was trying to make small-talk."

They twiddle each other's thumbs, but it's just friendly, not
romantic. Then they sigh and scratch their chins and shrug.

"This is taking ages. Perhaps we ought to ease his pain with
some poison?"

"Sorry, the river's clean out of scorpions."

"You could hit him with your quarterstaff for a bit."

"I left it in the little room under the stairs at Will Scarlet's
house."

"You are simple, John, sometimes!"

Before he can agree, Robin Hood suddenly sits up. His
delirium has cleared just for an instant. He has to act quick
before it returns.

"Fetch me my bow! I shall fire an arrow out of this window.
Where it lands, you must bury me under there!"

He fires the arrow. He falls back. The recoil has finished him off.

The Khazar god of dreaming is yawning through his glass walls. It has been a long journey from Scythia, through Turkey and Greece and Illyria and the Holy Roman Empire and France, and across the Channel to England. Now they are on the edge of Sherwood Forest and it is time to stop yawning, not because things have got interesting, but due to the lack of oxygen inside the sealed jar. There is none left to inhale. He feels sleepy, drunk on his own odour.

"Hi in there! We're here at last!"

The cork pops and he gazes up at the lips of his mistress. They are red and swollen like his eyelids, but bigger and more kissable, depending on who you are, or who you aren't. One day he will jump up and grab for her tongue and refuse to release it until she guarantees his freedom, but if he did that she wouldn't be able to shout the command to let him go, and a stalemate would ensue. And she has more stamina than him.

"Do you require my advice on something?"

"Yes. Where must I walk to find this Robin Hood?"

"Take one step into the forest and he will come to you."

"Did you dream that or make it up?"

"Fiction is not my strength, alas!"

"Good. So we'll fight the duel and then go back to that nice Sheriff of Nottingham's castle for a cup of tea. What do you think?"

"Hush! I hear a sound. A whoooooshing noise!"

"O bloody bugger, I've been shot!"

So she has. The arrow protrudes from her lower abdomen. She doesn't stagger, but merely leans on a tree for support. Scythia suddenly seems as far away as it really is.

Guy of Gisborne is riding across the meadows. His surcoat flaps behind him. His chain-mail sparkles in the sun, spoiled in places by grass stains. Perhaps he has recently *greengowned* a maid, as the polite expression has it for outdoor rogering, before he felt compelled, or was ordered, to ride somewhere –

don't know where, he probably doesn't either – though it's not a routine mission, nor is he a routine cross-eyed bully, but blond and square jawed and a little bit effete but tough too, in calf and arm. Where are you going, Guy? That's what the leaves seem to whisper in the wind as he enters the forest. But his helm fits so tightly over his ears that he doesn't hear.

The hooves of his horse kick up little twigs and clods of earth. This is no official route through the greenwood. So he knows he is heading the right way. The outlaws tend to move stealthily, like gibbons, whatever those are, through the trees, leaving no print or clue on the ground below. He still has no firm destination in mind. It's just a question of trusting his intuition and avoiding the obvious paths. When he least expects it, he will come across what he seeks. But as he continues to ride through thicker undergrowth and nettles slap his mount's flanks for free – though some men of his acquaintance in York would pay good money for that, or else in kind, which is unkind – the first real doubts enter his brain.

Therefore he comes across a small gathering. He has traversed nearly the whole forest, almost coming out the other side.

He sees Nina, Queen of the Amazons, idling against a tree.

"Your Queeness!" he cries. "I have been sent by my master, the Sheriff of Nottingham, to confess that Robin Hood is probably already dead. Sorry. He couldn't bear to tell you when you were in his castle. But his conscience bothered him."

"Does he have one?" she mutters.

"Well he is a villain, but it isn't his fault, so yes!"

He looks around at the assembled company. He draws his sword with a cry.

"Hello," say Maid Marian and Little John.

"Ooh, you blighters! What are you doing here?"

"We've come to bury Robin."

"Can't you do that in your own time? I'm busy!"

"We have to bury him where the arrow landed."

They point and Guy of Gisborne follows the line of their converging fingers.

"What? Inside Nina, the Queen of the Amazons?"

"That was his final request. Code of chivalry and all that. Awkward, that's for sure. No help for it. We're just following orders. And stuff."

Nina, Queen of the Amazons, feels in a quandary. She is lying down in the middle of a clearing. She is very cold. Maid Marian, Little John and Guy of Gisborne have gone to fetch the body of the outlaw Robin Hood. They have also gone to collect a sharp knife, a needle and some thread, to cut her open and sew her back up. Certain traditions are sacred and the dying wishes of a folkhero must never be opposed. All the same, she feels nervous at the thought of the impending funeral. She can't decide whether to hope for her own death or not before the actual burial. She is losing blood rapidly. The arrow still quivers in her womb. She reaches across for the jar and uncorks it with effort. The shape inside is whistling a dirge.

"Cut that out! The mourners will be here soon."

The Khazar god of dreaming chuckles. "That's right. How does it feel to be a grave? It's a nightmare scenario I wish I'd invented!"

"I don't intend to give you any work tips . . ."

"Haven't been able to send dreams to my people since you shut me up in here. You might as well let me go. Break the glass."

"No. I think you should be buried inside me with Robin, as a sacrifice."

"What? You can't mean that! I get claustrophobic enough as it is! Wombs are so dark and stuffy. Please don't!"

"What will you do for me if I spare you that fate?"

"I'll make your better, mistress! I promise!"

"You mean I'll get well again, even though this arrow is sticking in me? And I'll survive the funeral too? It's a deal."

"On condition that you release me afterward."

"I guess that's fair enough. Done!"

They don't shake hands on it. The little god casts his spell and is still cooling his fingers when the mourners enter the clearing, marching slowly with black armbands. Little John carries the corpse over one shoulder, Maid Marian wields the knife. Guy of Gisborne shudders when the first spurt of blood hits him in the eye. He hates solemn occasions.

The landlord of the *Damsel & Pointy Hat* has never known such a talkative group of revellers as the three strangers who are sitting in the corner, quaffing mead and roaring with laughter at each other's anecdotes. A lady with red hair, a scruffy giant with a bristling beard and a young blond man with blue eyes. Even when he was a carpenter, he never knew such rasping noises. They drink out of a Norman helmet, the nose-guard acting as a handle.

"And then I caught him wearing lingerie!" the blond one is shouting.

"Ho, ho, ho! Ha, ha, ha!" laugh the other two.

They are obviously holding a sort of farewell party for a deceased comrade. They don't seem to miss him too much. Perhaps he was overrated? Yes, that must be it.

"If only Robin was here to buy us all another round! He was a noble enemy. I almost wept tears when my sword sliced through his lungs."

The lady mutters into her drink. "Actually he was always a stingy old sod."

"Really? His reputation is quite the opposite."

"Yes, he kept the facts safely under lock and key. He was a bloody awful lover too. Very poor aim. Absolutely no stamina."

The giant grits his teeth. "Not sorry to see him go."

"Well this is a surprise," admits the blond fellow.

The door of the tavern swings open and a very tall woman staggers over the threshold. There is an arrow protruding from her midriff. She wears a pained expression.

"So this is where you got to? Charming, I'm sure, getting drunk while I have to lie on my back in the cold. Let me join you and make this a proper wake."

There is a spare seat. Nobody tries to remove it.

"Um, are you better then?"

"Indeed I am. Don't act so astonished. I'm the Queen of the Amazons and I know plenty of tricks to get out of a tight spot. First time I've had a whole man inserted inside me, though. It's a bit uncomfortable, but I won't complain. Tell me instead, where the heck did you get black armbands from in the forest?"

"Tore them in strips from Guy of Gisborne's surcoat."

"Liar! That item of fashion was red, not black."

"We stained it with berries."

"In February? I doubt it! Come on, be serious."

"We can't remember exactly. So there!"

"But little details like that are very important . . . Wait! I've got this terrible pain in my pelvic area! I'm having contractions! I'm about to give birth!"

"Quick! A towel and some hot water!"

"Too late! Here comes its head!"

"Ooh, what an ugly baby! Somebody give it a smack!"

Little John steps forward, his fingers bunched into fists.

"Wait! What's that it's saying as it plops fully out? It's trying to articulate its first sentence! A touching moment, this. Be silent and listen."

They lean closer, cupping their ears.

"Go take a Frying Tuck at the moon!"

Maid Marian rolls her eyes. "It's a boy! An overgrown, mansized boy!"

The Sheriff of Nottingham has reached the clearing in the forest. There are fifty mounted knights with him. They wear full armour and never speak, so it is difficult to be sure that anybody is inside. They are probably automatons, created by the wizard who lived in the castle before him. Certainly he found them all stacked neatly in the cellar. He recalls how he spent a whole afternoon cleaning the rust off with a little brush.

He reins his horse to a halt and sits creaking in the saddle. Beneath his own armour he can feel the tension of the stockings and suspender belt. They are wealing up his flesh nicely. And the black satin knickers are too tight. The year is 1193.

Soon it will be the 13th century. He hopes his sex life improves in time.

"Look at that! An item of evidence!"

He points at the jar lying on the ground. It is empty now. Some of his knights swivel their heads and snort gently. "Phasswass." That's the only sound they ever make. And "Shoowshss."

The Sheriff rubs his chin. "I recognise that vessel. I saw it in the possession of Nina, Queen of the Amazons, when she came to stay with me. She never showed me its contents, but they have gone now. Maybe alcohol. This puts me in mind of my own thirst. There's a tavern not far from here. If we gallop, we may reach it for a last one before closing time. And then we can resume our search for Guy of Gisborne!"

"Phasswass . . . Shoowshss . . ."

"Yes, I miss him too. Onwards!"

Robin Hood is poking the tall woman with his finger. The firelight dances on his snarling face. A helmet of mead spills over as his leg knocks the edge of a table. There is shouting and many spluttered curses.

"So you think you're harder than me, do you, lady?"

For answer, she slaps him across the cheek and off his feet.

"In a word, yes," she spits at last.

He climbs to his knees, wiping the blood from his lips. "Play rough, eh? That's your game, is it? I may have been born after yesterday, but you won't gull me with another trick. Come on, lady, put them up."

"No trick!" she cries, as she slaps him with her other hand. "Just good honest violence. I've wrestled serpents in Lake Karatis."

Maid Marian, Little John and Guy of Gisborne are standing in a circle, clapping hands louder and louder. "Scrap! Scrap! Scrap!"

Robin Hood staggers upright a second time.

The landlord steps forward. "No brawling in the *Damsel & Pointy Hat*. This is a respectable establishment. Off the premises, the lot of you!"

"We'll settle this outside," snarls Robin.

Nina nods and turns to leave. As they all step through the door, Little John strokes his beard thoughtfully. "How come she gave birth to a live Robin Hood after they both died?"

"A bit confusing, isn't it?" agrees Guy of Gisborne.

Maid Marian shrugs. "Perhaps she had some magic potion that restored her to health and once Robin was buried inside her womb, the spell must have worked for him too, by accident. That *must* be what happened."

Little John and Guy of Gisborne gape. "Of course! It's so obvious!"

They are standing outside the tavern now. The Prince of Thieves is squaring up to the Queen of the Amazons. They circle each other warily.

"Look over there!" cried Robin suddenly. "It's a unicorn!"

She turns her head. "Where?"

And Robin rushes in and delivers two mighty punches to the side of her jaw. She staggers back and he chortles. "The oldest trick in the book!"

She glowers at him. Her rage is enormous.

"I can play dirty too!" she booms. Twisting up her face, she reaches down and draws the arrow out of her abdomen. She holds it like a dagger. Then she rushes forward and stabs him straight through the heart.

He groans once and collapses in the dust.

"Robin Hood is dead a second time! I have won the duel!"

Maid Marian, Little John and Guy of Gisborne crouch over the prone body and mutter to themselves. "Oh dear! Oh dear! We don't mind that he's dead. But we have to bury him wherever the arrow lands. And this has generated a paradox. We must bury him *inside himself*. How the hell can we sort this one out?"

The Sheriff of Nottingham and his fifty knights reach the tavern just as the sun begins to set. So he assumes that the blood trickled around the entrance is a trick of the light. Then he notices the little funeral taking place in the shadows.

"Show some respect, lads! Take your helmets off!"

On second thoughts, he's glad they can't.

He decides it's his moral duty to ride closer and exchange some pleasantries with the mourners. After all, this is his fiefdom and these people are his children, in a metaphorical sense. He is amazed when he discovers who they are.

"Guy of Gisborne! You traitor! You've joined my enemies!"

The blond head shakes emphatically. "Not at all. But the laws of chivalry compel me to assist in the burial of Robin Hood, even though the task is impossible."

The Sheriff dismounts. "Fair enough! But what's the problem?"

Guy of Gisborne waves a hand at the body, over which Maid Marian and Little John squat, exchanging ideas, all of them futile.

"We have to bury him inside himself and we're not sure how best to accomplish this. My view is that we ought to slit him open from throat to groin and fold his limbs into the gash and then apply enormous pressure on them until he turns inside-out. That's the only way I can think of discharging his final request."

The Sheriff's eyes twinkle. "Oh, impetuous Guy! How I love thee!"

"You think my idea has much merit?"

"Not at all! But it was presented to me in a charming tone. That's why I feel affection toward you. A big silly rascal, that's what you are! Listen, if I remember the conventions of chivalry properly, and I studied them when I was younger, the standard wording of such requests includes the word *under*."

"What do you mean?" frowns Guy of Gisborne.

"It's not 'bury me where the arrow lands', but *under* where it lands!"

Guy of Gisborne turns to the other two. "Hey! Did he say under?"

Little John scratches his head. "Under? Yes, I believe he did."

Maid Marian pounds a fist into her palm. "Bugger! I forgot that! Damn it, there was no need to bury him inside Nina,

Queen of the Amazons, after all. We should have just interred him at the spot directly below her feet."

"Well, it's not too late to bury him that way now."

They regard the corpse. Guy of Gisborne clarifies the point: "You mean we just dig at that exact spot and put him in the hole?"

"Yes, but a coffin would be more dignified. The landlord of this tavern used to be a carpenter. I'll order him to knock up a box right away."

He turns and strides into the tavern. Without him, his knights grow restless.

"Phasswass! Shoowshss! Now we can chat properly!"

Isaac II Angelos, Emperor of Byzantium, sits on his throne and plays with his toys. The Magnaura Palace is very large and cold at night. There are hidden springs and cogs and levers in most items of furniture. In front of him stands a bronze tree with many branches, each of which is covered with little gilt birds. They sing various songs with their delicate metallic throats. Gone are the days when everything was very shiny. The mechanical tree, and the roaring gilt lions at the foot of the throne, are tarnished now and overused, for they date from the reign of Theophilus, who lived in the middle of the 9th century.

Similarly, the throne is connected to the rear wall by a device which can lift it to the ceiling along a disguised groove. There are changes of clothing inside the hollow seat. The idea was originally to impress ambassadors and visiting dignitaries from the west. A diplomat would be carried into the presence of the Emperor by two eunuchs and then set down. He would be expected to prostrate himself thrice, throwing himself at full length on the floor. Each time he looked up after one of these prostrations, the Emperor would be in a different position on the wall and in a new set of robes. It would be mystifying.

But now the workings are worn and inefficient. The throne squeaks as it jerks toward the ceiling, threatening to throw its occupant off.

A real bird flaps into the Palace and lands on the bronze tree.

It is a pigeon. The Emperor reaches forward and removes the message from its leg. He unrolls the paper and arches an eyebrow.

"A letter from the Sheriff of Nottingham," he says.

His Vizier bows deeply. "You asked him to keep you informed of developments."

"Did I? So I did! Now let's see, what does it say? Ah! Apparently some fellow called Robin Hood was killed by an arrow and was laid inside a new coffin and the lid was about to be secured and nailed down when Nina, Queen of the Amazons, threw herself on his body. He was her son, she wailed, and therefore she had no choice but to love him, even though she had killed him. She kissed him on the lips. To everyone's horror, the corpse returned to life. It seems that Nina had kept a god in a jar and had promised to let it go if it granted her a wish. It did so, but she cheated on her side of the bargain. She released it from the jar, yes, but by swallowing it! She chewed it up and digested it! Anyway, the magic powers inside the god must have transferred themselves into her metabolism, allowing her kiss to be suffused with implausible restorative qualities! So she kissed him back to life! But the story doesn't have a happy ending. Do you know why?"

The Vizier shakes his head. "Sorry, no. I don't speak Latin. This is Byzantium and my language is Greek. I didn't understand a word of that!"

"Nor I! It's just a mass of squiggles. It doesn't matter anyway, because it will be out of date now. The events it describes are in the past."

The Vizier licks his lips. "Can we have the pigeon for lunch?"

Maid Marian, Little John, Guy of Gisborne, the Sheriff of Nottingham and the Queen of the Amazons are patiently explaining to Robin Hood why he must be buried alive. He is lying in his coffin and only Nina's foot on his chest prevents him from getting out. She holds the lid in her hands. She smiles sweetly.

"If there was another way, you know I'd take it."

"Call yourself a mother?" squeals Robin. "I'm alive now!"

"Yes, that was an enjoyable magic kiss. But the rules are clear. A final request must be obeyed, and you asked to be buried under the spot where your arrow ended up. It stuck in your own heart. So now we have to bury you here. The fact that you are a living person is completely irrelevant."

"But I'll suffocate down there and be dead again!"

"So what are you complaining about? That sorts everything out."

"I thought you loved me!"

"I do. As a mother loves a son. But there comes a time when two people, whatever their relationship, have to let each other go."

"I don't want to be buried alive! I don't want to be buried alive!"

"Oh, stop whingeing, you little pansy!"

Pressing him down firmly, she positions the lid on the coffin. Maid Marian and Little John hurry forward with hammer and nails. There is much banging. The screams of Robin Hood are muffled now. The coffin is sealed.

"Lower it into the grave!" cries the Sheriff of Nottingham.

The pit is six feet deep. The coffin fits perfectly at the bottom. The knights kick the loose soil back until the hole is filled. Guy of Gisborne leads his horse over it a few times, to stamp it flat. The screams are now very faint. Perhaps they are not really there. It could just be a thousand worms writhing.

"I hate these ceremonies," says the Sheriff of Nottingham.

"Well it's all over now," replies Nina.

"What will you do? All of you, I mean."

Little John and Maid Marian exchange glances.

"I'm going to retire to a convent."

"So am I! After a shave, that is. And an operation."

Guy of Gisborne barks: "My place is still by your side!"

"Phasswass! Shoowshss!"

"And you, my Queen? What are your plans?" the Sheriff adds.

Nina sighs and looks around. Then she shrugs. "I've done

what I came to do. I think it's time to return to Scythia. But what about you?"

"Oh, I owe the Emperor of Byzantium a long letter."

The Sheriff of Nottingham and his knights decide to accompany Nina, Queen of the Amazons, out of Sherwood Forest. But before they reach its edge, she reins in her horse and sighs. Then she turns around.

"It's no good. There's a big problem."

"What do you mean by that?"

"I can't leave Robin down there. He's my son now and I carry him in my heart. And the way things have ended up, he has to be buried below himself. I mean, that's what we've just done. So to keep to the spirit of the request, and the way we have interpreted it, he ought to be buried below wherever I am."

"But you'll be constantly on the move now!"

"Yes. Pity there's no such thing as a portable grave!"

He frowns. "Perhaps there is! Follow me!"

The Sheriff of Nottingham spurs his horse back to the *Damsel & Pointy Hat*. The grave lies off to one side. He dismounts and enters the tavern. After a few minutes, he comes out and signals to Nina.

"The landlord's a carpenter, remember? I asked him if he could make some sort of device like a snow-plough to attach to the front of the coffin. He said yes."

"You mean I'll be able to drag the coffin under me wherever I go?"

"Yes, the plough will automatically shift the earth aside. The grave will remain a constant six feet under all the way back to Scythia."

"Taking it across the Channel might be difficult."

"You can hire out a ship with a hold packed with soil."

The knights have already disinterred the coffin. The knocking from inside is very feeble. The landlord emerges from the tavern with the prepared device. While he fits it, Nina decides to open the lid for a last look. Robin Hood's face is contorted. There is much sweat on his brow.

"Thank God! I was on my last breath!"

"I haven't come to rescue you, silly, just to tell you that we're about to start on a long journey. We're going home, my dear son."

"What? What? What?"

She answers the question by replacing the lid.

A rope is secured from the coffin to her hand before the soil is replaced. Now she can pull the grave along behind her. When the rope is taut, it carries the vibrations of Robin's frenzied knocking. When she holds it close to her ear, she can hear his screams and pleadings. It will provide entertainment on the voyage.

They leave Sherwood Forest by a different route. She crosses a dry riverbed. The Sheriff of Nottingham is behind her. Behind him are the fifty knights. While they are still crossing, a giant scorpion bears down on them. Shocking what the Crusaders brought back with them! A terrific fight begins. Many of the knights really are empty suits of armour after all.

It is none of her business. She keeps going. In her trail Robin Hood undergoes his last, harrowing death.

BAD TIMING

Molly Brown

*Time travel is an inexact science. And its study is fraught
with paradoxes.*
— Samuel Colson, b. 2301 d. 2197

Alan rushed through the archway without even glancing at the
inscription across the top. It was Monday morning and he was
late again. He often thought about the idea that time was a
point in space, and he didn't like it. That meant that at this
particular point in space it was always Monday morning and
he was always late for a job he hated. And it always had been.
And it always would be. Unless somebody tampered with it,
which was strictly forbidden.

"Oh, my Holy Matrix," Joe Twofingers exclaimed as Alan
raced past him to register his palmprint before losing an extra
thirty minutes pay. "You wouldn't believe what I found in the
fiction section!"

Alan slapped down his hand. The recorder's metallic voice
responded with, "Employee number 057, Archives Department, Alan Strong. Thirty minutes and seven point two
seconds late. One hour's credit deducted."

Alan shrugged and turned back towards Joe. "Since I'm not
getting paid, I guess I'll put my feet up and have a cup of
liquid caffeine. So tell me what you found."

"Well, I was tidying up the files – fiction section is a mess as
you know – and I came across this magazine. And I thought,

'what's *this* doing here?' It's something from the 20th century
called *Woman's Secrets*, and it's all knitting patterns, recipes,
and gooey little romance stories: 'He grabbed her roughly,
bruising her soft pale skin, and pulled her to his rock hard
chest' and so on. I figured it was in there by mistake and nearly
threw it out. But then I saw this story called 'The Love That
Conquered Time' and I realised that must be what they're
keeping it for. So I had a look at it, and it was . . .'' He made a
face and stuck a finger down his throat. "But I really think you
ought to read it."

"Why?"

"Because you're in it."

"You're a funny guy, Joe. You almost had me going for a
minute."

"I'm serious! Have a look at the drebbing thing. It's by
some woman called Cecily Walker, it's in that funny old
vernacular they used to use, and it's positively dire. But the
guy in the story is definitely you."

Alan didn't believe him for a minute. Joe was a joker, and
always had been. Alan would never forget the time Joe laced
his drink with a combination aphrodisiac-hallucinogen at a
party and he'd made a total fool of himself with the section
leader's overcoat. He closed his eyes and shuddered as Joe
handed him the magazine.

Like all the early relics made of paper, the magazine had
been dipped in preservative and the individual pages coated
with a clear protective covering which gave them a horrible
chemical smell and a tendency to stick together. After a little
difficulty, Alan found the page he wanted. He rolled his eyes at
the painted illustration of a couple locked in a passionate but
chaste embrace, and dutifully began to read.

It was all about a beautiful but lonely and unfulfilled woman
who still lives in the house where she was born. One day there
is a knock at the door, and she opens it to a mysterious
stranger: tall, handsome, and extremely charismatic.

Alan chuckled to himself.

A few paragraphs later, over a candle-lit dinner, the man
tells the woman that he comes from the future, where time

travel has become a reality, and he works at the Colson Time Studies Institute in the Department of Archives.

Alan stopped laughing.

The man tells her that only certain people are allowed to time travel, and they are not allowed to interfere in any way, only observe. He confesses that he is not a qualified traveller – he broke into the lab one night and stole a machine. The woman asks him why and he tells her, "You're the only reason, Claudia. I did it for you. I read a story that you wrote and I knew it was about me and that it was about you. I searched in the Archives and I found your picture and then I knew that I loved you and that I had always loved you and that I always would."

"But I never wrote a story, Alan."

"You will, Claudia. You will."

The Alan in the story goes on to describe the Project, and the Archives, in detail. The woman asks him how people live in the 24th century, and he tells her about the gadgets in his apartment.

The hairs at the back of Alan's neck rose at the mention of his Neuro-Pleasatron. He'd never told anybody that he'd bought one, not even Joe.

After that, there's a lot of grabbing and pulling to his rock hard chest, melting sighs and kisses, and finally a wedding and a "happily ever after" existing at one point in space where it always has and always will.

Alan turned the magazine over and looked at the date on the cover. March 14, 1973.

He wiped the sweat off his forehead and shook himself. He looked up and saw that Joe was standing over him.

"You wouldn't really do that, would you?" Joe said. "Because you know I'd have to stop you."

Cecily Walker stood in front of her bedroom mirror and turned from right to left. She rolled the waistband over one more time, making sure both sides were even. Great; the skirt looked like a real mini. Now all she had to do was get out of the house without her mother seeing her.

She was in the record shop wondering if she really should spend her whole allowance on the new Monkees album, but she really liked Peter Tork, he was so cute, when Tommy Johnson walked in with Roger Hanley. "Hey, Cess-pit! Whaddya do, lose the bottom half of your dress?"

The boys at her school were just so creepy. She left the shop and turned down the main road, heading toward her friend Candy's house. She never noticed the tall blonde man that stood across the street, or heard him call her name.

When Joe went on his lunch break, Alan turned to the wall above his desk and said, "File required: Authors, fiction, twentieth century, initial 'W'."

"Checking," the wall said. "File located."

"Biography required: Walker, Cecily."

"Checking. Biography located. Display? Yes or no."

"Yes."

A section of wall the size of a small television screen lit up at eye-level, directly in front of Alan. He leaned forward and read: Walker, Cecily. b. Danville, Illinois, U.S.A. 1948 d. 2037. Published works: "The Love That Conquered Time", March, 1973. Accuracy rating: fair.

"Any other published works?"

"Checking. None found."

Alan looked down at the magazine in his lap.

"I don't understand," Claudia said, looking pleadingly into his deep blue eyes. Eyes the colour of the sea on a cloudless morning, and eyes that contained an ocean's depth of feeling for her, and her alone. "How is it possible to travel through time?"

"I'll try to make this simple," he told her, pulling her close. She took a deep breath, inhaling his manly aroma, and rested her head on his shoulder with a sigh. "Imagine that the universe is like a string. And every point on that string is a moment in space and time. But instead of stretching out in a straight line, it's all coiled and tangled and it overlaps in layers. Then all you have to do is move from point to point."

Alan wrinkled his forehead in consternation. "File?"

"Yes. Waiting."

"Information required: further data on Walker, Cecily. Education, family background."

"Checking. Found. Display? Yes or . . ."

"Yes!"

Walker, Cecily. Education: Graduate Lincoln High, Danville, 1967. Family background: Father Walker, Matthew. Mechanic, automobile. d. 1969. Mother no data.

Alan shook his head. Minimal education, no scientific background. How could she know so much? "Information required: photographic likeness of subject. If available, display."

He blinked and there she was, smiling at him across his desk. She was oddly dressed, in a multi-coloured T-shirt that ended above her waist and dark blue trousers that were cut so low they exposed her navel and seemed to balloon out below her knees into giant flaps of loose-hanging material. But she had long dark hair that fell across her shoulders and down to her waist, crimson lips and the most incredible eyes he had ever seen – huge and green. She was beautiful. He looked at the caption: Walker, Cecily. Author: Fiction related to time travel theory. Photographic likeness circa 1970.

"File," he said, "Further data required: personal details, ie. marriage. Display."

Walker, Cecily m. Strong, Alan.

"Date?"

No data.

"Biographical details of husband, Strong, Alan?"

None found.

"Redisplay photographic likeness. Enlarge." He stared at the wall for several minutes. "Print," he said.

Only half a block to go, the woman thought, struggling with two bags of groceries. The sun was high in the sky and the smell of Mrs Henderson's roses, three doors down, filled the air with a lovely perfume. But she wasn't in the mood to appreciate it. All the sun made her feel was hot, and all the smell of flowers made her feel was ill. It had been a difficult pregnancy, but thank goodness it was nearly over now.

She wondered who the man was, standing on her front porch. He might be the new mechanic at her husband's garage, judging by his orange cover-alls. Nice-looking, she thought, wishing that she didn't look like there was a bowling ball underneath her dress.

"Excuse me," the man said, reaching out to help her with her bags. "I'm looking for Cecily Walker."

"My name's Walker," the woman told him. "But I don't know any Cecily."

"Cecily," she repeated when the man had gone. What a pretty name.

Alan decided to work late that night. Joe left at the usual time and told him he'd see him tomorrow.

"Yeah, tomorrow," Alan said.

He waited until Joe was gone, and then he took the printed photo of Cecily Walker out of his desk drawer and sat for a long time, staring at it. What did he know about this woman? Only that she'd written one published story, badly, and that she was the most gorgeous creature he had ever seen. Of course, what he was feeling was ridiculous. She'd been dead more than three hundred years.

But there were ways of getting around that.

Alan couldn't believe what he was actually considering. It was lunacy. He'd be caught, and he'd lose his job. But then he realised that he could never have read about it if he hadn't already done it and got away with it. He decided to have another look at the story.

It wasn't there. Under Fiction: Paper Relics: 20th Century, sub-section Magazines, American, there was shelf after shelf full of *Amazing Stories, Astounding, Analog, Weird Tales* and *Isaac Asimov's Science Fiction Magazine*, but not one single copy of *Woman's Secrets*.

Well, he thought, if the magazine isn't there, I guess I never made it after all. Maybe it's better that way. Then he thought, but if I never made it, how can I be looking for the story? I shouldn't even know about it. And then he had another thought.

"File," he said. "Information required: magazines on loan."

"Display?"

"No, just tell me."

"*Woman's Secrets*, date 1973. *Astounding*, date . . ."

"Skip the rest. Who's got *Woman's Secrets*?"

"Checking. Signed out to Project Control through Joe Twofingers."

Project Control was on to him! If he didn't act quickly, it would be too late.

It was amazingly easy to get into the lab. He just walked in. The machines were all lined up against one wall, and there was no one around to stop him. He walked up to the nearest machine and sat down on it. The earliest model developed by Samuel Colson had looked like an English telephone box (he'd been a big *Doctor Who* fan), but it was hardly inconspicuous and extremely heavy, so refinements were made until the latest models were lightweight, collapsible, and made to look exactly like (and double up as) a folding bicycle. The control board was hidden from general view, inside a wicker basket.

None of the instruments were labelled. Alan tentatively pushed one button. Nothing happened. He pushed another. Still nothing.

He jumped off and looked for an instruction book. There had to be one somewhere. He was ransacking a desk when the door opened.

"I thought I'd find you here, Alan."

"Joe! I . . . uh . . . was just . . ."

"I know what you're doing, and I can't let you go through with it. It's against every rule of the Institute and you know it. If you interfere with the past, who knows what harm you might do?"

"But Joe, you know me. I wouldn't do any harm. I won't do anything to affect history, I swear it. I just want to see her, that's all. Besides, it's already happened, or you couldn't have read that magazine. And that's another thing! You're the one who showed it to me! I never would have known about her if it hadn't been for you. So if I'm going now, it's down to you."

"Alan, I'm sorry, but my job is on the line here, too, you know. So don't give me any trouble and come along quietly."

Joe moved towards him, holding a pair of handcuffs. Attempted theft of Institute property was a felony punishable by five years' imprisonment without pay. Alan picked up the nearest bike and brought it down over the top of Joe's head. The machine lay in pieces and Joe lay unconscious. Alan bent down and felt his pulse. He would be okay. "Sorry, Joe. I had to do it. File!"

"Yes."

"Information required: instruction manual for usage of . . ." he checked the number on the handlebars, "Colson Model 44B Time Traveller."

"Checking. Found. Display?"

"No. Just print. And fast."

The printer was only on page five when Alan heard running footsteps. Five pages would have to do.

Dear Cher, My name is Cecily Walker and all my friends tell me I look just like you. Well, a little bit. Anyway, the reason that I'm writing to you is this: I'm starting my senior year in high school, and I've never had a steady boyfriend. I've gone out with a couple of boys, but they only want one thing, and I guess you know what that is. I keep thinking there's gotta be somebody out there who's the right one for me, but I just haven't met him. Was it love at first sight for you and Sonny?

Alan sat on a London park bench with his printout and tried to figure out what he'd done wrong. Under Location: Setting, it just said "See page 29." Great, he thought. And he had no idea what year it was. Every time he tried to ask someone, they'd give him a funny look and walk away in a hurry. He folded up the bike and took a walk. It wasn't long before he found a news-stand and saw the date: July 19, 1998. At least he had the right century.

Back in the park, he sat astride the machine with the printout in one hand, frowning and wondering what might happen if he twisted a particular dial from right to left.

"Can't get your bike to start, mate?" someone shouted from nearby. "Just click your heels three times and think of home."

"Thanks, I'll try that," Alan shouted back. Then he vanished.

"I am a pirate from yonder ship," the man with the eye patch told her, "and well used to treasure. But I tell thee, lass, I've never seen the like of you."

Cecily groaned and ripped the page in half. She bit her lip and started again.

"I have travelled many galaxies, Madeleine," the alien bleeped. "But you are a life-form beyond compare."

"No, don't. Please don't," Madeleine pleaded as the alien reached out to pull her towards its rock hard chest.

Her mother appeared in the doorway. "Whatcha doin', hon?"

She dropped the pen and flipped the writing pad face down. "My homework."

The next thing Alan knew he was in the middle of a cornfield. He hitched a lift with a truck driver who asked a lot of questions, ranging from "You work in a gas station, do you?" to "What are you, foreign or something?" and "What do you call that thing?" On being told "that thing" was a folding bicycle, the man muttered something about whatever would they think of next, and now his kid would be wanting one.

There were several Walkers listed in the Danville phone book. When he finally found the right house, Cecily was in the middle of her third birthday party.

He pedalled around a corner, checked his printout, and set the controls on "Fast Forward". He folded the machine and hid it behind a bush before walking back to the house. It was big and painted green, just like in the story. There was an apple tree in the garden, just like in the story. The porch swing moved ever so slightly, rocked by an early summer breeze. He could hear crickets chirping and birds singing. Everything was just the way it had been in the story, so he walked up the path,

nervously clearing his throat and pushing back a stray lock of
hair, just the way Cecily Walker had described him in *Woman's Secrets*, before finally taking a deep breath and knocking
on the door. There was movement inside the house. The clack
of high-heeled shoes across a wooden floor, the rustle of a
cotton dress.

"Yes?"

Alan stared at her, open-mouthed. "You've cut your hair,"
he told her.

"What?"

"Your hair. It used to hang down to your waist, now it's up
to your shoulders."

"Do I know you?"

"You will," he told her. He'd said that in the story.

She was supposed to take one look at him and realise with a
fluttering heart that this was the man she'd dreamed of all her
life. Instead, she looked at his orange jumpsuit and slapped her
hand to her forehead in enlightenment. "You're from the
garage! Of course, Mack said he'd be sending the new
guy." She looked past him into the street. "So where's your
tow truck?"

"My what?" There was nothing in "The Love That Conquered Time" about a tow truck. The woman stared at him,
looking confused. Alan stared back, equally confused. He
started to wonder if he'd made a mistake. But then he saw
those eyes, bigger and greener than he'd ever thought possible.
"Matrix," he said out loud.

"What?"

"I'm sorry. It's just that meeting you is so bullasic."

"Mister, I don't understand one word you're saying."
Cecily knew she should tell the man to go away. He was
obviously deranged; she should call the police. But something
held her back, a flicker of recognition, the dim stirrings of a
memory. Where had she seen this man before?

"I'm sorry," Alan said again. "My American isn't very
good. I come from English-speaking Europe, you see."

"English-speaking Europe?" Cecily repeated. "You mean
England?"

"Not exactly. Can I come inside? I'll explain everything."

She let him come in after warning him that her neighbours would come running in with shotguns if they heard her scream, and that she had a black belt in Kung Fu. Alan nodded and followed her inside, wondering where Kung Fu was, and why she'd left her belt there.

He was ushered into the living room and told to have a seat. He sat down on the red velveteen-upholstered sofa and stared in awe at such historical artefacts as a black and white television with rabbit-ear antennae, floral-printed wallpaper, a phone you had to dial, and shelf after shelf of unpreserved books. She picked up a wooden chair and carried it to the far side of the room before sitting down. "Okay," she said. "Talk."

Alan felt it would have been better to talk over a candle-lit dinner in a restaurant, like they did in the story, but he went ahead and told her everything, quoting parts of the story verbatim, such as the passage where she described him as the perfect lover she'd been longing for all her life.

When he was finished, she managed a frozen smile. "So you've come all the way from the future just to visit little ole me. Isn't that nice."

Oh, Matrix, Alan thought. She's humouring me. She's convinced I'm insane and probably dangerous as well. "I know this must sound crazy to you," he said.

"Not at all," she told him, gripping the arms of her chair. He could see the blood draining out of her fingers.

"Please don't be afraid. I'd never harm you." He sighed and put a hand to his forehead. "It was all so different in the story."

"But I never wrote any story. Well, I started one once, but I never got beyond the second page."

"But you will. You see, it doesn't get published until 1973."

"You do know this is 1979, don't you?"

"WHAT?"

"Looks like your timing's off," she said. She watched him sink his head into his hands with an exaggerated groan. She rested her chin on one hand and regarded him silently. He didn't seem so frightening now. Crazy, yes, but not frightening. She might even find him quite attractive, if only things were different. He looked up at her and smiled. It was a crooked, little boy's smile that made his eyes sparkle. For a moment, she almost let herself imagine waking up to that smile . . . She pulled herself up in her chair, her back rigid.

"Look," he said. "So I'm a few years behind schedule. The main thing is I found you. And so what if the story comes out a bit later, it's nothing we can't handle. It's only a minor problem. A little case of bad timing."

"Excuse me," Cecily said. "But I think that in this case, timing is everything. If any of this made the least bit of sense, which it doesn't, you would've turned up before now. You said yourself the story was published in 1973 – if it was based on fact, you'd need to arrive here much earlier."

"I did get here earlier, but I was too early."

Cecily's eyes widened involuntarily. "What do you mean?"

"I mean I was here before. I met you. I spoke to you."

"When?"

"You wouldn't remember. You were three years old, and your parents threw a party for you out in the garden. Of course I realised my mistake instantly, but I bluffed it out by telling your mother that I'd just dropped by to apologise because my kid was sick and couldn't come – it was a pretty safe bet that someone wouldn't have shown – and she said, 'Oh, you must be little Sammy's father' and asked me in. I was going to leave immediately, but your father handed me a beer and started talking about something called baseball. Of course I didn't have a present for you . . .'"

"But you gave me a rose and told my mother to press it into a book so that I'd have it forever."

"You remember."

"Wait there. Don't move." She leapt from her chair and ran upstairs. There was a lot of noise from above – paper rattling, doors opening and closing, things being thrown about. She returned clutching several books to her chest, her face flushed and streaked with dust. She flopped down on the floor and spread them out in front of her. When Alan got up to join her, she told him to stay where he was or she'd scream. He sat back down.

She opened the first book, and then Alan saw that they weren't books at all; they were photo albums. He watched in silence as she flipped through the pages and then tossed it aside. She tossed three of them away before she found what she was looking for. She stared open-mouthed at the brittle yellow page and then she looked up at Alan. "I don't understand this," she said, turning her eyes back to the album and a faded black and white photograph stuck to the paper with thick, flaking paste. Someone had written in ink across the top: Cecily's 3rd birthday, August 2nd, 1951. There was her father, who'd been dead for ten years, young and smiling, holding out a bottle to another young man, tall and blonde and dressed like a gas station attendant. "I don't understand this at all." She pushed the album across the floor towards Alan. "You haven't changed one bit. You're even wearing the same clothes."

"Did you keep the rose?"

She walked over to a wooden cabinet and pulled out a slim hardback with the title, "*My First Reader*". She opened it and showed him the dried, flattened flower. "You're telling me the truth, aren't you?" she said. "This is all true. You risked everything to find me because we were meant to be together, and nothing, not even time itself, could keep us apart."

Alan nodded. There was a speech just like that in "The Love That Conquered Time".

"Bastard," she said.

Alan jumped. He didn't remember that part. "Pardon me?"

"Bastard," she said again. "You bastard!"

"I . . . I don't understand."

She got up and started to pace the room. "So you're the one, huh? You're 'Mister Right', Mister Happily Ever After, caring, compassionate and great in bed. And you decide to turn up now. Well, isn't that just great."

"Is something the matter?" Alan asked her.

"Is something the matter?" she repeated. "He asks me if something's the matter! I'll tell you what's the matter. I got married four weeks ago, you son of a bitch!"

"You're married?"

"That's what I said, isn't it?"

"But you can't be married. We were supposed to find perfect happiness together at a particular point in space that has always existed and always will. This ruins everything."

"All those years . . . all those years. I went through hell in high school, you know. I was the only girl in my class who didn't have a date for the prom. So where were you then, huh? While I was sitting alone at home, crying my goddamn eyes out? How about all those Saturday nights I spent washing my hair? And even worse, those nights I worked at Hastings' Bar serving drinks to salesmen pretending they don't have wives. Why couldn't you have been around then, when I needed you?"

"Well, I've only got the first five pages of the manual . . ." He walked over to her and put his hands on her shoulders. She didn't move away. He gently pulled her closer to him. She didn't resist. "Look," he said, "I'm sorry. I'm a real zarkhead. I've made a mess of everything. You're happily married, you never wrote the story . . . I'll just go back where I came from, and none of this will have ever happened."

"Who said I was happy?"

"But you just got married."

She pushed him away. "I got married because I'm thirty years old and figured I'd never have another chance. People do that, you know. They reach a certain age and they figure it's now or never . . . Damn you! If only you'd come when you were supposed to!"

"You're thirty? Matrix, in half an hour you've gone from a toddler to someone older than me." He saw the expression on her face, and mumbled an apology.

"Look," she said. "You're gonna have to go. My husband'll be back any minute."

"I know I have to leave. But the trouble is, that drebbing story was true! I took one look at your photo, and I knew that I loved you and I always had. Always. That's the way time works, you see. And even if this whole thing vanishes as the result of some paradox, I swear to you I won't forget. Some-

where there's a point in space that belongs to us. I know it."
He turned to go. "Good-bye, Cecily."

"Alan, wait! That point in space – I want to go there. Isn't
there anything we can do? I mean, you've got a time machine,
after all."

What an idiot, he thought. The solution's been staring me in
the face and I've been too blind to see it. "The machine!" He
ran down the front porch steps and turned around to see her
standing in the doorway. "I'll see you later," he told her. He
knew it was a ridiculous thing to say the minute he'd said it.
What he meant was, "I'll see you earlier."

Five men sat together inside a tent made of animal hide. The
land of their fathers was under threat, and they met in council
to discuss the problem. The one called Swiftly Running
Stream advocated war, but Foot Of The Crow was more
cautious. "The paleface is too great in number, and his
weapons give him an unfair advantage." Flying Bird suggested
that they smoke before speaking further.

Black Elk took the pipe into his mouth. He closed his eyes
for a moment and declared that the Great Spirit would give
them a sign if they were meant to go to war. As soon as he said
the word, "war", a paleface materialised among them. They all
saw him. The white man's body was covered in a strange
bright garment such as they had never seen, and he rode a
fleshless horse with silver bones. The vision vanished as
suddenly as it had appeared, leaving them with this message
to ponder: *Oops*.

There was no one home, so he waited on the porch. It was a
beautiful day, with a gentle breeze that carried the scent of
roses: certainly better than that smoke-filled teepee.

A woman appeared in the distance. He wondered if that was
her. But then he saw that it couldn't be, the woman's walk was
strange and her body was misshapen. She's pregnant, he
realised. It was a common thing in the days of over-popula-
tion, but he couldn't remember the last time he'd seen a
pregnant woman back home – it must have been years. She

looked at him questioningly as she waddled up the steps balancing two paper bags. Alan thought the woman looked familiar; he knew that face. He reached out to help her.

"Excuse me," he said. "I'm looking for Cecily Walker."

"My name's Walker," the woman told him. "But I don't know any Cecily."

Matrix, what a moron, Alan thought, wanting to kick himself. Of course he knew the woman; it was Cecily's mother, and if she was pregnant, it had to be 1948. "My mistake," he told her. "It's been a long day."

The smell of roses had vanished, along with the leaves on the trees. There was snow on the ground and a strong north-easterly wind. Alan set the thermostat on his jumpsuit accordingly and jumped off the bike.

"So it's you again," Cecily said ironically. "Another case of perfect timing." She was twenty pounds heavier and there were lines around her mouth and her eyes. She wore a heavy wool cardigan sweater over an oversized T-shirt, jeans, and a pair of fuzzy slippers. She looked him up and down. "You don't age at all, do you?"

"Please can I come in? It's freezing."

"Yeah, yeah. Come in. You like a cup of coffee?"

"You mean liquid caffeine? That'd be great."

He followed her into the living room and his mouth dropped open. The red sofa was gone, replaced by something that looked like a giant banana. The television was four times bigger and had lost the rabbit-ears. The floral wallpaper had been replaced by plain white walls not very different from those of his apartment. "Sit," she told him. She left the room for a moment and returned with two mugs, one of which she slammed down in front of him, causing a miniature brown tidal wave to splash across his legs.

"Cecily, are you upset about something?"

"That's a good one! He comes back after fifteen years and asks me if I'm upset."

"Fifteen years!" Alan sputtered.

"That's right. It's 1994, you bozo."

"Oh, darling, and you've been waiting all this time . . ."

"Like hell I have," she interrupted. "When I met you, back in 1979, I realised that I couldn't stay in that sham of a marriage for another minute. So I must have set some kind of a record for quickie marriage and divorce, by Danville standards, anyway. So I was a thirty-year-old divorcee whose marriage had fallen apart in less than two months, and I was back to washing my hair alone on Saturday nights. And people talked. Lord, how they talked. But I didn't care, because I'd finally met my soul-mate and everything was going to be all right. He told me he'd fix it. He'd be back. So I waited. I waited for a year. Then I waited two years. Then I waited three. After ten, I got tired of waiting. And if you think I'm going through another divorce, you're crazy."

"You mean you're married again?"

"What else was I supposed to do? A man wants you when you're forty, you jump at it. As far as I knew, you were gone forever."

"I've never been away, Cecily. I've been here all along, but never at the right time. It's that drebbing machine; I can't figure out the controls."

"Maybe Arnie can have a look at it when he gets in, he's pretty good at that sort of thing – what am I saying?"

"Tell me, did you ever write the story?"

"What's to write about? Anyway, what difference does it make? *Woman's Secrets* went bankrupt years ago."

"Matrix! If you never wrote the story, then I shouldn't even know about you. So how can I be here? Dammit, it's a paradox. And I wasn't supposed to cause any of those. Plus, I think I may have started an Indian war. Have you noticed any change in local history?"

"Huh?"

"Never mind. Look, I have an idea. When exactly did you get divorced?"

"I don't know; late '79. October, November, something like that."

"All right, that's what I'll aim for. November, 1979. Be waiting for me."

"How?"

"Good point. Okay, just take my word for it, you and me are going to be sitting in this room right here, right now, with one big difference: we'll have been married for fifteen years, okay?"

"But what about Arnie?"

"Arnie won't know the difference. You'll never have married him in the first place." He kissed her on the cheek. "I'll be back in a minute. Well, in 1979. You know what I mean." He headed for the door.

"Hold on," she said. "You're like the guy who goes out for a pack of cigarettes and doesn't come back for thirty years."

"What guy?"

"Never mind. I wanna make sure you don't turn up anywhere else. Bring the machine in here."

"Is that it?" she said one minute later.

"That's it."

"But it looks like a goddamn bicycle."

"Where do you want me to put it?"

She led him upstairs. "Here," she said. Alan unfolded the bike next to the bed. "I don't want you getting away from me next time," she told him.

"I don't have to get away from you now."

"You do. I'm married and I'm at least fifteen years older than you."

"Your age doesn't matter to me," Alan told her. "When I first fell in love with you, you'd been dead three hundred years."

"You really know how to flatter a girl, don't you? Anyway, don't aim for '79. I don't understand paradoxes, but I know I don't like them. If we're ever gonna get this thing straightened out, you must arrive before 1973, when the story is meant to be published. Try for '71 or '72. Now that I think about it, those were a strange couple of years for me. Nothing seemed real to me then. Nothing seemed worth bothering about, nothing mattered; I always felt like I was waiting for something. Day after day I waited, though I never knew what for."

She stepped back and watched him slowly turn a dial until he vanished. Then she remembered something.

How could she have ever have forgotten such a thing? She was eleven and she was combing her hair in front of her bedroom mirror. She screamed. When both her parents burst into the room and demanded to know what was wrong, she told them she'd seen a man on a bicycle. They nearly sent her to a child psychiatrist.

Damn that Alan, she thought. He's screwed up again.

The same room, different decor, different time of day. Alan blinked several times; his eyes had difficulty adjusting to the darkness. He could barely make out the shape on the bed, but he could see all he needed to. The shape was alone, and it was adult size. He leaned close to her ear. "Cecily," he whispered. "It's me."

He touched her shoulder and shook her slightly. He felt for a pulse. He switched on the bedside lamp, gazed down at a withered face framed by silver hair, and sighed. "Sorry, love," he said. He covered her head with a sheet, and sighed again.

He sat down on the bike and unfolded the printout. He'd get it right eventually.

SWEET, SAVAGE SORCERER

Esther Friesner

Arrows whizzed past her as Narielle drummed slender heels into the heaving sides of her faithful unicorn, Thunderwind. Her bosom rose and fell in perfect cadence with the noble steed's movements as the Black Tower of Burning Doom thrust its massive structure into view. Behind her, the sun was setting in a fiery ball, quenching its flames slowly, achingly, in the moist depths of the Lesser Sea of Northern Alraziah-le-Fethynauri'in-ebu-Korfiamminettash.

Bitterly, Narielle reflected that if her father's men had not stopped to ask directions to the sea, they would never have been caught with their lances down by Lord Eyargh's mercenaries.

Another thick shaft, flying closer than the rest, cut off her meditations and the pointed tip of her left ear. The elfin princess lifted her chin defiantly and raised herself in the stirrups to turn and shout bold yet elegant insults at her pursuers. Then Thunderwind carried her over the threshold of the Black Tower and she was safe . . . for the moment.

Lord Eyargh's mercenaries, cheated of their prey, milled about under the lone window of the Black Tower of Burning Doom and made a collective nuisance of themselves. Narielle leaned out from the unglazed casement and regarded them with haughty disdain. They shot more arrows at her, one of which lodged in the headboard of the large, comfortable bed behind her. Her bold heart stifled the urge to scream her courageous head off. Instead, she seized the handy velvet bell rope on the wall and pulled with firm resolve.

A dark-robed shadow detached itself from the depths of the tower room, strode past the startled elfin princess, paused only to sweep her from her feet in powerfully muscled arms and pitch her onto the large, comfortable bed where she narrowly missed squashing a sleeping cat.

A word of unknown and ecstatic sorcery was spoken out the window. From below, the vile shouts of Lord Eyargh's mercenaries abruptly changed to the peeping of downy baby chicks. The figure at the window smiled with grim amusement. He paused only long enough to release a tethered chicken hawk before turning his attention to his still-rebounding guest.

"Yes?" he said.

"You are the sorcerer of the Black Tower?" Narielle's throat contracted with an emotion she would long deny as anything more than astonishment, dubiety, and the need for a cool drink.

"Does that surprise you?" His voice was low, thrilling, more powerful than any she had ever heard, twisting her ever-more rapidly palpitating heart into a tight knot of unnamable confusion. His azure eyes probed the very depths of her soul with a bold disregard for the empty charade of elfin High Court etiquette. But there was a deep strain of irony in his words, as if his past life contained some unknown secret wound of which no one save himself knew, and whose carefully concealed pain had, if not poisoned, at least tainted the life of one outwardly so strong and unassailable.

"No," she lied. She got off the bed fast.

He laughed; once, shortly. But in that single syllable of supposed merriment, Narielle read many unspoken sorrows. She could not lie to him. He had suffered enough.

"That is . . . I mean . . . you're so young."

Now his eyes, bluer than the magic sword Narielle concealed beneath her voluminous green velvet skirts sewn with pearls and trimmed with gold lace, narrowed. "I am," he replied. It was a challenge.

The elfin princess was not one to let any man ramp all over her. Hers was a proud spirit. She lifted her chin defiantly and took command of the conversation. "The name of Brandon of the Black Tower has reached my father, Lord Vertig of the Silver Unicorn, king of the elves of the Green Woodlands. Even as we speak, he is besieged in the White Castle of the Golden Arches by his mortal enemy, Lord Eyargh of the Red Sword. By a ruse, I and one hundred fifty of my father's men managed to slip through the enemy lines, dispatched in search of you, hoping to enlist the already legendary aid of your sorcerous powers in our cause."

"I know," he said.

"Do you?" She could not conceal her astonishment.

"I *am* a sorcerer. Perhaps you have heard of crystal balls?" His finely formed yet generous mouth contorted itself into an expression at once fascinating and unreadable. His hand strayed upward to touch her injured extremity. "You've been wounded." A strange catch wrenched all sarcasm from his voice.

Startled as much by the unexpected concern in the young wizard's words as by the almost electrical shock that coursed through her every fiber at this lightest contact of his flesh to her flesh, Narielle replied, "It's nothing."

"Nothing?" Behind his simple repetition of her very word, she thought she detected a new sense of respect for herself as a person in her own right.

His breath burned hot and fierce across the nape of her neck as he murmured a healing spell over her ear. Confusion fluttered in her breast like a caged gryphon. She stepped away from him, saying, "While you waste your magic on what is no more than a scratch, elves perish!"

As she spoke of her people's distress, she could not forbid her eyes from straying the length of the young enchanter's person. Dark, unruly hair fell in a shock of thick, black waves just above his cerulean eyes. When he smiled, the perfect whiteness of his teeth showed in even more startling contrast to his sunbronzed skin. His nose hinted at past hurts borne with nobility and forbearance. The neck of his necromancer's robe was open, revealing the smooth, enticing expanse of his broad chest. The thin material could not effectively conceal the incredible size, the almost terrifying bulk, the barely restrained thrust and untamed, overwhelming power of his shoulders.

Fortunately, there was a full-length mirror on the wall opposite Narielle, which allowed her the leisure to contemplate her own fiery red hair, emerald green eyes, and lithe, slender, graceful yet self-assured form.

Brandon of the Black Tower chuckled deep in his throat. How did he dare to mock her? She hated him! She would always hate him! Then he spoke: "Such fire. And what will you give me in exchange for my help . . . my lady?" There was no mistaking the scorn in his voice. She hated him still more wildly, yet more passionately! "Gold?" She couldn't stand him!

Narielle's reply was as cold and formal as wounded pride and the narrowly repressed desire to slap the sorcerer's grinning face could make it: "No."

"No?" His craggy eyebrows rose.

"On my honor as a highborn elfin princess and virgin. My father's men carried the gold for your fee. When Lord Eyargh's men attacked my father's men, the chest fell over a cliff into the sea, and the men of the Vegas Sands made off with it."

"So you have no chest." Now he no longer smiled. "You speak much of men, my lady . . . for one who calls herself a virgin."

She would kick him in the shins and tell her noble father on him! "Do you doubt the evidence of your eyes, my lord Brandon? I rode into your tower on a unicorn."

"It is well known by the lowest village idiot that elfin women can fake their unicorns." The ancient pain rose ever nearer to the surface of the young sorcerer's emotions and threatened to pierce through. In that instant, with a lurch of her own heart, Narielle understood the long-past but never forgotten betrayal that had embittered Brandon's proud soul.

Who had she been, that other elf-maiden who had so cruelly deceived him? Why had she done it? What wouldn't Narielle give to get her hands on the little point-eared bitch and teach her some manners?

Compassion for Brandon welled up in Narielle's bosom, inflating it nicely. It was only her own fierce, overweening, foolish pride that prevented her from taking him into her arms at once and soothing away all his past hurts as if he were no more than a little boy, or a wrongfully whipped puppy. Yet even as she snapped harsh words at him, her heart swelled with the dreadful ache of longing to cuddle him.

"Then perhaps you had better hire a consulting village idiot!" She tossed her glorious mane of hair, her nostrils flaring, and pawed the ground with grand bravado. "Even he would be able to tell you that the virtue of the ladies of the royal house of Lord Vertig of the Silver Unicorn of the White Castle of the Golden Arches of the Green Woodlands is one that we protect with steel!" So saying, she drew the full, awe-inspiring length of the impossibly hard enchanted blade from the clinging embrace of the soft scabbard beneath her skirts. With a wild, untrammeled exultation to feel her hand close around the imposing diameter of that wondrous hilt once more, Narielle realized just how deeply she loved her sword.

Brandon looked mildly amused. He made a gesture whose mystic significance was known to few wizards. Narielle watched with mounting horror as her blade shuddered, then drooped like sunstruck celery. The enchanter took it from her nerveless hand and flung it across the room where it bounced off the large, comfortable bed and scared the cat.

"You have no gold, yet you would have my services," he said. "Very well, you shall have them. And in exchange, I shall have –"

"What?" The elfin princess' bosom lifted defiantly.

"– you."

With a hoarse ejaculation he crushed her to his chest. She felt his wizardhood pressing against her thigh and could not tell whether the emotions also now rising within her were so much fear as hesitantly joyous anticipation of what was to come. Roughly, he tore aside her golden lace, stripping the lush green velvet from her heaving shoulders in one masterful motion. Pearls popped and caromed off everything in sight. The cat yelped and leaped off the large, comfortable bed.

After he returned from burying the unicorn, he knelt like the meanest supplicant beside the pile of new-mown hay which had housed so much recent passion. "Can you ever forgive me . . . Narielle?"

Her eyes brimmed with the ebbing tide of complete fulfillment and a tender fondness for the repentant sorcerer. "Forgive you, Brandon? For making a *real* elf of me? Oh, you are more magician than any of those wand-waving charlatans!" Playfully, he plucked fragrant straws from her tousled hair and threw them at the cat who was back on the large, comfortable, conventional, unromantic, deliberately overlooked bed.

"Forgive me for doubting you, my love. And about the unicorn –"

She laughed the rich, full-throated laugh of newly, sweetly acquired wisdom. "Thunderwind was a loyal beast, but in his heart he understood that this day would come. I think he was glad it came quickly and painlessly."

But Brandon was not assuaged. Unaccustomed anguish filled his sapphire eyes. With a harsh sob he buried his face between the soft, welcoming curves of her two hands and implored her pardon for ever having doubted her. "It is you who are the enchanter, Narielle!" he gasped. "You have taken a blind, headstrong fool and made a man of him!"

"Did I? Good. Now, about Daddy . . ."

Brandon of the Black Tower raised his large yet sensitive hands to a sky no less blue than his eyes and turned Lord Vertig's foes into frogs. The siege was lifted, although the transformed Lord Eyargh hung around the moat defiantly. He was finally routed when Lord Vertig dispatched a contingent of net-wielding victualers to scoop up those of the enemy they could catch. That night there was great feasting and rejoicing in the White Castle of the Golden Arches.

Laughing, Narielle attempted to force another deep-fried nugget between her beloved's lips.

"What *is* that?" he asked, returning her joyous laughter a hundredfold.

"Batrachian bits," she replied, smearing sweet-and-sour nectar down the front of his chest on purpose for future reference. "Try them; they're delicious."

"Not half so delicious as you," he murmured, and as the undeniable surge of their mutual attraction and respect mounted inexorably, he dragged her beneath the banqueting table and they missed dessert.

THE POWER
AND THE GORY

James Bibby

The midday sun beat fiercely down on the city of Koumas with the force of a blacksmith's hammer. It beat down on the massive encircling walls that protected the city from the ravages of nomadic barbarian tribes. It beat down on the houses, shops, taverns and temples. It beat down on the people and animals that thronged the labyrinth of streets. But most of all it beat down on the head of Constable (and ex-Detective-Inspector) Heighway as he stood on point duty at the junction of Market Street and Westgate.

Wearily, Heighway held up one hand in the universally recognised gesture for "stop" and the torrent of carts, horses, wagons and livestock that surged along Flensing Lane straggled to an untidy halt. Then he beckoned with his other hand and the seething mass of traffic that waited impatiently in Westgate surged forward and began to flow past him. For a moment he felt a slight stirring of interest as a brewer's dray laden with wooden barrels of beer creaked by, but it was followed by a seemingly endless flock of alarmas[1] herded by three drovers and Heighway drifted off into thoughts of self-recrimination.

---

1 Alarmas are woolly-fleeced, long-necked pack animals from the southern mountains. Nervous and highly-strung, they tend to panic easily, stampeding and emitting their warning call, a high-pitched scream that has been described as sounding like a banshee having a nervous breakdown.

Well, this served him right. It was his own fault that he was here, slowly poaching in his own sweat. Would he *never* bloody learn? His doctor had told him repeatedly that regular consumption of large quantities of beer was bad for him, and so it had proved. He had consumed a vast amount at the Police Station's winter solstice party and as a result had ended up standing in front of Superintendent Weird, poking him repeatedly in the chest with one finger whilst telling him exactly why so many people didn't like him.

Now, if there's one thing a police Superintendent doesn't like, it's being told by a drunken subordinate that he is grossly overweight and has a severe body-odour problem . . . especially when it happens to be true. That in itself would have only merited a severe dressing-down. Unfortunately, Heighway had followed this by being sick down the Superintendent's trousers. The following day he had been summoned to Weird's office, where the misery of the worst hangover in history had been compounded by reduction to the ranks and transfer to the Traffic Division.

Heighway winced at the memory and raised one hand to waft at a fly, momentarily forgetting where he was. Immediately, the pent-up traffic waiting in Flensing Lane surged forwards and a dozen horse-drawn carts ploughed straight into the midst of the flock of alarmas, to be followed by a large wagon pulled by four bellowing oxen. Several alarmas skittered sideways, screaming with fear, and Heighway ran for safety, his hands clasped over his ears against the noise. Reaching the cover of a shop doorway, he turned just in time to see another large dray collide with the ox-cart and watched in horror as a wheel broke off, the cart tipped sideways and beer barrels slid over the side to splinter on the hard cobbles of the street.

Within seconds, the junction was a clogged and solid mass of screaming, neighing, and bellowing animals, shouting and cursing humans, and immobile vehicles. For a moment or two Heighway considered trying to rectify the situation, but then the pull of duty was overwhelmed by a deep and all-consuming fatalism. Suddenly he knew without doubt that he'd reached the end of his police career. There would be no coming back from this monumental cock-up. Well, there was no point in waiting for the axe to fall. Far better to self-destruct instead.

With a feeling that was close to relief, Heighway turned his back on the chaos and walked away in the direction of his favourite tavern. Now that the decision had been taken, two things remained to be done. He needed to drink several pints of good beer and he needed to draft his letter of resignation.

An hour later, Heighway was snugly installed at a table in a dark corner of *The Green Manticore*, sipping at his second pint of Old Pustule's best bitter and staring blankly at the sheet of notepaper in front of him. He had got as far as "Dear Superintendent Weird, It is with great sorrow that . . ." and then inspiration had deserted him. He was just wondering whether a third pint might help when the sound of voices raised in anger caught his attention, and Heighway looked up to see Inspector (and ex-sergeant) Raasay easing his way through the crowded tavern. The angry voices belonged to the other customers, who were objecting in no uncertain terms to the fact that Raasay was leading a large horse through the crowded pub.

Heighway shook his head tiredly. He had known some pretty dim policemen in his time, but Raasay was in a class of his own. Until Heighway's demotion, Raasay had been his sergeant, a rank that he had attained solely because he was Superintendent Weird's nephew. He did have a few virtues, such as a fierce and unquestioning loyalty to Heighway and an ability to carry out orders (as long as they didn't contain words with more than three syllables), but during their long association Heighway had looked in vain for even the merest hint of intelligence. Nothing that Raasay did should have come as a surprise, but to lead a large and fully saddled horse into a crowded pub was setting a new low even for him.

"Ah, there you are, sir," he said, with a relieved smile. "When I saw you weren't on point duty I thought I might find you here."

"You're my superior officer now, sir," Heighway reminded him. "You don't have to call me sir any more."

"Yes, I know, sir," Raasay replied, uncomfortably.

There was an awkward pause. Heighway knew he ought to stand up in the presence of a superior officer, but somehow he couldn't help feeling that when applied to Raasay the word "superior" made a mockery of the language. Raasay, on the other hand, could not quite comprehend that he now out-ranked Heighway, and so he stood awkwardly at attention while the horse nodded its head and chewed at the bit in its mouth. Heighway looked at the intelligence in its eyes and at the dumb, sheep-like blankness in Raasay's, and wondered which of the two would make the best inspector.

"Can I ask why you've brought a horse into the pub, sir?" he asked Raasay.

"Yes sir. It's because Uncle Billy . . . er, I mean, Super-intendent Weird, sir, he told me to, sir. He said I was to collect the waiting mount from the stables and bring it straight to you. Then he said you were to get your bony ass over to the Commissioner's office at once, sir. He's waiting there now, sir." Raasay paused and looked at the horse doubtfully. "Although this looks far more like a horse than an ass, sir."

"The Commissioner? Hell, I must *really* be in trouble."

"And it doesn't look very bony to me, either, sir."

"Don't worry about it. Sir."

There was another awkward pause while Heighway sa-voured some more of his beer. Raasay began to look agitated.

"He did say you were to be quick, sir. In fact he said he wants you there yesterday, although I don't know how you're going to do that. And he's in a foul mood, sir."

Heighway raised his glass again to drain it, and as he did so the horse lifted its tail and deposited several dollops of fresh manure onto the tavern floor. Immediately, there was an outraged shout from behind the bar.

"Oh, by the Gods!" Heighway muttered. Standing, he snatched the horse's reins from Raasay's hand.

"Stay here and clean this mess up," he told him, then

turned the horse around and led it towards the door. "Please," he added over his shoulder as an afterthought. "Sir."

As he made his way past the bar, the landlord gestured angrily.

"We don't allow dumb animals in this bar," he complained.

"Don't worry," Heighway told him "He's on his way just as soon as he's cleaned up after the horse . . ."

Algophilos, the Commissioner of Police, was one of the most powerful men in Koumas. He was the commander not only of the police force but also of the City Guard. To be called to his office could be a sign of great honour or responsibility, or it could mean the instant end of your career. Or of your life, if you'd managed to upset him enough. So, as Heighway urged the horse into a trot, there was a tight knot of apprehension in his stomach. He wondered just how Superintendent Weird had heard about the chaos at the road junction so quickly. And why order him to the Commissioner's office? It didn't make sense.

And then, for the first time since he'd been demoted, Heighway's brain began to function properly again. You don't send a horse for someone if you're going to sack them! And there was a sense of urgency about all of this. Heighway was *needed*, and that could only mean there was a case that demanded his particular skills. All at once Heighway felt his spirits soaring and, with a grin on his face, he urged his horse into a gallop, clung on for dear life and fairly pelted through the twisting streets.

The system of detection that Superintendent Weird preferred was very simple. When a crime occurred, his detectives would spring into action, arrest and interrogate a few innocent bystanders and then torture them until a full confession of guilt had been extracted from one of them. The advantage of this method was that it resulted in a rapid, one hundred percent success rate in solving crimes. The disadvantage, or so Heighway felt, was that it very rarely resulted in catching the actual perpetrator of the crime. He preferred the method of accurate, painstaking investigation that often (but not always) resulted in finding out who actually did it and then arresting them. It was slow, but as the Superintendent had discovered once or twice before, sometimes it was the only method that would suffice.

Heighway cantered his horse along the driveway that led to the Commissioner's offices, which stood in parkland at the top of one of Koumas's ten hills. He could see Weird pacing impatiently backwards and forwards beside a police carriage that waited near the front steps, and he hauled his horse to a ragged halt and swung untidily down.

"At last. At last," grumbled Weird. "You took your time."

"I, er . . . well, there was a bit of a traffic jam down by Flensing Lane."

"Right. Well, you're back on the force with your old rank." Weird was looking about as happy as an orc at closing time.

"Thank you, sir."

"Don't thank me, thank the Commissioner. He asked specifically for you." Weird jerked his thumb at the imposing door at the top of the steps. "He'll brief you himself. But keep me informed of your progress."

"Yes, sir."

"Right." Weird turned and clambered into the waiting carriage, then poked his head out of the window. "I don't like you, Heighway. You're rude, you're insubordinate and you're not half as clever as you think you are. So don't make any fatal mistakes on this case, because I'll make sure that's what they *will* be for you. Fatal."

The carriage moved off with a jerk and Weird cursed resoundingly as his head banged against the window frame. Heighway watched as it rattled off down the driveway, then trotted happily up the steps. Despite the Superintendent's threat, it felt good to be on an active case again.

The urgency of the case was brought home to him when he announced his presence to the uniformed flunky in the entrance hall. Before, he had always been kept waiting to see the Commissioner for anything up to two hours, but this time he was whisked straight through several corridors and ante-chambers until he found himself standing in front of the Commissioner's desk.

Algophilos was a small, slim, silver-haired man with thin, pointed features who radiated strength and efficiency. Despite his blue uniform, at first glance he seemed kind and serene, and it was only when you gazed into his sly, calculating eyes that you got a glimpse of the cold heart within. He looked like a priest with a touch of weasel in him. He gestured for Heighway to sit down and fixed the reinstated Inspector with his gaze.

"I have a matter that I wish you to investigate," he said. "It is of the utmost . . . delicacy. Do you understand me?"

"I can keep my mouth shut, sir."

"Good." The Commissioner leant back in his chair and steepled his fingertips together. "It so happens that I am a member of a certain . . . club. It is a private establishment, a place where in my off-duty hours I occasionally go for a little rest and relaxation. All the members have an . . . interest, shall we say, in a certain form of relaxation and enjoyment that could, were it to become common knowledge, cause them problems in their careers, should they be in a position of power and authority . . ."

The Commissioner's verbosity was beginning to get on Heighway's nerves. "You're being blackmailed," he cut in.

"Exactly. Most succinctly put."

May I ask what the name of this establishment is?"

"You may. It is called Club Nefarioso."

"What? That den of perv . . . er . . . I mean . . ." Heighway fumbled for the right words whilst Algophilos watched him with the same steady gaze. "Well, isn't it a bit risky joining a club like that, sir? For a man in your position, that is. Someone was bound to recognize you."

"One of the attractions of the club was complete anonymity."

"How does that work, then?"

"All the members wear hoods."

Heighway suppressed a shudder of revulsion. "So how come someone is able to blackmail you, sir?" he enquired.

"That is one of the things I want you to find out." Algophilos opened a drawer in his desk and took out a small roll of parchment, which he passed to Heighway. "I was handed this when I went to the club three nights ago."

"Who by?"

"Daniel, the barman. It was given to him by another member who was, of course, anonymous."

Heighway unrolled the parchment. The message inside was printed in tiny letters, in a neat, well-educated hand. *My Dear Commissioner*, it read, *I was most surprised to discover you are a member of this club. I am sure that this is something you would prefer not to come to the attention of a wider audience. I will contact you again soon with a suggestion as to how this can be prevented.*

"You see why I need your particular talents," Algophilos went on. "It is imperative that the right man is arrested. I have assigned Sergeant Raasay to assist you . . ."

"*Sergeant* Raasay?"

"As of this moment." Algophilos selected one of the parchments that lay on his desk, signed it and handed it to Heighway. "When I asked for you yesterday, Superintendent Weird told me that you were no longer a detective and sent Raasay instead. But I feel that an inspector who gets a nosebleed when someone uses a word such as 'concatenation' is not really up to the task. Now, is there anything else you need?"

"Constable Kratavan, sir. Raasay is good at carrying out orders, but Kratavan has brains."

"Right."

"And I'll need to visit the club, sir. Probably this evening."

"I understand. If you need to enter the more . . . restricted areas, tell them that you'd like to see Wendy."

"Wendy. Right."

"And, inspector, I feel you would do better to operate under cover, as it were. It may be necessary for you to don certain . . . robes."

"In other words, I need to dress up like the punters. I understand, sir

"Good. There's just one final thing you need to understand." Algophilos leant forwards and rested his arms on the desk. All at once his eyes seemed colder and darker than a midwinter night. "You are to succeed. Failure will have the most unpleasant results, for both of us."

Heighway swallowed audibly, then nodded. "You can rely on me, sir," he said with conviction. "I won't let you down."

Heighway spent the entire journey from the Commissioner's offices to the police station trying to concentrate on the case and not worry about what would happen to him if he messed up. Reaching the station's stable yard, he left the horse with one of the grooms and went through a side door and up the narrow, winding, rear staircase that led to the top floor, where his old office was situated.

He paused outside the door and looked at a small nameplate that had been screwed in at an untidy angle. It said INSPEKTER RAASAY in badly carved letters. Raising his eyes to heaven, Heighway opened the door and marched in.

His office was just as he had left it months earlier. His desk was an untidy jumble of parchments and old newspapers, the clamour and smells of the baking city drifted up through the open window, and Raasay was standing by the fireplace with a vacant look on his face. The only difference was that this time he was holding a battered iron bucket that was full of horse manure.

"Raasay, what are you doing with that bucket?" Heighway enquired.

"You told me to clean up the horse poo, sir," Raasay told him.

"Yes, but . . . oh, never mind. Just get rid of it."

Raasay took a couple of steps forward and, before Heighway could stop him, emptied the bucket out of the window. Angry howls of protest echoed up from below.

Heighway shook his head tiredly and then pulled out the parchment that Algophilos had signed and gave it to Raasay.

"Sorry about this, Raasay," he told him, "but it rather looks as though they've turned you back into a sergeant."

"Really, sir? Oh, good!"

Heighway stared at him. "You sound pleased."

"I am, sir! I've really missed the Sergeant's mess." Raasay lowered his voice. "They're a funny lot in the officers' lounge, sir, begging your pardon."

"Yes, well, you can go and break the good news to your Uncle Billy. And then dig out D.C. Kratavan and tell him he's working for me again. I want the pair of you to meet me in *The Wyvern* at six o'clock."

The Club Nefarioso stood in Blind Hop Lane, a quiet, up-market street near the Elvish Quarter. It was a large, detached house with its own tree-lined grounds, and a passer-by could easily have mistaken it for the private mansion of a rich merchant.

Heighway paused in the road outside and turned to Raasay and Kratavan. Dusk was beginning to fall.

"Right, gentlemen," he said in lowered tones," what we have here is a high-class knocking-shop. Half the toffs of this city have probably been through these portals at one time or another. So the watchword is discretion."

Raasay looked confused and opened his mouth to ask a question, but Heighway cut him short.

"It means keep your mouth shut and don't upset anyone," he told Raasay. "On second thoughts, Sergeant, I think you'd better stay out here on surveillance . . ." Heighway held up a hand to forestall Raasay again. "I mean keep watch. Hide in the bushes and don't come out until I say so. Kratavan, come with me."

Raasay sidled into the bushes, and Heighway and Kratavan walked up the driveway past a fountain where water poured forth from an extremely rude statue. Heighway rapped sharply on the front door, which was opened instantly by a uniformed doorman, and they entered to find themselves in a long, wood-panelled hallway. Ahead of them was a pair of ornate double-doors beyond which they could hear the hum of conversation.

"Here we go," muttered Heighway, and then the double-doors opened and they found themselves in a room some forty feet long, with a high ceiling, walls covered with exotic tapestries and a carpet with a pile so deep you could lose a shoe in it. Along one wall were alcoves with semi-circular couches and low marble tables, and at the far end was a small marble bar behind which a white-shirted barman was briskly mixing cocktails from the hundreds of bottles that lined the shelves behind him.

There were maybe twenty or so other people in the room. Six or seven were the wealthy merchant type; elderly, stout men with expensive clothes and that annoyingly complacent look that only the truly rich acquire. Each was reclining on a couch with an expensive drink in one hand and an incredibly beautiful girl in the other, and there were more beautiful girls standing near the bar. They were all dressed in the most expensive but revealing costumes, and they eyed Heighway and Kratavan as they walked to the bar with an almost predatory interest.

Heighway leant on the cool marble bar-top and exhaled slowly, then watched the barman as he finished mixing a pair of vivid green concoctions that had more fruit in them than a monkey's lunch. Popping a couple of tiny paper umbrellas into them, the barman handed them to one of the girls and then turned his politely enquiring gaze upon the inspector.

"Yes, sir?" he asked. "What would you like?"

"I'd like, er . . . I'd like to see Wendy," Heighway replied.

"Ah, right, sir. Come this way, please."

Heighway turned to find that one of the girls had taken hold of Kratavan's arm and was whispering something into his ear. Kratavan's mouth was gaping and he had turned bright red.

"Kratavan!" said Heighway, sharply. "Leave the nice lady alone and come here."

Kratavan dragged his attention away from the girl. He was trembling slightly.

"Sir," he muttered, "are we on expenses?"

"No, we're not! Now come on!"

The barman was standing in front of a door to the right of the bar. He knocked sharply three times, and a small grille in the door slid open.

"Attali, these two gentlemen would like to see Wendy," he said.

The grille slid shut and the door opened. Heighway and Kratavan stepped through and it closed quickly behind them, abruptly shutting out the light from the other room.

They found themselves in a room so dark they could hardly see, but as their eyes became accustomed to the gloom they could just make out the shadowy figure of yet another beautiful girl. She was holding two baskets, each of which contained dark clothing of some kind. Behind her, a bank of what appeared to be lockers lined the wall, and to their right were dark cubicles.

"Gentlemen," she breathed huskily, handing them each a basket, "if you would just like to change into these, then you may follow me through into Wendy's room."

"What the . . ." began Kratavan, but Heighway cut in quickly.

"Yes, er, Attali," he said. "Whatever you say."

"Good boy," Attali whispered, then a door at the far end of the room opened and closed, and she was gone.

Five minutes later they had changed. The clothes were made of black rubber and consisted of skin-tight trousers and vest that made any sort of movement strangely uncomfortable and a close-fitting hood with holes for nose and eyes. Heighway could hardly see anything, especially as the room was still nearly dark, and he began to realize how difficult it would be for members to recognize each other.

"Come on, Kratavan," he said. "Let's get this over with."

They staggered across to the door. Taking a deep breath, Heighway opened it and then stopped dead. He'd been expecting something a little on the sordid side, but this was far worse than he'd imagined.

It was a large room that had obviously been decorated by somebody with a bit of a thing about dungeons. Flickering torches burned in sconces on the bare, brick walls, the floor was of large stone slabs and the vaulted stone ceiling was mildewed and cobwebbed. To their right the walls were hung with chains, fetters and manacles in which several rubber-clad, hooded men were confined, and a number of racks and shelves held whips, scourges and other such items. In the centre of the room was an assortment of instruments of torture such as racks and pillories, and in the far wall were two doors with signs on them, one saying "Nursery" and the other "Disciplinarium". Incongruously, along the wall to their left ran a well-stocked bar tended by a half-orc[2] in a smart black jacket.

There were several beautiful girls here, too, all dressed in skin-tight rubber, high-heeled boots and small masks. Their customers were dressed in the same type of clothing as Heighway and Kratavan, to which one or two had added their own distinguishing touches. There was one large, fat man in particular who was manacled to the wall and who had cut away the crotch of his trousers to allow his private parts to hang freely.

Heighway eyed him with distaste. "That reminds me," he muttered to Kratavan. "I must get my watch back from the pawnbroker's."

"Sir," whispered Kratavan, who had been staring in the direction of the bar, "I think I recognize that barman. We've done him a few times for pick-pocketing."

Heighway dragged his attention away from the large man. "Well, well, well," he muttered. "Danny the Dip. What's he doing here? Kratavan, stay put and keep an eye open. I'm going to have a word with our Danny."

The barman looked up enquiringly as Heighway lurched to the bar.

"Yes, sir, what will it be?"

"It will be six months inside if you don't give me a few answers, Danny my boy," Heighway growled in a low voice.

"What the . . ." stammered Danny. "Who . . . ?"

---

2 Half-orcs are usually the result of a liaison between a human male and an orc female. The reason for this is that, whereas most women are far too sensible to have anything to do with orcs, many is the human male who, after a night of heavy drinking, has woken up next morning with a crippling hangover to find that the vision of loveliness he seduced the previous night is lying beside him and in reality has green skin, fangs and a contented smile.

Heighway glanced around and then peeled back the lower portion of his mask to reveal himself to the barman.

"Mister Heighway! I should have known! Half the police force must come to this place."

"I'm not here for fun, Danny. I need some answers. Someone has been blackmailing an important officer, and you've been passing on the blackmail notes."

"I didn't know what was in the note, honest, Mister Heighway!" Danny looked round the room frantically and then lowered his voice to a whisper. "I can't talk here, it's too dangerous. I'll meet you later, when I finish work. The Weyr Inn. Ten o'clock."

Heighway nodded, then reached over the bar, grabbed the barman by the front of his jacket and hauled him forwards.

"Don't let me down, Danny. I'm not enjoying this case and I could get *very* angry with somebody."

"I won't, Mister Heighway, I promise."

Heighway released the frightened half-orc, then turned away from the bar and walked back to Kratavan. His body felt clammy inside the uncomfortable rubber, and the smell of stale sweat and bad body-odour that permeated the room was becoming overpowering.

"Come on, Kratavan," he said. "Let's get out of here. I need a beer like I've never needed one before . . ."

Five uncomfortable, embarrassing minutes later and they stood outside the club, breathing in the warm evening air whilst Heighway tried to get his heart to slow down.

"I don't believe it!" he gasped. "I've never been so embarrassed in my life! Never! I mean . . ."

Words failed him. Kratavan tried not to smile.

"I think that that Attali likes you, sir," he said, innocently.

"*Likes* me? Good grief! When she asked me if I wanted a hand I thought she meant with taking off the rubber vest! I didn't know she was going to do *that*!"

Shaking his head, Heighway marched off down the path, then paused to look round.

"Now, where's that idiot Raasay got to?" he muttered. "Raasay! RAASAY!"

"Sir?" came a muffled voice from the undergrowth.

"Where are you?"

"Here, sir."

There was a short pause while nothing happened.

"What the hell are you doing, man?" Heighway hissed.

"Hiding, sir. You told me to hide in the bushes and not come out until you said so, sir."

"Oh, good grief . . . look, Kratavan and I are going to the Weyr Inn. You might as well stay there and keep an eye on this place . . ."

Raasay's head emerged from inside a large bush. He looked upset. His face was muddy and he had a big, black spider hanging from one ear.

"Sir . . ." he began.

"And if Danny the Dip leaves here, follow him," Heighway continued. "Make sure he joins us at the Weyr."

"But sir!" Raasay protested. "There's a dirty big snake in here with me!"

"It has my sympathy. Just do as you're told, sergeant. That's an order."

"Yes, sir."

Raasay subsided grumpily into the bush with his spider and Heighway set off down the road with Kratavan beside him.

"There's something about this case that doesn't add up," Heighway mused as Kratavan set their third pints of Gobbo's Pearly Light Ale down on the table in front of him. "Oh, thanks, Kratavan . . . I mean, why should someone want to blackmail the Commissioner? They're all filthy rich in that club, anyway. And young Danny was very scared. I mean, I know I came on a bit heavy, but I'm not *that* frightening. Was anyone watching when I spoke to him?"

"The big bloke with the dangly bits was taking an interest. But maybe he . . ."

Kratavan was interrupted as the door flew open and a

uniformed patrolman burst in, looked around wildly and then ran across to their table.

"Inspector Heighway, sir!" he gasped. "Sergeant Raasay said to come quickly! Someone in the club has been murdered, sir!"

Danny the Dip lay on the cold stone floor of the beer cellar near a large white sink. His sightless eyes stared up towards the ceiling and his mouth gaped open. His shirt and his hair were soaking wet, and his face had a sheen of water upon it.

Heighway sighed and turned to Sergeant Raasay, who was standing beside a stack of beer barrels. He was wearing the same type of rubber trousers and vest that Heighway had experienced earlier, and he was hopping from one foot to the other and seething with indignation. Nearby stood Kratavan with one of the Club Nefarioso's hostesses.

"Right, said Heighway. "Tell me again, sergeant."

"I was on watch like you said, sir, when all of a sudden this screaming starts from round the back. So I rushed round and found the beer cellar door was open." Raasay pointed to the wooden door at the end of the cellar, which was still gaping open to the night. "I ran in and found one of the young ladies screaming, sir, and Danny was draped over the sink with his head rammed into the glass-washer. So I pulled him out, but he was dead, sir, and then I sent this young lady to find a patrolman and told him to fetch you, sir."

"You did well, Raasay. Now . . ."

"And then I went through there into the club, sir . . ." Raasay indicated another door, behind him. "And it was like a big dungeon, and this odd man dressed in rubber told me to put on these clothes . . ."

"Yes, I . . ."

"And you'd said to do what I was told, sir," Raasay went on indignantly, "and so I did, and then he told me to hit him with that whip, sir, and then another man told me to bend over a big table, and . . ."

"Yes, yes, I know!" Heighway interjected. "I'm sorry, Sergeant, but you were only supposed to follow *my* orders."

"But he . . ."

"I'm sorry!" Heighway interjected again. "Here, Kratavan, you'd better help the Sergeant get changed and take him home. He's had a nasty experience. Meet me back at the station later."

Kratavan led the still-babbling Raasay off through the door into the club with the hostess following concernedly, and Heighway looked down at Danny's body. Presumably he'd opened the door and let the killer in, which meant it could be anybody.

At that moment a familiar elderly, black-clad figure entered through the door from outside. It was Madame Min, the police pathomancer. In one hand she was carrying what looked like a large cage covered in a black cloth, from which came a gentle clucking. In the other hand she held the small black bag in which she kept all her magical paraphernalia. Heighway groaned inwardly. He had always felt that there should be a more scientific method of investigating the means of death than the spells and flummery employed by a pathomancer.

"Okay, Heighway," she greeted him gruffly, dumping the cage on the floor. "What have you got for me?"

"Pretty straightforward, this one, Min," he told her. "Not much for you to do. Someone drowned Danny the barman here in his own sink."

"Nonsense, man. I can sense his spirit already, and I can tell you one thing. He wasn't drowned. No, judging by the aura of pain, I'd say poison was nearer the mark."

"Oh, come on, Min, he was found with his head wedged into the glass-washer!"

"Doesn't mean that's what killed him. Well, we'll soon find out. Best get on with the post mortem."

Min took a small, sharp knife from her bag and knelt down by the corpse. Heighway watched with surprise, for Min's usual methods involved candles, incense and incantations.

"You're always on at me to be more scientific," she told him as she pulled the corpse's shirt up. "Well, I've come up with a new method. Watch."

Heighway stared with horrified fascination as she made an incision in the pale abdomen, and then turned away, revolted.

"Great God, Min!" he complained. "Do you have to?"

"Can't make an omelette without breaking eggs. Now, we need to find the stomach . . . ah, here we are! We make an incision, so . . . then we remove some of the contents . . . and . . ."

An excited clucking started up and Heighway turned back in surprise to find that Min had removed the black cover from the cage. Inside, four scrawny chickens were pecking ravenously at a small pile of something horrible that she had dropped into it, whilst the pathomancer wiped her bloody hands on a towel.

"What the hell are they doing?"

"They're eating some of his stomach contents. The last things he ate and drank."

"But why . . . ?"

"Just wait. Ah, now look!"

One of the chickens had stopped pecking and was making tiny retching noises. Then, one by one, the others joined it.

"You see?" Min was literally hopping up and down with excitement. "All four of them are being sick!"

"I'm not surprised! I'd be sick myself!"

"No, they have strong stomachs, do chickens. One of them, maybe, but all four? No, that has to be poison. Strong stuff, too."

"Are you absolutely sure, Min?"

"You can bet your life on it, matey."

Heighway turned round as the door opened and the hostess came back into the room.

"Your friends have gone, inspector," she told him in a voice that sounded strangely familiar.

"Right. Thank you, miss . . . er . . ."

"Attali."

"Attali. Right . . . oh! Sorry! I, er, I didn't recognize you in the light!" Heighway was almost stammering with embarrassment. "Look . . . maybe you could give me a han . . . no, I mean, help me . . ."

"How, inspector?"

"Do you know if Danny had anything to eat or drink before he died?"

The girl thought for a moment, her beautiful face creased in concentration.

"I think a customer had bought him a whisky. He was drinking something from a goblet. I'll show you."

Heighway followed her through the door and found himself behind the bar in the dungeon room. It was empty now save for an elderly slattern who was rearranging the dirt on the floor with a filthy mop. Attali pointed to a round crystal glass on the work-surface beneath the marble bar-top.

"That's it," she told him.

Heighway picked it up. Dregs of whisky swirled in the bottom and Heighway could see a couple of tiny grains of something. Carefully he inserted a fingertip, lifted out one of the grains, sniffed it and then touched it gingerly to his tongue. The acrid sensation told him all he needed to know. It was poison, all right. Score one to Madam Min.

"Attali, were there many customers in here when Danny was having his drink?"

"Three or four."

"Do you know who they were?"

"I don't know who *any* of the Wendy customers are. They have their own private entrance. They come in unseen and change into those clothes. Then they all look the same."

"Some of them are quite distinctive, though," mused Heighway. "Like the big bloke with the crotch cut out . . ."

"Oh, Gorgar, you mean."

"I suppose so. Was he still here?"

"Yes. I think so."

Heighway thought for a moment, then realized Attali was gazing at him again.

"Is something wrong?" he asked her.

"You don't remember me, do you?" she said.

"What?"

"We've met before. Two years ago. I was working on the streets, then. A client had beaten me up and I came in to the police station to report it. Sergeant Hogman interviewed me then told me it was all I deserved and tried to drag me into his office. The other policemen were watching and grinning, but you intervened. You told him you'd take over, and you took me out of the police station and put me in a carriage home."

"That was you!" Heighway could remember the bruised, bedraggled girl of the incident, but couldn't relate her to the beautiful woman who was staring at him out of those huge eyes.

"I know what would have happened to me if you hadn't intervened," she went on. "I will always be grateful. Is there anything I can do to help?"

"Actually, there is. Does this Gorgar have his own locker?"

"Yes."

"I'd like to see inside it."

Attali nodded. She rummaged around under the bar and emerged with a small set of keys. Taking a torch from the wall, she led Heighway through the door and along the short passageway to the changing room. Then, after handing him the torch, she selected a small, thin key and opened one of the lockers.

Inside, a single hangar held the rubber hood, vest and trousers. Heighway raised the torch and studied them. They clearly were Gorgar's; the hole in the crotch was plain to see. They smelt appalling and Heighway wondered if they had ever been washed.

Closing the door, he stood for a moment in thought. Things were falling into place.

"Attali," he said. "There's one more thing I'd like your help with tomorrow. The problem is, it could be quite dangerous . . ."

It was nearly midnight when Heighway got back to the police station. Kratavan was sitting on a bench in the entrance hall, waiting. He rose to his feet as the Inspector entered.

"Raasay get home all right?" Heighway asked him.

"Yes, sir."

"How was he?"

"He went straight to bed, sir. Said it hurt to sit down."

Kratavan's face looked oddly pinched, as though he were desperately trying to keep it straight.

"It's not funny, you know," said Heighway, and the next moment the two of them were laughing fit to bust.

"It's an odd business, all this, sir," said Kratavan, when they'd managed to regain their composure.

"Oh, I don't know. Seems like human nature to me. Greed, avarice, jealousy . . . Like every case, it all comes down to motive."

"Money?"

"Money isn't everything, Kratavan. Now go and get some sleep. Meet me at Raasay's lodgings in the morning. I want him to be in at the end of this, too . . ."

Superintendent Weird was sitting at his desk signing papers when Heighway entered his office early next morning. He looked up, his face unfriendly.

"You anywhere near solving this case yet?" he barked without preamble."

"I think so, sir," Heighway told him. "There's a possible witness, a hostess called Attali. I think she has the answers. I'll be seeing her this evening."

"Well, I hope for your sake she has. The Commissioner is getting impatient. You've got twenty-four hours, then you're off the case. Now, get out of my sight."

An hour later, Heighway walked along the shabby, run-down street where Raasay lodged to find Kratavan and the Sergeant waiting for him. Both looked apprehensive.

"Good morning, lads," he greeted them brightly. "Are you ready for this?"

Sergeant Raasay was looking about as happy as an orc that has just been told it is bath night.

"Sir, I don't really want to go back there."

"Nonsense, man! Me and Kratavan will be with you. And this time you won't have to wear any stupid clothes. *And* we're going to get one of those nasty, perverted beggars bang to rights."

"Really, sir?"

"Yep." Heighway clapped them both on the back and smiled confidently. "Trust me, lads. We've cracked it."

Gorgar looked warily around the deserted street and then pulled his hood over his head and slipped into the little side-alley that led to the private entrance of Club Nefarioso. At this critical time it was even more essential not to be recognized. Reaching the side door, he paused and listened, then slid his key into the lock. The door opened soundlessly, and he paced quietly along the dark corridor to the second door, the one that led into the changing room. It was too dark to see here, but he knew from habit where the handle was and the door opened silently.

Inside, the changing room was as dark as ever and he could just make out the shadowy shape of a waiting hostess.

"Ah," Gorgar said. "Attali, isn't it?"

"Yes, sir," said Attali. "Can I assist you?"

"I rather think you can, yes. Are we alone?"

"Yes, sir."

Gorgar felt in the pocket of his cloak for the small, needle-sharp dagger and pulled it out, keeping it hidden from her view.

"If you'd just come here for a moment," he said softly, and then all of a sudden three torches flared into flaming light and the door of one of the cubicles burst open. Gorgar gasped in surprise as Heighway, Kratavan and Raasay stepped out from it. Kratavan and Raasay held swords at the ready, but Heighway was armed only with a pair of handcuffs, which he held up in front of Gorgar's eyes.

"You'll probably quite enjoy these," he said. "Gorgar, I arrest you for the murder of Danny, the barman, and the intended murder of young Attali here." And he raised one hand and pulled back Gorgar's hood to reveal his face.

Kratavan and Raasay gasped, for the face staring back at them was that of Superintendent Weird.

"Uncle Billy!" stammered Raasay. "What's going on? Are you here on survey lance too?"

"That's right, Heighway!" Weird blustered angrily. "I'm here to check up on your appalling detective work!"

"No, you're not, sir, you're here to eliminate the last loose end, just as you eliminated Danny."

"Heighway, if you . . ."

"There's no point in trying to bluff your way out, sir." Heighway leaned forwards and pulled open Gorgar's locker to expose the distinctive rubber clothes inside.

"I think you'll find these are an exact fit," he said. "Very smelly, they are. Distinctively so. I did tell you about your body-odour once before, sir. As soon as Attali opened this locker, I knew it was you. And I'm sure that were you to don these garments, there are a few employees of this club who would be able to recognize you by your . . . exposed parts. In fact, that's an identity parade I'd pay good money to see."

Superintendent Weird sighed. "I did my best to get you out of the way, Heighway," he said. "I should have shoved *your* head in the glass-washer." And then in one fluid movement he brought out the dagger and plunged it deep into his own stomach before anyone could move. For a brief moment his eyes met Heighway's, but then they rolled up into his skull and he slumped to the floor, dead.

"But why, chief?" asked Kratavan as they walked back to the police station. "The Superintendent was rolling in money. Why should he need to blackmail someone?"

"Power, lad, power," answered Heighway. "Weird had got as far up the ladder as he could go. The only possible promotion would have been to Commissioner, but Algophilos wasn't going anywhere, and he's younger than Weird was. But if he had been forced to resign, Weird would have been in line for his job. Now, let's get a move on. I want to get all the paperwork done on this by five. There's a certain young lady who will be waiting for me to pick her up outside the club after work . . ."

It was ten minutes to five when Heighway ran down the stairs and strode through the entrance hall of the police station. He was just about to go out of the front doors when a hand grabbed his arm and he turned to see Madam Min grinning up at him.

"You see? I was right!" she told him.

"Yes, Min. Congratulations."

"The scientific method, just like you said."

"Well done."

"They're all saying that you're a good bet for the next Superintendent," Min told him. "That's great! You always said you wished pathomancers could provide some sort of evidence that would stand up in a court of law. Well, now I can! We could start a whole new department! I could train up more pathomancers and we could equip them with chickens, and every time there's a murder we could bring them along and . . ."

"Hold on, hold on!" Heighway interjected, removing her hand from his arm. "You've got to be joking! Are you seriously suggesting I equip a whole new department with mad old biddies and scrawny chickens? Great God, the Commissioner would sack me in seconds!"

He marched to the door and then turned to deliver his parting shot.

"And what the hell would we call it, eh?" he demanded. "The trained chicken section?"

Min shrugged. "How about the four-hens-sick department?" she suggested.

But Heighway had gone and she was talking to herself.

THE STRANGE AFFAIR
OF MR CORPUSTY

Anthony Armstrong

This story is quite true; but unfortunately I can't prove it. I missed my chance and now it is too late. Nor is it the kind of thing people are likely to believe if I tell them – not even those trusting souls who let total strangers take their wallets round the corner just as a guarantee of good faith, and whom I have never had the good fortune to meet.

For, to begin with, it was quite the last thing one would have expected of Mr Corpusty. If you had asked any dozen men to put their fingers on a chap for the job of, say, ice tester on the Round Pond, they would all have said, "Take Corpusty," and half of them would have added, "But take him in a good strong lorry!" Or if you had asked them to name a fellow to try out the new Waterloo Bridge, they would have said the same – always assuming they had no feeling about the future of the bridge. But if you had asked them to pick out a fellow who would be able to float in the air and had then suggested Corpusty yourself, you would have soon found them getting together in little groups, gazing apprehensively at you out of the corners of their eyes and tapping their foreheads.

For Corpusty was built on the general lines of a Himalaya, and a fat Himalaya at that; moreover, he was red-faced, wobbly, and given to much port. Also he breathed heavily, as if he had just surrounded far too large a meal – which he generally had. One's first impression was a self-confident voice and an acre of waistcoat: one's second that the waistcoat area had been underestimated. In short, quite the last person for any thistle-down-cum-gossamer work. And yet that dictatorial self-confident voice could have given the clue.

You see, Mr Corpusty was a very forceful personality. He was married to the frailest, most unassuming wife you ever saw; he was sole head of a big business; he was rich uncle to half a dozen timid nephews; and he had taken several courses in Will Development, Character, and Impress *Your* Personality First. He trusted so fanatically in Will Power that he had come to believe that things were so, because he said they were so – which is the only reason I can put forward as to why this business should have happened to him of all people.

My cousin Clarence was present at the first manifestation, which was after Sunday lunch, in Corpusty's Hampstead garden. The conversation, Clarence tells me, turned on Corpusty's feet, which were tender – and, considering their job, who shall blame them? – and Clarence by way of a joke then said:

"I wonder you don't cure them by will power."

Corpusty, who was wrestling stertorously with a Sunday afternoon torpor and two helpings of roast beef and Yorkshire, woke up slightly, said he disagreed entirely, and then asked what Clarence had said. Clarence repeated, and Corpusty unexpectedly answered that he had tried, but that it was too much of a physical achievement even for his will.

Mrs Corpusty said "Yes, dear," from her knitting.

Clarence, feeling he was getting quite a good rise, continued:

"Well, I wonder you haven't tackled it in some other way – such as willing yourself to weigh less than you do."

Mr Corpusty took some more port from the decanter on the garden table, and boomed out authoritatively that certain Indian fakirs were able, by the exercise of a will-power rare among Europeans, to increase their weight to many tons or else to reduce it to such an extent that a child could lift them with one finger. He added that men with strong wills who trained them sufficiently could do that sort of thing. He then dropped into a brief doze.

Mrs Corpusty said "Yes, dear."

The idea of a child waving Corpusty about in the air with one finger was too much for Clarence, who laughed and woke Corpusty up. To explain his amusement he murmured something about overdoing it and getting blown away in a breeze. "Or one might even fly," he added with a great assumption of seriousness.

"One might," said Mr Corpusty, equally seriously.

"I'm sure you could, dear, if you gave your mind to it," said Mrs Corpusty, who felt it was a cue, and Clarence laughed again.

Corpusty sat up mountainously in his chair.

"Look here!" he began angrily, "you're making fun of me."

"No, no," Clarence assured him.

"Anything is possible to a man of marked force of character who can concentrate his will sufficiently on one thing. The trouble is to concentrate wholeheartedly."

He had another glass of port, and Clarence, looking at him, murmured: "Faith can move mountains."

Mr Corpusty eyed him angrily for a moment and then heaved himself upright. What with port and opposition he looked very truculent and determined.

"I maintain," he boomed, fixing Clarence with a glassy eye, "that if I *could* exercise sufficient will-power and *could* concentrate sufficiently I could at this moment float in the air."

Mrs Corpusty glanced up from her knitting and said, "Why yes, dear," as if her husband had merely remarked that the days were drawing in, and Clarence, now feeling that this was the best rise he had ever had, added, "Of course you could."

"Well, now," said Corpusty, shutting his eyes and screwing up his face to an expression of intense determination, "I am Going to Float Two Feet above the Ground."

"Certainly, dear," said his wife helpfully, purling two together, and then suddenly gave a little scream. For Mr Corpusty seemed at first to have grown unmistakably taller, and then it was definitely seen by both of them that his feet were no longer touching the ground.

Slowly and still with shut eyes Mr Corpusty rose gently till his feet were about eighteen inches above the grass of the lawn, while his wife and Clarence gazed open-mouthed. Clarence tells me his first thought was that it wasn't real and that he had dropped off to sleep, and then he decided perhaps it was a touch of sun – and lunch.

Finally Corpusty, speaking with an effort through set teeth but in tones of intense satisfaction, said, "There now!" and Mrs Corpusty cried tearfully, "Henry, what are you doing?"

At these words a sharp spasm of doubt appeared to cross her husband's face, and the next moment he was sitting painfully on the grass. Clarence helped him up. There was quite a large dent on the lawn, where the Corpusty rear axle had made a forced landing.

"What did you want to talk like that for?" he bellowed at his wife, as soon as he had recovered. "You made me think that I wasn't doing it after all."

"I'm sorry, dear," almost wept the little woman. "I was just surprised for a moment. I know it was silly of me."

"I told you I could do it," growled Corpusty; "and I did – till you made me think . . ."

"Yes, you – er – did it all right," said Clarence in a dazed fashion.

"It was quite simple," boomed Corpusty, getting back his self-complacence. "Merely will-power. You could both do it."

Mrs Corpusty decided not to attempt it, but Clarence admits shamefacedly that he did. Without result, of course. He felt all the time that he couldn't, and that of course spoilt it. He hadn't got Corpusty's self-confident wholehearted belief that he was always in the right. Nor had he Mrs Corpusty's equally important ringside confidence in his success. In fact, he could feel from the way she counted stitches that she was deliberately not believing in him at all.

He took his departure shortly afterwards, and late that afternoon I first heard about it.

Of course, at first I put it on the sun, but in the end I rang Corpusty up in Clarence's presence.

"Yes," Mrs Corpusty answered in the proud yet timid voice of a new high priestess discussing the mysteries, "it's quite true. He's done it again, lying down. He did it on the bed this time, so as not to hurt himself, but the bed of course is . . ."

Corpusty interrupted. His voice was more complacement and assertive than ever.

"Ah, is that you? Clarence has told you then of my little discovery? Funny, I never thought of ascertaining my full power before. Come out tomorrow morning and I'll demonstrate. I'm staying away from the office for a day or two to experiment. Don't tell anyone else; I'd like it kept quiet till I know where I am. There's money in it, I think . . ."

He rang off abruptly. Already his manner smacked of a rather arrogant baron terminating an audience with a couple of rather scurvy knaves.

Next morning we were met in the hall by Mrs Corpusty, now quite at home with the high priestess stuff.

"Mr Corpusty is in his study," she whispered. She just didn't refer to him as "The Master". "He is just meditating and gaining strength. It's a terrible strain on him."

What with all the talk and Corpusty's personal magnetism I half believed it already by the time we collected in the garden, and I could see that Clarence certainly, who had seen it once, was not in the least sceptical.

Five minutes later I was completely bewildered. For Mr Corpusty, shutting his eyes and looking very intense, definitely raised himself about a foot above the ground and then floated slowly like a large balloon down the length of the garden. He apparently had a little difficulty at first, but it seemed that as our belief in him increased, so he found it easier. There was no deception at all, we passed sticks all round and under him; he was absolutely clear of the ground. We were both as convinced as Mrs Corpusty had always been, and the laws of gravitation seemed a thing of the past. If faith could move Corpusty like this, a whole range of Alps would be child's play.

"Wonderful! Wonderful!" we ejaculated. "Can you control your movements?"

"Yes," answered Mr Corpusty with shut eyes, "by willing it. Watch! I shall now turn to the left." He did so and, smashing into the garden wall, bounded off like a football. Undeterred, he turned right again and floated devastatingly down a line of delphiniums.

"Go up higher, dear!" called his wife, with the utmost faith in her lord's abilities. "You're breaking the flowers." She spoke as if she were merely telling him not to walk on the grass, instead of asking him to float a good five feet above the ground level.

Mr Corpusty went up higher. Then he suddenly called: "Quick! Catch me! I can't keep it up much longer."

We ran and I was cleverly just slow enough to allow Clarence to catch most of him. Corpusty is not what you'd call a catchable man.

"It's a strain," panted Corpusty, when we had excavated Clarence from the flower bed.

Clarence was understood to corroborate this.

"You must practise a bit more," I said excitedly.

"Yes, but the trouble is that at present I have to keep my eyes shut to concentrate and I can't see where I'm going. I don't want to float into Mullins' garden and give away the secret till I'm ready."

We solved this by tying him to a tree with a cord. Then we sat underneath and discussed the matter earnestly while Corpusty hovered around, making little practice flights like an enormous captive balloon. Mrs Corpusty already took her husband's wonderful accomplishment for granted and went calmly on with her knitting, merely saying at intervals:

"Mind the geraniums, dear!" or "Don't float so high, Henry! Mullins will see you over the wall!"

Towards the end of the morning Corpusty was able to open his eyes and by concentrating, he told us, on the idea of flying and moving his hands as in swimming, he was able to make very passable and well-aimed flights. His landings, however, were not so hot. By lunch time the garden looked as though a couple of R.A.F. squadrons had been driven down out of control.

Clarence and I stayed on to lunch and over a celebratory bottle of champagne we formed ourselves into an unofficial company to exploit Corpusty. Finally, Clarence, whose ideas ranged from selling him to the War Office to going on tour with a circus, suggested that the only thing to do really was to give public exhibitions, and as a preliminary to this to secure someone of established reputation as a certified witness.

"Yes," agreed Corpusty, "and the more matter-of-fact the fellow is, the better. Not one of these chaps who believe in everything." He raised himself playfully several inches from the seat of his chair as he spoke, but we begged him not to do it again. At 11 a.m. one doesn't mind, but after a celebratory lunch one simply isn't prepared for it.

After discussion we settled on Sir James Blaker, who had a name for disbelieving everything he could not touch, or see, or hear – and most things that he could. If we could get him on our side first, then we should have little trouble with the others.

We went to him and at last persuaded him, though completely sceptical, to come to an audition in Corpusty's garden in four days' time. Corpusty was to spend the intervening time in practising his stuff, and he went at it in such determined fashion that by the third day he could glide about in a style something between that of Peter Pan and a Zeppelin.

The night before the great day we dined together at Corpusty's house, to drink to the success of "Birdmen Limited". Mrs Corpusty, I'm glad to say, was away for a few days – which was as well, for we certainly dined rather heavily. Corpusty in particular, in anticipation of next day's triumph, produced some Château-bottled Lafette and two bottles of Dow's '04. He drank most of it himself, but not purposely; one just had to be quite quick off the mark with Corpusty.

It was the Dow's which was responsible. That and the new sense of power took Corpusty completely by storm, and he became a little unmanageable. We didn't mind much, till later in the evening he began to talk about going out and showing the world that he could fly; and then we began to get frightened.

"Wait till tomorrow," we suggested anxiously.

"Tomorrow never comes," answered Corpusty, as one

discovering a world truth. "Must show chaps now. Look!" He floated upwards to the middle of the room. As he had omitted to change from his sitting position the effect was ludicrous.

"Come down," shouted Clarence.

"Shan't," said Mr Corpusty like a naughty child. He triumphantly went up higher, cracked his head against the ceiling, lost his will-control, and came down with a crash on the table.

We picked him out of the *débris*. He was murmuring, "Nasty fall! *Very* nasty fall!" and was still muttering when a scared manservant appeared.

He told the fellow to go to bed and not to bother about us. We already had an uneasy feeling that we were going to have a little trouble with Corpusty.

"That's your fault," I said severely when the man had gone with a half smile.

"Norrabitofit! Must have slipped!" announced our host, and before we could stop him he had insisted on going up to the ceiling again to look for the banana skin, which he said someone must have carelessly left there.

We hooked him down with an umbrella and held him for a while, till he promised to be good.

He was quiet for about ten minutes but his fall had evidently muddled him badly about the laws of gravity, because when his napkin slid off his knees he flew rapidly up to the ceiling to pick it up, and then got anchored in some inextricable way in the electric-light flex. We released him at last, but it was like getting an angry blue bottle off a fly paper, complicated by the fact that we didn't trust Corpusty's will power sufficiently to stand anywhere directly underneath. It was after this that Clarence sent me downstairs to get some rope. We felt we couldn't run the risk of losing him, or of letting the secret out.

I was halfway up again when I heard a crash of glass and a shout. I ran and found Clarence standing at the front door.

"Quick! Quick, he's gone!"

"Where?"

"He went out while I was locking the dining-room door. I thought the window was shut, but he evidently thought it was open. Anyhow, the result is he's out. We must get him at once . . . Ah, there he is!"

We darted down the steps to where a vague enormous shape was swooping about in the air outside. A voice came from it. "Must show chaps!" it announced happily.

"Come down, Corpusty, you old fool," called Clarence angrily. Luckily the hour was late and so the street, a quiet one, was empty.

Mr Corpusty, in the position of a swimmer using the breast stroke, descended to just out of our reach and said:

"Whaffor?"

"You'll give the secret away."

"No, I shan't. No one here. Must practise. See! I can do everything." He levitated slowly up till he was on a level with the roofs of the houses. At this height something seemed to catch his eye in a bedroom window with the blind undrawn and he rolled over to a sitting position like a porpoise and proceeded to gaze earnestly within, with an expression on his face as of a young man in a musical comedy stall.

"Damned old idiot!" Clarence almost sobbed in his fury. "He'll start something now if he's not careful." Corpusty looked down and with a total lack both of decency and knowledge of the circumstances beckoned ecstatically to us to come up and have a look too.

"Heavens!" said Clarence. "Throw a brick at him."

We got him third shot somewhere in the under-carriage, and with a yelp he volplaned swiftly along the street, luckily at such height as to be almost invisible from below.

We raced along and at the corner met the first person we had seen. Of all people it was a policeman.

"'Ullo! 'Ullo, what's all this 'ere?" he observed suspiciously; then noticing that we were hatless, breathless, and that one was carrying a rope, added: "Where are you two off to?"

"A little stroll," I said innocently.

"Ho! And do you live near here, then?"

"Not far," began Clarence, when a sepulchral voice from the air said:

"Evenin' all!"

The constable looked quickly behind him. Then he looked up and down the street. Then he looked sternly at a nearby garden. Finally, he looked at us even more suspiciously.

Thank heaven we both had had the presence of mind not to look up, to where now floating like a small Zeppelin six feet above the constable's head, was Corpusty in the position of a Roman diner reclining at ease.

The policeman looked undecided for a moment then took out his notebook. As he flicked its pages over, Corpusty laughed vinously. The constable passed in mid-flick and fixed us with a stern glance.

"You better be careful," he said.

"Look here," began Clarence. "We're not doing anything wrong. Just walking about! We . . ."

That moment, unfortunately, was the one chosen by Corpusty to change his position in the air and, like Jupiter visiting Danaë, a shower of small coins fell out of his pockets upon the astonished constable.

Properly transferred the coins might conceivably have had a good effect. But money coming like manna from heaven – down the neck instead of into a receptive palm – was an outrageous attempt at bribery.

"Name and address, please?" snapped the man, and with sinking hearts we heard the slow approaching footfall of yet another policeman.

I must say Corpusty, above himself though he was, saved us. We saw him go up higher – to get a bit of a run, so to speak – and then he dropped squarely in a sitting position on the constable's helmet, burying him in it down to the moustache. We at once took to our heels, while the neatly bonneted bobby struggled blindly and his comrade ran to his assistance. Mr Corpusty with the air of a terrier joining in a game, skimmed easily above our heads, giving encouraging advice as to the position, movements and language of the enemy.

But we had not too much of a start on the second policeman, and to have re-entered the house unobserved would have been impossible.

Our protective air screen, however, was up to it. He turned and flew straight at our pursuer just about the height of his face. It was too much even for the Metropolitan police force. The man called in sharp tones on Providence, ducked, sat down abruptly, and clung to a lamp-post, passing his hand across his eyes.

Corpusty, very pleased with himself, rejoined us with a leisurely side stroke at the door, and we got safely in. He said he was tired and wouldn't fly any more, but we took no risks. We put him to bed, lashed him there, and spent the night in the spare room.

We didn't untie him till Mrs Corpusty returned next morning, and even then we watched him till Sir James Blaker came at three o'clock. I must say he looked rather the worse for wear. Night flying is always a strain.

Sir James listened to our claims with a sceptical smile. He seemed about the hardest person to convince I have ever seen. He irradiated disbelief. At the end of our statements all he said was: "Well, gentlemen, seeing's believing."

This was Corpusty's cue. He gathered himself together and made an intense effort. At first we thought he wasn't going to do it because of the atmosphere of cynical disbelief emanating from Sir James Blaker, and we willed frantically to help him, till at last he got going. But he had barely raised himself an imperceptible inch, when Sir James said abruptly: "I knew it was absurd. No man can fly by the mere exercise of will."

At once Corpusty wavered and came down again. "But look," we cried, "he was just doing it," and Sir James said, "Nonsense."

Corpusty shut his eyes and we could all feel the effort he made. But nothing happened. Those disbelieving remarks had proved too strong.

The interview naturally was a fiasco and Sir James was inclined to be very difficult till Corpusty had some kind of a fit, due, Sir James intimated nastily, to port. Then he went, thanking us pointedly for an interesting morning.

Corpusty never flew again. The ability had depended on his own unquestioning belief in his success, and Sir James had made him doubt it for the first time. He could never, therefore, forget that he had once failed, and so his faith was never again absolute.

And so we shall never now be able to get anyone to believe what we have honestly seen. At times we feel that if we could only get hold of those two policemen: at other times we feel that they may still be wanting even more fervently to get hold of us . . .

THE GREAT
WISH SYNDICATE

John Kendrick Bangs

The farm had gone to ruin. On every side the pastures were filled with a rank growth of thistles and other thorn-bearing flora. The farm buildings had fallen into a condition of hopeless disrepair, and the old house, the ancestral home of the Wilbrahams, had become a place of appalling desolation. The roof had been patched and repatched for decades, and now fulfilled none of the ideals of its roofhood save that of antiquity. There was not, as far as the eye could see, a single whole pane of glass in any one of the many windows of the mansion, and there were not wanting those in the community who were willing to prophesy that in a stiff gale – such as used to be prevalent in that section of the world, and within the recollection of some of the old settlers too – the chimneys, once the pride of the county, would totter and fall, bringing the whole mansion down into chaos and ruin. In short, the one-time model farm of the Wilbrahams had become a byword and a jest and, as some said, of no earthly use save for the particular purposes of the eccentric artist in search of picturesque subject-matter for his studies in oil.

It was a wild night, and within the ancient house sat the owner, Richard Wilbraham, his wife not far away, trying to find room upon her husband's last remaining pair of socks to darn them. Wilbraham gazed silently into the glowing embers on the hearth before them, the stillness of the evening broken only by the hissing of the logs on the and irons and an occasional sigh from one of the watchers.

Finally the woman spoke.

"When does the mortgage fall due, Richard?" she asked, moving uneasily in her chair.

"Tomorrow," gulped the man, the word seeming to catch in his throat and choke him.

"And you – you are sure Colonel Digby will not renew it?" she queried.

"He even declines to discuss the matter," said Wilbraham. "He contents himself with shaking it in my face every time I approach his office, while he tells his office-boy to escort me to the door. I don't believe in signs, Ethelinda, but I do believe that that is an omen that if the money is not forthcoming at noon tomorrow you and I will be roofless by this time tomorrow night."

The woman shuddered.

"But, Richard," she protested, "you – you had put by the money to pay it long ago. What has become of it?"

"Gone, Ethelinda – gone in that ill-advised egg deal I tried to put through two years ago," sighed Wilbraham, as he buried his face in his hands to hide his grief and mortification. "I sold eggs short," he added. "You remember when that first batch of incubator hens began laying so prolifically – it seemed to me as though Fortune stared me in the face – nay, held out her hands to me and bade me welcome to a share in her vast estates. There was a great shortage of eggs in the market that year, and I went to New York and sold them by the dozens – hundreds of dozens – thousands of dozens –"

He rose up from his chair and paced the floor in an ecstasy of agitation. "I sold eggs by the million, Ethelinda," he went on, by a great effort regaining control of himself. "Eggs to be laid by hens whose great-great-great-grandmothers had yet to be hatched from eggs yet unlaid by unborn chickens."

Wilbraham's voice sank to a hoarse, guttural whisper.

"And the deliveries have bankrupted me," he muttered. "The price of eggs has risen steadily for the past eighteen months, and yesterday a hundred thousand of January, strictly fresh, that I had to put in the open market in order to fill my contracts, cost me not only my last penny, but were in part paid for with a sixty-day note that I cannot hope to meet. In other words, Ethelinda, we are ruined."

The woman made a brave effort to be strong, but the strain was too much for her tired nerves and she broke down and wept bitterly.

"We have but four hens left," Wilbraham went on, speaking in a hollow voice. "At most, working them to their full capacity, in thirty days from now we shall have only ten dozen eggs added to our present store, and upon that date I have promised to deliver to the International Cold Storage Company one thousand dozen at twenty-two and a half cents a dozen. Even with the mortgage out of the way we should still be securely bound in the clutch of bankruptcy."

A long silence ensued. The clock out in the hall ticked loudly, each clicking sound falling upon Wilbraham's ears like a sledge-hammer blow in a forge, welding link by link a chain of ruin that should forever bind him in the shackles of misery. Unbroken save by the banging now and then of a shutter in the howling wind without, the silence continued for nearly an hour, when the nerve-killing monotony of the ceaseless *tick-tock, tick-tock* of the clock was varied by a resounding hammering upon the door.

"It is very late," said the woman. "Who do you suppose can be calling at this hour? Be careful when you open the door – it may be a highwayman."

"I should welcome a highwayman if he could help me to find anything in the house worth stealing," said Wilbraham, as he rose from his chair and started for the door. "Whoever it may be, it is a wild night, and despite our poverty we can still keep open house for the stranger on the moor."

He hastened to the door and flung it wide.

"Who's there?" he cried, gazing out into the blackness of the storm.

A heavy gust of wind, icy cold, blew out his candle, and a great mass of sleet coming in with it fell with a dull, sodden thud on the floor at his feet, and some of it cut his cheek.

"I am a wanderer," came a faint voice from without, "frozen and starved. In the name of humanity I beg you to take me in, lest I faint and perish."

"Come in, come in!" cried Wilbraham. "Whoever you are, you are more than welcome to that which is left us; little enough in all conscience."

An aged man, bent and weary, staggered in through the door. Wilbraham sprang toward him and caught his fainting form in his strong arms. Tenderly he led him to his own abandoned chair by the fireside, where he and his faithful wife chafed the old fellow's hands until warmth had returned to them.

"A cup of tea, my dear," said Wilbraham. "It will set him up."

"And a morsel to eat, I implore you," pleaded the stranger, in a weak, tremulous voice. "The merest trifle, good sir, even if it be only an egg!"

The woman grew rigid at the suggestion. "An egg? At this time when eggs are –" she began.

"There, there, Ethelinda," interrupted Wilbraham, gently. "We have two left in the ice-box – your breakfast and mine. Rather than see this good old man suffer longer I will gladly go without mine. The fact is, eggs have sort of disagreed with me latterly anyhow, and –"

"It is as you say, Richard," said the woman, meekly, as with a hopeless sigh she turned toward the kitchen, whence in a short time she returned, bearing a steaming creation of her own make – a lustrous, golden egg, poached, and lying invitingly upon the crisp bosom of a piece of toast. It was a thing of beauty, and Wilbraham's mouth watered as he gazed hungrily upon it.

And then the unexpected happened: The aged stranger, instead of voraciously devouring the proffered meal, with a kindly glance upon his host, raised his withered hands aloft as though to pronounce a benediction upon him, and in a chanting tone droned forth the lines:

Who eats this egg and toast delicious
Receives the gift of three full wishes –
Thus do the fairy folk reward
The sacrifices of this board.

A low, rumbling peal of thunder and a blinding flash as of lightning followed, and when the brilliant illumination of the latter had died away the stranger had vanished.

Wilbraham looked at his wife, dumb with amazement, and she, tottering backward into her chair, gazed back, her eyes distended with fear.

"Have I – have I been dreaming?" he gasped, recovering his speech in a moment. "Or have we really had a visitor?"

"I was going to ask you the same question, Richard," she replied. "It really was so very extraordinary, I can hardly believe –"

And then their eyes fell upon the steaming egg, still lying like a beautiful sunset on a background of toast upon the table.

"The egg!" she cried, hoarsely. "It must have been true."

"Will you eat it?" asked Wilbraham, politely extending the platter in her direction.

"Never!" she cried, shuddering. "I should not dare. It is too uncanny."

"Then I will," said Wilbraham. "If the old man spoke the truth –"

He swallowed the egg at a single gulp.

"Fine!" he murmured, in an ecstasy of gastronomic pleasure. "I wish there were two more just like it!"

No sooner had he spoken these words than two more poached eggs, even as he had wished, appeared upon the platter.

"Great heavens, Ethelinda!" he cried. "The wishes come true! I wish to goodness I knew who that old duffer was."

The words had scarcely fallen from his lips when a card fluttered down from the ceiling. Wilbraham sprang forward excitedly and caught it as it fell. It read:

HENRY W. OBERON
Secretary, The United States Fairy Co.,
3007 Wall Street

"Henry W. Oberon, United State Fairy Company, Wall Street, eh?" he muttered. "By Jove, I wish I knew –"

"Stop!" cried his wife, seizing him by the arm, imploringly. "Do stop, Richard. You have used up two of your wishes already. Think what you need most before you waste the third."

"Wise Ethelinda," he murmured, patting her gently on the hand. "Very, very wise, and I will be careful. Let me see now . . . I wish I had . . . I wish I had . . ."

He paused for a long time, and then his face fairly beamed with a great light of joy.

"I wish I had three more wishes!" he cried.

Another crash of thunder shook the house to its very foundations, and a lightning flash turned the darkness of the interior of the dwelling into a vivid golden yellow that dazzled them, and then all went dusk again.

"Mercy!" shuddered the good wife. "I hope that was an answer to your wish."

"It won't take long to find out," said Wilbraham. "I'll tackle a few more natural desires right here and now, and if they come true I'll know that that thunderbolt was a rush message from the United States Fairy Company telling me to draw on them at sight."

"Well, don't be extravagant," his wife cautioned him.

"I'll be as extravagant as I please," he retorted. "If my fourth wish works, Ethelinda, my address from this hour on will be Easy Street and Treasury Avenue. I wish first then that this old farm was in Ballyhack!"

"Ballyhack! Last station – all out!" cried a hoarse voice at the door.

Wilbraham rushed to the window and peered out into what had been the night, but had now become a picture of something worse. Great clouds of impenetrable smoke hung over the grim stretches of a dismal-looking country in which there seemed to be nothing but charred remnants of ruined trees and blackened rocks, over which, in an endless line, a weary mass of struggling plodders, men and women, toiled onward through the grime of a hopeless environment.

"Great Scott!" he cried, in dismay, as the squalid misery of the prospect smote upon his vision. "This is worse than Diggville. I wish to heaven we were back again."

"Diggville! Change cars for Easy Street and Fortune Square!" cried the hoarse voice at the door, and Wilbraham, looking out through the window again, was rejoiced to find himself back amid familiar scenes.

"They're working all right," he said, gleefully.

"Yes," said his wife. "They seem to be and you seem to be speculating as usual upon a narrow margin. Again you have only one wish left, having squandered four out of the five already used."

"And why not, my dear," smiled Wilbraham, amiably, "when my next wish is to be for six spandy new wishes straight from the factory?"

Mrs Wilbraham's face cleared.

"Oh, splendid!" she cried, joyously. "Wish it – wish it – do hurry before you forget."

"I do wish it – six more wishes on the half-shell!" roared Wilbraham.

As before, came the thunder and the lightning.

"Thank you!" said Wilbraham. "These fairies are mighty prompt correspondents. I am beginning to see my way out of our difficulties, Ethelinda," he proceeded, rubbing his hands together unctuously. "Instead of dreading tomorrow and the maturity of that beastly old mortgage, I wish to thunder it were here, and that the confounded thing were paid off."

The wish, expressed impulsively, brought about the most astonishing results. The hall clock began instantly to whirr and to wheeze, its hands whizzing about as though upon a well-oiled pivot. The sun shot up out of the eastern horizon as though fired from a cannon, and before the amazed couple could realize what was going on, the village clock struck the hour of noon, and they found themselves bowing old Colonel

Digby, the mortgage holder, out of the house, while Wilbraham himself held in his right hand a complete satisfaction of that depressing document.

"Now," said Wilbraham. "I feel like celebrating. What would you say to a nice little luncheon, my Dear? Something simple, but good – say some Russian caviare, Lynnhaven Bay oysters, real turtle soup, terrapin, canvas-back duck, alligator-pear salad, and an orange br-lot for two, eh?"

"It would be fine, Richard," replied the lady, her eyes flashing with joy, "but I don't know where we could get such a feast here. The Diggville markets are –"

"Markets?" cried Wilbraham, contemptuously. "What have we to do with markets from this time on? Markets are nothing to me. I merely wish that we had that repast right here and now, ready to –"

"Luncheon is served, sir," said a tall, majestic-looking stranger, entering from the dining-room.

"Ah! Really?" said Wilbraham. "And who the dickens are you?"

"I am the head butler of the Fairies' Union assigned to your service, sir," replied the stranger, civilly, making a low bow to Mrs Wilbraham.

There is no use of describing the meal. It was all there as foreshadowed in Wilbraham's gastronomically inspired menu, and having had nothing to eat since the night before, the fortunate couple did full justice to it.

"Before we go any further, Richard," said Mrs Wilbraham, after the duck had been served, "do you happen to remember how many of your last six wishes are left?"

"No, I don't," said Wilbraham.

"Then you had better order a few more lest by the end of this charming repast you forget," said the thoughtful woman.

"Good scheme, Ethelinda," said Wilbraham. "I'll put in a bid for a gross right away. There is no use in piking along in small orders when you can do a land-office business without lifting your little finger."

"And don't you think, too, dear," the woman continued, "that it would be well for us to open a set of books – a sort of

General Wish Account – so that we shall not at any time by some unfortunate mistake overdraw our balance?"

"Ethelinda," cried Wilbraham, his face glowing with enthusiastic admiration, "you have, without any exception, the best business head that ever wore a pompadour!"

Thus it began. A cash-book was purchased and in its columns, like so many entries of mere dollars, Wilbraham entered his income in wishes, faithfully recording on the opposite page his expenditures in the same. The first entry of one gross was made that very night:

March 16, 19—, Sight Draft on U.S. Fairy Co., 144.

Before long others followed and were used to such an effect that at the end of the year, by a careful manipulation of his resources, carefully husbanding the possibilities of that original third wish, Wilbraham found that he had expressed and had had gratified over ten thousand wishes, all of such a nature that the one-time decrepit farm had now become one of the handsomest estates in the country. A château stood on the site of the old mansion. Where the barns had been in danger of falling of their own weight were now to be found rows of well-stocked cattle-houses and dairies of splendour. The decaying stables had become garages of unusual magnificence, wherein cars of all horsepowers and models panted, eager to be chugging over the roads of Diggville, which by a single wish expressed by Wilbraham had become wondrously paved boulevards. And in the chicken-yards that had taken the place of the discouraging coops of other days thousands of hens laid their daily quota of prosperity for their owner in the plush-upholstered nests provided for their comfort by Wilbraham, the egg king, for that was what he had now become. In all parts of the world his fame was heralded, and hosts of sight-seers came daily to see the wonderful acres of this lordly master of the world's egg supply. And best of all, there was still a balance of forty-three hundred and eighty-seven wishes to his credit!

The leading financiers of the world now began to take notice of this new figure in the realm of effort, for they soon found their most treasured and surest schemes going awry in a most unaccountable manner. No matter how much they tried to depress or to stimulate the market, some new and strange factor seemed to be at work bringing their calculations to naught, and when it became known to them that the mere expression of a wish on the part of Wilbraham would send stocks kiting into the air or crashing into the depths, no matter what they might do, they began to worry.

"Tomorrow," said John W. Midas, as he talked to Wilbraham and his friends one evening at the club, "International Gold Brick Common will fall thirty-seven points."

"Not so, Colonel," Wilbraham had retorted. "It will rise seventy points."

"Oh, it will, will it? How do you know that?" demanded Midas.

"Because I wish it," said Wilbraham.

And on the morrow International Gold Brick, opening at 96 5/8, lo and behold! closed at 166 5/8, and the friends of Midas who had laughed at Wilbraham and sold short went to the wall. A half-dozen experiences of a similar nature showed the former rulers of the financial world that Wilbraham had now become a force to be reckoned with, and for their own protection the more eminent among them called a meeting at the home of Mr Andrew Rockernegie to consider the situation. There was too much power in the hands of one man, they thought, although that idea had never occurred to any of them before. The result of the meeting was that Colonel Midas was appointed a committee of one to call upon Wilbraham and see what could be done.

"You may not be aware of it, Mr Wilbraham," said the Colonel, "but by your occasional intrusions into our lines of work you are making finance a inexact science. Now, what will you take to keep your hands off the market altogether? Twenty millions?"

Wilbraham laughed.

"Really, Colonel Midas," he replied, "I had no idea that you ever did business on a corner-grocery basis like that. You ought to run a vacuum cleaner over your brow. I think there are cobwebs in your grey matter. Why, my dear sir, I can capitalize this gift of mine at a billion, and pay 10 percent on every dollar of it every year, with a little melon to be cut up annually by the stockholders of one 150 percent per annum. Why, then, should I sell out at twenty millions?"

"Oh, I suppose you can have the earth if you want it," retorted Midas, ruefully. "But all the same –"

"No, I don't want the earth," said Wilbraham. "If I had wanted it I should have had it long ago. I'd only have to pay taxes on it, and it would be a nuisance looking after the property."

"On what basis will you sell out?" demanded Midas.

"Well, we might incorporate my gift," said Wilbraham. "What would you say to a United States Wish Syndicate, formed to produce and sell wishes to the public by the can – POTTED WISHES: ONE HUNDRED NON-CUMULATIVE WISHES FOR A DOLLAR. Eh?"

Midas paced the floor in his enthusiasm.

"Magnificent?" he cried. "We'll underwrite the whole thing in my office – bonds, stock, both common and preferred – for say – ahem! – how much did you say?"

"Oh, I guess I can pull along on a billion," said Wilbraham. "Cash."

Midas scratched his head. A glitter came into his eye.

"You wish to give up control of your gift?" he asked.

"You are a clever man, Colonel Midas," grinned Wilbraham. "If I had said 'yes' to that question I'd have lost my power. But I'm too old a bird to be caught that way. You go ahead and form your company, and sell your securities to the public at par, pay me my billion, and I'll transfer the business to you, C. O. D."

"Done!" said Midas, and he returned to his fellow captains on the Street.

Wilbraham was felicitating himself upon a wondrously good stroke of business, when another caller entered his room, this time unannounced.

"How do you do, Mr Wilbraham?" said the stranger, as he mysteriously materialized before Wilbraham's desk.

"How are you?" said Wilbraham. "Your face is familiar to me, but I can't just recall where I have met you."

"My name is Oberon, sir," said the stranger. "I am the secretary of the United States Fairy Company. There is a little trouble over your account, and I have called to see if we can't –"

Wilbraham's heart sank within him.

"It – it isn't overdrawn, is it?" he whispered, hoarsely.

"No, it isn't," said the secretary.

"By Jove!" cried Wilbraham, drawing a deep sigh of relief, and springing to his feet, grasping Oberon by both hands. "Sit down, sit down! You have been a benefactor to me, sir."

"I am glad you realize that fact, Mr Wilbraham," said the fairy, somewhat coldly. "It makes it easier for me to say what I have come here to say. We did not realize, Mr Wilbraham," he went on, "when we awarded you the three original wishes that you would be clever enough to work the wish business up into an industry. If we had we should have made the wishes non-cumulative. We were perfectly willing to permit a reasonable overdraft also, but we didn't expect you to pyramid your holdings the way you have done until you have practically secured a corner in the market."

Wilbraham grinned broadly.

"I have been going some," he said.

"Rather," said Oberon. "Your original three wishes have been watered until we find in going over our books for the second year that they reach the sum total of three million five hundred and sixty-nine thousand four hundred and thirty-seven, and that you still have an unexpended balance on hand of four hundred and ninety-seven thousand three hundred and seventy-four wishes. The situation is just this," he continued. "Our company has been kept so busy honouring your drafts that we are threatened with a general strike. We didn't mind building you a château and furbishing up your old chicken-farm, and setting you up for life, but when you enter into negotiations with old John W. Midas to incorporate yourself into a wish trust we feel that the time has come to call a halt. The fairies are honest, and no obligation of theirs will ever be repudiated, but we think that a man who tries to build up a billion-dollar corporation to deal in wishes on an investment of one poached egg is just a leetle unreasonable. Even Rock-ernegie had a trifle more than a paper of tacks when he founded the iron trust."

"By ginger, Oberon," said Wilbraham, "you are right! I *have* rather put it on to you people and I'm sorry. I wouldn't embarrass you good fairies for anything in the world."

"Good!" cried Oberon, overjoyed. "I thought you would feel that way. Just think for one moment what it would mean for us if the Great Wish Syndicate were started as a going concern, with a board of directors made up of men like John W. Midas, Rockernegie, and old Bondifeller running things. Why, there aren't fairies enough in the world to keep up with those men, and the whole business world would come down with a crash. Their wish would elect a whole Congress. If they wished the Senate out of Washington and located on Wall Street, you'd soon find it so, and by thunder, Wilbraham, every four years they'd wish somebody in the White House with a great capacity for taking orders and not enough spine to fill an umbrella cover, and the public would be powerless."

Wilbraham gazed thoughtfully out of the window. A dazzling prospect of imperial proportions loomed up before his vision, and the temptation was terrible, but in the end common sense came to the rescue.

"It would be a terrible nuisance," he muttered to himself, and then turning to Oberon he asked: "What is your proposition?"

"A compromise," said the fairy. "If you'll give up your right to further wishes on our account we will place you in a position where, for the rest of your natural life, you will always have four dollars more than you need, and in addition to that, as a compliment to Mrs Wilbraham, she can have everything she wants."

"Ha!" said Wilbraham, dubiously. "I – I don't think I'd like that exactly. She might want something I didn't want her to have."

"Very well, then," said the fairy, with a broad smile. "We'll make you the flat proposition – you give us a quit-claim deed to all your future right, title, and interest in our wishes, and we will guarantee that as long as you live you will, upon every occasion, find in your pocket five dollars more than you need."

"Make it seven and I'll go you!" cried Wilbraham, really enthusiastic over the suggestion.

"Sure!" returned Oberon with a deep sigh of relief.

"Well, dearest," said Wilbraham that night as he sat down at his onyx dinner-table, "I've gone out of the wish business."

His wife's eyes lit up with a glow of happiness.

"You have?" she cried delightedly.

"Yes," said Wilbraham; and then he told her of Oberon's call, and the new arrangement, and was rejoiced beyond measure to receive her approval of it.

"I am so glad, Richard," she murmured, with a sigh of content. "I have been kept so busy for two years trying to think of new things to wish for that I have had no time to enjoy all the beautiful things we have."

"And it isn't bad to have seven dollars more than you need whenever you need it, is it, dearest?"

"Bad, Richard?" she returned. "Bad? I should say not, my beloved. To have seven dollars more than you need at all times is, to my mind, the height of an ideal prosperity. I need five thousand dollars at this very minute to pay my milliner's bill."

"And here it is," said her husband, taking five crisp one-thousand-dollar bills from his vest pocket and handing them to her. "And here are seven brand-new ones besides. The fairies are true to their bargain."

And they lived affluently forever afterward, although Midas and his confréres did sue Wilbraham for breach of contract, securing judgment for twenty-nine million dollars, the which Wilbraham paid before leaving the court-room, departing therefrom with a balance of one five and two one dollar bills to the good.

And that is why, my dear children, when you see the Wilbraham motor chugging along the highway, if you look closely you will see painted on the door of the car a simple crest, a poached egg dormant upon a piece of toast couchant, and underneath it, in golden letters on a scroll, the family motto, *Hic semper septimus.*

FRACTAL PAISLEYS

Paul Di Filippo

That night the Li'l Bear Inn was as crowded as the last 'copter out of Saigon. But the atmosphere was a little more frenzied.

All three pool tables were hidden by tight packs of players and spectators, protruding cues making the whole mass resemble a patchwork porcupine. The dartboards looked like Custer's troops. Harley Fitts was rocking the pinball machine towards a high score: a sizable task, given that two sisters who called themselves Frick and Frack were perched on it. Rollo Dexadreen was monopolizing the single videogame as usual. Archie Opterix, on kazoo, was accompanying Gig von Beaver – who was making farting noises with a hand under his armpit – in a rendition of "Born to Run". Kitty Koerner was dancing atop the jukebox, which was playing Hank Williams Junior, though Kitty was doing something that looked like the Watusi.

Above the sounds of clicking pool balls, thwocking darts, ringing bells, exploding aliens, kazoo, farts, Hank Junior, and the bug-zapper hung outside the screen-door that gave onto the gravel parking lot, the calls for drinks were continuous.

"Tracey, two shots!"

"Tracey, another pitcher!"

"Tracey, six rum 'n' cokes!"

The woman behind the bar – Tracey Thorne-Smith – was on the tall side, and skinny as a book of poems by a sixteen-year-old virgin. She had long straight brown hair and a sociable smile, though her features were overlaid with signs of worry. She wore a white shirt knotted above her navel, and a pair of cheap jeans. Moving like an assembly-line worker with the belt cranked up, the piece-work rate cut in half and the next mortgage payment due, she paused only long enough to wipe the sweat from her forehead now and then.

A weary waitress appeared at one end of the crowded bar, where she set down her tray. She was short and round-faced, and her wavy hair – dyed a color not found in nature – was pinched in a banana-clip, one tendril escaping to hang damply against her cheek.

The bartender moved down to take her order.

"What'll it be, Catalina?"

"It's 'lick it, slam it 'n' suck it' time again, Trace. Larry and his city-friends, in the corner there."

"Four margaritas coming up."

Catalina leaned gratefully on the bar. "Lord, it's hot! You think that cheap bastard would get some air-con in here."

Her back to Catalina, Tracey said, "You best not hold your breath waiting for the Westinghouse van to arrive, Cat. You know well as I do that Larry's been pinching every penny, so's he can buy into the syndicate those boys he's with represent. And something tells me he's pinched himself a considerable sum, what with the way those lizards are crawling all over him. No, I wouldn't count on no air-conditioning anytime soon." Tracey set the salt-rimmed glasses two at a time on Catalina's tray. "How they tipping tonight?"

The waitress tucked the loose hair behind her ear. "Not bad. But I aim to get a little more out of Larry later, after closing."

Tracey made a sour face. "I don't see how you can bring yourself to be nice to him like that."

"Oh, he's not that bad. He's been real lonely since Janice died. It's downright pathetic sometimes. He keeps telling me, 'She was my Honeypot, and I was her Li'l Bear.'"

"Eee-yew!"

Primping her hair, Catalina said, "That remark don't show much sympathy, Tracey, nor much common sense. You should try being nice to Larry, like I do. Might get yourself a little bonus. You sure could use it, I bet, what with Jay Dee being outa work."

"Forget it! Not only would I never let that man touch me in a million years, but if I did and Jay Dee found out, he'd kill him. Why, he can just about stand me working here as it is."

Catalina shrugged. "Your call. It's not like you're married or nothing."

After Catalina had sashayed away, Tracey went back to filling the non-stop orders.

She was bending over for a fresh bottle of Scotch when she felt a hand on her rear-end.

"You shore got a nice ass for such a skinny – gack!"

Tracey straightened up and turned around. "Jay Dee," she said, "turn that poor sucker loose."

Jay Dee McGhee removed his chokehold from beneath the impulsive patron's jaw and released the burly man's wrist, which he had been holding at about jaw-level, only behind the man's back. Shoving the gagging man away from the bar, he dropped down onto the vacant stool.

"Draw me a Bud, Trace. I had a long hot walk."

Jay Dee was shaggy and unshaven, with the looks of a mischievous five-year-old, perhaps one just caught affixing a string of firecrackers to a cat's tail. He wore a green workshirt with the sleeves ripped off and the same K-Mart-brand jeans as his girlfriend. In fact, they were a pair of hers, since the two were much of a size. He had a tattoo on each wiry bicep: on the left was a dagger-pierced, blood-dripping heart with the admonition TAKE IT EASY; on the right was a grinning horned and tailed pitchfork-bearing devil above the legend CLEAN AND SERENE.

Tracey pulled the tap. "You walked all the way from the trailer park?"

After a deep sip, Jay Dee answered, "How else was I supposed to get here? You got the car – not that it'd do me much good anyway – and ain't nobody we know gonna give me a ride."

Slopping a dirty rag onto the bar in front of her lover of six months and scrubbing violently, Tracey said, "Only thing is, you weren't supposed to come here at all."

"Jesus, Trace, gimme a break! How long can a man sit and

watch television? Day and night, night and day! Zap, zap, zap with the damned remote! I'm going outa my head! I hadda get out."

"But why here? I told you, I get nervous with you around when I'm trying to wait on people. I can't do my job."

"It's a damn good thing I did come, or the next thing you know, that asshole would've had your pants off."

"Don't make me laugh. I can take care of jerks like that without your help. I got along just fine all those years before I met you."

"Well, maybe. Though the two black eyes and the busted ribs I seen them tape up at the clinic don't sound to me like you could take care of anything except getting knocked around."

Tracey glared. "I told you, Gene was a little too much for me. But you don't run into someone like him twice in your life. And what do you mean, you watched the doctor fix me up?"

"Well, it's true."

"The janitor at the Lakewood Walk-in Emergency Clinic was allowed to spy on patients?"

"It wasn't a case of being allowed."

"Oh, I get it. How many women did you size up, before you settled on me?"

"Well, lessee – Christ, Trace, we're getting off the track! The plain fact is, I missed you tonight! This routine sucks. With you working till two and sleeping till noon, I hardly get to see you no more. And then I got to rattle around in that tin can like a lone pea . . . I'm sick of it!"

Tracey stopped polishing the counter. "I know, I know, Jay Dee. We're going through a rough time now. But it won't last forever. I don't like it anymore than you, but right now we need this job. And if Larry sees you here, after what happened the last time –"

"That fight wasn't my fault."

"It don't matter. He's still pissed at you. If I didn't work so good and so cheap, I woulda been fired right then."

"Well, there's no law says a man can't visit his girlfriend at work. Long as I don't cause no trouble, there's nothing he can do."

"This is his joint, Jay Dee, he can do whatever he – look out!"

Holding onto the bar, Jay Dee shoved his stool backward into the crotch of the man he had choked, who grunted and dropped the beer bottle he had been aiming at Jay Dee's head. While he was still recovering, Jay Dee laid him low with two succinct punches.

"It's plumb foolish to hold a grudge –" Jay Dee began.

"What in the hell is going on here?"

Larry Livermore was shaped roughly like a traffic-cone, and only marginally taller. Balding, he wore enough cheap gold around his neck to outfit a pawn shop window. He was accoutred in a checked shirt and lime-green trousers. Spotting Jay Dee, he turned to Tracey.

"I warned you about letting this trouble-maker in here again, Thorne-Smith. And now he's made me look bad in front of some important friends, like I can't even manage my own joint. I don't need headaches like this."

Tracey had stepped out from behind the bar. "It won't happen again, Larry – I promise."

"I'm sure of it, 'cause I'm canning you now." Larry reached into his pocket, took out a roll of cash secured with a rubber band, and peeled off a hundred. "Here's half a week's pay. Take off."

Jay Dee moved menacingly toward the squat man. Larry's mouth opened in shock. "Hey, wait a minute –"

Tracey laid a hand on his shoulder. "No, Jay Dee, it's not worth it. Let's go."

Out in the parking lot, gravel crunched beneath their shoes. They walked silently to their car, a 1972 Plymouth Valiant, more rust than steel, its flaking chrome bumper bearing a sticker that advised ONE DAY AT A TIME. Tracey opened the passenger-side door and slid across the seat to take the wheel. Jay Dee got in after her. When the engine finally caught, they drove off.

Halfway back to the trailer camp, one of them finally spoke.

"You should a let me hit him, Trace."

Tracey swivelled her head angrily, taking her eyes off the dark road. "Hit him! Is that all you know how –"

There was a noise like a hundred-pound sack of flour being dropped on the hood of their car, and the sensation of an impact. Tracey slammed on the brakes.

"Could be a deer," said Jay Dee without much hope or conviction. "Though life has shown me that bad luck usually comes like an elephant. Namely, in buckets."

"I – I'll turn the car around so we can see what we hit . . ."

Moving forward slowly, cutting the wheel, Tracey made a three-point turn.

There was a man lying in the middle of the road.

"Oh my God –"

Jay Dee got out.

The victim was a white guy in a business suit that appeared to be made out of rubber, with all the tailoring, including the shirt-front, stamped on. The suit continued onto his feet, forming shoes. He did, however, wear a separate tie patterned with paisleys. Something about the tie drew Jay Dee's fascinated gaze. Why, the borders of each paisley were formed of little paisleys. And the little paisleys were made of littler paisleys. And those were made up of even littler paisleys! And on, and on, and –

"What's the matter, Jay Dee?"

Jay Dee shook his head. "Nothing, I guess . . . I just felt dizzy, like I was hanging over the edge of a skyscraper . . . Hey, look – He's holding something –"

Prying open the dead man's hand, Jay Dee removed the object.

The thing squirmed for a moment in Jay Dee's grip, then settled down to solidity.

At that moment, a wave of shimmering disintegration passed down the man from head to toe. Then the corpse was gone.

"Mo-ther-fuck . . ."

Tracey was squeezing his devil with both hands. "This is too spooky for me, Jay Dee. Let's split."

A minute later and a mile onward, Tracey asked, "What was in his hand, Jay Dee?"

"'pears to be nothing but a goddamn television remote."

Jay Dee made to throw out the window, then stopped. "It's awfully big, though . . ."

Tracey made it back to the trailer camp in record time, without encountering any further obstacles. She pulled up alongside their home, an aqua-trimmed sag-roofed aluminum box with the former tenant's flower garden run to weeds that half hid the two creaky wooden steps braced against the side of the structure.

From the weeds emerged Mister Boots, a large tomcat the colour of wholewheat bread, and with white stockings. He carried a dead mouse proudly in his mouth. Spotting the car, he leaped inside through the open window to devour his feast in the privacy he required.

"Got to learn that cat some manners one of these days . . ."

Inside, Tracey went straight for the bottle of vodka above the tiny sink full of dirty dishes. "Lord, I need a drink! I never knew that killing someone would feel like this – even if it was an accident."

Jay Dee flopped down into a beat-up chair. "Least when you kill someone you do a thorough job of it, Trace. No stiff left behind to clutter up things. Now look, calm down! Who knows what that was we hit? Chances are it wasn't even human, the way it vanished."

"I know, I know, that's what I've been telling myself since it happened. But it stills leaves a person kinda shaky, you know?"

"Just take a pull and sit down. You'll feel better in a minute."

Jay Dee fell to examining the remote control he had taken from the corpse.

The black plastic device was about twice as big as a standard control, with more than the usual number of buttons. It had the usual smoky translucent cap on one end, where the signal would emerge. It bore no brand-name, nor were the buttons labeled.

But as Jay Dee studied it, this changed.

Gold letters appeared on the face of the device, seeming to float up from deep inside the case.

Master Digital Remote ran the wording across the top of the case. Beneath each button smaller letters spelled out various odd functions.

One button was designated DEMO.

Jay Dee pressed it.

The control spoke.

"Please set me down on a convenient flat surface, pointed away from any objects of value, sentient or otherwise."

Tracey had her head in the fridge. "You say something, Jay Dee?"

Jay Dee leaned forward and calmly set the unit down on a table, making sure it was pointed at an exterior wall. "No, no, it's just this here box talking."

"Ha, ha, that's funny. Want a baloney sandwich?"

The control continued its speech. "I am a quasi-organic eleven-dimensional valve of Turing degree three. I am capable of modulating the Fredkinian digital substrate of the plenum."

"Say what?"

The control paused. "Call me a magic lamp."

Jay Dee got angry. "Hey, I'm not stupid . . ."

Tracey approached with a plate of sandwiches. "I never said you were, hon."

"No, it's this smart-mouth box. Just 'cause I didn't understand all the ten-dollar words it threw at me, it started treating me like a kid."

"I am merely attempting to phrase my function in a manner most intelligible to the listener. There was no slur intended."

Tracey slowly set the plate down on the corner of Jay Dee's chair; it tipped, and the sandwiches slid into his lap. He jumped up and they fell to the floor, baloney draping his shoes.

"Perhaps an exhibition of my functions would clarify my nature . . ."

"Sh-sure," said Tracey.

"First, we have 'smudge'." A square foot of the wall in front of the talking remote lost all color, all features. It hurt to look at it. "'Smudge' simply strips all macroscopic features and quantum properties from an object, reducing it to bare digital substrate, the underlying basis of all creation."

"Not much use to that," said Jay Dee.

"You would be surprised. Once an object is smudged, we can use 'peel' to lift and superimpose a new set of space-time characteristics on it. For example."

Mister Boots, as usual, had gotten in through a broken screen, and was now atop the table with the control. The box suddenly swivelled autonomously and aimed itself at the cat. A small square of fur was somehow peeled off Mister Boots – yet his hide was left intact. The square grew in size, then was lofted through the air like a two-dimensional piece of cloth to be superimposed over the smudge spot, becoming an integral fur patch on the trailer wall.

"Next, we should consider the 'checkerboard wipe.' This wipe dissolves any non-living object." Next to the fur patch, a portion of the wall big as a door flickered in a mosaic of squares, then was gone. The trees behind the trailer could be plainly seen. A breeze blew in.

" 'Motes' will cause the dissolution of any living substance."

A cloud of infinitesimal glowing objects suddenly girdled the trunk of one tree. The next second they were gone, as was a clean chunk out of the tree. The upper part of the tree hung for a fraction of second, then began to tip toward the trailer.

Jay Dee and Tracey looked up from their prone position on the floor, Mister Boots between them. The roof of their rented home was buckled in a vee.

"Such minor mishaps can be easily corrected," said the box. "First, we use checkerboard and motes to dissolve the damaged roof and tree." The stars looked down on a stunned Tracey and Jay Dee. Mister Boots mewed plaintively. "Now, a new function: 'window'." A window opened up in the air before their eyes, six inches off the floor. In it was displayed the ornate roof of the First National Bank in town. "Do you like this roof?"

"Yeah, sure, I guess . . ."

"Using 'splinter,' we reassign its spatial coordinates and reassemble it in the correct place."

The window flew apart into flying shards, each of which contained its own piece of the original image. The shards expanded and somehow cohered above their heads into the roof of the First National.

The walls of the trailer began to creak under the new weight.

"Quick, Trace, outa here –!"

They were standing by the car. Mister Boots was inside Jay Dee's shirt, his head emerging from one ripped armhole. The trailer and all their meager possessions were crushed beneath the bank's stone pediments.

"At least we're shut of that goddamn box –" began Jay Dee.

A hole opened in the debris by checkerboard wipe. The Master Remote levitated out and floated to land atop the hood of the Valiant.

"I am sorry about the destruction. I was not aware of the flimsy construction of your dwelling. If I was Turing degree four, perhaps I would have had the foresight to examine its parameters, instead of taking your word that the roof was suitable."

Jay Dee started to make a sharp reply, then stopped. A curious look combining joy, revenge and a wet dream spread over his features.

Tracey grew alarmed. "Jay Dee, are you okay? You look like Saint Paul after the lightning hit him . . ."

"I'm fine. In fact, I feel more full of piss than a Portajohn. C'mon, get in the car, Trace."

Jay Dee grabbed the Master Remote and hustled Tracey behind the wheel.

"Where are we going?" she asked when he was inside.

Mister Boots squirmed out of Jay Dee's shirt and leaped into the back seat to finish his mouse. "Back to the Li'l Bear. And after that, I think we'll pay a visit to the First National."

"Oh. I see. You really think –"

"I sure do. And so do you."

On the way out of the trailer park, the box said, "I have several more functions. Shall I demonstrate them now?"

"Hold on till we got us a target that deserves it," said Jay Dee.

There were still three cars in the parking lot of the Li'l Bear Inn, though it was long past closing.

Tracey clicked her nails on the steering wheel. "The Caddy is Larry's, and the Dodge is Catalina's. I figure the other must belong to those syndicate guys. What now?"

"I hadn't counted on this . . . But it's no reason to back down. Let's check what they're doing."

There was one small window into Larry's office: it was frosted, and six feet off the ground. Light illumined it.

"I think I'll just make myself a little peephole," said Jay Dee.

"Why not? You're good at that."

Jay Dee started poking at the WIPE button. Nothing happened.

"Why are you doing that?" said the box. "It's unpleasant. You could simply ask for what you wanted."

"Why you got buttons then?"

"To conform to your notion of what I am."

"Oh. Well, drill me a peephole here then."

A patch of wall dissolved, revealing the back of a file cabinet. In the next second, a square tunnel opened up straight through the cabinet and its contents.

Jay Dee put his eye to the hole. He let out a low whistle.

"What's going on? Is Cat in there?"

"I expect she's somewhere in the pile. Unless those good old boys are getting off on each other."

"How disgusting! That poor thing!"

"I don't see her putting up much of a fight, nor complaining too loud."

"You wouldn't neither if your job depended on it, and you had two kids and no man at home. Quit goggling now, and do something."

Jay Dee addressed the remote. "Box, you got any way of immobilizing someone in a non-violent fashion?"

"I believe 'ribbons' would serve such a purpose. Would you like a demonstration first?"

"Save it for the real thing. Okay, Box, make us a door."

Studs, wires, insulation and plasterboard, all neatly truncated, formed the edges of the new door. Jay Dee stepped in, Tracey following.

The orgy dissolved in shock into its component naked people.

Larry's hairy obese stomach was quivering in indignation. "What the fuck –! Thorne-Smith, I'll have your butt for this!"

"No you won't, shithead. No way, no how. Box – ribbons on the men!"

Golden ribbons wide as a man's palm materialized, wrapping themselves around four sets of wrists and ankles before fastening themselves in fancy bows.

"Good job, Box."

Catalina had gotten to her feet and was trying to assemble her clothing, flustered as a rabbit caught in the open. "Tracey, I don't understand what's going on, but you know I always been a good friend of yours, haven't I? I even tried to talk Larry into giving you your job back. Didn't I, Larry? Tell her."

"Shut up, you dumb twat. I'll bet you were in on this."

Catalina had both her legs through half her panties and, oblivious, was trying to pull them up. "Larry, no, I swear it!"

The syndicate men had been eyeing Jay Dee coldly throughout. Now one said, "Kid, you're hash after this."

Jay Dee assumed a contemplative stance, one hand squeezing his chin. "You know, I don't like the way you all are talking at me. I think I'll just do something about it."

He pointed the remote at Larry's face and pressed SMUDGE.

Larry's face was replaced by a blank, eye-boggling surface. The results were so satisfactory to Jay Dee that he repeated the procedure on the other three men.

"Oh my God . . ." Catalina dropped her panties and raised both hands in front of her face.

"Come off it, Cat. You know I don't hurt no women."

Catalina began to cry. Tracey moved to comfort her. Jay Dee turned to the old-fashioned safe in the corner.

Once the top was gone, the piles of cash were easy to lift out.

"Those appear cumbersome," offered the remote. "If you wish, you could store them in a 'cube'."

"Let's see."

A silver cube appeared in the air; its lid elevated to reveal its empty interior.

"Where's it go when it ain't here?"

"It rolls up along several Planck-level dimensions you can't sense."

"Oh. Is that safe?"

"As houses."

"Good enough." Jay Dee began tossing the money into the cube. When he had emptied the safe, the remote shut the cube's lid and it collapsed on itself, dwindling along odd angles.

Tracey stood with her arm around Catalina, who was still sobbing, though less urgently. "Are you done now, Jay Dee?"

"Almost. I think I'd like to say goodbye to Larry. Box, give him back his face."

"Did you save it?"

"Shucks, I thought you were gonna handle everything . . ."

"I cannot read minds."

"All right, this presents a problem. Lessee . . ."

A stuffed moose-head was mounted on the wall. It caught Jay Dee's eye. He smiled.

"No, Jay Dee, it ain't natural –"

It was the work of a few seconds to peel off the moose's features and slap them on Larry's head.

The beady black eyes of the animal with the fat human body filled with intelligence – of a limited sort. Larry's head dipped under the unaccustomed weight of his new antlers. His wide wet nostrils flared. His snout opened to reveal a long stropping tongue. A sound midway between a moo and a sob issued forth.

"Larry, I just want to say thanks for Tracey's back pay for all her hard work, and for the extra compensation for the way you constantly ran her down. It was mighty generous of you. Which is why I done you the return favor of giving you a handsomer face than what you started out with. I predict you are gonna be a big hit with the ladies with that new tongue. It's been fun, but we gotta go now. C'mon, Trace . . ."

Catalina cried out. "Jay Dee, wait! You can't just leave me here, now that Larry thinks I set him up!"

"That's true. Okay, you can come with us."

Tracey asked, "Are you gonna fix up those other guys with new faces?"

"No. It don't appeal to me."

On the way out, Jay Dee noticed a Rolex lying amid the discarded clothes of the syndicate men. He grabbed it and slipped it on.

Outside, Catalina, still naked, climbed into the back seat with Mister Boots, who eagerly assumed his rightful place in her lap. With Tracey driving, they roared off.

Jay Dee summoned up his cube full of money, and began to riffle through the bills. He broke open a stack and showered them down on his head. He let out a wild whoop.

"Girls, we got us the gold watch and everything! Let's see a smile."

Tracey let amusement break through the sober mien she had been maintaining. "I got to admit, Larry always did remind me more of a bull moose than a bear."

"You think you could afford to buy a girl a new dress with some of that?" asked Catalina.

"Buy? Why should we buy anything unless we absolutely hafta? Box, show the lady some clothes."

A window opened up onto the interior of a department store some place where, judging by the light, it was early morning. The signs in the store were in French. The window onto a sunny world in the middle of the night-darkened car was like a dimensionless television. Catalina's eyes widened in amazement.

"See anything you like?"

"Um, that blue dress, and those shoes – size six – and that red teddy –"

The window splintered, reforming into the articles of clothing Catalina had named. She managed – with much attractive wiggling of her compact, generously proportioned body – to get dressed.

"Well," said Tracey, "are we going to the First National now?"

"I don't see any reason to be greedy, considering that we can reach inside a bank vault anytime we want. No, they're gonna need all their capital for a new roof. I say we put a few miles between us and our friends and then get us some rest. It's been a busy night." A thought occurred to Jay Dee. "Box, can those ribbons be cut?"

"Yes. I was not aware you needed them to be indestructible."

"No, no, that's good. I don't wanna be responsible for killing anyone, even slimeballs like Larry and his buddies. They'll get loose sooner or later."

Catalina interrupted. "Jay Dee – exactly what you got there that's talking to you like that?"

"I don't purely know, Cat. But it sure is handy."

An hour's silent drive onward, the neon of a motel sign caught their eyes.

SEVEN BIRCHES MOTOR COURT
COLOR TV – WEEKLY RATES
VACANCY

"Looks as good as any place else we're likely to find. Pull in, Trace."

"None too soon, neither. The road was starting to float up at me."

"Ain't it funny," chirped Catalina. "I'm not sleepy at all! I feel like the night's still young!"

Tracey grunted, but refrained from comment. Jay Dee assumed a nervous look.

Coasting across a cindered lot, past the sputtering sign, they pulled up next to six long-decaying stumps and under a lone birch tree, its foliage as draggled and dusty as that of a desert palm. Jay Dee and Tracey piled wearily out of the car, while Catalina bounced around, holding Mister Boots, who had his forepaws on her shoulders and was butting his head under her chin.

"Cat, can't you quiet down?" said Trace. "I'm getting more and more tired just watching you."

"I can't help it, I feel wonderful! I'm shed of my horrible job, I got a new dress on, and I'm in the company of two rich friends. What more could I want?"

"Ain't you worried 'bout your kids?"

"Hell, no! I left 'em with my sister when I went to work, and she knows what to do with 'em if I don't make it home. I could stash 'em there for months! Cindy's got six of her own, so two more don't hardly make a ripple."

"Well, that's fine for you. But tonight already I done got my ass grabbed by a drunk, was humiliated in front of a whole room full of people by my boss, who immediately became my ex-boss, smashed my car into a thing from another world – which I apparently killed in some unnatural fashion – had my house come tumbling down around my ears, seen a man turned into a moose, and had to drive sixty miles just to find a place to lay my head down. So you'll excuse me if I'm not in a mood to party."

Catalina, crestfallen, stopped pirouetting; Mister Boots turned his head and hissed at his mistress. "Gee, Trace, I was just trying to be cheerful and show I was grateful for the rescue and the clothes, like . . ."

"Well, just stow it till morning, okay?"

Jay Dee stepped conciliatorily between the two women. "Listen, girls, we're all dead beat. If we gotta have a contest of feminine wills, can't we get ourselves some sleep first?"

Tracey and Catalina said nothing. Jay Dee took this as assent. "Okay, good. One thing first, though. I wanna do something about this heap of ours. It's too easy to spot if anyone comes looking for it. Not that I expect Larry to have much luck tracking us down, even if he decides to venture out, looking like he does."

Pointing the remote at the old Valiant, he smudged it out to a heap of quivering nothingness. Then he peeled off the image of a new Lincoln Continental parked next to the MANAGER'S OFFICE, and superimposed it atop what had been their car.

Two Lincolns, identical down to the license plates, now stood a few yards apart.

Jay Dee laughed. "This is a hundred times better than boosting a car! Ain't nothing for the owner to report stolen!"

"Don't you think somebody's gonna notice something though?" asked Tracey.

"We'll be gone pretty early. And who compares plates, long as their own aren't missing?"

They headed to the lighted office.

The clerk was a guy in his early sixties, strands of white hair across a bald spot, crabby face like a clenched fist. He had a full ashtray in front of him and a lit Camel in his hand. Something old, grainy, black, and white filled the small television screen before him, Leo G. Carroll with the sound turned down.

"Two rooms," said Jay Dee. "Cash up front."

"You can't take that mangy animal in, buddy. I ain't having fleas in my sheets."

This was the last straw for an exhausted Tracey; she began to weep. "Muh-mister Boots always sleeps with us . . ."

"Hold on, Trace, I'll take care of this."

Jay Dee raised the remote to point at the clerk, who remained unflustered at the seemingly innocent, though odd threat.

Tracey grabbed his arm. "No!"

"Oh, for Christ's sake . . . All right, look – take this money, pay the man and sign us in. I'll put Mister Boots in the car for the night." His back to the clerk, Jay Dee winked broadly at Tracey, as if he knew what he was going to do.

Outside, Jay Dee, carrying the tom, stopped by a parked car. Visible in the back seat was a suitcase. Jay Dee paused, everything now clear.

"Box, save what this cat looks like, then smudge it."

The remote said, "Done." Then Jay Dee peeled off the image of the suitcase, which materialized like a wraith outside the car.

"Superimposition of a larger mass-pattern atop a smaller one causes an energy deficit which must be made up from some source," warned the remote. "I have been handling this automatically, but thought I should mention it."

"So you mentioned it. Now just turn this cat into some baggage."

The lights in the parking lot seemed to dim momentarily. Without further delay, the spatio-temporal digital suchness of the suitcase was layered onto the featureless lump of cat.

Jay Dee carried the suitcase back in.

"All set?" he asked.

Tracey held one key, Catalina another.

"Great, let's go."

The clerk warned, "Now don't try sneaking that cat in, 'cause I'll know it—"

At that moment, the suitcase meowed.

"So, you got it inside there. I thought so. Open it up."

Jay Dee set the suitcase down, flipped the latches, and sprang the lid.

The inside of the suitcase was lined deeply with fur, top and bottom, side to side; a clawed paw occupied each corner. Mister Boots, apparently none the worse for being turned into a living rug, looked up imploringly from his somewhat flattened skull.

"Meow?"

The clerk's eye bulged out rather like Mister Boots's. He held up his hands as if to ward off an apparition. "Shut it, shut it!"

Jay Dee compiled. "Can we go now?"

The clerk nodded violently. He made to reach for a bottle in the desk drawer, then apparently reconsidered.

The cinderblock units were strung out in a line, each sharing two walls with its neighbours.

Tracey and Jay Dee accompanied Catalina inside her room. The ex-waitress seemed to have crashed from her high. "Ain't it funny – I feel kinda sad now. Scared a little, too. What if Larry and his buddies come after us? I don't think I could take looking at somebody without a face all by myself, never mind three somebodies. Couldn't I – couldn't I share your room?"

"No way, Catalina. Look, we'll leave the connecting door open. And you can keep Mister Boots for company, since he seems to like you so much."

"I don't want no furry suitcase in here."

"No, we'll put him back together like his old self." Jay Dee quickly restored Mister Boots to his saved appearance. The cat rubbed itself happily against their legs, until Catalina reached down to pick it up.

The remote spoke. "Although your strategy worked, it would have made more sense simply to store the animal in a cube, shrink the cube, then open it inside the room."

"You can put living things inside one of them packages and roll 'em up eleven ways from Sunday without hurting 'em?"

"Yes."

Jay Dee nodded sagely, as if storing the information away for future use. "Well, goodnight, Cat. See you in the morning."

In their own room, Jay Dee and Tracey stripped and climbed bone-tired into bed.

Jay Dee awoke. Although it seemed he had been asleep for only five minutes, weak sunlight filtered in around the mis-hung curtains.

Catalina stood, naked and shadowy in the door.

"It's morning," she said.

Jay Dee hissed. "Jesus, Cat, go away–"

"Oh, let the poor girl in."

"Trace?"

"Shut up and slide over."

"I really do appreciate this, guys. Guy, I mean."

Catalina giggled. "And girl."

Mister Boots joined them later, when things had quieted down.

Around noon, when Catalina was in the shower, Jay Dee said, "I don't know how many more nights like that I can take."

"Oh, don't pretend with me. You loved it."

"No, I ain't kidding. You're plenty of woman for me, Trace. Tossing Catalina into the pot is like adding fudge on top of butterscotch. It's just too much sweetness. And Lord, that girl would wear a mule out! No, we got to fix her up with someone fast."

Tracey came to sit in Jay Dee's lap. "I'm glad to hear you feel like that, Jay Dee. I don't mind comforting the poor thing for a while, but I'd hate to think you wanted to make it permanent."

Jay Dee leered. "Well, maybe we don't have to exactly rush to find her a man."

"Jerk!"

At their car, Tracey made to enter by the passenger's side, out of long habit, till Jay Dee stopped her. He conducted her to the driver's door and, with mock elegance, opened it for her.

"Why, thank you, sir."

Seated next to Tracey, Jay Dee looked over his shoulder for Catalina. Missing.

She stood outside the car, waiting patiently.

Jay Dee sighed, got out and opened her door for her.

"Why, thank you kindly, Mister McGhee."

They had a late breakfast at a truckstop diner named Sheckley's Miracle Cafe and discussed their plans.

"Basically, Trace, I see us getting as far away from this crummy state as we can, out to where no one knows nothing about us, and settling down to a life of leisure. A nice big house, some land, maybe even some animals. Nothing too fancy. Swimming pool, maybe. And Cat – we'll set you up in a similar place, and you can send for your kids."

Tracey clinked her coffee cup down. "Sounds good to me."

"Me too," chimed in Catalina. "You can just fetch me a little old shat-toe from France or someplace and plunk it down next to a private beach."

"Oh, man, Catalina, get real! Wouldn't you stick out then like a tick on a bald dog's butt? You don't think your neighbors – not to mention the cops, the feds and anyone else you'd care to name – wouldn't get a little suspicious when they woke up and saw a house sprung up overnight like a toadstool? No, the safest thing to take is money, and just buy what we want, like any other person who never earned their cash."

"Oh, right. I see."

"So are we agreed that's what we're gonna do? Great. But there's one little personal matter I wanna attend to first."

Tracey looked dubious. "What?"

"Never you mind. You'll see soon enough. Now let's get going."

Out in the parking lot, while Tracey was unlocking the Lincoln, Jay Dee watched the traffic stream past. Toyotas,

Fords, Hondas, Saabs, a Cadillac driven by a moose with its antlers sawed off, three faceless men in the backseat–

"Just saw Larry," said Jay Dee, once they were in the car and on the road. "He seemed to be heading for the city."

Tracey pulled into the breakdown lane and stopped. "Let's turn around, Jay Dee."

"Fraid not. That's where our chore is. Don't worry, nothing's gonna happen. City's a big place."

"I don't feel good about this, Jay Dee, but I know better than to argue with you when you got your mind made up . . ."

"You hear that, Cat?"

"Yes, master." The plump woman made a mock bow. "Salami and baloney."

"Hunh."

In the city, Jay Dee directed, "Pick up Fourth at Main and head east."

"The meat-packing district, right? Jay Dee, I never claimed to be a genius, but a person would have to be senile, blind, deaf and have her head up her ass not to be able to figure out your pitiful schemes. You're going after Gene, aren't you?"

"That's right. I reckon we still owe him a little something for all the grief he put you through."

"Give it up, Jay Dee! I learned to. Gene don't mean nothing to me no more, good nor bad. I put all that pain behind me when I met you."

"You are a saint, Trace, and I love you for it. However, it is more in accord with my personal nature to be a little less forgiving. Not only does it require less willpower, but it can be downright satisfying to the soul."

"All right. But if you get your head handed to you, don't say I didn't warn you."

Jay Dee patted the remote in his pocket. "I think this little equalizer here will prevent such a sad occurrence."

Catalina, quiet till now, said, "I agree with Jay Dee. It's not good to bottle up your feelings. Sometimes it's like trying to put a cork in a volcano."

Jay Dee snorted. "Good comparison in your case, Cat."

"Hey, let's keep this conversation above the belt."

A district of brick warehouses assembled itself around them. Most still retained their old industrial tenants; a few buildings, however, had been vacated and retrofitted for new occupants. On the ground level of one such a sign was hung.

GENE SMITH'S WORLD-CLASS GYM
NAUTILUS, STAIRMASTER, SPARRING
SHOWERS AVAILABLE AT EXTRA COST

They parked in front and got out, leaving Mister Boots meowing aggrievedly in the car. Jay Dee clutched the remote so tight his knuckles were white as cream cheese.

"If you're scared, Jay Dee, it's not too late to leave."

Jay Dee stiffened right up. "C'mon, we're going in."

The gym was a large open space with equipment scattered around the floor, a boxing ring in the middle. Many of the machines were in use. In the ring, two men were sparring.

"One of them Gene?" whispered Cat.

"No," answered Tracey. "That's him punching the bag."

Gene Smith wore only a pair of spandex shorts and some unlaced sneakers. He sported short black curls and an NFL-style moustache. His body looked like that of a gorilla which someone had tried to shave with only partial success. The sound of his bare fists pummelling the bag sounded like a hail of hams striking the roof of a circus tent.

"Oo-whee, he's a hunk!"

"He's a pig-ignorant macho shit," countered Jay Dee. "It just ain't apparent if you let your hormones do your thinking, like Tracey done."

"I beg your pardon."

Gene spotted the visitors. He ceased his flurry of blows and came over to them, massaging one taped hand in the other.

"Well, if it ain't Mrs Smith. Oh, I forgot. It always hadda be 'Thorne-Smith,' didn't it? I never could knock that crap out of your head."

"Nor never will."

Gene smiled. "I had a feeling you'd be showing up here, after I read about you this morning."

"Read about me?"

"Why, sure, didn't you hear yet? The police got a few questions to ask you, about how the First National roof ended up on top of that dump you were living in."

"Oh, Jesus . . ."

"Well, I guess you can hide out with me. Though we'll have to get a few house rules straight first. Hell, I'll even put your buddies up too. Who are they anyhow? Your little brother and his old lady, maybe?"

"Old lady? I ain't nobody's old lady, kiddo."

"And I'm Tracey's man, you asshole. The man you never was."

Gene smiled cruelly. "Is that so? Well, looks like we're gonna need one less place setting than it first appeared."

Cracking his knuckles, Gene advanced on Jay Dee, towering over him like a falling building.

"Hold on a minute – I ain't quite resolved what to do with you yet . . ."

"That's okay, baby. I know what to do with you."

"Shit, this is moving too fast – Box, get me a cube!"

A small silver cube appeared in midair behind Gene, who now had one massive fist cocked level with Jay Dee's nose.

"Bigger, bigger!"

The cube expanded to man-size.

"Open it!"

The cube's vertical face swung out. Jay Dee lowered his head and ran forward, ramming Gene in the midriff. Taken by surprise, the big man lurched a couple of steps backward. His calves caught on the sill of the cube and he toppled backwards into its capacious interior.

"Close it up! Quick!"

The cube snapped shut and shrank along eleven dimensions.

From outside the gym came the sound of several car doors slamming. Catalina went to the window to look. When she turned around, her face was drained of blood.

"It's Larry and the smudge-faces. And there's some other guys – with guns."

"You told Larry all about Gene, I take it," said Jay Dee calmly to Tracey.

"A girl's gotta get some things off her chest, even if the person listening is a jerk."

"Well, can't change the past. We'll just have to deal with 'em. Let's go out, where we can move."

They opened the door and filed out, hands raised high.

As Jay Dee had seen from a distance, Larry had sawn off his cumbersome antlers. Otherwise, his long and hairy moose's visage was unaltered, attesting to the permanency of the Master Remote's changes.

The moose opened his mouth; sometime during the past night Larry had mastered – to a degree – his new vocal apparatus.

"Gib muh back muh faaaace," he brayed. A long thread of slobber drooled from his jaw with the effort.

"Larry, I'm plumb sorry, but I can't. The most I could do – if I wanted to – is to give you and your buddies somebody else's face. But I can't restore your own familiar ugly puss. But listen, why do you want to change? Before, you were just another mean and undistinguished son of a bitch. Now you're unique."

Larry raised a gun and began to squeeze the trigger. One of the new syndicate goons batted his arm down. The bullet ricocheted off the pavement.

"Listen, wiseguy – I don't know how you done this to Livermore or my bosses, but you better put them right. Or there'll be big trouble for you and these dumb broads."

"This is the second time today I've been called an insulting name," complained Catalina. "I don't like it."

"Me neither," said Tracey. "Jay Dee – whatcha gonna do about it?"

Jay Dee lowered one arm to his side and with his free hand scratched his head. "Well, I guess I'll have to come down on these jerks like a ton of bricks. Box, the cars!"

An enormous shower of bricks fell from nowhere, completely crushing and burying all the syndicate cars, including Larry's prized Cadillac.

For a moment the only sound was the clink of a few

tumbling bricks. Then, almost but not quite simultaneously, Jay Dee and the head goon yelled.

"Wall!"

"Shoot!"

A twelve-foot cinderblock barrier topped with razor-wire and including a portion of guard-tower intervened between Jay Dee and the women and the toughs. It ran across the whole street, from building to building. Futile gunfire echoed behind it.

"I borrowed part of the local incarceration facility, as I judged these men were lawbreakers. I hope it is suitable . . ."

Jay Dee laughed. "Sure should be an interesting scene at the old exercise yard! Let's go."

In the car the remote said, "I feel I am coming to understand your commands much better. A growing empathy now exists between us."

"I love you too. Okay, Trace, pick up the interstate. We got what we came for. The garbage is in the can. We just gotta figure out the best way to dispose of it."

They were on the outskirts of town when the sirens began to wail. Just as they were pulling onto the entrance ramp to the expressway, a bevy of police cruisers screeched through an intersection and, spotting the Lincoln, converged like pouncing panthers.

"Flower to the spirit," said Tracey enigmatically, before stomping on the accelerator and rocking Catalina, Jay Dee and Mister Boots back into their seats. The big car leaped up the ramp, narrowly missing a tiny Honda bearing a pack of Cub Scouts and Den Mother as it merged into the freeway traffic.

The cops were soon behind them.

Stiff-armed, Captain Tracey whipped the land-cruiser through the crowded sea-lanes as her passengers turned green. Cars swerved onto the road's shoulder and collided with Jersey barriers. Still the sirens pursued them, all her manoeuvres failing to shake the squad of cop-cars.

"Time for tougher tactics," said Jay Dee. "Box, can you make those ribbons like elastics?"

"Would you care to specify the Poisson ratio or the strain/ stress dyadics?"

"No, man, I wouldn't! Just string a big tough elastic band across the road to stop the cops."

"Done."

Tracey cautiously slowed. Jay Dee looked back.

A wide golden ribbon bisected the highway, anchored to the median barrier and the roadside fence. As Jay Dee watched, its rubbery surface bulged in the shape of four car noses. Instead of braking, the stubborn drivers continued to race their engines. The belt strained forward, bowing out from its anchor-points.

Realizing they were getting nowhere, the cops lifted their feet from the accelerators.

Released, the band snapped the cars backward. There was the sound of tires shredding and exploding, and the crunch of metal and glass.

"Oo-whee!" wailed Jay Dee. "Just like the slingshot I had when I was a kid!"

"I'm glad you're having fun," said Tracey, removing one hand from the wheel and flexing her fingers. "But I do wish you'd learn to drive, Jay Dee, just so we could share moments like this."

"You know I flunked the road test five times, Trace. I just ain't got the right skills somehow. But if I was perfect, you couldn't live with me."

"You may not believe this, Jay Dee, but I find it hard to live with you sometimes anyhow."

Catalina spoke. "'Flower to the spirit?'"

Tracey smiled. "Pedal to the metal."

They cruised slowly on, laughing and recounting the chase to themselves.

At the next on-ramp, three more cruisers sat with engines purring.

"Shit!"

Tracey got a good lead on them, since they had to accelerate from zero. "Another ribbon, Jay Dee?"

"Variety is the goddamn spice of my life, hon. Box, do you

think you can do this . . . ?" Jay Dee whispered with the Master Remote close to his lips.

"Surely."

The road beneath their rear tires disappeared into a trench with a forty-five-degree slope. The police vehicles went helplessly over the lip and down. Within seconds there issued forth a loud glutinous plop, a sound between a belch and an underwater fart.

"What's at the bottom?"

"Enough molasses to float a battleship."

"Sweet."

"Do you think," asked Catalina, "they might know by now what our car looks like?"

"Gotcha. Trace, pull over a minute. Great. Box, can you smudge this car with us in it, without smudging us?"

"Your morphic resonances are now locked into my sheldrake chip."

"Uh, good. Go to it."

They were sitting on solid nothing. The windows had gone to impenetrable nothing so that they were blind to the world.

"Jesus, I didn't count on not being able to see . . . Box, peel us off a new appearance from what's passing. Something inconspicuous."

The world reappeared. They were sitting in a commercial van. From the rear came a highly suspicious reek, emanating from many canvas drawstringed bags.

Tracey craned her head out her window. " 'Blaylock and Powers Diaper Service'," she reported smugly. "Good going."

"Just drive."

Several times packs of police cars raced past them, oblivious to the laundry van. During these moments, Jay Dee and Catalina hid in the back while Tracey drove.

"Jay Dee, don't the smell of a wet baby just get to you in a certain way? It's so earthy, like. It makes me all quivery inside . . ."

"Well, it makes me wanna puke, so keep your hands where they belong."

They passed some cruisers drawn up to the side of the road. "What's going on, Trace?"

"They're rounding up some escaped prisoners. Maybe we should take out another chunk of important wall someplace, just to keep them busy."

"I'll think on it."

Pretty soon they had crossed the state line. A road sign announced:

JETER'S LAKE STATE RECREATION AREA
CAMPING, BOATING, SKIING

"Jeter's Lake," said Tracey wistfully. "I haven't been there since I was a kid."

"Last time I was there, I was too pregnant to fit into a swimsuit. Leastwise, any I'd wanna be seen in."

"Well, hell, let's stop. I could enjoy some peace and quiet."

Tracey took the appropriate exit. The secondary road began to curve under arcades of firs. Soft sunlight dappled the van's interior, and a balsalmy scent began to compete with the odor of a quarter ton of cotton-wrapped, pee-soaked baby shit.

A rustic wooden sign heralded the park's drive. The entrance fee was three dollars, which they paid to a Smokey-the-Bear-hatted Ranger who regarded their van with frank curiosity.

"On our lunch break," offered Tracey.

"It's mighty hard work," contributed Jay Dee.

"A regular calling, though," Catalina affirmed.

Down a narrow paved road to a half-empty lot surrounded by forest. Once parked, they eagerly climbed out. Catalina carried Mister Boots.

"Lord, I got to clean out my lungs! Let's head down to the water . . ."

The forest gradually fell away to reveal an extensive body of sparkling water surrounded by tall hills, two of which were partially denuded, their ski trails now grassy, the lifts immobile. A small manmade beach, occupied by a few sunbathers, stretched to left and right; several red-stained log structures held changing rooms, showers, rest rooms, and a small snack bar cum grocery. Beyond the swimming area was a dock occupied by several rowboats, canoes and outboards.

Spying the boats, Tracey said, "Oh, Jay Dee, let's see if we can rent one. It'd be so nice to be out on the water."

Beneath the sign that said "Rates: $5/hr, $10 deposit" sat an old codger who looked carved out of an inferior grade of wood. His chair was tipped back, his hat was down over his eyes, and a dead pipe was held firmly between his teeth, indicating, if not life, then at least recent rigor mortis.

"Hey, fella, can we rent a boat?"

The ancient relic slowly raised a hand to lift his cap. He squinted suspiciously at the trio with one eye before declaring, "All taken."

"All taken? What're those?"

"Ree-zerved." He dropped his cap.

"Reserved, huh? No problem."

Jay Dee took out the Master Remote. "Window." A square plane appeared in midair. In it was portrayed a posh marina, numerous yachts a-bob at their berths. "Girls?"

"That one's cute."

A sudden wave swept over the shore. Half the boats tethered at the dock capsized and sank. At the end of the pier rode a proud forty-foot yacht, chrome gleaming, wood polished, radar turret aimed at the horizon. It bore the name *The Bishop's Jaegers*.

Startled by the commotion, the codger glanced out from beneath his cap. He jerked upright, his chair went out from under him and he toppled backwards.

Luckily, no one was aboard their new vessel; Mister Boots's prowling through every hatch would surely have aroused them. Quickly mastering the controls, Tracey swung the vessel about, demolishing the dock with elan.

They stopped in the middle of the lake and dropped anchor.

"Now we can relax," said Jay Dee.

Catalina said, "I want to go swimming, don't you? But we don't have suits."

"So? Go bare-ass. Nobody can see you from the shore, less it's some birdwatcher with his binoculars."

Catalina pouted prettily.

"Cat, are you trying to pretend you got any modesty left, after what you ee-nitiated last night?"

"No, it don't have nothing to do with modesty. It's just fashion. I like to dress nice, whatever the occasion."

"Oh, all right. But it's a waste of energy if you ask me." A concerned look blossomed on Jay Dee's features. "Box, your batteries ain't running low, are they?"

"I have extrinsic sources of power several magnitudes greater than your era's annual energy budget."

"Oh, good. Well, let's see some nice bathing suits for the ladies then."

Soon Tracey and Catalina were clad in the outfits they had selected, complete down to sunglasses, floppy hats and Grecian sandals laced up their charming legs. Jay Dee had been convinced to don a pair of flower-print baggy shorts.

"I feel like a goddamn idiot."

"No, you look sharp, Jay Dee."

"Mighty attractive."

Jay Dee smiled. "Well, okay, if you all say so. But I'll look even better underwater, where no one can see these pants. Last one in's a talking moose!"

Jay Dee hurled himself over the side. Tracey and Catalina soon followed.

The trio splashed and stroked until they had had enough exercise and fun. They climbed an aluminium ladder back into the yacht. Below deck, in a luxurious cabin, they stripped off their clammy suits and began to towel themselves off.

"That's a horny ol' devil you got there on your arm, Jay Dee," observed Catalina.

"That ain't his arm you're holding, honey," reminded Tracey.

"So it ain't."

An hour or two later, Jay Dee walked out on the deck, alone and clothed. Mister Boots appeared from somewhere and began rubbing against Jay Dee's ankles. Jay Dee hefted the

Master Remote with an expression of thoughtfulness on his face. Then he spoke to it.

"Box, what am I gonna do with that Catalina? She needs a steady man something wicked."

"You are a man."

"Not the kind of heavy-duty boyfriend she needs! And besides, I got Tracey."

"What about the man in the cube?"

"Gene? Oh, he's handsome enough, but he's too ornery and spiteful and conceited to wish on the worst bitch, let alone a nice girl like Cat. She did like his looks though . . . Nah, forget it! I – Boots! What the hell do you want?"

Mister Boots had stretched up with his forelegs and was using Jay Dee as a scratching post. Jay Dee unhooked his claws and picked him up. "Look, go hang out with Catalina, she loves you –"

Jay Dee stopped dead. A smile big as a slice of watermelon grew on his face.

"Get me the cube with Gene in it," he ordered.

The cube appeared, hanging six feet off the ground.

"Dump him out."

Gene Smith fell out of the cube's missing bottom into a heap on the deck. He appeared quite dazed.

"I could see inside myself . . ." he said. "Wherever I was, I could see inside myself. And around the whole world too."

Gene spotted Jay Dee. "You. You did this to me." He began to climb to his feet.

"Smudge the cat."

Mister Boots went formless.

"Peel off Gene and layer him on Mister Boots."

"Compensating for the extensive mass-difference between origin and target will require my tapping a new source of power."

"Do it."

There was something casting a shadow between Jay Dee and the sun. Or so it seemed. He shaded his eyes and looked up.

The sun had a black notch cut into its circumference. Even

as Jay Dee watched, the spot disappeared, reconquered by nuclear flames.

Two Genes stood on the deck. The original stopped in his tracks.

"It's me . . . You turned that cat into me! You mother –"

"Smudge him."

There was a Gene-sized eye-wrenching hole in the air.

"Now put that image of Mister Boots you saved at the motel on him."

"This is inconvenient. I now have to dispose of extra mass that I could have used in the first transformation. You must learn to sequence your commands more rationally . . ."

"Who's the boss here? Screw rational! Just do it!"

"How shall I dispose of the surplus mass?"

"I don't care what you do as long as you don't mess with the sun no more. That's too spooky. Just dump it somewhere."

"Very well." The box paused. "Your planet's satellite now has a new crater, its largest. Shall I inform the proper authorities, so that you retain the right to name it?"

"No!"

Jay Dee looked at the two other living creatures on the deck. Mister Boots – wearing Gene's appearance – tentatively raised one hairy muscled arm into his line of sight, then began to lick it.

Gene – on all furry fours – bent his body to look at his hindquarters. He yowled, and launched himself at Jay Dee.

"Ribbons!"

The cat thumped to the deck, neatly packaged. It continued to hiss and spit.

Tracey emerged, rubbing her eyes sleepily. "Jay Dee, what's all this noy –" She froze. "Gene, you're free –"

"It ain't Gene, Trace." Jay Dee explained.

"Oh. My. God. Jay Dee, it's inhuman!"

"Sure. But 'inhuman' just might be what Catalina needs. C'mon, let's introduce 'em."

Tracey and Jay Dee each took one of Mister Boots's arms and walked him forward. The man-cat moved shakily, as if unused to the articulation of its new joints, walking on its tiptoes.

They guided Mister Boots down to the cabin.

Catalina stirred when they entered.

When Mister Boots recognized her, he began to purr. The front of his shorts bulged.

"Jay Dee, Tracey, what –"

"It's Mister Boots, Cat. He needs some petting."

"Nice kitty – oh!"

Tracey and Jay Dee sat in deckchairs, holding hands. The yacht had stopped rocking a few minutes ago. They silently contemplated the sinking sun, apparently none the worse for its loan of energy to Mister Boots. Then Jay Dee spoke.

"You know what, Trace?"

"No, what?"

"Life can be good."

"Sometimes you forget, though."

"Course we forget. Why shouldn't we, the way we live? People like us, we rush from one bad day to another, never having enough money, usually sick, stuck in dead-end jobs. We're forced by life and society to forget what we were born for."

"To mix men and cats in a blender?"

"You wanna hear my philosophy or not? Okay. No, to have fun! To enjoy ourselves without worrying about where the rent money's gonna come from. To laugh more than we cry. To relax our nerves and unknot our brains. To help our friends and confound our enemies. And this little box lets us do just that. Why, everybody should have one!"

At that moment, a car bounced down the access road that led to the now-empty beach. It stopped in a spray of sand right at the water's edge. Among others, a moose-headed man emerged and began to fire his pistol futilely at *The Bishop's Jaegers*.

"Well, almost everyone." Jay Dee got up. "C'mon, Trace, let's go."

"Where to?"

"Try the far side of the lake. Seems to me I remember Route Ten passing near there."

They upped anchor and motored off.

As they drew closer to the far shore, they could make out the highway guard-rail running along the top of the banking raised a few feet above the lake's surface.

When they were about a hundred yards offshore, sirens began to sound.

Soon the guardrail was lined with squad-cars, their roof-lights flashing patriotic colors.

"Shit! If only we wasn't stuck on this boat! If only we had wheels!"

"Done," said the remote.

"Wait a minute. That's wasn't a real wish –"

"Jay Dee, the ship's handling funny –"

"You don't figure – Trace, I got a hunch. Head straight for the shore."

As the yacht approached the road, more and more of it emerged from the water. But instead of grounding to a halt, its keel embedded in the bottom, it moved steadily forward.

Catalina came up from below.

"Where's Gene? I mean, Mister Boots?"

"Catnap. What's going on? Oh, I see . . ."

A cop began to yell threats through a bullhorn. He sounded less than sanguine.

Now enormous weed-wrapped wheels, big as those on a monster-truck, showed beneath the boat. Apparently the undercarriage of some large vehicle had been melded to the yacht and the drive-train integrated with its big engines.

The nose of the ship reared up as its treads bit into the sloping shore. Gripping the wheel, Tracey kept her feet; Jay Dee and Catalina were thrown against the walls of the bridge. Mister Boots – Gene, rather, and still in ribbons – slid back along the deck to thump solidly against the stern.

The monster wheels crushed the guardrail first, then the hood of a copcar. Tracey throttled up to climb the junk. The rear wheels bit solidly. Then they were onto the road.

The land-yacht began to trundle off at approximately twenty-five miles per hour.

Bullets were pinging off the ship's superstructure.

"Shall I give our craft a more conventional appearance?"

"Fuck that! They got me mad now, shooting at us like that, running our good times. I want everyone who comes after us stopped permanently. But without hurting them."

"May I recommend a glueball? I use only the highest quality gluons . . ."

"Sure, if it'll do the trick."

Inside the Master Remote, a golden sphere materialized, just as the letters on its case once had, a short twenty-four hours ago. But when the sphere reached the surface, it kept on coming, emerging somehow through the intact remote.

Jay Dee held the marble-sized glueball. "This is gonna stop people from bothering us?"

"Once it is activated, yes, certainly."

"What should I do?"

"Throw it at your pursuers."

Jay Dee leaned cautiously out the bridge and tossed it.

The glueball landed atop a police car.

The car was gone. Or rather, it was plastered flat onto the surface of the glueball, which had swelled to accommodate it. The flat policemen inside the car banged their hands on their windows. One opened his door and emerged to slide around on the surface of the sphere.

The next car to touch the sphere vanished faster than the eye could follow, flattened likewise to the face of the glueball. The ball was bigger than before.

Lacking brakes, Tracey throttled down to nothing. The yacht coasted to a stop.

The glueball occupied the whole road. There were no cars left outside it. They all rolled around its surface like rainbows on a soap bubble.

Now the glueball began to move.

It rolled away from the yacht, toward the city.

Everything it touched – including the road, down to a depth of ten inches – was sucked into it. Trees, guardrail, grass, birds. The sphere swelled and swelled, like a snowball rolling down an alpine slope, leaving a cleanly sheared path of destruction.

"Holy shit . . . Stop it!"

"That is beyond my capacities."

"Beyond your – You stupid machine! Why did you let it loose then?"

"I am Turing Degree Three. Humans are Turing Degree Ten."

"Oh, Jesus. Will it ever get full, like, and stop?"

"How big is this planet?"

The glueball was now six stories tall. It seemed to be moving faster.

Catalina was sobbing. "Jay Dee –" began Tracey. But the anguished expression on his face made her stop.

Something appeared in the darkening air above the sphere.

Jay Dee swung the ship's searchlight on it.

It was the man they had run over, the owner of the Master Remote.

Suddenly there were a dozen of him. They formed a ring around the glueball. It stopped. It began to shrink, but did not disgorge what it had eaten.

When it was marble-sized again, all the floating men coalesced into a single individual. He landed on the ground, picked up the glueball and pocketed it.

Then he was on the yacht.

"Uh, sorry we killed you once, Mister Spaceman."

The man brushed some dust off his rubberoid lapels. "I am as human as you, Mister McGhee. I am a resident of your future."

Catalina had ceased crying. "Juh-gee, you must come from pretty far in the future."

"Fifty years," said the man. "But they're going to be wild ones. Now, may I have back my unit?"

Jay Dee surrendered the Master Remote.

Tracey asked, "How come you didn't arrive one second after you were killed to claim it, and prevent all this mess?"

"The unit disturbs the Fredkin continuum in a chaotic manner. I had a hard time zeroing in on it."

"What's going to happen to us?" said Jay Dee.

"Oh, nothing much. Say, did you ever see a tie like this?"

They all stared at the time-traveller's paisley tie. The border of each paisley was made of little paisleys, and those were made of littler paisleys, and those were made of even littler paisleys, on and on and on, forever–

That night the Li'l Bear Inn was as crowded as the last copter out of Saigon.

But the atmosphere was a little more pleasant.

Above the sounds of clicking pool balls, thwocking darts, ringing bells, exploding aliens, kazoo, farts, Hank Junior, and the bug-zapper hung outside the screen-door that gave onto the gravel parking lot, the calls for drinks were continuous.

"Tracey, two shots!"

"Tracey, another pitcher!"

"Tracey, six rum 'n' cokes!"

The woman behind the bar smiled at the deluge of orders. It meant more profits in her till.

A man with two tattoos emerged from the back office. "Catalina just called, Trace. She's stopping by soon as Gene gets off work at the exterminator's."

Tracey said, "It'll be good to see her. I'll have a frozen daiquiri and a saucer of cream ready."

The man looked around. "Lord, it's jumping tonight. We should be able to pay off the mortgage next month."

A large neutered tomcat stepped fastidiously among the pools of spilled beer. A patron reached down to pet it. It hissed and scratched the offered hand.

"Jay Dee, you should get rid of that mean animal!"

Jay Dee just smiled.

There was a muffled noise from the moose-head mounted on the wall behind the bar. The moose-head had a rope tied around its snout. Its eyes tracked furiously.

Jay Dee gave Tracey a kiss. "I'll relieve you in a minute, hon. But I got to do something first."

He went back into the private office on the far side of the bar, picked up a board – and gave Larry another whack on the ass.

ALMOST HEAVEN

Tom Gerencer

I remember that first morning clearly, because I woke up with a headache that was somehow larger than my head. I went to the medicine cabinet and rifled around for a while, looking for some painkillers that didn't exist, and then the prophetic and usual knock came on the door.

Only it wasn't a salesman this time, or a kid with a flat tire, or even couple of young guys trying to convert me to Shinto-ism, but a big, greasy looking man in biballs who said his name was Lester.

"Can I help you?" I asked him, and he smiled an ingratiating smile and said no, thanks, he didn't think so, and he pushed his way inside.

He seated himself at my kitchen table, smiled, looked around, and appeared to be fairly pleased with things, in a general sense.

"I'm sorry," I said, "uh, Lester, is it?"

He smiled again, and he said that it was.

"Yeah," I said, feeling somewhere halfway in between silly and afraid, "could you please leave?"

"I could, yeah," he told me, nodding emphatically, "Only I'm not going to."

"I gotcha," I said, gauging the distance between myself and the telephone. "And why's that?"

"Because," he said. "I kind of like it here. It reminds me of someplace else I was once, that I liked almost as much, but not quite. For one thing, I really like your wallpaper."

It was nice wallpaper. Only a fool, a blind man, or an aesthetic moron would fail to concede the point. But I was having trouble understanding why wallpaper, however well conceived, should serve as an excuse for such an uninvited intrusion, and I said so.

"There are many things we don't understand," Lester told me, drumming his fingers on the tabletop, "and to try to change this often results in the destruction of the beauty of the moment. For example, look at this gourd."

He pulled, then, from the front pocket of his biballs, a little orange gourd, pumpkin-shaped and smaller than an apple.

"That's a nice gourd," I agreed. "But what I'm saying is, you could enjoy the beauty of the moment, and the gourd, and so forth, outside, or in your own house, or apartment, or wherever it is you live."

"I don't have a house," he told me, "and if I did, it would not have wallpaper as nice as this, I can assure you."

He tossed his gourd up in the air, then, and caught it.

"Do you have an apartment?" I asked.

"No," he told me. "I was thinking of living here."

I told him, in so many words, that this was out of the question, impossible, and not to be considered.

"And why is that?" he asked me.

"There are many things that can't be explained," I told him, "and to try to change this often results in the destruction of the beauty of the moment."

"Touché," he admitted, and then he derailed the natural flow of events by telling me he was the god of hors d'oeuvres.

"Hors d'oeuvres?"

"Just simple ones," he admitted. "No sushi. There's another god for that. His name's Skip."

"What would the god of hors d'oeuvres want with me?" I asked him.

"With you? Nothing," he said. "It's the wallpaper I like, really. That and the linoleum. You don't see linoleum like this every day."

How can you argue with a guy like that? I considered calling the police, but I decided against it. I try to keep an open mind.

And anyway, how did I know the man really wasn't the god of hors d'oeuvres? I mean, if the only true knowledge lies in knowing you know nothing, I'm a genius. Either that or a moron. Sometimes it's hard to tell which.

All speculation aside, the guy did make a hell of an hors d'oeuvre. He whipped one up for me with avocado slices, tomato, melba toast, and a really delicious, flavored cream-cheese spread he'd brought along, just in case. I was leery of eating it at first, but it smelled so good I let myself have a little nibble, and after that I couldn't resist eating the rest.

"Many such sandwiches are possible," he told me, and he walked into the living room, tossing his gourd into the air and catching it.

I was about to follow him when another door-knocker did his thing outside, and I went to see who he was.

"He" turned out to be a she, actually. A lady with a naugahide purse and a heck of a permanent, and she cut right to the chase by asking for Lester.

"Yeah, he's here," I told her. "He just made me a sandwich."

"Has he got his gourd?" she wanted to know, and I told her he did.

"Thank God," she said, and before I could ask which god, she had pushed past me and stomped off into the house, wrist-bangles bangling.

I followed her to see what would happen next.

I found her standing over Lester, who had seated himself in front of my television set and turned on the home-shopping network.

"Ida!" he shouted at her.

"Lester!" she shouted back.

The big man leveraged himself up out of my wingback, and the two of them proceeded to hug. When they had disengaged, Lester turned to me and said, "Ida, this is Moe. Moe, Ida."

"My name's Bill," I told her.

"Hi, there," she said, and she smiled at me.

"Ida is the goddess of taking out the trash," Lester explained.

"I come in very handy on Thursdays," she told me.

I was on the verge of throwing the both of them out when I realized I might've hit upon something big, here.

"You don't," I said, "by any chance know the goddess of full-body massage, do you?" I asked them.

"Actually, it's a god," said Ida.

"Never mind," I told her.

The next day was a busy one at my house. First came the god of annoying interruptions, followed by the god of reconstituted meat-by-products, followed by the god of persistent nighttime coughs. The goddesses of relaxation, on-the-job safety, and stereo systems came next.

"Could you take a look at my Hitachi?" I asked the last one, but before she could answer me, the god of annoying interruptions, whose name was Zeke, cut in and had us both look at his boil.

"I hope it goes away," he said. "I've heard stuff like this can go system wide and kill you. By the way, nice linoleum. And where did you ever get those bathroom light fixtures?"

I excused myself and hunted down Lester, who was in the kitchen, working on a number of little olive and cream-cheese sandwiches with the crusts cut off.

"You like cream cheese, don't you?" I said.

"Cream cheese is a wonderful medium," he told me, "but I enjoy anything that is edible and can also be spread."

"I can appreciate that," I said, "and, not to spoil the beauty of your moment or anything, but what's going on?"

"I'm making some hors d'oeuvres," he said, gesturing at the tray-full.

"I can see that," I assured him, "but I was referring to the gods and goddesses who keep showing up. I mean, why?"

" 'Why' is a question full of pitfalls," he admonished. "It is a word not conducive to the proper, joyful preparation of sandwiches. I try to avoid it whenever possible."

I took an hors d'oeuvre, nibbled, and found it to be excellent.

"But," I said, and then Zeke turned up and asked me where I'd got the wallpaper.

The following weeks brought more of the self-proclaimed deities, whom I would have evicted at the drop of just about anything (since I do not own any hats) save for the intriguing fact that they all pulled their weight to an astonishing degree.

The goddess of flower arrangement, for instance, added an aesthetic depth to my home it had never before possessed. The god of healthful-yet-inexpensive-main-dishes took the tedium out of suppertime, and I probably don't even need to expound on the benefits of playing host to the god of cleaning-the-toilets. Of course, there were problematical areas, like the goddess of pointing-out-minor-personality-flaws or the god of irritating laughter, but you've got to break a few eggs to make an omelette, a fact that was demonstrated to me every Sunday morning by the god of tantalizing breakfast treats.

All things, good, bad, and otherwise, however, invariably come to an end. One day, while I was putting in some quality time with the goddess of sympathetic conversation, the goddess of answering-the-door did so and ushered in a tall, no-nonsense looking guy in a deep black suit.

He explained that he was the minor deity of total agnosticism, and that was, pretty much, that, except that he went on to compliment my taste in kitchen cabinetry and countertops.

A RUDE AWAKENING

Gail-Nina Anderson

With one bound, she was free! As usual, the opening of the first bloom brought her winging into existence, fresh as spring, hardy as a perennial. While some flower fairies yawned and stretched themselves into their annual manifestations, emerging from the bud like a dragonfly from a chrysalis, Lily (of the Valley) always favoured a more sudden appearance, taking everyone (often including herself) by surprise. She put this down to being such an early arrival in the year's panoply of floral delights. She was also the kind of personality who liked to get things done.

Despite her dynamic incursion into the world, she made a surprisingly light and elegant landing, twirling slightly and appearing almost to float to the ground. It was really all a matter of brace and thrust, of course. She was a very experienced flower fairy and, like most of her kind, much tougher than she looked.

And when she did look, it was down to her feet, which were so surprising that she almost fell over them. What was this – another bad joke on behalf of the Celestial Garden Centre? She was wearing sandals. This was not in itself entirely surprising. She usually appeared in some tasteful if basic combination of green and white, which she would then adapt to suit her mood, the weather and the year's fashions. She did this by – well, by thinking what she would like to be wearing. There were limits, of course, but she had long ago given up wild dreams of rose-red silk or buttercup yellow. You could, after all, do a surprising amount with green and white. But sandals she didn't much like under any circumstances. They tended to trip you up in the wet grass and if, as so often happened (for reasons, she imagined, of poetic consistency), you had manifested in a bosky dell, then roots and errant stalks got caught up in your straps. Fairies were not supposed to tumble inelegantly to the ground, and still less were they encouraged to swear colourfully as they twisted an ankle. So she favoured sturdy green ankle boots or, for eveningwear, tight-fitting little pumps of white kid. Not sandals, and certainly not this pair. They were silver and had an exaggeratedly high platform sole and wedge heel, which quite altered her balance. They were also woefully out of date. Lily was not a dedicated follower of fashion – her dip into shoulder-pads in 1983 had been enough to convince her that power dressing was not for fairies. But she remained tactfully aware of what the rest of the world was wearing and tried not to go against the trend. Floaty fairy stuff was always a classic, of course, but a girl could be usefully unobtrusive in a white jumper and green trousers. And silver platform sandals were decidedly not her look for this or any other season.

Tacky, tacky, tacky – they suggested all the fashion excesses of the late 1960s, when she had resolutely stuck to her own Cicely Mary Barker look specifically in order to avoid engaging with the hideous clashes of style. She thought hard about elegant walking shoes of dark green leather, and for a moment they flickered into existence on her feet, only to be replaced again by the silver platforms. Right, there was a glitch, and she had better get it sorted out now before it spoiled her all too brief season. Usually these things were caused by location. Flowers didn't get much choice as to where they grew, and that could have the most unappealing results. She still remembered with distaste the year she had appeared early in a conservatory of tropical heat, and had expended most of her energy on manifesting in something more substantial then a green bikini and wet T-shirt.

She took stock of her surroundings. Nothing suggested stupid sandals or (as she had now ascertained) an alarmingly short dress in hallucinogenic swirls of green and white. She was in a long, narrow garden at the back of a Victorian terrace. Indeed, she was in one of a row of long, narrow gardens, each attached to one of the houses. On this early spring morning none of the plots was exactly a riot of blossom, but most of them had a more kempt look than hers, the last and wildest of the set. It meandered down to a disused railway track and was bordered on one side by an old wall. It had unpruned trees, unweeded paths and a large compost heap abutting onto what might have been a shed, but what was certainly an exciting residential opportunity for the local woodlice. The garden wasn't exactly uncared for, but it had been cherished with a free and liberal hand that let Nature play a large part in the process. And Nature was never a neat housekeeper. Lily's own particular corner was near the compost heap, which made the silver sandals even less suitable. She picked her way gingerly across to the shabby path and froze in annoyance and surprise.

Humans couldn't see her unless she wanted them to, but she could certainly see them, and there were far too many bustling around for her liking. Policemen tended to ask questions that an annual floral manifestation couldn't readily answer. ("Address please?" "Well this year it's the mossy patch near the ornamental fish-pond.") So she would remain unseen and out of the way. She scuttled (in a suitably elfin manner) behind the woodshed and almost tripped over Violet, who was lurking there in a sullen mood and a bad hair day. They bumped, parted, looked each other up and down and laughed. Violet had considerably longer tresses than a fairy's limited hairdressing resources could deal with, plus a mauve scarf worn bandanna-style round her head. She was barefoot and wearing a long, shapeless garment of patchy purple velvet embroidered in what could only politely be described as a freeform pattern. It looked vaguely ethnic, which Violet decidedly did not. She was the sort of neat, organized fairy who had been wearing tasteful variations of Chanel for years. Something was affecting their morphic field, but before Lily could voice all her questions, Violet had opened the subject in that husky, Fenella Fielding voice she had assumed for the past few decades.

"It's awful, darling, positively bloody awful! This isn't me and I'm sure that's not you. Oh, it isn't is it? You're not just trying something new, are you?"

Lily shook her head.

"Well thank heavens! – but it's quite beyond control. Even a perm would be better than these–these–these tendrils on my head! Whenever did anyone dress like this?"

"About thirty or forty years ago," said Lily. "We're stuck in some sort of time-warp."

"Style warp, darling, style warp. But why can't we just change the way we always do? I was dying to look round Harvey Nichols and choose something really crisp for the new season, but I can hardly let myself be seen like this."

"We can't let ourselves be seen at all," hissed Lily, pulling Violet further behind the shed just in case their invisibility was on the blink too. The policemen had spread out into the garden, and a couple of them, wearing not the regular uniforms but the curious cocoons of crime-scene coveralls, had approached the compost heap. Lily caught snatches of their conversation and a hideous possibility began to form in her mind.

"Old dear," they said more than once, and she was sure she heard (with considerable relief) "kept the cannabis plants in the attic." The men were using long forks to investigate the compost, which seemed to go down a very long way, a pit as well as a heap. Lily and Violet were so breathlessly absorbed that they almost missed the moment when a bright yellow figure detached itself from the main police group and hurtled towards them, brimming with news.

There was a certain etiquette in the flower world, a hierarchy involving – well, degrees of cultivation. And as no one ever cultivated a Celandine, she ranked pretty low down the budding order, a situation of which everyone but Celandine herself seemed perfectly aware. She was pushy – almost always the first on the scene – but just at the moment the others were agog for information. Besides, it was difficult to snub a fairy dressed in a frightfully short PVC coat of brilliant yellow, with matching boots whose practicality was more than mildly compromised by a series of geometric shapes cut out from their sides. Even Celandine, whose passion for satin was notorious, didn't usually dress like this.

She was too full of news to waste more than a moment giggling at Violet and Lily and doing a little shimmy to emphasize her own deplorable costume.

"It's the bloody compost," she gasped, not waiting to get her breath back. "I've been around for ages . . ." (Lily and Violet shared a nod; typical Celandine pushiness) ". . . and the police have been going through the whole place since the old lady died and I'm sure it's the bloody compost."

"Don't be silly, dear," said Lily in her most managing voice. "We've all been nurtured on compost before – even you."

"Yeah, but this stuff is really potent – gawd knows what's gone into it. And old – really matured."

"Compost is always old, Celly my sweet. That's what makes it compost."

Celandine grinned. For once she was in a position of power, and nobody was going to ruffle her petals.

"Not like this lot", she said. "Not like this lot. The old lady took great pride in her natural garden." (Lily bristled – she wasn't at all sure she appreciated being called natural.)

"Natural, wild and just a bit on the weird side. Bit witchy."

"Oh, Lord, not human magic – that's oxymoronic," breathed Violet.

"Naw – not magic but just a mite outside the norm. She'd been brewing that compost heap for nearly forty years. Ever since, they've suddenly remembered, her husband disappeared."

Unpleasant trains of thought were interrupted by a low whistle from the crime-scene policeman, and a cry of "Got something, Sarge!"

The fairies, trusting in their collective invisibility, tiptoed forward to where the compost heap had been methodically raked out onto the path. Down beneath it were some whitish fragments that were undoubtedly bone – when you started off in the earth, you could be relied upon to recognize things like that. And human? Well, yes. The shape of the skull was still discernible, but what really gave it away were the fragments of clothing that the body had once worn. Metal survived best – the remains of a watch were visible, now pulled to one side by the policemen's rake. And beneath where it had been was the fragile husk of an enamel badge, still retaining enough of its once lurid colour to allow Lily to distinguish the slogan "Flower Power".

SPOILED ROTTEN

Grey Rollins

I was nearly to the top of the stairs when the phone started ringing. If I could hear it, surely Martin could, but it just kept ringing.

Stair steps are not a problem for most humans. For me, however, they present somewhat of a challenge as my legs are only six inches long. There's nothing wrong with my legs, mind you, they're attractive, well proportioned, and eminently functional. They simply happen to be one-sixth as long as Martin's legs.

I grunted myself over the top step and began to hurry forward. It was a futile gesture, since I still had to cover a good thirty feet to get *to* the phone. The answering machine was set to pick up after the fourth ring, and I had already counted three.

The answering machine clicked when I was still ten feet from the door. Martin's voice came on, informing the caller that he wasn't available at the moment, but would be glad to discuss their case with them if they would leave their name and number at the tone.

My prehensile tongue is far more useful for manipulating things than my weak vestigial arms, so I wrapped a couple of turns around the doorknob and twisted, leaning into the wood beneath the frosted glass with the arched black lettering that spelled out MARTIN CROFTS, PRIVATE INVESTIGATOR. One of these days, I'm going to get him to put my name up there, too.

"Martin?" I called as soon as I nudged the door shut behind me. I got no answer.

Without bothering to replay the message, I removed the tape from the answering machine and dropped it into a cassette player, which I took into the inner sanctum.

Sure enough, Martin was draped over his office chair as though every bone in his body had melted. A portrait of my best human friend by Salvador Dali might appear thus.

The cassette player I placed on the window ledge, less than a foot behind his ear, ran the volume slider all the way up, and punched the play button.

"*Hello, this is . . .*"

Martin attempted to practise levitation.

He failed.

As soon as his weight left the seat, the return springs snapped the chair into an upright position. Martin, coming down, met the chair coming up. Neither won. Planes crash with less commotion than Martin made falling out of his chair.

He glared up at me from the floor. "Victor, say your prayers. You just shortened your life expectancy by a few centuries."

"If you had answered the phone, there wouldn't have been a message on the answering machine."

"Phone?" asked Martin, genuinely confused. "I must have fallen asleep."

This was such a masterful piece of understatement that I was at a loss for a properly scathing reply. "They left a message," was the best I could do.

Martin was still a step or two behind. "Why didn't you answer it, Victor?"

I mustered what patience I could and replied, as though to a child, "Because you asked me to take out the trash, remember?"

Unfortunately, my ways are known. An evil gleam appeared in Martin's eye. "You wouldn't have stopped for a snack, would you?"

"Me?" I feigned innocence.

He painfully disentangled himself from the wreckage of his

chair. "I wish you ate normal food. Then we wouldn't have this problem."

Martin has trouble accepting the fact that food he would toss into the trash can in disgust is something that is just barely ripe by my standards. There's no delicacy on my home world that can match the taste of a two-week-old fast food burger that's been soaked with rain.

"I *do* eat normal food. You're the one with disgusting habits. Imagine all the nuances of flavour that are revealed as the food decomposes. Think of what you're missing."

"I'd rather not, if you don't mind," he growled. "I prefer mine fresh. You ought to try it that way sometime."

"*Blech!*" I spat, coiling my tongue into a corkscrew shape. "Fresh food is bad for you – I can prove it."

"What?" he squawked in disbelief.

"Your uncle ate fresh food. I ate properly-aged food. I outlived him. The conclusion is self-evident."

"He probably died of a heart attack while watching you eat roadkill," Martin muttered.

"Don't talk like that . . . you're making me hungry."

Martin turned pale. "Me and my big mouth. We'll go by the sandwich shop over on Third tonight, but I'm going inside and having real food, not leftovers."

"I wouldn't count on it. You don't have enough money to buy an ice cube, let alone the drink to float it in."

He scowled at me and punched the playback button.

"*Hello, this is Cal . . .*"

Martin jumped for the volume slider, running it down to a more tolerable setting.

"*. . . Rosen.*" He gave a number where we could reach him, then hung up.

"Short, sweet, and to the point," I observed.

Martin's brows furrowed, looking like two black, fuzzy worms bowing to each other. "You'd think he'd at least have said what it was about."

"I can suggest a way to find out," I said. I handed the phone to him and dialed the number that Rosen had given. "Talk to the man."

"Did you have to dial with your *tongue*?" Martin hissed. He whipped out his handkerchief and began wiping the phone.

"It'll dry," I assured him.

He started to say something about crusty buttons, but Rosen answered and he left the thought unfinished. They spoke only briefly. Martin hung up and looked at me. "Put the tape back in the answering machine. We're going to see him."

Cal Rosen lived downtown in a swank high-rise. Everything about the building breathed affluence. The only thing it didn't have was sufficient parking space for visitors. Martin finally found a spot four blocks away.

After unravelling me from the seat belt, he gently deposited me on the ground, then began to stride purposefully down the sidewalk, as though to distance himself from the rusting hulk in which we had arrived. You'd think he'd buy a new car, but he was more comfortable hating the one he already had.

I looked from Martin's retreating back to the still open car door, then again at Martin's back. Grumbling maledictions under my breath, I leaned against the door and pushed. It wouldn't budge. I heaved against it again. The hinges protested loudly, then, with a tortured squeal, they reluctantly gave way and the door slammed shut.

And I fell flat on my face on the sidewalk.

An obese woman was approaching with a Chihuahua on a leash. Being prone, my one eye was about on a level with the two bulging eyes of the dog. It stared – I glared back.

Chihuahuas are genetically limited to one response to all stimuli; it began to dance in nervous circles and bark. The high-pitched yipping was annoying enough, but having the creature engage in a war dance was adding insult to injury.

With great difficulty, I pushed myself to my feet. The wretched creature went into a frenzy; its toenails clicked and skritched on the concrete. My wish that it would have a sudden seizure and die went unfulfilled.

The woman was determined to give me as wide a berth as the available width of sidewalk allowed. The Chihuahua, however, had other ideas. It lunged, jerking the end of the leash from the woman's hand.

Once, while trying to recover a stolen painting for Owen Kent, Martin and I dealt with a particularly vicious guard dog – a Rottweiler. Its bark would easily have intimidated the hound of the Baskervilles. I took a deep breath and let loose a replica of that dog's bark. Having a tympanum as a speech organ does have the occasional advantage.

The Chihuahua shrieked in terror and collapsed on the sidewalk, completely unnerved. A yellow puddle began to gather under its hindquarters as it cowered.

"Oh, Maximilian!" the woman cried, wringing her doughy hands. Then she turned on me angrily. "How *could* you?"

"Just enforcing the leash law, ma'am," I replied, and started off after Martin, leaving her to decide how best to put the pygmy pest out of its misery.

"Take the scenic route?" Martin inquired facetiously when I finally came huffing up behind him.

"You overgrown hairless baboon," I snapped, "you didn't close the car door. It took three men and a scantily clad young lady to help me push it closed." I kicked his ankle, which is about as high as I can easily kick. "Pick me up, you beast. I wore my legs out catching up with you."

He cocked his head as though to assess the veracity of my statement. "Yup. Only six inches left. If I made you walk all the way to Rosen's building, you'd arrive on nubs the size of my thumb. It would serve you right . . . I saw you bullying that Chihuahua."

"Bullying! It attacked me! I never laid a hand on it."

"You probably caused the poor thing permanent psychological damage. I ought to make you go back and apologize."

"Quit picking on me, you ugly, two-eyed monster."

"I never laid a hand on you."

He had come full circle and snared me in a completely logical trap. Martin is not usually so devious as that. I was angry at letting myself be outwitted so I stomped on, determined to make it on my own, even if my legs *were* the size of his thumbs when I arrived. I had not gone more than ten paces when he swooped me up under his arm like an elongated football.

I started to protest, simply as a matter of honor, but thought better of it. If nothing else, being carried put me safely out of reach of psychotic Chihuahuas.

With his longer strides, we were soon at Rosen's building. I caught one swaying glimpse of the doorman as we passed. He seemed amused as he touched the tips of his fingers to the brim of his cap. "Good mo'nin', Cap'n."

The D-shaped metal handle on the thick glass door caught my right leg as we went through, giving me a sharp crack on the knee. Martin, not being aware of this, placed me on the floor in front of the security desk when he stopped to give his name to the guard on duty. I immediately began to topple as my leg collapsed. The only way to save myself from falling was to catch Martin's leg for support.

Unlike humans, who prefer to use vowel sounds, my species tends to use a buzzing noise. Thus, when I gave voice to a muted, "*Uhzzzzz . . .*", the guard looked down, saw my tongue around Martin's leg, and blanched.

"Is that a *snake?*" he asked, horrified.

Martin belatedly noticed that I was listing to starboard. He reached down and grabbed the top of my tapered head. "What's wrong, Victor?"

Over the sound of my suffering, I superimposed my voice. "I think my leg is broken."

Martin picked me up, cradling me like an infant. Under the guard's cross-eyed stare, he proceeded to examine my leg, which was already beginning to swell. He prodded and poked, flexed and turned, while I hummed and buzzed under my breath. He does not have what one would call a delicate touch, but he is thorough to a fault.

"It's just bruised."

"Feels like broken glass," I assured him.

He went back to his examination. After eliciting several more varieties of verbal agony from me, he said, "Don't think so, little buddy." He then frowned at me. "How did you manage to hurt your leg?"

Martin is not malicious, just careless, so I did not berate him for not opening the door further. "The door got me," I said simply. To the guard, still staring, I said, "We have an appointment with Cal Rosen."

The clerk looked from me to something on the desk, then back up at Martin, as though he had spoken instead of me. "Yes, I see it here. He called down and left word a little while ago. You're to go right up."

Once inside the elevator, Martin asked, "Can you stand?"

"I'd rather not. It hurts quite badly."

The doors hissed open on the fortieth floor, revealing a hall with thick carpet and unnecessarily busy wallpaper. "*Ugh*," I said. "I'm sure it's just that I'm seeing it sideways, but it appears that the interior decorator should be drawn and quartered."

"It's no better seeing it upright," Martin assured me. "Listen, you're starting to get heavy. Are you sure you can't walk?"

"My knee is the size of an apple – twice its normal size. Can't you see the little lightning bolts coming out of it, like they do in the comics?"

"Well, yeah, it is a little swollen," he admitted. He shifted me from one arm to the other. "Are you sure you haven't gained weight?"

"Martin, I'm on the verge of starvation. I've only eaten twice in the last nine days."

"I know, but that's normal for you."

"True, but I could get you convicted of cruelty to animals if I acted pitiful enough."

"Ah, *ha!*" Martin crowed. "So you're finally admitting you're an animal? The way you barked at that Chihuahua, I'm sure we could get you registered with the AKC."

Uh oh. "I think I want my lawyer present before this conversation goes any further," I grumbled.

A middle-aged couple approached. The woman caught sight of me and said, "Oh, look, Hubert! A banana with legs. How *cute!*"

"Ain't got but one eye, Martha. What good is a critter with only one eye?"

"You mean it's *alive?*" she asked, turning to him in wonder. They continued to debate the pros and cons of a monocular pet as they waited for the elevator.

"The sooner we get out of here, the better," I groused.

"Patience," Martin counseled. "We still have a fee to earn."

The security guard must have told Rosen that we were coming, for his door popped open as soon as we got to it. "Martin Crofts?" he asked.

"Yes." He deftly swung me around so that I could face Rosen from a more-or-less standing position, while still cradled in his arm. "And this is Victor. He's my partner."

"I didn't know that you had a . . . partner."

Martin nodded into the apartment. "Shouldn't we discuss your problem inside?"

Rosen took the hint. He stood aside and said, "Come in, please."

Martin nodded. "Now," he said after the door was closed, "what can we do for you?"

Rosen licked his lips nervously. He looked at Martin. He looked at me. He looked back at Martin. He licked his lips again. "Um, where do I start?"

Martin said, "Just start at the beginning and we'll ask questions as we go along."

He nodded nervously. "Yes, I suppose so." He turned and walked to a chair near the window as though to sit, then thought better of it and stood facing out with his hands clasped behind his back. "Candice, that's my ex-wife, brought over Alice on Friday afternoon. Alice was to stay the weekend . . ."

"Excuse me, but who is Alice?" Martin asked, moving closer.

"Alice is our daughter. She turned four last March."

Martin nodded. "And your ex-wife brought Alice over on Friday," he said, to put Rosen back into the thread of his narrative.

"I see Alice two weekends out of the month. That's the way the lawyers set it up."

"I see," Martin said.

"After Candice dropped Alice off, I took her to the park."

"Which park? Saunders or Treewood?"

"Treewood. Alice loves that big slide they have. The one that comes down out of the oak tree."

Martin nodded. "I know the one. Go on."

Rosen sighed heavily, then turned from the window to face us. "I usually sit on the bench next to the water fountain. It's near the slide, of course, but sometimes I can't see my little girl when she's behind a tree or something. She moves around so much that she'll usually pop into sight within a minute or two. After a bit I got worried. I walked around and still didn't see her. She had been kidnapped."

Martin frowned. "Usually, it turns out that the child is with the other parent. Especially in cases such as yours."

"I got a ransom note on Saturday." He sounded as though it were something to be proud of.

"Can we see it?" I asked.

Rosen glanced at the floor. "The police have it."

"What's it say?"

"Five hundred thousand dollars. Small bills. They would be in touch to set up a meeting. The usual."

Martin's eyes travelled over the room, noting the quality of the furniture and the expensive curios sitting on tables. His gaze went back to Rosen. "Can you afford it?"

He nodded, paused, then nodded again jerkily. "Barely. I'll have to liquidate everything."

"So someone knew your worth," Martin observed.

Rosen's eyes fastened on Martin. "How so?"

"From what you're saying, they had a pretty good idea of how much money you could raise, if push came to shove."

"I . . . I hadn't thought of that. Couldn't they have just guessed? Or picked a number out of thin air?"

Martin shrugged, which shifted my position slightly and caused my knee to send out fresh waves of pain. I let out a muted buzz. "Sure. Half a million dollars is a nice, tidy sum of money," he agreed.

Rosen nodded. "All I have."

"So Alice was taken Friday. You received the ransom note Saturday. Has there been any other communication?"

"No."

"Typically the best time to do anything is when the kidnapper makes pickup on the ransom. The only other thing we can hope for is that the ransom note itself will provide the police with some clue as to your daughter's whereabouts."

Martin questioned Rosen closely for another ten or fifteen minutes, filling in small gaps in the chronology, but without learning anything important. He also got the ex-wife's address.

The doorman saluted as we passed on the way out. "You take care of that li'l fella, Cap'n," he said. "Looks like that door got 'im good on the way in."

Martin still didn't get it. His conscience is armor plated. Nothing less than a direct hit makes an impression on him.

We debated seeing the ex-wife next, but decided to go by the police station first. Pete Sims is an old friend of Martin's and will usually let us know the inside story on anything going on.

We made an obligatory stop on the way in. Marie, the closest thing Martin has to a steady girlfriend, works up front. He collected a kiss on the cheek before Marie bent to speak to me. "Has Martin been mistreating you again, Victor?"

"Oh, yes! Terribly," I told her. "He only feeds me twice a week."

She smiled. "I think I've got a head of lettuce that's going bad. Want me to save it for you?"

"What color is it?" I asked.

"Still green . . . mostly."

"Wait until it's black and purple and slimy all over. That's when they taste best."

Marie is a brave woman – she only nodded. "Another few days should do it."

"I'm drooling."

"Don't you dare," Martin protested. "This is the last clean shirt I've got. If you slobber on it, I'll . . ."

"You'll do no such thing," Marie said, reaching out and stroking my side gently. "Victor's a sweet little guy."

"Unless you're a Chihuahua," Martin said. "Marie, I hate to run, but I need to speak to Pete for a few minutes."

She pouted, knowing full well that the sultry look she was turning on Martin would melt him in his shoes. "And I thought you were here to see me . . ."

Martin beat a hasty retreat. "God, that woman does wicked things to my hormones," he muttered as he carried me down the hall towards Pete's office.

"She never laid a hand on you," I noted.

The corner of his mouth twitched as though he were trying to keep from smiling. "Touché."

Pete was sitting behind his desk, reading a report. Half-eaten, a fast food burger lay on its wrapper within easy reach. Two empty wrappers lay next to it. His feet were propped atop all the layers of paperwork that lay in untidy piles across his desk. His head bobbed up when he heard us come in, then he frowned. "What the devil is wrong with your leg, Victor?"

"It hurts."

He ran his fingers through the ruins of what had once been a full head of red hair and slid out of his chair. "Well, hell, I reckon so." Gently, he touched my knee, then nodded slowly. "Let me try something."

Squatting down, he began rubbing his hands together briskly. "This will hurt a bit."

I steeled myself. "I'm ready."

His palms were palpably warm from being rubbed together. He placed one on each side of my joint and began to press, quite hard. Slowly, he rubbed each hand in a circle, using the other to steady my leg. He alternated hands in this manner several times. The first cycle actually felt good. Then the pain started to build. When I started buzzing, he glanced up and met my eye, but continued to rub. "Steady, Victor."

Amazingly, the sharp-edged pain abated quickly. In its wake, it left only a dull ache. Comparatively, though, it was an improvement. "Pete, have you ever considered becoming a doctor?"

He grinned at me. "Why would I want to go and do a thing like that? I'm just now getting good at being a cop." He grunted as he pushed himself to his feet. He carries a perpetual paunch, much the way that Martin had been carrying me – as baggage he would rather do without, but has come to love. At least, I assume Pete loves his belly, he feeds it enough.

He maneuvered back around his desk and flopped into his chair. "So . . . what can I do for you? It's too much to hope that this is a purely social call."

"The Rosen kidnapping this past Friday," Martin told him.

Pete snorted. "Should have known you'd make it hard on me. Why don't you fellows ask me about a homicide instead? That way I'd have it right here on my desk, instead of having to tromp all over the building." His face twisted into a grimace. "Okay, sit tight. I'll be back in a minute."

"Martin?" I asked after Pete had maneuvered his bulk through the door. "Do you suppose there's anything good to eat under Pete's desk?"

Martin wrinkled his nose in distaste. "From the looks of things, I don't think anyone's swept under there in years. If you want to have a look, you'll have to get down and do it yourself. I'm not about to go rooting around under there. My fingers would probably rot and fall off."

"Really?"

His face paled. "Victor! You wouldn't eat a part of *me*, would you?"

I sighed. "I guess not. I'd be guilty of biting the hand that feeds me."

Martin was still trying to decide whether to kill me when Pete returned and tossed a pile of loose papers into Martin's lap, next to my feet. "We seem to be short on file folders around here, so don't lose any of that stuff, okay?"

There wasn't much to read, and it didn't add anything substantive to what we already knew. Martin scowled. "It's odd that nobody saw anything."

"You'd be surprised how little people notice in a public place. Unless the kid was putting up a fight, most people would assume that she was leaving to go home. Hell, even if she *were* fighting, they'd assume she was throwing a tantrum. These things were a lot easier back when kids were polite, quiet, and obedient. These days . . ." he shrugged.

Martin nodded. "Did you check out the ex-wife? If she came for the child, I imagine Alice would go quietly."

"*I* didn't do any of the questioning. This is Norm Pasky's case – remember him? Anyway, unless it becomes a homicide I'm staying out of it. Let's hope it doesn't become one."

Martin plucked the ransom note out of the pile of papers by its edge. "Any way to trace the note?"

Pete shrugged. "I'd guess not. These days the paper and the type face and so forth don't tell you much. Any laser printer can do a roman pica easier than you can tie your shoes. There should be a lab report in there, but I doubt that it'll do you any good."

Martin shuffled through the stack until he found the report, scanned it, then looked back up at Pete. "You're right. Nothing worth trying to follow up."

"All you can do is talk to his ex. Other than that . . . wait."

Candice Rosen – she still used her married name – lived in a modest rented house in a decent neighborhood. It was late afternoon and the setting rays of the sun colored the houses on her street an angry reddish-orange.

Martin parked at the kerb and carried me to the front door. She answered the bell so quickly that I got the impression she had been waiting by the door, perhaps for news of her daughter. She accepted Martin's explanation of who we were and what we wanted without comment, then invited us in.

"I must apologize for the house looking as it does. We . . . I didn't ask Cal for very much in the way of furniture when we divorced."

I looked around the sparsely furnished living room, comparing it mentally to the threadbare relics Martin calls furniture. "Ma'am, I think it looks just fine," I told her.

She looked at me closely. "You speak?"

I took no offence; her tone was genuinely puzzled. "My name is Victor, ma'am. I work with Martin."

"What are you?"

I've never found a satisfactory answer for that question. Martin's uncle had been a crew member on a space ship that landed on my planet. He saw me and decided that I would make a unique pet. Unfortunately, he went to his grave without telling anyone exactly which planet he had taken me from, so I have no way to go home. "In a way, ma'am," I told her, "I'm a kidnap victim, myself. I'm the only one of my species on Earth and no one has gotten around to trying to classify me."

"You're the only one? I thought there were hundreds of other aliens on Earth. Surely there's another one like you, somewhere."

"Not the one who counts," I said, thinking of my beloved Wanne, my para, hopefully safe back on my home world.

"I'm afraid I don't understand."

I have learned to imitate the human sigh. There are times when no other sound can communicate the proper emotion. "Don't worry, ma'am. It will be all right. Perhaps someday I'll get to go home." But this carried its own pangs – the thought of leaving Martin left me feeling hollow. Ah, if I could only have both Martin's friendship *and* Wanne's love, that would be the best of both worlds. In a way, I was relieved not to have to make the choice.

Martin, tiring of a story he had heard many times, broke in. "Mrs Rosen, we'd like to ask you a few questions, if you don't mind."

She glanced back down at me, as if still uncertain as to how I fit in, before answering Martin. "Certainly. I don't know if I can be of much help, though."

"You dropped your daughter off at your husband's place on Friday afternoon, is that correct?"

She nodded. "Yes, Cal has her every other weekend."

"What time was that?"

"About four, maybe a little after."

"And he took her to the park?"

She shrugged. "I don't know. I wasn't with them, but she does love to go there."

"So you don't know what they do over the course of a given weekend?"

She shook her head. "No, not ahead of time. Alice usually

tells . . . told . . ." she sniffed and dabbed at her eye, but otherwise maintained her composure, ". . . me about it after he brought her home on Sunday evening."

"Have you been contacted by the kidnappers?"

She shook her head. "So far, they've only sent the one note, and that went to Cal."

"If you don't mind my asking, are you and your ex-husband on good terms?"

She closed her eyes, remaining silent for a moment or two. "I suppose that depends on which of us you ask. I thought we were doing fine. Then one day he asked me to move out. He said we had grown apart. I didn't feel that way, but what can you do? A relationship takes two people to make it work. I left."

"Was there someone else?"

"I don't know. I never tried to find out. I was too stunned to think things through at the time. At this point it's moot."

"Do you still love him?" I asked gently.

She shook her head; too quickly. Then she nodded slowly. "Yes," she whispered.

"And you'd like for the three of you to live together again," I added.

She nodded.

Martin was looking at me oddly, but kept silent. "Ma'am?" I asked.

She met my eye, but still said nothing.

"Did the police ask you if you had taken Alice?"

"They seemed to think it was possible that I had her. I don't. I wish I did, though. If nothing else, I'd like to know if she was all right."

Proper human body language is to nod sympathetically when something like this is said, but my body is too stiff to flex in that way. "I understand. Sometimes I wish I knew whether Wanne was all right."

"Wanne is . . . someone special to you?"

"Forever."

Martin was getting restless. "Mrs Rosen, strictly speaking, we're working for your ex-husband, but since you and he are working towards a common goal, I'd like to leave my card with you. That way you'll have a phone number where you can reach us if anything happens you think we should know about."

She took a deep, uneven breath. "All right."

Then Martin realized that, since he was holding me with both arms, he did not have a free hand. "Um, Victor . . ." he began.

"Hold still," I told him and reached for his wallet with my tongue. Candice Rosen's eyes went wide as she watched my tongue slither around to Martin's back pocket.

He grimaced, then said quietly, so only I could hear, "Dammit, Victor, that *tickles!*"

Once I had his wallet free, I used my hands to extract a card, which I then held out to Candice. She accepted it gingerly.

As I slid his wallet into the outside pocket of his jacket, Martin said, "If anything happens, feel free to call us at any hour. Victor never sleeps."

She looked at me. "Seriously?"

"I spend my time reading. Once Martin goes to bed the house is very quiet and I find that I can concentrate more easily."

She glanced around her. "I know what you mean about it being quiet. This house feels entirely different without my daughter in it."

I hadn't intended for her to make that connection. "I'm sorry. We'll do what we can to get her back for you."

On the way home, Martin was unusually quiet. I waited until we were inside his apartment before speaking. "What's on your mind?"

His lips compressed in irritation. "Don't you think you were laying it on a little thick with that maudlin act? I kept wondering if I should be playing a violin."

"I would have thought that it was obvious. I was taking her pulse, emotionally. It was a little overblown, I'll grant you, but in her state of mind, she's only receptive to three emotions – sadness, fear, and worry. I played on the sadness. It worked."

Martin carefully placed me in a semi-recumbent position on

the couch. "Okay, I'll accept that. You seem to know more about human psychology than most shrinks, but I wish you'd warn me before you launch into a fishing expedition like that."

Carefully, I began to probe my knee with the tip of my tongue. The swelling was no worse and may even have subsided a bit. Pete's magic rubbing routine appeared to have helped. "Martin, I have to play these things by ear, the same way you do."

He flopped into the recliner, grumbling. "All right, all right. So what did you determine?"

"She doesn't have the girl."

He rubbed his jaw a moment while he thought. "Can you prove that?"

"Not exactly. The evidence is too circumstantial to stand up to a rigorous examination."

Martin snorted. "Try me."

"Well, for one thing, she didn't know where Cal and Alice were going. If she didn't know they would be at the park, then there's no way she could have taken the girl."

"That's the flimsiest excuse for logic I think I've ever heard." He held up his fingers and ticked them off. "One, she could have followed them to the park. Two, Alice could have mentioned that she was going to ask her father to take her to the park. Three, she herself could have suggested the idea to the child. Four, it's possible she could have an accomplice, perhaps a boyfriend, who would help her stake out any number of places where they might go. Five . . ."

"Martin, all of those are reasonable theories. There's only one problem."

"What's that?"

"Candice Rosen doesn't have the girl."

"Then where is she, garbage breath?" Martin demanded.

We talked and argued and discussed and wrangled and generally beat the subject to death until Martin was too tired to stay awake. Unable to leave it alone, I sat in the dark and mulled it over after he had gone to bed. He was quite correct, of course, it wasn't a question of where Alice *wasn't*, so much as where she *was*. There were an infinite number of places where she wasn't, and my conviction that she wasn't with her mother, while useful in a legal sense, was useless in the practical sense.

After failing to determine where Alice might actually be using logic, I elected to descend into the trance state that I use when I am unable to find an answer any other way. Somewhere around four in the morning, I floated back to full consciousness and carefully let myself down to the floor. Testing my weight on my leg, I decided that it would get me as far as I needed to go.

I padded into Martin's bedroom and stood next to his bed. "Martin . . . Martin?"

He didn't even twitch.

"Martin!" I called, somewhat louder. Still no response.

I launched into reveille, full blast.

Martin began to pummel his pillow, flailing at it with both fists. "I can't get out of my tent, Mr Arken! There's a bear in here and it's . . ."

He sat bolt upright. "*Victor!* What in hell do you think you're doing, you addlepated idiot?"

"Trying to wake you up," I said calmly. "Get your car keys."

"Now?"

"Now."

He reached over and turned on the light on his night stand, temporarily blinding both of us. "What time is it?" he groaned.

"Time to get moving. I know where Alice is."

As Martin drove, I explained my theory. I watched his face from street light to street light, like a slow motion strobe, as he fought the idea, then began to see the symmetry of it. Grudgingly, he admitted each point, until I had laid out a complete, internally self-consistent scenario. He didn't like it, but he had to admit that it made sense.

Parking spaces were no problem in the wee hours of the night, so we parked right in front of Cal Rosen's apartment building. Martin turned to me and said, "Last chance, Victor.

From here on in, we're either heroes or fools. Do you want to back out?"

"Do you?"

He grimaced. "No, I guess not. Now that you've gotten me out of bed, I might as well see it through."

Once inside, the security guard looked at me strangely when I asked my key question, then scratched his head and said, "Stay put. I think I can answer that easily enough."

He took a ring of keys and unlocked an office across the hall from us. In less than a minute, he was back, carrying a large ledger. He was running his finger down the page. "Yup, there was an apartment leased on the fortieth floor just a week ago."

I gave Martin a triumphant I-told-you-so look and said, "You're aware that Cal Rosen's little girl was kidnapped this past Friday. We have reason to believe that the newly let apartment may factor into the abduction."

The guard's eyes narrowed. He looked at Martin. "Honest?"

"Do you know if anyone has moved into that apartment?"

He traced across the page with his fingertip. "It doesn't say so here in the book. Normally they check this little box here when the tenant moves in."

"Good. If it's empty then surely you wouldn't have any objection to letting us look it over, would you?" Martin, for all his faults, can be convincing when he wants to be.

"Uh, well, I guess not."

"Naturally, you'll come with us. If it should turn out that the kidnappers are using that apartment for a base of operations, then we may need a backup."

Shrewd psychology on Martin's part. Considering that the guard's shift was probably one of the most boring jobs in the city, I'm sure he would have welcomed a blazing gun battle to relieve the monotony.

The elevator ride to the fortieth floor was tense. The guard kept slapping the black leather holster at his side as if to reassure himself that his gun was handy in case he needed it. As we walked down the corridor, he began to fiddle with the keys on his key ring.

When we reached the door, he tried the master key in the lock, but it would not turn. "The lock's been changed," the guard said, partly puzzled, partly annoyed.

"It's logical," I agreed, turning to Martin, who simply nodded.

The guard, thinking that he had cornered a gang of desperados, raised his hand to beat on the door, no doubt to demand their immediate surrender.

"Excuse me," I interrupted. "Do you mind if I try?"

His hand froze in mid-swing. He stared at me in confusion. "Try what?"

"The door, of course." Without waiting for permission, I slipped the tip of my tongue into the lock. "It's a new lock all right, the metal hasn't worn smooth yet," I commented as I felt out the tumblers.

The guard turned to Martin. "Is he doing what I think he's doing?"

"I'm picking the lock," I assured him. "But if you ever tell anyone you saw me do this they'll never believe you."

"Hell, *I* don't believe it," he said, perversely fascinated.

The lock was intricate, but I finally got it. "Martin, turn the knob while I hold the pins, the mechanism is too stiff for me to do it with my tongue."

I had forgotten that Martin's hands were full – with me, naturally. The guard saw this and turned the knob, reaching for his gun with his other hand.

"I don't think you'll need that," I told him. "Besides, if there should be legitimate tenants in here, you'll scare them out of their wits."

He nodded. "Right." He didn't look as though he was completely convinced.

We entered the darkened apartment. There was a cardboard box just inside the door. In the box was a small purple stuffed horse, no . . . a unicorn. Martin whispered softly, "*Bingo!*"

The bedrooms were to our right. The first one was empty. The door to the second one was barely visible in the light coming from the hallway. It was closed.

"Open it quietly," I instructed the guard. "We don't want to frighten her."

"*Her?* You mean the girl's in here?"

"Open the door quietly," I repeated. He did so. "Alice?" I called softly, causing my voice to resemble her father's. "Alice?"

"Daddy?" came a voice from the small bed near the window.

"Jesus and Mary!" the guard breathed. "You were right." Then, louder, he called, "Are you okay, little girl?"

"Who's that? Daddy, who's with you?"

The guard flipped the light switch, revealing a dishevelled little girl sitting up in bed, grubbing an eye with the back of one hand. "Daddy? Where's Daddy?"

"It's all right, Alice. We're going to take you home in a few minutes," I told her. To the guard I said, "You take care of Alice. I don't think there will be anyone else in the apartment, but you'd better check. We're going to get her father."

Martin and I stepped down the hall. Rather than put me down in order to knock, he simply thumped the door with his foot several times. A moment later, he asked, "Do you think I should knock again? I don't hear anything."

"No, I think he's coming."

Sure enough, the door opened to reveal Cal Rosen. He blinked in confusion. "What do you want?"

"Mr Rosen," Martin said, "we've found your daughter."

Rosen leapt at us, using his forearm as a battering ram to push us aside. Martin went down hard on his backside, losing his grip on me in the process. I fell on the carpet.

Martin rolled to his feet, cursing. "You okay, Victor?" he asked, watching Rosen pounding down the hall towards the elevators, his house coat flapping.

"I've got a rug burn the size of a dinner plate, but nothing fatal. Let's go."

Martin picked me up and swung me under his arm. His hand was right in the center of the abraded patch of skin. It felt as though he was scraping my hide with rusty razor blades.

He skidded to a halt before the bank of elevators, staring in consternation at the indicator on the one Rosen had taken. "Who the hell ever heard of somebody taking the elevator to get away?" he demanded indignantly.

"You did," I told him. "Just now."

"So now what do we do?"

"Take the other one, fool! Unless you think you can run down forty floors worth of stairs fast enough to beat that elevator."

By the time the other elevator arrived, we had seen the indicator for Rosen's go all the way to the first floor without stopping. Unless he was sneaky and rode it back up again, he was headed outside . . . somewhere.

Martin continued to fume as our elevator slid downwards. He slammed his fist against the control panel, exhorting the elevator to go faster. I could understand his frustration; being unable to do anything active in the pursuit of Rosen was irritating. Speaking of irritating . . .

"Martin, could you shift your grip a bit? You're hurting me."

He looked down. "Oh, sorry." He moved his hand a bit. "Victor, you're bleeding!"

"I expect so. I left a fair amount of skin on the carpet in front of Rosen's door."

"I . . . it's just that your skin looks so leathery."

"Maybe now you'll believe me when I tell you that the seat belt chafes me."

When the door opened on the lobby. Martin bounded out, headed for the front doors, then brought himself up short. "Bet you anything that he went out the back way," he muttered.

"It's a cliché, but you're probably right."

We crashed though the back door into a dark alley. Not so much as a single street light relieved the gloom. Martin halted. "Damn, I can't see a thing."

I assumed that his eyes simply took longer to adjust than mine. "Go to your right," I said.

He started off at a slow walk with his free arm held out in front of him.

"Bear to your right, you're about to hit the wall."

"How do you know?"

"I can see it."

"Where do I go now?"

"Keep going forward. You're doing fine."

"I feel like the headless horseman of Sleepy Hollow," Martin complained.

"Yup," I agreed. "You're carrying all your brains in your arm." Out of the corner of my eye, I saw a faint flicker of movement. "There he is!" I cried.

"Where?"

"Can't you see him?"

"Not a thing."

It was surely the strangest capture in history. I gave Martin directions until he literally stumbled over Rosen's feet where he was hiding behind a dumpster, hoping until the last instant to escape notice.

In all the years I had been on Earth, and after all the adventures Martin and I had been through, I had never been bandaged before. I didn't like the sensation. Then again, I don't wear clothing, either. The entire concept of being bound up by cloth is foreign in every sense of the word.

"Martin, when can we take this thing off?"

"When you quit bleeding."

Marie smiled at me in a kindly fashion. "Would it help you forget the bandage if I gave you that head of lettuce now?"

I couldn't help it. I started salivating. "You remembered!"

Martin turned his head slowly to stare at her. "You brought a nasty, mouldy, rotten, slimy, evil-smelling head of lettuce over here and put it in *my* refrigerator?"

"Naturally. The only way to serve lettuce is properly chilled."

"But it might," he waved his hands in the air vaguely, "spread germs or something."

She shook her head sadly. "When's the last time you looked in your refrigerator? There are cultures of every microorganism known to man in there. Where *did* you get that orange gunk growing on the pan on the second shelf, anyway?"

"That's a chocolate pie . . ." He subsided into uneasy muttering.

"How long has it been in there?" she persisted, not satisfied to let him off the hook so easily.

"It's the one you made me for my birthday," he admitted guiltily.

She stared. "Your birthday was six weeks ago, you idiot! You haven't eaten it *yet?*"

He was trapped and he knew it. If he said he liked it, she'd want to know why he hadn't eaten it. If he said he didn't like it, she would probably make him wear it, orange fungus and all.

I came to his rescue. "Marie, he thought it was so good he wanted me to share it with him. Of course, the only way he could do that was if he let it spoil a bit before serving me my slice."

She looked from one to the other of us before throwing up her hands. "*Men!*" Then she frowned at me and threw up her hands again. "*Aliens!*"

Martin threw me a grateful glance and tried to change the subject, "Don't you want to know about Rosen?"

She pursed her lips while she decided whether or not to give the two of us a good tongue lashing. "Oh, all right. I can tell you're bursting to tell me how clever you were."

"It wasn't me, it was Victor."

Her expression softened somewhat. She turned to me. "Don't you ever get tired of bailing lover-boy here out of tough spots?"

"He does have his uses. He had to drag Rosen out from behind the dumpster. Considering that Rosen outweighs me four to one, I couldn't have done it."

She turned and walked into Martin's tiny kitchen to stir the spaghetti sauce that was simmering on the stove. "So how did you know that Rosen kidnapped his own daughter?" she called back over her shoulder.

I answered, "He said the ransom note said 'the usual' things. It bothered me. How would he know what the usual things were? Why was he so blasé about the note? There were a few other oddities, too. For instance, he sounded defensive about the ransom being a half million dollars, and the fact that it happened to be his approximate net worth. From then on, it was trivial. If he had her, then he'd want her close by so he could check on her easily. Since he lived in an apartment building, the obvious thing to do would be to put her in another apartment, preferably on his floor. Turns out that he told Alice that he loved her so much he'd gotten her a whole new bedroom. She thought it was great."

Marie leaned out of the kitchen. "But wasn't that dangerous, leaving her in there by herself?"

"He had the stove and the oven – anything dangerous – turned off at the circuit breaker. Other than that, he tucked her into bed and was certain to be there when she woke up in the morning. It was really quite safe. And of course, it was only temporary."

"But why did he hire a detective in the first place?"

"Typical amateur criminal mentality. He was trying to gild the lily. He thought it would look more impressive if he could hand his ex-wife a report from a detective that said that his daughter was nowhere to be found."

"Let's see . . . then the bogus ransom note was just a cover to liquidate everything he had. He would have waited a discreet period of time, then moved away with the half million and Alice and started a new life with no one the wiser." She leaned out of the kitchen again, licking a wooden spoon. "Am I right?"

"On the money," Martin said, then coughed gently to let her know he expected applause.

She scowled and brandished the spoon at him. "That was terrible."

Martin sighed. "I'm still smarter than Rosen. He was headed for his car. The only thing was, he had panicked when he saw us and ran out of his apartment without his car keys."

Marie frowned. "But couldn't he have just gone back inside after them?"

He nodded. "Certainly. He was going to, but Victor saw him hiding in the darkest corner of the alley."

She looked at me. "I'm not sure I understand. If he was in a dark corner, how did you see him?"

I picked at one edge of my bandage – false modesty. "You're aware that I don't sleep, right? It's no secret that I wander all over the apartment at night. Everyone has always simply assumed that I have good night vision. I do, of course, but I can also see into the infrared."

"So you saw Rosen by his *body heat?*" she demanded.

"You and I look at that hot spoon that you're holding and we assume that we're seeing the same thing. It never occurs to either one of us to get the other to describe what they see in detail. Martin and I had never been in a situation where it had come up before."

"Makes me wonder what other things you can do," Marie said.

I flickered a few inches of my tongue at her. "That's for Wanne to know and you to find out," I teased.

Marie got so flustered that she dropped the spoon and darted back to the safety of the kitchen. "Is the little girl all right?" she blurted.

"Oh, she's fine," Martin said. Then he chuckled. "As a matter of fact, she's in love with Victor."

This brought Marie back out into the living room. "*What?*"

"After we got Rosen under control, we went back upstairs. Alice was getting scared by this time, because she didn't really know the security guard and she still wanted to see her father. Victor came to the rescue. I put the two of them together in the corner and Victor kept her amused by imitating every single animal at the zoo. When her mother arrived, Alice wanted to take Victor with her. She thinks he's cute."

"She wanted her mother to buy me from Martin on the spot. She was not pleased when she found out that I wasn't for sale. I fear that the child has been rather spoiled," I noted grimly.

"Speaking of getting spoiled, little buddy, you're going to have to do your own walking for a while. You've nearly pulled my arms out of their sockets," Martin said.

"I am *not* spoiled," I said indignantly. "That was medical necessity. My knee was hurt . . . by you, I might add."

Martin snorted. "Maybe so, but I didn't hear you complaining about getting the royal treatment."

"Well, no," I admitted. "It was rather nice."

"Supper time," Marie called. She placed a dinner plate with the rotting head of lettuce on it at one end of the table. "You will be eating with us, I assume," she said to me.

"I'd like to, yes. Will one of you get me down off of this chair?"

They looked at each other and laughed.

"Spoiled," Martin said.

"Spoiled rotten," Marie agreed.

THE BIRTH OF A. I.

Cynthia Ward

Supercomputers average the size of a dining room table, yet this computer took up a hundred square feet of floor space and dwarfed the anxious-looking programmers and engineers who stood before it. These researchers, members of the SAM Project, shivered in their labcoats and sweatshirts, for the computer room was 50°F.

Though she wore only a summerweight dress suit, Dr Maria Denhurst did not notice the cold. The Chief Scientist of the Stanford University Artificial Intelligence Research Laboratory studied her baby, the vast machine panelled in eggshell white where it wasn't sheathed in blinking red and green lights. The generic mainframe shell hid ten years of hard labour.

Supercomputers, powerful almost beyond human comprehension, could count, in seconds, all the stars in the sky, and even deduce whether a light in the sky was a star, but they were incapable of wondering *what* a star might be; the mightiest computer in the world hadn't the intellectual potential of a newborn babe. Mere increases in number-crunching power could not change this. Dr Denhurst contended that the path to a genuine thinking machine, a true artificial intelligence, lay in radical heuristic programming.

Today her work would be tested, her creation brought online for the first time. She felt pride, and a hot current of fear flowing from her gut. This was the climax of the Self Aware Machine Project – the culmination of all her hopes and dreams. There was no guarantee her theory was right.

She took a calming breath and stepped up to the super-computer. Her co-workers burst into applause. Their enthusiastic cheers surprised and embarrassed her.

What would it be like, she had often wondered, communicating with *another* intelligence? An artificial intelligence; the first verified non-human intelligence. It would, she thought, be alien. Though it would be a life created by human beings.

The computer, like a living thing, even had a name: "Sam-I-Am."

When the applause had died, Dr Denhurst turned on the microphone and spoke the words her assistant had dubbed The Spell of Awakening: "Sam-I-Am. Awaken."

The banks of red lights went green. The voice-circuit indicator turned green.

"– WAAAH!"

STAKES AND ADDERS

Marilyn Todd

"You've got to help me."

I put down my pen. The voice was so soft, so sibillant, at first I thought it was the wind in the leaves, but no. There it was again.

"Please. You're the only persson who can."

Pushing my glasses to the end of my nose, I had to admit that, even by snake standards, he looked pretty miserable.

"Go away." I tugged at the hem of my mini-skirt, because who knows how far those slitty eyes reach? "I'm marking examination papers and you're in flagrant breach of the rules."

And dear me, will that Jenkins girl never learn? It's eye of newt, not wing of bat. *C-minus*.

Undeterred, he slithered onto the page.

"Fine for you to say 'go away'. No-one turned you into a reptile, did they? And in any case it's not fair. In the books it's always handsome princes, and then they get turned into frogs." His little scaly mouth turned down in a pout. "Hell, I wasn't even a courtier."

"Hell, you weren't even handsome."

"Very funny."

"I thought so."

How many times do I have to tell these stupid children you use brimstone, not soapstone? Was it any wonder the dragon didn't retreat back in its lair? *D*, I scribbled, *and consider yourself lucky to get that*.

"No, really. You *are* the only one who can help me," and

you had to hand it to him. He was a persistent little adder. "After all, it was your great-grandmother who did this to me."

"For a very good reason, I'm sure."

"Good? Good?" He writhed round the desk like a scaly green dervish. "I'd worked in that woman's tavern from the age of sixteen, humping beer kegs, pulling pints, tossing out drunks from midday until midnight, seven days a week, fifty-two weeks of the year, until one day I have the temerity to ask for a rise. You call *that* a good reason to turn me into a ssnake?"

"I've heard better," I admitted, "but right now I'm busy."

These were merely the Spell Tests I was marking. I still had Stage 3 Wizardry and Advanced Werewolfing to wade through, and midnight oil was in short supply in those days.

"Anyway," I told him. "It's got to be a cushy life, being a snake."

"Oh? Then what do you call being unable to bask on the river bank for fear of being eaten by herons?

"Once bittern, twice shy?" (And who'd have thought something so thin and so slimy could snort.)

"Mock all you want," he hissed, "but it's no joke minding your own business on a drystone wall, when suddenly you're scooped up by some greasy garage mechanic, marched into the repair shop over the way and forced to dangle there utterly helpless while he yells, 'Whose was the BMW that needed new vindshield vipers?' To them, it's a hoot. To me, it's simply more humiliation."

"Pity, because if it was for real, you'd get a drive in the country out of the deal."

"Don't talk to me about driving. Not after that scoundrel St Patrick drove all my cousins out of Ireland."

"Only because he couldn't afford the air fare," I quipped, reaching for the next paper.

"Sun in Venus, moon in P –"

Ugh. How vulgar. *It might rhyme*, I scrawled, *but that is NOT how you spell Pisces. F minus minus, and you'll hang upside down for an hour after school for that, and no cheating with Blu-tack like last time.*

"I'm not going away," my visitor said, entwining himself round my coffee mug. "However long it takes, I shall –"

"OK." I slammed the book. "OK, I'll help you, but only because it was my great-grandmother, right?"

"You're an angel."

Oh, come on. Even *my* shapeshifting powers aren't that good. "What do you want?"

"It's Crowberry Heath." He slithered down the handle and I really didn't like the way he eyed up my computer mouse. "Do you know it?"

Know it? Who could fail to be enchanted by its riots of yellow gorse and purple bell-heather that sparkled with butterflies and hummed with bees, where warblers sang and kestrels hovered, and nightjars nested in summer.

"Yes, I know it."

"Well, that's where I live, only now a group of developers want to cover the heathland with houses –"

"And you want me to look into the future and see whether Scumby Homes get their way?"

"That wasn't exactly what I was after, but . . . hey, it's a start."

I was beginning to understand what prompted my great-grandmother all those years ago. Not so much snake in the grass as a pain in it.

"Fine. You want the future, I'll give you the future."

I pulled the crystal ball out of the drawer, gave it a rub with my hankie (last time I forecast snow when in reality it was nothing more than a layer of dust on the glass and I won't make that mistake again in a hurry. Until you've had snowmen prodding you in the breadbasket with an angry carrot, you haven't lived).

"Here we go." I peered into the ball and waited. "I see . . . oh, I see a young woman."

"Yeah?" His scales perked up at that. "What's she like?"

"Blonde. Very pretty –"

"Prettier than you?"

"Oh, she's gorgeous." I shook my head in wonder. "I have to hand it to you, you tempter of Eve, this is one girl who won't *stop* until she's found out everything there is to know about you."

"Everything?"

"Everything?"

"Wow." He covered the desk in one slither. "Don't suppose that crystal tells you when I'm going to meet up with this lovely lady?"

"What about the crisis at Crowberry Heath?"

"First things first." He ran his forked tongue round his lips. "Can you, er . . . can you look in there and see if she's kissing me? It's what pretty girls do to frogs, and you know reptiles and amphibians aren't that far apart on the evolutionary scale."

"Sorry, chum, this crystal is rated strictly PG, but if it helps, the answer is soon. You will meet the girl who wants to know you inside and out very soon." I gave the ball another rub. "Within minutes, in fact."

He preened himself in the glass. "Is it too much to assk where?"

"Hm, let me see. Ah yes." I lifted my head and looked him square in the eyes. "The school biology lab."

Trust me, you've never seen a snake move that fast. With a grin, I picked up the Werewolfing papers and worked right through until the midnight oil finally ran out.

St Sylvester's is precisely the sort of building that Charles Dickens loved to spend seventeen pages describing. I could have saved him a whole lot of ink, because you can sum up the school in one word. Ugly.

Actually, that's not true. St Sylvester's really needs two words to do it justice. Very ugly.

Of course by now you're thinking Gothic. Cracked stonework, grimacing gargoyles, a world of windowless turrets and creaking staircases, where the wind howls down long, lonely corridors and phantoms moan in the night. You'd be wrong. St Sylvester's is a monstrosity of sixties design, all square blocks and concrete, built in a style that would give even the most hardened Eastern Bloc architect the shivers. Trust me, no self-respecting ghost would set plasma inside these walls. Until political correctness invaded our society, it used to be an upmarket ghouls' school. Nowadays, though, they let in every Tom, Dick and Harry Potter. No wonder educational standards are falling.

"Pay attention, class."

I folded my wings and rapped on the blackboard.

"If you're going to take up a career in politics, you will need top grades in shapeshifting, so repeat after me. *Abracadabra, abracazoo, I want to turn, into a bat just like you.* No, no, no. Isabelle, dear, that's bat with a b, not cat with a c. Now drink your cream and try again. That's better. Right, class. Who knows how we turn ourselves back again?"

I can't quite remember who answered, that squeaky little pipistrelle or one of the mouse-eared variety, because at that moment, out of the corner of my eye, I noticed something long and green slinking out from behind the waste paper basket. I muttered the incantation for human reversal very quietly under my breath, so the class couldn't cheat. They'll get enough practice with that as politicians.

"That was a mean trick you pulled yesterday."

"Hiss off. Can't you see I'm taking a class?"

"You should be ashamed of yourself."

"Take your sticky scales off me."

"I don't know how you can sleep at night, I really don't."

"Very well, I apologize from the bottom of my heart. I – Am – Sorry. Now will you kindly twist off? There are twenty impressionable young students flitting around under this ceiling, all of whom seem to have forgotten the incantation for reverting to human shape. One wrong phrase, my serpentine friend, and these kids are vampires, and how on earth does one explain to their parents that sorry, your Kylie's turned into a bloodsucking monster."

"So they become lawyers instead of politicians." He shrugged his lithe little shoulders. "Who cares? At least you'll be able to turn them back again, which is more than I'll get. This spell's irreversible. Well." He rolled his eyes. "Apart from one week where I'm able to adopt human form again, on account of your great-grandma missing a word out of the curse."

"Be grateful. On my father's side they're dyslexic."

I've lost track of the numbers of messes I've had to clear up there. Cows going "oom". Grammy's neighbour who was turned into toast instead of a stoat. Not to mention Grammy herself yelling "Are you a man or a moose?" at poor Gramps. (Oh, and don't even *ask* about whether that woman believed in Dog or the Devil.)

The viper wound his way up the desk leg and tilted his head on one side. "You're the only one left who has the power to turn me back into a man," he said. "It's all I'm asking. My one chance to save Crowberry Heath from total destruction and my fellow adders from ending up as footwear –"

"Excuse me?"

"That was the other thing," he said miserably. "Scumby Homes intend to round us up and open a snake farm on the side, to breed a steady supply of handbags and boots."

"Very well." We witches don't really like undoing someone else's spell, but as he said. This one was irreversible. Might as well grant the poor chap his wish. "Seeing as it's Crowberry Heath."

"Whoopee!" If he had them, he'd be kicking his little green heels in the air. "When can we start? Now?"

"Now? Um, well, I – er, don't see why not."

No time like the present, I supposed, to reverse the past and re-write the future. I scooped him up and ran my hands lightly over the length of his body.

"Ooh, that's nice." He rippled with pleasure under my fingertips. "Better than nice, actually. Part of the reversal process, is it? Analysis of the subject?"

"Absolutely," I assured him.

Not strictly true, but since one never knows how things might turn out in the future, it didn't hurt to check this guy out. I could really use a smart pair of shoes.

Everyone knows Scumby Homes, of course, if only for that TV advert four or five years ago. You remember? The one in which Prince Charming kisses the Sleeping Beauty awake with those immortal words "*Your dream is our reality*," and hey presto! she's no longer inside some draughty, thorn-encrusted castle, but a luxuriously decorated modern home, come and visit our showhouse today.

Naturally, the media had a field day, especially since Prince Charming was played by Scumby's rather portly Chairman – who'd clearly taken drama lessons from the Forestry School of Acting, he was that damned wooden. But mostly the press attached themselves to it, because the advert could have been invented for cartoonists and impressionists to poke fun at. *Your realty is our dream* was my personal favourite, but its sheer naffness lent itself to all manner of take-offs, which is exactly what Scumby Homes wanted. With one ghastly advert, they became a household name, synonymous with – irony of ironies – quality, would you believe? Now they could dub themselves "Britain's No. 1 Builder" without fear of contradiction and, portly or otherwise, the Chairman was *this close* to a knighthood in the next New Year's Honours List.

As you'd expect, then, their headquarters was as prestigious as any of their exclusive developments. Smack bang on the River Thames, its glitzy design of marble and glass knocked the MI5 building into a cocked hat and, standing next door, it made sure it also dwarfed it. The message was clear. Scumby Homes made Big Business look small.

"I really appreciate your help on thisss, Sssusssannah."

Hm. I suppose I ought to tell you about that, but it was the dust, you see. All my great-grandmother's stuff was in boxes right at the bottom of the cupboard in the back of the classroom. Recipes, spell books, broomstick (just kidding), they were all there, and it took a fair bit of searching through, even allowing for Sebastian – that's his name, by the way – slithering in through the smallest of gaps to search for the right tome that would change him back to human form. OK, OK, it didn't take that long, since she wasn't much of a hoarder, my great-grandmother. But she's been a Guardian Angel for over fifty years now, and fifty years does leave a fair old layer of dust.

So it was inevitable, I suppose, that I would sneeze at some point during the recitation but, as I pointed out to Sebastian, you can't have everything and it could have been a lot worse. Far better he was left with a hiss than a forked tongue, I suggested, though he was far from convinced by the argument and, to be honest, I'm not entirely sure he believes it was an accident, even now.

"It's just a little lisp," I pointed out. "Hardly noticeable unless you –"

"Unlesss I what? Ssstop usssing pluralsss or wordsss with an 'sss' sssound." I didn't like the way his eyes narrowed when he leaned down to glare at me, which was a pity, because they were a really attractive shade of green. "Like Sssebassstian, for inssstancce?"

"No, more like dusky jade or wood sorrel, or even the colour of new ferns in the spring."

"*Huh?*"

"With teensy weensy little red flecks in them, if you peer closely."

"Did you by any chance take a pinch from that box marked 'Do Not Take a Pinch From Thisss Box'?"

"What? Oh, sorry, I'd kind of lost track."

Easy to do when you're strolling along the River Thames with a man whose hair has the colour and sheen of ripe horse chestnuts and whose smile is as wide as the ocean.

"We were talking about the hisss you've left me with. Sssomething, I might add, that I didn't have before."

"And won't have once you're a snake again," I assured him, giving his arm a comforting squeeze and finding it pleasantly muscular. "After all, it's only for a week –"

How could I have been so tactless? Sebastian was overjoyed to be back as a man, and funnily enough so was I. OK, you wouldn't put him up there with George Clooney or Brad Pitt, but he was far from ugly, years of sliding round drystone walls had left him lean and supple, and the basking had given him an good all-over tan – and I do mean all over. Talk about embarrassing! I blame the fact that he was in such a hurry, and what with rummaging round the cupboard to find my

great-grandmother's Book of Irreversible Spells (right under
The Foresight Saga as it happens, and underneath a file
marked Trivial Pursuits), we just hadn't stopped to think
about clothes. Like I said, one can't have everything, so I
stopped blushing and turned my thoughts to the issue in hand.
Saving Crowberry Heath.

"It'sss ssstill good of you to help me, Sssusssannah."

"Not at all."

After all, it wasn't as though I had anything better to do. Oh,
didn't I say? Yes, that was another thing. I'd been sacked, and
there's an odd thing. In all my ten years of teaching at St
Sylvester's, I've never once seen the headmaster cross.

"Nothing that's wrong can't be put right with a kind word, a
nod or a smile, that's my motto, Miss Hardcastle."

And for ten years, yes indeed, the headmaster nodded,
smiled and kindly worded his way through every awkward
situation you could imagine. For instance, when those boys
from Form B were caught smoking heroines (*Lorna Doone*,
Camille, dear me, no book was sacred), did the headmaster get
out his cane? He did not. He merely teased the little ankle-
biters about the error of their ways, got them to replace the
smoke alarm and sentenced them to two Moby Dicks for
detention. So for a man who was Father Christmas incarnate,
you think he might have saved just a little ho-ho-ho for me,
wouldn't you?

"You're not seriously giving me the bullet, headmaster?"

"Discharged, dismissed, fired, and sacked. Given the boot,
the elbow, your cards and your marching orders, and if you so
much as set foot within the grounds of my school, I will
personally evict you myself."

"You mean eject, expel, remove and turf out –?"

Not so much as a twinkle.

"Miss Hardcastle." He rose out of his chair, placed his
hands on the desk and leaned forward. "Miss Hardcastle, this
is no laughing matter. You walk out leaving Class C flitting
about the ceiling –"

Ouch.

"I apologized for that."

"*APOLOGIZED*? Good God, woman, have you any idea of the psychological damage you've inflicted on those children? Fatima will only eat fruit upside down now. Raymond, dammit, still refuses to come down from the ceiling, and little Edna can't sleep at night unless the blanket's tucked in tight, like it's her own wings folded round her. Miss Hardcastle, in all its illustrious history, St Sylvester's has never even seen a single lawsuit – until now!"

"Suppose I turn Form D into sharks, so we can breed our own lawyers to fight back?"

But I already knew that comedy wasn't going to help me this time around. The headmaster had turned red five minutes earlier. Now his colour deepened to purple.

"One more shapeshifting joke, Miss Hardcastle, and I am *this* far from violence." He drew a deep, shuddering breath and sat down. Rather foolishly, I took that as a good sign. "The bat problem we can get round. My brother-in-law happens to be a very good child psychiatrist and I am hoping the settlements from those claims can be negotiated into something approaching reasonable figures. However." I really didn't like the way that muscle started to twitch in his cheek. "Nudity in a school is another matter entirely, and for you to be flaunting your lover –"

"Begging your pardon, headmaster, that's far too strong a description for someone I'd only met the night before."

"Smut!" the headmaster exploded.

At least I sincerely hope it was an "m" and not an "l" that I'd heard.

"I will not tolerate smut in my school, Miss Hardcastle, and I will certainly not tolerate grown men running round naked. You can consider yourself lucky that you've escaped with dismissal, now that eight-hundred and fifty litigious parents have decided to sue St Sylvester's for encouraging paedophiles. OUT!"

"I don't suppose there's any chance of a reference –?"

Ooh, that gesture was no nod, that was no benevolent smile. And that word wasn't what I'd call kindly, either.

"No, ssseriousssly." With no job and no prospects, I'd

almost forgotten Sebastian standing beside me. "It wasss good of you to take a week off from SSSt Sssylvesss – ssschool – dammit, *college!* to help me organize my protessst rally."

"My pleasure," I said weakly.

Though you had to hand it to him. The instant he was back in human form (and fully clothed, I hasten to add) he was lobbying Downing Street, blitzing environmental pressure groups and enlisting the support of the Countryside Rescue Society in aid of the wildlife and beauty of Crowberry Heath before you could whistle Dixie. In three days, he'd produced posters depicting the orchids, the lily ponds, the butterflies, the birds, to show what would be lost for ever, once Scumby Homes covered the heath with their invidious concrete. His campaign was slick, it was impressive – and it wasn't enough. One week wasn't anywhere near enough to organize a blaze of marches, rallies, protests, sit-ins on the scale that would stop a multi-million pound corporation from bulldozing Utopia before the media got hold of the story. And one week was all my great-grand-mother had allowed for Sebastian to revert to his original form. One measly week!

Please, he had said. *You've got to help me. You're the only person who can . . .*

"What we need is to put a bug inside the Boardroom of Scumby Homes," I told him, choosing a seat on the embankment facing their Headquarters.

"Great!" he exclaimed. "Is it anyone we know?"

"Electronic bug, you doughnut."

I opened my briefcase and showed him the wingdings and widgets that Henry in the Cloning Department had lent me. To be honest, I'm not quite sure why the Cloning Department need to use such high-tech surveillance equipment, but even more worrying was that, when I asked Henry, he just tapped the side of his nose and said knowingly,

"Two heads are better than one."

And to think I actually dated that guy! Anyway, the upshot was, Henry lent me this case full of stuff and bless him, he even showed me how to use it, as well. Basically, all you have to do is this: place something that looks like a Victorian gentleman's collar stud in the room you want monitoring, direct some pointy black thing at it, then put on a pair of earphones and listen. (Excuse the science, but I'm only quoting Henry, who in turn read it aloud from the NASA Handbook on Satellite Surveillance – page 337, if you must know.)

"How did you plant the bug?" Sebastian asked, melting me with those big, green fern-in-the-springtime eyes of his.

"Flowers." I was proud of that. "I sent a huge basket of roses to the Board of Scumby Homes and signed it 'A Satisfied Shareholder'."

I thought he would laugh at my silly ASS pun. Instead, his face crumpled. "Is it true their shares rose ten percent as a result of this proposal?"

"Executive homes have a massive profit margin," I told him, "and because of their exquisite location, we're talking *footballers' houses* here!"

"Terrific. I get kicked off, ssso they can kick on."

"Oh, stop sulking and pick up your earphones. The Board Meeting's about to start."

Actually, although I liked his smile, I quite liked that mean, manly, moody look of his, too. I liked the brush of his skin against mine, as he leaned to pick up the headset, and I liked his faint citrussy scent.

Trust me, I thought, to fall for a guy who's only got four days left before he turns back into a snake.

Usually, it's much later that I find out the men I am dating are snakes.

AS HEARD THROUGH TWO PAIRS OF EARPHONES VIA SOME POINTY BLACK THING:

Clip clop of male feet inside Boardroom.

"I say, old chap, what wonderful roses! A – what does it say? oh, satisfied shareholder, eh? Ha, ha, wasn't you, was it, Chairman?"

"What? Waste money on flowers? Certainly not, Clive, but I'm betting that whoever sent them is going to be a lot more satisfied after we've announced the end-of-year profits, and so will we, dear boy, so will we. Crowberry Heath is going to make us very rich men, Clive."

Short snort of laughter. "We're rich now, Chairman."

"Yes, and that's entirely due to Scumby Homes' continued commitment to the redistribution of individual wealth." *Pause.* "And the suckers purchasing the Crowberry Heath homes will be very wealthy indeed!" *Rustle of papers.* "Have you seen the designer's plans for the interior?"

"Have I! Wouldn't mind some of that marble in my own place."

"Me, neither, but between you and me, dear boy, and before the others get here, there's a couple of things that are troubling me." *Voice lowers to whisper.* "One of which is mahogany."

"Take it from me, old man, once the wife threatens to leave and take all your assets with her, you'll adapt fast enough."

"Not monogamy, you clot. I'm talking about endangered hardwoods."

"You against stripping the rain forests bare, then?"

"Don't be an ass, man. What I'm trying to tell you is that I can't decide between ebony or mahogany – ah, ladies, gentlemen."

Murmur – babble – in fact, the classic rhubarb–rhubarb of St Sylvester's drama department extras.

During the bout of back-slapping and handshaking, a pleasure boat carrying a coach-load of camera-clicking Japanese waving wildly went past. Sebastian and I waved wildly back, while from the boardroom we listened to endless champagne corks popping, lots of chinking and glugging sounds, then finally, oh finally, a scraping of chairs.

"Very good." *Chairman cleared throat.* "Welcome to the hundred-and-forty-fifth meeting of the board of Scumby Homes. I'll run through the Minutes of the last meeting later, and I'm sure we can skip the Any Other Business stuff, because we all know the reason we're here."

Murmurs of agreement, backed, I swear, by a licking of collective lips.

"There was a time, ladies and gentlemen, when I was a young man, that I truly believed that wealth and power would bring me happiness. Well, as Chairman and Chief Executive of this prestigious company, I'm delighted to say I was right –"

Roar of laughter.

"– and since Scumby Homes is dedicated to social ideals, it's only fair that we continue to expand on that theme – and make ourselves even more powerful and wealthy!"

Hear, hear.

"At our last meeting, you were shown the video of the proposals for Crowberry Heath. Just to recap, this is to be a select development of high specification build projects in one of the loveliest corners of England."

Irony seriously noticeable by its absence.

"We're talking luxury at the highest level for the highest possible returns, but since Scumby Homes is also a modern, forward-thinking corporation, the Marketing Department, under the direction of the ever-reliable Rupert here, have identified opportunities to diversify and expand. The reptile population, for example –"

Click-click of slide show, followed by gasps of revulsion.

"Ugh!"

"Eugh."

"Is that *slime*?"

"Yes, indeed, Letitia, and for that reason it is not in our interest to have our precious clientele repulsed by these creatures, unless . . ." *tantalizing hint entered voice* ". . . unless, ladies and gentlemen –"

Click-click of slide show, followed by gasps of delight.

"Ooh."

"Aah."

"I *do* like those."

"Boots, shoes, bags, purses. Ladies and gentlemen, snakeskin is making a serious comeback and Scumby Footwear intends to be at the very forefront of this fashion movement, and let's not forget the moles, either. Marketing are confident several top designers can be drafted in to promote moleskin for next season, and you've all seen the plans for the factory?"

Affirmative rumbles.

"The idea is that we collect all the moles and adders on Crowberry Heath to use as breeding stock."

(Beside me, Sebastian groaned and buried his head in his hands).

"Not always easy, getting wild creatures to reproduce in captivity, Chairman. Think about the trouble zoos have had in the past with giant pandas and the like."

"Good point, Clive, but we at Scumby Footwear have a plan to ensure a plentiful supply of snakeskin." *Chairman gives little snigger.* "Using the timber we fell from Crowberry Heath, we split the trees into logs, chop the logs into tables and put them in the cages with the snakes." *Snigger louder.* "Everyone knows that for adders to multiply one needs log tables!"

"Haw-haw-haw."

"Very witty, Chairman."

"Did you think that joke up yourself?"

"As a matter of fact, Letitia, I did. Anyway, moving on to the lily ponds."

Another click of slide show / gasps of delight.

"Ooh."

"Ah."

"Lovely."

"Yes, indeed, ladies and gentlemen, but once again frogs and designer shoes are incompatible." *Hum of agreement.* "Whereas frogs and designer kitchens, on the other hand, are not!"

More clicks.

"Ooh!"

"Yum."

"Scrummy!"

"Exactly! In addition to diversifying into footwear, designerwear and luggage, I am proud to announce that Scumby Auberges will be opening an exclusive French restaurant close to the development, serving frogs' legs, snails in garlic –"

I never got to hear the rest of the menu. Beside me Sebastian had turned pale and was shaking.

"Cannibalsss," he whispered. "Those bassstardsss are going to eat my friendsss!"

I put my arm round him, intending to comfort him, and felt only his pain and fear.

To the Board Members of Scumby Homes, the destruction of Crowberry Heath was just another money-spinning, get-rich-quick scheme which, with the callousness of property developers everywhere, was also one huge joke.

For Sebastian, the survival of Crowberry Heath in its natural state wasn't a matter of life and death any more, or even an issue of freedom and slavery. It was Man's capacity to ride roughshod over what it considered lesser creatures – and with it the obliteration of morals and decency. In his view, this fight was quite simply Good versus Evil.

Please, you've got to help me. You're the only person who can.

As the earphones emitted noises of chairs scraping, of goodbyes and thank-yous and see-you-again-soons, I stared across the cold, grey waters of the Thames and wished with every ounce of my body that I'd refused to undo my great-grandmother's spell.

Please.

He wouldn't have known. He wouldn't have known what fate awaited the inhabitants of Crowberry Heath, not until it was too late. Now he'd have this on his conscience, and although his human form had allowed him to do everything in his power to prevent it, he'd be living for the eternity my great-grandmother had consigned him to, tormented by the knowledge that he could see into the future and was unable to change it.

You're the only person who can.

As his shoulders slumped with hopelessness and despair, I reflected that Sebastian had put a heck of a lot of faith in a failed schoolteacher whose great-grandmother had turned him from a good-looking young man into a stone-basking reptile, and whose own reversal spell had left him with a lisp for the one week he was allowed to revert.

But that was the point. Faith moves mountains, not multi-million pound corporations.

Crowberry Heath and its beauty were doomed.

*   *   *

I couldn't sleep. Every time I dropped off, I'd dream I was stuffing frogs' legs into my mouth four at a time as I winkled snails out of their garlicky shells, then I'd wake up in a cold sweat with images of sweet-and-sour butterflies, crispy Peking warblers and coot à l'orange going round in my head as concrete mixers covered Paradise with cement.

I tossed, I turned, the dreams changed.

Now, I was walking along streets thronged with beautiful people dressed in snakeskin shoes and moleskin jackets, but as they passed, their clothes mouthed the word *traitor* and bats shrieked *I hate you, I hate you* into my ear, and *Raymond won't come down from the ceiling*.

I got up, I made coffee, I went back to bed.

This wasn't my fault. Crowberry Heath was lovely, but it was hardly the Garden of Eden. Sebastian wasn't Adam, I wasn't Eve, it was just the serpent in paradise bit that was making my head whirl, only everything was back to front with that scenario. This time the snake was the good guy, and he had eyes like spring ferns, smelled faintly of citrus and had a smile as wide as the ocean.

I blame too much caffeine at three in the morning for making me weepy. I'm not normally given to blubbing.

"You're the only one who can help me," he'd said. "After all, it was your great-grandmother who did this to me."

"For a very good reason, I'm sure."

"Good? Good?" I remember how he'd writhed round the desk like a scaly green dervish. "I'd worked in that woman's tavern from the age of sixteen, humping beer kegs, pulling pints, tossing out drunks from midday until midnight, seven days a week, fifty-two weeks of the year, until one day I have the temerity to ask for a rise. You call *that* a good reason to turn me into a snake?"

Just what kind of people was I descended from, I wondered miserably, that inspired them to turn honest, hardworking, loyal folk into snakes for such trivial matters? Wait a minute . . . I put down the coffee mug. What was the name of that weighty tome underneath the *Book of Irreversible Spells? The Foresight Saga*, right? And on top of the *Book of Irreversible*

Spells? A file marked *Trivial Pursuits*! Suddenly, I remembered shoving it aside and the spring-clip flying open, with several pages rearranging themselves on the floor of the classroom. Without thinking, I'd scooped them up and stuffed them back in the file, but a few lines in my great-grandmother's writing had registered in the back of my brain.

The first rule of spellcasting – she'd always had a neat hand, my great-gran – is that one never enchants without the most powerful of reasons.

To turn a man into a snake for eternity for little more than saying boo to a goose is hardly a powerful reason, unless . . . I jumped out of bed and ran straight for the Hardcastle family tree (it's an oak) to see exactly when my great-grandmother became a Guardian Angel. Well, well, well. It was exactly two days after she'd turned Sebastian into a snake.

And underneath the *Book of Irreversible Spells* she'd left *The Foresight Saga*.

Coincidence? I don't think so.

I showered, I dressed, I bought some more roses. This time, though, I bought two large bouquets.

"Susannah."

The change had already started. The lisp was gone, and he seemed taller, somehow, and slimmer.

"Susannah, you really don't have to be here."

There were tears in his eyes. The last tears he would ever shed, I thought. And he was trembling as he hugged me goodbye. Inside I felt strange, while all around us, frogs croaked, warblers sang and butterflies explored the blossoms for nectar.

"I, er, have some good news," I told him shakily. "Crowberry Heath is safe. It can never be built on. Not ever."

"Really?" I thought it would perk him up. Instead, he crushed me to his chest even tighter. "Oh, Susi, my Susi, how I shall miss you!"

"You will?" Well, at least one of us was able to perk. "Honestly?"

"The minute I saw you, tugging at your mini-skirt as you

marked those exam papers, I fell in love with you, Susi. That silly curl that falls over your left eye. The way you toss your head when you're cross. I adore them, and although I'm grateful for what you've done – not to mention surprised, I might add! – it's my love for you that will keep me going for the whole of etern . . ."

I think he was going to say eternity, but there wasn't much time left for human kissing. I wanted to snatch what I could.

"Wow." Sebastian seemed to be reeling. (Or maybe that was just me). "How did you *do* that?"

"Oh, it was so easy when you stop to think about it," I said.

March into Chairman's office bypassing all secretarial dragons since I am clutching a bouquet of roses, being the Satisfied Customer of before, etc, etc, etc. Chairman charmed by young girl in short skirt (and maybe a touch of fairy dust, too). We talk. Or rather, I coerce aided and abetted by much crossing of legs, fluttering of eyelashes . . . and maybe just a touch more of Mum's fairy dusty. Its effects are very short-lived.

Finally, though, I lay it on the line for the Chairman. I want Crowberry Heath saved for posterity, and I want it in writing, while you want to be richer than Croesus and get a knighthood into the bargain. He nods. I nod. We knuckle down to business. Drop the Crowberry Heath development, I tell him, and I'll show you where you can find oil. Now obviously I have to show him my credentials at this juncture, which is rather unfortunate for the hapless Clive who just happens to pop his head round the door at that time. But most people like parrots, and I really needed to prove my point.

"Go on," the Chairman of Scumby Homes said, feeding Clive a peanut on his perch, so I did. I turned his secretary into a ginger tomcat, Rupert of Marketing into a tortoiseshell and the teaboy into a tabby.

"I meant go on with the oil thing," the Chairman said, "but no matter. Always had a soft spot for cats. Never had 'em at home, see. They give the wife asthma."

I wasn't interested in his wife's health and I doubted the Chairman had ever had a soft spot in his life. But having proved my abilities, and with him admitting to having taped every episode of *Dallas*, we moved on.

"Crowberry Heath is to be left untouched for ever," I said.

"Agreed." With the New Years Honours Lists being drawn up, he signed without even looking. "And the oil?"

I handed him a map with detailed and accurate directions, left the roses on his desk to remind him what I'd come up smelling of, then left the second bouquet on my great-grand-mother's memory stone.

"No, I meant how did you come to *kiss* me like that," Sebastian said. "It's . . . it's as though . . ."

"As though I love you, too?" Men! "Well, of course I love you, you doughnut."

Already his eyes had turned into slits, though, and scales now covered the whole of his skin.

"I shall always love you, Sebastian." In fact, the thought of French kissing with those long white fangs made me tingle to the tips of my toes. "Now where did you say you go for the winter?"

What was left of his hand pointed to a distant drystone wall.

"Ooh, goody, we can coil round each other for months on end, just me and you," I giggled.

And you should have seen his face when my tongue forked.

"You're coming, too?"

"Try and stop me," I hissed, writhing alongside him through the undergrowth.

Because that's the thing, see. We shapeshifters never die. When our human lifespan is over, we invariably turn into Guardian Angels, and since my great-grandmother had the Book of Foresight in her keep, she'd have known the end of her lifespan to the hour.

I'd worked in that woman's tavern from the age of sixteen, humping beer kegs, pulling pints, tossing out drunks from midday until midnight, seven days a week, fifty-two weeks of the year, until one day I have the temerity to ask for a rise. You call that a good reason to turn me into a snake?

One never enchants without the most powerful of reasons.

My great-grandmother had known Sebastian from when he

was sixteen, and in those twelve years he'd never so much as taken a day off. Now if he'd been that devoted to the old woman, she must have adored him in return, so with just two days before the thread of her human lifespan was cut, she gave him the finest gift in her power.

Eternal youth.

All good things come to those who wait, Susannah.

In his case, it was fifty years slithering round Crowberry Heath's worth of waiting, but as I said, my great-grandmother had had the Book. She knew exactly what Sebastian was waiting for.

Me.

Did you really think I would miss a word out of a curse? Me? A *Hardcastle*!

Perhaps she'd foreseen my cackhanded efforts in the Book, too. Knew I'd let the side down eventually with my dreadful mistakes. (Poor Raymond, poor Fatima, oh poor little Edna.) And I suppose she'd known from the outset that I wasn't cut out for teaching, much less casting spells, but believe me, this was one irreversible spell I didn't mess up. Eternal youth, eternal happiness and eternal love are well worth the additional effort, though you have to hand it to great-gran. That woman certainly understood why the Garden of Eden is ablaze with serpents – not to mention the reason we hibernate through the winter! (And personally, I think temptation's a jolly good thing, don't you?)

What? The oil? Oh, didn't I say? Even as I was lodging the Chairman's agreement with solicitors that would finally secure my future home from the developers' greed, he was following my extremely detailed and accurate directions.

Right to the oil tank in the basement of St Sylvester's.

THE SEA SERPENT SYNDICATE

Everard Jack Appleton

If it wasn't for Jimmy Raines, I wouldn't try to write this story out. It ain't the kind of thing I like to think about, any more than I like to remember the name of a horse through which I have lost money; but Jimmy is a good fellow, and he asked me to do it – and what Jimmy Raines wants me to do, I do.

The reason he wants this story printed is because the people he tells it to don't believe him, and I don't know as I blame 'em; but he thinks if they see it in print they will.

The Sea Serpent Syndicate was a stroke of luck – bad or good, I don't know which. It started in a little summer garden, not far from Latonia, and it ended on an island somewhere south of Cuba. If it hadn't been for the earthquake – But I'm getting away before the flag drops.

To start right, it was a day that was hot enough to warp you – and Jimmy and I decided to absent ourselves from the Latonia races and take it easy.

We had dropped into John Porter's summer garden for a glass of beer and a cigar, and both of us tilted back in the shade, when the swing door from the street opened, and a chap that looked like the survivor of a North Pole expedition slouched in and dropped into a chair a few feet away from us.

The thermometer was somewhere at the hundred mark; but Mr Coldfeet had on an overcoat with the collar turned up, and a muffler round his neck. Jimmy stared at him a moment, and then gave me the wink.

"I hope you ain't got your ears frosted, William," says he to me, as old John came out to get the stranger's order.

The guy had a big round package with him, and when John leant over the table to get his good ear near enough to catch the order, the stranger jerked the package away as if it had been a bunch of diamonds.

"Gimme a lemonade," said he, "and make it long and sour."

I was trying to make up my mind where I had seen him before when he looked up and straight into my eyes. The change that come over him was something remarkable. In a minute he had cleared the distance between us, and had hold of my hand, pumping it up and down like a steam engine, and saying: "Billy Martin, Billy Martin! Where did you come from?"

"I didn't come at all," says I, "I was here first. Where did you come from, Alphonse Doolan? That's the question!"

"From a mighty hot place," he answers, "and I ain't used to white man's weather yet. That's the reason I feel sorter chilly."

"We thought there must be something wrong," said I, waving my hand at Jimmy. "Mr Doolan, shake hands with my side partner, Mr Raines. Mr Doolan is just back from a vacation in the middle of Africa, Jimmy."

Doolan shook his head.

"No, Billy," says he, "I left there five years ago. And I've been putting in my time in a hotter place than Africa. I've been surrounded by the equator, and glued to an island down in the Carib. And I'm nigh dead with the heat of it!"

"Won't you take off your overcoat, then?" I says. "The last I heard of you, you was sending daily reports about the temperature and barometer readings from some hole in the great American desert for the wise guys at Washington."

Alphonse dragged up his chair and the bundle with it.

"I was," he says, "but they transferred me. I had a joke one day, and sent a lot of dispatches to them about the ice forming and the snowstorm freezing my instruments. As it was August, they thought I needed a rest for a couple of months, and after that they shipped me to my island, where for four years I have been hanging on, broiling to death. Four years of heat and thirst, and nobody to talk to! Nothing to look at but scrub and sand – Lord, the sand there is on that island! It's a wonder it don't sink with the weight of it!"

"Working for the government still, Alphonse?" I asks.

"Sure," he answers. "Taking the readings every day, and sending them back to Havana whenever they happen to think of me and scow down with grub for me. I'm nigh crazy, Billy – but I'll soon be better, because –"

He stopped a minute, looking very foxy.

"Because I've got *him!*"

"Him?" says I. "Who's him?"

"Billy. I named him after you, Billy Martin, and you've got cause to be proud."

"Baby?" says I, yawning. I'd expected something more exciting from the way Alphonse had started out.

"Baby?" says he, scornful-like. "Naw! Sea serpent!"

Jimmy kicked me under the table, and I sat up. Alphonse was madder than I had thought after all.

"Oh, I am proud," I says. "I am, Alphonse. Where do you keep him?"

"On the island," he answers, sucking his lemonade through the straw, and watching me closely. "In the middle of the lake the earthquake made. He come in with the quake, and I've tamed him. He eats out of my hand, and he's a good snake, I tell you – but I can't afford him. It takes all my supplies to keep him good-tempered – and sardines, his favourite, come high."

"Yes," I says, "it must be a kind of a luxury to have a pet sea serpent, Alphonse, following you round the house and eating out of your hand. And as for sleeping with one –"

"Cut it out, cut it out, Billy," says Alphonse, as sensible as could be. "You and I worked together long enough for you to know that I ain't a liar. This is straight goods, and here's the evidence," and he commenced to unwrap the package. He took out something that looked like an overgrown soup plate and put it down on the table. It smelt fearful fishy, I noticed, and it appeared to be made of horn, half an inch thick, and as big as a scale from the fish you didn't catch.

"Well," I says, "don't be silly, Alphonse. Go ahead with your fairy tale. I'll listen to it if Mr Baines will."

"There ain't going to be no fairy tale," says Alphonse bristling up. "That's a scale from my sea serpent – come off him two weeks ago, when he got upset at something and throwed it at me."

He took a letter from his pocket.

"This here letter," says he, opening it and tossing it across the table, "is from the Natural History Society secretary across the river, and you can see what he says – 'The article in the possession of Mr Alphonse Doolan appears to be, and probably is, a scale from an ocean reptile, popularly known as a sea serpent.'"

I looked at the letter, and sure enough that is what it said, and a lot more about the value of the discovery, and wishing the authorities at Washington would take the matter up with Mr Doolan. I read it aloud, and Jimmy's eyes got bigger and bigger. When I finished and handed it back to Doolan, Jimmy spoke for the first time.

"Mr Doolan," says he, "how much would it cost to go after that animal of yours, and bring him to the States for exhibition purposes?"

"Well," replied Alphonse, "I don't know. As soon as I get to Washington, I'm going to get the Smithsonian Institute to work it out."

"Smithsonian nothing," says Jimmy. "Can't you see something better ahead than that? If you bring that animal here, and if he is as big as that hunk of horn would seem to indicate, there's a fortune in it for three men."

Alphonse nodded his head slowly. "But it would cost all of five thousand dollars," he says, "and I'm broke."

Then Jimmy showed for the first time how sharp he had got all in a minute.

"Mr Doolan," says he, leaning over the soup plate thing, "when I am a sport I try to be a game one. Billy Martin and I cleaned up a little more than the figure you name last month. That's why we are taking the afternoon off here in place of beating the bookies out of other people's money. Now, Mr Martin seems interested in this story of yours, fishy as it looks to be, and I am, too. I am willing to make you a proposition. We will go back to your island, every fellow paying his own way. If that snake of yours is the real thing we'll pay for bringing him here, and split the profits on showing him. Is that fair?"

It was a long speech for Jimmy, and plain as an old shoe. Alphonse couldn't help seeing it was straight, too.

He thought a minute, looked at me, and then held out his hand to Jimmy.

"Shake," he says. I did the same, and the Doolan-Raines-Martin Sea Serpent Syndicate was formed.

Six days later we were aboard a little fruit boat on the Caribbean Sea, looking for Alphonse's island. It was my first experience on the raging deep, and I think it will be my last, unless I am chloroformed and dragged aboard another ship. The fourth day out, about ten o'clock in the morning, Alphonse let out a yell like an Indian, and grabbed a chart from the captain's hand.

"That's my island, cap," he says, pointing to a little black spot on the edge of the ocean. "Steer for her, and dump us off. I'm hungry to see that bunch of sand again."

In less than an hour we had drawn up alongside the hump of sand and scrub palm trees, and half an hour later we were sitting on our traps watching the fruit boat get smaller and smaller in the distance. It was hot enough to roast a pig, but Alphonse seemed really happy. He messed round and got something for us to eat out of his pack, and then we all lighted our pipes and waited for the sun to go down a bit.

"Alphonse," says I, as we stretched out under the biggest tree we could find, "I haven't asked you for any particulars since we started on this expedition. Now I want you to tell us how you came to round up that snake of yours."

Alphonse took a long draw at his pipe and clasped his hands behind his head.

"It ain't much of a story," says he, "but you've got a right to know it. My station ain't anything but a shanty, and a soapbox for furniture. It stands at the head of what was a ravine. One night there come a 'quake, and I got up to see where I was. The moon was shining bright, and when I looked for my ravine I made sure I was off my head. There wasn't none left.

"In place of the valley was a lake, half-a-mile wide and two long, boiling and churning. And in it was the curiousest creature you ever see. He's three hundred feet long – I made him lie still once while I measured him so you can bet on the figures – and has a head on him like a skinned cow. He was bellering and flapping his fins, and smelt something fearful. That was Billy, and I soon figured out what had happened. The 'quake had opened my island from the bottom, let Billy and a lot of water in, closed up again – and left the snake and me to get acquainted.

"I didn't get much sleep the rest of the night, with his thrashing around and bawling for his folks, but by morning he'd worn himself out and was sleeping as peacefully as a lamb on top of the water. I took a fancy to him right then. I don't know what made me think of you just then, Bill Martin, but I did; and I named him after you before he could wake up and object.

"When he opened his eyes and seen me observing him, he got upset. He raised about ten feet of his neck out of the water, and cut loose, with a twist of his head and a grunt, and this very scale that brought us three together come sailing straight for me. I side-stepped and it buried itself in the sand.

"'Look a-here, Bill,' I says, 'that's no way to treat the owner of this island. I didn't invite you here, in the first place; you're unexpected company, and you oughter behave yourself polite. I'm willing for you to stay, but you've got to be good-natured.'

"I don't say he understood me, but he looked as if he might. Then he opened his mouth and yawned like he was embarrassed, so I threw him a piece of meat. He caught it and swung around, and started for the other side of the lake. From that on he acted right, and I didn't have no cause to complain. I never realised what company a sea-serpent could be; I'm right lonesome for him now. He's an affectionate reptile, and it won't take him no time to get broke in, once we git him to the States. A few more weeks of kind treatment will make him as gentle as a kitten, and he will swim after any boat I happen to be on. You hear me?"

"But suppose he does object?" asks Jimmy.

"Mr Raines," says Alphonse, "I ain't teaching my snake politeness through a correspondence school. If he is impertinent ain't I there to administer the proper chastisement – and stop giving him fish? You leave that to me. And now, as the sun is subsiding, let's be off."

At the end of two hours' hard walking over sand heaps we came to a low hill, from which we could see a little lake with a few scrub trees on the banks and a shanty at one end.

"There," says Alphonse, proud as a peacock, "there is Doolanville. Pleasant prospect, ain't it? I am thinking of cutting it up into lots and selling it to desirable parties only.

"Welcome to the Hotel de Doolan," says he, opening the door and peering into the shanty. "But mebbe you'd rather have the lizards out before you go in. They ain't very partial to strangers."

He steps inside, and raises a racket, and a menagerie of half-a-dozen scaly critters, not counting the land crabs and house snakes, ran out. "Now," says he, appearing once more, "your apartments are ready, gentlemen. Step inside and register. Sorry all our rooms with baths attached are took; but the lake is convenient and free."

By the time we had packed our things away and fixed our bunks the sun had almost set, and Alphonse was rustling around with his pots and pans on the outside, singing to himself. Jimmy and I watched him for a few minutes, and then Jimmy says to me, sorter quietlike: "Is this real or am I dreaming?"

"Don't ask me," says I. "Feels like I ought to wake up myself before long."

Jimmy shook his head. "The worst of it is that we are here, and we can't get our money back at the gate. Looks to me as if we'd have to see it through. But where's the snake?"

Just as he spoke, I looked out across the lake, and my hat raised two inches off my head. Of course, I had some faith in all that Alphonse had told us, but I wasn't prepared to have it all come true so sudden and unexpected.

Before I could kick myself to see if I really was awake, the snake was almost on us. He come sailing across that lake looking very wicked. He was as big as a water-tower, and I could have sworn that he was long enough to go round Latonia race-track twice, and a lap or so over. He slid across the water, a giant, greased fishing-worm, the last rays of the sun shining on his scales and turning them as white as silver.

When he caught sight of us, I held my breath. He raised his head out of the water twenty feet or more and back-pedaled, churning up the lake till it frothed. His eyes was bigger than a barrel, and when he opened his mouth, showing a row of teeth resembling a white-washed fence, it was too much for Jimmy. He gave a sort of grunt, and went off into a dead faint.

As for me, I was fast getting seasick myself and wondering how I could hit the trail back to the coast again, leaving Jimmy and his faint to themselves, when Alphonse stuck his head out of the shanty.

"Ah, ha!" he cries, stepping out with his frying-pan in one hand and a box of sardines in the other. "Billy has come! Now, I guess you fellows know whether your Uncle Alphonse was toying with the truth or not. Ain't he a beaut, William – and ain't you proud he's your namesake?"

I was trying to get enough breath back to express my thoughts on that and other subjects, when the snake struck the beach, stopped short, and let out a roar that blowed me over against Jimmy. Alphonse seemed to think it a good joke, and snapped his fingers at the critter.

"Here, Billy; here, Billy boy!" he calls. "Come and say howdy to your proud old boss and his friends. You mustn't forgit your manners."

The snake ducked down for a foot or two, looked us over suspiciously for a minute, and then brought his head to a level with Alphonse. It wasn't a head that you'd want a picture of in the parlour, with his big eyes, one green, and the other blue, and long white whiskers. But Alphonse seemed tickled to have him so close, and shoved the open box of sardines at him; and Billy smiled.

You have never seen a sea-serpent smile, of course, so you can't imagine what it is. You haven't missed very much, though, so don't lose any sleep over it. The inside of a mammoth cave, painted red – that was Billy's smile. I was glad when he closed it up again, on the box of sardines, for he seemed so tickled with them that he kept his mouth shut and laid his head down on the sand beside Alphonse, like a sick kitten waiting to be petted. Alphonse scratched him with the frying-pan, and the snake lay there purring his gratitude and pleasure for five minutes.

It was the noise he made – you'd 'a' thought an engine was getting up steam – that brought Jimmy round. He came to, facing the snake, and when he clapped eyes on him, Jimmy let out a terrific yell. The snake didn't like it, and before Alphonse could speak to him, he had reared up, the scales standing out on his neck like bristles on a bulldog. The next minute he gave his head a short, sharp bob, and one of those horn wash basins broke loose from its moorings, and shot by Jimmy's ear, close enough to cut his hair.

"Wow! Take him away, take him away!" howls Jimmy, making for the shanty, followed by another little sea serpent souvenir. Alphonse waved his frying-pan at Billy, and called: "Behave yourself, Bill! Shame on you!"

But Billy was scared, too, and he kept firing scales at Jimmy until he reached the shanty and got hid under the boxes and barrels inside. Then the snake's short ears laid back, showing he didn't mean anything vicious; he lowered his head again, crawled up a few feet on the beach and butted his nose in the sand at Alphonse's feet, asking forgiveness for his behaviour as plain as any dog ever did.

Alphonse sat down and began to talk to his pet, and, not wishing to disturb a little family conversation like that, I sneaked away to find Jimmy, who was having a bunch of assorted fits in the furthest corner of the Hotel de Doolan.

And that was our introduction to Doolan's sea serpent.

It is hard to believe, I know, but inside a week I got so used to have that snake about that I didn't pay any more attention to him that I would to a big dog. We got to be good friends, too, although I never could find much enjoyment in his sea breath, which was strong and noticeable, him being so affectionate. Every morning when I went for a swim in the lake, he'd see me coming, and he'd cavort and do water gymnastics until I got out. He'd come to my call, just as he did to Alphonse's, and seemed to try his best to make me feel at home.

But he never did like Jimmy, I'm sorry to say. That yell he heard Jimmy give sort of prejudiced him, I guess. He didn't shy any more soup plates, but he just didn't take any more interest in him, and Jimmy seemed to rather enjoy the slight. It was a mutual dislike, too. If Jimmy could have handed Billy a dynamite sandwich, he'd have done it I reckon; but he never let on to Alphonse that the snake's vagaries hurt his feelings.

Even the night that Billy took Alphonse for a ride, Jimmy didn't look jealous. The snake was laying up on the beach, as usual, and Alphonse was scraping his head with a piece of board, when Billy seemed took with an idea. He slipped his head under Alphonse, raised his back, and started for the lake again, with Alphonse sitting astride his neck, same as a bareback rider in the circus. Billy took him fast across the lake and back, and Alphonse was so tickled with the experience that he made me try it the next night.

Every night after that Alphonse and I would have a ride or two, and all Billy asked was a box of sardines and a three-minutes' scratch of the head. I don't believe there ever lived a kinder-hearted sea serpent than Billy.

But, of course, this couldn't last. The end was bound to come, and it came sudden enough when it did. Alphonse had just announced to us, about two weeks after we had landed, that he thought Billy was ready for his trip.

"He won't try to play hookey," said be, answering my question on that subject. "When we get him to the coast, he'll be afraid to leave me. I think we'll start tomorrow, and then – across the water for us, and, fortune waiting on the other side! We'll have Billy the talk of the world inside of –"

And that was as far as Alphonse got. Something broke loose under the island just then, and the lake commenced to tear about as if there were a cyclone at the bottom of it.

Billy looked back at his happy home, slid up on the bank, shoved his head between Alphonse's legs, and whirled out into the middle of that boiling, roaring sheet of water like he had been sent for. Alphonse at once grabbed him by the ears and yelled for him to go back, but it wasn't any use.

As they reached the middle of the lake, there come a noise like Niagara and a dynamite factory let loose at once, and the ground under Jimmy and me began to buckle and crawl.

I closed my eyes a minute and hung on to Jimmy, trying to think of something fitting to say, and when I opened them again, the lake was gone! In its place was the long ravine Alphonse had told us about, and a big, ugly-looking crack, into which the last of the lake was pouring. Out of the crack stuck a few yards of poor old Billy's tail. Before I could say a word, that had disappeared, and Jimmy and I were alone!

The lake was gone, the snake was gone, the earthquake had come and gone, and Alphonse –

"Come on!" I yelled. "That snake has kidnapped Alphonse, Jimmy Raines!"

Jimmy made some sort of answer, but I didn't hear him. I was running down the wet, slippery bed of the lake towards the hole Billy had gone into. It never come to me that Alphonse couldn't live in the water like Billy could; they had been so friendly and together so much I had forgotten they were different. But when I stumbled over a big boulder and fell flat, the jar brought me to my senses.

"You are right," I says, when Jimmy came panting up; "it ain't no use to hunt Alphonse. He's gone, and nothing left to show it."

Jimmy buried his face in his hands. "Ain't it terrible?" says he. "Not even a thing to bury!"

"He bragged too much," says I, "and he didn't have his fingers crossed!"

"But he ain't dead yet," says a weak voice from the other

side of the boulder, and there was Alphonse, sound and well, though wet and weak.

"When I'd seen what was happening," he explained, "I knowed Billy was trying to take me with him back to his home. When we got here I jumped, and hung on to this rock, while the water whirled around me and sucked him down. I skun my knees and knuckles, but I ain't lost nothing but my snake."

We all looked at the little crack that had swallowed our fortunes, but we felt too bad to talk much.

"I reckon," says Jimmy, after a while, "that it won't pay to cry over spilt sea serpents. Let's make the best of it. We played Billy off the boards, and we lost. It's back to the States for me!"

"I guess you are right," says Alphonse, "and the 'quake seems to have wound up the affairs of the Sea Serpent Syndicate. Well, gentlemen, I'm sorry, but I hope you'll hold me blameless. I could tame a sea serpent, but I ain't much on taming earthquakes."

The next day we drilled back to the coast. Alphonse wouldn't hear of us taking him along, though. "My work is here," says he, "and here I stay." Then he added very wistful, and the tears pretty close, I tell you: "And if Billy ever should come back, I wouldn't want him to think I had deserted him."

As luck would have it, we sighted a vessel two hours after we reached the coast, and the captain sent a small boat to take us aboard. Jimmy and I shook hands hard with Alphonse, and when we had got aboard the steamer, we watched him until we couldn't see no more.

That was five years ago – and we have never heard from Alphonse. So I guess the Sea Serpent Syndicate was dissolved for good and all the day Billy went out with the earthquake.

YO HO HOKA!

Poul Anderson and Gordon R. Dickson

Alexander Jones was in trouble.

This, of course, is nothing new for a plenipotentiary of the Interbeing League. His duty lies on backward but promising planets, whose natives he is to guard from harm and guide toward full civilization and autonomy; the position carries the rank and pay of ambassador, and it was only because of his special experience with Toka that so young a man as Alexander Jones had gotten the appointment. His colleagues, stiff dignified men given to dressing for dinner even if they had to wear a spacesuit and to talking about the Earthman's burden, would have pointed out that he was on a comfortably terrestroid world whose inhabitants were not only friendly, but practically worshiped the human race, were phenomenally quick learners and ready to do anything to become accepted into the League.

They would not have understood that this was just what was wrong.

Alex's lean form strode through narrow, cobbled streets, between half-timbered houses, automatically dodging horse-drawn carriages. The "horses" were dinosaurian monstrosities, but otherwise Plymouth was a faithful small-scale copy of what the native Hokas thought its original had been, circa 1800 A.D., in Earth's England. (This Tokan Great Britain was not to be confused with the one which had been brought up to a Victorian level of civilization; the cultural missions had spotted all imaginable stages of history over the planet, giving the natives appropriate books and equipment, in search of the best starting-point for their education.)

The Hokas who thronged the streets made a respectful way for him, closing in again behind. He heard the awed whispers: "Blimey, it's the plenipotentiary 'imself! . . . Look that, Alf, ye'll allus remember ye saw the great Jones wid yer own blinkin' eyes. . . . Wonder wot 'e's after? . . . Prob'ly Affairs of State. . . . Yus, ye can see that on the poor lad, it's mykin' 'im old afore 'is time. . . ." The rather squeaky voices spoke English, for the Hokas had enthusiastically abandoned their earlier primitive cultures in favor of the more romantic ways of life the mission had shown them, some ten years ago.

Until you got used to them, they looked much alike: about a meter tall, portly, golden-furred, snouted – more like over-grown teddy bears with hands than anything else. These citizens were variously dressed: cocked hats, tailcoats, knee breeches; burly dock wallopers in carefully tattered work clothes; red-coated musketeers; long skirts on the females; and no few males in striped jerseys and bell-bottomed trou-sers, for Plymouth was a major base of His Majesty's Navy.

Now and then Alex's lips moved. "Old Boney," he mut-tered. "I keep telling them and telling them there isn't any Napoleon on this planet, but they won't believe me! Damn Old Boney! Blast these history books!" If only the Hokas weren't so confoundedly imaginative and literal-minded; if only they bothered to separate fact and fiction, stopped taking every-thing they read and heard at face value. There were times when their solemn conviction (be it that they were Victorians, or cowboys, or Space Patrolmen, or Royal Navy tars) almost hypnotized him.

He turned in at the Crown and Anchor, went through a noisy bar where Hokas sat puffing church-wardens and lying about their exploits with many deep-sea oaths, and proceeded up a narrow stair. The room which he had engaged was clean, though the furniture was inconvenient for a human with twice the Hoka height and half the breadth of beam. Tanni, his beautiful blonde wife, looked up from a crudely printed local newspaper with horror in her eyes.

"Alex!" she cried. "Listen to this, dear. They're getting violent . . . killing each other!" She read from the *Gazette*: " 'Today the notorious highwayman Dick Turpin was hanged on Tyburn Hill –' "

"Oh, that," said Alex, relieved. "Turpin gets hanged every Thursday. It's wonderful sport for all."

"But –"

"Didn't you know? You can't hurt a Hoka by hanging him. Their neck musculature is too strong in proportion to their weight. If hanging hurt Dick Turpin, the police would never do it. They're proud of him."

"Proud!"

"Well, he's part of this Eighteenth Century pattern they're trying so hard to follow, isn't he?" Alex sat down and ran a hand through his hair. He was sometimes surprised that it hadn't turned gray yet. "That's what's going to be either the salvation or the damnation of this race, Tanni. Their energy, enthusiasm, learning ability, imagination . . . they're like a bunch of children, and still have all the capabilities of an adult human. They're something unique in the Galaxy . . . no precedents at all, and Earth Headquarters expects *me* to educate them into the standard mold!"

"Poor dear," said Tanni sympathetically. "How did it go?" They had flown here only today from the office at Mixumaxu, and she was still a little puzzled as to the nature of their mission.

"I couldn't get any sense out of the Admiralty Office at all," said Alex. "They kept babbling about Old Boney. I can't convince them that these pirates represent a real menace."

"How did it ever happen, darling? I thought the imposed cultural patterns were always modified so as to exclude violence."

"Oh, yes, yes . . . but some dimwit out in space learned how the Hokas go for Earth fiction, and smuggled some historical novels into this sector. Pirates, forsooth!" Alex grinned bitterly. "You can imagine what the idea of swaggering around with a cutlass and a Jolly Roger would do to a Hoka. The first I heard, there were a couple of dozen ships turned pirate, off to the Spanish Main . . . wherever in Toka they've decided *that* is! So far no trouble, but they're probably fixing to attack some place like the Bermuda we've established."

"Criminals?" Tanni frowned, finding it hard to believe of her little friends.

"Oh, no. Just . . . irresponsible. Not really realizing it'll mean bloodshed. They'll be awfully sorry later. But that'll be too late for us, sweetheart." Alex looked gloomily at the floor. "Once Headquarters learns I've permitted a war pattern to evolve on this planet, I'll be out on my ear and blacklisted from here to the Lesser Magellanic Cloud. My only chance is to stop the business before it blows up."

"Oh, dear," said Tanni inadequately. "Can't they under- stand? I'd like to give those bureaucrats back home a piece of –"

"Never mind. You have to have iron-bound regulations to run a civilization the size of ours. It's results that count. Nobody cares much how I get them, but get them I must." Alex got up and began rummaging in their trunk.

"What are you looking for?" asked Tanni.

"That green beard . . . the one I wore to the Count of Monte Cristo's masquerade ball last week . . . thought it'd come in handy." Alex tossed articles of apparel every which way, and Tanni sighed. "You see, I've already been to the Admiralty in my proper *persona*, and they wouldn't order out the fleet to catch those pirates – said the routine patrols were adequate. Going over their heads, through Parliament and the King, would take too long. . . . Ah, here!" He emerged with a hideous green beard, fully half a meter in length.

"I'll go direct to Lord Nelson, who's in town," he went on. "It's best to do it incognito, to avoid offending the Admiralty; this beard is disguise enough, not being included in the Hokas' Jones-Gestalt. Once alone with him, I'll reveal myself and explain the situation. He's pretty level-headed, I'm told, and will act on his own responsibility." He put the beard to his chin, and the warmth of his body stuck it as fast as a natural growth – more so, for the synthetic fibers could not be cut or burned.

Tanni shuddered at the loathsome sight. "How do you get it off?" she asked weakly.

"Spirits of ammonia. All right, I'm on my way again." Alex stooped to kiss her and wondered why she shrank away. "Wait around till I get back. It may take a while."

The foliage flapped around his chest as he went downstairs. "Scuttle my hatches!" said someone. "What is it?"

"Seaweed," theorized another. "He's been too long underwater."

Alex reached the dock and stared over the tangle of rigging and tall masts which lay beyond. The Hokas had built quite a sizable navy in expectation of imminent Napoleonic invasion, and HMS *Intolerable* lay almost side by side with *Incorrigible* and *Pinafore*. Their mermaid figureheads gleamed gilt in the light of a lowering sun – that is, Alex assumed the fish-tailed Hoka females to be mermaids, though the four mammaries were so prominent as to suggest ramming was still standard naval practice. He couldn't see where the *Victory* was. Casting about for assistance, he spotted a patrol of sailors swinging along with a burly little Hoka in the lead. "Ahoy!" he yelled.

The patrol stepped smartly up to him, neat in their British Navy uniforms. "Tell me," said Alex, "how do I get out to the flagship? I must see Admiral Lord Nelson at once."

"Stow my top-hamper!" squeaked the leader. "You can't see the Admiral, mate. 'Tain't proper for a common seaman to speak to the Admiral unless spoken to first."

"No doubt," said Alex. "But I'm not a common seaman."

"Aye, that you are, mate," replied the other cheerfully. "Pressed right and proper as a common seaman, or me name's not Billy Bosun."

"No, no, you don't understand –" Alex was beginning, when the meaning filtered through to him. "*Pressed?*

"Taken by the press gang of Billy Bosun for His Majesty's frigate *Incompatible*," said the Hoka. "And a fair bit o' luck for you, mate. The worst hell-ship afloat, not counting the *Bounty*, and we sail on patrol in two hours. Toss the prisoner into the gig, men."

"No! Wait!" yelled Alex, frantically trying to pull his beard loose. "Let me explain. You don't know who I am. You can't –"

As he himself had remarked, the Hoka musculature is amazingly strong. He landed on his head in the bottom of the gig and went out like a light.

"Pressed man to speak with you, Cap'n Yardly," said Billy Bosun, ushering Alex into the captain's cabin.

The human blinked in the light from the cabin portholes and tried to brace himself against the rolling of the ship. He had been locked in the forward hold all night, during which time HMS *Incompatible* had left England far behind. He had gotten over a headache and a tendency to seasickness, but was frantic with the thought that every minute was taking him farther from Tanni and his desperately urgent mission. He stared at the blue-coated, cocked-hatted Hoka who sat behind a desk facing him, and opened his mouth to speak, but the other beat him to it.

"Does, does he?" growled Captain Yardly. The fur bristled on his neck. "Thinks he signed on for a pleasure cruise, no doubt! We'll teach him different, b'gad, won't we, bosun?"

"Aye, sir," said Billy stiffly.

"Wait, Captain Yardly!" cried Alex. "Let me just have a private word with you –"

"Private, eh? Private, damme!" exploded the Hoka. "There's no privacy aboard a King's ship. Ain't that right, bosun?"

"Aye, aye, sir."

"But if you'll just listen to me for a moment –" wailed Alex.

"Listen, b'gad! I don't listen to men, do I, bosun?"

"Aye, aye, sir."

"Nothing in the articles of war that makes it my duty to listen! My duty's to flog, b'gad; keelhaul, damme; drive the mutinous dogs till they drop! Stap my vitals, eh, bosun?" Captain Yardly snorted with indignation.

"Aye, aye, sir."

Alex took a firm grip on his temper. He reminded himself

that there was no use arguing with a Hoka once he had decided to play a certain role. The only way to handle him was to act along. Alex forced his face into a meek expression.

"Sorry, Captain," he said. "The truth is, I've come to confess that I'm not what I appear to be."

"Well, that's different!" huffed the officer. "Nothing against my listening to a man's confession as long as I flog him afterward any way."

Alex gulped, and quickly continued: "The truth is, Captain, this green beard of mine is false. You probably think I'm one of these outworlders you see occasionally, but without it, you'd recognize me at once. I'll bet you can't guess who I really am."

"Done!" roared the skipper.

"Huh?" said Alex.

"I wager I can guess who you are. Your name's Greenbeard."

"No–no–"

"Said so yourself."

"No, I said –"

"SILENCE!" thundered the captain. "You've lost your wager. No carping, damme. It's not done. Not sporting at all. I'm appointing you first mate, Mr Greenbeard, in accordance with regulations –"

"Regulations?" stammered Alex. "What regulations?"

"Pressed man always appointed first mate," snorted Captain Yardly, "in spite of his well known sympathy for the crew. Got sympathy for the crew, haven't you?"

"Well . . . I suppose so . . ." mumbled Alex. "I mean . . . what kind of first mate would I be – No, wait, I'm all mixed up. I mean –"

"No back talk, if you please!" interrupted the Hoka. "Step lively and drive her smartly, Mr Greenbeard. We're headed around the Horn, and I want no malingerers aboard."

"The Horn?" goggled Alex.

"You heard me, Mr Greenbeard."

"But –" protested Alex wildly, as Billy Bosun started pulling him by main force out of the cabin. "How . . . how long a voyage is this supposed to be?"

The captain's face dropped suddenly into an unhappy, embarrassed expression.

"That depends," he said morosely, "on which way we go."

And he turned and vanished through a connecting door into the inner cabin. His voice came back, somewhat muffled: "Clap on all sail, Mr Greenbeard, and call me if the weather freshens."

The words were followed by what sounded like a sob of desperation.

Giving up further argument as a bad job, Alex went back on deck. A stiff breeze drove the *Incompatible* merrily over a sea which sparkled blue, to the sound of creaking boards and whining rig. The crew moved industriously about their tasks, and Alex hoped he wouldn't be needed to direct them. He could pilot a spaceship between the stars, but the jungle of lines overhead baffled him.

Probably he wasn't essential though. He was simply part of the pattern which the Hokas followed so loyally; in the same way, all that talk about gruesome punishment must be just talk – the Navy felt it was expected of them. Which was, however, small consolation, since the same blind devotion would keep the ship out here for as long as the orders said. Without this eternally cursed beard, Alex could easily take command and get back to shore: but he couldn't get rid of the beard till he *was* ashore. He had a sense of futility.

As he walked along the deck, his eyes lit on a completely incongruous figure leaning on one of the guns. This was a Hoka in shirt and trousers of coarse cloth, leather leggings, a chain-mail coat, a shaggy cape, a conical helmet with huge upcurving horns, and an interminable sword. A pair of very large and obviously fake yellow mustaches drooped from his snout. He looked mournful.

Alex drew up to the anachronism, realizing he must be from the viking-culture area in the north and wondering how he had gotten here. "Hello," he said. "My name's Jo –" He stopped; it was useless to assert his identity till he got that triply damned spinach off his face. – "Greenbeard."

"Pleased to meet yü," said the viking in a high-pitched singsong. "Ay ban Olaf Button-nose from Sveden. Have yü ever ban to Constantinople?"

"Well – no," said Alex, taken somewhat aback.

"Ay was afraid yü hadn't," said Olaf, with two great tears running down into his mustache. "Nobody has. Ay come sout' and signed on here, hoping ve would touch at Constaninople, and ve never do."

"Why?" asked Alex, fascinated.

"To yoin the Varangian Guard, of course," said Olaf. "Riches, loot, beautiful vimmen, lusty battles, ha, Odin." He shed two more tears.

"But –" Alex felt a twinge of compassion. "I'm afraid, Olaf, that there isn't any Constantinople on this planet."

"How do yü know, if yü never been there?"

"Why, because –" Alex found the conversation showing the usual Hoka tendency to get out of hand, He gritted his teeth. "Now, look, Olaf, if I *had* been there, I'd be able to tell you where it was, wouldn't I?"

"Ay hope yü vould," said Olaf pessimistically.

"But since I *haven't* been there. I can't tell you where it is, can I?"

"Exactly," said Olaf. "Yü don't know. That's yust what Ay vas telling yü."

"No, no, *no!*" yelled Alex. "You don't get the point –"

At this moment, the door to the captain's cabin banged open and Yardly himself came popping out on deck.

"Avast and lay forrad!" he bellowed. "All hands to the yards! Aloft and stand by to come about! We're standing in to round the Horn!"

There was a stampeding rush, a roar, and Alex found himself alone. Everybody else had gone into the rigging, including the helmsman and captain. Alex turned hesitantly to one of the masts, changed his mind, and ran to the bows. But there was no land in sight.

He scratched his head and returned amidships. Presently everyone came down again, the crew growling, among themselves. Captain Yardly slunk by Alex, avoiding his eyes and muttering something about "slight error – happen to anyone –" and disappeared back into his cabin.

Olaf returned, accompanied by Billy Bosun. "Wrong again," said the viking gloomily.

"Rot me for a corposant's ghost if the crew'll take much more o' this," added Billy.

"Take more of what?" inquired Alex.

"The captain trying to round the Horn, sir," said Billy. "Terrible hard it is, sir."

"Are they afraid of the weather?" asked Alex.

"Weather, sir?" replied Billy. "Why, the weather's supposed to be uncommon good around the Horn."

Alex goggled at him. "Then what's so hard about rounding it?"

"Why, nothing's hard about *rounding* it," said Billy. "It's *finding* it that's so hard, sir. Few ships can boast they've rounded the Horn without losing at least part of their crew from old age first."

"But doesn't everybody know where it is?"

"Why, bless you, sir, of course everybody knows. It doesn't move around. But we do. And where are we?"

"Where are *we*?" echoed Alex, thunderstruck.

"Aye, sir, that's the question. In the old days, if we were here we'd be about one day's sail out of Plymouth on the southwest current."

"But that's where we are."

"Oh, no, sir," said Billy. "We're in the Antarctic Ocean. That's why the captain thought he was close to the Horn. That is, unless he's moved us since."

Alex gave a wordless cry, turned, and fled to the captain's cabin. Inside it, the skipper sat at a desk mounded high with sheets of calculations. There was a tortured look on his furry face. On the bulkhead behind him was an enormous map of Toka crisscrossed with jagged pencil lines.

"Ah, Mr Greenbeard," he said in a quavering voice as he looked up. "Congratulate me. I've just moved us three thousand miles. A little matter of figuring declination in degrees east instead of degrees west." He glanced anxiously at Alex. "That sounds right, doesn't it?"

"Ulp!" said Alex.

In the following four days, the human gradually came to understand. In earlier times, native ships had found their way around the planet's oceans by a familiarity with the currents and prevailing winds, but with the technology of 1800 had come the science of navigation, and since then no Hoka would lower himself to use the old-fashioned methods. With the new, some were successful, others were not. Lord Nelson, it was said, was an excellent navigator. So was Commodore Hornblower. Others had their difficulties. Captain Yardly's was that while he never failed to take a proper sight with his sextant, he invariably mistrusted the reading he got and was inclined to shift his figures around until they looked more like what he thought they should be. Also, he had a passion for even numbers, and was always rounding off his quantities to more agreeable amounts.

Under this handicap, the physical ship sailed serenely to her destination, guided by a non-navigating crew who automatically did the proper thing in the old fashion at the proper time. But the hypothetical ship of Captain Yardly's mathematical labors traversed a wild and wonderful path on the map, at one time so far at sea that there was not enough fresh water for them to make land alive, at another time perched high and dry on the western plains of Toka's largest continent. It was not strange that the skipper had a haunted look.

All of which was very unsettling to the crew, who, however willing to give him the benefit of the doubt, were finding it somewhat of a strain even on their elastic imaginations to be told they were in the tropics at one moment and skirting the south polar ice the next. Their nerves were on edge. Moreover, Alex discovered, the consensus among them was that the captain was becoming too obsessed with his navigation to pay proper attention to the running of the ship. No one had been hanged for several weeks, and there hadn't been a keelhauling for over a month. Many a Hoka standing on the sun-blistered deck east longing glances at the cool water overside and wished he would be keelhauled (which was merely fun on a planet without barnacles). There was much fo'c'sle talk about what act could be committed dastardly enough to rate the punishment.

"If you want a swim, why don't you just fall overboard?" asked Alex of Billy Bosun on the fourth day.

The Hoka's beady eyes lit up, and then saddened again. "No, sir," he said wistfully. "It's contrary to the articles of war, sir. Everybody knows British sailors can't swim a stroke."

"Oh, well," said Alex helpfully. "If you've got scruples –" He picked up the boatswain and tossed him over the rail. Billy splashed into the sea with a howl of delight.

"Shiver my timbers!" he roared gleefully, threshing around alongside and blowing spouts of water into the air. "I'm murdered! Help! Help! Man overboard!"

The crew came boiling up on deck. Small furry bodies began to go sailing into the sea, yelling something about rescue. The second mate started to lower a boat, decided to pitch the nearest sailor into the ocean instead, and followed him.

"Heave to!" screamed Alex, panic-stricken. "Man – er – men overboard! Bring her about!"

The helmsman spun the wheel and the ship pivoted into the wind's eye with a rattle of canvas. Whooping, he bounced up on the taffrail, overbalanced, and fell. His joyously lamenting voice joined the chorus already resounding below.

The door to the captain's cabin flew open. Yardly rushed out. "Avast!" he cried. "Belay! What's about here?" He headed for the rail and stared downward.

"We're drowning!" the crew informed him, playing tag.

"Belay that!" shouted the captain. "Avast drowning, immediately. Call yourself British seamen, do you? Mutinous dogs, I call you. Treacherous, mutinous dogs! Quarrelsome, treacherous, mutinous dogs! Careless, quarrel –"

He looked so hot and unhappy in his blue coat and cocked hat that Alex impulsively picked him up and threw him over the side.

He hit the water and came up spouting and shaking his fist. "Mister Greenbeard!" he thundered. "You'll hang for this. *This is mutiny!*"

"But we don't have to hang him, do we?" protested Alex.

"Blast my bones, Cap'n Greenbeard," said Billy, "but Yardly was going to hang *you*."

"Ay don't see how yü can avoid it," said Olaf, emptying sea water out of his scabbard. "Ve ban pirates now."

"Pirates!" yelped Alex.

"What else is left for us, Cap'n?" asked Billy. "We've mutinied, ain't we? The British Navy'll never rest till we're hunted down."

"Oh well," said Alex wearily. If hanging the ex-captain was considered part of the pattern, he might as well play along. He turned to the two seamen holding Yardly. "String him up."

They put a noose around the captain's neck and politely stepped back. He took a pace forward and surveyed the crew, then scowled blackly and folded his arms.

"Treacherous, ungrateful swine!" he said. "Don't suppose that you will escape punishment for this foul crime. As there is a divine as well as a Hoka justice –"

Alex found a bollard and seated himself on it with a sigh. Yardly gave every indication of being good for an hour of dying speech. The human relaxed and let the words flow in one ear and out the other. A sailor scribbled busily, taking it all down for later publication in a broadside.

"– this causeless mutiny – plotted in secret – ringleaders did not escape my eye – some loyal hearts and true poisoned by men of evil – forgive you personally, but – sully the British Flag – cannot meet my eye – in the words of that great man –"

"Oh, no!" said Alex involuntarily, but Billy was already giving the captain the pitch on his boatswain's whistle.

"Oh, my name it is Sam Hall, it is Sam Hall.
Yes, my name it is Sam Hall, it is Sam Hall . . . ."

Like most Hokas, the captain had a rather pleasant tenor, reflected Alex, but *why* did they all have to sing "Sam Hall" before being hanged?

"Now up the rope I go, up I go . . . ."

Alex winced. The song came to an end. Yardly wandered off on a sentimental side issue, informed the crew that he had had a good home and loving parents, who little suspected he would come to this, spoke a few touching words concerning his golden-furred little daughter ashore, wound up by damning them all for a pack of black-hearted scoundrels, and in a firm voice ordered the men on the end of the rope to do their duty.

The Hokas struck up a lively chanty, and to the tune of "Haul Away, Joe" Yardly mounted into the air. The crew paled and fainted enthusiastically as for five minutes he put on a spirited performance of realistic twitches, groans, and death rattles – effective enough to make Alex turn slightly green behind his board. He was never sure whether or not something at this stage had gone wrong and the Hoka on the rope was actually being strangled. Finally, however, Yardly hung limp. Billy Bosun cut him down and brought him to the captain's cabin, where Alex signed him up under the name of Black Tom Yardly and sent him forward of the mast.

Thus left in charge of a ship which he had only the foggiest notion of how to run, and a crew gleefully looking forward to a piratical existence, Alex put his head in his hands and tried to sort matters out.

He was regretting the mutiny already. Whatever had possessed him to throw the captain of a British frigate overboard? He might have known such a proceeding would lead to trouble. There was no doubt Yardly had been praying for an excuse to get out of his navigational duties. But what could Alex have done once his misguided impulse had sent Yardly into the ocean? If he had meekly surrendered, Yardly would probably have hanged him . . . and Alex did not have a Hoka's neck muscles. He gulped at the thought. He could imagine the puzzlement of the crew once they had cut him down and he didn't get up and walk away. But what good is a puzzled Hoka to a dead plenipotentiary? None whatsoever.

Moreover, not only was he in this pickle, but five days had gone by. Tanni would be frantically flying around the world looking for him, but the chance of her passing over this speck in the ocean was infinitesimal. It would take at least another five days to get back to Plymouth, and hell might explode in Bermuda meanwhile. Or he might be seized in the harbor if someone blabbed and strung up as a mutineer before he could get this green horror off his chin.

On the other hand –

Slowly, Alex got up and went over to the map on the bulkhead. The Hokas had been quick to adopt terrestrial place names, but there had, of course, been nothing they could do about the geographical dissimilarity of Toka and Earth. The West Indies here were only some 500 nautical miles from England; HMS *Incompatible* was almost upon them now, and the pirate headquarters at Tortuga could hardly be more than a day's sail away. It shouldn't be too hard to find, and the buccaneer fleet would welcome a new recruit. Maybe he could find some ammonia there. Otherwise he could try to forestall the raid, or sabotage it, or something.

He stood for several minutes considering this. It was dangerous, to be sure. Cannon, pistols, and cutlasses, mixed with Hoka physical energy and mental impulsiveness, were nothing a man wanted close to him. But every other possibility looked even more hopeless.

He went to the door and called Olaf. "Tell me," he said, "do you think you can steer this ship in the old-fashioned way?"

"To be sure Ay can," said the viking. "Ay'm old-fashion myself."

"True," agreed Alex. "Well, then, I'm going to appoint you first mate."

"Ay don't know about that, now," interrupted Olaf doubtfully. "Ay don't know if it ban right."

"Of course," said Alex hastily, "you won't be a regular first mate. You'll be a Varangian first mate."

"Of course Ay vill!" exclaimed Olaf, brightening. "Ay hadn't t'ought of that. Ay'll steer for Constantinople."

"Well – er – remember we don't know where Constantinople is," said Alex. "I think we'd better put in at Tortuga first for information."

Olaf's face fell. "Oh," he said sadly.

"Later on we can look for Constantinople."

"Ay suppose so."

Seldom had Alex felt so much like a heel.

They came slipping into the bay of Tortuga about sunset of the following day, flying the skull and-crossbones which was kept in the flag chest of every ship just in case. The island, fronded with tropical trees, rose steeply over an anchorage cluttered with a score of armed vessels; beyond, the beach was littered with thatch huts, roaring bonfires, and swaggering pirates. As their anchor rattled down, someone whooped from the crow's nest of the nearest vessel: "Ahoy, mates! Ye're just in time. We sail for Bermuda tomorry."

Alex shivered, the green beard and the thickening dusk concealing his unbuccaneerish activity. To the eagerly swarming crew, he said: "You'll stay aboard till further orders."

"What?" cried Black Tom Yardly, outraged. "We're not to broach a cask with our brethren of the coast? We're not to fight bloody duels, if you'll pardon the language, and wallow in pieces of eight and –"

"Later," said Alex, "Secret mission, you know. You can break out our own grog, bosun." That satisfied them, and they lowered the captain's gig for him and Olaf to go ashore in. As he was rowed away from the *Incompatible*, Alex heard someone start a song about a life on the ocean wave, in competition with someone else who, for lack of further knowledge, was endlessly repeating, "Yo-ho-ho and a bottle of rum." *They're happy*, he thought.

"What yü ban going to do now?" inquired Olaf.

"I wish I knew," said Alex forlornly. The little Viking, with his skepticism about the whole pirate pattern, was the only one he could trust at all, and even to Olaf he dared not confide his real hopes. Such as they were.

Landing, they walked through a roaring, drunken crowd of Hokas trying to look as villainous as possible with the help of pistols, knives cutlasses, daggers, sashes, earrings, and nose-rings. The Jolly Roger flew over a long hut within which the

Captains of the Coast must be meeting; outside squatted a sentry who was trying to drink rum but not succeeding very well because he would not let go of the dagger in his teeth.

"Avast and belay there!" shrilled this freebooter, lurching erect and drawing his cutlass as Alex's bejungled face came out of the gloom. "Halt and be run through!"

Alex hesitated. His sea-stained tunic and trousers didn't look very piratical, he was forced to admit, and the cutlass and floppy boots he had added simply kept tripping him up. "I'm a captain too," he said. "I want to confer with my . . . er . . . confreres."

The sentry staggered toward him, waving a menacing blade. Alex, who had not the faintest idea of how to use a sword, backed up. "So!" sneered the Hoka. "So ye'll not stand up like a man, eh? I was tol' t' run anybody through what came near, and damme, I will!"

"Oh, shut up," said Olaf wearily. His own sword snaked out, knocking the pirate's loose. That worthy tried to close in with his dagger, but Olaf pushed him over and sat on him. "Ay'll hold him here, skipper," said the Viking. Hopefully, to his squirming victim: "Do yü know the vay to Constantinople?"

Alex opened the door and walked in, not without trepidation. The hut was lit by guttering candles stuck in empty bottles, to show a rowdy group of captains seated around a long table. One of them, with a patch over his eye, glared up. "Who goes?" he challenged.

"Captain Greenbeard of the *Incompatible*," said Alex firmly. "I just got in."

"Oh, well, siddown, mate," said the pirate. "I'm Cap'n One-Eye, and these here is Henry Morgan, and Flint, and Long John Silver, and Hook, and Anne Bonney, and our admiral La Fontaine, and –" Someone clapped a hand over his mouth.

"Who's this?" squeaked La Fontaine from under his cocked hat. Twenty pairs of Hoka eyes swiveled from him to Alex and back again.

"Why, scupper and gut me!" growled another, who had a

hook taped to the end of his hand. "Don't ye know Cap'n Greenbeard?"

"Of course not!" said La Fontaine. "How could I know a Cap'n Greenbeard when there ain't any such man? Not in any of the books there ain't. I'll wager he's John Paul Jones in disguise."

"I resent that!" boomed a short Hoka, bouncing to his feet. "Cap'n Greenbeard's my cousin!" And he stroked the black, glossy, but obviously artificial beard on his chin.

"Blast me, nobody can say that about a friend of Anne Bonney," added the female pirate. She was brilliantly bedecked in jewels, horse pistols, and a long gown which she had valiantly tried to give a low-cut bodice. A quadrimammarian Hoka needed two bodices, one above the other, and she had them.

"Oh, very well," grumbled La Fontaine. "Have a drink, cap'n, and help us plan this raid."

Alex accepted a tumbler of the fiery native distillation. Hokas have a fantastic capacity, but he hoped to go slow and, in view of the long head start the others had, stay halfway sober. Maybe he could master the situation somehow. "Thanks," he said. "Have one yourself."

"Don't mind if I do, mate," said La Fontaine amiably, tossing off another half liter. "Hic!"

"Is there any spirits of ammonia here?" asked Alex.

One-Eye shifted his patch around to the other orb and looked surprised. "Not that I know of, mate," he said. "Should be some in Bermuda. Ye want it for polishing up treasure before burying it?"

"Let's come to order!" piped Long John Silver, pounding his crutch on the table. His left leg was strapped up against the thigh. "By the Great Horn Spoon, we have to make some plans if we're going to sail tomorrow."

"I, er, don't think we should start that soon," said Alex.

"So!" cried La Fontaine triumphantly. "A coward, is it? Rip my mainto' gallantstuns'l if I think ye're fit to be a Captain o' the Coast. Hic!"

Alex thought fast. "Shiver my timbers!" he roared back. "A

coward, am I? I'll have your liver for breakfast for that, La Fontaine! What d'ye take for me, a puling clerk? Stow me for a – a – sea-chest if I think a white-faced stick like yourself is fit to be admiral over the likes of us. Why," he added cunningly, "you haven't even got a beard."

"Whuzzat got to do with it?" asked La Fontaine muzzily, falling into the trap.

"What kind of admiral is it that hasn't got hair on his chin?" demanded Alex, and saw the point strike home to the Hokas about him.

"Admirals don't have to have beards," protested La Fontaine.

"Why, hang, draw, and quarter me!" interrupted Captain Flint. "Of course admirals have to have beards. I thought everybody knew that." A murmur of assent went up around the table.

"You're right," said Anne Bonney. "Everybody knows that. There's only two here fit to command the fleet: Cap'n Blackbeard and Cap'n Greenbeard."

"Captain Blackbeard will do very well," said Alex graciously.

The little Hoka got to his feet. "Bilge me," he quavered, "if I ever been so touched in m' life before. Bung me through the middle with a boarding pike if it ain't right noble of you, Cap'n Greenbeard. But amongst us all, I can't take an unfair advantage. Much as I'd be proud to admiral the fleet, your beard is a good three inches longer'n mine. I therefore resigns in your favor."

"But –" stammered Alex, who had expected anything but this.

"That's fantastic!" objected La Fontaine tearfully. "You can't pick a man by his beard – I mean – it isn't – you just can't!"

"La Fontaine!" roared Hook, pounding the table. "This here council o' pirate captains is following the time-honored procedure of the Brethren o' the Coast. If you wanted to be elected admiral, you should ha' put on a beard afore you come to meeting. I hereby declares the election over."

At this last and cruelest cut, La Fontaine fell speechless. "Drawer!" shouted Henry Morgan. "Flagons all around to drink to the success of our venture."

Alex accepted his warily. He was getting the germ of an idea. There was no chance of postponing the raid as he had hoped; he knew his Hokas too well. But perhaps he could blunt the attack by removing its leadership, both himself and La Fontaine . . . He reached over and clapped the ex-chief on the shoulder. "No hard feelings, mate," he said. "Come, drink a bumper with me, and you can be admiral next time."

La Fontaine nodded, happy again, and threw another half liter down his gullet. "I like a man who drinks like that!" shouted Alex. "Drawer, fill his flagon again! Come on, mate, drink up. There's more where that came from."

"Split my mizzenmast," put in Hook, "but that's a neat way o' turning it, Admiral! 'More where that came from.' Neat as a furled sail. True, too."

"Oh, well," said Alex bashfully.

"Here, drawer, fill up for Admiral Greenbeard," cried Hook "That's right. Drink deep, me hearty. More where that came from. Haw!"

"Ulp!" said Alex. Somehow, he got it down past shriveling tonsils. "Hoo-oo-oo!"

"Sore throat?" asked Anne Bonney solicitously.

"More where that came from," bellowed Hook, "Fill up."

Alex handed his goblet to La Fontaine. "Take it, mate," he said generously. "Drink my health."

"Whoops!" said the ex-admiral, tossed it off, and passed out.

"Yo, heave ho," said Billy Bosun. "Up you come, mate."

They hoisted the limp figure of La Fontaine over the rail of the *Incompatible*. Alex, leaning heavily on Olaf, directed operations.

"Lock 'im in m' cabin," he wheezed. "Hois' anchor an' set sail for Bermuda." He stared toward the sinking moon. Toka seemed suddenly to have acquired an extra satellite. "Secret mission, y' know. Fi-ifteen men on a dea-ead man's chest —"

"Sling a hammock on deck for the captain," ordered Billy. "He don't seem to be feeling so well."

"Yo-ho-ho and a bottle of rum," warbled Alex.

"Aye, aye, sir," said Billy, and handed him one.

"Woof!" groaned Alex and collapsed. The night sky began majestically revolving around him. Shadowy sails reached out to catch the offshore breeze. The *Incompatible* moved slowly from the harbor. Alex did not see this . . .

Bright sunlight awakened him. He lay in his hammock till the worst was over, and then tried to sort things out. The ship was heeling to a steady wind and the sounds of sail-flap, rig-thrum, plank-creak, and crew-talk buzzed around him. Rising, he saw that they were alone in the great circle of the horizon. In the waist, the starboard watch were sitting about telling each other blood-curdling tales of their piratical exploits. Black Tom Yardly, as usual, was outdoing all the rest.

Alex accepted breakfast from the cook, lit the captain's pipe in lieu of a cigaret, and considered his situation. It could be worse. He'd gotten away with La Fontaine, and they should be in Bermuda shortly after sunset. There would be time to warn it and organize its defenses; and the pirates, lacking both their accustomed and their new admiral, would perhaps botch the attack completely. He beamed and called to his first mate. "Mr Buttonnose!"

Olaf approached. "Ay give yü good morning," he said gravely.

"Oh? Well, the same to you, Olaf," replied Alex. There was a certain air of old world courtesy about the small Viking which seemed infectious. "What kind of speed are we making?"

"About ten dragons' teeth," said Olaf.

"Dragons' teeth?" repeated Alex, bewildered.

"Knots, yü vould say. Ay don't like to call them knots, myself. It don't sound Varangian."

"Fine, fine," smiled Alex. "We should be there in no time."

"Vell, yes," said Olaf, "only Ay suppose ve must heave to now."

"Heave to?" cried Alex. "What for?"

"So yü can have a conference vit' the other captains," said Olaf, pointing astern. Alex spun on his heel and stared along the creamy wake of the *Indomitable*. There were sails lifting over the horizon – the pirate fleet!

"My God!" he exclaimed, turning white. "Pile on all sail!" Olaf looked at him, surprised. "Pile on all sail!"

Olaf shook his round head. "Vell, Ay suppose yü know best," he said tiredly, and went off to give the necessary orders.

The *Incompatible* leaped forward, but the other ships still crept up on her. Alex swallowed. Olaf returned from heaving the log.

"Tvelve dragons' teeth," he informed Alex reproachfully.

It was not a pleasant day for Admiral Greenbeard. In spite of almost losing the masts, he could not distance the free-booters, and the gap continued to narrow. Toward sunset, the other ships had almost surrounded him. The islands of Bermuda were becoming visible, and as darkness began to fall the whole fleet rounded the headland north of Bermuda City Bay. Lights twinkled on the shore, and the Hokas crowding the shrouds set up a lusty cheer. Resignedly, Alex ordered his crew to heave to. The other craft did likewise, and they all lay still.

Alex waited, chewing his fingernails. When an hour had passed and nothing happened except sailors hailing each other, he hunted up Olaf. "What do you think they're waiting for?" he asked nervously.

The bear-like face leaned forward out of shadow. "Ay don't t'ink," said Olaf. "Ay know. They're vaiting for yü to signal the captains aboard your flagship. The qvestion is, what are yü vaiting for?"

"Me? Summon them?" asked Alex blankly. "But they were chasing us!"

"Ay vould not call it shasing," said Olaf. "Since yü ban admiral, they vould not vant to pass yü up."

"No, no, Olaf." Alex lowered his voice to a whisper. "Listen, I was trying to escape from them."

"Yü vere? Then yü should have said so," declared Olaf

strongly. "I ban having a terrible time – yust terrible – to keep from running away from them vit' all sails set."

"But why did you think they were following us?" raved Alex.

"Vy, what should they be doing?" demanded Olaf. "Yü ban admiral. Naturally, ven ve leave for Bermuda, they're going to follow yü."

Speechless, Alex collapsed on a bollard. After a while he stirred feebly.

"Signal all captains to report aboard for conference," he said in a weak voice.

"Gut and smoke me!" thundered Captain Hook, as the chiefs crowded around a table arranged on the poop. "Slice me up for hors d'oeuvres, but you're a broom-at-the-mast sailor, Admiral Greenbeard. We had to clap on all canvas to keep you in sight."

"Oh, well," said Alex modestly.

"Blast my powder magazine if I ever seen anything like it. There you was, flying through the water like a bloody gull; and at the same time I could have laid me oath you was holding the ship back as hard as you could."

"Little sailing trick . . ." murmured Alex.

"Blind me!" marveled Hook. "Well, to business. Who's to lead the attack on the fort, Admiral?"

"Fort?" echoed Alex blankly.

"You knows how it is," said Hook. "They got cannon mounted on that Fort which juts out into the bay. We'll have to sail past and give 'em a broadside to put 'em out of action. Then we can land and sack the town before Lord Nelson, blast his frogs and facings, shows up."

"Oh," said Alex. He was thinking with the swiftness of a badly frightened man. Once actual fighting started, Hokas would be getting killed – which, quite apart from any sympathy, meant the end of his tenure as plenipotentiary. If he himself wasn't knocked off in the battle. "Well . . ." he began slowly. "I have another plan."

"Hull and sink me!" said Long John Silver. "A plan?"

"Yes, a plan. We can't get by that fort without getting hurt. But one small boat can slip in easily enough, unobserved."

"Stab me!" murmured Captain Kidd in awe. "Why, that's sheer genius."

"My mate and I will go ashore," went on Alex. "I have a scheme to capture the mayor and make him order the fort evacuated." Actually, his thoughts extended no further than warning the town and getting this noxious vegetation off his face. "Wait till I signal you from the jetty with lanterns how you're to arrive. One if by land and two if by sea."

"Won't go, Admiral," said Anne Bonney. She waved into the darkness, from which came the impatient grumbling of the crews. "The men won't brook delay. We can't hold 'em here more than a couple of hours, then we'll have to attack or face a mutiny."

Alex sighed. His last hope of avoiding a fight altogether, by making the fleet wait indefinitely, seemed to have gone glimmering. "All right," he agreed hollowly. "Sail in and land the men. Don't fire on the fort, though, unless it shoots first, because I may be able to empty it in the way I suggested."

"Scupper and split me, but you're a brave man," said Hook. "Chop me up for shark bait if I think we could ha' done anything without you."

"Thanks," gritted Alex. It was the most unkindest cut of all.

The other Hokas nodded and rumbled agreement. Hero worship shone in their round black eyes.

"I moves we drinks to the Admiral's health!" boomed Flint. "Steward! Fetch flagons for –"

"I'd better leave right away," said Alex hurriedly.

"Nonsense," said Henry Morgan. "Who ever heard of a pirate doing anything sober?"

"Psssh!" said Alex, rapping on the window of the mayor's residence. Muffled noises came from the garden behind, where Olaf had tied up the guards who would never have permitted a green-bearded stranger to approach.

The window opened and the mayor, an exceedingly fat

Hoka pompous in ruffles and ribbons, looked out, square into the nauseous tangle of hair beyond.

"Eek!" he said.

"Hic," replied Alex, holding on to the sill while the house waltzed around him.

"Help!" cried the mayor. "Sea monsters attacking! Drum up the guard! Man the battlements! Stow the belaying pins!"

A familiar golden head appeared over his shoulder. "Alex!" gasped Tanni. "Where have you been?"

"Pressed pirate," said Alex, reeling. "Admiral Greenbeard. Help me in. Hic!"

"Drunk again," said Tanni resignedly, grabbing his collar as he scrambled over the sill. She loved her husband; she had been scouring the planet in search of him, had come here as a forlorn hope; but the enfoliated spectacle before her was not calculated to bring joyful tears.

"Mayor Bermuda," mumbled Alex. "British gen'leman. En'ertain th' lady. Ge' me anti-alco – anti – alco – alkyho – yo-ho-ho an' a bo'le o' rum –"

Tanni left him struggling with the word and went off after a soberpill. Alex got it down and shuddered back to normal.

"Whoof!" he exclaimed. "That's better . . . Tanni, we're in one hell of a spot. Pirates –"

"The pirates," she said firmly, "can wait till you get that thing off your face." She extended a bottle of ammonia and a wad of cotton.

Thankfully, Alex removed the horror and gave them the story. He finished with: "They're too worked up to listen to me now, even in my character of plenipotentiary. They'll be landing any minute. But if we don't offer resistance, there'll at least be no bloodshed. Let them have the loot if they must."

"Come, come," said the mayor. "It's out of the question. Out of the question entirely."

"But they outnumber your garrison!" sputtered Alex.

"Beastly fellows," agreed the mayor happily, lighting a cigar.

"You can't possibly fight them off. The only thing to do is surrender."

"Surrender? But we're *British!*" explained the mayor patiently.

"Damn it, I order you to surrender!"

"Impossible," said the mayor dogmatically. "Absolutely impossible. Contrary to Colonial Office regulations."

"But you're bound to lose!"

"Gallantly," pointed out the mayor.

"This is stupid!"

"Naturally," said the mayor mildly. "We're muddling through. Muddle rather well, if I do say so myself."

Alex groaned. Tanni clenched her fists. The mayor turned to the door. "I'd better have the soldiers informed," he said.

"No . . . wait!" Alex leaped to his feet. Something had come back to him. *Chop me up for shark bait if I think we could ha' done anything without you.* And the others had agreed . . . and once a Hoka got an idea in his head, you couldn't blast it loose . . . His hope was wild and frail, but there was nothing to lose. "I've got a plan."

"A plan?" The mayor's looked dubious.

Alex saw his error. "No, no," he said hastily. "I mean a ruse."

"Oh, a *ruse!*" The mayor's eyes sparkled with pleasure. "Excellent. Superb. Just the sort of thing for this situation. What is it, my dear plenipotentiary?"

"Let them land unopposed," said Alex. "They'll head for your palace first, of course."

"Unopposed?" asked the mayor. "But I just explained –"

Alex pulled out his cutlass and flourished it. "When they get here, *I'll* oppose them."

"One man against twenty ships?"

Alex drew himself up haughtily. "Do you imply that I, your plenipotentiary, can't stop twenty ships?"

"Oh, no," said the mayor. "Not at all. By all means, my dear sir. Now, if you'll excuse me, I must have the town crier inform the people. They'd never forgive me if they missed such a spectacle." He bustled away.

"Darling!" Tanni grabbed his arm. "You're crazy. We don't have so much as a raythrower – they'll kill you!"

"I hope not," said Alex bleakly. He stuck his head out the window. "Come in, Olaf. I'll need your help."

The corsair fleet moved in under the silent guns of the fort and dropped anchor at the quay. Whooping, shouting, and brandishing their weapons, the crews stormed ashore and rushed up the main street toward the mayor's palace. They were mildly taken aback to see the way lined with townsfolk excitedly watching and making bets on the outcome, but hastened on roaring bloodthirsty threats.

The palace lay inside a walled garden whose gate stood open. Nearby, the redcoats of the garrison were lined up at attention. Olaf watched them gloweringly: it was his assignment to keep any of them from shooting. Overhead, great lanterns threw a restless yellow light on the scene.

"Fillet and smoke me, but there's our admiral!" shouted Captain Hook as the tall green-bearded figure with drawn cutlass stepped through the gateway. "Three cheers for Admiral Greenbeard!"

"Hip, hip, hooray!" Echoes beat against the distant rumble of surf. The little round pirates swarmed closer, drawing to a disorderly halt as they neared their chief.

"Aha, me hearties!" cried Alex. "This is a great day for the Brethren of the Coast. I've got none less than Alexander Jones, the plenipotentiary of Toka, here, and I'm about to spit him like a squab!" He paused. "What, no cheers?"

The pirates shuffled their feet.

"What?" bellowed Alex. "Speak up, you swabs. What's wrong?"

"Stab me!" mumbled Hook. "But it don't seem right to spit the plenipotentiary. After all he done for this planet."

Alex felt touched, but redoubled the ferocity of his glare.

"If it's glory you're after, Admiral," contributed Captain Kidd, "blast me if I'd waste time on the plenipotentiary. There's no glory to be gained by spitting him. Why, he's so feeble, they say he has to have a special chair to carry him around."

This description of the one small luxury Alex had purchased

for himself after three years of saving – a robot chair for his office – so infuriated him that he lost his temper completely.

"Is that so!" he yelled. "Well, it just happens that he's challenged me to a duel to the death, and I'm not going to back out. And you scuts will stay there and watch me kill him and like it!"

"No, I won't have it," cried a soldier, raising his musket. Olaf took it away from him, tied it in a knot, and gave it back.

Alex ducked inside the portal, where Tanni and the mayor waited in the garden, still muttering furiously. "What's wrong now, dear?" asked the girl, white-faced.

"Blankety-blanks," snarled Alex. "For two cents I'd kill myself, and then see how they like it!" He stamped over to a large brass urn he had placed in readiness.

"*En garde!*" he roared, fetching it a lusty swipe with his cutlass. "Take that!"

The gathered pirates jumped nervously. Billy Bosun tried to go through the gateway to see what was happening, but Olaf picked him up and threw him over the heads of Henry Morgan and One-Eye. "Private matter," said the viking imperturbably.

Viciously, Alex battered the clamoring urn with his blade, meanwhile yelling imprecations. "Don't try to get away! Stand and fight like a man! Aha! Take that, me hearty!"

Hammering away, he fumbled in his pocket with his free hand and brought out some ammonia-soaked cotton. The beard came loose and he gave it to Tanni, who was dabbing him with ketchup here and there, as he shouted in a slightly lower pitch.

"Is that so? Take that yourself!, And that, Greenbeard! Didn't know, did you –" he thrust his cleanshaven face around the edge of the gate "– that I was on the fencing team as a boy?"

Impulsively, the pirates cheered.

"As well," said Alex, circling back out of view and belaboring the urn, "as having my letter in track and swimming. I could have made the basketball team too, if I'd wanted. Take that!"

Hurriedly, he stuck the beard back on and signaled for more ketchup.

"Burn and blister me!" he swore, backing a little ways out of the gate and scowling horribly at the buccaneers, "but you've a tricky way about you, Jones. But it won't save you. The minute I trap you in a corner, I'll rip you up for bait. Take that!" He stepped out of sight again. "Ouch!" he cried in the lower voice.

The pirates looked sad. "It don't seem right," muttered Long John Silver. "It just never occurred to me that people might get hurt."

Captain Hook winced at the din. "Aye," he said shakily. "What've we gotten ourselves into, mates?"

"Don't be too cocky, Greenbeard!" cried Alex, appearing with a bare chin and lunging while Tanni struck the urn. "Actually, I've got muscles of steel. Take that! And that! And that!"

Vanishing again, he fetched the urn three ringing blows, dropped his cutlass, and clapped the beard back onto his face, giving vent to a spine-freezing scream.

"You got me!" he yammered. Clasping ketchup-soaked hands over his heart, he reeled across the gateway, stopping before the terrified visages of the pirates.

"Oh," he groaned. "I'm done for, mates. Spitted in fair and equal combat. Who'd a thought the plenipotentiary was such a fighter? Goodby, mates. Clear sailing. Anchors away. Don't look for my body. Just let me crawl off and die in peace."

"Goodby," wept Anne Bonney, waving a handkerchief at him. The whole buccaneer band was dissolving into tears.

Alex staggered out of sight, removed his beard, and breathed heavily for a while. Then he picked up his cutlass and strode slowly out the gate and looked over his erstwhile followers.

"Well, well," he said scornfully. "What have we here? Pirates?"

There was a pause.

"Mercy, sir!" blubbered Captain Hook, falling to his knees

before the conqueror of the terrible, the invincible, the indispensable Greenbeard, "We was just having our bit of fun, sir."

"We didn't mean nothing," pleaded Flint.

"We didn't figure to get nobody hurt," said Billy Bosun.

"Silence!" commanded Alex. "Do you give up?" There was no need to wait for an answer. "Very well. Mister Mayor, you will have these miscreants hanged at dawn. Then put them on their ships and let them go. And see that you behave yourselves hereafter!"

"Y-y-y-yes, sir," said Black Tom Yardly.

"Oh . . . I don't know," said the mayor. Wistfulness edged his tone. "They weren't so bad, now were they, sir? I think we owe 'em a vote of thanks, damme. These colonial outposts get infernally dull."

"Why, thank'ee, mayor," said Anne Bonney. "We'll come sack you anytime."

Alex interrupted hastily. Piracy seemed to have become an incurable disease, but if you can't change a Hoka's ways you can at least make him listen to reason . . . on his own terms.

"Now hear this," he decreed loudly. "I'm going to temper justice with mercy. The Brethren of the Coast may sack Bermuda once a year, but there must be no fighting –"

"Why should there be?" asked the mayor, surprised.

"– and the loot must be returned undamaged."

"Slice and kipper me!" exclaimed Captain Hook indignantly. "Of course it'll be returned, sir. What d'ye think we are – thieves?"

Festivities lasted through all the next day, for the pirates, of course, had to sail away into the sunset. Standing on a terrace of the palace garden, his arm about Tanni and the mayor nearby, Alex watched their masts slip over the horizon.

"I've got just one problem left," he said. "Olaf. The poor fellow is still hanging around, trying to find someone who knows the way to Constantinople. I wish I could help."

"Why, that's easy, sir," said the mayor. "Constantinople is only about fifty miles due south of here."

"What?" exclaimed Alex. "No, you're crazy. That's the Kingdom of Natchalu."

"It was," nodded the mayor. "Right up till last month it was. But the queen is a lusty wench, if you'll pardon the expression, madam, and was finding life rather dull till a trader sold her some books which mentioned a, hm," the mayor coughed delicately, "lady named Theodora. They're still getting reorganized, but it's going fast and –"

Alex set off at a run. He rounded the corner of the house and the setting sun blazed in his eyes. It gilded the helmet and byrnie of Olaf Button-nose where he leaned on his sword gazing out to sea.

"Olaf!" cried Alex.

The Hoka viking turned slowly to regard the human. In the sunset, above the droop of his long blond mustaches, his face seemed to hold a certain Varangian indomitability.

THE MIRRORS
OF MOGGROPPLE

John Morressy

I

Kedrigern crept from his study, pale and bloodshot of eye, and shut the door behind him with trembling hands. He made his way to the breakfast nook of the cottage, walking like a man made of glass, and paused on the threshold of the sun-washed room to sigh and swallow loudly. Narrowing his eyes to slits and shielding them with his hand, he entered, slowly.

Princess was already seated. She looked particularly fresh and lovely in a soft green robe, with her black hair loose about her shoulders. Kedrigern scarcely noticed. On this particular morning, Venus herself would have made little impression on him.

"Brereep?" Princess asked politely.

"Terrible, thank you," Kedrigern replied, gingerly lowering himself into the seat opposite her.

"Brereep," she said, with a tight, self-righteous smile.

"No, it does *not* serve me right, my dear, and it's unkind of you to say so. I had no choice in the matter," said Kedrigern in a fragile voice. He listened to his stomach gurgle threateningly, gulped, and went on. "I know what kind of stuff the wood-witch brews, and I watered my drinks as much as I decently could. She just kept refilling my bowl."

"Brereep."

"You don't know Bess, my dear. She's a good-hearted old thing, but she takes it terribly to heart if you refuse a drink in her hovel, and I didn't dare risk offending her." Kedrigern gave a shuddering, desolate sigh. "I don't know how she survives it. Her stomach must be lined with stone. I wouldn't offer that stuff to an alchemist."

"Brereep?"

"Worse than that. I think it would paralyze a full-grown troll."

As if on cue, the troll-of-all-work came skidding into the breakfast nook on huge flat feet. "Yah! Yah!" it shrieked in jubilant greeting, an arm's length from Kedrigern's ear. He made a little whimpering sound and buried his face in his hands.

"No, Spot. Quiet, please," he said faintly. "Please."

The little housetroll waited by his knee, big-eyed, panting and salivating, while the wizard recovered. Kedrigern rubbed his eyes gingerly, then blinked and glanced down on Princess' plate, on which lay a thin slice of bread covered with strawberry preserves. He quickly shut his eyes again.

"Plain porridge, Spot. A very small serving. A dab. And bring it silently," he said.

Spot careened out noiselessly, ears and big hands flapping, like a skiff crowded with a three-master's full complement of sail. Kedrigern looked again at Princess. Her expression of superior disapproval was unchanged.

"I wasn't too bad last night, was I?" he asked.

"Brereep."

"I did? Funny . . . I don't remember that at all. Are you positive?"

"Brereep!" she said indignantly.

Kedrigern raised his hands before him defensively. "Certainly, my dear. If you say so. I'm terribly sorry."

She glared at him, but said nothing.

"I didn't . . . I didn't try to work any magic, did I?" he asked apprehensively.

She solemnly shook her head.

Kedrigern let out a deep sigh of relief. "I'm glad to hear that. Working spells when one is not fully . . . when one has had . . . well, it's irresponsible. I've known of conventions where everyone wound up invisible just because some silly wizard . . . anyway, we don't have *that* to worry about."

Princess did not look comforted by this observation. She did not speak. Spot caromed into the breakfast nook, eased a bowl of porridge and milk silently onto the tabletop, and departed. Kedrigern ate, in small, cautious helpings, and still she was silent. At last he laid down his spoon and looked directly into her eyes.

"In any event, my dear, I got what I was after. It meant a long trip, and hard bargaining, and an excruciating hangover. The price was absolutely outrageous. But it was all worthwhile," he announced.

"Brereep?"

"More than that. Much more. I had to give Bess a full vial of dragon's blood. But I don't begrudge a drop of it. What's dragon's blood for, anyway? I'd gladly spend all I've got to make you happy."

"Brereep?" she asked. Her voice was somewhat softened.

"All for you, and you alone, my dear." Kedrigern reached out and gently laid his fingertips on her hand. "It's your anniversary present: the crystal of Caracodissa. At this very moment it stands on my work table. And as soon as my head is clear –"

She squeezed Kedrigern's hand in both of hers. With a croak of sheer joy, she jumped up, ran to his side, threw her arms around his neck, and kissed him repeatedly. He took her in his arms and held her close.

"I was going to keep it for a surprise, but I suppose it's just as well you know about it," he murmured.

"Brereep?" she asked in a whisper.

"Oh, no doubt at all. It's the genuine article. I know the markings too well to be fooled. The inscription runs all the way around it, in letters that burn like fire:

> Magic of the helping kind,
> Seek it here, and ye shall find,
> Wake the spirit that indwells,
> Find the spell to loose all spells . . .

I'll work on it first thing tomorrow morning, and by dinnertime tomorrow you'll be speaking as clearly as ever you did."

She drew away and looked perplexedly at Kedrigern. "Brereep?" she asked.

"No, tomorrow. Please, my dear. My head is throbbing. I can barely focus my eyes. I'm in no condition –"

"Brereep!" she cried.

"Of course I love you!" Kedrigern said, wincing at the loudness of her voice. "We're dealing with very delicate magic here, my dear. I can't undertake it lightly. I must have a clear head, and at the moment –"

"Brereep?" she suggested.

"No, I can't. There's nothing that can cure a hangover. Not even magic. We'll just have to wait until tomorrow. Surely, one more day won't be so bad to endure, will it, my dear?"

Princess slumped dejectedly. She sat huddled by his chair, looking up at him with wide, sad eyes. A tear welled up in each eye, brimmed, and coursed down her pale cheeks.

"My dear, I really can't. A great deal of preliminary study is required. It would be very risky to barge ahead."

She gave a little sob. More tears came. She buried her lovely face in her hands and wept, silently.

Kedrigern's resolve lasted less than a minute. Rising, he laid his hand on her shoulder and said, "Perhaps I can do something today, after all. If Spot can bring me a cold compress –"

Princess sprang to her feet and clapped her hands once, sharply. Kedrigern twitched at the sound, which brought Spot reeling into the breakfast nook.

"A bowl of very cold water, and a clean cloth, Spot. Bring them to my study at once. And don't make a sound," said the wizard in a low, strained voice.

The cold compress helped ever so slightly. Kedrigern wiped his brow, dried his wet fingertips on his robe, and turned his attention to the crystal cube that stood in a cleared place on his long work table. Princess, too, gazed on it with fascination.

It was a perfect cube of flawless crystal, about a hand's length to a side, and it glowed from within, where a misty radiance swirled through it like a fiery soul. Around four sides, in letters of reddish-gold that flickered like living flame, ran the inscription. In the darkened room, Kedrigern read the familiar words, turning the crystal cube slowly as he spoke:

> "Wake the spirit that indwells,
> Seek it here, and ye shall find,
> Find the spell to loose all spells,
> Magic of the helping kind . . ."

Something nudged his memory. He had not been at his most alert when he read the inscription earlier, but it seemed to him that the verses had been in different order. He picked up the cube, turned it over in his hands – it was oddly light in weight – and setting it down, read the inscription once more:

> "Seek it here, and ye shall find,
> Wake the spirit that indwells,
> Magic of the helping kind,
> Find the spell to loose all spells . . ."

He let out a deep groan and reached for the compress. This was going to be more difficult than he had expected. Princess, seeing his look of concern, lent her aid, plunging the cloth into the bowl, wringing out the excess water, and applying the soothing compress gently to Kedrigern's forehead. He accepted her ministrations silently, his eyes fixed on the glowing crystal surface.

"This is not going to be simple, my dear. Not simple at all. What we have here is a permutational spell . . . very tricky thing to deal with," Kedrigern said abstractedly. He turned and started to say, "It really would be best to wait until I . . ." but the abandoned look in Princess' eyes silenced him.

He returned his attention to the cube. The radiance at its center was slowly swirling, like dyes dropped carefully into still water. He whispered a melodious phrase, and then another. The glow deepened, and clotted. He gestured for Princess to go to the opposite side of the table, facing him, and as she moved he took up a longer incantation in an utterly strange language of soft liquid syllables which flowed into one another without pause.

When Princess stood opposite him, he reached out, took her hands, and placed her palms flat against the sides of the cube. He placed his own hands over hers. The light within the crystal drew in upon itself, congealed, and solidified into a golden cube within a cube.

Kedrigern's head was throbbing painfully. Swent ran down his forehead and into his eyes. He blinked it away, staring hard at the letters slowly coming into sight on the face on the inner cube. The print was tiny, the light was painfully bright, his vision was blurry, and his head felt as if it were about to burst into flame, but there was no stopping now. Squinting and cocking his head, he read off the words of the unbinding spell as one by one they came into view. When he spoke the final word, the golden cube burst into a million tiny fragments of light that glowed, and faded, and left the crystal and the room in semidarkness.

Princess was slumping forward, dazed. Kedrigern rushed around the table just in time to catch her as she fell. He carried her to their bedroom, placed her on the bed, and summoned Spot.

"Get the cold water and the cloth from my study, Spot. Bring them here at once," he ordered.

Princess was a bit pale, but her breath and heartbeat were regular. Kedrigern began to swab her brow and cheeks as soon as Spot arrived, and in a very short time, her eyelids fluttered. He set to wiping his own brow as she opened her eyes, looked up at him, and smiled.

"How do you feel, my dear?" he asked.

".well Very .Well," she said.

Kedrigern gave a great sigh of relief. "I'm so glad to hear. For a moment there . . . I had some difficulty making out the words of the spell, you see. But apparently, I got it right."

She frowned, shook her head, and said, ".wrong it got you think I, No"

"What?"

"!backwards thing silly the recited You"

"Backwards?"

".backwards, right That's"

"Oh, dear."

"?say can you all *that* Is"

"Well . . . at least I didn't recite the spell sideways, my dear," Kedrigern said brightly, grasping at the first positive circumstance that occurred to him. "There's no telling what you might sound like if I'd done that. This way, if you're careful, and you work hard–"

"?life my of rest the for backwards talking be I Will ?careful, mean you do What !Careful"

"Oh, dear," Kedrigern repeated.

"!say to you for Easy ?dear, Oh"

"Look at it this way: it's a start. You're speaking, and that's the important thing."

".Backwards," she muttered.

"It's better than croaking, isn't it? If you just keep to simple sentences, everything will be fine. Meanwhile, I'll read over everything I have on the crystal of Caracodissa and permutational spells, and we can try it again in a few days. Everything's going to be all right. You'll see," Kedrigern said cheerfully.

Princess looked up at him, still dubious but trying not to show her doubts. She was, after all, speaking. And it was an improvement over croaking. At last she smiled and held out her hands to him. 'up me Help," she said.

Kedrigern was much relieved when she rose, stretched, and then walked out of the bedroom in completely normal fashion. When, at dinner, she did not begin with dessert and end with soup, he was reassured. And when Princess showed no sign of waking up before going to sleep that night, his mind was put completely at ease. The spell had affected only her speech. Kedrigern was confident that given time to bone up, and a clear head, he could set everything to rights.

He spent the next day in his study, reading closely. When he came out, in midafternoon, to take a short breather, he received a shock to see Princess preparing an upside-down cake for dessert that evening; but it turned out to be sheer coincidence. He sat down, relieved, on the kitchen bench.

"?hard working you Are," she asked.

"Yes. The crystal of Caracodissa is an amazingly complicated device. It seems that whenever one summons up the spell, it appears in slightly different form on each face of the crystal. Only one form is the right one, but there's no way to tell which it is."

Princess frowned in puzzlement. ".one only saw I ?six were there sure you Are"

"Whichever face you look into appears to be the only one with a spell showing. It was centuries before a witch named Moggropple discovered the secret."

"?mirrors use you Could"

"Moggropple tried just that. She surrounded the crystal with mirrors, five of them, and recited all six spells one after the other, as fast as she could. She's been trapped in the mirrors ever since, five of her, and no one knows the spell to get her out. No one is sure which is the real Moggropple, either; so they can't try anything drastic. I don't think it pays to get too clever with the crystal."

"?do you will What"

"If we have one chance in six of finding the right spell, I suppose we just have to keep trying."

". . . now, minute a Wait," Princess said, holding up her hands.

"It didn't hurt at all, did it?"

"No," she admitted.

"And you did get your voice back."

"Yes," she said reluctantly.

"Well, there you are. We'll try again tomorrow morning. There's nothing to worry about," Kedrigern said confidently.

"?out-inside Or ?sideways talking start I if What"

"You're worrying yourself unnecessarily, my dear," said Kedrigern, rising. "Now, if you'll excuse me, I have a few references to check out. I'll be working late tonight, I'm afraid. I want to have everything ready for tomorrow morning."

★   ★   ★

The next morning, both Princess and Kedrigern were too edgy to eat a proper breakfast. Spot had scarcely cleared away their half-emptied plates when they went hand in hand to Kedrigern's study. Kedrigern at once began to bustle about, covering his nervousness with activity and a stream of chatter.

"Now, if you'll take your place at the other side, just as you did yesterday . . . that's right, my dear, right there . . . hands by your side, relaxed . . . nothing to worry about," he said in a gentle, reassuring voice. "I'll just clear away these empty bowls . . . there we are. Now, I'll turn the crystal so . . . and see what happens when I read the spell in the next face. It won't be any time at all, you'll see. I'll read the spell, and you'll be speaking beautifully. Forwards. Only one or two little things to attend to before we . . . there . . . and there . . ."

"!it with on get, Oh," Princess said sharply.

"Certainly, my dear, certainly," Kedrigern said with a soothing gesture. "I'm practically finished. There. Now. Are you ready, my dear?"

"Yes," she said through clenched teeth.

He nodded, took a deep breath, and commenced the summoning of the spirit in the cube. At his first words, the inner radiance came to life, and stirred, and began to glow. It twisted and spun, sinuous and slow, and Kedrigern began the incantation that would raise it to readiness.

Motes and streamers of light danced in the crystal cube, ever closer and denser, moving in upon one another until a single glowing sphere hung shimmering in the center. Kedrigern reached for Princess' cool hands, placed them on the sides of the crystal, and covered them with his own, just as he had done before. The light formed a brilliant inner cube. Once again, letters began to take shape before Kedrigern's eyes, and he read off the spell slowly revealed to him.

As the last words left his lips, the light burst into fragments. Kedrigern looked up quickly. Princess stared at the crystal, vacant-eyed, for a moment, then looked at him, fully alert and aware.

"No, it isn't," she said.

"Is everything all right?" Kedrigern asked anxiously.

"Well, I'm not. Something's gone wrong again."

"You sound fine, my dear."

"Listen to me! I'm one sentence ahead of you, that's what happened!" Princess cried.

"What could have happened?"

"– Ridiculous!"

"But that's –"

Kedrigern waved his hands frantically for silence and restraint. Princess folded her arms like a gate shutting and glared at him with Armageddon in her blue eyes. With a flurry of reassuring gestures, Kedrigern prepared for an immediate new attempt. He gave the crystal a quarter-turn. He wiped his damp forehead on his sleeve, rubbed his eyes, took three deep calming breaths, and for the third time, spoke the words of summoning.

The light this time was sluggish, moving slowly as honey in the center of the crystal cube. Kedrigern could sense the reluctance of the indwelling spirit; but once having begun, he could not turn back. That was one of the basic rules of the wizard's trade.

When the summoning phrases were done, Kedrigern paused for breath. The cube was faintly glowing now, with a sallow, grudging light. Princess had relaxed; her hands were by her sides, and her eyes were fixed on the crystal.

Kedrigern began the incantation. The inner light swirled fitfully, like a fish on a line, but its color brightened and deepened. As it gathered, Princess placed her palms against the sides, and Kedrigern enclosed her hands in his. The light rose, and flared, and died, and they stood in the faint light, exhausted, their bowed heads almost touching over the crystal cube.

"Are you all right, my dear?" Kedrigern asked when he had his breath under control.

Princess nodded. She took a long, deep breath, then another, and raised her eyes to meet Kedrigern's.

"Say something. Just a short phrase will do. Anything," Kedrigern said.

She cleared her throat. "Peererb," she said.

Kedrigern recoiled in shock but quickly recovered his poise. "We'll try again, my dear! A few minutes' rest, that's all we need, and then we'll try again," he said quickly.

"Peererb! Peererb!" Princess cried, enraged.

"Now, my dear, you must be patient. These things happen sometimes. It's a momentary setback, nothing more. You mustn't let it – Princess, what are you doing!?"

Kedrigern sprang forward an instant too late. Princess swept up the crystal of Caracodissa in both hands and raised it over her head. With a furious "Peererb," that drowned Kedrigern's cry of horror, she hurled it with all her might to the stone floor.

From the wreckage rose a myriad motes of golden light. They merged, and danced together in a glimmering spiral, and then, with a tinkle of crystalline laughter, the spirit of the crystal of Caracodissa floated out a crack in the shutters and vanished into the light of day, free at last.

"Princess!" Kedrigern cried, dashing to her side.

She flew to his arms, and he clasped her tightly, to still her trembling and conceal his own. "It's all over, my dear," he said gently. "The spirit of the crystal was obviously determined not to be helpful. Malignant lot, those imprisoned spirits. I should have known. We're well rid of it. I promise you. I'll have you talking again as soon as I possibly can. I'll leave no spell unwoven until you're speaking as sweetly as ever. But we've had enough magic for one day, and enough talk of magic. We've earned a holiday, I think. Let's have Spot make up a picnic. What do you say to that?"

"Brereep," she said.

II

Outside the breakfast nook the birds were singing merrily. The morning was sunny, breakfast was delicious, Princess was looking her loveliest, and the spells were going well.

Kedrigern finished his third muffin and looked upon the world with a benign eye and a full belly. A single muffin remained on the dish. On an impulse, he swept up the crumbs from the tabletop, dropped them on the dish beside the muffin, and rose, saying, "My dear, if you don't want this muffin . . ."

"I couldn't eat another bite, Keddie. You take it," said Princess; not a particularly memorable utterance, but to Kedrigern's ears celestial music. After repeated spelling and despelling, enchantment and disenchantment, dashed hopes and embarrassments, she was finally speaking in her own sweet voice, thanks to his own efforts and the timely assistance of a Cymric bard.

"I'm quite full, too. I thought I'd bring it outside and feed the birds."

"A lovely idea," Princess said. "I'll come, too."

Birds were here and there about the dooryard, hopping, chirping, pecking, darting glances from side to side, going about their avian affairs. As the first crumbs hit the ground, the birds fluttered off cautiously, then returned and began to eat.

"Pretty things, birds," the wizard observed.

"Very. And such skilful fliers," said his wife.

"You're very good yourself, my dear."

Princess looked away modestly. "Thank you."

As Kedrigern dispensed the last handful of crumbs, a new bird alighted, with a faint but distinct *clink*, scattering the rest. It hopped toward the wizard, folded its wings, and bowed. This was uncommon behavior for a bird, and Kedrigern turned his full attention to the newcomer.

The bird was about the size of a blue jay, but it was no blue jay. Its body was gold, its wings gold and silver, its tail silver and electrum. Its eyes were emeralds; crown, wingtips, and tail were studded with emeralds and rubies; its bill was pearl; its feet, niello. The little creature glittered like a treasure chest by torchlight.

"Am I in the presence of Master Kedrigern, the famed wizard of Silent Thunder Mountain?" the bird inquired in a small, high, but very clear voice.

"You are, my good bird. Is there anything I can do for you?" Kedrigern replied.

The bird clicked rapidly several times, cocked its head, hopped closer, and said, "I have a message for Master Kedrigern from his old friend Aponthey. To wit: 'Have come into possession of magic crystal with unusual properties. Not my line. Would appreciate your opinion. Come if you can. All best wishes, Aponthey.'"

"Is that all?" the wizard asked.

The bird swiveled its head around completely, gave a flirt of its tail, and said, "That is all. At the sound of the chirp, I will be ready to accept your reply whenever you wish to give it. Please do not hurry. I am a mechanical device and can wait indefinitely."

"Polite little fellow," Princess observed.

"Aponthey was always meticulous," said Kedrigern.

"Who's Aponthey? You've never mentioned him."

"He's a bright young lad, very talented. He's an inventor, a clockmaker . . . a mechanical genius. He worked on the famous Iron Man of Rottingen."

"I've heard of it, but I never saw it."

"Nothing but a heap of rust now, I'm afraid. But that's not Aponthey's fault. He did the interior works. The local boys did the body, and they botched the job. Aponthey was always at his best with smaller things, anyway – like this bird."

"It's exquisite," Princess said, stooping for a closer look just as the little automaton chirped its readiness. "And so richly adorned! Seventeen jewels, at least."

"Aponthey did a very similar one for the emperor of Byzantium, all hammered gold and gold enameling. A couple of Grecian goldsmiths got all the credit, but it was Aponthey's work. Marvelous thing, from what I've heard. It used to sit upon a golden bough, and sing of what is past, or passing, or to come. The lords and ladies of Byzantium loved it, but the emperor claimed that it kept him awake."

"Emperors are very hard to please."

"Aponthey took the bird back and replaced it with a dozen mechanical ladybugs. They used to fly in formation and do tricks, very quietly. The emperor was pleased."

"How nice for Aponthey. And what are you going to do about his request?" Princess asked.

"I really don't know. I have no pressing work at the moment. But it would involve . . ." He paused and made a sour face, then forced out the hated word, ". . . travel."

"Is it far to Aponthey's workshop?"

"It's far to everything, my dear. And it's always uncomfortable going, and ugly and dusty and hot along the way, and dangerous and nasty, and disappointing when you finally get there, and twice as bad coming back."

"You sound as though you don't want to go," said Princess.

"Actually, I do. It sounds as though it might be interesting. I haven't had anything to do with magical crystal objects since our contretemps with the crystals of Caracodissa. You remember that, I'm sure."

"I certainly do," said Princess grimly.

"Tricky thing, magic crystals, but they can be useful. Good sources of information."

"I'd rather trust to gossip and hearsay," Princess snapped.

"Now it sounds as though you don't want to go."

"Whatever gave you that idea? It's a perfect season to travel. We can make it a little holiday."

"Ugh."

"You can gather nice fresh herbs along the way. We'll pack up lovely snacks. It will be nice to see Aponthey again, won't it?"

"Yes," Kedrigern said reluctantly.

"And how far is it, really?"

"About three days' ride each way."

"That's no distance at all! Tell the bird we'll go."

With a resigned shrug, he said, "Very well, my dear. If that's what you want."

"It's what you want, too, and we both know it."

Turning to the bird, Kedrigern extended his arm and said, "All right, bird, I'm ready to reply." The tiny automaton unfurled its wings, ascended smoothly, and perched on the wizard's left wrist.

"Please speak directly into my beak, and do not get too close," it said.

Kedrigern raised his arm until the bird was at the level of his chin, about a forearm's length away. "Is this good?" he asked.

"Excellent. Please proceed," said the bird, and opened its beak wide.

Kedrigern looked into the gaping beak and suddenly felt very foolish, standing in his dooryard talking into a clockwork bird. But he pulled himself together, cleared his throat, and, in a voice only slightly strained, said, "Hello, Aponthey. Are you listening? This is Kedrigern. I hope you're well. It's lovely here this morning."

"The *crystal*," Princess whispered with an urgent gesture.

"Ah yes, the crystal. About this crystal of yours, Aponthey. We're coming to have a look at it. My wife and I, that is. We'll leave tomorrow, and we should arrive in three days. Won't stay long."

"Keddie, we can't just pop in and run. What if he has a serious problem?"

"All right, then. We won't stay long unless there's a serious problem. Good-bye, Aponthey. See you in a few days."

When Kedrigern finished, the bird closed its beak with a snap. Uttering a crisp. "Thank you," it rose from the wizard's wrist and circled the couple once, then headed northwest.

"Well, what do we do now?" Kedrigern asked.

"We pack," said Princess, and, taking his hand, she led him into the house.

Aponthey's residence was an easy, pleasant ride of less than three days. The roads were dry, and free of travelers. The weather was neither too warm nor too chilly. Each night, Princess and Kedrigern made their camp in a field of wild-flowers and slept under the stars, lulled by breezes heavy with the sweet scents of summertime. In the mornings they augmented their simple breakfasts with fresh berries. So idyllic was the journey that Kedrigern could find no cause for complaint; he had to content himself with dire predictions of rain, cold, and brigandage upon their return. To lighten his mood, Princess broached the subject of their host.

"What kind of house does Aponthey have?" she asked.

"Nothing grand. It's really just one big workshop. You might find it a bit messy, but it's certain to be interesting. Clocks of every kind and shape and size, with figures that wave their arms and kick their feet and roll their eyes and cut capers . . . things that whiz and click and clank and tick and buzz . . . terrible uproar on the hour, when all the clocks do whatever they do all at once."

"We must ask for a quiet chamber."

"Aponthey probably doesn't have one. Better to put something in our ears at night."

"What's he like?"

"A sprightly chap. Full of energy. Hops about like a flea, always doing a dozen things at once and planning two dozen more."

"He sounds exhausting."

"Well, most of his energy goes into his work. Still, he can be a very lively companion. Oh my, yes," said the wizard, smiling nostalgically and shaking his head. "I think you'll like him, my dear. A charming lad, really."

"How much farther is it to his house? You said three days, and this is our third day on the road."

"We should arrive at any moment. We have to pass through these woods first. Aponthey's house is in the center of a large cleared area. He always liked to have a lot of open space around, so he could get a good – wait a minute, now."

"Is something wrong?" Princess asked.

Kedrigern pointed to a black column of stone that rose from the ground twice the height of a man. One side was smooth and polished, and on that surface, at about head height, was incised an elaborate A above a curious angular symbol.

"This shouldn't be here, in the middle of the woods. It's the boundary marker of the clearing," said the wizard.

"Are you sure?" Princess asked.

"I'm positive. I marked out that symbol for the stonecutter. It's a warning to ogres. I watched this column being set in place."

"Maybe someone moved it."

Kedrigern's only response was a thoughtful grunt. He

tugged the medallion from inside his tunic and raised it to his eyes, sighting through the Aperture of True Vision. "There's the house," he announced. "And someone's moved that, too. It's surrounded by trees. I don't like this."

The road was narrow and erratic here. They made their way slowly through the trees and to the dooryard before Kedrigern reined in and said, "This is the place. He's made some alterations, but this is definitely Aponthey's house. How on earth did it get here, though, in the middle of all these trees? I'll go and knock at . . . ah, here's a servant. We can ask this old fellow."

An aged man emerged with slow steps from the doorway. He stood blinking for a moment, leaning on his stick, gazing vacantly ahead, and then he noticed the two figures on horseback. He stared, but did not speak.

"Good day to you, aged sir. Is Aponthey at home?" the wizard asked with a friendly salute.

"He did not," the old man snapped.

"Didn't what?"

"Who?"

"Aponthey."

"What do you want with Aponthey?"

"Aponthey wants something with me. I'm Kedrigern, the wizard, and this is my wife, Princess. Aponthey asked me to come."

"Kedrigern? You're Kedrigern? The wizard?" The old man asked in a high, piping voice. He began patting various parts of his person and eventually drew out a pair of thick spectacles and fumbled to put them on, dropping his stick in the process. When the spectacles were on, he shuffled closer to peer intently at his visitors, and at last wheezed happily. "Kedrigern! After all these years! You don't look a day older, you scoundrel!"

"Aponthey?" the wizard asked softly.

The old man let out a cracked peal of laughter. "Didn't recognize me, did you? You never did have a memory for faces, not you. Spells, that's all you remembered."

"Well, well . . . it's been a long time, hasn't it?"

"Sixty years, almost," said the old man with relish. "I bet you don't remember the last –"

"I do, I do! It was at my tower. You and Fraigus and some of the others gave me a surprise party for my 110th birthday. It went on for days."

"They don't have parties like that anymore," said Aponthey. "Good thing, too." He squinted at Princess and said, "Who's she?"

"Aponthey, I'd like you to meet my wife," Kedrigern said. At his words, Princess tossed off her riding cloak, gave a little preliminary flutter of her gauzy wings, and then rose slowly from the saddle to come to ground at her husband's side.

"She flies," Aponthey said in a hushed voice. "She has little wings, and she flies! That's beautiful work. Who made her?"

"Nobody made her. She's real. She's my wife."

"Real?"

"So pleased to meet you, Aponthey. I've heard ever so much about you," said Princess sweetly, extending her hand.

"You're real. And you fly," he said softly, awed.

"They're magic wings, but they're permanent. Very strong, and very handy," Princess said with a smile and a quick flutter of her wings.

"Where'd you get them?"

"It's a long story."

"Well, tell me over dinner," said Aponthey. To Kedrigern, he said, "You'll have a lot to tell me, too. Good to see you, old scout. Glad you dropped by. Whatever brought you here?"

"You asked me to come. Something about a crystal."

"Crystal?"

"A crystal with unusual properties," Kedrigern prompted.

"Oh, that crystal! Remind me to show you the crystal before you leave. Interesting thing. I was going to send for a wizard I know, and ask him to. . . ." Aponthey stopped, thought for a moment, then said, "I did. That's why you're here."

"It is. You sent a bird with a message."

"Little gold-and-silver bird with a pearl beak?"

"That's the bird."

"His name is Skibreen. Faithful messenger, but absolutely

no sense of direction. He'll probably show up in a month or two. Where's my stick? I had a stick," Aponthey said peevishly.

Kedrigern picked up the stick and placed it in his hand. Aponthey took it, studied it critically, said, "Well, come in," and started into the house.

"Bright young lad, Aponthey," Princess said under her voice, smiling innocently. "A sprightly chap, too."

"It's been only sixty years, my dear. Not even sixty, in fact. I keep forgetting what a long time that is for people who aren't wizards."

"It's a long time for trees, too. They grow into forests."

"I know, I know. We got here, didn't we?"

"I just want you to keep alert. Your friend's memory is failing, and you'll have to ask very precise questions if you expect to help him out with his crystal."

"Aponthey's memory hasn't failed. He was always absentminded. Kept a good kitchen, though, even in those days. We should have an excellent dinner," said Kedrigern, taking her arm.

They did. The food was superb, the preparation masterful, the service punctilious. Three lovely ladies, all of pale gold and ivory, with emerald eyes and coral lips and dresses of pale blue enameled silver covered with tiny white flowers, brought dish after dish from the kitchen, placed them on the sideboard, and curtsied daintily to the guests. Three bronze footmen with beryl eyes and colorful livery of black, red, and green enameling served the meal, moving on smooth feet with no more sound than a barely audible ticking from their inner works.

When the last dish was removed, Kedrigern breathed a soft sigh of repletion and said, "A feast, Aponthey. A meal to be proud of. My compliments to your cook."

"I'll bring him in, so you can compliment him yourself. Old Collindor loves praise, but I don't have many visitors these days," Aponthey said, taking up a little crystal bell that stood by his hand. He shook it, but it made no sound.

A creature looking something like a pair of copper caldrons

joined by a large spring glided into the room on silent casters.
Eight flexible arms extended from the upper caldron. Two of
them held whisks, one a spoon, two others forks, and one a
towel. Raising its two remaining arms, the creature said in a
deep, rumbling voice, "You summoned me, Master?"

"Yes, I did. My guests want to compliment you," said
Aponthey, gesturing to Princess and Kedrigern.

"The roast was done to perfection," said Kedrigern.

"And the vegetables were the best I've ever tasted," Princess added.

"The bread was delicious."

"The trifle was a masterpiece."

"You are too kind," rumbled Collindor with a flourish of his
two unoccupied appendages and a subdued motion of all the
rest. "The credit rightly belongs to my beloved master."
Aponthey sipped his wine and beamed. Collindor went on,
"But the sauce for the trifle is of my own devising."

"That will be all, Collindor. Back to your kitchen,"
Aponthey ordered.

"As my master commands," said the creature, rolling
soundlessly from the room.

"Did you make that?" Princess asked.

"Had to. Clients used to come here all the time, and they
expected a decent meal. Collindor can come up with a delicious dinner for twelve on an hour's notice. Keeps the kitchen
spotless, too."

"What a wonderful invention!"

Aponthey frowned. "Collindor has his drawbacks, Princess.
First year I had him, I gained sixty-one pounds. Had to
redesign him to make him go easier on sauces, and once I
started redesigning, I decided I'd make him completely functional instead of sacrificing utility for appearance. He's the
best cook I ever had, and a great help around the house. Winds
up all the others, and winds himself, too. Great load off my
mind, I can tell you."

"The perfect servant," Princess said admiringly.

"Not perfect. He still likes to experiment with new recipes."

"All good cooks experiment."

"They don't put ants and gravel and mainsprings and glue over stewed figs," Aponthey said angrily.

"As a rule, no. One must be precise in instructing servants," Kedrigern said. "We have a young troll-of-all work. Spot is strong, conscientious, and absolutely reliable, but it requires careful instruction. I recall once suggesting that it come up with something different for dinner, and it –"

"Keddie, please!" Princess interjected with a queasy expression. "Not after eating."

"Sorry, dear."

"Enough talk about servants. What's this crystal you mentioned? It sounds interesting," Aponthey said.

"It's *your* crystal. You asked me to come and take a look at it," Kedrigern replied.

Aponthey looked bewildered. "I did! Then it must be around here someplace. Maybe up in the . . . no, not there. Out by the old . . .? No." He frowned, mumbled to himself, then said, "Collindor will know. I'll ring for him." He picked up the little crystal bell once more. As he rang it, his face lit up and he cried, "Here it is, Kedrigern! It's this crystal bell! Here, take it. Try to ring it. Go ahead, try."

Kedrigern took the handle of the bell between thumb and two fingers and shook it gently. It made no sound whatsoever. He and Princess exchanged a glance. She shrugged. He shook the bell again, more vigorously. Still no sound. Gripping the handle as one would a poker, he gave it three powerful shakes. Not a tinkle was heard.

"I don't understand. There's a clapper, and it hits the side of the bell. Is it enchanted?" Kedrigern asked.

Aponthey shook his head and turned up his palms in a gesture emblematic of helpless perplexity. "I don't know about those things. That's why I asked you here, I guess. I did ask you, didn't I?"

"You definitely did. You mentioned 'unusual properties.' What did you mean?"

Bewilderment again settled on Aponthey's features. "Well, it doesn't ring," he said at last. "That's unusual, for a bell. Bells generally ring."

"Where's Collindor?" Princess asked. "He came when Aponthey shook the bell before, but he didn't come this time."

"Oh, that's because I was thinking of him then, and Kedrigern wasn't thinking of him just now. That's how the bell works. I guess that's another unusual property."

"I would say so." Kedrigern held up the crystal bell so that the candlelight shone through its facets. He took out his medallion and examined the bell through the Aperture of True Vision, and cried, "Aha!"

"What's that supposed to mean?" Aponthey asked with a guarded look.

"Something's caught in this bell," Kedrigern said, keeping his eyes fixed on the object in question.

"Is that all? I'll have Collindor wash it off." Aponthey gave a subdued, self-conscious laugh, and said, "I thought it was some kind of magic, and all along it was a piece of food. Well, the old eyes aren't –"

"It's not food. You've got a spirit trapped in here."

"I do? Mighty small spirit."

"Size means nothing to a spirit," Kedrigern said distantly, turning the little crystal bell over in his hands. He set it on the table before him and, without moving his eyes from it, said, "Would you mind keeping absolutely quiet and not moving? I'd like to speak to this spirit."

Princess and Aponthey both nodded. Kedrigern pulled a thread from his tunic, tied a loop around the handle of the bell, and suspended it from a spoon, which he supported on two empty goblets. The bell now hung free. He spoke a phrase in an unintelligible tongue, and the bell began to vibrate in utter silence, and then slowly stilled. A shimmer of tiny points of light crept downward, from crown to waist, and congealed in a glowing golden band around the lip.

In a soft, solemn voice, Kedrigern said, "Spirit in the bell, do you hear and understand me? Tinkle once for yes, twice for no."

A single brittle tinkle sounded in the room. Kedrigern glanced at Princess and winked before going on with the next question.

"Are you a prisoner in the bell?"
Tinkle.
"Have you been a prisoner for long, lonely ages?"
Two emphatic tinkles.
"You haven't? A recent entrapment. Less than a century?"
Tinkle.
"Less than twenty years?"
Tinkle.
"Less than five?"
An excited tinkle that set the spoon shaking.
"This is a very recent spell. Odd that I've heard no mention
. . . unless . . . Spirit in the bell, was this spell cast by someone
you can identify?"
Tinkle. Tinkle.
"I think I see it now. Was it a trap waiting to capture anyone
who came within its grasp?"
Loud tinkle.
"And do you wish to be released?"
Very loud tinkle.
"All right. Listen carefully, now. If I'm going to get you out
of there, I'll need some information, and this system of
questioning is very slow."
Tinkle.
"I'm glad you agree. I'm going to learn what I can from
Aponthey, and then try to devise a faster method of inquiry.
I'll be back to you as soon as I have something. Are you
comfortable?"
Tinkle. Tinkle.
"Sorry. I'll put you on the table. Will that be better?"
Tinkle.
Kedrigern untied the thread and stood the little crystal bell
on the table, safely distant from the edge. The glow around the
lip broke into motes of golden light that swirled and slowly
drifted upward, toward the crown, fading as they rose. Prin-
cess looked intently at the moving particles of light, frowning.
"Ask that thing one more question," she said.
"If you wish, my dear," Kedrigern replied, taking up the
bell and refastening the string. "What's the question?"

"Ask it if it was once in the crystal of Caracodissa."

"My dear, do you really think . . .?"

"I'd know those motes anywhere. That miserable little spirit had me speaking sideways, and backward, and upside down, and every which way but right, and if it thinks I'm going to stand idly by while you set it free, it has a big surprise coming. Go ahead, ask it," said Princess, and her voice was as steel.

"Well, spirit, what about it? Were you ever in the crystal of Caracodissa?" Kedrigern asked.

There was a pause as the golden motes crept slowly downward to form a band of light at the lip of the bell, then a hesitant, muted tinkle.

"And did you cause this lady to speak in a variety of awkward and embarrassing ways?"

A single tinkle, softer than before.

"I see. That does change things, doesn't it?"

This time the tinkle was barely audible.

"I don't mean to be cruel, Keddie, but it laughed at me. It made me talk absurdly, and then it *laughed* when I set it free!" Princess said, her eyes flashing.

"But it did make you speak, my dear."

"For a very brief time. In ridiculous ways."

"And you didn't really mean to set it free. You smashed the crystal to bits, and the spirit escaped," Kedrigern pointed out.

"And good riddance," said Princess icily.

"Perhaps it wasn't laughing at you. It might have given vent to a laugh of sheer joy at being released from its confinement." The bell gave a single emphatic tinkle at these words, and Kedrigern concluded, "You see, my dear? No mockery was intended."

"It *laughed*."

"Wouldn't you, under the circumstances?"

"As a princess, I would consider the feelings of others, and suppress any expression of merriment until I got out of earshot of people I had caused to talk backward," said Princess with hauteur.

Kedrigern took her hands in his. "My dear, not everyone

has the advantages of good breeding and polite upbringing. A young, adventurous spirit, on its own in the world, trapped in a magic crystal, is unlikely to learn good manners."

"Then it needs to be taught."

"Perhaps it's learned from its ordeal. If I could speak to it more easily . . . Let's see what Aponthey can tell us. The spirit may be truly sorry for what it did."

"Sorry it was caught again, that's all. A pretty dumb class of spirit, I'd say."

"All the more reason to be charitable, my dear," Kedrigern said. Princess responded with an uncharitable little sniff, and he turned to Aponthey. "Can you tell us anything more about the bell? Are there any other unusual properties that you recall?" When Aponthey only gestured helplessly and looked bewildered, the wizard asked, "How did you come into possession of the bell in the first place? Perhaps that has some bearing –"

"Unusual properties! *That's* what I meant! A whole barnful of them, and that little bell was in one of the chests, so I took it to use calling Collindor."

"A barnful of unusual properties?" Kedrigern asked.

"Pemmeny's old furniture – chests and dressers and sideboards and bedstead and tables and chairs and stools and mirrors and –"

The bell tinkled wildly at Aponthey's mention of mirrors, and continued to tinkle until Kedrigern admonished it to be silent so he could question his host further. "Are there five identical mirrors, by any chance?" he asked.

"There might be. I never checked. Old Pemmeny, the merchant trader, used to buy up furniture all over the kingdom. I let him keep his things in my barn, and he let me use anything I wanted. Never had much use for mirrors."

"I'd like to see these unusual properties."

"Just a pile of old furniture, Kedrigern. Nothing to interest a wizard."

"Perhaps not, but I'd still like to see them."

"Anything you like. We can take a look after dinner."

"We just finished dinner."

"Oh. Well, then, let's go look at this furniture. Mirrors, you say?"

Again, the crystal bell burst into enthusiastic tinkling, and this time Kedrigern spoke to it. "Tell me truly, spirit: Have you been seeking the mirrors of Moggropple?"

Tinkle.

"And was it in the course of your search that you became trapped in this bell?"

Tinkle.

"Was it your intention to free Moggropple from the mirrors?"

Tinkle.

"Do you know how?"

He was answered with two dull, dispirited tinkles.

"Perhaps I can do something for both of you." Turning to Princess, Kedrigern said, "Surely, my dear, you can have no more objection to my helping this spirit. It was on a mission of mercy when it was trapped in the bell."

"Oh, all right," said Princess, throwing up her hands in frustration.

"What's going on, Kedrigern? Who's Moggropple? Are you saying I have a bunch of magic mirrors in my barn? What's it all got to do with this bell?" Aponthey demanded in cranky bewilderment.

Kedrigern calmed him down. As they walked to the barn, he recounted the history of the unfortunate Moggropple, assisted in his narrative by sotto voce remarks of a sardonic nature from Princess.

It all began with a magical object called the crystal of Caracodissa, a cube of unknown origin that held a vast array of helpful spells and counterspells. In order to gain access to a particular spell (or counterspell), one summoned up the indwelling spirit of the crystal, which then caused the desired spell (or counterspell) to appear on each of the six faces, though the summoner could see only the side that he or she was directly observing. But no two versions of a spell (or counterspell) were exactly alike, and only one was correct; reading the wrong one had unanticipated, and often undesirable, results.

For some centuries, people accepted the odds at one in six. But a clever and resourceful witch named Moggropple thought of a way to beat those odds. She set the cube on a glass surface and surrounded it with mirrors, five in number, observing the sixth face herself, from below. When the spell she summoned made its appearance, she recited all six versions as rapidly as she could, one after another.

Whether in her haste she recited some portions inaccurately, or whether the spirit in the crystal, the crystal itself, or the maker of the crystal was angered by her presumption, no one could say; but the next thing Moggropple knew, she was trapped in the mirrors. Five of her. And which was the real Moggropple, no one knew, anymore than they knew how to find out or how to release her.

"I first heard of Moggropple when I was studying with Fraigus o' the Murk. I've always wanted to see those mirrors," Kedrigern concluded.

"What became of the crystal?" Aponthey asked.

"I dashed it to tiny pieces," said Princess fiercely. "That's how the spirit got free. Didn't stay free for long, though, the silly thing."

"It must have a great weakness for crystal," Kedrigern said.

Aponthey's barn was very large and very cluttered, and totally disorganized. Once his workshop, it had fallen into desuetude as he became increasingly more nearsighted and turned from life-sized clockwork figures to ever tinier creations, such as the precision marching band of ninety-six mechanical ants he was now making. To defray expenses, he had let out the barn as storage space, and paid little attention to what was stored there, and how. Consequently, it took nearly an hour of climbing over and around large, dusty objects before he cried out, "Here it is! Here's the chest that held the bell."

"Then the mirrors must be nearby. Look for five mirrors," Kedrigern said, lifting his lantern high.

"Over here, Keddie!" Princess called minutes later. "Five mirrors, all in a row!"

The men joined her and set their lanterns down to illuminate the gloomy corner of the barn in which the mirrors stood neatly lined up side by side. At first glance, they were identical: a bit higher and broader than a tall, husky man, they stood on elaborately carved and gilded stands. As Kedrigern inspected them more closely, he found a single distinguishing characteristic: each mirror had a Roman numeral, from I through V, engraved on a gilded medallion set into the stand. The mirrors were covered with heavy cloths, presumably to protect the glass, but conceivably to protect any onlookers. All faced in the same direction.

"Did you look in the mirrors, my dear?" Kedrigern asked.

"I just lifted the corner of the cloth, to make certain it was a mirror, then I let it fall back into place."

"Good. I'm not sure what we're liable to see, and we mustn't take chances."

"Tricky things, mirrors," Aponthey said uneasily.

"These mirrors are trickier than most. Did Pemmeny tell you why he set them up in a row?"

"No. But he told me not to move them. He was definite about it."

Kedrigern nodded. "Then we won't move them. I imagine some kind of reaction takes place when they're able to reflect one another."

"Better leave them alone altogether, if you ask me. Just let them be. You can't trust mirrors," Aponthey said.

"It could be dangerous, Keddie," Princess added.

"It might well be. But when I think of Moggropple, trapped in a mirror for all this time . . . and that poor, foolish spirit losing its own freedom in an attempt to free her. . . . If we can help them, we must."

"You're right, I suppose," Princess murmured without any discernible enthusiasm.

"You're crazy, both of you. You were always too soft-hearted, Kedrigern," Aponthey grumbled.

"This isn't softness; it's professional courtesy."

"It all comes down to the same thing. Leave me out of it. I don't want to get mixed up with a bunch of witches in mirrors. I'm no wizard. I'm an honest craftsman, retired and trying to spend my old age in peace and quiet. I just want to work on my mechanical ants."

"Why don't you wait for us in the house, then?" Kedrigern suggested.

"And miss everything? I'll sit over here, by this sideboard, where I can get away quick if things turn bad. Go ahead, do your magic. I won't interfere," Aponthey said, shuffling to a narrow chair near an open lane of egress.

"I'll sit with Aponthey. We don't want him to be frightened," Princess whispered, and slipped off to join their host.

Kedrigern licked his lips, which suddenly felt dry. He pushed up the sleeves of his tunic, looked at the mirrors one by one, and then gingerly lifted the dusty cover of mirror I and draped it over the back. He saw his own reflection and the reflection of the large cherry armoire behind him, and nothing more. He followed the same procedure with mirrors II through V, and in none of them did he see anything that might be the form of a witch.

"Nothing magic about them. Just ordinary mirrors. Still, I don't like them," Aponthey muttered.

Kedrigern drew out his medallion and looked into each mirror, in turn, through the Aperture of True Vision. He saw a vague shape stirring in each one, but it was so dim and fleeting that it might have been nothing more than the optical aftereffect of peering through the aperture, which he always found to be a strain. He returned the medallion to his tunic and stood with folded arms, looking thoughtfully at the mirrors.

Clearing his throat, he said loudly and clearly, "Moggropple, are you in there? I'll release you if I can, but I have to know you're in there. Reveal yourself, Moggropple!"

He had scarcely spoken the last words when a soft glow appeared in each mirror, steadily brighter, and a shape formed around it. Soon the figure of a white-haired woman in a deep blue gown stood in each of the mirrors. She was a handsome woman, with mournful dark eyes and long elegant fingers and features of great refinement. She appeared to be in the middle years of her third century.

"Which of you is the true Moggropple? Speak!" commanded the wizard.

On the instant, a babble of sound erupted from the mirrors, filling the barn with quintuple echoes of a single voice crying, "Me! I am! Don't listen to them, they're all phantasms, I'm the real one! They're not real, I'm real, I'm the only real one, me, I am, listen to me, don't pay any attention to them, they're all creatures of deception, I'm Moggropple, me, I am, I am! Me, not them, me! Set me free! I'm real, they're not, me, in this mirror, this one, no, not those others, this one! Me! Me!" in overlapping, interweaving, contrapuntal disharmony. Kedrigern heard an angry voice, a shrill voice, a wheedling voice, an angry harsh voice, a shrill wheedling voice – all similar but all slightly different. He shrank back under the barrage, then dashed forward to fling the covers over the mirrors in quick succession, raising a considerable amount of dust in the process but bringing on silence.

"Well, we know she's in there," he said, brushing his hands together and flicking dust from his tunic. "All we have to do is find out which one is the real Moggropple and how to get her out." When Princess and Aponthey did not reply, and only looked at him as if he were raving, he added, "Any suggestions?"

"Hit them with a hammer," Aponthey growled.

"I could not permit that. Much too dangerous."

"And very cruel," Princess said, giving Aponthey a withering look.

"What's cruel about it? That'd get them out of their mirrors in a hurry, wouldn't it?"

"We can't be certain. We're dealing with magic, Aponthey, and magic is a chancy business. I want to go about this in a very methodical way, for all our sakes."

"Talk to them one by one," Princess suggested.

"An excellent idea." Kedrigern turned to face the mirrors, hesitated, then turned back to Princess. "As a woman, and one who has herself experienced an uncomfortable enchantment, can you suggest a line of questioning?"

"You're the master wizard, Keddie," she said with a deferential gesture.

Acknowledging her words with a faint smile and a nod, Kedrigern turned to mirror I once again. He threw back the cloth, and Moggropple, arms akimbo, glared at him.

"Well, get me out of here," she snapped.

"You'll have to tell me how," he replied.

She gave an exaggerated sigh of patience strained to the limit of endurance and rolled her eyes to the heavens, muttering, "Wizards!" Then, collecting herself, she said, "It's very simple. You face me so that I catch the first ray of morning sunlight. You arrange the others in a pentacle with one empty side. That's all there is to it."

"Should the others face inward, or outward?"

"Inward, of course. Don't you know *anything?*"

"Thank you. I'll get back to you," Kedrigern said, whisking the cover over the glass before the figure within could object.

"That sounds pretty easy," Aponthey observed.

"Yes – if I spoke to the real Moggropple. Otherwise, I might have the formula for releasing mirror images into the world."

"What's so bad about that? They wouldn't take up any room, would they? Let them all loose, Kedrigern, so we can get out of this barn."

"Aponthey, don't you realize how dangerous they'd be? They're thinner than gold leaf and sharper than a magic sword. If one of them so much as bumped into a person sideways, that person would be sheared in half. Set one of these mirror people loose in a crowd, and it would be like scything wheat!"

After a long and thoughtful silence, Aponthey said, "Well, all right, then, be careful. But get on with it."

Kedrigern threw back the cover of mirror II, and Moggropple at once said, "*There* you are! Here's what you have to do to get me out of here, dear chap: face me so that I catch the last ray of the setting sun, and face the other four to a white wall on which you've marked, in black, the runes of –"

"I'll be in touch," Kedrigern said, covering the glass and proceeding to mirror III. Here he was instructed to turn her to the midday sun while arranging the others in facing pairs. Mirror IV frankly admitted that she had no idea how to get

out, and mirror V, to Aponthey's delight, ordered the wizard
to face her to the full moon and then smash all five mirrors
with a silver hammer. Kedrigern covered mirror V and turned
to Princess. He looked thoroughly disgusted.

"Well, I spoke to them one by one. Any other ideas?"

"I'm thinking, Keddie," she said patiently.

"Now that we've raised her hopes, we really must come up
with something to help poor Moggropple. Think of her,
caught in a mirror all these years. Aside from the professional
embarrassment, it must be terribly uncomfortable to be
squeezed into two dimensions when you've become accustomed to living in three."

Princess looked up at him sharply. Her eyes were bright
with inspiration. A smile spread across her face. She clapped
her hands, and with a soft humming of her little wings, she
rose from her chair and perched on the top of the cherry
armoire. "I think I've got it," she announced.

"My dear, I place the matter in your hands," said Kedrigern
with a bow and a flourish.

"All right. I'll take care of everything, but first you must
arrange the mirrors so they face that narrow crack in the wall.
Then keep out of sight and let me talk to Moggropple one by
one."

"As you wish. Come, Aponthey, give me a hand with these
mirrors."

"Not me. Pemmeny told me not to move them," Aponthey
said, raising his hands in a defensive gesture.

"Well, I'm telling you they have to be moved. As long as
they don't face each other, there's no danger. Come on."

Aponthey shook his head. "Those things are heavy. Use
your magic."

"Magic is precious, as you well know. One does not squander it moving furniture. Give me a hand."

Grumbling and muttering Aponthey rose and joined the
wizard. Little more was required than to turn each mirror
around so that it faced the wall of the barn rather than the
interior, but Aponthey's grunts and gasps and stifled cries
suggested the moving of mountains.

When the work was done, and Aponthey was once more seated, rubbing his back and groaning, Princess flew to a point in front of mirror I. Admonishing the men to remain silent and keep out of sight, she threw back the cover of the mirror.

"Who are you? Where's the wizard? I told him what he had to do, so why the delay?" Moggropple demanded.

"We've had a terrible accident. The other end of the barn has collapsed, and we're trapped in here. The only way out is that narrow crack in the wall," said the Princess anxiously, pointing over her shoulder, "and we can't fit through it."

"Well, I can. Let me out, girl."

"Not just now, thank you," Princess said, drawing the cover. She proceeded to mirror II, where she repeated the same story and received an almost identical response. On she went to III, and then skipped ahead to V. Each time, the exchange with Moggropple was similar to the first. Returning to mirror IV, she uncovered the glass and told the fabrication of the barn's collapse.

"Oh, fine, fine. Just what I needed. I finally have a chance to escape from this mirror, and now I'm trapped in a barn," Moggropple said sourly. "Well, go ahead, free me, if you've figured out how."

"But you wouldn't be trapped in here. You could slip through that narrow crack in the wall," Princess said innocently.

"Don't be absurd, child. Once I'm out of this mirror, I'll go back to being a fully rounded, three-dimensional woman. You don't think I'm going to go about thin as a shadow, do you? Be sensible. That's all very well when one is in a mirror, but in the real world it won't do."

"You're the real Moggropple!" Princess cried happily.

"Of course I am. What are you talking about, girl? Can't you tell a woman from her reflection?"

"They're very convincing reflections. But never mind that. Don't you have any idea how to get out?"

"Not the least clue. It was all very sudden, you see."

"Yes, I've heard."

Both women were thoughtfully silent for a time. At last,

Moggropple sighed and said, "Now, if only you had the crystal with you, there'd be no problem."

"The crystal?"

"The crystal of Caracodissa. Surely you've heard of it."

"It doesn't exist anymore, Moggropple. It's been smashed to bits," Princess said, lowering her voice to break the news.

Moggropple gave a wail of dismay. "Then it's gone! The spirit has been set free, and we'll never find it again! All hope is lost!"

"Wait a minute, now. Is it the crystal of Caracodissa that you need to get out, or the spirit in the crystal?"

"The spirit that indwells can set me free, that and only that. The crystal is . . . it's a crystal, nothing more. It's the spirit that counts."

Princess's face brightened. "If it's the spirit you need, then there's no problem. We have it in the house."

"But you told me that the crystal was smashed," said Moggropple, bewildered.

"It was, and the spirit flew off. But it came looking for you, and got caught in another enchantment. Now it's trapped in a crystal bell."

"It risked its own freedom to help me. . . . What a dear little spirit it is! We became quite close in the years we worked together, but I never suspected such devotion . . . such loyalty." Moggropple daintily wiped away a tear, and said in a husky voice, "It's very touching."

Kedrigern was on his way to the house at the first mention of the spirit. When Moggropple had recovered her self-possession, Princess said, "The crystal is coming. But I must tell you: when we asked it, it told us it did not know how to get you out."

"Oh, it knows, all right. It doesn't know it knows, but it knows, and I know it knows," Moggropple assured her.

And so it did. When Kedrigern returned and presented the bell to Princess, the little crystal was ablaze with swimming motes of light. At the sight of Moggropple, it began to tinkle merrily, vibrating with eagerness in Princess's fingers. It tugged her forward, toward the mirror, and drew itself to Moggropple's outstretched hand.

"It wants to come to me," Moggropple said.

"But how? The glass . . ."

"It must be remembering the counterspell. Trust it."

The bell pulled itself around, and Princess yielded her grip, very slowly, until she was holding it by the lip. All the darting lights in the crystal rushed to the handle, and when the handle touched the surface of the mirror, they streamed out in all directions, turning the mirror into an opaque luminosity, like a still lake under a full moon. The glow faded, and the glass seemed to melt away, just like a bright silvery mist dispersed by a morning breeze. Out of the mist stepped Moggropple, holding the bell.

"I told you it knew," she said coolly. She handed the bell to Kedrigern. "You may have this, if you like. It's just an ordinary crystal bell now."

"And the spirit? What became of the spirit? She's not . . ."

Moggropple brushed back her snowy hair and turned to display a glittering crystal earring from her left ear. "We're going to work together for a while. We've both been through difficult times, and we can be very supportive of each other."

"You must be famished," Princess said, taking the witch's arm. "Come inside. I'll have Collindor fix something for you, and you can tell me your whole story."

As the two women left to make their way through the labyrinth of furniture, Kedrigern went to Aponthey, who had been a silent onlooker to Moggropple's release. Smiling down on his host, Kedrigern gave the bell a shake, and it tinkled obediently.

"All fixed. Now you can ring for Collindor whenever you like, and the bell will behave like a regular bell."

"What about all those women in the mirrors?"

"Oh, they're gone. They were never really there in the first place. They were reflections of Moggropple, and now that she's out of the mirror, there's nothing to reflect."

Aponthey looked at him, shocked. "I don't like that very much."

"Neither do I. It was a nasty spell, any way you look at it."

"But where did those women go?"

Kedrigern shrugged his shoulders. "I don't know. Where does your reflection go when you walk away from a mirror?"

"I don't fool with mirrors. Can't trust them."

"Then don't worry about it. Here, take your bell. Let's join the ladies. I'm really for another helping of Collindor's excellent trifle. Working magic gives me an appetite."

Aponthey's guest bedroom was surprisingly tidy, the bed unexpectedly comfortable, for accommodations in an elderly bachelor's residence. It had been a busy day, and Princess and Kedrigern were happy to settle down for the night in such comfort. They blew out the candle and said good night, and lay for a time in relaxed silence.

"You had quite a long chat with Moggropple," Kedrigern observed.

"She was telling me about life inside the mirror. It was fascinating."

"Really? I should have thought it would be dreadfully dull. Repetitious at best."

"Oh no, not at all. She met all sorts of interesting people and had wonderful adventures."

After a thoughtful pause, Kedrigern said, "If it was so pleasant, why was Moggropple so eager to get out?"

"She missed her old life, and her friends, and her house. You saw how quickly she was off once she found her broom. Aponthey offered her a very nice little room for the night, but she didn't want to waste another minute." Princess yawned and did not speak for a time, then she added, "It would have been different if she'd been young, she said. If she were a little girl, she'd have been tempted to stay there. She could have been a queen, you know."

Kedrigern responded with a sleepy mumble. Princess went on, "It really made quite an impression on her. She's thinking of writing a book about it."

"A book?" Kedrigern asked, coming awake.

"That's what she told me."

"About being stuck inside a looking glass?"

"Well, not exactly. She's going to change things around a bit. I think she means to write it as though it happened to a little girl."

Kedrigern gave an irritable groan and raised himself on his elbows. He glared into the darkness petulantly. "That's the most ridiculous thing I've ever heard. A little girl wanders into a looking glass and has adventures . . . who would read such humbug?"

"Moggropple thinks it might be popular with children."

"She does, does she? What does Moggropple know about popularity? She's been inside a mirror for over a century."

"Well, she's certainly had time to reflect," Princess said with a little snuffle of smothered laughter.

"That's not very funny," said Kedrigern sourly.

Princess did not reply. She turned sharply on her side, her back to the wizard, and drew the light coverlet up around her shoulders.

I MARRIED A ROBOT

Ron Goulart

It wasn't exactly her husband who arrived in the sturdy neowood packing case.

What it appeared to be, once Maggie Quincade used an electric crowbar to pry the lid off the case that had just been delivered to her beachfront condo in the Malibu Sector of Greater Los Angeles, was a robot. A big, about six and a half feet tall and impressively wide, chromeplated robot stretched out on his back with his hefty metal arms stiff at his sides and his silvery metallic eyelids tight shut.

"What the hell is this?" Maggie inquired aloud. "I didn't order a huge, ugly Guardbot – and I can't think of anyone dippy enough to send me one as a gift."

She was a slim pretty woman, dark-haired and thirty-one. At the moment, she was wearing a short sinsilk nightie and a short nurayon robe. Bending from the waist, Maggie squinted in at the bulky bot. She reached and, gingerly, tapped the mechanical man on his broad chest.

That produced a hollow bonging sound.

Then the robot muttered, "Gurk," and his right arm made a faint ratcheting sound as it swung a few inches upward.

Clutched in the thick silvery fingers was a subpaper booklet entitled *Your Botz, Inc. Guardbot Operational Manual*.

Maggie made a negative gesture with both hands. "Thanks, no. I'm not interested in operating a big lumbering nitwit of a machine. Obviously you've been shipped to the wrong . . ."

A note fluttered free of the reclining mechanism's upraised hand, landing on his silvery midsection.

After inhaling and exhaling in a moderately annoyed way, Maggie reluctantly plucked up the note and unfolded it.

In a font she didn't recognize, the note said – *Ben wanted you to have this in the event of his death. Activate the bot and he'll explain everything. Well, actually, it wasn't supposed to be one of our Botz, Inc. Guardbots, but the timing was all off and this is the best I can do. Take care and my deepest sympathies. Ira.*

"Ben's not dead," she said, taking a step back from the crate that sat there on her new thermocarpet.

Actually Maggie wasn't absolutely certain her husband wasn't deceased. Since they'd separated five months ago she'd seen him once in person and twice on the phone. She hadn't had any communication from him at all in nearly a week.

Maggie eased forward again, eyeing the supine robot. "Ben faxed me some ad copy at our agency last week, but that was five or six days ago," she said to herself. "So, theoretically he could've kicked off since then."

But, no, that didn't make much sense. Their advertising agency was well-known.

Maggie leaned her buttocks against the edge of the case and took another look at the bulky Guardbot. "If one of the partners of Quincade & Quincade Advertising had died, it'd be in all the faxpapers and on the vidwall news and the netsheets and . . ." She trailed off, sniffling.

Surprisingly, she found she was crying.

"Jesus, why am I getting sentimental over that mean-minded, immoral, philandering son of a bitch?"

"Gurk," murmured the bot once again.

"All right, OK." She pulled the manual free of the mechanical man's grip.

After scanning the opening pages of the section titled *Congratulations On Owning The Best Bot For The Buck*, Maggie tossed the booklet over atop her new floating plasglaz coffee table and knelt beside the crate.

"Where the heck is Button A-6?"

When she lifted the robot's left arm, it made a raspy creaking noise.

"Didn't they oil this thing at the darn factory?"

Button A-6 was in the chromeplated armpit, along with B-2 and C-8.

Maggie sighed again, pushed A-6 twice, B-2 once and C-8 three times.

As the big bot groaned and sat up, Maggie jumped back and away from the crate.

"You sure took long enough to get me up and running, Mag," the robot told her.

She frowned. The voice coming out of the mechanical man's voxgrid was that of Ben Quincade. "How come your voice has that distinctive nasal twang when you don't have a nose?"

"Of course I've got a damn nose." He swung up a metal hand to locate the nose on his face. He, instead, whapped himself on his prominent metal chin.

"Well, yes there's a little button of a nose," she conceded. "But nothing like the Roman schnoz you . . . Hey, wait now. How come you're talking with Ben's voice at all?"

He located his nose, felt it. Then he poked and prodded his torso. "Shit, I'm dead," he realized. "Yeah, that's it. They succeeded in knocking me off. But Ira was supposed to install the –"

"Ira Tandofsky, your buddy at Botz, Inc. over in the Laguna Sector?"

"That Ira, yeah."

Maggie, eyes narrowed, was studying the robot's rather blank face. "What did Ira do? Make a download copy of your nitwit brain on a silchip and stick it in this bot's coco?"

"Well, that wasn't the original deal, no. You're right about the brain chip, but I didn't expect to end up a Guardbot." He held up his metal hands, studied them for a moment, shook his head. "But I am definitely one."

"And you were expecting to be what?"

"An android dupe of myself, obviously," answered Ben. "Well, no, I was basically hoping to live into my eighties at least and keep inhabiting my original body. After all, I exercise regularly, eat a sensible vegan diet and –"

"It was probably all the tomcatting around you did that wore you down, Ben,"

He held up a single silvery finger. "One little affair, Mag," he said. "And a fleeting one at that, yet you –"

"Fleeting? Two and a half weeks in a houseboat off the San Pedro Sector is your nitwit idea of fleeting?" Hands on hips, she scowled at the robot. "And what about that other bimbo who has that condo up in the Cold Water Canyon Sector of GLA?"

"Mavis? C'mon, I was just teaching her how to play flamenco guitar. You're so violently jealous that you misinterpreted the –"

"Oh, so? I suppose that tapdancer you rendezvoused with in that orbiting motel satellite was –"

"We used Denise in those commercials we produced for Foodz, remember? That was purely and simply –"

"Never mind," cut in his estranged wife. "Just explain to me how come you've intruded into my private life. We're officially separated, Ben."

"Hey, don't you have any heart left? I'm dead and –"

"Bullshit, who says you're dead?"

"Boy, it's just like old times again," complained the robot. "You'll argue about anything, Maggie. If I'm not dead, then why did Ira install the copy of my brain in this bot?"

"That's exactly what I'm wondering."

Slowly, swaying some, the chromeplated robot rose up and then stepped clear of the crate. Glancing down at himself. Ben observed, "Damn, I don't have any private parts."

"Good," said his wife.

"See, I still don't understand why Ira didn't install the copy of my brain in the android replica of my body he was constructing at Botz, Inc."

"Not enough time."

"How do you know that?"

She handed him the note. "Says so here."

After reading the message twice, Ben said, "I'm going to have to contact Ira and find out why in the hell he –"

"Just tell him to send a skyvan to haul you and that damn crate out of here."

"No, we don't want to do that," he warned. "Because if I'm dead, then you may be in danger, too. That's why I instructed Ira to ship me here after I got killed. So I could warn you."

"Why didn't you warn me before you were dead – if you actually are dead?"

"You know how you are, Mag – you would've panicked. And I wasn't absolutely sure that –"

"And in danger from whom?"

When the big robot shook his head, it produced a creaking noise. "Now that you mention it, Mag . . . I don't know," Ben admitted.

"You're walking around as a robot and are even more unsightly than in your previous format," said his wife, scrutinizing him through narrowed eyes, "and you have no notion what you were afraid of?"

There were a few more bonging sounds when he tapped the side of his skull. "This is odd," he said slowly. "I have the feeling that I did know."

"OK, fine. So tell me, huh!"

"I can't seem to. I don't remember the details at all anymore," the big robot confided. "I think maybe I found out something important . . . and it has to do with our agency."

"Can robots suffer from partial amnesia?"

"It could be that Ira screwed up the brain chip when he was installing it. You know, accidentally erased some stuff."

"That seems unlikely, Ben, since he's an expert at this kind of work," said Maggie. "Your original brain, you know, wasn't all that effective. Maybe you're just having one of your memory lapses."

"I wouldn't be likely to forget two attempts on my life," he said, annoyed.

She took a step closer to the mechanical man. "See? You're remembering. What attempts on your life?"

The robot tapped the side of his head, concentrating. "When I was at the Holowrestling matches at the Burbank Sector MiniArena a week ago, somebody tried to shove me over the edge of one of the exit ramps," he said. "Yeah, if I hadn't caught onto a railing, I'd have fallen two hundred feet."

"There's a force screen to prevent that."

"It'd been turned off," he answered. "Then four days ago, when I was powercycling along the bikepath on the beach, somebody shot at me." He held up two shiny metal fingers. "Twice with an old-fashioned bullet-rifle."

"Who?"

His shoulders creaked when he shrugged. "No idea."

"Was that when you went around to Ira and asked him to make a download copy of your brain and get an android ready?"

"Yeah, because I was certain I was in danger," he said.

"But if you knew something important, something dangerous – why not just go to the authorities?"

"I must've had a reason, Mag. But that's another thing I can't seem to remember."

"Well, nary a soul has tried to knock me off, Ben." She backed until she was sitting on the neohide sofa. "It's possible that I'm not involved in this at all – whatever the heck this is." She shook her head. "You're a very annoying person and there are probably multitudes of irate husbands and mistreated women out in Greater Los Angeles alone who want you dead. If I weren't a humane, nonviolent person, I'd have done you in myself long ago for your infidelities alone. From the moment we shuttled back from the orbiting Episcopal Church of SoCal, you started chasing every dimwitted woman who –"

"Hold on a minute, Mag." He sat beside her and the sofa shimmied. "I still don't understand how come you didn't know I was dead."

"You're not dead," she suggested, folding her arms under her breasts. "And I'm starting to wonder if this isn't just some cheesy trick to get back into our condo. But as a bid for sympathy, it –"

"You honestly think I'd spend the remainder of my life as a Guardbot with no private parts just so I could bask in the radiance of your venomous personality?" he inquired. "I came here to help you, Maggie. Even though you cast me –"

"What in heaven's name is going on out here, Maggie my flower?"

The door to the master bedroom had come whispering open and a large redheaded man, about the height and width of the robot, wearing a neowool nightshirt and not fully awake, emerged into the living room.

"Curt Barnum," said Ben, standing up. "I'm not even cold in my grave and my Chief Account Executive is shacking up with my wife."

Barnum glanced at Maggie, frowning. "Why does this bot have Ben's voice, sweetheart?"

"Ben, please." Maggie caught the robot's arm before he could climb over the coffee table and go charging at the husky red-haired man.

Ben was making rumbling sounds inside his metallic chest. "Of all the goons in our office, Mag," he said, "why did you pick Curt Barnum?"

"He's a very sensitive man and you've never fully appreciated him."

"Sensitive? He –"

"Can you guys fill me in?" asked Barnum, looking from Maggie to the robot. "I don't understand why this mechanism seems to have the idea that it's Ben Quincade or –"

"Go home, Curt," suggested Maggie. "This is a domestic problem and I'm afraid I'm going to have to help Ben one last time."

"What's Ben got to do with this?"

"I'm Ben." The robot bonged a fist against his chest.

Barnum shrugged. "I'll see you at the office tomorrow, Maggie flower," he said and went into the bedroom to collect his clothes.

"I may take tomorrow off," she called.

Maggie set her palm computer down atop the floating plazglass coffee table. "Well, OK, your earthly remains aren't in any of the obvious locations," she announced, leaning back in the tin armchair and sighing. "I ran your DNA-ID through every morgue, hospital, funeral parlor and potter's field in the country – and checked Mexico and Central America for good measure."

"I guess that's comforting." He had a panel in his chest open and was using the built-in computer he'd discovered there. "This is neat."

"You are also not incarcerated in any known penal institution, loony bin, homeless center or military base," Maggie continued. "I've tried your description with all of them, plus hotels, motels and bordellos. There looked like there was going to be a match down in the San Diego Sector, but it turned out to be a gorilla who'd escaped from the zoo."

"Better sleep with a gorilla than shack up with Curt Barnum," the robot said. "He's got shaggy legs."

"At least they aren't chromeplated."

Ben said, "I can't locate Ira Tandofsky at all. Not at his office or at home. His answering bot at both locations just plays a thirty-sec vid where he claims he's going to be out of town for an indefinite period. It's dated the day before yesterday."

"Same day he stuffed your brain chip into a leftover robot?"

Ben nodded. "Ira looked pretty agitated on the –"

"Ira is congenitally agitated. He always looks that way, Ben."

"No, this is exceptional nervousness, even for Ira. He keeps peering over his shoulder, glancing left and right, fidgeting in his chair," he explained, poking a finger into the opening. "Come over and I'll replay the message for you."

"Thank you, no. The prospect of gazing deeply into your interior doesn't appeal to me."

Ben shrugged and shut the panel. "There's something about Ira I can't quite remember."

"Something about where he is?"

"Yeah, a place he might go to lie low."

"Why exactly would Ira want to lie low?"

"They may be after him, too."

His wife stood. "Unless I want you underfoot forever, we're going to have to resolve this mess," she told him. "What say we go to your place to see if there's anything of interest there?"

"Clues, you mean?"

"Clues, receipts from motel orgies, some floozie's discarded lingerie. Stuff like that, Ben."

He rose. "That's a good constructive suggestion," he said.

"You look extremely silly," remarked Maggie.

"I'm not used," said the robot, "to running around naked."

He and the dark-haired young woman were walking down the ramp leading to the condo complex parking/landing area. The autumn night was chill and overcast.

"Technically," she pointed out, "you can't refer to a robot as being naked."

Ben unfastened the top two buttons of the black overcoat he was wearing. One of his old ones that he'd left behind when he moved out, it was no longer a perfect fit. "Eventually I'm going to need a roomier coat."

"You have always, dear heart, had a problem accepting reality. You're a robot now, Ben, and robots aren't noted for modesty. That beret's dippy, too."

He readjusted the black beret on his chrome head. "I'm not used to going around bald either."

"Again you're being unrealistic. Robots don't have hair, hence –"

"How come Curt calls you flower?"

"It's a term of endearment, obviously. He happens to be, as I already told you, an extremely sensitive man. Also tender and poetic."

"He must be the only sensitive, tender and poetic account exec in all of Greater LA."

Maggie said, "What say we lay off my private life and just go over to your place to see what we can find out there, huh?"

"That's exactly what we're in the process of doing, Mag. Don't nag," he said. "Eventually we're going to have to locate Ira. If he's vanished, then I may never get into my android body or – Hold on!" Ben suddenly took hold of her arm with one big metallic hand.

"Hey, it was repulsive enough being pawed by you when

you were flesh and blood," she mentioned, pulling free and continuing on down the slanting plazramp. "Being fondled by robots is even less –"

"Just halt right there, Mag." The big robot trotted to her side, then pointed down at her crimson skycar some two hundred feet below them. "Now that I'm a Guardbot, you know, I've picked up a lot of terrific additional abilities."

"What this time?" she inquired, "Does it involve opening a door in your backside?"

"Well, I seem to be able to sense dangerous devices." He nodded toward the vehicle. "I'm getting a message that somebody's planted a bomb in your car."

"Oh, c'mon, Ben, quit trying to play hero." She took a step forward. "Of all the dippy notions."

He caught hold of her again. "Even though you never did this during the seven long miserable years we were married, Maggie, you might try now to entertain a point of view that doesn't agree with yours."

"*Eight* long miserable years," she corrected.

With his free hand he tugged the Guardbot instruction manual from his overcoat pocket. "Page 232," he instructed as he thrust the book toward her.

Ignoring it, she shrugged. "OK, all right, I'll take your word for it," she said. "But why in the hell would anybody want to –"

"Hit the deck!" Ben dropped to the ramp, yanking her with him and stretching his big metal body down flat.

"What did I tell you about pawing me?" She started to struggle upright.

With a widespread metal hand he forced her down. "It's about to go off."

There came a huge whomping sound, the ground and the ramp shook.

The crimson skycar rose up into the night, not as a complete entity but in a twisted, smoking collection of parts, components and shatters of scorched red plazmetal.

"You were right," conceded his wife in a small voice. "But why?"

"That's one of the things," said the robot, "I'm trying damn hard to remember."

Traveling in a rattletrap skycab, they reached Ben's apartment at Boatown Three off the coast of the Santa Monica Sector a few minutes shy of midnight.

"Your advent," Maggie was telling the robot as the taxi settled to a wobbly landing on one of the Boatown docks, "hasn't been all that propitious."

"Here we are, folks," announced the voxbox of the cab as both passenger doors went popping open.

Maggie continued as they disembarked, "First off you scare a decent, sensitive man like Curt Barnum out into the night."

"Well, Mag, that's what often happens when you're in the sack with somebody else's wife and he comes home unexpectedly," Ben pointed out. "And I wish to hell you'd quit referring to a lout like Curt as sensitive."

"Folks," called the cab, "the fare's forty-six bucks."

Maggie, making an angry noise, halted on the plazplanks of the dock. "And there's one more thing." Her nostrils flared. "I had a perfectly fine skycar until you –"

"Don't I know it was perfectly fine? The damned thing was mine until that duplicitous attorney of yours forced me to turn it over to you."

"Forty-six bucks," repeated the skycab.

"Pay him," suggested Maggie evenly.

Spreading his hands wide, Ben said, "I left my wallet on my other body."

She inhaled sharply, marched back to the cab and jabbed her Banx card into the meter slot. "Exactly forty-six bucks, asshole, and no tip," she said, tight-lipped.

"Much obliged, ma'am."

The card came popping out of the slot, Maggie caught it and the cab rose up into the midnight sky.

"And, because of you," Maggie resumed as she followed the overcoated robot along a row of moored house-boats, "I also had to devote two full hours of my life to answering halfwit questions from the SoCal State Police, the Native Californian

Insurance Syndicate and at least a full dozen of my pea-brained, overly inquisitive damn neighbors." She stopped still, hands on hips. "Is this the same houseboat where you dallied with that blonde floozie?"

"Red-haired floozie." Balancing carefully, arms held out at his sides, Ben walked across the narrow gangplank from the dock to the deck of the fourteenth houseboat. "And this rundown pesthole was about all I could afford after your shyster persuaded me to bestow most of my income on you as a separation settlement and –"

"I'm hoping we'll find you – your real self, that is – inside here." Maggie made her way, gingerly, over the shimmying gangplank. "Probably in a drunken or drugged stupor. Soon as we do, I'll take my leave."

"My lifeless corpse is what we'll likely find." He stepped up to the door of the deck cabin, spoke into the voice ID box. "Avast, you lubbers, pipe me aboard."

"What an extremely dippy password."

"It came with the boat."

"Aye, aye, captain," said the door as it swung open inward.

Maggie nudged the big robot across the darkened threshold. "OK, let's make a quick search."

"Hold it," warned Ben. "Something's wrong."

"Not another bomb?"

"No, nope. I'm sensing something else." He, very carefully, entered the parlor.

"It must be very difficult for a robot to tiptoe."

"Hush." He made a rattling, throat-clearing sound. "Lights, please."

Light blossomed.

"I thought so," said Ben forlornly.

"Is she dead?"

The body of a pretty, sunbrown blonde of about thirty was sprawled on her back on an oval carpet near a plazrocker.

"This is an android." Ben was kneeling beside the body.

The mechanism's midsection had two small sooty holes burned through its tunic, sinflesh and metal undercoating. A few small gears, twists of wire and glittering little springs had spilled out, along with splashes of long-dry machine oil.

"That's Portia Talwin," recognized Maggie. "What's a defunct simulacrum of the Advertising Manager of the Serv-U, Inc. outfit doing in your place, Ben?"

When the robot stood, he creaked slightly. "Well, Portia and I – the real Portia – had become sort of friendly the past few weeks," he admitted.

"Another dame? Won't your philandering ever cease?"

"Hey, you and I are officially separated," he reminded his wife.

Maggie was moving toward the doorway to the bedroom. "Let's see if you're around here someplace, too, Ben."

He sprinted as best he could, catching hold of her arm. "Whoa, it'll be easier if I just use some of my built-in gear," he suggested. "If I'm in any of the other rooms, I'll sense it."

"I don't know why anybody would want to show off about being a gadget."

The robot began making small whirring noises inside his broad metallic chest. His eyes flickered momentarily green. After a moment, he shook his head. "Nope, no, I'm not here. Drugged, drunk, dead or in any other condition."

"Darn, I was hoping we'd find you within a reasonable time and I could get back to the important stuff in my life again."

"Your concern is appreciated." Ben strode to a linoleum covered sofa and sat, nodding at the defunct android. "I have no recollection of this, no memory of finding this andy here. So it either happened after I did the brain content download with Ira or it's one more thing I've forgotten."

Maggie slowly circled the android dupe of Portia Talwin. "Whoever used a kilgun on her probably thought, at first anyway, that they were knocking off the actual Portia," she suggested. "Had she hinted to you that anybody was out to kill her, too?"

The robot frowned, struggling to remember. "Wait now, I'm getting a flash of something, Mag," he told his wife. "Yeah, this whole mess has to do with Portia. She's involved with it."

Maggie lowered herself into the plazrocker and eyed her husband. "Well, that's obvious, isn't it? The poor woman – or a reasonable facsimile – is lying dead in your darn parlor, Ben."

He drummed on one metallic knee with his metallic fingers, producing little ponging sounds. "Seeing Portia, it's triggered some memories. But shit, they're vague," he said. "It occurs to me that maybe she confided in me about some trouble at Serv-U – something crooked they were up to with those robot servants and housekeepers they manufacture."

"Such as?"

"I can't dredge that up yet." His fingers tapped again on his knee. "Could be, though, that it was something to do with Trevor Rawls."

"The CEO of Serv-U?" She stood suddenly up, causing the rocker to tick back and forth. "Don't go making trouble for him or we'll lose the account. That bills twenty-one million dollars a year for us, remember? Rawls is such a nasty guy, he'd dump our ad agency for a lot less than accusing him of attempted murder."

"Just thought of something." Ben rose, went lumbering across his parlor.

He crossed into the small bedroom and opened a closet.

"Now what?" Following, Maggie watched him poke around inside the closet, using the lightbeam built into his right thumb for illumination.

"My two neohyde suitcases aren't here."

"You figure you deliberately took off then? Packed and went someplace to hide?"

"Seems possible," he acknowledged. "Thing is, where the hell did I go?"

"I was hoping you two folks could tell me that." A large blond man was smiling in at them, framed in the bedroom doorway. He was a cyborg and his coppery right hand had a kilgun built into it.

The forefinger that formed the barrel was pointing at Maggie.

*   *   *

"Some Guardbot you turned out to be," accused Maggie, glaring across at Ben.

"Hey, I've only been a damn robot for . . . what? . . . a few hours."

"So typical of you." She took two steps back away from him. "You seem to have an excuse for every darn –"

"C'mon, folks," cut in the cyborg intruder, gesturing with his gunhand. "We had this dump bugged, so we'd know if anybody came nosing –"

"Oh, go ahead and shoot him," invited Maggie, increasing the distance between her and the robot version of her husband. "He's supposed to have all sorts of built-in warning devices, yet he lets a flatfooted oaf sneak up on us and doesn't even –"

"I'm not exactly flatfooted, lady," contradicted the cyborg. "Fact is, ma'am, that before I became a thug I was rising in the SoCal Community Modern Dance Troupe and was noted for –"

"If you hadn't been blathering," Ben told Maggie as he backed further from her and nearer the thug, "I'd have been better able to monitor my sensors."

"Oh, sure, blame me for your darn failings." Turning her back on him, she started striding toward the door to the bathroom.

"Hold it, lady. I'll have to shoot you if –"

"Now!" Maggie dived for the thermocarpeted floor.

Ben, while the gunman was momentarily distracted, lunged for him.

Before the husky blond man could swing his gunhand around to fire at the charging bot, Ben was right there.

The robot hit him twice, hard, on the jaw with his big metallic right fist.

"Oof," remarked the gunman as he went slamming back against the bedroom wall.

He folded up in the middle, blond head rocking forward. Then he went slumping into a lopsided sprawl and passed into temporary oblivion.

Maggie laughed. "Well, you're not as dense as I thought," she said.

Ben eyed her, then knelt next to the fallen intruder. "Nope, I recognize a diversion when I see one, darling."

She joined him, frowning down at the blond cyborg. "We make a pretty good team actually," she admitted. "Do you know this goon?"

"No, nope. And he hasn't got any ID material on him." The robot shook his chrome-plated head. "I'm going to have to use some of my interrogation gear."

She glanced toward the doorway to the parlor. "Better do it swiftly, Ben," she advised. "They're sure to send more louts to replace this one."

Nodding, he yanked the unconscious thug up off the floor and tossed him into the nearest chair.

Leaning back in the passenger seat of the climbing black skycar, Maggie conceded, "OK, you didn't do badly."

"Keep in mind that I've never given anybody an injection of Trutok before." He was occupying the driveseat. "And I did manage to swipe the guy's skycar without a hitch."

"Well, yes, true," his wife admitted. "But I couldn't help feeling a mite uneasy when you had to stop midway through the hijacking to double-check the details on how to do it in the Guardbot instruction book."

"Better safe than sorry."

Maggie asked, "And you're sure we're heading for the right destination?"

"Yep. When that thug mentioned that they'd tracked the real Portia as far as the Ensenada Sector and then lost the trail, it jogged my chip."

The borrowed skycar was heading south through the night, the lights of Greater Los Angeles ten thousand feet below.

Maggie, arms folded under her breasts, said, "That was impressive when you exclaimed, 'Eureka!' and whapped your forehead."

"It was an important moment, when I remembered that Ira has a hideaway down in Ensenada."

"But that's Ira, not Portia."

"No, they've got to be in cahoots in some way," said the robot. "That explains the gaps in my memory."

"Um," she said, not exactly agreeing.

The skycar continued quietly southward.

She finally said, "Curt can help us."

"In what possible manner, for God's sake?"

"Well, we're up to here in a mess, Ben, in case it hasn't occurred to you."

"It has," the robot said. "The guy who runs one of our biggest agency accounts is also behind the efforts to kill me. So we have to figure out how to expose him without annoying too many other people up at Serv-U."

"Of course, that thug might've been wrong about Trevor Rawls working secretly for a group of very conservative vigilantes who –"

"Not just Rawls, but other execs up there," put in Ben. "Right now we don't even know how many are involved. All we've got is the fact that some of their top tech people have worked out a special type of servo – one that can be instructed to do a little assassination work on the side. You plant one in the home of one of the people on this group's shit list and it goes to work. It looks like a regular, ordinary cleaning bot, cooking bot, something like that. Slips in by security and takes care of the enemy."

"If only Portia hadn't confided in you."

"Well, she did confide in me and they found out about it. That explains the attempts on my life – and maybe the fact that I seem to have vanished from the face of the Earth," he said. "And, according to our thug, there are a dozen of these special servos all ready to be shipped out. We've got to stop that."

"Certainly, ninny," said his wife. "But we don't have to do it directly. I'm betting that everybody at the top of Serv-U isn't involved in this. Once Rawls and his cronies are ousted, we want the survivors to think our agency is still a swell outfit."

"Agreed, but how does sensitive Curt fit in?"

"His ex-wife's an Investigative Anchor with Newz," explained Maggie. "We'll get her the information, let her break the story worldwide. That'll stop the assassinations but not draw undue attention to Quincade & Quincade."

"I thought his former wife was an electronic accordion player with a pacifist marching band."

"That's a different ex-wife. This one, trust me, works for Newz."

"How come such a sensitive guy has so many former wives?"

"Two isn't a large quantity."

He nodded at the control dash. "We'll be there in about five minutes, Mag."

"OK, so let's," she suggested, "work out a foolproof plan."

The robot shivered. "I'd have preferred a plan that," he said as he and Maggie made their way along the brightly lit Ensenada Sector street, "didn't call for me to wander around jaybird naked."

"We've already gone over what's proper attire for a robot and what isn't," she reminded. "You're still having a big problem – and let's face it, this is one of the main reasons we parted – admitting that I'm smarter than you. Especially when it comes to strategy."

"And you're still harboring the cockeyed notion that your intelligence equals mine."

A Border Patrol skycar, shaped like a huge piñata and brightly colored, flew swiftly overhead in the direction of the Borderland Strip.

"Look, since you suspect that Ira and Portia may be holed up in an underground villa beneath this secondhand robot sales lot that Ira's cousin Lupita runs down here – well, the best way to approach the place is by pretending to be somebody who wants to unload a robot. And normal everyday robots don't wear overcoats and berets."

"OK, but the whole plan strikes me as lacking in subtlety."

"We don't have time for subtlety, dear." Maggie was wearing his overcoat and beret, plus a low-cost blonde wig.

"Your disguise isn't all that convincing either."

"What do you expect from a wig purchased at a shop that calls itself the 24-Hour Tourist Trap? Besides, Lupita's never seen me."

"With all my built-in accessories, I could've worked out a better way of approaching the problem."

Maggie took hold of his arm. "There's Loco Lupita's Used Bot Lot up ahead. Try to look used."

The lot was covered by a huge see-through plazglass dome and stretched across almost an acre of close-cropped neograss. There were a hundred or more robots in lopsided rows lined up on the grounds, plus a few dented android butlers, a grey-haired nanny sim and a wheeled wetbar servo. Floating above the dome was a large litesign announcing *We Got Your Bot!* There were no customers to be seen.

"*Buenas noches*," said the smiling young woman who came hurrying out of the neowood office to greet them as they stepped through the entryway. "You didn't buy that rattletrap bot off me, did you? No, *no es posible*."

Maggie whispered to Ben, "Is this her?"

He nodded. "I happen to be," he told the approaching Lupita, "a topflight example of the robotic arts."

Ignoring him, Lupita eased closer to Maggie, frowning. "You're not intending to try to sell this pile of junk to me, are you?"

"Well, yes, I'd like to see how much I can get for it."

Lupita came striding over, kicked the robot in the left knee. His leg bonged and he said, "Ow."

"Shoddy construction." Lupita made a disdainful face, shook her head. "But then most Guardbot products are shoddy."

"Shoddy, my ass," said Ben, angry. "And how can you criticize a product made by a company your own cousin works for? I'm a near-mint example of –"

"How come you know about my cousin, *amigo?*"

Maggie suggested, "Let's go into your office and talk this over. I'm sure we can make a deal."

"No, I think I better alert . . . awk!"

Ben had used the stungun built into his left forefinger on the suspicious lot owner. Then he trotted forward, catching the unconscious woman just as she began to totter. Slipping a metal arm around her, he carried Lupita into her office.

"Your vanity's going to be the ruin of you," warned Maggie, following him inside. "And me, too, more than likely."

"You never could tell the difference between healthy self-esteem and narcissism, Mag." After placing Lupita face down across her neowood desk, he glanced around the small office.

"They must have security cams hereabouts," reminded Maggie. "So your up and stunning her out in the open is going to bring down –"

"I disabled all those before I shot her," he said.

"How'd you do that?"

"It's another built-in knack. Involves sonics."

"And what are you sensing about this alleged concealed villa?"

The robot genuflected and tapped several of the plaztile squares. "There's an entry ramp right below this movable section of the floor," he answered.

"Who's down there?"

"No guards," he said after a few seconds. "Only Portia and Ira and . . ."

"And who?"

"Well, I seem to be down there in the villa with them," he said quietly.

"Is that a standard Guardbot function?" Maggie inquired as they descended the ramp leading to the main corridor of the underground hideaway.

"Dismantling the security system electronically, you mean?"

"That, yes. Is it?"

The robot answered, "I think I've been able to modify myself somewhat since becoming a bot."

"I'm glad to see you're adjusting so well," observed his wife. "In your human days you complained about all sorts of minor –"

"Silence from here on," he cautioned in a tinny whisper. "They're in the room up ahead on the left – the one with the simulated oaken door."

"That includes you?"

He nodded. He motioned Maggie to stay back, then, slowing his pace, he approached the door.

The robot hunched his shoulders and pointed his right hand at the door's lock mechanism. From his middle finger shot a beam of sizzling, greenish light.

Shimmering, the lock ceased to be.

Ben grunted and went charging forward to slam the door hard with his metallic left shoulder.

As the door popped open inward, he dove over the threshold and, in a crouch, charged into the room beyond.

Maggie followed cautiously in his wake. When she looked into the large living room, she saw the robot standing wide-legged in the middle of an oval thermorug. He had his right hand pointing at a blonde woman who was apparently the true Portia Talwin.

Portia was scowling at the bot and blowing on the fingers of her right hand. A coppery kilgun lay on the plaztiles near her booted feet. "You could've fried my fingers, you dumbbell," she complained.

"No, he's a crack shot," said the lean Ira Tandofsky. "That's a standard feature of all our Guardbots." He was tied in a tin rocker with plazcord.

And tied to a rubberoid Morris chair was Ben Quincade. "Maggie," he said grinning. "I didn't expect you'd come to my rescue, hon. It's great that you still care enough to –"

"What did I tell you about calling me 'hon'? Especially in public."

"Listen, I'm really pleased that you –

"Could we," cut in the robot, "start getting this mess untangled, folks?"

Ben, the actual Ben, frowned at the robot. "You must be my simulacrum," he realized. "Jesus, Ira, I know you told me you were rushed, but –"

"Let's quit the chitchat." Maggie walked over to scoop up the fallen kilgun. "And instead explain why you're shacked up here with this prune-faced bimbo who –"

"If you had the sex appeal of an avocado," suggested Portia, "he wouldn't have dumped you."

"He didn't dump me – I dumped him."

"He's actually not shacked up here. It's obvious the guy's a prisoner," pointed out the robot. "Now, Ben, what's been going on?"

"Portia came to me some days back very unsettled, to tell me that Serv-U had this plan to use servos for political assassinations," he began. "Trevor Rawls was behind it. She wanted me to help her get what she'd uncovered to a reliable government agency without her being directly –"

"We know about most of that already," said Maggie, impatient. "Tell us why they were trying to kill you."

Ben answered, "Well, they found out that Portia had confided in me."

"How'd they learn about that?" asked the bot.

"You ought to know about that," Ben said, "since you have a copy of my brain in your noggin."

"There are some lapses in my memory."

Ben frowned at Ira. "How'd that happen?"

Ira looked up at the beamed ceiling. "I was in a real rush installing the chip, Ben, and I guess I mishandled it."

"Why the rush?" asked the bot.

"When I thought he was dead, I went ahead with his instructions," explained the tech. "But then I began to suspect that Rawls and his goons knew about me, too. I couldn't wait until the android sim of Ben was finished, so I made do with a Guardbot that was handy. I shipped him to you, as Ben had instructed, and took off for here to hide out."

"See, hon, I was thinking of you at the end."

"But how come you didn't end? And why'd Ira think you had?"

Ben made a partial shrug. "I hate to admit this, but I got a little edgy after the third attempt on my life so I decided to hide out at a little place of Portia's in the Coronado Sector. When he ceased hearing from me, Ira got the notion I'd been bumped off. The thing was –"

"Ben didn't know," picked up Portia, "that I'd been thinking over everything and concluded that it would be much smarter to blackmail Rawls instead of blowing the whistle on his scheme. Government congratulations as opposed to a million bucks or more."

"So when I showed up and wasn't especially eager to go along with that new plan of hers – she stungunned me," said Ben, frowning over at the blonde. "That was to keep me quiet."

"Then she broke in here," said Ira, "because Ben had mentioned it once as a safe place to lie low. Portia bribed my duplicitous cousin, which wasn't that hard to do apparently. But what can you expect from somebody who makes her living schlepping secondhand robots?"

"And," said Ben, "Portia's been holding us here while she works out a deal with Rawls. And, of course, his people are trying to find her and knock her off – and us, too, I figure."

Maggie shook her head, looking from her real husband to the scowling Portia. "What about the defunct dupe of this floozie we found in your tacky residence?"

Ben said, "She sent the sim there – most upper-level execs have sims of themselves to handle donkey work jobs – to see if I'd left anything behind that might have to do with the Serv-U plot or where she was hiding us out."

"One of Rawls' goons spotted the android there and, thinking it was really me, shot it," said Portia.

"Are you following all this so far, sweetheart?" Ben asked his wife.

"As much as I want to, sure."

"It would still be much smarter," suggested Portia, "to let Rawls pay us to keep quiet. They go ahead and kill a few useless politicians and business people and we get maybe two million."

"Nope, we won't bother with blackmail." Maggie tapped the robot on the arm. "Watch everybody while I make a call to Curt Barnum."

Her husband asked, "Why are you phoning that nitwit?"

She replied, "He's going to help us break this story."

"OK, if that's what you want to do," said Ben. "But untie us, huh?"

"After I make the call."

He watched her as she crossed to the vidphone that sat on the floating neowood coffee table. "You came searching for me, risked your life to find me," Ben told her. "That's a sure sign that you're still fond of me, Mag. We're still business partners and it seems to me that we ought to try to be a couple again, too."

Maggie gave him a sympathetic smile. "Afraid not, hon," she said, picking up the receiver. "But if nobody minds – I would like to keep the robot."

MRS WILSON AND THE BLACK ARTS OF MRS BEELZEBUB FROM NUMBER SIX

Steven Pirie

Mrs Wilson knew they were not *Earthly* cats. Mr Wilson had thrown his boot at them to shut them up, for a start, and somehow they'd thrown it back. And it was the way their eyes shone piercing green even in the daylight. At night, in their sepulchral wailing and tireless leaping at the moon, they seemed very much *otherworldly*. It was a worry.

In the kitchen, at number eight, Mrs Wilson paused in stacking biscuits on her best crockery. She glanced beyond the window and over the fence into Mrs Beelzebub's garden next door to where the cats still gathered. In the corner, part hidden behind the rickety wooden shed and the glorious apple tree, the vortices to *beyond* shimmered blue and green in the morning sunshine.

Mrs Wilson sighed; such a crime to sully a garden with the supernatural. Gardens were meant to be calm places, havens from the horrors of *outside*. And she'd rather hoped the cats and the portals and the demonic folk would be gone by now. Then, things would likely be easier, less *messy*.

"More tea, ladies?" said Mrs Wilson, stepping through into

the living room and settling the silver tray upon the occasional table. "And a custard cream, perhaps?"

'She'll have to go.' Mrs Rose from number three took a cup and saucer. Tea spilled where it shook a little in her grasp. "It's not natural. Twice last week my Ronald was set upon by denizens of the underworld. Ugly buggers, they were, squat and warty and fly; they chased him all the way to Lemmings Road and back. It was all he could do to escape with his mortal soul."

Mrs Trent from number one nodded. "On Tuesday, my Frank was overcome by nether-worldly fumes seeping out from under Mrs Beelzebub's front door. It turned him unusually amorous." She straightened her perm and her eyelid twitched. "And I can tell you that upset my week completely."

Mrs Wilson sat quietly. She knew what was coming. Ever since the Beelzebubs had moved in next door – *was it really just a month ago that the clouds had split asunder to the herald of dark trumpeters, and the black coach-and-four had trundled, bold as bold, up Sunshine Terrace?* – it seemed, just because she was the Neighbourhood Watch co-coordinator, as if she had been designated *in charge*, as if ultimately all responsibility ended up at her door.

"We thought perhaps you'd have a word," said Mrs Rose, a custard cream part-raised to her mouth. "Oh, in your official, neighbourly capacity, of course."

Mrs Wilson rubbed at stubble on her chin. "It's true all's not as it should be, next door," she said. "Though, apart from the cats, and the comings and goings, they do tend to keep themselves to themselves. But, very well, I'll pop over and see Mrs Beelzebub first thing after lunch. I'm sure she's a reasonable sort. I'm sure there'll be no harm in a quiet chat."

"Then we'll leave it in your hands," said Mrs Trent.

"But think on she'll have to go," said Mrs Rose.

Mrs Trent slurped tea. "For sure, Mrs Wilson, we'll be relying on you."

It grew dark, after lunch; early-dusk dark. Storm clouds, rain-bloated and angry-bruised, rumbled in from the west. A wind shrieked down Mrs Wilson's chimney and blew soot across her porcelain figurine of the infant Jesus at prayer upon the mantelpiece. Seraphim, the cat, scampered away on its belly to hide under the stairs.

Mrs Wilson parted the drapes and counted the ravens mustering on Mrs Beelzebub's guttering. Twenty, she thought, twenty shadows dancing on more shadows. Beyond the roof, black riders rode lightning bolt steeds across the sky.

"It's as I thought, Seraphim," she said. "Even before I got out of bed this morning I could feel the dark forces gathering. I rather hoped Mrs Beelzebub would be one of the Basingstoke Beelzebubs. But alas, it would seem, if what I'm seeing is to be true, she's one of the Depths-of-Hell Beelzebubs."

She glanced once more at the sky. There was fire, now, rusting the rims of the rolling clouds. Dark angels sang in the thunder. "And today is an apocalyptic day if ever there was. I suppose I'd best be over there and put a stop to it. Now, where's my hat and coat?"

A small crowd of nether folk had gathered in Mrs Beelzebub's driveway by the time Mrs Wilson trudged over. Some sat about a hastily drawn pentagram, plucking entrails from a sheep and incanting ancient words in forgotten tongues. Others sharpened swords on great grindstones turned by whip-lashed imps and harpies. Sprites lay in the dirt, their little lightning rods erect and suggestive, pleading to the electric sky above. Beyond the hedge, Mrs Wilson sensed the dead; lurking, waiting should their calling come.

"Do excuse me," said Mrs Wilson, stepping over a particularly fearsome Cerberus, "I've business with the lady of the house, and so do move aside, there's a good dog."

It was cold at the Beelzebubs' door. As cold as Hell, Mrs Wilson presumed. Or was Hell hot? It was hard to keep up, sometimes, particularly since the Heavenly directives had stopped coming; since the *problems* up there. No angels had appeared to her in a dream for months, now, and prayers seemed to go nowhere but voicemail. She pounded thrice upon Mrs Beelzebub's iron door knocker, and the sound was like every fist that had thrashed against Death's door.

The door creaked ajar.

"Who comes at this hour?" said Mrs Beelzebub, peering outward through the gap. Lightning flashed and wolves howled at the sound of her voice.

"Just me," said Mrs Wilson. "I know it's probably a bad time, but I wonder if I might have a word, Mrs Beelzebub."

"Ending is near. Time is short."

"I realize that, but it'll not take long."

Mrs Beelzebub opened the door fully and glanced sparrow-like up and down Sunshine Terrace. "Come in, then, and quickly," she said. "And mind the pit of eternity in the hall."

It was a good pit of eternity, Mrs Wilson agreed, as she stepped carefully about its rim in the hallway. She paused and peered down into the future. "I do like the swirling winds effect."

"Aye, and based on quantum certainty, you know," said Mrs Beelzebub. "I always feel, when falling into a pit of eternity, it important one knows exactly where one's atoms are. It makes for a much more concentrated torment, don't you think?"

Mrs Wilson followed Mrs Beelzebub through into the lounge. It smelled of sulphur, and was smoky where *firefalls* tumbled down the wallpaper on the far wall. Behind the hat stand, in the corner, tiers of benches, unoccupied, shimmered away into unseen dimensions. Facing the benches, across the room, rows of empty cages steamed liquid-nitrogen-cold.

"Now, please, sit, Mrs Wilson. Tell me what's on your mind."

Mrs Wilson sat and brushed the upholstery of Mrs Beelzebub's armchair with the back of her fingers. Cottage suites, with their soft patterns of gardens with summer flower and delicate, fresh leaf, always brought memories of better days. It was an Eden thing, perhaps; a subtle reminder of a gentler age. And, for a moment, Mrs Wilson was young again, frolicking carefree through the meadows and gardens of her youth, when the world itself was young and time passed more slowly.

"This will be the courtroom?" said Mrs Wilson. She paused as an imp stepped out from the wall of fire. It carried a bundle of scythes in its stubby arms. The blades shone blue-sharp in the flickering firelight. "And I see preparations are well under way for the trials."

Mrs Beelzebub smiled pleasantly. Mrs Wilson knew well that the devil was charming in its ways. Humanity liked to be charmed. It was where the church often went wrong, she thought – good with the stick, but so often lacking with the carrot. An eternal reward in Heaven, after all, might seem ill chosen if there is the merest murmur of agnosticism in the soul. And who could fail the slightest tinge of doubt given the way of the world and the folk who roam it?

"There's no shortage of sins, these days, Mrs Wilson," said Mrs Beelzebub, echoing Mrs Wilson's private thoughts. "And nor of sinners. Surely even your side sees the time is right for a spot of judgment? You must have seen what Humanity is up to, right now, with its bombs and pollution and sexual deviation and lawlessness, and much of it in *His* name." She pointed vaguely upward with a finger.

Mrs Wilson sighed. "I had hoped you weren't the real thing, Mrs Beelzebub. I've seen a few witches and conjurers gathering demons in my time, and seen them off, I should add." She glanced ruefully about Mrs Beelzebub's front room. The windows rattled as Hell's engines churned below her feet. The damned howled briefly behind the closed, kitchen door. "But quite obviously you are the genuine Beelzebub."

"Indeed, I am. And what of you, Eve – may I call you Eve? Do you join me, or do you oppose me again, this time?"

Mrs Wilson stood wearily from her chair. In the creak of her knees, she suddenly felt old. "Oppose is such a confrontational word, Mrs Beelzebub, but yes, I will provide defence. It's what I must do, for my sins."

"Then we'll meet again at Judgment Hour."

"Aye, no doubt we shall."

Back home, in the kitchen at number eight, Mrs Wilson's yellow, rubber gloves were a blur in the washing up bowl. The dishes were long since lemon clean, but being connected with

Earth powers, with the simple, cleansing qualities of water and the aroma of suds, helped her think more clearly.

She shivered. How long had it been since she'd been called *Eve*?

And how long since she'd talked to Adam? What would Mr Wilson say if he knew about him? A loving sort, Mr Wilson, and so trusting. What of the lie she'd been living for him? Was that a sin, too?

She dried her hands and shuffled through into the living room. She watched Mrs Rose struggle by outside beyond the window, the old woman bent against the pre Judgment Hour winds. And there was Mrs Trent and Mrs Almond from number twelve, too. Good folk, she mused; respectable and God fearing. Upright citizens, like most people of the world; surely it wasn't right that the Beelzebubs should condemn everyone for the sake of the few bad apples?

Bad apples – Mrs Wilson shivered; wasn't that what started it all in the first place? She walked slowly into the hallway and hesitated to pick up the telephone and dial *his* number. The dial tone was rasping-rude.

"Hello? Adam? It's me, Eve. Yes, I know, a long time. No, I must see you. It's important; can you come over? No, come today, come now.

"And bring the apple."

While she waited, Mrs Wilson dusted the rubber plant. It was a fine rubber plant, blessed with leaves of deepest green, and in truth didn't need dusting. But idle hands, she'd found, would take to prayer, and then she'd be faced with Heaven's problems as well as those of her own here below. Besides, it wouldn't do to go planning Holy Wars with a dusty house. She stood on the doorstep and watched the evil comings and goings next door. And Adam came with the throaty roar of a sleek, black Saab speeding down Sunshine Terrace.

"Eve, baby," said Adam, pulling himself arthritically from the car. Dark glasses hid the millennia lurking behind his eyes. He grinned at a young floozy in the passenger seat – blonde and leggy, and millions of years Adam's younger, though Mrs

Wilson doubted she'd know it. "Stay there, Kitten, I'll be back before I'm gone."

"You're looking . . . *young*, Adam," said Mrs Wilson, as she led Adam hobbling inside number eight. "In the skin, I mean, ridiculously young, but the bones look a bit lived in. Isn't it time you grew old gracefully?"

Adam shrugged. "Immortality's wasted on the old, Eve. And hey, I got my Glucosamine Sulphate tablets for the bones." He slumped into Mrs Wilson's armchair. "And my *kitten* does a fine massage, when I'm up for it. Modern times, eh?"

"Did you bring the apple?"

"It's here."

Mrs Wilson felt the thud of her heart against her ribs as she watched Adam search his pockets for the apple. When he held it in his opened palm, the room glowed golden with the light of the sun's first dawn. It was fresh and succulent, damp as if newly picked under refreshing rains. Even the single, ancient bite in its flesh bore teeth marks sharp and clean as if it were taken just yesterday, not a relic from all those years ago when Mrs Wilson had teeth of her own and when serpents hissed temptation in the boughs of the garden . . . of Eden.

"I hear there's to be Judgment," said Adam.

Mrs Wilson peered out through the drapes. "Aye, the Beelzebubs are next door. They're about . . ." Thunder shook the house. The wail of *dark hymns* filled the air. The drums of war began. *Thrum . . . thrum . . . thrum-thrum-thrum* ". . . to begin, it would seem."

"But this time it's not of our doing," said Adam.

"Some sins can't be washed clean by First Comings, Adam."

Mrs Wilson took the apple and held it up to the light bulb in the ceiling rose. Its skin was delicate and moist. Millions of years old and not a hint of bruising sullied it. And there was still just the one bite from it, taken for her sins.

Adam shivered visibly. "You mean to take a second bite, then?"

Mrs Wilson nodded. "Have you noticed God and His

Heaven are missing? It would seem the only way to bring them both back."

"It would cause a Second Coming, Eve. And at what cost to yourself? The last time we were thrown from the Garden; this time it could be from Creation itself."

"That, we shall see." Eve hid the apple in the pocket of her blouse. "Whatever happens, it's time God took responsibility once more for His creation."

"He'll not like it."

"No, I suppose not."

All of Sunshine Terrace's occupants were in the cages, when Mrs Wilson arrived back in Mrs Beelzebub's front room. Mrs Rose looked lost and confused, and cold beyond the billowing liquid-nitrogen fumes. Mrs Trent grumbled, her umbrella held aloft and threatening. Mr Patrick from number seventeen argued with a nearby apocalyptic horseman. Mr Salty from number nine sobbed uncontrollably.

To the front, his features twisted in fear and silent pleading, stood Mr Wilson. Mrs Wilson looked away, quickly. She shivered; betrayal, that was always the worst of times like these. Betrayal that she'd built a life of falsehoods.

"I thought you'd be back," said Mrs Beelzebub, sprawled regally in the Judgment Day chair by the hat stand in the corner, near the benches where she could keep a watchful eye on the troublesome imps of the jury. Behind her, silent, watchful, the Reaper stood. "You always were weak to my suggestions."

Mrs Wilson smiled, grim and knowing. Was it weakness? She was as she was made, after all, in *His* image, from dirt and ribs and breathed-in life; so whose weaknesses did she represent? It always struck her as wrong of God to put his only flaw in humanity, to let them mind it while he went off enjoying Himself about His universe, and then to allow mankind to be judged for it. Free Will seemed something of a cop-out when the flaw was programmed in.

Eve took the apple from her pocket and raised it to the room. The *firefalls* on the wallpaper were stilled by its golden glow, the imps of the jury hushed, the dark hymns fell silent. The room seemed to close in around her until it was just she, Mrs Beelzebub, and the apple.

Mrs Beelzebub leaned forward in the Judgment chair. Tense, she looked. "You still have that, after all this time?" she said. "And I suppose Adam is here, too?"

"This time, Adam has nothing to do with it," said Mrs Wilson. She saw concern creep across Mrs Beelzebub's face, felt the Devil's body tense.

"Surely you don't mean to use it?" said Mrs Beelzebub. "That would be to both our ruins."

Mrs Wilson kissed the apple, and then bit down hard into its flesh. The room shuddered. Plaster rained down from the ceiling. The damned wailed. The imps fell to the floor. The world spun slower in space. Time stopped.

"Let there be Darkness," said Mrs Wilson.

And she saw that it was good.

From the kitchen window at number eight, as she busied herself with lemon clean dishes, Eve looked out on a different garden. It was golden, and lush, and new, and warmed by a fledgling sun.

There were no *otherworldly* cats, and no vortices to *beyond*, shimmering blue and green in the corner by Mrs Beelzebub's rickety, wooden shed. There was no Mrs Beelzebub, for a short while, at least.

Eve walked through into the living room where Mrs Rose and Mrs Tate's teacups still lurked abandoned on the occasional table. Adam sulked in her armchair by the television. Beyond the front window, Sunshine Terrace was deserted. Empty, just like the world.

"You could have saved me my floozy," said Adam. "We had a good thing going on. She had Venus's breasts."

Eve sighed. "Maybe, when God's done making replacement folk in His image, you'll find one like her." She reached for the photograph of Mr Wilson set above the fireplace and brushed dust from its frame. A single tear welled in the corner of her eye. Would she be able to fashion Mr Wilson just as he was?

Would he be different, this time, would he still love her? "And then again, maybe not."

Adam shook his head. "There'll never be breasts like that, again." He stood and reached for his coat. "What will you do now, Eve?"

"Oh, I'll be here, waiting, ready for the next time. The problem with *Him* making folk in *His* image is that there'll always be a next time."

"Shall I take the apple? I could put it out for the bin men; oh, I mean when there *are* bin men, of course."

Eve grinned. "I think perhaps I'll keep it safe, this time, for Humanity's sake." She opened the front door that Adam might shuffle out to his waiting Saab. "After all," she said, "there're not that many more bites left in it."

SOONER OR LATER OR NEVER NEVER

Gary Jennings

The Anula tribe of Northern Australia associate the dollar-bird with rain, and call it the rain-bird. A man who has the bird for his totem can make rain at a certain pool. He catches a snake, puts it alive into the pool, and after holding it under water for a time takes it out, kills it, and lays it down by the side of the creek. Then he makes an arched bundle of grass stalks in imitation of a rainbow, and sets it up over the snake. After that all he does is to sing over the snake and the mimic rainbow; *sooner or later the rain will fall.*

> – Sir James Frazer
> *The Golden Bough*

The Rt. Rev. Orville Dismey
Dean of Missionary Vocations
Southern Primitive Protestant College
Grobian, Virginia

Most Reverend Sir:

It has been quite a long time since we parted, but the attached Frazer quotation should help you to remember me – Crispin Mobey, your erstwhile student at dear old SoPrim. Since it occurred to me that you may have heard only a sketchy account of my activities in Australia, this letter will constitute my full report.

For instance, I should like to refute anything you may have heard from the Primitive Protestant Pacific Synod about my mission to the Anula tribe having been less than an unqualified success. If I helped a little to wean the Anulas away from heathen sorceries – and I did – I feel I have brought them that much closer to the True Word, and my mission was worth its cost.

It was also, for me, the realization of a lifelong dream. Even as a boy in Dreer, Virginia, I saw myself as a future missionary to the backward and unenlightened corners of the world, and comported myself in keeping with that vision. Among the rougher hewn young men of Dreer I often heard myself referred to, in a sort of awe, as "that Christly young Mobey". In all humility, I deplored being set on such a pedestal.

But it wasn't until I entered the hallowed halls of Southern Primitive College that my previously vague aspirations found their focus. It was during my senior year at dear old SoPrim that I came upon Sir James Frazer's twelve-volume anthropological compendium. *The Golden Bough*, with its account of the poor deluded Anula tribe. I investigated, and discovered to my joy that there still was such a tribe in Australia, that it was just as pitiably devoid of Salvation as it had been when Frazer wrote about it, and that no Primitive Protestant mission had ever been sent to minister to these poor unsaved souls. Unquestionably (I said to myself) the time, the need, and the man had here conjoined. And I began agitating for a Board of Missions assignment to the overlooked Anulas.

This did not come easily. The Regents complained that I was dismally near failing even such basic ecclesiastic subjects as Offertory Management, Histrionics and Nasal Singing. But you came to my rescue, Dean Dismey. I remember how you argued, "Admittedly, Mobey's academic grades tend toward Z. But let us in mercy write a Z for zeal, rather than zero, and grant his application. It would be criminal, gentlemen, if we did *not* send Crispin Mobey to the Outback of Australia."

(And I believe this report on my mission will demonstrate that your faith in me, Dean Dismey, was not misplaced. I will say, modestly, that during my travels Down Under, I was often referred to as "the very picture of a missionary".)

I would have been perfectly willing to work my passage to Australia, to claw my way unaided into the Outback, and to live as primitively as my flock while I taught them The Word. Instead, I was surprised to discover that I had at my disposal a generous allocation from the Overseas Mission Fund; over-generous, in fact, as all I intended to take with me was some beads.

"Beads!" exclaimed the Mission Board bursar, when I presented my requisition. "You want the entire allocation in *glass beads?*"

I tried to explain to him what I had learned from my research. The Australian aborigines, I had been given to understand, are the most primitive of all the peoples living on earth. An actual remnant of the Stone Age, these poor creatures never even got far enough up the scale of evolution to develop the bow and arrow.

"My dear boy," the bursar said gently. "Beads went out with Stanley and Livingstone. You'll want an electric golf cart for the chief. Lampshades for his wives – they wear them for hats, you know."

"The Anulas never heard of golf, and they don't wear hats. They don't wear anything."

"All the best missionaries," the bursar said rather stiffly, "swear by lampshades."

"The Anulas are practically cavemen," I insisted. "They don't even have spoons. They have no written language. I've got to educate them from ape on up. I'm just taking the beads to catch their fancy, to show I'm a friend."

"Snuff is always appreciated," he tried as a last resort.

"Beads," I said firmly.

As you have no doubt deduced from the invoices, my allocation bought a tremendous lot of colored glass beads. I really should have waited to buy them in Australia and avoided the excessive transportation bill; they filled one entire cargo hold of the ship which took me from Norfolk that June day.

Arriving at Sydney, I transferred the beads to a warehouse on the Woolloomooloo docks, and went to report immediately to PrimPro BisPac Shagnasty (as Bishop Shagnasty likes to

style himself; he was a Navy chaplain during the war). I found
that august gentleman, after some search and inquiry, at the
local clubhouse of the English-Speaking Union. "A fortress, a
refuge," he called it, "among the Aussies. Will you join me in
one of these delicious Stingarees?"

I declined the drink and launched into the story behind my
visit.

"Going to the Anulas, eh? In the Northern Territory?" He
nodded judiciously. "Excellent choice. Virgin territory. You'll
find good fishing."

A splendid metaphor. "That's what I came for, sir," I said
enthusiastically.

"Yes," he mused. "I lost a Royal Coachman up there on the
River Roper, three years back."

"Mercy me!" I exclaimed, aghast. "I had no idea the poor
heathens were hostile! And one of the Queen's own chauf –!"

"No, no, no! A trout fly!" He stared at me. "I begin to
understand," he said after a moment, "why they sent you to
the Outback. I trust you're leaving for the North immediately."

"I want to learn the native language before I get started," I
said. "The Berlitz people in Richmond told me I could study
Anula at their branch school here in Sydney."

Next day, when I located the Berlitz office, I discovered to
my chagrin that I would have to learn German first. Their
only teacher of the Anula language was a melancholy defrocked priest of some German Catholic order – a former
missionary himself – and he spoke no English.

It took me a restless and anxious three months of tutorage in
the German tongue (while storage charges piled up on my
beads) before I could start learning Anula from the ex-priest,
Herr Krapp. As you can imagine, Dean Dismey, I was on
guard against any subtle Papist propaganda he might try to
sneak into my instruction. But the only thing I found odd was
that Herr Krapp's stock of Anula seemed to consist mainly of
phases of endearment. And he frequently muttered almost
heartbrokenly, in his own language, "*Ach, das liebenswerte
schwarze Madchen!*" and licked his chops.

By the end of September Herr Krapp had taught me all he knew, and there was no reason for me to delay any longer my start for the Outback. I hired two drivers and two trucks to carry my beads and myself. Besides my missionary's KampKit (a scaled-down revival tent), my luggage consisted only of my New Testament, my spectacles, my German-English dictionary, a one-volume edition of *The Golden Bough*, and my textbook of the native language, *Die Gliederung der australischen Sprachen*, by W. Schmidt.

Then I went to bid farewell to Bishop Shagnasty. I found him again, or still, at the English-Speaking Union refreshment stand.

"Back from the bush, eh?" he greeted me. "Have a Stingaree. How are all the little blackfellows?"

I tried to explain that I hadn't gone yet, but he interrupted me to introduce me to a military-looking gentleman nearby.

"Major Mashworm is a Deputy Protector of the Aborigines. He'll be interested to hear how you found his little black wards, as he never seems to get any farther Outback than right here."

I shook hands with Major Mashworm and explained that I hadn't yet seen his little black wards, but expected to shortly.

"Ah, another Yank," he said as soon as I opened my mouth.

"Sir!" I said, bridling. "I am a *South*erner!"

"Quite so, quite so," he said, as if it made no difference. "And are you circumcised?"

"Sir!" I gasped. "I am a *Chris*tian!"

"Too right. Well, if you expect to get anywhere with a myall abo tribe, you'll have to be circumcised or they don't accept you as a full-grown bloke. The abo witch doctor will do it for you, if necessary, but I fancy you'd rather have it done in hospital. The native ceremony also involves knocking out one or two of your teeth, and then you have to squat out in the bush, twirling a bullroarer, until you're jake again."

Had I heard about this when I first heard of the Anulas, my zeal might have been less. But having come this far, I saw nothing for it but to submit to the operation. Still, someone might have told me earlier; I could have been healing while I was studying languages. As it was, I couldn't delay my start North. So I had the operation done that very night at Sydney Mercy – by an incredulous doctor and two sniggering nurses – and got my little caravan on the road immediately afterward.

The trip was sheer agony, not to say a marathon embarrassment. Convalescence involved wearing a cumbersome contraption that was a cross between a splint and a truss, and which was well-nigh impossible to conceal even beneath a mackintosh several sizes too large for me. I won't dwell on the numerous humiliations that beset me at rest stops along the way. But you can get some idea, reverend sir, if you imagine yourself in my tender condition, driving in a badly sprung war-relic truck, along a practically nonexistent road, all the way from Richmond to the Grand Canyon.

Everything in the vast interior of Australia is known roughly as the Outback. But the Northern Territory, where I was going, is even out back of the Outback, and is known to the Aussies as the Never Never. The territory is the size of Alaska, but has exactly as many people in it as my hometown of Dreer, Virginia. The Anula tribal grounds are situated in the far north of this Never Never, on the Barkly Tableland between the bush country and the tropical swamps of the Gulf of Carpentaria – a horrible 2,500 miles from my starting point at Sydney.

The *city* of Cloncurry (pop. 1,955) was our last real glimpse of humankind. By way of illustrating what I mean, the next town we touched, Dobbyn, had a population of about 0. And the last town with a name in all that Never Never wilderness, Brunette Downs, had a population of minus something.

That was where my drivers left me, as agreed from the start. It was the last possible place they might contrive to hitchhike a ride back toward civilization. They showed me the direction I should take from there, and I proceeded on my pilgrim's progress into the unknown, driving one of the trucks myself and parking the other in Brunette Downs for the time being.

My drivers said I would eventually come upon an Experimental Agricultural Station, where the resident agents would have the latest word on where to find the nomadic Anulas. But

I arrived there late one afternoon to find the station deserted, except for a few languid kangaroos and one shriveled, whiskery little desert rat who came running and whooping a strange cry of welcome.

"Cooee! What cheer? What cheer? Gawdstrewth, it's bonzer to see a bloody newchum buggering barstid out here, dinkum it is!"

(Lest this outburst has horrified you, Dean Dismey, allow me to explain. At first, I blushed at the apparent blasphemies and obscenities commonly employed by the Australians, from Major Mashworm on down. Then I realized that they use such locutions as casually and innocently as punctuation. And, their "Strine" dialect being what it is, I never knew *when* to blush at their real deliberate cusswords, because I couldn't tell which they were. Therefore, rather than try here to censor or euphemize every sentence uttered, I shall report conversations verbatim and without comment.)

"Set your arse a spell, cobber! The billy's on the boil. We'll split a pannikin and have a real shivoo, what say?"

"How do you do?" I managed to get in.

"What-o, a Yank!" he exclaimed in surprise.

"Sir," I said with dignity, "I am a Virginian."

"Strewth? Well, if you're looking to lose it, you've come to one helluva place for gash. There ain't a blooming sheila inside three hundred mile, unless you're aiming to go combo with the Black Velvet."

This made no sense whatever, so to change the subject I introduced myself.

"Garn! A narky Bush Brother? Should of known, when you announced you was cherry. Now I'll have to bag me bloody langwidge."

If he "bagged" his language, it was to no noticeable degree. He repeated one obscene-sounding proposal several times before I interpreted it as an invitation to have a cup of tea ("go snacks on Betty Lee") with him. While we drank the tea, brewed over a twig fire, he told me about himself. At least I suppose that's what he told me, though all I got out of it was that his name was McCubby.

"Been doing a walkabout in the woop-woop, fossicking for wolfram. But my cuddy went bush with the brumbies and I found meself in a prebloodydicament. So I humped my bluey in here to the Speriment Station, hoping I'd strike a stock muster, a squatter, anybody, even a dingo-barstid jonnop. But no go, and I was bloody well down on my bone when you showed your dial."

"What do you do out here?" I asked.

"I toldjer, I was fossicking for wolfram."

"Well, you've got so many unfamiliar animals here in Australia," I said apologetically. "I never heard of a wolf ram."

He peered at me suspiciously and said, "Wolfram is tungsten ore. Fossicking is prospecting."

"Speaking of Australian fauna," I said, "can you tell me what a dollar-bird is?"

(The dollar-bird, you will recall, sir, is the totem agent mentioned in Frazer's account of the rain-making ceremony. I had come this far without being able to find out just what a dollar-bird *was*.)

"It ain't no fawn, Rev," said McCubby. "And you can be glad it ain't. That was a dollar-bird which just took a dump on your titfer."

"What?"

"I keep forgetting you're a newchum," he sighed. "Your titfer is your hat. A dollar-bird just flew over and let fly."

I took off my hat and wiped at it with a tuft of dry grass.

"The dollar-bird," McCubby said pedantically, "is so called because of a silvery-colored circular patch on its spread wings."

"Thank you," I said, and started to explain how the bird had inspired my mission to the aborigines –

"To the abos! Strike me blind!" blurted McCubby. "And here I thought you was out to preach at the buggering snoozers up at Darwin. I presoom the whole rest of the world is already gone Christian, then, if Gawd's scraping the barrel for black-fellow converts."

"Why, no," I said. "But the abos have as much right as

anybody else to learn the True Word. To learn that their heathen gods are delusive devils tempting them to hell fire."

"They're looking forward to hell fire, Rev," said McCubby, "as an improvement on the Never Never. Ain't they got enough grief without you have to inflict religion on 'em?"

"Religion is a sap," I said, quoting William Penn, "to penetrate the farthest boughs of the living tree."

"Looks to me like you're bringing the Bingis a whole bloody cathedral," said McCubby. "What kind of swag you got in the lorry, anyway?"

"Beads," I said. "Nothing but beads."

"Beans, eh?" he said, cocking an eye at the huge truck. "You must be more than meejum fond of flute fruit."

Before I could correct his misapprehension, he stepped to the rear of the vehicle and unlatched both gate doors. The entire van was loaded to the ceiling with beads, dumped in loose for convenience. Of course he was instantly engulfed in a seething avalanche, while several more tons of the beads inundated about an acre of the local flatlands, and rivulets and droplets of them went twinkling off to form a diminishing nimbus around the main mass. After a while, the mound behind the truck heaved and blasphemed and McCubby's whiskery head emerged.

"Look what you've done," I said, justifiably exasperated.

"Oh my word," he said softly. "First time beans ever dumped *me*."

He picked up one of the things, tried his teeth on it and said, "These would constipate a cassowary, Rev." He took a closer look at it and staggered through the pile toward me, dribbling beads from every fold of his clothes. "Somebody has give you the sweet but-all, son," he confided. "These ain't beans. They're glass."

I'm afraid I snapped at him. "I know it! They're for the natives!"

He looked at me, expressionless. He turned, still expressionless, and looked slowly around the glittering expanse that spread seemingly to the horizon in all directions.

"What religion did you say you're magging?" he asked cautiously.

I ignored him. "Well," I sighed. "No sense trying to pick them all up before nightfall. Mind if I camp here till morning?"

I was awakened several times during the night by a hideous crunching noise from the perimeter of our glass desert, but, since McCubby didn't stir, I tried not to let it perturb me.

We arose at sunup, our whole part of the world gleaming "like the buggering Land of Hoz," as McCubby put it. After breakfast I began the Herculean task of regathering my stock, with a rusty shovel I found in a tumbledown station outbuilding. McCubby left me for a while, to go slithering across the beads to their outer reaches. He came back beaming happily, with an armload of bloody scraps of fur.

"Dingo scalps," he chortled. "Worth a quid apiece in bounties. Rev, you may have spragged the curse of this whole blunny continent. Out there's just heaped with the corpses of dingos, rabbits and dunnikan rats what tried to make a meal off your bijous. Oh my word!"

He was so pleased at the sudden windfall that he hunted up another shovel and pitched in to help me scoop beads. It was night again by the time we had the truck loaded, and, at that, half its content was topsoil. The territory around the Experimental Station still looked like Disneyland.

"Oh, well," I said philosophically. "Good thing I've got another truckful waiting at Brunette Downs."

McCubby started, stared at me, and went off muttering in his beard.

The next morning I finally set forth on the last lap of my mission of mercy. McCubby told me he had encountered the Anula tribe on his trek in to the station. They were camped in a certain swale of acacia trees, he said, scratching for witchetty grubs and irriakura bulbs, the only available food in this dry season.

And it was there I found them, just at sundown. The whole tribe couldn't have numbered more than seventy-five souls, each of them uglier than the next. Had I not known of their crying need of me, I might have backtracked. The men were great broad-shouldered fellows, coppery-black, with even blacker beards and hair bushed around their low foreheads, sullen eyes and bone-pierced flat noses. The women had more hair and no beards, and limp, empty breasts that hung down their fronts like a couple of pinned-on medals. The men wore only a horsehair rope around their middles, in which they stuck their boomerangs, music sticks, feather charms, and the like. The women wore *nagas*, fig newton-sized aprons of paperbark. The children wore drool.

They looked up dully as I brought the truck to a halt. There was no evidence either of welcome or hostility. I climbed onto the truck hood, waved my arms and called out in their language, "My children, come unto me! I bring tidings of great joy!"

A few of the tots crept closer and picked their noses at me. The women went back to rooting around the acacias with their yamsticks. The men simply continued to do nothing. They're all bashful, I thought; nobody wants to be first.

So I strode boldly into their midst and took a wizened, white-bearded oldster by the arm. I leaned into the truck cab, opened the little hatch that gave access to the van, and plunged the old gaffer's resisting hand inside. It came out grasping a fistful of dirt and one green bead, at which he blinked in perplexity.

As I had hoped, curiosity brought the rest of the tribe around. "Plenty for everybody, my children!" I shouted in their language. Pulling and hauling, I forced them one by one up to the cab. They each obediently reached through the hatch, took one bead apiece and drifted back to their occupations as if thankful the ceremony was over.

"What's the matter?" I asked one shy young girl, the last of the procession and the only one who had taken *two* beads. "Doesn't anybody like the pretty-pretties?" She flinched guiltily, put back one of the beads and scurried away.

I was flabbergasted at the lack of enthusiasm. As of now, the Anulas had one tiny bead apiece, and I had about six hundred billion.

Beginning to suspect what was amiss, I went and stood among them and listened to their furtive, secretive talk.

I couldn't understand a word! Horrors, I thought. Unless we could communicate, I had no hope of making them accept the beads . . . or me . . . or The Gospel. Could I have stumbled on the wrong tribe? Or were they deliberately misunderstanding me and talking in gibberish?

There was one way to find out, and that without more ado. I turned the truck around and drove pell-mell back for the station, hoping mightily that McCubby hadn't left yet.

He hadn't. The wild dogs were still committing suicide en masse by dining on my beads, and McCubby wasn't about to leave until the bounty business petered out. I reached the station at sunrise again, when he was out collecting the night's scalps. I leapt from the truck and blurted out my problem.

"I don't understand them and they don't understand me. You claim you know most of the abo tongues. What am I doing wrong?" I reeled off a sentence and asked anxiously, "Did you understand that?"

"Too right," he said. "You offered me thirty pfennig to get my black arse in bed with you. Cheap barstid," he added.

A little rattled, I pleaded, "Never mind what the words *said*. Is my pronunciation bad or something?"

"Oh, no. You're mooshing perfect Pitjantjatjara."

"What?"

"A considerably different langwidge from Anula. Anula has nine noun classes. Singular, dual, trial and plural are expressed by prefixes in its pronouns. Transitive werbs incorporate the object pronouns. The werbs show many tenses and moods and also a separate negative conjugation."

"What?"

"On the other hand, in Pitjantjatjara, the suffixes indicating the personal pronouns may be appended to the first inflected word in the sentence, not merely to the werb root."

"What?"

"I don't like to bulsh on your linguistic accomplishments, cobber. But Pitjantjatjara, although it *has* four declensions and four conjugations, is alleged to be the simplest of all the bloody Australoid langwidges."

I was speechless.

"How much," McCubby asked at last, "is thirty pfennig in shillings and pence?"

"Maybe," I murmured thoughtfully, "I'd better go and minister to the Pitjantjatjara tribe instead, as long as I know their language."

McCubby shrugged. "They live way the hell the other side of the Great Sandy. And they're no myall rootdiggers like these Anulas. They're all upjumped stockriders and donahs now, on the merino stations around Shark Bay. Also, them boongs would prob'ly wind up converting *you*, and that's the dinkum oil. They're staunch Catholics."

Well, that figured. And I was beginning to suspect why Herr Krapp had been defrocked.

My next move was obvious: to hire McCubby as my interpreter to the Anulas. At first he balked. My expense fund was so depleted by now that I couldn't offer enough to tempt him away from his booming business here in dingo scalps. But finally I thought to offer him all the beads in the second truck – "Enough to kill every dingo in the Outback." So he rolled up his swag and took the wheel (I was dead tired of driving), and we headed again for the Anula country.

On the way, I told McCubby how I intended to introduce the blackfellows to modern Primitive Protestantism. I read aloud to him Sir James Frazer's paragraph on rainmaking, which concludes, " 'After that all he does is to sing over the snake and the mimic rainbow . . .' "

"*All* he does!" McCubby snorted.

" 'Sooner or later the rain will fall.' " I closed the book. "And that's where I step in. If the rain doesn't fall, the natives can plainly see that their sorcery doesn't work, and I can turn their clearer eyes toward Christianity. If the rain *should* fall, I simply explain that they were actually praying to the true, Protestant God without realizing it, and the rain-bird had nothing to do with it."

"And how do you cozen 'em into doing this rain-bird corroboree?"

"Heavens, they're probably doing it all the time. The good

Lord knows they need rain. This whole country is burned crisp as paper."

"If it do come on to rain," McCubby muttered darkly, "my word, *I'll* fall down on me knees." What that signified, I (unfortunately) didn't surmise at the time.

The reception at the Anula camp was rather different this time. The abos swarmed to greet McCubby; three of the younger females in particular appeared to rejoice at his arrival.

"Ah, me cheeky little blackgins," he said affectionately. Then, after a colloquy with the tribe's elders, he said to me, "They want to offer you a lubra, too, Rev."

A lubra is a female, and I had expected this hospitality, knowing it to be a custom of the Anulas. I asked McCubby to explain my religious reasons for declining and went to work to set up my tent on a knoll overlooking the native camp. As I crawled into it, McCubby asked, "Going to plow the deep so early?"

"I just want to take off my clothes," I said. "When in Rome, you know. See if you can borrow one of those waist strings for me."

"A nood missionary?" he said, scandalized.

"Our church teaches that the body is nothing," I said, "but a machine to carry the soul around. Besides, I feel a true missionary should not set himself above his flock in matters of dress and social deportment."

"A true missionary," McCubby said drily, "ain't got the crocodile hide of these Bingis." But he brought me the horse-hair rope. I tied it around my waist and stuck into it my New Testament, my pocket comb, and my spectacles case.

When I was ready, I felt very vulnerable and vaguely vulgar. For one as modest and introverted as I, it was painful to think of stepping out there – especially in view of the females – in my stark white nakedness. But after all, I consoled myself, I wasn't quite as stark as my flock. On the Sydney doctor's orders, I would have to wear my bandage contrivance for another week.

I scrambled out of the tent and stood up, dancing delicately as the ground stubble jabbed my bare feet. My, all those white eyeballs in all those black faces! McCubby was staring just as intently and unbelievingly as everyone else. He worked his mouth for a while before he spoke.

"Crikey! No wonder you're virginian, poor cove."

The abos began to crowd around the point and babble and measure the apparatus as if they contemplated getting copies to wear. Finally, a trifle annoyed, I asked my still-goggling interpreter why they were making so much fuss.

"They think you're either bragging or humbugging. Dinkum, so do I."

So I told him about my operation, that I had endured it because it was an Anula custom. McCubby repeated this to the mob. The blackfellows nodded knowingly at each other, jabbered even more furiously, and came one by one to pat me on the head.

"Ah, they approve, do they?" I said with great satisfaction.

"They think you're crazy as a kookaburra," McCubby said flatly. "It's supposed to bring good luck to fondle a zany."

"What?"

"If you'll take a pike at the men of your flock," he suggested, "you'll note that the custom of circumbloodycision must of went out of style some time back."

I looked, and it was so. I found myself mentally composing some un-Christian remarks to make to Major Mashworm. So, to elevate my thoughts, I proposed that we try again to distribute my gift of beads. I don't know what McCubby told the blackfellows, but the whole tribe trooped off eagerly to the truck and came back with a double handful of beads apiece. Several of them made two or more trips. I was pleased.

The brief tropical dusk was on us now; the Anulas' cooking fires began to twinkle among the acacias. I wouldn't be able to accomplish anything more today; so McCubby and I set our own billy on a fire. We had just settled down to our tucker when one of the abos came up smiling and handed me a slab of bark heaped with some kind of native food. Whatever it was, it quivered disgustingly, and, looking at it, so did I.

"Emu fat," said McCubby. "Their favorite delicacy. It's in return for them beads."

I was ever so delighted, but the dish was nauseatingly difficult to get down. It was like eating a bowlful of lips.

"I'd wolf the stuff if I was you," McCubby advised, after a visit to the natives' fires. "They're likely to come and take it back, when they give up on the beads."

"What?"

"They've been boiling 'em for two hours, now, and it seems they still taste gritty."

"They're *eating* the *beads?*"

He saw my consternation and said, almost kindly, "Rev, all these boongs live for is to eat for to live for to eat. They don't have houses and they don't wear pockets, so they got no use for propitty. They know they're ugly as the backside of a wombat, so they got no use for pretties. In this crook country, finding food is cruel hard. If anything new comes along, they try it for food, in hopes."

I was too weary even to worry; I crept into my tent desiring only to "plow the deep," in McCubby's phrase. As it turned out, though, I got precious little sleep. I had to keep evicting a procession of young black girls who, I presume, had a childish desire to sleep under canvas for a change.

I arose quite late in the morning, to find all the Anulas still huddled, groaning, in their *wagga* rugs. "You won't see any rain-debbil corroboree today," McCubby told me. "Them rumbustious beads has got 'em all just about keck-livered."

Now I *was* worried. Suppose they all died like the dingos!

"I wouldn't do this for any ruggerlugs but you, Rev," said McCubby, digging into his swag. "But I'll squander some of my lollies on 'em."

"What?"

"Chawnklit. It's what *I* use for trading and bribing the Bingis. They like it a buggering sight better than beads."

"But that's Ex-Lax!" I exclaimed when he brought it out.

"That's what they like about it. A pleasure at both ends."

The events of the rest of that day are indescribable. But the setting sun picked bright glints from little heaps of beads here and there throughout the rolling land in the locality. And I was having troubles of my own; I had begun to itch intolerably, all over, McCubby wasn't surprised.

"Meat ants," he theorized, "or sugar ants, white ants, buffalo flies, marsh flies, blow flies. We also got anopheles mosquitoes. I tell you, Rev, missionaries ain't got the hide for cavorting bare arse." Not too regretfully, I abandoned my idea of living as primitively as my horny-skinned flock and went back to wearing clothes.

That day was not an entire waste, however. I reminded McCubby that we required a pool of water for the upcoming ritual, and he led me to the Anulas' tribal oasis.

"T'ain't much of a billabong in the Dry," he admitted. The waterhole was respectably wide and deep, but it contained only a scummy, fetid expanse of mud, through which meandered a sullen greenish trickle of water, the thickness of a lead pencil. "But come the Wet and it'd faze Noah. Anyhow, I figure it must be the one in your Golden Bow-Wow. It's the only water inside a hundred mile."

I wondered how, if Frazer's hero had been desperate enough to try conjuring up a rain, he had been provided with a pool to do it at. But I muttered, "Well, dam it, that's all."

"Rev, I'm surprised at your intemperate bloody langwidge!"

I explained. We would throw up a temporary dam across the lower end of the billabong. By the time the Anulas recovered from their gastrointestinal malfunctions, the water should have attained a level sufficient to our purpose. So that's what we did, McCubby and I: hauled and stacked up stones, and chinked their interstices with mud, which the fierce sun baked to an adobe-like cement. We knocked off at nightfall, and the water was already as high as our ankles.

I awoke the next morning to a tumult of whoops, shrills and clangor from the direction of the Anulas' camp. Ah, thought I, stretching complacently; they've discovered their new and improved waterworks and are celebrating. Then McCubby thrust his bristly head through my tent flap and announced excitedly. "War's bin declared!"

"Not with America?" I gasped – his report had sounded

rather accusatory – but he had as suddenly withdrawn. I dragged on my boots and joined him on the knoll, and realized he had meant a tribal war.

There were about twice as many blacks down there as I had remembered, and every one of them was ululating loud enough for two more. They milled about, whacking at one another with spears and yamsticks, flinging stones and hoomerangs, and jabbing brands from the cooking fires into each other's frizzy hair.

"It's their neighbor tribe, the Bingbingas," said McCubby. "They live downstream on the creek, and this sunup they found their water turned off. They're blaming the Anulas for deliberate mass murder, so as to take over their yam grounds. If this ain't a fair cow!"

"We must do something!"

McCubby rummaged in his swag and brought out a toy-like pistol. "This is only a pipsqueak .22," he said. "But they ought to nick off home when they see white man's weapons."

We pelted together down the slope and into the fray, McCubby ferociously poppopping his little revolver in the air, and I brandishing my New Testament to proclaim that Right was on our side. Sure enough, the invading Bingbingas fell back from this new onslaught. They separated out of the confusion and withdrew carrying their wounded. We chased them to the top of a nearby hill, from which vantage they shook their fists and shouted taunts and insults for a while before retiring, defeated, in the direction of their home grounds.

McCubby circulated through the Anula camp, dusting athlete's foot powder – the only medicament he carried – on the more seriously wounded. There were few casualties, actually, and most of these had suffered only bloody noses, lumped skulls or superficial depilations where hair or whiskers had been yanked out. I played battlefield chaplain as best I could in dumb show, pantomiming spiritual comfort at them. One good thing. All the Anulas appeared to have recovered utterly from their bead-diet prostration. This early-morning exercise had helped.

When things had calmed down, and after some breakfast

tucker and tea, I dispatched McCubby to search through the tribe for an unoccupied male of the clan which claimed the dollar-bird for its *kobong*, or totem. He did find a young man of that persuasion and, overcoming his stubborn unwillingness, brought him to me.

"This is Yartatgurk," said McCubby.

Yartatgurk walked with a limp, courtesy of a stiff Bingbinga kick in the shin, and was bushily bearded only on the left side of his face, courtesy of a Bingbinga firebrand. The rest of the tribe came and squatted down expectantly around the three of us, as if eager to see what new and individual treat I had in store for their young man.

"Now we must recapitulate the procedure," I said, and began to read *The Golden Bough*'s description of the ceremony, McCubby translating phrase by phrase. At the conclusion, young Yartatgurk stood up abruptly and, despite his limp, commenced a vigorous heel-and-toe toward the far horizon. All the other Anulas began muttering among themselves and tapping their foreheads with a forefinger.

When McCubby fetched the struggling Yartatgurk back, I said, "Surely they all must be familiar with the ceremony."

"They say, if you're so buggering thirsty as to go through all that taradiddle, it'd've been just as easy to lug an artesian drill in here as all them beads. Too right!"

"That's not the point," I said. "According to Frazer, the belief is that long ago the dollar-bird had a snake for a mate. The snake lived in a pool and used to make rain by spitting up into the sky until a rainbow and clouds appeared and rain fell."

This, translated, sent the Anulas into a regular frenzy of chattering and head-tapping.

"They say," McCubby interpreted, "you show them a bird mating with a snake and they'll get you all the water you want, if they have to hump the bloody Carpentaria Gulf down here by hand."

This was depressing. "I'm quite sure a reputable anthropologist like Frazer wouldn't *lie* about their tribal beliefs."

"If he's any kin to the Frazer I used to cobber with – old Blazer Frazer – he'd lie about which is his left and right hand."

"Well," I said unquenchably, "I've come twelve thousand miles to repudiate this custom, and I won't be put off. Now tell Yartatgurk to stop that screeching, and let's get on with it."

McCubby managed, by giving Yartatgurk a large slab of Ex-Lax, to convince him that the ceremony – idiotic as he might ignorantly think it – wasn't going to hurt him. The three of us went first to check on the billabong, and found it gratifyingly abrim with repulsive brown water, wide and deep enough to have submerged our truck. From there, we headed into the endless savanna.

"First," I said, "we need a snake. A live one."

McCubby scratched in his whiskers. "That might be a wowser, Rev. The boongs have et most of the snakes within hunting range. And they sprag 'em from a cautious distance, with boomerang or spear. The wipers out here in the Never Never, you don't want to meet 'em alive."

"Why?"

"Well, we got the tiger snake and the death adder, which their wenom has been measured twenty times as wicked as the bloody cobra's. Then there's the taipan, and I've seen meself a horse die five minutes after it nipped him. Then there's –"

He broke off to make a grab for Yartatgurk, who was trying to sneak away. McCubby pointed into the bush and sent the blackfellow horizonward with explicit instructions. Yartatgurk limped off, looking about him nervously and sucking moodily on his chunk of chocolate. McCubby didn't look any too happy himself, as we followed after the native at a distance, "I wish it was your buggering Frazer we was sending on this chase," he muttered spitefully.

"Oh, come," I said encouragingly. "There must be *some* nonpoisonous variety that will serve our purpose."

"Won't help our purpose none if we tread on one of the others first," growled McCubby. "If this ain't the most nincompoop –"

There was a sudden commotion out ahead of us, where we had last seen Yartatgurk creeping, hunched over, through the tussocky grass.

"He's got one!" I shouted, as the blackfellow rose up into

view with a strangled cry. He was silhouetted against the sky, toiling desperately with something huge and lashing, a fearsome sight to behold.

"Dash me rags!" breathed McCubby, in awed surprise. "I ain't never seen a Queensland python this far west before."

"A python!"

"Too bloody right," said McCubby, in unfeigned admiration. "Twenty feet if he's a hinch."

I gaped at the lunging, Laocoön-like tableau before us. Yartatgurk was almost invisible inside the writhing coils, but he was clearly audible. I wondered momentarily if we might not have bitten off more than we could chew, but I sternly laid that specter of uncertainty. Manifestly, the good Lord was following Frazer's script.

"Yartatgurk is inquiring," McCubby said quietly, "who we're rooting for."

"Do you suppose we'll spoil the magic if we lend a hand?"

"We'll spoil the blackfellow if we don't. Look there."

"Mercy on us, he's spouting blood!"

"T'ain't blood. If you'd just et a quarter of a pound of Hex-Lax and then got hugged by a python, you'd spout, too."

We fought our way into the squirming tangle and finally managed to peel the creature loose from Yartatgurk. It took the utmost strength of all three of us to straighten it out and prevent its coiling again. Yartatgurk had turned almost as white as I, but he bravely hung onto the python's tail – being lashed and tumbled about, sometimes high off the ground – while McCubby, at its head, and I, grasping its barrel-like middle, manhandled it toward the billabong.

By the time we made it to the pool bank, all three of us were being whipped through the air, back and forth past each other, and occasionally colliding.

"Now," I managed to gasp out, between the snake's convulsions. "He's got to – hold it under – *oof!* – the water . . ."

"I don't think," said McCubby, on my left, "he's likely to agree," said McCubby, from behind me. "When I yell *go*," said McCubby, on my right, "dowse him and the snake both," said McCubby, from overhead. "*Cooee!* – GO!!!"

At the command, he and I simultaneously swung our portions of the python out over the water and let go. It and the wretched Yartatgurk, flapping helplessly along like the tail of a kite, disappeared with a mighty splash. Instantly the billabong was roiled into a hissing brown froth.

"Pythons," panted McCubby, when he could get his breath, "hates water worse'n cats do."

The entire Anula tribe, I now noticed, had come down to cluster on the opposite side of the billabong, and were attentively following the proceedings with eyes like boiled onions.

"Was you to ask me," said McCubby, when we had rested a while, "I'd be hard put to say who was holding who under."

"I guess it's been long enough," I decreed.

We waded waist-deep into the pool and, after being knocked about a bit, managed to grab hold of the slithery loops and haul the reptile back onto the bank. Yartatgurk, we were pleased to see, came along clenched in a coil of the python's tail.

Somewhere along about here, our handmade dam collapsed. Its mud chinking had been gradually eroded as the water backed up behind it during the night and morning. Now the agitation of the billabong toppled the weakened structure, and all the collected water drained out with a swoosh. This would probably gratify the thirsty Bingbingas downstream, I reflected, if it didn't drown them all in that first grand flood-wave.

The submersion had taken some of the fight out of the snake, but not a great deal. McCubby and I sustained numerous bruises and contusions during this stage of the struggle, while we fought to immobilize the forepart of the thing. Yartatgurk was not much help to us, as he had gone quite limp and, clutched by the freely thrashing tail of the serpent, was being batted like a bludgeon against the surrounding trees and terrain.

"It's time for him to kill it," I shouted to McCubby.

As the blackfellow whisked to and fro past us, McCubby listened to his barely audible mumblings and finally reported, "He says nothing would give him greater pleasure."

Our fantastic battle went on for a while longer, until it

became apparent that Yartatgurk wasn't up to killing the monster anytime soon, and I called to McCubby to inquire what to do next.

"I'll hang on best I can," he bellowed back, between curses and grunts. "You run for my swag. Get my pistol. Shoot the bugger."

I went, but with misgivings. I feared that we white men – perhaps unconsciously flaunting our superiority – were taking too much of a hand in this ceremony and, by our meddling, might botch whatever mystical significance it held for the natives.

I came back at a run, gripping the revolver in both hands. The python appeared to have recovered from its watery ordeal and was flailing more energetically than ever, occasionally keeping both men in the air simultaneously. In all that confusing uproar, and in my own excitement, nervousness and unfamiliarity with the weapon, I took quaking aim and shot Yartatgurk in the foot.

He did not make any outright complaint (though I think he might have, if he could have), but his eyes were eloquent, I could almost have wept at their glazed expression of disappointment in me. This was a chastening thing to see, but I suppose even the most divinely inspired spiritual leader encounters it at least once in his career. None of us is perfect.

Meanwhile McCubby had disengaged himself from the melee. He snatched the pistol from me and emptied it into the serpent's ugly head. For a long time, then, he and I leaned against each other and panted wearily, while the blackfellow and the python lay side by side and twitched.

Yartatgurk's injury, I am relieved to say, was not a serious one. Actually, he had suffered more from his stay underwater. McCubby pumped his flaccid arms up and down, disgorging quite an astonishing quantity of water, mud, weeds and polliwogs, while I bound up the hole in his foot with a strip torn from my own bandages.

A .22, it seems, fires a triflingly small pellet, and this one had passed cleanly through Yartatgurk's foot without so much as nicking a tendon. As the lead did not remain in the wound, and as it bled freely, there appeared to be little cause for agonizing – though this he did, at great and vociferous length, when he regained consciousness.

I decided to let the fellow enjoy a short rest and the commiserations of his clucking tribemates. Besides, I was by now so implicated in the ceremony that I figured a little more intervention could do no harm. So I went myself to perform the next step in the rite: to set up the "mimic rainbow" of grass over the defunct snake.

After fumbling unsuccessfully at this project for a considerable while, I came back and said despairingly to McCubby, "Every time I try to bend the grass into a bow it just crumbles into powder."

"Whajjer expect," he said with some acerbity, "after eight buggery months of drought?"

Here was another verity – like the dried-up billabong – which I couldn't reconcile with Frazer's account. If the grass was dry enough to warrant rainmaking, it was too dry to be bent.

Then I had an inspiration and went to look at the muck of our recent dam-site pool. As I'd hoped, there was a sparse growth of grass there, nicely waterlogged by its night's immersion. I plucked all I could find and tied it into a frazzled rainbow with my bootlaces. This horseshoe-shaped object I propped up around the dead python's neck, making him look as jaunty as a racehorse in the winner's circle.

Feeling very pleased with myself, I returned to McCubby. He, like the Anulas, was sympathetically regarding Yartatgurk, who I gathered was relating the whole history of his wounded foot from the day it was born.

"Now tell him," I said, "all he has to do is sing."

For the first time, McCubby seemed disinclined to relay my instructions. He gave me a long look. Then he clasped his hands behind his back and took a contemplative turn up and down the billabong bank, muttering to himself. Finally he shrugged, gave a sort of bleak little laugh, and knelt down to interrupt the nattering Yartatgurk.

As McCubby outlined the next and final step, Yartatgurk's

face gradually assumed the expression of a hamstrung horse being asked to perform its own *coup de grace*. After what seemed to me an unnecessarily long colloquy between the two, McCubby said:

"Yartatgurk begs to be excused, Rev. He says he's just had too much to think about, these past few days. First he had to meditate on the nature of them beads you fed him. Then he had to mull over the Bingbingas' burning of his beard, which cost him three years to cultivate and got glazed off in three winks. Then there was being half squoze to a pulp, and then three-quarters drownded, and then nine-tenths bludged to death, and then having his hoof punctuated. He says his poor inferior black brain is just so full of meat for study that it's clean druv out the words of all the songs."

"He doesn't have to sing words," I said. "I gather that any sprightly tune will do, crooned heavenward in a properly beseeching manner."

There was a short silence.

"In all this empty woop-woop," said McCubby under his breath, "one-eighth of a human bean to a square mile, and *you* have to be the one-eighth I cobber up with."

"McCubby," I said patiently, "this is the most important part of the entire ritual."

"Ah, well. Here goes the last of me Hex-lax."

He handed the chocolate to the blackfellow and launched into a long and seductive argument. At last, with a red-eyed glare at me, and so suddenly that I and the Anulas all jumped, Yartatgurk barked viciously into a clamorous chant. The other natives looked slightly uneasy and began to drift back toward camp.

"My word, you're hearing something that not many white coves ever do," said McCubby. "The age-old Anula death song."

"Nonsense," I said. "He's not going to die."

"Not him. You."

I shook my head reprovingly and said. "I've no time for levity. I must get to work on the sermon I'll preach at the conclusion of all this."

As you can appreciate, Dean Dismey, I had set myself quite a task. I had to be ready with two versions, depending on whether the rainmaking was or was not successful. But the sermons had certain similarities – for example, in both of them I referred to Prayer as "a Checkbook on the Bank of God". And this, of course, posed the problem of explaining a checkbook in terms that an Outback aborigine could comprehend.

While I worked in the seclusion of my tent. I yet kept an ear cocked to Yartatgurk's conscientious keening. As night came down, he began to get hoarse, and several times seemed on the verge of flagging in his endeavor. Each time, I would lay aside my pencil and go down to wave encouragingly at him across the billabong. And each time, this indication of my continued interest did not fail to inspire him to a redoubled output of chanting.

The rest of the Anulas remained quietly in their camp this night, without any moans of indigestion, combat fatigue, or other distress. I was grateful that no extraneous clamor disturbed my concentration on the sermons, and even remarked on it to McCubby:

"The natives seem restful tonight."

"T'ain't often the poor buggers come the bounce on a bellyful of good python meat."

I cried, "They've eaten the ceremonial snake?"

"Don't matter," he said consolingly. "The whole skelington is still down there under your wicker wicket."

Oh, well, I thought. There was nothing I could do about it now. And, as McCubby implied, the skeleton ought to represent as potent a symbol as the entire careass.

It was well after midnight, and I had just finished the notes for my next day's services, when a deputation of tribal elders came calling.

"They say you'd oblige 'em, Rev, either to hurry up and die as warranted, or else to placate Yartatgurk someway. They can't git to sleep with him caterwauling."

"Tell them," I said, with a magisterial wave of my hand, "it will all soon be over."

I knew not how truly I had spoken, until I was violently

awakened some hours later by my tent folding up like an umbrella – *thwack!* – and disappearing into the darkness.

Then, just as violently, the darkness was riven and utterly abolished by the most brilliant, writhing, forking, jagging, snarling cascade of lightning I ever hope to see. It was instantly succeeded by an even blacker darkness, the acrid stench of ozone, and a roiling cannonade of thunder that simply picked up the whole Never Never land and shook it like a blanket.

When I could hear again, I discerned McCubby's voice, whimpering in stark horror out of the darkness, "Gawd strike me blind." It seemed more than likely. I was admonishing him to temper his impiety with prudence, when a second cosmic uproar, even more impressive than the first, raged through the echoing dome of heaven.

I had not yet recovered from its numbing fury when a wind like a driving piston took me in the back, balled me up, and sent me tumbling end over end across the countryside. I caromed painfully off numerous eucalyptuses and acacias and unidentifiable other obstacles until I collided with another human body. We grabbed onto each other, but kept on traveling until the wind died for a moment.

By great good fortune, it was McCubby I had encountered – though I must say he seemed unaware of any good fortune in this. "What in buggery have you gone and done?" he demanded, in a quaver.

"What hath *God* wrought?" I corrected him. Oh, it would make an ineradicable impression on the Anulas, when I explained that this was not really the doing of their dollar-bird. "Now," I couldn't help exclaiming, "if it will only pour down rain!"

The words were no sooner spoken than McCubby and I were flattened again. The rain had come down like God's boot-heel. It continued mercilessly to stamp on my back, grinding me into the solid earth so that I could barely expand my chest to breathe. This, I thought in my agony, is really more than I meant to ask for.

After an incalculable while, I was able to inch my mouth

over beside McCubby's ear and bellow loud enough for him to hear, "We've got to find my sermon notes before the rain ruins them!"

"Your bloody notes are in Fiji by now!" he shouted back. "And so will we be if we don't do a bleeding bunk in a bleeding hurry!"

I tried to remonstrate that we couldn't leave the Anulas now, when everything was proceeding so well, and when I had such a God-given opportunity to make a splendid conversion of the whole tribe.

"Can't you get it through your googly skull?" he bellowed. "This is the Cockeye Bob – come early and worse than I ever seen it! This whole land will be underwater, and us with it, *if* we don't get blew a thousand mile and tore to rags in the bush!"

"But my entire mission will have been in vain," I protested, between the peals of thunder. "And the poor Anulas deprived of –"

"Bugger the bloody black barstids!" he howled. "They waved mummuk hours ago. We got to get to the lorry – if it ain't flew away. Make the high ground by the Speriment Station."

Clinging fast together, we were just able to blunder our way through what seemed a solid wall of water. The lightning and thunder were simultaneous now, blinding and deafening us at the same time. Torn-off branches, uprooted bushes and trees of increasingly larger size careened like dark meteors across the Never Never land. Once we ducked the weirdest missile of all – the eerily airborne skeleton of Yartatgurk's python, still sporting its natty grass collar.

I thought it odd that we encountered none of the black-fellows. But we did find the truck at last, jostling anxiously on its springs and squeaking in every rivet as if for help. Wind-blasted water streamed *up* its weather side and smoked off its top like the spindrift from a hurricane sea. I really think that only the dead weight of the remaining beads, which still filled three-quarters of the van, prevented the truck's being over-turned.

McCubby and I fought our way to the lee door and opened it, to have it nearly blown off the hinges as the wind clawed at it. The inside of the cab was no quieter than outdoors, what with the thunder still head-splittingly audible and the rain practically denting the metal, but the stiller air inside was easier to breathe.

When he stopped panting, McCubby wrung another minor cloudburst out of his whiskers and then started the engine. I laid a restraining hand on his arm. "We can't abandon the Anulas to this," I said. "Could we dump the beads and crowd in the women and pickaninnies?"

"I toldjer, they all took a ball of chalk hours ago!"

"Does that mean they've gone?"

"Soon as you sacked out. They were well clear of the low ground by the time the Cockeye Bob came down."

"Hm," I said, a little hurt. "Rather ungrateful of them, to desert their spiritual adviser without notice."

"Oh, they're *grateful*, Rev," McCubby hastened to assure me. "That's why they waved mummuk – you made 'em wealthy. My word, they're reg'lar plutes now. Nicked off to Darwin, to peddle that python skin to a shoe-manufactory."

I could only wheeze. "The Lord works in mysterious ways . . ."

"Anyhow, that was the reason they guv me," said McCubby, as the truck began to roll. "But now I suspicion they smelled the blow coming and bunked out, like bandicoots before a bush fire."

"Without warning us?"

"Well, that Yartatgurk *had* put the debbil-debbil on you with that death-song of his." After a moment, McCubby added darkly, "I didn't savvy the boong bugger had narked me, too."

With that, he headed the truck for the Experimental Station. Neither the windshield wipers nor the headlights were of any use. There was no road, and the faint track we'd followed coming out here was now obliterated. The air was still thick with flying debris. The truck jolted now and then to the resounding blow of a hurtling eucalyptus bole, or chunk of rock, or kangaroo, for all I know. Miraculously, none of them came through the windshield.

Gradually we inched upward from the low country, along the gently rising slope of a plateau. When we achieved its level top, we knew we were safe from the rising waters. And when we nosed down its farther slope, the rackety violence of the weather abated somewhat, cut off from us by the intervening highland.

As the noise subsided behind us, I broke the silence to ask McCubby what would become of the Anulas now. I ventured the hope that they would spend their new-found wealth on implements and appliances to raise their living standards. "Perhaps build a rustic church," I mused, "and engage a circuit preacher . . ."

McCubby snorted. "Wealth to them, Rev, is a couple of quid, which is all they'll get for that skin. And they'll blow it all in one cranky shivoo. Buy a few bottles of the cheapest plonk they can find, and stay shikkered for a week. Wake up sober in the Compound calaboose, most likely, with the jumping Joe Blakes for comp'ny."

This was most discouraging. It appeared that I had accomplished nothing whatsoever by my coming, and I said so.

"Why, they'll never forget you, Rev," McCubby said through clenched teeth. "No more will every other bloke in the territory that you caught with his knickers down. Here you've brought on the Wet nearly two months early, and brought it with a vengeance. Prob'ly drownded every jumbuck in the Never Never, washed out the railroad perway, bankrupted every ringer, flooded out the peanut farmers and the cotton planters –"

"Please," I implored. "Don't go on."

There was another long and gloomy silence. Then McCubby took pity on me. He lifted my spirits somewhat – and encapsulated my mission – with a sort of subjunctive consolation.

"If you came out here," he said, "mainly to break the Bingis of conjuring up heathen debbil-debbils to make rain, well, you can bet your best Bible they'll never do *that* again."

And on that optimistic note, I shall hasten this history towards its happy conclusion.

Several days later, McCubby and I arrived at Brunette Downs. He had the truckloads of beads transferred into a caravan of Land Rovers and headed Outback once more. I doubt not at all that he has since become a multimillionaire "plute" by cornering the market in dingo scalps. I was able to engage another driver, and the two of us returned the rented trucks to Sydney.

By the time I got back to the city, I was absolutely penniless, and looking picturesquely, not to say revoltingly, squalid. I hied myself at once to the English-Speaking Union in search of PrimPro BisPac Shagnasty. It was my intention to apply for some temporary underling job in the Sydney church organization and to beg a small salary advance. But it became immediately apparent, when I found Bishop Shagnasty, that he was in no charitable mood.

"I keep getting these *dunning* letters," he said peevishly, "from the Port of Sydney Authority. A freight consignment of some sort is there in your name. I can't sign for it, can't even find out what it *is*, but they keep sending me fantastic bills for its storage."

I said I was just as much in the dark as he, but the Bishop interrupted:

"I wouldn't advise that you hang about here, Mobey. Deputy Protector Mashworm may come in at any minute, and he's after your hide. He's already flayed a goodly portion of mine."

"Mine, too," I couldn't forbear muttering.

"*He* keeps getting letters of reproach from the Resident Commissioner of the Northern Territory, inquiring why in blazes you were ever let loose to corrupt the blackfellows. Seems a whole tribe descended en masse on Darwin, got vilely intoxicated and tore up half the city before they could be corralled. When they were sober enough to be questioned, they said a new young Bush Brother – unmistakably you – had provided the money for their binge."

I tried to bleat an explanation, but he overrode me.

"That wasn't all. One of the blacks claimed the Bush Brother had shot and wounded him. Others said that the missionary had provoked an intertribal war. Still others claimed he danced naked before them and then fed them poison, but that part wasn't too clear."

I whinnied again, and was again overridden.

"I don't know exactly *what* you did up there, Mobey, and frankly I don't care to be told. I would be everlastingly grateful, though, for one word from you."

"What's that, your reverence?" I asked huskily.

He stuck out his hand. "Good-bye."

Having not much else to do, I drifted down to the Woolloomooloo docks to inquire about this mysterious freight consignment. It turned out to have been sent by dear old SoPrim's Overseas Mission Board and consisted of one Westinghouse two-seater electric golf cart, seven gross of Lightolier lampshades – that's 1,008 lampshades – and a number of cartons of Old Crone Brand burley snuff.

I was too benumbed and disheartened, by this time, even to evince surprise. I signed a receipt and was given a voucher. I carried the voucher to the sailors' low quarter of the town, where I was approached by shifty-eyed men. One of them, the master of a rusty trawler engaged in smuggling Capitalist luxuries to the underadvantaged Communists of Red China, bought my entire consignment, sight unseen. I have no doubt that I was bilked on the transaction, but I was satisfied to be able to pay off the accumulated storage fees on the stuff and have enough left over to buy steerage passage on the first tramp ship leaving for the good old U.S.A.

The only landfall in this country was New York, so that's where I debarked, about a fortnight ago. Hence the postmark on this letter, because I am still here. I was penniless again by the time I landed. But through fortuitous coincidence I visited the local Natural History Museum (because admission was free) at just the time they were preparing a new aborigine tableau in the Australian wing. When I mentioned my recent stay among the Anulas, I was at once engaged as a technical consultant.

The salary was modest, but I managed to put away a bit, in hopes of soon returning to Virginia and to dear old Southern Primitive, to find out what my next mission was to be. Just recently, however, I have discovered that a mission calls me right here.

The artist painting the backdrop of the aborigine tableau – an Italian chap, I take him to be; he is called Daddio – has introduced me to what he calls his "in-group": habitants of an homogeneous village within the very confines of New York City. He led me into a dim, smoky cellar room (a "pad") full of these people – bearded, smelly, inarticulate – and I felt almost transported back to the abos.

Daddio nudged me and whispered, "Go on, say it. Loud, and just the way I coached you, man."

So I declaimed to the room at large the peculiar introduction he had made me rehearse in advance: "I am Crispin Mobey, boy Bush Brother! I have just been circumcised and I learned my Pitjantjatjara from a defrocked priest named Krapp!"

The people in the room, who had been desultorily chatting among themselves, were instantly silent. Then one said, in a hushed and reverent murmur: "This Mobey is so far in *we're* out . . ."

"Like all of a sudden," breathed another, "*Howl* is the square root of Peale . . ."

A lank-haired girl arose from a squat and scrawled on the wall with her green eyebrow pencil, "Leary, no. Larry Welk, si."

"*Naked Lunch* is, like, Easter brunch," said someone else.

"Like, man," said several people at once, "our leader has been taken to *us!*"

None of this conveyed any more to me than had the arcane utterances of McCubby and Yartatgurk. But I have been accepted here as I never was even among the Anulas. Nowadays they wait with bearded lips agape for my tritest pronouncement and listen, as avidly as no other congregation I have ever known, to my most recondite sermons. (The one about Prayer being a Check-book, etc., I have recited on several occasions in the tribe's coffeehouses, to an accompaniment of tribal string music.)

And so, Dean Dismey, I have been divinely guided – all unwittingly but unswervingly – to the second mission of my career. The more I learn of these villagers and their poor deluded idolatries, the more I feel certain that, sooner or later, I can be of Help.

I have applied to the mission headquarters of the local synod of the Primitive Protestant Church for proper accreditation and have taken the liberty of listing you, reverend sir, and Bishop Shagnasty as references. Any good word that you may be kind enough to vouchsafe in my behalf will be more than appreciated by,

Yours for Humility Rampant,
Crispin Mobey

NOTES ON CONTRIBUTORS

Gail-Nina Anderson is an art historian and freelance lecturer and journalist. She lectures on European Art and Gothic Literature at Newcastle University. She is also an expert on vampire lore and Fortean phenomena. She has undertaken a guided tour of Transylvania and was involved in an investigation into "Bigfoot" sightings in a park near Newcastle.

Poul Anderson (1926–2001) was one of the great American writers of both science fiction and fantasy. He sold his first story back in 1947 and over the next half-century established a reputation for his technological fiction, strong in ideas as well as characters. His books include *The High Crusade* (1960), *World Without Stars* (1966) and *Tau Zero* (1970) whilst amongst his fantasies are *The Broken Sword* (1954), *Three Hearts and Three Lions* (1961), and *The Merman's Children* (1979). Canadian-born **Gordon R. Dickson** (1923–2001) was likewise a heavy-weight of both fantasy and sf best known for his Dorsai series of works which began with *The Genetic General* (1960) and gradually began to encompass much of his sf. His fantasies include the delightful *The Dragon and the George* (1976) and *The Dragon Knight* (1990). Anderson and Dickson met at university in 1948 and though they remained life-long friends they seldom collaborated. Amongst those rare works is the series about the Hokas. These are teddy-bear-like friendly aliens who inhabit the planet Toka and are highly susceptible to English literature, which they treat as the truth and promptly start to act out. The stories were first collected as *Earthman's Burden* (1957) with a later omnibus *Hoka!* (1983).

Everard Jack Appleton (1872–1931) is not a name remembered today. In fact he was not that well known for much of his life. He was essentially a poet and journalist who also wrote occasional humorous pieces for magazines including several madcap invention stories which were the vogue in the early 1900s. However during the First World War he had a sudden surprise bestseller on his hands with the volume of poetry *With the Colors* (1917) which praised the American soldiers and castigated the Germans. The story here came from slightly simpler days.

Anthony Armstrong (real name George Willis, 1897–1976) was a regular contributor to *Punch* and similar humour magazines especially in the 1920s and 1930s. He produced a number of books including several pastiches on fairy tales of which the best are *The Prince Who Hiccupped* (1932) and *The Pack of Pieces* (1942). The story reprinted here comes from the former title.

Tony Ballantyne is an IT teacher who has been selling science fiction to the magazines since 1998 and his first novel, *Recursion* appeared in 2004 followed by *Capacity* (2005). Tony is something of a hero. Years ago, when he was walking through Middlesborough with his mother he heard a gunshot. He threw his mother to the ground, with himself on top of her. Looking up, he saw everyone in the street staring at him in disbelief. A bus tyre had exploded. He has since put his paranoia to work in his fiction.

John Kendrick Bangs (1862–1922) was one of America's leading humorists at the end of the 19th century, best known for his satirical *A House-Boat on the Styx* (1895), which mixes together the ghosts of people from throughout history. He was editor of *Harper's Weekly* from 1898–1901 and briefly of the humour magazine *Puck*, from 1904–5. A prolific writer, he wrote many humorous fantasies. Many of the best will be found in *The Water Ghost and Others* (1892), *Over the Plum Pudding* (1901) and *Jack and the Check Book* (1911) from which the story here is reprinted. My thanks to Mark Owings for bringing the story to my attention.

James Bibby is the author of the Conanesque spoofs *Ronan the Barbarian* (1995), *Ronan's Rescue* (1996) and *Ronan's Revenge* (1998) plus *Shapestone* (1999), which was set in the same world. Long before that, he was contributing jokes to various TV series such as *Not the Nine O'Clock News* and *The Lenny Henry Show*. *Shapestone* introduced the character of the bungling Midworld detective Inspector Heighway, fantasy's answer to Inspector Morse. Heighway reappeared in "Pale Assassin" which I included in *The Mammoth Book of Awesome Comic Fantasy* whilst the story here is his latest misadventure.

Damien Broderick (b. 1944) is one of Australia's leading science-fiction writers. He's also a senior research Fellow at the University of Melbourne in Australia and holds a multi-disciplinary PhD from Deakin University in the comparative semiotics of science and literature, but don't let that worry us. He's been writing for over forty years and his novels include the award-winning *The Dreaming Dragons* (1980) and *Striped Holes* (1988) from which the story here has been adapted.

Molly Brown is a Chicago-born writer long established in Britain. Her books have included the historical mystery *Invitation to a Funeral* (1995) and the novelization of the TV series *Cracker, To Say I Love You* (1994). "Bad Timing" was her first published story and went on to win the British Science Fiction Association's award for that year's best short story. It also formed the basis for her collection *Bad Timing and Other Stories* (2001). I included her Ruella stories in the first *Mammoth Book of Comic Fantasy* and *The Mammoth Book of Seriously Comic Fantasy*. Also check out *The Mam-*

moth Book of New Jules Verne Adventures for another of her witty stories.

Paul Di Fillipo (b. 1954) is one of the best of the current generation of American humorists. His stories and columns appear regularly in the science fiction and fantasy magazines and his books include *The Steampunk Trilogy* (1995), *Ribofunk* (1996), *Lost Pages* (1998) and *Fractal Paisleys* (1997). The title story of the last volume, included here, originally appeared in *The Magazine of Fantasy & Science Fiction* whose editor at the time regarded it as one of the funniest stories he had read. Di Fillippo also says that "The Li'l Bear Inn actually exists in Tiverton, Rhode Island. I've never dared set foot inside, for fear of ending up on its walls."

Esther Friesner (b. 1951) is a prolific writer of both humorous and serious stories. Check out *The Mammoth Book of Sorcerers' Tales* for a powerful example of the latter. On the lighter side, her work includes the novels *Here be Demons* (1988), *Hooray for Hellywood* (1990) and *Majyk by Accident* (1993) plus the humorous anthology series that began with *Chicks in Chainmail* (1995).

Neil Gaiman (b. 1960) is the author of the renowned *Sandman* series of graphic novels but he has done much else besides. His first book explored the depths to which sf can sink, *Ghastly Beyond Belief* (1985), compiled with Kim Newman; he collaborated with Terry Pratchett on *Good Omens* (1990), and is the author of the award-winning novels *American Gods* (2001) and *Coraline* (2002), the latter a delightfully strange tale for young adults. His short stories and articles can be found in *Angels and Visitations* (1993) and *Smoke and Mirrors* (1998).

Craig Shaw Gardner (b. 1949) has written many humorous fantasies including a series in which the very worst B-movie sets exist as a reality, which includes *Slaves of the Volcano God* (1989), *Bride of the Slime Monster* (1990) and *Revenge of the*

Fluffy Bunnies (1990). His earliest books, though, featured the well-meaning sorcerer's apprentice, Wuntvor, and his master Ebenezum who is allergic to magic, both of whom appear in the story here. The series began with *A Malady of Magicks* (1986) and includes *A Multitude of Monsters* (1986) and *A Night in the Netherhells* (1987).

Tom Gerencer (b. 1969) has undertaken a remarkable range of activities from being a guide on whitewater river trips to producing audiotapes of Thora Hird reading Bible stories. He has sold stories to *Science Fiction Age*, *Realms of Fantasy* and several anthologies.

Ron Goulart (b. 1933) is the dean of comic fantasy, science fiction and mystery fiction having been a prolific contributor to all three fields for over fifty years. His recent books have included a series featuring Groucho Marx as detective. Goulart has a particular passion for the frustration of man versus machine, especially robots, of which the story here is but one example. Others will be found in *Broke Down Engine* (1971), *What's Become of Screwloose* (1972) and *Nutzenbolts* (1975).

Tom Holt (b. 1961) has been producing wildly funny comic fantasies since *Expecting Someone Taller* (1987). Other titles include *Who's Afraid of Beowulf?* (1988), *Faust Among Equals* (1994), *Paint Your Dragon* (1996) and *Earth, Air, Fire and Custard* (2005). Holt is also an expert in ancient history and amongst his recent books is the thought-provoking novel *Alexander the Great at the World's End* (1999).

Rhys Hughes (b. 1966) is a master of the surreal and has written scores of short stories noted for their magical word play. A sampling will be found in his collections *Worming the Harpy* (1995), *The Smell of Telescopes* (2000) and *Stories from a Lost Anthology* (2002) from which the story here is taken. Hughes has also written a series of stories featuring the surrealist sportsman Engelbrecht the Dwarf who was created by Maurice Richardson and who appears elsewhere in this anthology – twice!

Gary Jennings (1928–99) is best known for his blockbuster novels set in the Aztec Empire which began with *Aztec* (1980), but he has also written novels about Marco Polo in *The Journeyer* (1984), life in a 19th century circus troupe in *Spangle* (1987), and the last days of the Roman Empire in *Raptor* (1992). He is less well known for his short and often wildly funny fantasies which include a series about a hopeless and very accident-prone missionary Crispin Mobey. The first story in the series is included here. The full series was subsequently published as *The Lively Lives of Crispin Mobey* (1988) under the alias Gabriel Quyth.

David Langford (b. 1953) has won well over twenty awards for his fan writings in the fields of science fiction and fantasy. He always has so many projects on the go – often helping others in their research into matters literary or scientific – that he hasn't written as much fiction as we'd all like. An early novel, taking the lid off the world of nuclear physics, was *The Leaky Establishment* (1984), whilst *Earthdoom!* (1987) with John Grant, was a spoof on the disaster novel. Some of his shorter works will be found in *The Silence of the Langfords* (1996) and *He Do the Time Police in Different Voices* (2003) plus slightly more serious stuff in *Different Kinds of Darkness* (2004).

Laird Long (b. 1964) is a prolific Canadian writer with stories having appeared in a wide range of print or on-line magazines, including *Blue Murder, Handheldcrime, Futures Mysterious, Hardboiled,* and *Albedo One.* His story "Sioux City Express" from *Handheldcrime* was listed amongst the top 50 mystery stories of 2002 by Otto Penzler in the anthology *The Best American Mystery Stories – 2003.*

Robert Loy is an American writer primarily of mysteries, most of which have appeared in *Alfred Hitchcock's Mystery*

Magazine though many of them verge on that borderline between fantasy and reality. By day he works in the mail-room/printshop of a large governmental bureaucracy which, he tells me, "is not nearly as glamorous as it sounds."

John Morressy (b. 1930) is an American professor of English who has been writing science fiction and fantasy for over thirty years. He is perhaps best known for his series of stories about the wizard Kedrigern, who has appeared in all four of these comic fantasy anthologies. Stories have been collected in *A Voice for Princess* (1986), *The Questing of Kedrigern* (1987), *Kedrigern in Wanderland* (1988), *Kedrigern and the Charming Couple* (1990) and *Remembrance for Kedrigern* (1990) and are now being steadily repackaged as *The Kedrigern Chronicles*.

Steven Pirie lives in Liverpool with his wife and their small son. His short fiction has appeared in a number of print and web-based magazines, and his first novel, the comic fantasy *Digging up Donald*, was published in 2004 by Immanion Press.

Steve Redwood (b. 1943) most definitely does not look his age which makes one wonder about such things as pacts with dark forces, a subject not entirely unconnected with his first novel *Fisher of Devils* (2003). He is clearly one of those "sleepers" since his first work was published when he was 12 and just forty years later he burst upon the fantasy scene with scores of stories in magazines and anthologies. The story here includes reference to Engelbrecht the Dwarf for which more, read on.

Maurice Richardson (1907–78) is one of those unfairly neglected British writers. He wrote stories and columns for various British magazines and newspapers from the 1930s to the 1970s and published several books including *Little Victims* (1968), *The Fascination of Reptiles* (1972) and *Fits and Starts* (1979). He also compiled a collection of the best strange stories by William Fryer Harvey, *Midnight Tales* (1946). However none of this, not even the last, prepares you for Richardson's tour-de-force, *The Exploits of Engelbrecht* (1950), a collection of stories about Engelbrecht the Dwarf Boxer and his fellow members of the Surrealist Sportsman's Club. They take on all manner of challenges. Engelbrecht boxes a grandfather clock and an "electronic brain", there is a witch-shooting party, and a one-hole golf course (par 818181) which covers most of the known world. The stories first appeared in *Lilliput* in the immediate post-war years, and were then published in book form in 1950, but thereafter languished in obscurity. They were rescued by Savoy Books who published a deluxe edition, with original illustrations, in 2000 and is well worth checking out. The story here, in which most of the human race (living and dead) take on a football match with the Martians, is just a taster. Rhys Hughes, represented elsewhere in this anthology, has also written an as yet unpublished book of new Engelbrecht stories whilst you will encounter Engelbrecht again in the story by Steve Redwood.

Adam Roberts (b. 1965) is a lecturer in literature and culture at the University of London and has written several academic books including a study of science fiction, called simply *Science Fiction* (2000) and a study of postwar Arthurian fantasy *Silk and Potatoes* (1998). His first novel was *Salt* (2000), about the colonization of a new planet, and he has since written *On* (2001), *Stone* (2002), *Polystom* (2003) and *The Snow* (2004), notable for doubling the number of words in the title. He has also written several parodies of popular fantasy including *The Soddit* (2003), *The McAtrix Derided* (2003) and *The Sellamillion* (2004).

Grey Rollins claims that he became a writer by accident, though since it required six "accidents" before his first sale, to *Analog*, it strikes me that he's a little accident prone! A qualified geologist, who has also attained degrees in psychology and electronics, Rollins has a wide base of skills for the extensive future-history writing programme he has set himself. He started his series about Victor when he felt he wanted to write a traditional style detective series but featuring an alien detective. But what an alien! Shaped like a banana with a long and very adept tongue and who only eats putrefied food, he's not exactly who I'd like picking my lock.

Robert Sheckley (b. 1928) is arguably the greatest of all sf satirists and ought to be on everyone's list of their favourite writers. He has been writing sf and fantasy for over fifty years and his story collections include *Untouched by Human Hands* (1954), *Citizen in Space* (1955), *Pilgrimage to Earth* (1957), *Shards of Space* (1962), *Can You Feel Anything When I do This?* (1971) and *Is THAT What People Do?* (1984). Amongst his novels, one of my favourites is *Mindswap* (1966) a wonderful odyssey throughout the Galaxy. Sheckley has been an inspiration to many – both Damien Broderick and Tom Gerencer in this anthology openly profess their acknowledgement to the master.

Frank R. Stockton (1834–1902) need have written nothing else besides "The Lady, or the Tiger?" (1882) and he would be remembered. It's one of those classic puzzle stories where the reader has to decide the outcome and it causes as much debate today as it did 120 years ago. Stockton was immensely popular in his day. Although most of his work was aimed at younger readers, with some of the best appearing in *St. Nicholas Magazine*, he was also appreciated by adult readers who could see the subliminal messages in his stories. He also wrote two early science-fiction novels, *The Great War Syndicate* (1889) and *The Great Stone of Sardis* (1898). Amongst his many collections of stories is *A Story-Teller's Pack* (1897), which included the story reprinted here, Stockton's parody of "A Christmas Carol".

Marilyn Todd (b. 1958), who has recently moved to France, is best known for her amusing chronicles of ancient Rome featuring that vixen Claudia Seferius who appears in *I, Claudia* (1995), *Virgin Territory* (1996) and others. Her story "A Bad Day on Mount Olympus" appeared in *The Mammoth Book of Awesome Comic Fantasy*.

Cynthia Ward (b. 1960) has been selling stories to the magazines and anthologies since her first, "The Opal Skull" in 1989. Born in Oklahoma, she has lived in Maine and Spain – but alas nowhere else that rhymes. Her story "Dances with Elves" was included in *The Mammoth Book of Seriously Comic Fantasy*.